D1234014

HUNTER

JAMES BYRON HUGGINS

WILDBLUE
PRESS

WildBluePress.com

HUNTER published by:

WILDBLUE PRESS
P.O. Box 102440
Denver, Colorado 80250

WILDBLUE PRESS is registered at the U.S. Patent and Trademark Offices.

ISBN 978-1-947290-65-5   Trade Paperback
ISBN 978-1-947290-64-8   eBook

Interior Formatting/Book Cover Design by Elijah Toten
www.totencreative.com

HUNTER

To Sylvester Stallone
This book is dedicated to your genius,
for genius, it is.

PROLOGUE

"That boy dies in four hours."

The words were all but lost beneath the roar of a low-soaring helicopter that swept across the darkening sky before vanishing into cloud. Thundering past the encircling tree line, it whirled thick cold air as the big man cast a cigar to the ground, grinding it angrily.

"Sheriff Cahill," a radio barked inside a patrol car and he turned, staring. His square face had been chaffed by the bitter winter wind. He reached through the window and palmed the microphone. "This is Cahill."

The voice at the other end was cautious: "Sheriff, volunteers searching the trailhead haven't found any sign of the kid. And the Guard is spread out all the way to Cedar Pass but they ain't found nuthin' either."

The frown deepened on Cahill's broad face. "Listen," he growled, "We have four hours 'til dark. If we don't find that boy before then, he's gonna freeze to death. Weather report says we got heavy snow coming. How many birds we got in the air?"

"Six." Static on the line increased. "But it's hard to see through the trees 'cause the clouds are cuttin' the light pretty bad."

Cahill cursed under his breath and leaned against the car, which tilted at his imposing weight. "Keep everybody moving," he said. "We don't stop, not even if we lose the light. If the rest of us are hurtin', think how a four-year-old boy feels out there."

A black pickup stopped beside him as Cahill tossed the mike onto the seat. He turned to the sound of sliding gravel and his mouth opened in surprise as a man, followed by a great black wolf, stepped from the door. The man came around the front of the vehicle, staring hard at Cahill.

"What do you have, Frank?" he asked.

The gigantic wolf turned its huge head toward the tree line.

Clearly shocked, Cahill took a moment to reply. "Damn, Hunter. I thought you was out of the country or somethin'."

"I got back a couple hours ago." Hunter bent to tighten knee-high moccasins worn over faded blue jeans. His shirt was leather, brown and worn. "Tell me quick what you've got, Frank."

Cahill stepped forward, seemingly galvanized. "Well, Hunter, we got a four-year-old boy lost out there somewhere who's gonna be dead by true dark if we don't find him. I've got deputies, three hundred volunteers and a thousand National Guardsmen out there on the north ridge. We got dogs on the track, six birds in the air. But we can't find hide nor hair. It's like the kid just vanished."

Moving with grim purpose and almost frightening speed, Hunter snatched a portable radio from Cahill's squad car, strapping it quickly to his belt. His voice was cold. "Where was the boy last seen?"

"There." Cahill pointed with a burly arm. His voice was excited. "Up near the trailhead. He was there one minute and then, his parents say, he just vanished in the trees."

"What was he wearing?" Hunter placed food and an emergency kit in a leather bag slung from one shoulder. He carried a single canteen on a leather case at his belt.

"A red shirt, blue coat, old jeans and tennis shoes," Cahill answered. "He was warm enough to last the day but he ain't gonna make it tonight."

Hunter threw a coat over his shoulders. It was leather and strangely designed, coming midway down his thighs. It had double hoods that draped over the shoulders, as if one could be used to protect his head from the wind while the other shed rain from his back. Cahill, who had always been amazed at the design, knew Hunter had made it himself.

"Dogs been over the tracks?" Hunter asked.

"Yeah. Dogs. Volunteers. Hell, every damn body."

"Tell everyone to stay where they're at." Hunter frowned at the forest, which was darkening quickly. "The tracks are gonna be messed up enough."

He looked at the huge wolf.

"Ghost," he said.

With primordial strength—a terrifying animal strength brought to life with the single word—the enormous wolf turned, massive muscles bunching and hardening beneath the heavy black coat. The huge head, as broad as an anvil, went to the ground as it padded toward the treeline.

"Hey, Hunter," Cahill called after them, his voice revealing a faint nervousness. "You really think you have a chance? I mean, what with the tracks all messed up like they are?"

Hunter hesitated, and his stern eyes—eyes a strange blue— revealed a determination that chilled even more than the blast of freezing wind that rushed over them.

Hunter turned away.

Vanishing into wild.

***

Winter whispered in a gathering wind as snow drifted over his small form. And he could feel the darkness gathering, could sense the sun was almost gone.

So cold . . .

The boy cried and held himself and wished desperately that he was someplace else, someplace warm. As he cried, he trembled and rocked back and forth on the snow-covered ground, his teeth chattering. There was no place to go, and nothing he could do but cry.

He wished someone would find him.

Deep in the forest, Hunter moved like a human tiger, bending to study the ground with a quick, keen alertness. In the distance behind him, he heard National Guard helicopters flying in a wild and desperate pattern.

He paid them no heed as he moved quickly forward, knowing that Cahill was right. The boy would die with night, probably within a few hours. Then, hurtling a log that the child had slid beneath, Hunter bent down, studying the ground again.

The boy was wandering left, right, left again—as a child had the frustrating habit of doing. That's what made a child far more difficult to track than a full-grown man. A man would generally move in a fast straight line. But a child would just venture aimlessly, no true sense of purpose or direction as he became distracted by the tiniest things.

Also, Hunter could tell from the dragging tracks that the boy was perilously fatigued. And with the cold slowing his blood, he would be even more disoriented.

Hunter bent and read the tiny, almost indiscernible tracks. If the boy weighed more it would have been far easier. But the kid was so light, the tracks so vague, that he had to be careful not to miss them in the fast fading light. Then he raised his face against the descending sun and frowned, imagining what the boy would be feeling, scared and lost and alone in this harsh wilderness.

Hunter's gaze hardened.

No, boy, you ain't gonna die . . .

It had taken him an hour to find tracks that hadn't been marred by search parties. Then, tracking for another hour, he saw where the search party had lost the boy's prints. And for the last two hours Hunter had pushed himself without remorse, allowing no rest.

He knew he was close, just as he knew he was almost out of time. Nor did he think the child had gone too much farther because his tracks—prints left by the tiny shoes—were beginning to drag severely, a dangerous sign of fatigue. He saw where the kid was resting more and more often.

Racing a dying sun, Hunter moved more quickly, bending and searching, anticipating the child's moves more effectively because he had tracked so many children and knew basically how they moved. He raised his eyes toward a nearby slope and read the almost invisible scuff marks left where the boy scampered up the ridge. Trying to think ahead of the game, Hunter searched ahead for the path a child would take.

Almost instantly he saw a break in the ridge—a path of light— and knew it was the most likely direction. He moved quickly forward again, making sure he didn't lose even the faintest print because he had no time to backtrack. And as he neared the ridge he saw where the boy had fallen and he paused, staring down. He felt tempted to rush, but a practiced discipline gave him patience to study the ground, making certain.

There . . .

Examining the tiny print closely, Hunter saw it sloping on the right and knew the boy had turned left, wandering again. He followed it, ignoring the brutal cold enveloping him.

With Ghost running lightly beside him, Hunter moved in a loping crouch; fast but cautious, always cautious because he knew the child could wander away from the path at any point. He didn't cast another glance at the last crimson light of the sun as he moved along the ridge.

Fatigue from moving ceaselessly for hours and expending extraordinary concentration to read the almost invisible tracks was beginning to take a toll. But Hunter knew in his heart that it had come to this moment. He was only minutes from last light and minutes from the boy. But he had to find the child before last light because even he couldn't track in the dark.

I ain't gonna let you die, kid . . .

I ain't gonna let you die . . .

***

Something huge, dark and frightening suddenly and silently loomed out of the shadowed granite slab above him. And the boy looked up to see ... a man?

A man and ... a wolf?

Yes, it was a man. And it was a wolf.

The boy beheld the beast's black eyes staring over him with such intensity, saw the slightly distended fangs that glinted sharp-white even in moonlight, and felt new fear.

Then the man and wolf dropped without a sound from the rock and bent over him, man speaking soothingly as the huge wolf pressed a warm nose against his cheek, making him smile. The boy raised a shaking hand, touching the warmth of the thick black mane.

Without another word, the man gently wrapped him in his coat and lifted him from the hateful ground, and then they were moving through the trees with the sound of a great roaring of wind—the shadowed leaves and limbs sliding over them but never touching them because the man held him so close and so strong.

He was warm again and, reaching up, he felt the man's great strength, and knew he was safe.

***

"By God." Cahill shook his head. "I never thought you could pull it off, Hunter."

Cut by branches and covered with bruises, Hunter was silent a moment as he took a sip of coffee, sitting against Cahill's desk. He stared into his cup as he spoke.

"The boy's gonna be all right?"

"Yeah." Cahill rose from his chair, pouring himself another cup. Burly and deep chested with blacksmith arms, the sheriff moved with the square grace of a heavyweight boxer.

"The doc says he's dehydrated and in shock, but they already got him in a room. Ain't got no frostbite." Cahill sat and leaned heavily back, taking a slow sip. "The parents called. They wanted to thank you."

Hunter took a sip. "Tell them I'm glad their boy's okay."

Silent for a while, Cahill studied the face of the man who stood before him.

Muscular with a ragged mane of black hair that fell slightly to his shoulders, Hunter seemed to have stepped out of another, more primitive age. His eyes were dark beneath a low, hard brow burned brown by years of living in the wild. His cheeks were sharp above a mouth deeply cast in a bronze frown. His broad shoulders, deep chest, and heavy arms were evidence of great strength but, Cahill had noticed before that Hunter seemed to possess a greater strength than was visible there. He had long suspected that Hunter's best, greatest, and truest strength was something he purposefully hid. He had always wondered why he hid so much of himself.

Cahill spoke. "You really don't have much use for people do you, Hunter?"

He waited. Hunter didn't reply.

Cahill continued, "But you risk your life finding these people when we got a thousand people in the woods that don't have a chance." Cahill didn't seem disturbed by Hunter's silence. "Like last year when you found that couple lost down below the Sipsey. You tracked 'em for four days with no food, no shelter." He grunted. "They got lucky. So did you. That track almost killed you."

Hunter sighed, raised his eyes slightly in agreement. "Once you get on a track, it's best not to take a break. The more single-minded you are, the better your chances." He paused. "But you're right. That one was tough. So was this one. The little guy kept wandering on me."

Cahill nodded, thoughtful. "So where you headed off to?"

"Manchuria."

Cahill laughed out loud. "Manchuria! For what?"

"The Tipler Institute wants me to try and capture a Siberian tiger."

Hunter shook his head. "They're pretty rare, but a recent expedition said they saw one." He shrugged. "I doubt it's there, but it's possible. I'll find out if I don't get myself killed."

Cahill smiled. "So, ol' Doc Tipler is still alive." Then his smile thinned, disappeared. "You know, kid, I hear a tiger is the meanest thing on four feet. Meaner than a Grizzly. And they're kinda like a Griz, too. They like to sneak up on you."

Hunter smiled. "Yeah, Siberians are the best stalkers in the world. They don't make a sound 'til they move, and they always attack from ambush. I've captured them before, but I think this might be different."

"What's gonna be different?"

'Just the range." Hunter set the coffee on the desk, stretched his arms. "Because of the foliage I'll have pretty limited range for a shot. Maybe thirty, forty feet."

"Think you can get that close to a tiger and stay down wind?"

"Guess we'll have to find out." Hunter's face was contented and easy as he spoke. He rose and reached for the door and Cahill could have sworn he heard half a laugh as the man went out the door.

***

He moved through the night, at home with the darkness.

Cold wind separated around his form, swaying the surrounding spruce, birch, and pine. He paused, breathing slowly and rhythmically, reminded of so much, and knew that the moss beneath his feet had survived here for ten centuries. The scent of a dozen flora concealed by the night rose to greet him, he knew them all. The bark of this nearby tree could quell pain, and the root of that plant could fill his stomach. He knew their secrets, their uses, even merely as food, though this was not the land he had known, was far from the land he had known. He could survive here.

And he could do even more than survive.

The guard drew near the gate.

It is time.

He knew that he must move before the dog could sense his presence. A hunting instinct that was clearer than human intelligence, purer than any purpose, pulled him forward.

His human intelligence reigned, yet it was reinforced by the instincts of this fantastic evolution of his flesh. Crouching low, he padded forward with silent steps, emerging ghostlike from the forest—a phantom rising from a dark mossy silence and gloom into the light of a dead moon to near the gate almost undetected. Only at the last did a guard turn to behold the phantasmic shape taking horrific form from darkness—an image beyond fear—and screamed in disbelief before whirling to wildly chamber a round in his rifle.

It was too late.

A single horrific blow tore the first guard's head from his neck and another clawed hand rent a lung from the second before the dog's howl burst from the fence. Snarling, the beast turned to see the German shepherd hurling itself forward with a fury beyond anything human.

A clawed hand arched through dark air to tear away the animal's heart and then he cast the lifeless body aside. It required no effort—so easy was it—and he leaped forward to finish, evading the panicked rifle fire of the last guard before he slew again.

It was over quickly.

Growling, he stood over smoking red snow and turned, glaring bale-fully at the heavy metal doors that secured the facility. He stalked forward and when he reached the portal he roared, hurling up gigantic arms to bring them down against the steel, thunderously sundering the panels.

Night eyes narrowing instantly at the light, he saw a white-coated mob screaming and running, running and screaming. He struck again and again as he moved through them to slay, and slay . . .

And slay.

CHAPTER 1

"Vicious little beasts, aren't they?"

The words, spoken with ominous disaster, came from a white-haired old man in a white lab coat. Seated patiently, he watched as a host of red army ants, some as large as his thumb, attacked what he had dispassionately dropped into the aquarium. The ants overwhelmed the rat in seconds, killing it almost instantly with venom, then devouring it. In three minutes a haggard skeleton was all that remained.

Dr. Angus Tipler clicked a stopwatch, staring down. "Yes," he frowned, "utterly vicious."

He turned to others in the laboratory of the Tipler Institute, the leading crypto-zoological foundation in the world. His face portrayed consternation. "What are we to do with them?" he asked, almost to himself. "They kill with venom long before they dismember their prey." He looked back. "Yes, and so we must therefore devise some type of ... serum, if for no other reason so that people will stop bothering us all the time. Has anyone concluded the molecular weight of the poison?"

A woman bent over an enormous electron microscope positioned neatly in the center of the room muttered in reply. "Not yet, Doctor. I need another minute."

Dr. Tipler said nothing as he turned back to the aquarium where the ants were safely—very safely—contained. The rest of the laboratory was filled with virtually every poisonous animal in the world, insect and mammal and reptile. There were black scorpions, Indian cobras, adders and stonefish, brown recluse spiders and the lethal Sydney funnel web, the most dangerous spider in the world. A single unfelt bite from the tiny arachnid would kill a full-grown man within a day. It was Tipler himself who had created the anti-venom.

"It seems this venom is neuromuscular in nature," he said in a raspy, harsh voice into a recorder. He waved off the video technician who had recorded the grisly episode. "The venom, no matter the location of injection, seems to infiltrate the ligamentum denticulatum, thereby bridging the pons Varolii to decussate the involuntary respiratory abilities of the medulla oblongata. Now, if we can—"

"Dr. Tipler?"

Tipler raised bushy white eyebrows as he turned, seeing a young woman scientist with long black hair. The Asian woman was obviously apprehensive at the intrusion, despite the old man's well-known patient nature.

"Yes, Gina?" His voice was gentle. "What is it?"

"There are some men to see you, sir."

Tipler laughed, waving a hand as he turned away. "There are always men to see me, lass. Tell them to wait. The commissary should still be open. They serve an excellent roast chicken. It is my best recommendation."

"I don't think these men will wait, sir." She stepped closer, lowering her voice. Her eyes widened slightly. "There are three of them, and they're wearing uniforms."

Tipler barked a short laugh. "Uniforms! What sort of uniforms?"

"Army uniforms, sir."

Tipler laughed again and shook his head as he rose. "All right, Gina. Assist Rebecca in discovering the molecular weight of this venom. And, also, if you would be so kind, extract venom from, oh ... let's say fifty of these infernal creatures. Just sedate them with chloroform and use the electroshock method—the same procedure we use for the black widows." He removed his glasses with a sigh and stood up. "And I will deal with these impatient men in uniforms."

"Yes, sir. They're waiting in the observation room."

"Thank you, lass."

Upon seeing the three, Dr. Tipler stopped short. He had been told often enough that, upon first impression, he was not an imposing figure, so he had no illusions. At seventy-two years of age he was short and thick with a wide brow and snowy hair laid back from the forehead. But he knew that his eyes, blue like Arctic ice, distinguished him from other men both with their startling color and their equally startling intelligence. And equally their quickness to perceive the heart of a mystery. And it was that perceptiveness, a blending of art, science and intuition that had made the world's eminent paleontologist and crypto-zoologist.

Crypto-zoology was in itself an almost unknown area of biological expertise. Fewer than a dozen distinguished scientists in the world practiced it with any measure of dedication. And, for the most part, few scientists realized that it was practiced at all. But, in essence, it was a systematic and highly rigid system of investigation designed to determine whether species thought to be extinct still inhabited the planet.

Tipler had known significant success in various stages of his career, discovering the last surviving Atacama condors in the Andes Mountains of Chile in 1983, and later discovering a species identified as the blind stone-fish, off the northern coast of Greenland. The deep-water fish had been thought extinct since the Paleolithic Period, but Tipler had pieced together a theory that they still existed in the south-flowing East Greenland Current, which drew directly from the Arctic Sea. He held even further suspicions that the fish existed higher in the Arctic Circle, protected by the vast ice caps of the pole. But a lack of funding had prevented further exploration.

However, his startling discoveries had earned him a modest measure of global recognition, which consequently delivered the attention of several wealthy philanthropists who deemed his unique nonprofit enterprise worthy of endorsement. So, with significant funding and a larger, better-trained staff, he had founded the Tipler Institute. Now, a decade later, he was recognized universally as the world's leading expert on unknown species, and their extinction or survival. Along the way he had also gained significant exposure to deadly snakes, fish, and spiders and discovered, to his own surprise, that he had a remarkable acumen for pinpointing the molecular characteristics of each type of venom.

Studying venom was, at first, simply a means of aiding those few medical institutions already overwhelmed trying to keep apace with the new strains of poison. But through a working relationship with the Centers for Disease Control, Tipler also joined the crusade, synthesizing over a dozen effective anti-venoms over the past decade. Nor did he find it distracting. Although he was an increasingly sought-after author, lecturer, and researcher, his greatest pleasure remained the simple pursuit of biological science.

From time to time, however, agencies not academic had sought his aid. And he had assisted. Once the Central Intelligence Agency had requested that he do what their physicists could not; develop a counteracting agent for a deadly poison in use by Middle Eastern countries. Tipler had succeeded and consequently heard no more of it. And last, the U.S. Army had asked him, rather sternly, if he could not identify a substance in their own anti-germ warfare serums that tended to incapacitate soldiers. In this, too, Tipler was successful, and modifications were made in the synthesis of the serums. Again, he heard no more of it. Yet he knew they would return, as they had.

A thin smile creased his squared face.

Before him, he knew from his World War II days as an infantryman, was an army lieutenant colonel, whose rank he identified from the silver oak leaves on his uniform. There was another man in uniform, a major, and an unknown representative who wore nondescript civilian clothes. But, as always, it was the man in civilian clothes who commanded Tipler's attention, for he was accustomed to subterfuge. Tipler greeted them as the man in the rear silently lit a cigarette, settling into a chair.

"Dr. Tipler, I'm Lieutenant Colonel Bob Maddox," the short, gray-haired man said distinctly. "This is Major Preston Westcott. And that "— the colonel gestured vaguely—" is Mr. Dixon. He's a liaison with the Department of the Interior."

Tipler smiled as he weighed the colonel; the army officer carried himself with an air of indisputable authority, as if his self-worth relied upon his rank. His insignia were so highly polished they couldn't be overlooked, even by civilians. His face was slightly pudgy and his stomach strained against his uniform. He held his hands behind his back as he spoke. "Thank you for seeing us on such short notice, Doctor. I assure you that we won't take up too much of your time."

Something in the voice intimated to Dr. Tipler that he had no choice in the matter, but he revealed nothing as he moved to sit at a table directly opposite the mysterious Mr. Dixon. "Oh, I am always ready to assist the military, Colonel," he said with exacting courtesy. "In fact, as you are probably aware, I just finished working with an army research team to design new protocols for Arctic survival. So please, continue."

Maddox was obviously in charge, Tipler realized, and Prescott was present to verify the meeting or take mental notes. He hadn't yet concluded a purpose for Dixon.

"That's part of the reason we're here—your experience in the Arctic. We also understand that you're the world's leading authority on crypto-zoology." Maddox strolled before the table. "So we hoped you'd be able to help us with ... a situation."

Tipler decided to play their game for now. He did not look at Mr. Dixon. "Perhaps," he replied casually.

Clearly, Maddox was proceeding with caution. "Doctor, we would like to ask you some questions about species of predators found in the Arctic Circle. Specifically, species that inhabit the deep interior of Alaska and the North Face region." He stepped forward, almost delicately. "Recently we lost several members of an elite military training squad to an animal. They were killed. And we want to determine what manner of animal it was."

Tipler absorbed it without expression.

"Surely," Tipler said finally, "Alaskan wildlife officials can be of more use to you than an old gaffer such as myself. And I am not certain in what aspect my credentials in crypto-zoology are related. Crypto-zoology is the study of animals long presumed to be extinct but which are, in fact, not. Such as some of the marine reptiles like the one the Japanese fishing vessel, the Zuiyo Mam, snagged on a line nine hundred feet below the surface of the Pacific near Christchurch, New Zealand, in 1977. Or," Tipler could not resist adding, "perhaps like the beast of unknown species that attacked the U.S.S. Stern in the early 'eighties, disabling its sonar system with hundreds of teeth driven deeply in the steel. It was documented with the Department of the Navy and the ship was examined by the Naval Oceans Center. They reached the fascinating conclusion that damage to the sonar was caused by the attack of a large and unknown ocean-dwelling species."

Maddox stood in silence. His face tightened. "Yes, Doctor. We are aware of those incidents. It is certainly verification of... something. But those cases are not why we have come."

"I presumed." Tipler smiled. "So, shall we get to the reason? I am a bit overwhelmed by my work."

Gravely, even apprehensively, Maddox laid a gory series of full-sized color photographs on the table. And Tipler precisely set glasses on his nose, leaning on broad hands to examine them. So total was his concentration, it was as if, in seconds, he had physically removed himself from the room.

The old man made no sound as he studied the photographs, but his brow hardened frame by frame. His lips pursed slightly and he began to take more time with each, returning often to the first, beginning over. Finally he lifted a single eight-by-ten and studied it inches from his face, peering at the details. "Colonel," he said, casting a slow gaze over the massacred bodies. "These wounds, were they all inflicted by the same creature?"

There was no hesitation. "Yes."

"You are certain of this?"

"Yes, Doctor, we are certain."

"And how can you be certain? In science, certainty is determined by exceedingly strict criteria."

Maddox grimaced slightly. "There were obscured video images. Nothing too revealing, but it gave us glimpses of whatever this was. We couldn't make out the species. And, despite what I said earlier, we can't be, uh, absolutely certain on whether it was one or two of them. It's just that the evidence, except for some of these photographs, seems to indicate that."

Without reply, Tipler shifted several of the photographs of massacred soldiers until he had the most vivid, the ghastliest. He placed a hand on it and touched the image of wounds as delicately as if the soldier were before him. Finally, he mumbled, "This is not the work of Ursus arctos horribilis."

Clearly, Maddox was trying to be patient. "Could you be more specific, Doctor?"

"This is not the work of a ... a Grizzly." Tipler was again staring at the photo he had lifted, a close-up image of tracks leading across hard sand. The elongated footprints moved in a straight run down a strand to disappear in the distance, but some of the tracks were disjointed, as far as three feet to the side. It was not a straight line of tracks, though clearly the creature had been running straight. Rocks littered the stream.

"Now ... " the old man continued in a genuine tone of confusion, "this is somewhat curious."

"What?" Maddox asked.

"The way that the tracks are broken."

"That's what our own trackers said, Doctor. I mean, despite the cameras, we want to know about this. Do you think there could be two of them?"

Tipler took a long time to consider. "I am not an expert in tracking, Colonel Maddox. I cannot say. But I do not think that there were two creatures involved in this ... this catastrophe."

"Then how do you explain the way some tracks are so far to the side from others?"

"As I said, sir, I cannot explain such a phenomenon."

Maddox concentrated. "You're certain this isn't the work of a Grizzly, Doctor? Or maybe a polar bear? A tiger, maybe?"

"No, not a Grizzly, nor a brown bear," the professor expounded in a low tone. "For one matter, a Grizzly has five claws. And whatever did this had four predominant claws, and a smaller one. But the paw print is distinctly ...humanoid. Now this," he paused, "is damn peculiar." A long silence lengthened. "No, gentlemen, not a bear of any kind. Perhaps a tiger could have caused this much carnage to your team, but the tracks are ... just ... they just appear to me to be somewhat too manlike. In fact, *far* too manlike."

"But clearly no human being could do something like this, Doctor." Dixon spoke for the first time.

Tipler raised his eyes, gazing over bifocals. "I would not make a determination of any fact until I had obtained the information necessary to make the determination of that fact, Mr. Dixon." He smiled. "That is the discipline of science."

Dixon leaned back, smoked in silence.

The army officials were, indeed, leaning forward as Tipler raised a magnifying glass from his pocket, studying the photograph more closely. Finally he lowered it with the glass, but continued to stare profoundly. His voice was quiet. "These tracks ... how far did your men follow them, gentlemen?"

"Why?" Maddox asked.

"Because they do not 'register.' "

"Register?" the colonel asked. "What does that mean?"

"They ... they are not in line." The scientist gestured. "A tiger, which is the only terrestrial beast that could have struck with such fury, registers when it walks or runs. Which is to say that both paws on the left side are in a line, as they are on the right. There should be two paw prints set closely together, in a straight line, left side and right side. And, clearly, they are not the tracks of a Grizzly, though they resemble one in size."

"Yes," Maddox said. "Our military trackers told us that. But they lost the trail when it moved to high ground. They said no one can track across rock. This animal seemed to know it was being hunted."

"Most creatures are more intelligent than we presume, Colonel," Tipler replied, casting a narrow glance at Dixon, who was smoking quietly. "No," Tipler added finally. "It was not a tiger. The fury of the attack is commensurate with a tiger, but it is not feline or canine. Nor is a larger species of Ursus. No. Whatever did this ... was distinctly bipedal."

They waited, but the old man merely placed his glasses back in his lab coat pocket. Then he bridged his fingers, capping them, allowing them to continue the conversation.

"Bipedal?" Dixon asked without friendliness. "Does that mean what I think it means?"

"Quite probably," Tipler smiled. "It means that whatever killed your men walks on two legs, Mr. Dixon."

"That's preposterous." Dixon leaned back again. "Humans are the only animal that walks on two legs, Doctor. What do you suggest left these tracks? *Bigfoot*? This thing must have been registering! It's just that the tracks are too difficult to read."

"Difficult, yes," Tipler scowled. "But not impossible. Is that why you called me here? Because your men have already told you that they know of no creature that could have done this? And now you wish to know if, perhaps, there is an undiscovered species?"

"To be honest, I'll admit it occurred to us," Maddox replied. "And let me add that this is a situation of some seriousness, Doctor. We've got dead soldiers near secure facilities and we want to know how they died. We want to know why they died."

Tipler gazed over the photos of carnage. "I cannot give you the answer, gentlemen," he said finally. "There were species of beasts that are presumed to have been exterminated hundreds of thousands of years ago, yet we still find evidence of their continuing existence. But I am not familiar with this paw print, or footprint." He paused and strolled a short distance away before turning back. "In order to answer your question—to even attempt to answer your question—we would need a scientific expedition, saliva samples, blood samples, plaster casts of the prints, hair samples, video surveillance records. If you are willing to fund an expedi-"

"We can't do that." Dixon stood up. "There are factors which preclude that option. We just wanted your best opinion, Doctor." He paused for effect. "We still do."

Tipler held the stare.

"My best opinion, Mr. Dixon, is that whatever did this has the strength of a Grizzly, the speed of a Siberian tiger and, quite probably, the stalking skills of a tiger. Which happens to be the most skilled predator on Earth. Further, if it managed to evade the initial pursuit of your military, I would confidently surmise that it has unnatural intelligence."

"So," Maddox asked, asserting some kind of vague authority, "what do you think it is? I want your best guess."

Tipler sighed once more and glanced at a photo of the tracks. "Your best guess will be revealed by these tracks, Mr. Dixon. But I don't understand why some of them"—he pointed at several—"are so far to the left of these others. It makes no sense that I can see."

They exchanged glances as the old man stared over them. Then, after a moment, they began wordlessly gathering papers.

"Will you be hunting this beast again?" the scientist asked, interested.

"Yes," Maddox replied solidly. "We will."

"Then I suggest you find a man who can possibly track it," said Tipler.

He hesitated, as if scientific passion and personal loyalty were competing with something more hidden, staring at the photograph.

"I know the man," he said softly, "who could do this? If anyone could. But I do not know if he will cooperate. He has his own reasons ... for why he does things."

Maddox stepped forward. "Who is he?"

Tipler stared slightly to the side, brow furrowed.

"His name," he said finally, "is Nathaniel Hunter."

CHAPTER 2

The sunset breeze carried a sweet tang of mountain laurel. Nathaniel Hunter was emptying his simple leather pack onto the table. The door of his cabin was wide open, allowing the green sound of rushing water to move over him. And yet it wasn't sound, but a sudden silence, that made him lift his head.

Where there had been a communicative chorus of bird surrounding his backwoods home, there was now an unnatural quiet. He turned to stare out the door, listened, and heard a car coming slowly up the one-lane dirt road. It was still a mile away.

It took them more than ten minutes to arrive. He met them on the porch wearing old blue jeans, a leather shirt, and knee-high moccasins.

One of the contingent—a portly army colonel—spoke first. But it was the man in civilian clothes, standing in the rear that drew Hunter's sullen attention. Quiet but close, the man was dressed in a suit you would have forgotten without even trying, and dark sunglasses protected his eyes from any probing. Hands clasped behind him, he followed the others like a schoolteacher ensuring that the students perform the assigned task. It was clear who was truly in charge.

"I am Lieutenant Colonel Maddox of the United States Army," said the man in uniform. "We would like to speak with Nathaniel Hunter, if that's possible."

"I'm Hunter," he said, his voice low.

"Well." The colonel stepped forward, an ingratiating smile on his lips.

"We'd just like to get your opinion on some photographs, if you don't mind. Of course, if there is a problem, we can arrange a more formal appointment."

Hunter took his time before turning toward the door, motioning vaguely. "Come into the cabin," he said.

It took only a few minutes for them to recount their story of blood and death in the snow. Then they displayed a series of photographs on the cabin's crude wooden table. They wanted his best guess as to what the killer was, they said, and they wanted to know if there was more than one of them. Hunter bent over the photographs and studied them for a moment. His eyes narrowed as he examined the tracks, as well as the terrain.

Maddox began, "We want to know why these tracks here are so far from the others."

"Wind," Hunter said simply.

Hunter heard the man introduced as Dixon step forward. But Maddox only stared as he said, "Excuse me, did you say 'wind'?"

"Yeah." Hunter had expected this confusion. "These tracks to the side were in a straight line with these others. But the wind moved them, inch by inch. The other tracks weren't moved because they were shielded from the northeastern breeze by this boulder."

Maddox seemed astounded. "Wind can do that?"

Hunter pointed to the tracks. "These to the side were originally over here, like the others. You can see the gap that was left when they were moved. The wind just edged them to where they are here." He shrugged, gave the picture to Maddox. "It's a common phenomenon on sand like this. Is that what you wanted to know?"

"Uh." Maddox started. "Uh, actually, no. We wanted you to—"

A sudden, silent atmospheric change in the cabin stopped him short. It was as if the room had been instantly charged with a primal force, something utterly savage. Hunter watched as Maddox slowly turned his head. He almost smiled at the nervous expression on Dixon's face as he began to sense what was behind him. Slowly, moving only his head, Dixon managed to look down stiffly. Hunter saw sweat glisten suddenly on his forehead.

Massive and menacing, Ghost stood less than a foot behind Dixon and Maddox, slightly to the side. The gigantic wolf was almost entirely black, touched with gray only on his flanks.

Ghost's jet-black eyes seemed to possess a primal and predatory glow. Black claws clicked on the wooden floor as he took a single pace forward, head low, again unmoving. Ghost's uncanny silence seemed more terrifying than a roar.

Hunter made them suffer for only a moment. With a slight smile he snapped his fingers.

"Ghost," he said.

The wolf glided innocently through the men and sat beside Hunter.

Hunter spoke politely. "You were saying, Colonel?"

Maddox had trouble speaking. "I, uh, I was saying that...uh, we wanted you to help us with ... with ... something."

Hunter smiled at the trembling tone and noticed that Major Prescott's fists were clenched. All of them were sweating, and Maddox's face was pasty, whitening by the moment. He knew this would take all day with Ghost in the room. He looked down, speaking so low that none of the others could catch the word.

"Outside," he said.

Treading with an air of shocking animal might, the wolf moved fearlessly through the three of them. Then it reached the door and angled away, disappearing with haunting silence and grace. The air silently trembled with the wildness, the power, the very scent of it as it was gone. But Hunter knew Ghost would remain close, just as he knew they wouldn't see the wolf again—not ever—unless it wanted them to.

"Good Lord," whispered Maddox as he took out a handkerchief, wiping his face. "Is that ... is that your dog?"

"He's a wolf."

"Yes ... yes, of course." The colonel cast a nervous eye to the doorway and involuntarily backed up. "But ... but what does it do?"

Hunter stared, almost laughed, but suppressed it; there was no need to mock them, even incidentally. They weren't at home in his world, though he had managed to become both prosperous and respected in theirs. He added, "He does whatever he wants to do, I guess. He comes, he goes."

"I mean, do you own him?" Maddox added. "Is he trained? Does he always come and go like that?" All three of the men had repositioned themselves so they could keep an eye on the door.

Hunter half-shrugged. "No, he's not trained, Colonel. And nobody owns him. He comes when he wants. Goes when he wants."

"But ... but how much does the thing weigh?" Maddox asked. "I didn't think wolves got so ... so huge."

"That depends on bloodline," Hunter answered, continuing to unpack. "Most male wolves go a hundred or so. Ghost is about a hundred and fifty, more or less. He won't get much bigger."

Maddox began to recover degree by degree and Hunter tried to move it along. He knew they were still dancing around the central issue. He continued quietly. "Now, gentlemen, if you're ready to talk, maybe we can get down to why you wanted to see me. What do you want?"

Fortifying himself, Maddox stepped forward. He pointed at the photographs of slaughtered soldiers.

"We want to know," Maddox said in a stronger tone, "what kind of creature could have done this? What kind of creature could have walked through an entire platoon like this, killing such heavily armed men?"

Frowning slightly, Hunter shifted the photos and finally shook his head. "Maybe a Grizzly," he muttered, but with obvious uncertainty. "But I doubt it."

"Why do you doubt it?"

"Because a Grizzly will usually maul its victim," Hunter answered, more certain. "It'll hit over and over, tear off your scalp, your face. And whatever did this struck once, maybe twice, with each kill." He pointed at a photo. "This man was killed with one blow. So whatever did this didn't attack out of fear or rage." He paused, eyes narrowing. "Whatever did this ...had a reason."

"But what animal would ... I mean, what animal could do something like this for a reason?"

Hunter shook his head. "I don't know."

"But aren't you supposed to be an expert on—"

"Colonel," Hunter cut him off, "I don't consider myself an expert in anything at all. I just do what I do, the best way I can do it. And I don't think I can help you. I can't tell you what killed your men." He waited; they were stoically silent. "I can say, however, that whatever killed these men didn't kill for food. It didn't kill out of defense. And it didn't kill to defend territory."

"Like a tiger might have done?"

"It's not a tiger."

"But how can you be certain?" Maddox was openly disturbed. "You just said that you're not certain what did this."

"Because these men were attacked on level ground with open field all around them." Hunter was relaxed and certain. "Tigers don't do that. They'll attack from an elevated position or from ambush. A tiger will never put itself in a position where it might have to chase prey. They don't chase."

"Tigers won't chase prey? Why?"

Hunter shrugged, went back to removing equipment from his pack. "No one knows. Instinct, maybe. Maybe because they're so heavy. But if a tiger doesn't catch you within three or four bounds, you're probably a free man."

Struck by a stray thought, he pointed vaguely to a grainy photo. "See these tracks?" he continued. "This ... thing ... was moving fast, and in a straight line. It's as if ... I don't know ... as if it was trying to reach something." Drawn to direction of his own words, Hunter studied several photos, quickly arranging them in a new order. "Do you see this? All of these men went down in sequence. It moved through them, killing quick and moving to the next, always headed in the same direction." For a long time he paused. When he spoke again, his voice was flat. "I'm not sure that this is an animal."

Slowly Dixon stepped forward, almost indulgent. "Mr. Hunter, this has got to be an animal. Certainly, and this should go without saying, no human being could have done this."

"Believe what you want." Hunter was unaffected. "But I've never seen an animal that killed like this. Animals have reasons, like fear or rage or defense, when they kill. And there's no evidence of that here. Not that I can see. It didn't maul, which would indicate anger. It didn't eat. It just killed and moved on to the next victim." With a faintly fatigued sign, he stood back. "You wanted my best guess, gentlemen. That's it."

"What about the tracks?" Dixon pressed. "You're certain they're not bear tracks?"

"No, they're not bear tracks. They're not even close. Your own people can tell you that." Hunter stared at him. "In fact, if I had to make a determination, I'd say they were human."

Dixon blinked. "Have you ever seen an animal leave tracks like this?"

"No."

"Never?"

"No."

Dixon seemed slightly agitated, but cast a quick glance to the door. "Look, Mr. Hunter," he began, "we were told that you're an expert at tracking. And please don't tell me you're not. We've checked you out."

Hunter laughed soundlessly.

"Yeah, we do that with everyone," Dixon continued, as if he'd seen the expression a thousand times. "Nathaniel Hunter. Grew up in the wilds of Wyoming. Your father died before you were born and an old trapper and a Sioux Indian woman raised you. The trapper taught you to track when you were just a kid, and you're supposed to be the best in the world. Some kind of legend. They say you can track a ghost through fog, and you've been used by police departments to find kids lost in wilderness areas when everyone else has failed. And that you've located animals so on the brink of extermination that there were only a handful left. Then, when you were twenty, you found a tree in the Amazon that provided a better treatment for spinal meningitis. You sold it to a pharmaceutical company for about twenty million. And since then you've discovered a dozen plants that provide antibodies against various bacterial infections. Yeah, and I know this old shack isn't your only place. You have a penthouse in New York filled with about twenty million in art and rare books, a place in Paris that rivals the Smithsonian for rare artifacts. You go wherever you want, do whatever you want. Got a private jet on standby at JFK Airport and high friends in high places in both government and private business. You're the money behind the Tipler Institute." Dixon shook his head.

"You're a kick in the head, Hunter. You've got all that damn money and you hardly spend a dime on yourself. All those luxury spots of yours sit empty while you spend most of your time at this old shack." He grunted. "You're an interesting guy, all right, but the one thing everybody agrees about is that you're some kind of wilderness guru. So surely you have some clue of what this might be. Even if it's just a suspicion."

Hunter held Dixon's stare, not bothering to look friendly. "I've already studied them, Dixon," he said. "They're vaguely like a bear but the tracks are badly marred and mulled, so it's hard to tell. And then this thing is bipedal, so it doesn't move like a bear when it's either running or loping or walking. This thing, whatever it is, probably weighs about three hundred, and it's right-handed. It looks to the right a lot and pauses about every fifty feet. It's hunched when it moves, as if it's stalking. And when it turns it pivots both feet at the same time. When it kills it tends to strike from right to left, placing its weight on its left front leg, like a boxer."

A stunned silence.

Maddox was the first to speak. "You can tell all that from those photographs?"

Hunter nodded.

"But ... how?"

Hunter waved a hand at the photos. "Sideheading, dulling and compression, pressure release marks, wave and pitch, curving. Simple things, Colonel."

"But our pathfinders, our trackers ...they couldn't tell us all that."

Hunter sighed. "Well, I'm sure that your people are good, Colonel. But that's what I see. You can take it or leave it."

Maddox said nothing for a moment, turning and strolling across the room, cupping his chin. He seemed to be pondering. After a moment he looked at Dixon. "Mr. Dixon, I'd like a word with you," he said. "In private."

Dixon, black glasses concealing his eyes even here, held Hunter's stare for a long moment before he turned away, walking across the room. Hunter leaned against the table and watched them whisper. He didn't know what they were discussing but he had an idea. He had no plans to cooperate.

"Mr. Hunter." Maddox walked back slowly. Clearly, he was attempting to phrase his words carefully. "I would like to make a request, and I would like for you to genuinely consider it before you reply." He lifted his face, honest for all Hunter could tell.

He nodded. "Go ahead."

"This, uh, this situation," Maddox continued, "is not exactly what it seems. I'm sure you consider it to be a tragedy that our soldiers were killed. And remember, these were all good men. Men with families. But there is more to it than that."

Hunter said nothing.

"In truth, Mr. Hunter, this creature, whatever it is, has killed many times in the past three days—mostly military personnel, bodies that we can conceal, in a sense. But it seems to be headed south. And soon, if it continues on its current course, it will reach a populated civilian area."

"Why can't you find this creature by triangulating infrared signatures from satellite?" Hunter asked. "The technology exists for a hunt like this through the global imaging system. Seems like you could isolate its heat signature."

"We're not fools, Mr. Hunter. We've tried that. But there is an abundance—an overabundance—of large animal life in that area. There's moose, bear, elk, wolf, so many creatures that tracking by heat signature is futile. What we need is someone who can track this one, specific creature. Because if it reaches a populated civilian area, I am not certain how successful we will be in containing it. Tens, perhaps hundreds of people would die." Maddox raised his hands, almost plaintively. "Now, I realize that you're not under, nor have you ever submitted to, military command. Nor, should you decline, can I compel you against your will to assist. But I am asking you as a man—as an honorable man—to help us. I am asking you to help us track this thing down. I'm asking you ... to help us kill it."

Hunter absorbed it awhile in silence.

"Your people aren't sufficient?" he asked.

"No," Maddox replied flatly. They've already tried and they failed. In fact, they died. The results were ...discouraging, to say the least."

Hunter stared at nothing, said nothing for a long time.

"We have a killing team assembled," the colonel continued. "You need not be involved in that aspect. If you can only track this creature through those mountains, somehow give our people an opportunity to confront it, then your job will be done. You will be present as an observer. And the team that we have assembled is extremely proficient. You will be quite safe. In fact, it may be the safest action you've undertaken in some time. One other thing we learned was that you are a man prone to taking risks."

Hunter rose slowly, turned away.

He stared out the window and searched the surrounding tree-line, already dark. And he half-scanned for Ghost but knew the wolf would remain invisible unless he wanted to be seen. Yet he would be there, un-moving, waiting, listening to every word. And if Hunter were attacked, the great black image of pure animal fury would roar into the cabin like a storm with flashing fangs and claws, and God help anything mortal that got in his way. Somehow Hunter knew he had already made the decision but he waited, sensing something that troubled him.

"All right," he said finally. "But for this I'll need Ghost."

A pause.

"Whatever you want," Maddox said, nervousness entering his voice at the mere mention of the wolf.

"And I won't submit to military command or authority." Hunter turned back with the words. "If I lead the track, then I'm the one that leads. Nobody countermands my decisions or my methods. This is gonna be hard enough as it is. I don't want someone who doesn't understand what I do trying to give me orders."

"Of course not. I will ensure your authority in certain areas. This ...this support team will be present only for the confrontation."

Hunter turned away again, staring into a slowly gathering dark. He could tell from the air that a cold front was coming, rain not far behind. But there was something else, something that continued to hover over him—a premonition.

He felt it, but couldn't identify it. Yet he had made his decision, realizing that, if innocent lives were truly compromised by a creature as obviously powerful as this, there was really no choice.

"Set it up," he said, low. "Let me know."

Maddox swayed. "Good. Just be aware this is going to happen soon. Perhaps as early as tomorrow."

"That's fine," Hunter said, glancing at Dixon one last time.

Utterly concealed, Dixon's eyes were reflectionless pools of black, revealing nothing. And Hunter sensed rather than read the faintest apparition of a smile on the haggard face. And he knew that whatever disturbed him was hidden in that darkness.

CHAPTER 3

It's where the map ends; an unforgiving, heavily forested frontier of permafrost, tundra, glacier and air that froze skin at the touch. Hunter had been here once before, and knew it was an easy place to die.

Countless hikers, adventurers, and even native Alaskans had lost their lives in the merciless terrain of the Brooks Range. And Hunter didn't underestimate its brutality. He knew that it was through respect and caution that a man stayed alive in these mountains. And a lack of either would have only one outcome; the land was littered with legends of those who failed to heed advice and went unprepared into the high country, never to be seen again.

Hunter knew what equipment was essential for the average trapper or camper: a large-caliber scoped rifle, a shotgun, plenty of ammunition for both, an oversupply of preserved food, an ax, hatchet, sheath knife and a smaller folding blade for skinning, a tent, topographical map of the areas with federal emergency stations marked, a compass, rope, rain slick, matches and flint for making fires, a ball of leather twine, emergency medical equipment, grain for two pack mules and a horse, and a radio.

But Hunter traveled light, trusting his life to his skills. He never challenged the forces of nature, he respected them. But he knew he could effortlessly live off the land for weeks at a time and could improvise shelter in even the most hostile weather. So he carried all he needed in a compact belt rig that rested at the small of his back. He also had a pouch on a leather strap that went over a shoulder in the style of ancient Apaches. Inside it he carried air-dried beef jerky, herbal pastes for either cooking or wounds, a compass and map, and lesser-known tricks of the trade for tracking—chalk, a marking stick, pebbles.

He had a single canteen on his right side, though he rarely used it because he would drink at almost every stream, knowing dehydration was a lightning-fast killer this high. A large, finely-honed Bowie knife and hatchet were on his belt and he carried extra cartridges on the strap of the un-scoped Marlin 45.70 lever-action rifle that he carried over his shoulder.

He wore wool pants, a leather shirt and jacket, and knee-high moccasins lined with goose down, and carried no other clothes. The extra insulation in the moccasins would protect his feet against the cold, dry quickly, and allow him to move soundlessly. And he always wore leather while tracking because, unlike polyester or cotton, it made almost no sound when it scraped branches or leaves.

Long ago, inspired by an idea he'd obtained from studying ancient Aztec priests, he had sewn a double hood for the shoulders of his jacket. The lower layer protected his shoulders from rain. The upper layer, descending over his broad shoulders like a short cape, could be drawn up in a hood to prevent excessive heat loss from his head, which accounted for sixty percent of heat loss in the open air. It was a unique and functional design, and Hunter had learned from experience that a hood was indispensable in frigid temperatures.

Traveling so light, he resembled an early American frontier scout—an appearance made all the more apparent when contrasted to the high-tech profile and weaponry of the Special Response Squads he often worked beside.

For shelter and food he would simply live off nature. He would forage as he went, kill quickly and efficiently when necessary, but always moving. At night he would take fifteen minutes to rig a simple but effective fish trap in a stream which would capture a half dozen mountain trout for breakfast before morning. The fish that he didn't immediately eat he would eat as hunger came on him through the day. From years of practice he had discovered that it was a simple, effective means of traveling quickly across cold, high country.

He assumed that this mysterious military team would bear the standard forty pounds of survival gear necessary for Arctic survival. In general, that included a load-bearing vest, or LBV, probably armored with Kevlar. Then they would have a small backpack that held individual water purifiers, cold-weather tents, Arctic sleeping bags, extra clothes and socks, de-hydrated food, propane ovens, field radios and microphones, night-vision equipment, teargas, and flares, as well as bionic listening devices—either those worn as earphones or the laser-guided sort for pinpointing distant disturbance.

In addition to that, they would be heavily armed with a variety of weapons from M-16's to Benelli shotguns and MH-40 cylindrical grenade launchers. And, doubtless, they would rely upon the Magellan Global Positioning System for orientation—a fist-sized device that triangulated off satellites to provide exact location, accurate to within six feet. It was standard equipment for maneuvers.

Hunter was familiar with the technology and had used it himself. But it was still a machine, and machines could break down in primitive conditions. So he preferred to rely upon a map and compass and had cultivated his skills at dead reckoning so that he could accurately navigate using only the sun and stars, or nothing at all.

But Hunter knew that the most essential ingredient for survival in this land wasn't something so simple as equipment: it was mindset. For it was all too easy to panic when disaster struck and there was no one to rely upon for assistance.

He had learned long ago, mostly by necessity, to be supremely self-reliant under any circumstance. And up here there would be no substitute for a lack of strength or willpower.

He remembered a conversation he had with a grizzled old trapper during his first trip to Alaska. As he was preparing to venture into the mountains, he asked the old man if it was possible to survive a winter in the mountains with only a knife and rifle. Experienced with the lethal brutality of the wilderness, the trapper had taken a surprisingly long time to reply.

"Well," he said finally, turning a weathered face, "I reckon it could be done." His tone indicated that he had no intention of trying. "But you'd have to have Injun in you. You'd have to be an animal. 'Cause there ain't no God nor mercy up there, boy. Damn sure ain't." He paused. "When I go up high, I got my horse and two pack mules, 'cause a mule is worth any three horses in them woods. I break camp late and set up early, and I don't break at all if it looks like a hard cold might be settin in." He chewed a toothpick. "You ain't planning to try nuthin' like that, are ya?"

"No," Hunter assured him. "Just asking."

The old man nodded slowly and pointed toward the mountains. "The big ol' Out There ain't no place for a human bein', son. I seen some go in and winter it out, and them that made it home ... well, they wudn't the same. It changes a man, more ways 'an one."

Hunter knew the words were true.

There were few areas in the world as brutal with rain and cold, and as unforgiving of fools. He knew that if he was injured and forced to survive in those mountains for months, sheer determination would be his greatest ally. Pain could be ignored but any wound must be very carefully tended. Just as food would have to be attentively protected and harbored; it would be endless work to stay alive.

Patience and discipline would be vital, as would whatever tenuous grip he managed to maintain on his sanity. Although under the current conditions of this trip there would be little chance of a disaster, he had learned to always be prepared: conditions, no matter how certain they seem, could change completely and without warning.

As Hunter surfaced from his thoughts he was suddenly aware of the dull thundering engines of the military C-141, its four huge jet engines roaring outside the fuselage.

He smiled at the sudden awareness, for absolute concentration to the point of ignoring everything else was a faculty he had unconsciously perfected. And it was a vital skill when he was tracking.

Amazingly, although Hunter could effortlessly ignore a loud conversation directly behind him, he could simultaneously pick up the whispered clicks of a woodlark a quarter mile away. To the uninitiated, the sound would mean nothing, but it could tell Hunter what the bird was experiencing, what it was looking at, whether it was searching for its mate or just frightened, and of what.

For instance, the woodlark, more than any bird, hated water snakes like cottonmouths. So when a viper was moving in the water the woodlark would virtually set the forest on fire with that distinctive, hysterical high-pitched cry—a sound far different from its other songs and calls.

And, just as Hunter could identify the call to know that a snake was moving close, he knew that particular snakes would not be moving at all during certain times of the day unless something was forcing them. So, in a thousand ways similar to this, the forest could tell you about hidden movement and unseen activity. One had only to know the language of the forest, the native calls of the wild.

Ghost, sleeping soundly, lay beside him on a tarp and Hunter reached out to caress the wolf's thick mane.

Military officials had refused to allow Ghost among the other passengers, fearing the massive wolf's potential for violence if, for some reason, he decided to demonstrate his prowess. And, rather than engage them in a doomed debate, Hunter elected to travel in the cargo hold with what he knew was his closest and most loyal friend.

He remembered when he had found Ghost. The wolf was only three weeks old, and his sire, an enormous gray wolf, had been killed by poachers, along with the mother and siblings.

Though wounded by a bullet graze, Ghost had survived by hiding beneath a deadfall, buried deep beneath tons of logs. Starving, sick and wounded, the cub would have died within days but Hunter coaxed him out with a piece of raw meat and carried him back to the cabin.

It was a month before the malnourished cub could clamber around the three-room structure, but after that he grew rapidly, eventually surpassing the strength and size of his gigantic father. Yet it was his spirit that caught Hunter's early attention and made him laugh; something he rarely did.

Hunter had never attempted to train him, but the wolf's keen intelligence was evident from the first moments. Without being taught, Ghost knew where to find food, how to communicate his needs, when he wanted to go outside. And his curiosity was endless, as was his unconcealed joy every time Hunter returned from a trip.

When he was six months old Hunter let him sleep on the porch, sheltered by a fairly luxurious doghouse that Hunter built from spare lumber. Hunter filled the bottom with a thick layer of straw and an old blanket and installed a heat lamp for cold nights, but he never leashed the wolf. If Ghost wished to leave, he was free to go.

For endless nights Hunter went to bed knowing Ghost was staring and listening to the calls of the wild, summoned by the wolf packs that surrounded the cabin. And then when Ghost was two years old, near full size, he began disappearing for days at a time, often returning with bloody wounds—slash marks of other wolves.

Hunter suspected that during the nocturnal forays, Ghost had declared his own dominion over a part of the forest—of which the cabin was the heart. And after those nights, Hunter distinctly noticed, the surrounding howls of wolf packs came from a far greater distance. Ghost had, alone, won his territory.

His relationship with Ghost had not so much developed as it seemed to flourish full-born. And Hunter suspected it was because he himself had never been close to anyone or anything, except perhaps the old trapper who half-raised him. Just as Ghost had never really had a family. So it came naturally and easily that each had simply accepted the other, each of them needing someone.

In fact, Hunter had mostly raised himself, spending long endless days trapping and tracking, living more like an animal than a child. Before he was ten years old he could see a single track and identify the species, the size, how old it was, and where it was going. He could lift his head and find the scent of what had passed this way hours ago, or make shelters that would keep him warm in frigid winter nights. At twelve he could snatch fish from a stream with his hand, or silently sneak up on a deer so that he could touch its flank before it could sense his presence. Yet it was not until he was sixteen that he did what every true tracker considers the ultimate challenge. It had been a misty summer night, and he had come upon a slumbering Grizzly, laid his hand softly on its massive side, and then stolen away, having never awakened it.

Sometimes, lying in the somber light of the cabin with Ghost beside him, Hunter remembered the days when he would spend more time in the wild, alone and living—truly living—than among people. He remembered how, as a child, the white look of bone would catch his eye in the bright light of day, and even now the fascination felt fresh. He could still feel the coarseness of red dirt as he sifted it from the white pitted relic of bear or elk or wolverine.

He remembered how he would craft barbaric ornaments and necklaces of bear claws or wolverine fangs, looking not unlike a long-haired ten-year-old wild child of prehistoric Homo sapiens as he walked half-naked out of the forest. The thoughts made him laugh; he ruffled Ghost's mane.

Hunter made no demands—Ghost knew he was free—but they were each other's ally. And, in time, Ghost had taken to sleeping inside the cabin again, sometimes clambering slowly and massively into Hunter's bed in the middle of the night to lay a paw as wide as a plate on Hunter's chest. Or sometimes Hunter would simply awaken to feel Ghost's nose at his throat; the wolf checking to ensure he was all right.

House patrol, Hunter called it with a laugh. But he realized it was only once in a lifetime that a man found an animal he truly loved, just as he knew he could never replace the great wolf. But, then, Ghost was only three years old, and would live a long time.

In a sense, Hunter regretted bringing him on this trip. But he knew that in the harsh terrain of that hostile interior he would need every advantage. Because, while he himself could be deceived, it would be much more difficult for this thing—whatever it was— to deceive Ghost. Together, Hunter thought, they stood a good chance of tracking this thing to ground before it reached more innocent victims.

Before it killed again.

As he knew it would.

***

In darkness ... no, not darkness, he awoke.

He wasn't naked, as he had anticipated. But he was shirtless, and his boots were gone. The prickly green of forest was beneath him and the deserted shade thick, almost gloom, as he slowly rose. He touched his head, feeling, and noticed nothing amiss; no alteration, no transformation. But he knew what it ...what he ...had done.

What he had become.

He laughed.

Memories of last night were like an unfocused, scarlet-lit dream. But he recalled the visions much better than before; the sight of men running wildly across his perfect red-tinted vision, screams that roared with flame. He remembered how he could visually register the body heat caused by their stark terror, could palpably scent and taste their horror as he struck, and struck, and killed, moving through them to slay without effort. And in the long quenching slaughter he had found bestial pleasure in the power much, much more than before. He realized that he was gaining with each transformation, becoming stronger, purer.

The first transformation, brought about by his maniacal violation of procedure, had been a shocking and painful experience—a black blazing maze of taloned hands sweeping laboratory equipment aside and devastating whatever or whoever had been unfortunate enough to encounter his fury. Yet there had also been addictive exultation in the pure animal pleasure, fed with adrenaline and lust, and a thirst that was quenched only with killing. It had lasted long, and longer, bringing him on that tide of bestial might into the next day when it faded and he fell, leaving him alone among the dead in a facility in ruin and aflame.

He understood now that, yes, his risky experimentation had been a success. He had not expected to take on the fullness of the creature, not in feature and form. But he did not regret it, though he felt somehow that he was losing more and more of his personal identity—whatever he could be called—as the infection continued. Just the glory, the triumph of possessing such bestial supremacy made him feel like a lion among sheep. Yes he had been successful, no matter the unintended after-effects that seemed to become more progressive with each transformation.

He laughed as he recalled his shocked mind when he had recovered from the first unexpected alteration, not knowing that he would soon glory in it more than he ever gloried in his old life.

Stunned at the carnage he had wrought, he had transmitted a hasty emergency message to the command center and informed them that the experimental DNA had been successfully fused with his own. And further, he had told them that further testing would confirm that their secret goals had been satisfied. Although they were shocked and enraged that he had grossly and dangerously violated procedure by injecting himself, they had been openly pleased that the serum could indeed be transferred to humans.

Within hours a secondary team arrived to replace the dead. And although they were also shocked at such a gory spectacle of wanton, wholesale murder, they were indifferent to the loss of life when measured against the stunning success of the experiment.

Yet they did take prudent measures to ensure that they would not follow the fate of their colleagues. So restraints were set in place to contain him should the transformation occur before the expected hour.

A steel-reinforced concrete room was selected and locked with a steel door that was in turn reinforced with a niobium-titanium brace. Then blood samples were taken for analysis as he waited through the long day, wondering what night would bring.

Deep beneath the level where he had been imprisoned, they would be feverishly searching the DNA strand for the genes that had evolved so rapidly, and had indeed evolved without warning to doom his former coworkers.

Thinking of their deaths, he sensed faint remorse over their coldblooded execution, but strangely did not feel the full measure of regret that he anticipated. It intrigued him as the hours passed, and then his ruminations were broken.

The massive steel door opened wide, and within the frame stood the white-haired man who was responsible for the operation. He knew the man well, just as he knew the man did not approve of his reckless violation of proper procedure. But it did not matter. He had what he wanted, the power of the creature . . .

Without words, the man departed.

He thought back to how it had all begun, remembering the unexpected discovery of the creature. Clearly an ancestor of early homo-sapiens, it had been miraculously and magnificently preserved by the glacier that had hidden it for 10,000 years in an icy tomb.

Even without analysis of its DNA, the creature's superior qualities were obvious. Such as its fantastic strength and speed, or the size of its brain and the incredible ocular space dedicated to nocturnal vision. The only disappointment had been to discover the reduced size of its temporal lobes, which indicated a lack of higher thinking ability. But that was something nature had obviously sacrificed for the amazing physical attributes.

They classified it *Homo scimitar,* for 'man-beast.'

And when it was carefully chipped out of its icy coffin and the frozen carcass of a saber-toothed tiger was discovered beneath—a seven-hundred-pound predator whose neck had been snapped like a rotten branch—they knew it had been a creature of truly unimaginable physical power, undoubtedly the fiercest, strongest, most enduring ancient ancestor of modern Homo sapiens.

Debate ensued for a logical explanation to explain the startling presence of viable DNA after so many centuries, and they discovered that the creature's chemical composition at the time of its death consisted of a strange combination of unidentifiable organic substances. Probably part of its floral diet, the chemicals had acted within its system as a form of genetic antifreeze, preventing the cells from expanding as the water froze. Therefore it never completely froze, even despite sub-zero temperatures.

Yes, it was the discovery of the century, but it had not been for science.

It had never been for science.

Hunter knew they would be landing soon and reviewed what Maddox had told him about the support team.

It had been an informal and enigmatic briefing, the colonel volunteering as little as possible. But Hunter had gleaned enough to know that this Special Response Team wasn't standard military. Maddox had said, in a rather strange tone, that it was out of the CMC—the Central Military Commission—which was an operational center under the authority of the National Security Agency.

The CMC, he learned, was the only federal agency not restricted by *Posse Comitatus*—a doctrine that prevented the government from using U.S. military forces for active missions on American soil without congressional approval. That alone to Hunter was intriguing and distinctly disturbing. For some reason, it seemed, they were afraid this might require active military mobilization. And that didn't make sense.

Even stranger, this hunting party seemed bizarre. Hunter had perceived that much when he asked if this was a singularly American event. And Dixon, eyes hidden, had replied with even more vagueness that it was a unique team assembled from half a dozen nations. In essence, he said, they had recruited professional soldiers who were reputed to be highly trained at hunting not only men but animals as well.

Hunter hadn't pushed it. He suspected already that anything Dixon said was a lie. Even asking him a question indicated a lessening of awareness. Then it was intriguing how Maddox had seemed to spend an excessive amount of time assuring Hunter that helicopter transports would be on constant standby in case of a disaster.

Hunter grunted as he recalled it. Sure, seemed like they were spending more time preparing for a disaster than for success.

Rousing himself, Ghost sat and turned his huge wedged head for a brief moment before locking on Hunter. With unnatural alertness the wolf then scanned the empty cargo hold before it blinked, yawning.

Hunter wrapped an arm about the huge neck, feeling the iron strength locked deep as the stone of a mountain in the dark frame, and laughed. He turned his face away as Ghost tried to nuzzle him with his huge black nose.

"Lie down," Hunter laughed again. "I don't want your big ol' nose in my face." He nudged the wolf away. "Go on. Go on, now. Lie down. We ain't there yet. It'll be soon enough."

With the distinct impression of great weight, the wolf settled on the tarp. His eyes, wide-open now and as black as his mane, stared into the sixty-foot cargo hold, always alert.

Despite his self-confidence, Hunter felt safer knowing this great beast was with him, a bodyguard that never truly slept. Even when Ghost was asleep, which was rare, nothing could approach him without his acute senses bringing him to his feet.

Hunter had researched wolves after he adopted the cub and discovered that wolves were very much different from dogs or even coyotes. For one thing, far more of a wolf's brain was dedicated to hearing and vision.

Not only could they hear ranges far greater than any other animal except a cat, they also had the ability to purposefully block particular sounds that they didn't care to hear. It was an incredible natural endowment, as was their sense of smell—the scent pad within their snout was so large that, if removed and unfolded, it could cover their entire head. And their night vision was superior to every mammal but a bat, a necessary faculty for hunting at night that wolves were prone to do. But the most amazing ability of wolves, and what truly separated them, was their ability to hunt by either sight or scent, or both, simultaneously.

Most creatures depended upon one faculty or the other, sight or sound, to hunt prey; it was instinctive. But wolves could, and would, switch in the middle of a hunt from scent to sight, or back again. And they were the ultimate hunters—once they locked onto prey they wouldn't stop until they were successful. But Ghost was special even for a gray wolf. One of his distinctions was his strength, incredible by any standard. Another was his size.

Hunter knew from experience that most wolves were remarkably lean and limber because excess body weight diminished their ability to go for days and weeks without sustenance. But Ghost, by genetic design and perhaps partially because of the care Hunter had given him since birth, was far more muscular than the average wolf, almost overpoweringly muscular. His shoulders swelled with thick muscle, as did his flanks. And his neck was like corded iron humped behind a massive wedged head. Gingerly, Hunter reached out in the half light of the cargo hold and felt for the closed fangs, and Ghost lowered his head. Then Hunter touched the incisors—they were thick as a boar's tusks, sharp and set deep in hardened bone, and Hunter remembered when he had taken the wolf on a track last year in British Columbia.

Hunter had eventually found the tourists deep in the Kispiox Wilderness but it had been a difficult four-day track. The couple, not having the simple presence of mind to just bed down, conserve energy, and wait for help, had wandered dumbly, burning up precious calories in the cold and forcing Hunter to begin foraging to maintain his own energy level. He finally found them and called for a medical helicopter, but then Ghost had vanished.

Concerned, Hunter had tracked the wolf into a tall stand of birch to find Ghost squared off against another wolf—a large gray alpha, leader of the pack.

A bull elk had been brought down by the pack, and the alpha, by definition as leader, would eat first. But Ghost would have none of it. He waded in, and the alpha warned him off. Then Ghost emitted an ungodly growl that made even Hunter feel a thrill of fear, and the alpha attacked.

Ghost evaded the first lightning-quick lunge, struck a shoulder on the larger wolf and was gone again before it could react. And for an amazingly long and savage battle it was blow for blow, Ghost retreating and attacking, leaping and striking with feral fury.

Hunter watched in fascination as they joined in combat for six hours, neither surrendering, neither striking a mortal wound until Ghost finally slashed a crimson brand that savaged the alpha's neck and the gray wolf fell to a knee. But there was no mercy. Not now.

Ghost moved in, slowly at first, and then, in a movement too quick to follow, hit again, and there was a flare of blood, and the alpha lay deathly still. Ghost stood only a moment over the carcass before he went tiredly to the elk and began to feed.

The other wolves let him feast until he was done. Then, as he turned his back and moved away, the rest of them moved in and devoured what was left.

Hunter never forgot the episode, or the awesome, utter savagery Ghost had embodied. It had been a display of the purest primal fury, truly awesome in its power and awesome in its ferocity.

Hungry as he was, Hunter didn't interrupt as Ghost fed alone, though afterwards he fired a shot into the air to drive off the pack. Then he moved in cautiously beneath the uncaring gaze of Ghost to cut several large steaks from the hindquarter.

He ate one raw, cooked another, then air-dried twenty pounds of jerky for the long journey back. And by cutting off one of the massive legs, stripping the skin at the socket, and tying it back to the hoof, he made an efficient shoulder strap of raw meat— enough to sustain the wolf until they reached the Ranger base.

The forest, all that was in this land, would completely consume what remained of the elk; nothing was wasted.

Hunter had often thought of the incident, wondering what savage pride had driven Ghost to continue the fight. But, from the first day, it was clear that he would die before he walked away.

Hunter smiled as he reached out to ruffle Ghost's mane once more but noticed the wolf was staring away intently, as if perceiving a slowly approaching threat. Suddenly sensitive, Hunter turned his head to gaze into the cargo hold. But he saw nothing.

Nothing but darkness.

***

Standing half-naked in the shadowed gloom, he was amazed that he could not remember his name.

Faintly troubled by it, he slowly raised his hands before his face, frowning slightly, for they were slightly different than before. They were wider, thicker, and tipped with what remained of claws. The transformations were lasting longer, and taking longer to fade, he thought. But that was something to be expected. Soon, he assumed, they might not fade at all. That was well with him; he had grown to prefer that superior state of being—that matchless measure of might that he alone enjoyed.

No, never again would he be one of them—the weak, the puny, the prey. No, he would forever enjoy a higher realm of existence—a physical glory not seen on the Earth for ten thousand years, and which he alone possessed.

Strangely, though he could not remember his name, he remembered so much else. To test himself, he attempted to recall everything he knew about the alien DNA he had injected into his body.

Electrophoresis, he remembered clearly, had categorized the recombinant DNA as ninety-nine percent Homo sapiens. Yet it was the one percent that had demanded their attention and launched the first stage of the experiment.

An aggressive immunity to every disease tested against it had been discovered in that DNA, which contained the very building blocks of life. It was like a battery able to recharge endlessly. Yes, there was not just life, but virtual eternal life hidden within.

For death, he well knew, was simply the aging of cells—a progressive mutation of the body until the cells could simply no longer reproduce. But this creature, Homo scimitar, was not cursed with such a fate as modern man. Although the DNA hinted that there was ultimately an end to the recombinant strength, it was at a level far beyond modern Homo sapiens. Yes, this Lord of the North had possessed a life span of hundreds and hundreds of years. Theoretically, he realized that a thousand years was not beyond hope.

Although the true biochemical essence of its phenomenal longevity was, despite their calculations, a mystery, its immunity system had been readily understood.

A breakdown of the coding had revealed the astonishing level of restrictive enzymes that prevented a foreign agent, like a virus or bacteria, from infecting and interfering with the host DNA. Literally billions of various restrictive enzymes were locked in the helix, a clear indication that this creature had been as invulnerable to virus and bacteria as he was to age—a superior species from a superior realm.

Then the time came to see if the DNA could be copied in modern homo-sapiens. And after performing his own series of tests, he had decided to experiment on himself.

He never even debated his right to inject himself with the coding. He knew that, if successful, he would share those superhuman qualities, and he had judged the potential triumph worth the risk. His motives had not been pure, nor did he care. What he wanted for himself was justification enough for his actions.

But he had not anticipated the transformation to be so overpowering. And he could even now feel the strength growing again, flexing solid muscle that was increasing moment by moment. He could even sense the increasing bone density in his arms and chest and legs, and realized he would soon change again.

He did not know what had compelled his rampage on that first night when he changed within the chamber. He only remembered a dim transposing of visions, screaming faces and hands raised in appeal as his own hands—black claws there—swept left and right with the scarlet world falling before him. Then morning had come and he was himself, in his own mind and with his own eyes.

And after the next research team arrived, replacing those he had massacred so joyfully in his rampage, he had felt it building within him again and knew without question that, when night came, he would be as he had been.

And he was.

They screamed when the steel door exploded before his blow, and a cloud of concrete dust arose as the deep-set bolts were ripped from the wall.

It was a single thunderous impact of his forearm, smashing down with the irresistible force of a wrecking ball that reduced the concrete to chalk and laid the steel flat before him. Then he saw them through the familiar red haze. He saw them backing away in horror, screaming, always screaming.

And he had roared in among them.

But on that second occasion, everything was clearer, and he gained bestial satisfaction from the sheer exultation, the uncontainable exultation of his omnipotent power.

Yes, he smiled.

Like a god on the earth.

Nothing could stop him.

Nothing ...

He knew in that moment that he could bring down a charging rhinoceros with the strength of his arms, that he could kill anything living—any-thing—with the massive might and claws that found no resistance in earthly substance. It was the best of all worlds; human cunning, the fierce blood of the beast, and prehistoric power. But then his human mind was fading, he knew, with each changing. And the changes were becoming more frequent, the beast slowly overcoming what he had been until he would be man no more. He thought of it a moment, and decided he did not care.

Whatever he had been no longer mattered. Tests no longer mattered. Nothing mattered but the power, the endless life, and the freedom to kill, and kill, and kill.

***

It was midday when Hunter climbed off the plane. Standing stiffly in the bay, he stretched for a moment. Then he hoisted his small pack, shouldered the Marlin and, looking out, saw Maddox dressed in a camouflage uniform walking toward the ramp.

Authoritative but more casual than anticipated, the lieutenant colonel stopped and clasped his hands behind his back, nodding. Hunter saw a pistol holstered at his waist and glanced at the grip: a Colt .45 semi-auto. Standard army issue for World War II.

"Afternoon, Colonel," Hunter said as he walked slowly down the ramp, Ghost close beside him.

Maddox's expression altered slightly when he saw the wolf but he had the fortitude not to display the barely controlled nervousness of their first encounter. Still, his eyes shifted jerkily, as he tried to watch Ghost as well as Hunter.

"Welcome to the base, Mr. Hunter. How was your flight?"

" 'Bout like the rest," Hunter replied as he scanned the facility, observing with a wide, unfocused vision. It was a method he'd perfected in the forest, reading everything at once, concentrating on nothing in particular. If something important appeared, instinct or reflex would lock his gaze on it.

This place required no reflex or instinct to see what was important. The compound resembled a battle post more than a research station. Within a high wire-mesh fence sat six Blackhawk helicopters, all armed with rocket pods and M-60's hung from bungee cord in the open bays.

Squinting, Hunter counted eight Light Personnel Carriers—heavily armored vehicles mounted with deadly 25mm Bushmaster cannons. There were at least fifteen Humvees, each carrying an M-60 machine gun mounted on the roof, and maybe six personnel trucks. Hunter estimated at least sixty personnel, which was a lot for a research station. Tin-domed winter huts were set well within the compound in a tight square, and there was a single-level tin structure about two acres in size that was reminiscent of Arctic research outposts located farther north. Yeah, Hunter thought, they were expecting to be attacked soon. He could almost smell the fear in the wind.

Expressionless, he looked at the colonel.

"We have a briefing at twenty hundred hours," Maddox said pleasantly. "Would you like to rest?"

Hunter gently grabbed Ghost by the scruff of the neck. "A little food would be fine, Colonel," he said.

"Ah, very well. The commissary remained open for you and the crew. Please." Maddox gestured.

It caused slight consternation at the commissary when Hunter requested thirty pounds of raw meat for Ghost, but Maddox smoothed it over. And before he himself ate, Hunter stationed Ghost outside the door with a shank of beef, knowing the wolf would eat it through the long day and night, storing up for a time when food might be scarce.

It was a wolf's way, he had learned, to eat continuously on prey for a period of a day and night, knowing it might not eat again for as much as a week. So, leaving Ghost in view, Hunter listened to Maddox expound on the importance of the mission.

"Here we cannot speak plainly," the lieutenant colonel said in a low tone. "But make no mistake. We have assembled the best support team in the world. Every conceivable emergency is anticipated. All you are required to do is...well, what you do best. Track."

Hunter, chewing slowly on a steak, cast a glance at Ghost to ensure that no one was approaching him—an unlikely event in any case. He saw several soldiers standing about fifty feet away, staring with fear and curiosity. But he doubted anyone would bother him, which would be a tragic mistake. Suddenly Maddox raised his head and Hunter sensed a presence. He heard the voice and turned to see a short, square, white-haired figure behind him.

Dr. Tipler was dressed like he was going on safari, hands stuffed deeply in the pockets of a well-worn fishing vest. The chain of a pocket watch dipped on the right side. He was smiling broadly.

Hunter laughed as he stood, embracing the old man.

"Ah," Tipler said," 'tis good to see you again, boy." He patted Hunter's powerful shoulder with a pale hand, standing close. "I heard about Manchuria. Were you injured at all?"

Hunter had not had an opportunity to speak with the professor since returning from Manchuria, where he had narrowly escaped death after being trapped in a cavern by two Siberian tigers fighting for territory. Caught between them as they raged through the cave in battle, Hunter survived only because they had killed each other in the conflict.

Hunter shook his head. "No, I didn't get hit by either of them. But ... I guess it came close."

"Well, good." The old man nodded with satisfaction. "Yes, all very good." He noticed that Hunter had ceased eating. "Here now, sit down and eat, my boy. Please finish your meal. It might be the last time for a while that we might enjoy a calm moment of relaxation." He continued as Hunter took a bite. "So, what of the resemblance?"

"I tracked it for six days," Hunter answered, chewing. "It was ranging high on the Bureiskij Chrebet. For most of the year temperatures are freezing. Could have been genetic, or an adaptation to the cold, but it had a mane like a Caspian, right down to the color. The misidentification is understandable." He pondered it, shrugged slightly. "But it was just a Siberian. Big, though." He opened his eyes slightly at the memory of it. "And seventeen years old. Went about seven hundred, maybe thirteen feet. From a distance it might have looked a Caspian. But it wasn't."

Tipler nodded, solemn for a moment, as Hunter ate in silence. Hunter knew he would need the energy because he would burn more calories in the altitude and cold. In fact, up here he would probably burn four times as many calories just remaining warm as his body would consume in a temperate environment.

"So," the professor said finally. "Perhaps we should concentrate on the business at hand. We certainly have enough to deal with!"

Maddox broke in. "Professor, this is not the place to—"

Gesturing impatiently, Tipler continued. "Oh, I am far too old for subterfuge and lurking about in shadows, meeting under bridges at midnight and whatnot. In fact, I am probably too old to be accompanying your men on this trip. So do not deny me my eccentricities."

Hunter looked up sharply at the professor, then across at Maddox. "What is this?" he asked. He had suddenly realized the air of danger in his stillness. "You never told me the professor was coming on this track."

"Uh, well, Mr. Hunter." The colonel motioned kindly to Tipler. "The professor is, indeed, expected to accompany you, but only as an observer like yourself, of course. And, be perfectly assured, should any mishaps occur, we are very well prepared to deal with them. We can have him out of those mountains and to a hospital within thirty minutes." He made an attempt at utter confidence. "There is no question: his health will never be at risk."

Hunter gazed at Tipler. "Professor?"

The old man's hand settled on his shoulder. "Things will be all right, my boy. I have been, as you know, on several arduous expeditions in recent years." He laughed, leaning back. "Yes, I am somewhat old. And if I suspect at any time that I am slowing you down I will demand my, uh, what do you call it, a . . ."

"An extraction," Maddox contributed. "An emergency extraction."

"Yes." Tipler waved his hand. "An extraction, as they say."

"But Professor, this is going to be a hard track. And you know how I move. You can't keep up with me. Even this so-called support team couldn't keep up with me if I didn't allow them. Besides, we don't even know what this thing is. We just know it's dangerous. More dangerous than anything we've ever seen. Maybe more dangerous than anything anyone has ever seen. We don't know its habits, its instincts, whether it's territorial or nocturnal. We don't know what it will do when it's wounded or cornered. We don't know if it will counterattack or hunt us at the same time I'm hunting it. I know you're still in good shape for your age, but this isn't a bone hunt, Professor. We're going after something that can kill like a tiger. But this is worse because it plans to kill without any reason." Hunter paused, staring hard. "I think, Professor, this thing kills for the sake of killing."

Tipler laughed sympathetically.

"I appreciate your concern, Nathaniel. I truly do. You have always had my best interests at heart, and you have never disappointed me in your support. But the issue has been decided: I shall accompany you on this trip." He held Hunter's stare and leaned forward, seemingly taken by a thought. "Don't you understand what we may have here, my boy?" He paused. "I mean, have you truly imagined?"

Hunter didn't blink. "A killer is what we have, Professor. And it'll kill you or me as quick as it would kill anything else." In this, Hunter's certainty seemed to temper his tone. "This thing doesn't care about guns or greater numbers, Professor. It won't be driven like a tiger. And I don't think it can be baited or ambushed or trapped. Whatever this is, and right now I don't have a clue, is probably the most efficient killing machine on earth. And we'll be alone with it on its home ground. These people talk a lot about a backup team, but if this thing attacks us, we won't be alive when any backup team arrives. So make sure you're willing to die over this before you go into those mountains to find it."

Obviously grateful for the words, Tipler displayed his resolve. "I understand, Nathaniel. But I am committed to this adventure." He laughed gruffly. "Perhaps, at my age, it will be the last adventure of my life. No need to deny an old man one last stab at feeling alive."

After a moment, Hunter looked down. His jaw tightened almost im-perceptibly, and he nodded.

"There." The professor clapped his hands sharply. "It is settled. Now, where is that big horse you call a dog?"

Hunter shook his head with a faint smile. "He's outside."

With a laugh Tipler rose and walked up the slate-gray ramp to the double doors, and when he was outside they heard his booming voice. Through the window Hunter saw Ghost rear on hind legs, fully as tall as the professor as he licked the old man's face. Faintly he could hear Tipler's booming laugh.

It was Tipler who, so long ago, had helped Hunter nurse Ghost back from death. Without any charge the professor had liberally dispensed antibiotics and necessary drugs and vitamins as he tenderly cared for the cub's wounds. And when Ghost was ill with parvo it was Tipler who had kept him in his own home until the wolf wore out the infection.

For six weeks it was touch and go, but Tipler had vigilantly remained by the wolf's side with Hunter, sometimes injecting near-lethal doses of saline solution and Thorazine to prevent the endless convulsions from shredding the wolf's intestines. But in the end it wasn't science that defeated the plague; it was Ghost's pure brute strength and un-killable will. He had simply refused to die when agony and Nature had told him to die. And after three weeks he stood on weak legs.

Now Hunter watched Tipler laugh as he half-wrestled with the wolf, and knew some part of Ghost's animal mind had never forgotten the kindness. The old man was the only person besides Hunter who could touch him. Then Hunter's mind turned to other things. Darker things.

Finishing his meal, he stood.

"All right," he nodded. "Let's get on with it."

"This creature"—Maddox used a laser pointer on the topographical map—"is moving south in a straight line. It used the Anaktuvuk Pass to cross over the Endicott mountain range. Our trackers told us that much. Then it continued south. Pathfinders lost it somewhere around there." He pinpointed the Sistanche Gorge, located about a mile beneath the pass.

The support team had not yet arrived. Hunter gazed about the room. "You sending the professor and me in there all by our lonesome?" he asked mildly.

"Well." Maddox skipped a single beat that seemed somehow important. "This is not like any kind of team we have used before, Mr. Hunter. As you know, we were forced to assemble them from around the world. And, if I may reiterate, they are the best in the world at what they do, each handpicked for a specific skill. They are soldiers but they are also, to the last, men who are proficient hunters."

Hunter stared, saying nothing as Tipler laughed out loud. Then: "You make it sound as if it is a feat of remarkable engineering to assemble such a team, Colonel. Is it so difficult?"

"No, no," Maddox said convincingly. "We have the best people in the world, gentlemen. Be reminded, we are talking about the United States military, here. However the unnatural events of the past week have caused quite a, uh, a stir, and ... uh, in case of some contingencies we have recruited one or two foreign nationals for the team. It is only a precautionary action, and won't affect unit integrity or final authority."

"When do they arrive?" Hunter asked.

"Well ... why do you ask?"

"Because the tracks are getting old." Hunter leaned forward. "This soil is hard, good for tracking. But there's still gonna be erosion. Deterioration. And from the pictures, these tracks already have 5 curves in them, which makes them even harder to read. Plus that, a lot of them will be covered by leaves and debris. You've got severe temperature variations in the mountain range, and that's gonna age them even faster because the change in heat and cold will break down the edges. If you want me to go after this thing, then we need to move as soon as possible. Every day we wait makes it more difficult."

Maddox absorbed it, staring at Hunter for a long moment. "All right, Mr. Hunter. From our latest intelligence I believe the team will arrive by early morning. Then you can begin." He moved to the table. "Now, let me give you something to examine."

He lifted a plaster cast of the creature's footprint and almost gingerly presented it to Hunter, who laid it down. Professor Tipler removed his eyeglasses from the front pocket of his vest and leaned forward as they looked closely.

They studied it for a moment in silence.

"Well?" Maddox asked finally. "Now that you've seen a cast of the print, what do you conjecture? Surely the cast can tell you more than a mere photograph."

Hunter delicately ran fingers over the impression. "How long from the time of the attack to the time this cast was set?"

"Approximately six hours."

"Weather conditions?"

"Dry."

"Wind?"

Maddox paused. "It was relatively mild, I believe."

"Was this in sand or dirt or clay?"

"Simple dirt, I believe." Maddox appeared frustrated. "Why do you ask? Yes, yes, I remember what you said about time and age and erosion and how the tracks are affected by these things. But now, having seen the cast up close, surely you can give me some idea as to what we are dealing with."

Tipler cast Hunter a concerned glance.

"Gentlemen?" Maddox pressed. Frustration was quickly graduating to nervousness.

With a sigh, Hunter shook his head. "It's a plantigrade walk," he said simply. "It's bringing the heel of the foot all the way down to the ground, like a human. Normally, when you see a track, an animal is moving at its usual slow rate of speed. But this thing was moving fast. Running. It's probably male, because it pronates. Males tend to walk more on the outside of their feet while females tend to supinate, or put more pressure on the inside of the foot. And it's not very old, because there's not any mulling."

"Mulling?"

Hunter waved vaguely. "It's complicated. It takes years of practice before you can read something's age in a track. Don't worry about it. But I'm pretty sure this thing isn't more than five, maybe six years old."

"You still have no idea as to what it is?"

"No."

The colonel seemed vaguely stunned. "But surely by now you have some idea!"

Hunter was thoughtful. "I know how it moves, Colonel," he said. "I know how it thinks. How it attacks. How it kills. I know it's right-handed, and I'm pretty sure about its age. I know it weighs close to three hundred. I know it's strong and fast and dangerous. But, no, I don't know what it is."

"Yet you said the tracks were vaguely bearlike."

"Those tracks were severely marred, and that doesn't make it a bear," Hunter responded. "I also said they were vaguely humanlike. All I know is that it's not a tiger. And I don't see how it can be a man because no man can carry that stride width. Right now I think it's something I've never seen before. Maybe something none of us have ever seen."

Tipler lifted the cast and studied it before raising his eyes to Maddox. "Colonel," he began, "would you have any objections about sending this cast back to the Institute where we might analyze the indentations? It is an excellent reconstruction of the print, and my people might be able to discern clues that we may have missed by a simple visual examination."

"Of course not, Professor."

The colonel was clearly becoming frustrated at the continuing enigma. He strolled away for a minute. A decision was evident in his tone when he spoke again. "All right, gentlemen, the Special Response Team should arrive at first light. But since you've told me that time is such a vital factor, I'm going to change orders so that they will rendezvous with you at the first base that was destroyed. From there, we'll fly you to the second and third stations so you can study its habits. And from there, Mr. Hunter, it will be your responsibility to track it down."

Hunter shook his head. "Just drop us at the third base. The tracks at the first two stations will be useless. When was the last station attacked?"

"Twenty-four hours ago."

"Survivors?"

"None."

The answer was clipped.

Tipler's brow hardened with a slight scowl.

"Colonel," he asked, "you must have increased your security at these outposts. You must have had more men, more guns, more gadgets. Why is this thing still alive?"

"It seems ..." Maddox gazed down as he lightly touched a photo of red flesh on snow, "to understand ... things."

Tipler waited. "Things?"

"Yes, it seems to understand our, uh, tactics." The colonel didn't look up as he continued. "It seems to know how to penetrate a security screen, such as the timing of patrols, the formation of flanking. Apparently it does some kind of circular surveillance of an area before it attacks. And it appears to kill listening posts before it does anything else. It doesn't sneak past them, it kills them. Only then does it move into a compound."

There were so many questions floating in Hunters mind that he wasn't even tempted to ask the first one. Obviously, whatever had done this was nothing he'd ever seen. And if he hadn't seen it, it was a safe bet that nobody had.

He knew the only way to find any answers would be at the site. Only by learning to think like this thing could he harbor any hope of tracking it. He stared at the colonel, trying to determine whether something vital was being hidden behind that military mask.

Rising, he turned to Tipler.

"Try to get some rest tonight, Professor," he said. "Tomorrow's gonna be a hard day."

"Ah, my boy, most certainly." Tipler rose beside him. "Thank you, Colonel. We shall leave at ...?"

"0500 hours." Maddox nodded curtly. "We'll be on site by 0600."

"Very good. I shall retire now, so that I can prepare."

"Everything you need is in your quarters, Professor."

"Thank you," Tipler waved. "Good night."

With Ghost at his side, Hunter saw the professor to his room. Then he slipped silently into the night and, hidden in shadow, searched through a mound of discarded construction materials. It was a long while before he found what he needed: a long, pliable shoestring-thin wire of titanium alloy and a peg-sized section of solid steel. The steel fit perfectly in his hand, comfortable and cold.

Then he returned to his own room and made preparations through the long night, working till sunrise. When he was finished he carefully placed the improvised weapon inside his wide leather belt with a frown.

He thought that if this thing went as he feared, it might give him a last desperate chance.

CHAPTER 4

Thundering out of low dark clouds, the Blackhawk descended into a charred glade. Twenty-four hours after the carnage, the snow was still widely stained with red—trampled by military boots.

He quickly scanned the surrounding terrain for a quick orientation and in a breath memorized ravines and hills, what would be the natural approach, the most calculated line of an attack. It took him ten seconds to read the scene, proceeding more by instinct than by intense scrutiny.

The Blackhawk settled gently in the square and Hunter was out first, turning back to help Professor Tipler from the bay. Then, after the old man dusted himself off, they walked out a hundred yards or so and stared silently at the fire-scarred facility. Clearly, the unfortunate team trapped inside it when the creature attacked didn't stand a chance.

Entire portals constructed from fire-resistant steel had been ripped from the hinges as if by a hurricane.

Shaking his head at the devastation, Hunter turned and saw them; the support team. A group of five, they wore specialized forest-camouflaged BDUs. They also wore load-bearing vests packed with weapons and clips. Ignoring Hunter and Tipler, they were unloading equipment from a second Blackhawk.

Hunter observed that they moved with a certain cold economy; no emotion, no questions. They spoke little and each seemed to recognize his responsibility without instruction. Then he saw something else that attracted his attention.

It was a woman dressed in forest BDUs like the rest, but also wearing some kind of high-tech, obviously lightweight armor. She knelt on one knee beside the chopper, bent over a rifle of formidable size. Hunter had never seen one like it, but noticed how adeptly she managed it. When she had finished loading four oversized rounds in a clip and tapping it on her knee to seat the cartridges, she inserted it into the rifle and loudly chambered a round. When she was finished, she lifted it to her shoulder as if it were weightless and aimed across the scorched square, moving left, right, hesitating ...before centering on him.

For a moment, she held aim.

Hunter didn't move, gazing stonily into the glare of the sniper's scope. Then, expressionless, she lowered the massive rifle to her side and turned back to her work. Hunter ignored her and studied the devastated, windswept station.

An air of utter defeat was the first impression, then a lingering sense of horror: shattered steel doors, scars of explosions and fire, broken windows and red snow told the story.

Everywhere the ground was stained crimson, and Ghost was pacing busily across the compound, checking scents. Hunter knew he was attempting to separate the human from the inhuman.

Studying the tracks, Hunter determined easily that many of the men and women present here had fled wildly into the freezing night, heedless of the consequences. Obviously, facing what had been inside that facility had been infinitely worse than the grim fate of freezing to death in the dark.

Hunter moved toward the facility. He glanced at Maddox. "Tell everyone to stay where they're at until I get back."

The colonel turned. "What?"

"Tell everyone to stay where they're at." Hunter approached the shattered door. He knew that the discovery team, or sanitation team or whatever they had used, had already marred whatever evidence he could gain from the facility, but he would give it a try.

His best hope of picking up a track, he presumed, would be in the woods, in finding its mind through its approach. But if there were tracks inside the facility he might learn something of its habits. As he neared the door he saw a portal of solid steel blasted from the hinges by some incredible velocity of force. It was split widely at the top, as if struck by a foot-wide ax.

Carefully Hunter bent close to the ground, studying, but all the footsteps led away from the door. His jaw hardened.

Yeah, those who had fled the facility had obliterated whatever he might have discovered. Rising, he moved inside, turning back and raising a hand to indicate that no one should follow. Then he entered the shrouded darkness alone.

The scent of blood was everywhere, permeating the atmosphere, seeming to replace the air. Hunter bent, staring into the gloom. He sniffed, releasing a bit of the animal instinct within him. His eyes narrowed into the distant dark, but he sensed nothing. Only a cold scent of rusty copper hovered in the dead blackness.

Red lights flickered in the distance, and the scent of smoke was stronger there. And for a long time Hunter stood, staring at nothing, at everything, feeling the atmosphere, letting it speak to him.

Then he tried to imagine what he himself would have done if he were attacking, killing, slaughtering—something not completely alien from the wild animal side he had been born with and had cultivated through the years, yet kept in check.

Though he never fully released the animal within, he never forgot it was there, so much stronger in him than in most. And sometimes, in a long track, with the wind in his face and the cold and the wild surrounding him as he was running free, he felt it rise up, more alive than he was himself. But it was the part of him that he would never let go.

His enormous success in business, his wealth, his skills were a valued part of his life, but they were not his heart. No, the heart of his life would always be here, and free, where he was hunting and hunted ... at home.

Scowling, he turned his mind to the task.

He saw a wide corridor—the most obvious line of attack—and bent, searching the floor. Removing a flashlight from his side pack, he shone it over dry bloody footsteps, all heading toward the door. Then he moved farther into the corridor, trying not to step on anything, always searching. He was twenty feet inside when he found the first blood-dry print of the beast. It was moving hard to the left, as if with purpose.

It took only a moment for Hunter to read the pressure release marks that indicated its speed and lack of hesitation, and he followed it slowly. With the obscuring redness of the floor, it was difficult work, but he followed it deeper into the facility. Despite the frigid air, hot sweat beaded his forehead and chest, and he moved as silently as if he were close to a kill. He knew the beast had fled, but he could not help the instinctive fear that made him breathe deeper, oxygenating as if for a fight.

It was a jagged thin tendril of black that attracted his attention, high and to the right, and Hunter paused. He stared up and angled the flashlight, not rushing anything. And what he saw took a moment, his brow hardening degree by degree in concentration. He straightened. Then, carefully, he walked forward and stared at four long claw marks.

They were torn through steel in a movement of rage and nothing less—claw marks that had shorn metal like paper, as if it had not exhausted enough of its enormous energy by now, slaying the dozens that lay behind it. No, it was compelled to strike at anything living or dead—a vicious engine of unquenchable savagery.

Gently, Hunter lifted the flashlight higher and shone it into the smooth cuts. He saw that the steel was split by something far harder than itself, an edge that had torn through it with incredible velocity. All the cuts were the same, smooth in and out.

Except for one.

Hunter's eyes narrowed as he studied the ragged, stunted end of the gash, and he moved closer, shining the light into the crack.

And saw it.

It was obscure at first, but as he tilted the light just so, he knew what it was. He removed his pocket knife and gently pried it from the steel. Then he stared down at what he held, carefully raising it before his face to study the long curving sharpness. The edge was serrated, like a steak knife. Glancing over his shoulder, ensuring he was alone, he placed it in his pocket.

Step by step he found a silent path deeper into the facility until he arrived at what appeared to be a laboratory. He gazed about the dimly illuminated chamber and saw that it was demolished like the rest. Then a yawning steel door, framed by light within, drew his attention. Walking slowly, amazed at the dented steel doors and smashed machinery, he approached it and stared inside.

It took a moment, staring silently at the interior, for him to identify what was wrong. And then it was there, so obvious that he felt ashamed for missing it: The room was a storage vault with refrigerated sections neatly lining a wall. But the strangeness was that this room, and this room alone, hadn't been damaged by the creature's attack.

None of the glass doors had been shattered. None of the heavy doors had been torn from their hinges. The stainless-steel autopsy-like table in the center of the room was undamaged. So Hunter bent, staring at the floor, shining the flashlight at an angle.

Why did it destroy every other room and not this one?

He saw no bloodied tracks on the gray tile, no indication that it had even entered. But that wasn't right. This thing had purposefully moved through this entire facility releasing a rage that couldn't be quenched.

Something was wrong here.

Stepping carefully to the side to avoid marring near-invisible tracks, Hunter examined everything. He searched along the walls for scratches, smears, anything. And all the while, concentrated to the task, he kept alert to the slightest whisper of sound behind him. For, though his mind was engaged in pinpoint concentration, his reflexive survival mode prevented anything from approaching him without his knowledge.

It was a while before he found a thin line on the floor, a ghostly tendril of white powder as thin as a razor. And Hunter spent a long time examining it, studying it, reconstructing how it came to be. And then he knew. Nodding, he stood and opened a refrigerated door and examined the serums within. Despite the carnage, the unit was still functional.

He searched randomly, and then began to sense what had happened here. Then, after checking the manifest of inventoried fluids, he felt more certain, and left the door open as he exited.

Already he knew things were not as they seemed. But it would be dangerous to mention anything until he was certain of who, and why. He left with the same measure of alertness he had when he entered—a habit he had perfected from years of surviving in environments that were safe one day, lethal the next.

The undamaged chamber was not all that he would have to hold secret for a time. He knew it would also be unwise to tell them he'd found a broken claw.

***

Finding nothing more on the grounds, Hunter exited the facility and approached the colonel. He knew now that nothing else would be gained by a concentrated search. Only trampled tracks and blood remained of the holocaust that had consumed the building.

"You people can finish whatever they're doing in the building," Hunter said as he turned his head to the support team.

They were standing silently, and at his glance they stared back, implacable. There was a moment of testing, measuring. But one member of the team gave Hunter particular attention.

A large soldier, with a barrel chest and stout, muscular arms—he could have a heavyweight boxer—concentrated on Hunter the longest. His face beneath short white hair was viciously scarred on one side by fire, and a white eye gazed at Hunter from the ravaged section like a lifeless marble. His other eye was calculating, cold, and it glinted with an unconcealed wildness.

Expressionless, Hunter turned to Maddox. "From here, it's my call. I suppose they understand how things are going to work."

"They do."

"All right." Hunter looked at the surrounding landscape. "Well, let's get started. I'm going into the hills to see if I can pick up this thing's scent. Keep everyone inside the compound."

Silently, Ghost appeared at his side.

"Yes, of course," said Maddox. "And good luck. We'll back you up as soon as you find it."

Moving away, Hunter paused beside Tipler, who stood near the chopper. The old professor seemed to know from Hunter's expression that whatever needed to be said couldn't be communicated at the moment. Hunter wordlessly picked up the Marlin and strapped it across his back.

He was descending into his tracking mode, allowing a deeper concentration to command all his energy and mind, as he moved slowly for the open gate. Ghost, needing no instruction, paced head-down at his side. At the gate, Hunter paused, taking his time to study the terrain.

He saw patches of scattered snow and, between them, soggy ground. He lifted a handful of snow and squeezed a fist to see how it compressed, measuring its dryness. He watched the spruce as they swayed in a whispering wind, noting the direction of the breeze. For a long time he stood perfectly still, listening, watching.

Then he sensed a presence and heard the hard crunch of gravel beneath boots, but didn't turn even when the intruder was close. A gruff voice spoke down to him.

"We can get a move on any time, tracker."

Hunter gave no indication that he had heard.

"Jesus," the man said, "I hope this ain't gonna be one of them Indian things. This is a hunt, not a vision quest." Hunter felt the man turn his attention to Ghost. He laughed without any hint of humor. "Nice dog you got there."

Vaguely Hunter bent his head and saw the big man, the one with the fire-scarred face, raise a single hand at Ghost, holding two fingers as a pistol. "Click," he said. Then, after smiling with clear malice at Hunter, he walked away.

Hunter turned back to the ground, raising his eyes to the hills, letting every slight bend of leaf, each sway of bush or angle of slope, compose a mosaic of the terrain. He determined which ways were most easily negotiable in the dark; he knew too well that any animal, even a big cat, would select the path of least resistance—a natural path, if it was there.

A moment later he heard more steps, but different. These contained the softness of respect, of patience, as if the intruder did not want to disturb him. They halted about fifteen feet away to be followed by silence.

At last, sensing a general direction of its approach, Hunter rose and turned to see who had come up behind. Whoever it was—it didn't matter—had demonstrated a measure of respect; Hunter would do the same.

Standing less than ten feet behind him—surprisingly less than Hunter had estimated—was a large Japanese. The man was dark-haired with a chiseled, severe face, and there was no emotion whatsoever present in the coal-black eyes. He was big for a Japanese and dressed in BDUs. He carried a camouflaged MP-5 and a cut-down pump-action Remington shotgun. Then Hunter saw the leather hilt of a katana extending over his powerful right shoulder. After a moment the Japanese nodded curtly. Hunter returned the nod.

"I am Takakura," he rumbled.

His voice indicated a disciplined inner strength, both patient and tempered. Overall, he had the presence of a feudal samurai displaced to the twentieth century.

"I am the designated commander of this team," Takakura added. "I only wished to say that I am familiar with your skills and your instructions. We will wait here until you contact us." He handed Hunter a small radio, barely the size of his hand. "With that you can communicate, even in these mountains, for a distance often kilometers. I believe you will find it indispensable."

"Thank you." Hunter placed it in his hip pack, casting another glance at the team. "I'll call you as soon as I pick up a track."

"I understand," Takakura nodded.

Moving at a slow trot through the gate, Ghost ranging at his side, Hunter loped across a ridge and angled right, following a tree-line. He had a feeling that it had approached from somewhere along the northern slope where the spruce were thick. The lack of undergrowth would make stalking easier, and the spruce trees would still provide deep shadow to conceal it from electronic and human listening posts.

What Hunter needed to do first was find any kind of animal run, even a rabbit run, because animals tended to follow certain routes. So he moved into the tree-line and began searching for the thickest brush hidden behind the spruce.

Heavy undergrowth was always the best place to start because it offered smaller animals concealment while they moved from their dens to food or water. And within minutes Hunter found a slight depression in the ground and knelt to determine the species. The prints, about four days old, were half an inch long. They looked like a miniature bear track. He smiled: a lemming.

Moving quickly and silently, Hunter followed the run until it intersected with a general trail, the way a paved road intersects a highway. He studied the ground and saw elk, bear, and the five-clawed prints of a large wolverine. Hunter almost laughed; this was a popular route.

Staying off the trail as he walked parallel to it, he saw that it carved a safe swath around the military compound. He couldn't help but smile; it amused him to think that an entire convoy of animals moved up and down this trail in the morning and evening, so close to the compound and yet so hidden because the civilized personnel knew nothing of the wild. He had covered a half-mile circuit when he came across the first print of the beast.

Stopping suddenly in place, Hunter raised his face to search the forest. But he could determine by the natural chorus of activity that nothing was close. Two red squirrels were eating acorns of a white oak less than forty feet away, and a collared pika was barking down the trail, summoning her mate. For a moment he almost felt at home, then dismissed it in the shadow of what he had been caught in. Frowning, he bent to the print.

It took only a second to determine that it had been moving fast, as if enraged. The ground was almost torn by claw marks, and the front of each print was deeper than the back, like the beast had been running on the balls of its feet. Hunter estimated its weight and size and knew his earlier calculations had been close. It would go maybe two hundred fifty, slightly over six feet. It was right-handed, and it wasn't older than six years. He raised the radio: "This is Hunter."

Takakura replied, "Yes, Mr. Hunter."

"I'm on the northeastern ridge. Have the team move north from the gate and up this slope. I'll be at the top. I'll tell you when to stop."

"Understood."

Setting the radio in his belt, Hunter thought of the dauntless tone of the Japanese and felt the first faint sense of security. Though unemotional, the man's voice and attitude were both forthright and efficient. Then he remembered the severe face and wondered about what manner of man was leading this team, and why Takakura had been selected commander. Hunter had already decided that nothing involved in this situation happened without a reason. Suddenly angry, he shook his head at the distracting thought. Time enough to worry about that later.

Studying the track again, he determined its direction and moved up the slope to find a second print, and another, and another. Even beyond the force and weight of the impressions, he was amazed at the length of its stride, the almost casual demonstration of titanic power.

He concentrated on observation and tracking but slowly felt a thought—more of a fear—nagging him. And as he neared the crest of the ridge and saw that the beast had cunningly used a series of large granite boulders—hard stone that left virtually no tracks—to descend, he realized what it was.

This thing knew it would be hunted for what it had done.

**

Turning as he heard the careful approach, Hunter spoke in an even tone. "It's not close. You can come up."

It was a fire-scarred face that Hunter saw first, rising from beneath a low spruce limb to stare at him with open hostility. Hunter, for some reason, squared off, implacably returning the stare. If there were going to be trouble, he might as well settle it now.

Staring impassively for a moment, the man suddenly smiled, then laughed silently. He turned, holding a large automatic shotgun, and walked down the ridge.

Within minutes the rest of them emerged from the trees, each holding a different weapon. Without tactical instruction they automatically branched out across the rock-strewn crest in an efficient guard, poised and apparently unafraid. The Japanese came through the brush last, slightly behind Professor Tipler.

Hunter saw that the old man was keeping up well, and it assuaged some of his concern. But this had just begun. The first full day would be the primary measure of what the professor could endure, and Hunter felt fairly confident that the old man would maintain his strength for a while. But after that, mostly because of his advanced age, Hunter was uncertain.

After so many miles in the mountains, everyone, even those in excellent physical condition, would begin to crack at the strain. The back was generally the first thing to go, then the legs, then the feet, and then a general physical blowout that had no exact cause or remedy. And what put someone on his feet every morning wasn't brute physical strength; it was the pure and simple will to rise.

Hunter had seen hundreds of well-conditioned gym athletes crumble completely after ten days on the trail, unable even to roll out of sleeping bags to put on their boots, while other, less-conditioned hikers who had a simple but determined will just pushed themselves up and finished the task. Tipler had plenty of will, and Hunter wondered how far it could take him.

Dignified and solid, the Japanese paused. His curt nod could have indicated anything but Hunter sensed it was respect. Takakura's eyes, obsidian and impenetrable, flicked past Hunter and then down the ridge. "Is that the direction?"

"Yeah." Hunter adjusted the Marlin slung across his back; the leather strap crossed his chest, frontier-style. "It's moving south, like before. Tracks are about a day old."

Hunter once again noticed the katana strapped to Takakura's back, along with a sawed-off shotgun. The hilts protruded from behind either shoulder while the Japanese held the MP-5. Extra clips and shotgun shells were on a bandoleer, and a large combat knife was strapped to his leg.

Cold and concentrated, Hunter ignored Taylor and glanced at the other men on the team. Hunter didn't know where the woman had gone. He didn't know which of them he could truly trust, but for the moment Takakura appeared the safest bet. There would be time to learn more about them later. He squatted by the trail, staring at the last track and trying to imagine the route that he himself would have taken from this ridge in the dark. After a moment he found it and stood.

"We are ready to begin?" Takakura inquired, already seeming to understand a little of Hunter's style of tracking.

"We need to get some things straight," Hunter said, turning to face Takakura, who nodded curtly. "I lead," Hunter continued, "and your people stay back about a hundred yards. Simple as that."

"I have no objection." Takakura frowned. "But we have someone who might be able to aid you. Each of us, as you know, possesses specialized skills which you may, at your convenience, utilize to complete this mission."

Hunter considered it. "All right. Which one?"

Without hesitation—a man comfortable with authority—Takakura raised a hand. "Bobbi Jo!"

Hunter turned his head to see the team's female member trotting instantly and effortlessly up the ridge. She reached them in a few seconds, only slightly winded. Standing at port arms with the gigantic sniper rifle, she regarded Hunter without expression.

She was about five-eight, and slim. Her hair was a dark blond and tied in a ponytail. Her eyes were a vivid blue and her face was sharply angled, indicating that she was in excellent shape. She had a bandoleer stretched across her chest filled with huge metal-jacketed cartridges. Hunter estimated they were at least .50-caliber rounds.

Takakura began, "I have told Mr. Hunter that—"

"Just call me Hunter."

A pause, and the Japanese nodded. "*Hai*," he continued, staring back at Bobbi Jo. "I have told Mr. Hunter that you are also skilled at tracking. I informed him that you might be of some assistance."

Patiently Hunter asked, "How much do you know?"

Bobbi Jo's voice was young and confident. "I know who you are, Mr.—"

"Just Hunter."

"All right. I know who you are, Hunter. I've followed your work, and I'm not as good as you. I'll say that outright. But I've been through Tracker and Pathfinder. I've got five years in the program. And I grew up hunting. So, although I'm not as good, I can hold my own and I don't make stupid mistakes. And I'd like to take point with you." Her mouth made a firm line.

He studied her. "Okay, how may claws on a bear?"

"Five."

"Wolf?"

"Five."

"How do you tell a coyote from a wolf?"

"A wolf has a larger rear pad, and the digit claw doesn't print."

"How does the movement of a bear differ from the movement of a mountain lion?"

"A bear wanders. No path, just territory. A cougar follows a circuit. Usually about fifty miles in diameter. And it uses paths."

Hunter raised his eyes slightly. "Okay, but what difference does that make if you're hunting them?"

"You can anticipate a cougar because it stays on a ridge, in general, and if you lose the track you just crisscross the ridge until you find prints. But if you lose a bear track, you'll have to circle, widening the circle each time to find it."

Hunter nodded. Yeah, she was pretty good. He continued, "How can you tell if a man moves to the right or left?"

"There are at least fifty different kinds of pressure release marks," she said firmly. "But, in general, if a man moves to the right, the print will be impressed deeper on the left side. He was pushing himself in the opposite direction, so the print will be higher. Same for the man moving left, just the opposite effect."

"And if the track is on a ridge?"

"If the ridge slopes down to the left and it moved to the right, then the track would be deeper on the right. And vice versa."

Hunter was impressed but tried not to reveal it.

"How do you crosshead?" he continued.

"If you tell me to crosshead, I'll go ahead of you and crisscross for sign. If you were moving south, I would be moving east and west, trying to pick up anything that would indicate a change of direction."

"And sideheading?"

"Sideheading is when you move parallel to the track, keeping the sun on the other side so you can read faint indentations. You usually use it on hard ground or rock where the impressions are thin. The main thing is to keep the sun at an angle that pitches shadow just right." She paused, hefted the heavy rifle slightly. Hunter was again impressed by how easily she seemed to carry it. "It takes a lot of practice," she said. "I learned how to do it when I was a kid."

"I'll bet. So what have you tracked before?"

"Bear, cougar, coyote, wolf, elk – just about everything."

"And lately?"

"Lately," she said, looking into his eyes without discernible emotion, "I've tracked and killed men, Mr. Hunter."

Hunter studied her a moment. He knew he wouldn't really be able to tell anything until he saw what she could do in the field; whether she could read the age of a track, how delicately she observed everything else as they moved, how alert she was to the forest itself. But she obviously knew the basics.

"Okay," he said. "One last question. How can you tell if you're close to a snake when you can't see it?"

Her eyes narrowed. "You ... you can ..."

He waited patiently. From the corner of his eye he saw Takakura's hard gaze trade between the two of them. Then Bobbi Jo replied, un-intimidated, "I don't know, Mr. Hunter."

A nod, and Hunter tightened the strap on the rifle. "You can lead with me." He turned to Takakura. "Just keep your men far enough back not to mar tracks before I can study them. Is that good enough for you?"

Takakura nodded. "Most acceptable. But we shall remain close, in case of a confrontation."

"Let's go," Hunter said to Bobbi Jo, and moved down the slope. She was close behind him, placing her steps carefully. They were halfway to the base when she spoke again.

"So how can I tell if I'm close to a snake?"

Hunter lifted his head to the forest.

"It tells you."

CHAPTER 5

As they descended the slope it seemed unseasonably hot—a blinding sun blazing in a sky beyond blue—and Hunter felt his blood whitening with adrenaline as he tracked claw marks on stone.

By the time he and Ghost reached the base of the ravine he had already regressed to a pure and primal state of being. He was only dimly aware of Bobbi Jo moving quietly a few steps behind him.

He knew the others were farther back, letting him do his job, holding him with a measure of contempt because they believed no one could do this job as well as the military. But it was enough that they moved without speaking because animals—including their prey—would instantly pick up the alien sounds. And in this terrestrial environment the sound of a soft human voice would have the same effect as a shotgun blast.

No, they had to move as silently as possible if he was going to pick up anything from the forest itself. But he felt slight reassurance because of Takakura s presence. The team leader seemed ready to give unqualified cooperation. For now.

At the base of the slope, Hunter raised a hand and Bobbi Jo stopped, crouching quietly. Then Hunter himself crouched, studying the muddy ground, measuring its solidity, its composition, water-grade level—a dozen elements that would reveal to him a great deal more when he found this things prints.

Overall there was little growth in the area, only scattered vegetation. Scanning, he found a slight pool of water as large as his foot. But only one: a single depression. He placed a hand down to feel the slight ridges concealed by the muddy water.

It was the right age for a track; maybe a day. But the water had already eroded what was important so he would have to go without a direction. Bobbi Jo was moving so silently behind him, despite her boots, that he had almost forgotten she was there. He turned, motioned for her to move to the left, and he moved to the right. Together, twenty feet apart, they entered a long, wide glade covered with tall grass.

It took Hunter five minutes to find the second track angling on slightly higher ground. But it, too, was in poor condition from drainage. It was covered with leaves and he almost missed it but for the deep slicing of claw marks left in the harder soil. Those had not been eradicated by the storm and remained readable.

He turned, looking still and straight at Bobbi Jo, waiting to see if she would peripherally catch his sudden lack of movement, and she did. Slowly, she turned her head and he nodded once.

Not having sight or scent of prey, Ghost roved close behind him, sniffing, searching unsuccessfully.

Hunter moved up the slope and bent to study the old track. He was feeling a slight frustration. There was one long row of a forward pad with claws digging deep for traction, and what resembled the impression of a human heel. The next track on the slope—the left foot—was more than twenty feet away.

This thing had leaped twenty feet with a stride.

No way ...

No way that it could have done that ...

Even a tiger would have had trouble covering more than five feet on this slope. And it gave Hunter pause, forcing him to recheck, to make sure he hadn't missed anything. But after careful study he was certain. No, the forest doesn't care what you want or what you want to believe ...

Clearly this thing had leaped twenty feet.

Hunter tried to convince himself that it was only a temporary strength induced from the overflow of adrenaline that had been coursing through its system at the time. And when Bobbi Jo came up close, he moved forward again. He still couldn't identify the print, but knew it wasn't anything he had seen before.

Maybe something he never wanted to see.

At the Tipler Institute of Crypto-zoology and Paleontology, Rebecca Tanus and Gina Gilbert stared side by side, hands resting on chins, at the plaster cast that had been couriered to them by a military official. The cast, almost sixteen inches long, rested on the table. Their faces only barely concealed the fact that they were profoundly confused.

Rebecca, laboratory director until the return of Dr. Tipler, sighed. "I have a doctorate from Cambridge in ecosystems, a master's in paleontology. I graduated first in my class in historical geology and molecular theory of fossilization. I've spent a year at the most prestigious institute on earth under the tutelage of the greatest paleontologist of our age." She paused, her face only inches from the cast. "And I don't have the foggiest idea what this is."

Gina said nothing; silence lengthened.

With a quick breath that blew a lock of auburn hair out of her eyes, Rebecca continued, "Good grief, Gina. I don't even know where to start." She pondered it, tapping a foot. "Well, it looks human. But it has five non-retractable claws. So, it has claws, ergo—it's not human."

"No," Gina mumbled. "It's not human. But, then, it's not an animal. Because it looks human."

"Uh-huh," Rebecca murmured. She began tapping the table. "So ...it's not human. And it's not animal." Her smile had no humor. "I guess that doesn't really leave us a lot to consider, does it?"

Again, silence.

"Okay." Rebecca roused herself. "Let's try and think like the doc. When he can't identify a fossil, he categorizes it according to the number and shape of appendages, size, location, and age. He places it in a category or phylum and begins to find its family. Then he works down from there. Usually it's a related species of some determined genus we're only vaguely familiar with."

Gina joined in. "Okay. Let's do that. Species: Homo sapiens. Age: One week old."

Silence.

"Well, that didn't really get us very far," the older woman mused. "Look at these." She pointed with a pencil. "Those are five single claws. Big ones, too. Five clawed appendages on what appears to be the foot of a species related to Homo sapiens. Not too likely. So what other species has five appendages?"

Gina didn't really need to think. "Well, there's *Homo-habilis*, *Homo erectus*. Then there's apes and big cats and bears— Grizzly, Kodiak, brown and black—and, oh, most of the lower terrestrial mammals like wolverine, raccoon, chipmunk, squirrel, porcupine—" Her voice assumed a droning tone. "Then there's beaver, mink, skunk, badgers—"

"Okay, okay." Rebecca cut her a glance. "I got it already."

Neither spoke for a while.

"This is what we'll do," Rebecca started. "We know what it isn't, right? So we'll begin at zero and assume it's an unknown species."

"Like the old man does."

"Yeah, like Doc does. We'll take this and run a phosphorescent scan on it for any tracings that might have been picked up by the plaster. The plaster is already contaminated, so unless we find an actual hair or trace of hemoglobin, we'll never get a DNA trace. But let's look for it anyway. We'll start at the top of the list and work down. Then we'll worry about classifying it."

"Just go by procedure," Gina chimed in.

"Right. Just go by procedure. Like the doc says. But this is a rush job so put everything else on hold." Rebecca stood as she spoke, staring down at the mystery. "If we find a piece of this thing no bigger than a grain of sand, we own him."

"Chaney!"

Asleep at his desk at the U.S. Marshals Service in Washington, Chaney raised bloodshot eyes. He saw the haggard face of Marshal Hank Vincent, or "Skull" as they called him for his merciless expression, approaching. He could see that Skull held an expense voucher in his hand, crumbling it into a tight wad.

Chaney muttered, "Oh, shit."

Suddenly finding themselves needed elsewhere, a dozen Deputy U.S. Marshals surrounding Chaney's desk began wandering in separate directions. With a remarkable air of calm, Chaney said, "Hey, Chief, I was just about to talk to you about that little—"

Skull held the voucher before Chaney's face. "Explain to me," he said carefully, "how you can spend five thousand dollars on gas in a single month when you never left the city? I want to hear this one. It's got to be a classic."

"Travel expenses, boss."

"Travel expenses?" Skull stared, as if he'd never heard the term. "Travel expenses? Is that the best you can do?" He pointed.

"I want to see you in my office." Without waiting for a reply he turned away.

Chaney rose slowly, making a vague attempt to straighten his tie. Then to a chorus of murmured "good lucks" he walked slowly into Marshal Vincent's office, quietly closing the door. He stood with hands clasped, all dignity, and Skull stared back. Slowly, after a moment, the marshal shook his head. A thin smile creased his lips. It was a rare moment. He tossed the voucher on the desk and leaned back, shaking his head.

"So, travel expenses," he said finally. "But then you busted that cartel last week didn't you, Chaney? Arrested Lau Tai when he was cutting one of his better deals."

Chaney nodded, then looked away slightly as Skull lifted another invoice. "Says here that you maxed out your snitch allotment almost six weeks ago. How long you been working that case?"

"Six months, sir."

"So how did you buy off your snitches in the last month to find the location of the deal?"

After a pause, Chaney said, "Well, boss, I relied upon creativity and resourcefulness. Like we're supposed to."

At that, Skull actually smiled. "Yeah, Chaney, I'll bet you did." He waited a moment, barked a short laugh. "That," he motioned to the door, "is called 'street theater.' I did it because everyone knows what you did and I don't want them following your example.

"You took a big chance, Chaney, and you pulled it off. But you pulled it off only because of your street contacts, and there's not too many that have that. It's a forgotten art. So someone like you could take a chance and win. But the rest shouldn't even try." He frowned a little. "Some of them would, you know. They'd go for broke, spend the money, and still not get their puke. Then they'd burn for it. Even worse, I'd have to burn them for it. 'Cause I wouldn't be able to protect them."

Skull waited; Chaney was silent.

"You know." Skull contemplated a pen. "I caught some heat over that Lau arrest."

"Heat over it? Why? It was a good snag."

" 'Cause Lau was the responsibility of the DEA." Skull gestured with the pen as if, in truth, he really didn't give a damn. "Jurisdictional disputes ... that sort of thing."

"He was a known fugitive from justice, boss."

"Then he fell under our people in the Fugitive Program," Skull said, suddenly more serious. "Hell, Chaney, you're in intelligence and counter-intelligence. You were supposed to be investigating whether there was a current covert American intelligence operative working with the Golden Triangle heroin bands, not chasing rucking Lau. If you hadn't used your own special brand of creative writing in your weekly reports, I would have been on you a lot sooner. And to make it worse, the FBI is saying that you violated Lau's rights because you interrogated him pretty rough, trying to make him spit out his contacts. Then, cherry on the cake, he claims you didn't even read him his rights." He paused. "They're saying that you blew the entire arrest and that we can't charge him at all. They want a formal investigation."

Chaney revealed nothing but strolled forward to gently touch the desk nameplate. It was dark maple with "Marshal Hank Vincent" stamped squarely in the gold plate.

"Well, you know, boss," he began, "we don't need to charge Lau for this crime. He's a fugitive from justice with three other federal convictions. If he hadn't escaped from Lompoc, he was gonna do another fifty years without possibility of parole. Which he will, as soon as I escort him back. I admit, uh, that I interviewed him alone, and I may have even forgotten to read him all his rights, but now we have the names of all his American contacts." Chaney hesitated, shrugged. "We can make a dent with this information, boss. It was a good snag."

Skull crossed his arms. "And he wound up at the ER because ...?"

Raising hands to the sides, Chaney responded, "Well, hell, he resisted arrest. Simple as that."

"Uh-huh." Skull let the moment hang. "I'll take care of the college boys, Chaney. I'll tell them we're not initiating any Article 31 investigation, and if they don't like it, they can kiss my freckled butt." He shuffled papers. "All right, I've got another assignment for you. I want you on it right away."

Chaney was silent. It was one of his habits, when speaking to superiors, to say as little as possible. He figured it was hard to incriminate yourself when you don't talk, though he often rode the crest between caution and rudeness.

"This is it." Skull laid the file out. "It seems that we've had a military incident up in Alaska that—"

"The army?" Chaney looked up. He couldn't conceal his surprise. "They have their own marshals. What does that have to do with us?"

"Just hear me out." Skull gestured, uncommonly patient. "It seems that some oh-so-slightly more than classified research stations have had some serious trouble. Like dead people. A bunch of them. I want you to look into it."

"Why me? More important, why us?"

Skull said nothing for a moment, then rose slowly to stare out the window behind his desk. In the distance Chaney saw traffic moving slowly along the Beltway, which bordered the rear of the facility.

"Because some of our friends in Congress are worried about a rumor that the research stations may have been doing some off-the-books biological warfare research," Skull said finally. "That's not the jurisdiction of the FBI. It's not our jurisdiction, either. But the Hill wants us to take it."

"And you want me to take it?"

"Yes."

There was something about this that Chaney didn't like at all.

"Well, just what, exactly, am I supposed to investigate? I don't know anything about biological warfare. I wouldn't know a cold virus from Ebola. I could be up there investigating for a year and not find anything that—"

"Your assignment is in Washington," Skull said.

Chaney didn't even try to conceal what he felt. "Washington?" he asked slowly; the pause lasted a long time as he studied Skull's downcast face. "What's going on here, Marshal?"

For a long time, Skull was silent.

"Chaney, if someone is using government resources to develop biological weapons illegally, then that means people at the highest levels are involved in covert activity that directly countermands not only the mandates of the President but the

1972 United Nations agreement prohibiting the experimental development of such weapons systems." He paused. "I presume you understand the implications of that?"

A cold feeling settled on Chaney's spine. "Yeah, I understand. So you want me to investigate the Pentagon, the National Security Agency and the Central Intelligence Agency to determine if they're running a black operation in direct contravention of a presidential directive."

Skull nodded.

Chaney took his time to respond.

"All right," he said finally. "But I'll have to go outside procedures for this. Way outside. I want unlimited funds and my own crew, all of 'em handpicked by me. I also want written preceding authority to travel wherever I want, both me and my crew. And I want my own check vouchers." He was studious. "Plus, I want marshals in each district instructed that they will cooperate with me without hesitation, no matter what my requests entail. And, no offense, boss, but I want all that in writing or you can give the job to someone else." Chaney nodded. "That's my deal. You know what you're asking me to do."

The words hung heavy in the air.

Skull was obviously reluctant. "You've never let me down, Chaney. But I'll have to clear something like that with the Chief."

"Take all the time you want. We can talk about what a jerk I am later. If I live." Moving away, he paused at the door as Skull called after him.

"Hey, Chaney."

Chaney turned back.

"You asked why I selected you for this job." Skull's gaze never left Chaney's face. "The reason is simple. I got lots of guys smart enough to be a cop. I only got one who's smart enough to be a crook."

***

Hunter spun like a panther.

What he glimpsed—outlined in distant shadow for the fierce single beat of a heart—was unmistakable. Before it was gone.

Eyes narrowing at what was no longer there, Hunter stared with a frown at a ridge over a half mile distant. He knew that eyes could play tricks at that distance, with shadow and foliage joining to throw a myriad of threatening shapes amid the waving brush of movement. But something deeper told him no; he wasn't mistaken.

He had caught the most frantic, fleeting glimpse of a faraway shape—a manlike form that stood in the gloom and purposefully stared back, challenging. Engulfed in foliage, it was there and then turned—gone in a heartbeat as Bobbi Jo came up tiredly behind him, kneeling to rest. She had seen nothing, he knew, nor would he share the knowledge.

"What is it?" she whispered, sweating in the humidity.

He stared down a moment, shook his head.

"Take a break," he said without tone. "Have some water. You're gonna need it." He moved away as she recovered from hauling the monstrous sniper rifle through the deep brush.

Considering the horrific sight, Hunter shook his head: None of this was right. Whatever he had seen had stood upright. But nothing, nothing did that. Not if it could rip a steel door off hinges and separate a man's head from his body with a blow. Hunter tried not to let his consternation show.

Takakura and the rest, Dr. Tipler straggling slightly, came up beside them. The doc seemed to be narrowly holding his own, despite his age. But Takakura seemed slightly fazed by Hunter's unrelenting pace. And that spoke of extraordinary conditioning because Hunter hadn't yet rested, though it was nearing late afternoon.

Hunter himself didn't even feel the strain, and he had long ago ceased to wonder of his endurance, knowing that it was a specific kind of strength perfected by a brutal life. Just as he knew that he could go sleepless for days without feeling any effects or cover a hundred miles in a day by foot if needed. But he didn't expect that from others and was forced to remind himself frequently to slow down.

Takakura bent, fatigued, but glanced at the ground as if searching. Hunter smiled; even the Japanese was slowly learning to track. Then he glanced around the ridge, back at Hunter. "We are closing on the creature?" he asked.

"Yeah," Hunter said, debating what else to say.

He wouldn't withhold information to the point of endangering the team, but he wouldn't speak before he was certain. Losing credibility in this outlandish place, and under these conditions, could endanger the entire team.

"*Hai*, this is good," Takakura grunted, resting the rifle.

He knelt, staring out, and what Hunter saw in those coal-black eyes assured him that the Japanese, no matter what secrets were concealed in this mysterious operation, had only one purpose. The Japanese was a man committed to his work. He would do his duty, even if it killed him.

Remembering what he had discovered in the research station, scanning the rest of the team, Hunter was pleased there was at least one member he could trust.

***

Exhausted, Taylor sat and raised his head to see Hunter on the ridge. The tracker was unmoving, talking in muted tones to Bobbi Jo and Takakura.

The old professor was off to the side, wiping perspiration from his face. And the big wolf lying at Hunter's side was, as always, alert with black bat-like ears standing straight up.

Another team member, Buck Joyce, came up beside him and laid an M-203 on a jagged stump, the remnant of a lightning-blasted tree. Buck was much smaller but six years in Special Forces had burned him down to a lean wiry frame.

Taylor wiped sweat from the back of his neck. "That guy never stops," he mumbled, glancing at Hunter's powerful frame. "I ain't covered this much ground in a single day since I qualified for damn Delta. Fifty miles with a full pack." He shook his head. "That guy'd burn Bragg instructors to the ground in a week."

Buck laughed, glancing easily at Hunter and Ghost silhouetted on the ridge. "Yeah." He released a tired smile. "And that dog is something else, too."

"It's a wolf, moron."

Buck smiled. "Hell, Taylor, I know what it is." He laughed again, genuinely amused. "Biggest damn wolf I ever saw, that's for sure. Meanest looking one, too. I ain't getting close to it, myself. You can't tell about them things. They can turn on you."

Taylor's scarred face twisted as he shaded his eyes, measuring the height of the sun. "We gotta make camp and set up a perimeter in less than three hours or we're gonna lose this light. Dark comes fast in these mountains. I been here before."

"Yeah?" Buck was interested. "When?"

"Ah, back in the late 'eighties." He spit to the side. "Some big recon thing on the North Ridge. I didn't know what we was doing. Supposed to be looking for a cavern or something. We found nothing and froze our butts off."

"Well, you're back in the saddle again, my man." Buck stood as Hunter and the rest began moving from the ridge toward the valley below. "But then, chances are, with the way that thing moves, we won't get a shot at it anyway."

Taylor grunted. "Buck, you idiot. Don't you know nuthin'?" He gestured up the hills. "You're SF and you can't tell by now how good that guy is? That mother ... He is *tough*." He took a second to shoulder his shotgun. "Ain't never seen his kind and I seen army trackers; they're supposed to be the best but they can't do in a day in the sun with what this guy can do in fifteen minutes. He reads everything, son. And I mean *everything*." He paused. "No, he ain't gonna let it get away."

Casting a last glance at Buck, he moved forward.

"You better lock and load, son."

Hunter was staring at the ground as Bobbi Jo knelt beside him. When he spoke, his voice was so low she could barely hear it. Somehow, she realized, he had used the sound of rushing water in the stream to cover the words.

"This morning, they started out okay," he whispered. "Now they sound like a herd of buffalo." A pause. "Happens like that. People get comfortable. Then they get careless. They cross a stream ninety-nine times and don't see a snake. Then they don't look down for the hundredth time 'cause they think it's safe. And that's when it's there. And that's when it hits them. Habit. It gets you killed out here."

She gazed about, then turned to see the team on a far slope. She could hear nothing from their direction, but the sound of the creek dominated in the descending light of day. As she watched, it seemed that they still moved in silence, carefully placing their feet in a standard single-file advance, each man ten feet apart.

Wondering what had Hunter so alarmed, she moved up carefully beside him, leaning close. He was studying everything around him in silence. She saw a single track in the hardened bank and nothing else. It was as if the creature had simply disappeared from the face of the Earth.

Hunter turned his head slightly to the side.

"Ghost," he said softly.

Moving with uncanny grace, the huge black wolf crept forward, head bowed with a kind of eerie calm. Bobbi Jo couldn't help but clutch the rifle slightly tighter at the savage profile, the wide head and the black eyes that revealed no life at all.

Pointing to the track, Hunter said, "Search."

Within a moment the wolf vanished around a bend in the river, lost to the lesser blackness of this seemingly infinite forest. Bobbi Jo waited but Hunter said nothing more as he continued to stare intently at the print. Then, taking a chance on this man who seemed so at home in the forest, Bobbi Jo spoke. "What is it that's bothering you?"

Hunter didn't reply for a time.

Then, "It doesn't make sense."

"What doesn't?"

"The pressure release marks in this track." Hunter looked to the right, ahead of them. "This thing moved to the right, but there aren't any tracks to the right. Just that ridge."

A sharply angled rise was beside them, over a hundred and fifty feet high. It was edged shale, revealing no path. They could free-climb it easily enough but there were no signs that the creature had used it, so there was no purpose to follow.

Bobbi Jo whispered, "You know, Hunter, it's been staying close to water all day."

"That's what bothers me."

"What do you mean?"

"Animals this size don't stay close to water during the day," he said, using the water to cover his voice, and then she understood how he was doing it. He was altering the pitch of his voice to blend with that of the current, modulating his words to fit the slightly lower rushing of the water beside them. She was amazed that he could so perfectly blend into the environment. It was as if he himself were part of the wild.

He continued, "Big animals always drink at dawn, then they drink again at night like clockwork. And they don't stay close to water during the day. During the day they hunt and feed."

"But the thing hasn't fed yet," she responded, trying to lower her voice so it would blend in with the current. "It's been moving fast."

"Yeah," Hunter answered. "That bothers me too. It's moving too fast. And a big animal doesn't do that. They cover maybe ... three, five miles an hour. But this thing is making serious distance. None of this is right."

She leaned even closer. "Hunter, I think I might have a good idea on this. It's been moving beside water all day."

"Like a man would do," he said, not lifting his eyes.

She paused. "Yeah, well, maybe. But the fact is that it tends to stay close to water. And that's probably what it's doing now because it's not going to suddenly change its habits. This thing is strong beyond belief. But I think it's gonna continue doing what it's been doing."

Slowly, Hunter turned his head to look up the ridge, inch by inch. His mouth hung slightly open and his face was frozen, as if with revelation.

"No," he whispered, "this would do something ...else."

His hawk-like eyes roamed the ridge.

"Tell you what," Bobbi Jo said, "how about if I cross-trail about a hundred yards out? I'll be careful not to mar any tracks if I find them."

She waited a long minute before he spoke.

"Yeah," he murmured, studying the jagged ridge. "You do that. I'm gonna have a look around here." He turned back to her, face hardening. "Don't go any farther than that."

"I won't." She rose with the words, stepping lightly from rock to rock, moving down the stream.

Hunter studied the cliff for a long time, reading ridges, slabs, and crevasses. A good man could climb it in about twenty minutes. Then he stepped forward and grabbed an outcrop, hauling himself easily over the edge. He effortlessly picked a path up the ridge, setting his feet firmly, testing the rock before placing his weight on it, choosing the easiest route.

The procedure was in effect just an extension of the method he used for moving in silence. He knew that in order to move through the forest without sound you had to set the ball of the foot down first, then settle the foot slowly, front to back. Also, it was important that you knew the step wouldn't make any sound before you placed your weight upon it by choosing solid ground. And if nothing but twigs were present, placing the foot down parallel with them.

Cautiously, he reconnoitered the rock, searching, reading every disturbance of the gray-brown dust that settled on the rock. And after twenty minutes of careful investigation he found it: a deep impact of claws branded in rock.

Crouching, Hunter turned his head and gazed down at the stream. He measured the distance and shook his head at the overall, overpowering impression before he calculated the leap to be at least thirty feet. It was an incredible distance for any creature to jump, even a tiger.

To confirm that he was correct, he looked around and found claw marks clicked in stone, marks of incredible clenching strength. He saw where it had climbed from a hundred infinitesimal signs that would have easily been overlooked by an inexperienced tracker. He nodded; yeah, this is why there weren't any more tracks in the streambed.

He moved up the cliff, climbing surely to the summit. Staring down, he observed Takakura crouching at the head of the team, still far away.

He waved them closer and waited until Bobbi Jo entered the open from the far side of the stream. When he saw her, he waved an arm and she nodded, coming toward them.

When the team arrived at the base of the cliff, Hunter simply pointed to the top, and together they began climbing.

CHAPTER 6

Fangs distended beneath gleaming red eyes, he stalked into the light of a pale moon that hung like a haggard skull over the mountains. Hulking and horrific, his slouched shoulders swelled beneath a vaguely human face and savage glare.

With animal grace he reached up to brush a branch aside and moved into a wide grassy glade, now that his sleep was done—and that what he had once been was gone.

As he entered the light he could be seen—hunched, tremendously muscular, hands slightly clutched. Long black talons extended from his fingers. He was distinctly mannish, though his bulk and brutal muscularity surpassed anything that could be called human.

He would attack them at night, he had decided. And when the moment was right, he would kill them all. For he had expected them to follow, had known that they would follow and try to destroy him for what he had done. Yes, he would kill them all, but not yet. He would not kill them until he cornered them in a place where their helicopters and support teams could not be their salvation.

Another day, and perhaps another.

He thought back over what he had observed ...

During the day he had carefully watched the man who wore the moccasins, the one who moved with the wolf, following its steps so surely. And although he did not recognize fear as they knew fear, he knew he could not escape this one as he had the others.

Yes, he would have to kill the man first. Then the others would be chattel, slain at his leisure as he hunted them through the days and nights. Perhaps, if they were fortunate, some might escape. But he would kill the man with the radio quickly so they could not communicate; he understood this much of their ways.

Snarling, his mind returned angrily to the man . . .

Yes, he was dangerous; a hateful phantom of days when he had battled truly powerful enemies who had injured him. For certain, with the man he must strike quickly, and finish quickly.

The rest would be prey.

Although he was outnumbered, he was supremely confident because he was faster, stronger, and far more cunning than they. Nor did he fear pain, as he sometimes had when they had blanketed him with bullets and explosions.

Although he did not fully understand this new body, he knew that its hardened flesh was amazingly resistant to modern weapons. Now, all he needed was the rest of the serum to make himself complete, old man and new man; the perfect being.

The fact that he had won this hybrid rage from something lost to the earth for eons did not disturb him. Yes, it was enough to be alive, and if he could only retrieve the serum, he knew he would never know death as mortals knew death.

He stood in the deepest darkness, staring from a ridge over their camp where their fire burned.

Yes, he muttered, laughing, use your fire. As they did before. But we slaughtered you then.

We will slaughter you again.

***

Darkness shimmered on the edge of the campfire.

In the eerie silence, Taylor inserted and ejected .12-gauge double-ought rounds from a shotgun, working the gun with mechanical precision, almost an extension of the machine. Varied shotguns were positioned around him, and he wore a sawed-off double-barrel with a cut-down stock on his hip. On his other side was a large-caliber handgun. He was the most heavily armed man on the team, and the largest. The great weight of ammo and guns didn't seem to disturb him at all.

One of the weapons slung across his back was an M-16-type cut-down shotgun that exchanged clips filled with .12-gauge rounds, just as soldiers exchanged clips loaded with .223 cartridges. Across one shoulder was a bandoleer of shells. Across the other shoulder was a belt containing magazines for the automatic shotgun.

Hunter hadn't spoken to Taylor until he was preparing to bed down for the night. But he glanced up as Taylor approached and asked, "Why mess with all them sticks and leaves? Think that's gonna keep you from freezing to death?"

"Usually works well enough," Hunter said, simply.

A pause.

"You know, Hunter. You're good." He seemed to think about it. "Fact is, you're real good. Maybe the best I ever seen. But I don't like guys like you."

Hunter shrugged. "Doesn't make much difference, does it?"

"Does to me."

"Well," Hunter replied as he carefully placed a piece of bark, "look at it like this, Taylor. If you're as good as they say you are, you won't have to put up with me much longer, anyway."

Silence. Then Taylor grunted. "I knew a guy like you back in 'Nam. Real mystical. A tracker. Indian dude. Used to talk to spirits, all that shit. Everybody liked him. Until all them great spirits led us into an ambush and they ended up dog meat."

"Sorry about that, Taylor." Hunter finished his task with a curved piece of bark. "But, truth is, I don't do much talking to spirits, divine or otherwise. So you shouldn't have anything to worry about."

After a moment Taylor mumbled something low to himself and walked toward his tent.

Hunter had become accustomed to the sergeant's fire-scarred face. One half was permanently reddened and smooth, the dead eye gazing from a broad, determined brow, the other dark and fierce, changing in a breath from concentrated and distant to personal and close and threatening. Working through the aftermath of the conversation, Hunter sensed yet another presence approaching but didn't turn because he identified it by the familiar soft stride.

Each hour, he had noticed, his senses were becoming more acute, his eyes adjusting to a keenness he hadn't experienced in a long time. There was a renewed acuity for distant searching, and he could read the faintest ghost of a track without a magnifying glass. He could see distant ridges clearly while the rest relied upon cumbersome binoculars. And he knew his senses would sharpen even more as the track progressed.

It was a phenomenon that sometimes happened, sometimes not. For in thick jungle, where only limited vision was necessary, his eyesight never seemed to improve. But in this vast wilderness where a clear superiority of vision was required, he usually adjusted quickly. He heard Bobbi Jo behind him.

"What's that?" she asked.

"A leaf hut," he said without turning. "I learned how to make it when I was a kid."

"It's not very big."

"That's what makes it work."

"How's that?"

Hunter shrugged. "You create a small cocoon with leaves and sticks, place some bark on the outside to keep out the rain, insulate it good so there's nothing but dead air and you're set. Body heat warms the space, the dry leaves keep the heat inside. The bark keeps out the moisture. It works well in any environment."

She knelt, rifle in hand, and studied the structure. "But it's only closed on three sides. It's gonna get pretty cold tonight."

Glancing at her, Hunter gestured vaguely at the fire. "I'll heat a few stones and put them just outside the entrance. That'll do for the night."

"So this is why you don't carry any equipment?" She seemed more interested in him now than the hut. " 'Cause you can just live off the land?" She smiled, something Hunter hadn't yet seen; it won his attention. She added with a laugh, "A Tarzan kinda thing?"

He laughed with her. "I guess it's something like that."

Uninvited, she squatted beside him, watching him work. "Where did you learn to do all this, Hunter? I've had expert jungle training under covert programs where they allow women in combat and—"

"And where would that be?" Hunter asked.

She paused. "In the government," she said, a meaningful bluntness to it. "The only place where they'll take a woman in combat."

"Impressive," he replied. "I respect that."

"Do you really?"

"Sure," he continued. "Why wouldn't I?"

She wrapped her arms around her knees. "You know, seems to me somebody like you wouldn't respect much at all."

He smiled but didn't look. "Why's that?"

"Oh, I don't know," she remarked vaguely. "What they told us in the briefing was that you can survive out here or anywhere. You're rich. Famous. You come up with all those cures for diseases and stuff. You have mansions and penthouses and yet you prefer to live in that old broken-down log cabin. Like you don't really need any of that fancy stuff." She paused; the smile still hovered on his bronzed face. "They told us all that but they couldn't answer my questions. So ...what's the score?" she continued, watching closer. "That is, if you don't mind my asking."

He shrugged. "No special reason. You're right. I don't need the rest of that stuff. Neither does anyone else, either. But I have it: I use it for a good purpose."

"You think this is a good purpose?"

"Yeah," he said, a slight lifting of his brow. "Yeah, I do."

Silence.

Bobbi Jo leaned forward. "What'd you do before this?"

"Spent most of my life just surviving," he replied. "An old trapper taught me how to live off the land when I was just a kid. So I traveled out in the Northwest, just tracking, living in the wild. It's all the same as a city, anyway. 'Cause everything you need to survive is beside you. Food, shelter, clothing. A man could come out here with nothing but a knife and an ax and make a home for himself." He laughed. "Not real smart, but it's possible. This place is a lot harder than any other that I've seen. Hard country, for sure."

"I truly think you'd need more than just a knife."

Hunter turned his head. "Really?"

"Yeah, really." She gestured toward her pack. "That's my pack, and it's got the bare minimum for surviving in this terrain. And I'm someone who actually knows what she's doing. I can survive almost anywhere, but I need everything in that pack."

"Like a tent?" Hunter smiled.

Bobbi Jo looked at the structure he had completed in less than a half hour. It looked absolutely solid and, despite herself, she believed that it would be as warm as anything they had brought.

He continued, "You mean like all that food you carry?" He motioned vaguely. "You see that tree?"

"Yeah, I see it."

"That's a white oak. And a handful of those acorns, even the ones on the ground, will give you more protein than you'll find in a ten-ounce steak. They're not too bitter and you can eat them raw. And over there"— he pointed to the side—"is some purslane. Dig up the root bulbs and boil them just like potatoes and they'll give you vitamins and minerals." He continued speaking as he worked, not looking up. "We're surrounded by tamarack trees. Cut off the shoots and they're as good as any vegetable, and tastier. And you can use the stems as bow drills. Then on the other side of this clearing is some wintergreen. It's a plant."

"Yes, thank you. I know what it is."

With a patient smile he continued, "Yeah, well, anyway, boil winter-green and the leaves make a tea that reduces fever better than anything in a hospital. It's good for a sore throat and the tea is full of vitamins." He shrugged. "It goes on and on. You're surrounded by a pharmacy and all the food you would ever need. And if you need clothing there are plenty of places for snares, deadfalls, bow pits. We passed over about a hundred trails and runs and beds today with everything from bobcat to beaver, so there's an abundance of food. And they're easy enough to catch with your hand if you know how. And this place is alive with fish, which I've already built a trap cage for. In the morning, while you're preparing your MRJEs, I'll cook up a couple of trout and eat them. Or eat them raw. Doesn't matter. What hurts you and the rest of these guys is that you try to overcome the land instead of taking advantage of it."

Bobbi Jo was silent, but her eyes had narrowed as he talked. Then he was finished and rose, walked slowly around the hut. He shook it with his hand: It was solid. It would keep him warm for the night.

Kneeling, he removed three large stones from the fire and placed them near the entrance, covering them lightly with dirt. He did not seem fatigued by the work; it was as if he had lived this life for so long that his body could complete the movements by muscle memory alone. His face reflected nothing but effortless concentration; a purity of movement that came from the purest strength and patience ruled by a disciplined soul.

"You really are some kind of Tarzan, aren't you?" Bobbi Jo asked quietly. She shook her blond head as she added, "You're more at home in the wild than anyone I've ever seen." She paused. "But there's still something about you I can't figure out."

He raised his eyes with a faint smile. "What's that?"

A pause.

"I don't know," she remarked plainly. "It's something you seem to hide. But I can sometimes glimpse it in your eyes when you respond to a sound. You react with some kind of wild purity. Like a wolf. Or a tiger. It's like you've got this fantastic instinct that is just way beyond the rest of us. I ... I really don't know how to describe it and I don't know whether to be afraid of it or just be glad you're on our side."

Hunter gazed down at her, silent.

He blinked, considering her words.

Really, neither did he.

***

Lying quietly in her tent, Bobbi Jo stared at Hunter s hut, unable to forget the great black wolf that lay slightly to his side, ever on guard even in a thin semblance of sleep. Hunter was already asleep inside the enclosure. She had noticed that when he lay down he was asleep in seconds although she figured he could stay awake far longer than the rest of them, if he chose.

She wondered about what kind of man he was inside, and what he had found out here in the wild. Perhaps it was a simplicity of life that somehow escaped him in the cultured world, but she didn't think so. It was something more. Something deeper. And for the first time in a while, she felt an attraction. Even though she tried to shield herself from such thoughts in the field, she couldn't help but recognize the sensation.

She had read his dossier and was familiar with his documented history. Of the life he had led before he emerged in the public eye, little was known.

Yes, an unusual man ...

She blinked. Then she reached out and gently clutched her rifle, sensing somehow that the strength, the will, and the spirit of this enigma of a man was probably worth more than all of them and their weapons combined.

***

Crouching, monstrous hands clenching, he stared at the camp, studying all he could see in the moon's skull-like light. Silent and unmoving, he saw the big man who led at the front, the man who tracked with such remarkable skill. Then he studied the wolf that lay at the man's side, the black one.

Even in sleep, the wolf seemed alert. Its ears still stood straight and its face was away from the fire. He could not tell if it was gazing into the treeline. The canine black eyes melted into the utter blackness of its face but its posture was decidedly tense, as if it never relaxed. He knew that it was a creature that could possibly deliver a savage battle. As much, even, as the Grizzly he had killed earlier in the day.

But by now the wounds that branded him in that fierce fight had healed; only a thin pink scar marked the moment. With his frightfully dim human intelligence—what had been his name?—he estimated that he could recover from almost any wound within a day's time, the hybrid DNA in his system somehow synthesizing to accelerate cell replication and enhanced blood generation.

Slowly, outlined against the sky, he stood, still gazing somberly on the campsite.

No, he would not attack them tonight. He would wait. He would lead them across the forest tomorrow, allowing them to close. He would lead them and let them think they were cornering him, as he would corner them, in the end. Then, when his stalking was complete, he would launch his first attack, killing several of them before he escaped again.

He did not fear injury, or the soldiers, or the wolf. Though he did, somehow, fear the man.

They would fight fiercely, as all of them did, but the titanic might in his form, in his acutely enhanced senses and his superior intelligence would be more than enough to destroy them.

Yes, to destroy all of them.

He growled as he turned into the night.

CHAPTER 7

Bobbi Jo's voice seemed to come from a distance.

"What do you see?"

Hunter didn't move as he studied the tracks intently. The ground was soft on the ridge and he could read distinct impressions—dragging signs of where he had shuffled restlessly, thirsty. Hunter turned his head to stare down over the camp, estimating how long the beast had watched them during the night.

"Hunter?" Bobbi Jo leaned forward. "What do you see?"

"It was here."

"It was here? For how long?"

"Four hours, maybe." Hunter's brow hardened in concentration. "Early this morning."

Creeping up, she knelt beside him. Her dark blond hair fell forward to cover half her face as she stared at the tracks, and for a long time she was silent. Then she raised her head, scanning as her head moved in a precision pattern. "What is this thing, Hunter?" Her voice held the edge of subdued fear. "This isn't natural."

Hunter didn't move.

To lesser trackers, the footprints would only reveal that it had been here. Others could determine its approach, its retreat. But Hunter could determine more, using skills so long adapted into his very being that they were only slightly less than instinct.

He could tell how long it had stood before it shuffled its foot, measuring its patience. He could read from only the slight mulling that its balance was almost perfect, or that it had softly and silently clawed the loam in its silent vigil, and where it had watched the longest. He turned his head to stare down into the camp. And from the cliff's edge, he saw what it had watched the closest. What had been its highest priority. And knew it was him.

***

A low growl like subterranean thunder came from behind Hunter.

Really not so much a growl as a black vibration in the atmosphere—a dark rumbling inhabited by a pure and savage animal essence. They had been moving steadily, rapidly for hours, close on the beast's heels. Hunter turned his head and gazed back, watching Ghost's distended canines extend past his lower jaw. A snarl twisted the face beneath blazing black eyes.

"What is it, Ghost?"

Moving with massive, deep power, Ghost took a solid step forward. And the snarl continued to build in depth, blending growl and roar into an unusual, cavernous depth. Then a faint trembling tensed the great dark form and Hunter turned his head to search out what lay before them.

With the support team behind him and Bobbi Jo close, Hunter searched the thick stand of white poplars and evergreens that laid an almost impenetrable black wall. He was certain the creature had used this trail to travel south; it was obvious. But the tracks clearly indicated that it had not been hesitating, that it had been moving with purpose.

Holding the rifle tight, Hunter stood from a crouch and moved closer. Even though the sun was still high in the sky, the darkness was almost complete. It reminded him of the triple canopy jungles of South America where sunlight never saw the earth beneath the arboreal giants.

Shoulders humped, hackles rising along his neck and back, Ghost moved beside him. Although the wolf now made no sound, its jaws were distended, open fangs the only threat it gave before it hurtled forward. For now it was in a killing mode, and by instinct it would be silent until it struck. Bobbi Jo, turning slowly, continued to scan the flanks for an ambush.

Hunter spoke quietly. "Don't worry about the flanks right now." His eyes never left the darkness before them. "It's not going to ambush us here. It's moving fast, not even looking to the side."

She stared. "So what's got you so worried?"

"Because it doesn't do that."

"Why not?"

Hunter bent and studied the ground. He could see where an impression was deeper, almost gouging out the ground. The mark indicated clearly that the creature had made a sudden, volcanic move to the right, turning almost in midair.

Hunter stretched out a hand, feeling the age of the track as he subconsciously identified a myriad of smells: ferns, rotting vegetation, pine and mold and ferment, a faded, coarse animal pungency, and something else— something heavy and motionless and moist. It was scent he had come to know well from a life spent mostly in the harsh wild.

He looked down. "Ghost, stay here."

The great wolf stopped in midstride, but the burning black eyes never left the forest wall before it, nor did its tension fade. Slowly, Hunter turned to Bobbi Jo. "Stay with Ghost. Tell the others to hold position."

She tightened almost to a combat readiness; the barrel of the Barrett rose. "What are you going to do?"

Hunter was already moving away, angling deeply to the right. As he twisted a move between two mammoth ferns and into the bush he whispered back to her, "Something died here. I'm gonna find out what it was."

She brushed a lock from her face and looked to him again.

But he was gone.

***

Despite Bobbi Jo's hand signal to hold position, Takakura moved up silently to crouch beside her. Frowning, the big Japanese stared into the foliage, searching. His narrow black eyes revealed only fierce alertness when Bobbi Jo cast a slight glance. Obviously, the commander was at home in combat. His voice came to her calmly and coldly.

"What is it, Bobbi Jo?"

She shook her head. "I don't know."

Takakura gave a glance toward the wolf, but it had vanished without a sound in the space of three seconds. It had been here when he crouched and now it was gone; no sound, no sight. The Japanese's disciplined face revealed no surprise. "The wolf ... he is ... like ..."

"A ghost?" Bobbi Jo said, and despite an appropriateness in the reply, she didn't smile.

All that she had, emotion and intellect and will, were too tightly focused on what vague darkness—what shapeless threat—hovered on the far side of that green, mossy dark wall of impenetrable fern. Then Takakura bowed his head, slightly frowning, toward the gathering dark. He took one second to monitor the support team's stillness and nodded. Obviously, their readiness was acceptable.

"What did Hunter say as he moved?" he whispered.

"He doesn't generally say anything when he moves."

A moment, and Takakura seemed to read more into it. Without effort he seemed to understand what manner of man was leading them.

"He is a hard man," he muttered. "There is something in him that moves him. But it, in itself, does not move." He paused. "How long do you think he will be gone? We are losing what little light this canopy allows."

She waited, shook her head. "With him, you can never tell. Sometimes he won't move at all for an hour. He'll just stare at the terrain. Then sometimes he moves so fast you have to be half wolf to keep up."

Takakura grunted. "This I know."

"He'll come back when he's certain," she added, turning her head with mechanical precision to stay alert. "I've learned that much about him. He doesn't ever make a mistake. He says it takes too long to double back and pick up a track if he's wrong."

"The wolf, it helps him."

"Yeah." Bobbi Jo's hands tightened on the rifle at a slight rustling sound. She waited; possibly a falling branch. "Ghost helps him. Or he helps Ghost. One or the other. Either way, they work together."

"So I have seen. How long, do you think, before we are able to target this creature?"

Her voice was softer.

"Probably sooner than we'd like, Commander."

***

Slashed and disemboweled, the mammoth brown-black carcass with protruding white ribs lay before Hunter in the somber gloom.

He stood motionless, measuring the great Grizzly's size, judged it to be close to half a ton. Glistening black claws at the end of incredible huge forelegs lay still. Its fangs were fixed in a frozen roar. Its open eyes were glazed by the vicious impact of a sudden and unexpected death.

Circling the area, Hunter had easily discovered the creature's taloned tracks, the ones left after it had killed the Grizzly. Almost immediately he had known what had happened, but had done a careful reconnaissance to make sure that the thing, whatever it was, was not lying close to the dead Grizzly as a tiger would often do. All around the area he found the Grizzly's tracks, half-eaten bushes, and trampled berries. Then, after he was certain that he and the team were alone, Hunter angled carefully back to examine the corpse.

Clearly, reading the overlaying tracks, Hunter could see that it had been a ferocious fight. Not long, certainly, but ferocious— clearly a confrontation of two creatures each of whom struck with horrific force. And for a moment Hunter remembered the two Siberian tigers who had fought to the death as he rolled between them. It confirmed to him that the more powerful the enemies were, the shorter the fight.

The Grizzly, normally reluctant to challenge a creature of equal size, had put up a formidable defense. Its claws were caked in dried blood, confirming Hunter's suspicion gleaned from surrounding leaves that the creature he was tracking could indeed be wounded, and had been. And somehow it gave him comfort.

No, he thought to himself, it wasn't un-killable.

In a surreal silence Hunter bent and froze. Then removed his knife to examine the bear's wounds when he heard what could have been the soft nestling of a bird's wings, so close.

He followed the almost-silent approaching steps and knew what it was before he shook his head, smiling and turning. He angled his head toward the gloom and waited, but there was no more movement. Then, softly, in a voice no human being could have heard if they had been standing six inches away, he spoke into the darkness.

"Ghost. Come here, boy."

One second later a pair of glistening black eyes and a huge anvil-like head, wide muscular shoulders beneath, silently parted the leafy black ferns. Ghost didn't move as his dark animal gaze darted around the torn and trampled glade, rich with the scent of blood. From Hunter's aspect alone, he seemed to recognize that there was no battle to be fought.

Hunter smiled and shook his head. Then he turned to examine the gutted carcass of the Grizzly. Its intestines, liver, and heart were gone. And the massive injury wasn't slashed into the massive chest, it was torn, as if inflicted in some demoniacal killing rage. Then Hunter examined the great bear's huge neck and head and found a large indentation in the inch-thick skull. Gingerly, he ran his hand over the depression, attempting to feel through the armor-like fur, before he was certain.

Part of the Grizzly's skull had been crushed into powder. Slightly larger than a man's fist, the area ground jagged slices of bone beneath Hunter's probing grasp before he leaned back, shaking his head in amazement that approached disbelief.

Hunter was accustomed to death; it was the way of the wild, the way of his life. And he himself could kill efficiently and without emotion when necessary. And if he hadn't possessed that hard discipline, and will, and skill, the forest would have long ago claimed him. For in the end, always, the strongest survived.

He knew that a Grizzly would eat anything, plant or animal or fish or bark or even rotten meat, to sustain its great bulk. Nor did it suffer any adverse effects from the combination. Grizzlies were, quite simply, gigantic garbage disposals. Which is why they rarely challenged large animals; they simply didn't need such quantities of meat when the entire forest was alive with plenteous sustenance.

Reaching out with the Bowie, Hunter made a larger incision in the stomach and, turning his face from the gastric vapors released, methodically pulled out five handfuls of half-digested berries and the shredded, bony remains of at least six fish, all eaten within the last twenty-four hours.

The bear had obviously been gorging itself, as bears habitually did in late summer and fall to produce the huge layers of fat that would sustain them through hibernation and the harsh winter.

Hunter knew that it would have eaten omnivorously for another two months before it bedded down in what most called hibernation but which was really little more than a long and often interrupted sleep. Even with the protective foldings of fat, it would awaken daily to meander in its den for warmth. It would often clean itself or even spend hours staring into the snow to alleviate boredom, waiting and watching for the first signs of spring. Just as it would stoically endure hunger as its body began utilizing the fat for sheer survival.

Hunter knew what blow had probably killed the beast, though he found it difficult to believe. And, despite his resolute courage, Hunter felt his chest tighten. His skin felt chilled and the hairs along his arms and neck seemed to rise.

He had been gauging this creature's strength all along, but not yet had he seen any act that could approach this. This was monstrous. This was something he had never seen and never imagined. What had done this had no predator. What had done this stood at the top of evolution. Stood where even man himself was simply food; a puny, dying thing.

Unmoving, raising his face only, Hunter stared into the distant forest and searched, knowing he would find nothing. Deep within, he knew a semblance of a fear he had felt many times, but this time it was joined by something else. Something he refused to accept or recognize, because he knew it would make him weak.

Hunter stood slowly, his brow hardening beneath his ragged black mane as his blue eyes narrowed and hardened degree by degree until they were as opaque as a leopard crouching before an attack. Some instinct he had long ago come to trust told him battle was here, and there was no escape. It was instinct, or more, that he had come to know true.

Then he felt Ghost beside him, the great wide shoulders rising almost to his hips.

"Let's go, boy." Hunter ruffled the wolf's neck hair. "We've got some bad news for our friends."

***

Takakura seemed unfazed.

Holding his MP-5 in a strong hand, the Japanese stared at the slaughtered bear. His face revealed nothing but defiance and determination. He stood a long time in silence as Hunter described what had obviously happened.

"The bear came from the brush, as they generally do," Hunter continued uneasily. "It was probably surprised. Was probably just defending itself. But it was flat ground, and this creature moved faster." He motioned from a point in the brush to the body of the dead Grizzly. "They started there and they never quit. And it was probably a hard fight. Neither of them backed up, and they threw a lot of blows. The bear wounded it, I think, 'cause I found its blood on the trees. But right here the thing took it to the ground, got on top, and struck it hard in the head. Crushed its skull like a grape. Then it tore out its heart."

Takakura looked up. "Tore out its heart?"

Heavy pause.

"That was for pleasure, Commander." Hunter was expressionless. "It had already killed it."

Silent, Takakura looked to the rest of the squad.

Then Tipler, moving up from the edge, muttered almost to himself, "Damned peculiar, I must say ... Yes, *very* peculiar ..."

"What is it, Professor?" Hunter asked, attempting to conceal a faint depression he felt at this latest discovery.

"These, my boy," Tipler said with keen interest as he bent over the corpse. He lifted a short stick, pointing to wounds on the front section of the Grizzly's behemoth shoulders. "These," he murmured, "are holding marks, my boy. Not slashing marks. Which means ..."

Hunter stared a moment, eyes narrowing. Beneath the Grizzly's armorlike fur he had not noticed the dissimilarity of the multitude of ravaging wounds torn into the shoulders. "Yeah," he muttered, his own interest fired by the acute observation. "Yeah, I know what it means."

"Well, don't feel like you have to tell the rest of us," Taylor said, stepping up. "The only thing we have to lose is our lives."

Tipler continued, becoming more excited as he confirmed his observation. "Yes, yes, not for ten thousand years has there been a beast that killed as this. Not since Smilodon." He pointed and turned to the group. "You see! It was on the bear's back"—carried away with the drama, he raised his hands as claws—"holding tightly with its great massive claws deeply embedded in the shoulders, ravaging its neck from behind! And it was then that it raised its hand in the air and brought it down to crush its skull! Remarkable! Such strength! I have never seen its equal! A Smilodon would have embedded its incisors meant for slashing and holding, to kill as it held. But this creature was forced to use a somewhat hammer-like blow"—he began to pace in his excitement—"which tells us that its fangs, or whatever semblance of canine attributes it may possess, are not formidable or sufficient for this manner of physical confrontation. However, it does possess strength not in proportion to its already established physical weight. Strange, yes." He paused, staring down. "The mystery deepens, but this creature's rage reveals it. No, it is not a tiger, not a creature with customary predatory attributes. Yet even so, it is still to be feared. Its most formidable weapons may be somewhat conventional, but they are nevertheless deadly in effect."

Taylor mumbled, "Well, then, why don't we just give it a bleeping medal?"

Takakura turned his head. "Taylor," he said reprovingly. Then, to the professor: "Which means what, exactly?"

Tipler stepped slightly back. "Which means, Commander, that this creature kills in a strangely similar fashion to Smilodon—the saber-toothed tiger—which has been absent from the planet for millennia. Yet it walks as a man, and appears to think sometimes as a man. Which leaves yet another possibility to us."

"Yes?"

"A mutation," Tipler replied flatly. "A genetic mutation of either man or beast. How or why it came about I cannot say. But it is a theory which we must now consider. Without doubt."

Hunter followed the gazes and measured the men behind him more thoroughly than he had several days ago. Because now he had seen them in action, could estimate their wilderness skills. And some, he had already calculated, were out of their element.

First, there was Taylor, who seemed to care for nothing and fear nothing. He seemed relatively comfortable in the bush, and Hunter had determined that his overt propensity to antagonize was born from the simple fact that he was innately hostile. But in the field he was a consummate soldier, dependable and performing his duties professionally and without complaint.

Then there was Buck, a Stone Age cowboy who never complained and seemed to move with an easy economy of movement that belied an ingrained wilderness wisdom. And, somehow, Hunter felt Buck could be trusted, perhaps because he was one of the few team members who retained some sense of humor about the affair. As efficient as he seemed to be, Buck was easygoing and relaxed, and seemed to hide nothing. The only team member that Hunter had not yet spoken with was a British soldier named Arthur Wilkenson.

Wilkenson, Hunter had learned from Bobbi Jo, was a former member of the British Special Air Service. And Hunter knew that the SAS were considered the toughest of the tough. Stoic and aloof, Wilkenson had made no efforts to speak with Hunter, but Hunter had studied him quietly. Tall and lean, but clearly quite muscular, Wilkenson never seemed to tire. But Hunter didn't think it was from his native constitution; it seemed more a product of stern conditioning.

The Englishman's sharply angled face held piercing green eyes that glinted with quick intelligence, and Hunter remembered Bobbi Jo mentioning that he spoke five languages and was an expert in tactical analysis.

"What's that?" Hunter had asked.

"It's an SOP," she responded. "It's where someone is adept at analyzing defense strength and designing the appropriate tactic to countermine it." She had stared back as she thought more carefully about it. "In the army, you'd probably have to go to the National War College for something like that. At least to some kind of policy-making position training camp. I don't know how they do it in the SAS. But I know he's a high-level thinker. Maybe as high as it gets."

Slowly raising his eyes, Hunter studied the austere silhouette of Wilkenson. "Why do you think he was assigned to this?"

She hesitated, catching his vague disturbance. "The Pentagon doesn't know what to expect," she said finally, "so they might be covering every contingency." She stared over the forest. "I have to be honest with you, this weird-ass stunt isn't like anything I've ever done, Hunter. Throwing together a team for a high-risk mission like this instead of pulling in a group from Delta or the SEALs goes against good sense. We haven't seen any combat together so we don't know how the next person is going to react. I don't know why they did it like this. It almost guarantees failure."

As she spoke, Hunter heard something approach.

"Set all weapons on fully automatic fire," Takakura said sternly. "But there will be no firing unless we have a clear sight of the creature."

Another team member that Hunter had not come to know well— Riley—stepped forward. Also lean but with heavy arms and shoulders, Riley was brown-haired with brown eyes. He had a sharp angular face and high cheekbones. He spoke with a slight Irish accent. And, in addition to his M-16 rifle, he carried a climbing rope looped shoulder to waist with crampons, chocks, carabineers and pitons on a belt at his waist.

"I would like to ask Hunter a question," he said.

Hunter looked quietly at him. Waited patiently.

"Mr. Hunter." Riley stepped forward. "I have watched you track this creature. I respect you. I admire your skills. But I wish to know what you know. They say that you can tell much about this from how it moves. That you can think as it does." He paused. "I doubt, when we come face to face with this creature, that we will have time to learn from our mistakes. To me, now seems an appropriate time for you to prepare us."

Takakura turned toward Hunter at Riley's words, indicating that he agreed. Hunter wondered how much he should reveal, and quickly ruled out the claw and what he had discovered in the laboratory at the research center. But, clearly, they deserved to know everything else he could give them. He didn't know as much as he wished, but whatever he could tell them would be more than they knew now.

"All right," he said, glad for the opportunity. "I'll tell you what I think. This thing we're after doesn't move like an animal. And I know, 'cause I've tracked 'em all. It's not following a circuit and it's not roaming. It's killing whatever it finds." He paused, thinking, and tried to be concise. "Listen, this is what I think will happen," he continued. "It will ambush us. Probably from above. A ledge, a tree, something like that. It'll try and hit and get away quick. But it probably won't chase any of us. It'll wait 'til we're close, then it'll make its move. You've got to watch your surroundings at all times. And I mean at all times. And ... I think we're dealing with something that is faster and stronger than anything you've ever seen or imagined. If you see it coming, get off a shot fast. The rest of us will follow. If you hesitate, I guarantee you won't be around to regret it."

Frowning, Takakura bent his dark head. "How soon before we encounter this creature?"

Hunter hesitated, measuring the commitment burning in their faces before he lifted his rifle, turning away.

"Whenever it decides," he said.

CHAPTER 8

After reorienting from the discovery of the Grizzly and deciding to establish camp at the first available defensive position, Hunter led them down the ridge by dead reckoning. He didn't have time for a map or compass, and the Magellan system only revealed where you were, not the suitability of surrounding terrain for bivouac purposes.

Bobbi Jo was to his left, as usual, and Ghost moved to his right, often lifting his head to search by sight before he lowered his nose and sniffed, suddenly disturbed. Hunter paused but saw nothing, and had no time for a detailed examination, so they kept moving through a gathering dark that would fall like a phantom's cloak on these trees, making even the moon seem distant and weak.

Since discovering the bear, Hunter had carried in his hand the ragged claw he had retrieved from the steel panel of the destroyed research facility, trying to construct everything he knew about the beast into a cohesive picture. Although broken, it was thick as a bear's—long and slightly curving with a tip that razored to a wicked, hooked point. He wondered if it was used primarily for slashing or piercing or even holding; he couldn't decide.

It was strangely tapered, almost in a wedge. He had never seen one like it because most claws were task-specific, tailored to a particular job like digging, holding, slashing, or climbing. But this claw seemed to be unnaturally all-purpose, as if it could gouge, pierce, or tear; an effective weapon or tool.

It was also finely serrated, so no matter what, it retained an effective cutting edge. It reminded him of the teeth of those prehistoric sharks, the Carcharodon Megalodon, whose teeth, recovered 10,000 years later from the ocean floor, still retained a serrated razor sharpness. He turned his mind back to making a quick and secure camp. Found Takakura moving beside him.

"You have never seen anything like this?" he asked with some credulity. "Not ever?"

"No," Hunter replied. "I've tracked everything on earth, Commander, and I've never tracked anything that moved purposefully from stone to stone. Nothing that made sudden changes of direction without reason. Nothing that didn't move on a circuit or within a territory. And, strangely, this thing doesn't seem to hunt at all. It just kills whatever it encounters by chance, eats it and moves on. It kills a lot and eats a lot, but it holds to the direction it's going like a man. It knows exactly where it's heading, that much is clear. So it has purpose." Hunter paused, turned toward Takakura: "But the only purpose a normal animal has is survival, Commander. So this thing, whatever it is, doesn't think like an animal. It has some kind of ... plan." A pause. "Or something."

Takakura appeared disturbed, but he did not dispute Hunter's words. "Can you discern anything else? We must know as much as possible. What about its fight with the Grizzly? Did you learn anything of its methods?"

"I told you most everything I could read. It was short but ferocious. All I can say for sure is that it fights pure, with no hesitation. It doesn't have any mercy. But some part of it ..." Hunter shook his head. "Some part of it thinks like a man."

Takakura also shook his head, openly frustrated.

Hunter continued as they moved quickly. "Generally a bear won't fight on the ground because nothing is big enough to take it down. Even another bear. They fight on their back legs, strike with their forelegs." His face tightened. "No, I've never seen anything strong enough to take a Grizzly to the ground and kill it like that."

"I see," said the Japanese. He hoisted his rifle and adjusted a leather strap holding the katana. His dark eyes narrowed at the distant ridge, still lit by the crimson light of a descending sun. "We cannot make the ridge before dark. We will estab-"

Suddenly a thunderous god-roar of shocking animal might erupted violently from the ridge to crash over them, and they raised aim as one. And for the faintest split second an enormous manlike silhouette was half visible—snarling, raging, challenging. And then it was gone, turning and disappearing beyond the rocky ridge like a vaporous apparition.

Staring up, feeling the racing of his breath, the pounding of his heart, Hunter almost couldn't believe what he had seen—something he surely saw more clearly than the others because he had almost instantly separated it from the green mossy ferns and gloom.

He heard himself whispering, "God Almighty ..."

Vicious expletives were hurled up and down the rank, Taylor overpowering them all with, "What the hell was that! What the hell was *that*?"

Hunter lowered his rifle long before the others, knowing it wouldn't reveal itself again.

No, that hadn't been for conflict. That had been to officially announce the battle and the war about to come. And, probably most of all, to satisfy some kind of pure bestial pleasure, some latent need to display its superiority.

Hunter was certain: tonight.

And if it attacked them here in the open ground when they were without a defensible perimeter, they would be slaughtered as quickly as the Grizzly.

"Move quickly!" Takakura hissed. "We must make camp. Quickly! Quickly!"

Hunter was already moving, searching for clearing with easy access to the stream. They had covered a little more than three hundred yards when he found it, a fairly level section ringed on three sides by a wall of forest. Hunter didn't like the size of the perimeter and searched for a better place to camp, but they were out of time. This would have to suffice.

"This is the best we're gonna get for the night," he said, casting a glance at the low full moon, hazy and hauntingly large on the horizon. "In thirty minutes it'll be pitch dark."

"Fuck that!" Buck said, throwing a pile of wood he'd already grabbed down in the center of the clearing. "This place is gonna look like daylight!"

In two minutes he had a blazing fire going and was still feeding more wood. And he returned to the woods with his rifle close, quickly gathering more scattered branches to hurl a mound into a bonfire that would easily illuminate the small clearing through the night.

Takakura was hurling terse instructions for incendiaries, motion detectors, listening devices, occipital laser locaters and random intruder scanning devices to be set for the perimeter.

Working quickly, they had everything in place within twenty minutes.

Hunter, not involved in the military procedures, examined Tipler as they settled, concerned that the old man was breathing heavily and holding his left arm at the wrist. And Bobbi Jo stood watch in the center of the glade. She scanned left, right and back again like a machine, cold and focused.

Hunter knew that if the creature pierced the gloomy veil imprisoning them, especially while she still had light, she would hit it dead center before it made ten feet.

"You all right, Doc?" he whispered.

Breathing heavily, Tipler patted his hand. "I am fine, my boy. You'd best make your preparations as quickly as possible. You have little time. Hurry. You will need food in the morning."

"Forget the food. No time for it tonight."

Takakura spoke sternly to the team. "Buck! You take first watch with Wilkenson! We don't know what we are up against but we can be certain that it knows our location! From now, there will be a double guard on all shifts. The rest will sleep close to the fire with weapons ready at all times!"

Takakura expended the clip to the MP-5, tapped it, reset it quickly, and opened the bolt. His face was fierce as he turned to the surrounding forest. "A fortress of guards and security devices could not stop it from attacking the research facilities! Likely, this defense shall not stop it either! Our best strategy will be a concentrated wall of ordnance that might dissuade it from a full frontal attack."

Wilkenson spoke. "We actually have an advantage in the clearing that they did not possess at the compounds, Commander. For one, we can observe its approach. And, for the first attack, at least, we can target it easily. But that is an advantage that will exhaust itself after we hit it once or twice. More than likely, if it is effective, it will adopt a different strategy to avoid direct contact." The Englishman gazed about, seeming to measure distances. "I would project that we will defeat it earlier in the battle, but as the night progresses, I believe it will find a means of penetrating the perimeter."

Hunter felt a touch at his thigh and knew the silent familiar presence. Without looking he reached down and ruffled Ghost's mane, but the wolf didn't move. As usual, it had been scouting ahead and doubling back to ensure that Hunter was safe. But now they were making camp and Hunter knew Ghost wouldn't leave his side until morning.

No matter what.

"Rebecca?"

Gina s voice contained an edge of suppressed excitement and Rebecca Tanus turned. She saw the younger woman staring up at the electron microscope display screen. The power was set at three-quarter magnification for cytosine and thymine molecules. The pulsating blue light of the screen flicked as she adjusted half a dozen dials.

Holding a clipboard heavily laden with notes, Rebecca walked forward. "What is it, Gina?"

"This." Gina leaned back. "I think there's some sort of residue on the cast. Something indigenous."

Rebecca put down the clipboard and stared. It took her only a moment to see the microscopic tendril set against a blue-gray electric background. "What is it?" she asked quietly.

"I think it's hemoglobin," Gina said. "I've got *heme* tone and what appear to be iron atoms and some protein."

"Protein?"

"Looks like it."

"Well, what makes you think that it's not a blood particle from one of the victims?"

"Because of this." Gina adjusted the screen again, and an amazing blaze of electrons and virtual protons could be seen flickering in and out of focus as she gently turned the dials. Rebecca was reminded that mastering an electron microscope was as much an art as a science. After a moment a cluster of atoms was isolated. Then Gina increased magnification and after another fifteen minutes Rebecca saw the beginning of a DNA chart. She stared at it.

"It looks human, Gina."

"'Looks' is the pivotal word," Gina replied, adjusting the scope again. "Watch what happens when I use electrophoresis. I'm going to magnetize the segment and see if it curls away from the positive or negative electrons like human DNA would."

After a moment, the distinction was obvious.

"Nothing is happening," said Rebecca.

"Exactly. Nothing is happening. But it should be."

They stared at the DNA strand, which seemed remarkably resilient to the magnetic provocation. Gina delicately added a slight amount of phosphorescent dye to the sample. In technical terms it was called fluorescent in-situ hybridization, or "FISHing" for short. It was a process in which geneticists locate particular genes in much the same way as a computer could search and locate for a particular word in a text.

"I tried to find out why the segment was so resistant to electrophoresis," Gina added. "And I found a hybrid segment of restrictive enzymes that accelerate cloning. Actually, they don't just accelerate. They clone so quickly that an invasion, like a virus or bacteria, is almost instantly absorbed and destroyed. The only thing this DNA lacks is the ability to reproduce enough of itself to construct a consistent molecular polymerase chain."

Rebecca was bending toward the screen. "And what, exactly, does that mean, Gina?"

"It means that, it this strand were complete, which it isn't, it would be able to clone, or, rather, duplicate, polymerase genes indefinitely. Which means, in effect, that it would have almost unlimited cellular reproductive capabilities."

Rebecca was silent for a moment. "Okay, let's suppose you're right on this. But let's check the preliminaries. Have you used sanitation procedures to make sure the cast wasn't contaminated?"

"Since it arrived, yes."

"And do you think you can print this out?"

"Yeah. But some of the sample will be destroyed. It's going to be impossible to pull it through without damage."

"I know," Rebecca said slowly. "But we'll still have enough for a printout. That's all we've got and that's all we should need. When you get this into the spectrograph and give me a reading, I'll run it down to Langley."

Gina turned. "Langley? Why Langley?"

"Because those are the guys behind all of this," Rebecca said. "I've got a contact there, somebody that Doc put me in touch with before he left. He's supposed to help us out."

Absorbing it, Gina turned back to the microscope. "Okay," she said in a low voice. "I'll have it ready for you in about an hour."

"Good enough," Rebecca whispered. A disturbed frown creased her face as she gazed at the screen. "So, this is our mystery man." Her eyes narrowed. "What is it that scares me about this guy?"

Glancing across the small glade, Hunter saw Bobbi Jo tightly holding the Barrett sniper rifle. It was an awesome weapon, and the full metal jacket cartridges were each six inches long.

Hunter couldn't imagine her taking the recoil of the savage detonation required to hurl a three-hundred-grain bullet as far as two thousand yards. But now that he knew what it was, he remembered that he had heard accurate hits at that range, and even farther ones were not outside the ability of the weapon.

He remembered that an emergency shipment of Barretts had been ordered by the U.S. Marine Corps after the 1983 attack on their barracks in Beirut, Lebanon. And in days following the attack they had more than proven their effectiveness at long-range combat.

Since they had begun tracking together, Hunter had developed sincere respect for the sniper. She said little, never seemed to lose patience, and only challenged his judgment when she had good reason. Yet if he overruled her ideas, she didn't debate. With a silent nod she would quietly tall in beside him, and he noticed she was learning from his movements. In time, he thought, she could be vastly superior to the corps of army trackers that this thing defeated so easily at the research facility

And, somehow, he was beginning to wonder if it might not also defeat him, too. He had been frustrated before, mostly by bobcats who walked so softly and carefully, leaving no sign. But never by anything of such enormous size and weight.

Even large cats, like cougars and tigers, were much easier to track than a bobcat because their heavy paws, which enhanced silence, also left distinct impressions. But this thing ruled in the worst of both worlds. It rarely left a clear track because it selected the hardest surfaces, always made the smart move, and couldn't be predicted.

Hunter's face hardened as he pondered it, and then Bobbi Jo shouldered the rifle and pulled her hair into a tight ponytail, tying it with a deft move. Afterwards she paused, staring at the perimeter, motionless and concentrated.

Hunter anticipated the movement, saw it in her profile before she even turned and, slowly, bent her head to gaze steadily at him. She didn't blink, didn't smile. And he held her look for a long time before he frowned, turning his attention to the professor. He had prepared the old man a meal from a large trout he had cooked and smoked that morning, knowing he himself would need the energy. But he sacrificed it now because of the old man's health. He had also given him a generous amount of pemmican—a mixture of beef jerky and animal fat. It was highly nutritious and kept for long periods of time in even the most extreme conditions. It had been a favorite staple of mountain men and American Indians, and Hunter always carried a small supply.

After a while the professor seemed to regain a measure of strength, though his face was still whitened, glistening with a sheen of sweat. Hunter knew it was the sudden run through the forest to the clearing that had strained him.

"Drink some more water, Professor," Hunter said. "Dehydration kills quick this high."

"Yes, yes, so I've heard," the old man replied, smiling faintly. He took a sip. "Ah, yes, a rather ...electrifying experience, that was." After a moment he asked, "Will it attack tonight, do you think?"

Hunter shook his head. "No way to know."

"But what do you think, my boy?"

Raising his eyes to scan the extensive perimeter, Hunter saw everyone alert with weapons ready. "It could, Professor. But it's too unpredictable. This thing doesn't move or think like anything I've ever tried to—"

Hunter joined what happened next by reflex.

Buck had been the first to unleash, the shotgun shredding the night at a titanic and monstrous image of underworld might that had broken the south treeline, charging out of the dark with an imperious air of indestructibility. And not even a full second passed before they opened up together, six weapons blazing outward. But Hunter spun toward the center when Bobbi Jo finally fired—the Barrett detonating with at least five feet of flame mushrooming from the barrel in a tremendous concussion that made the other weapons seem insignificant.

Stunned, Hunter whirled back to the beast, still firing. But he saw that the incredible impact of the Barrett had stopped the beast in stride, wounding it in the collar. Then Bobbi Jo had fired again, the brutal collision of the round staggering it backwards into the brush as the rest continued to hurl a wall of heated lead.

Falling back awkwardly with a wounded roar, it rose again as the forest around it was devastated by multi-weapon fire. Then, holding a hand to its chest, it staggered away. They continued the attack for another moment before Takakura bellowed for them to cease fire. But he was forced to repeat his command a number of times before they fell silent in a swirling gray atmosphere of smoking rifles. The ground was littered with brass cartridges and spent shotgun shells, and echoes of the wild cascade reverberated off distant mountains.

Hunter had ceased firing before the rest, having expended the six rounds of the Marlin at the nightmarish form in seconds. Together, backing up, they reloaded, quickly dropping clips and inserting shotgun rounds.

"Jesus!" Buck shouted without removing his eyes from the shredded black wall of leaves. "Did you see the size of that thing?" He shoved a grenade into his weapon, shouldering instantly, unable to relax.

"Reload and watch the perimeter!" Takakura raged, quickly exchanging clips and raising his weapon to his shoulder.

Only Bobbi Jo moved with a deadly air of cold calm.

With a brief glance, Hunter saw the female sniper very methodically remove the clip from her weapon. Then she took two six-inch rounds from her vest and shoved them into the magazine with mechanical precision before smoothly reinserting it in the rifle. Her motion to rack one of them into the chamber took obvious effort and then she was alert once more, eyes icy and sharp. Lowering the bipod attached to the rifle's stock, she rested it on the ground before her.

In all, the confrontation hadn't lasted more than fifteen seconds, but it had seemed like a lifetime until the beast had taken the second massive round from the Barrett and fallen to its back. But when it staggered up, it appeared that the awesome rifle had wounded it. It must have hurt it. But in the gloom, with such uncertain light and the detonations of the rifles half-blinding him, Hunter had been unable to tell for certain. All he knew was that it had been Bobbi Jo's weapon alone that had defied the beast's charge.

Takakura was speaking, still backing toward the bonfire. "For some reason it is resistant to small arms!" he yelled, since their hearing was dulled by the blasts. "But it is not impervious to the pain inflicted when it is hit! So if we can concentrate a heavy enough wall of rounds, the shock might make it retreat once more!"

Hunter wasn't betting on that; he knew that Bobbi Jo's rounds had really been what deterred its attack. But she could miss, or her rifle could jam, or the beast could launch a rushing attack and kill her first, temporarily disabling their ability to injure it. And all it would need would be seconds before it waded through them as it had waded through the guards at the research stations, stoically enduring the small-arms ordnance as it killed with impunity. No, they needed to come up with another defense if they were going to survive the entire night in this glade.

Already, it was too late to call for an emergency extraction. Because by the time the chopper snaked a dangerous path through these night-shrouded mountains to locate them, it would probably be over. Hunter estimated it would attack again in minutes—as soon as it determined that its injuries were minor. Obviously, the Barrett had stunned it—probably the first time a ballistic weapon had ever caused anything more than annoyance.

And despite their apparent shock at its unique ability to resist low-caliber arms, Hunter was not stunned. He knew that many creatures possessed skeletal density and skin composition sufficient to completely defeat low-velocity ordnance. A Grizzly's skull could easily deflect a round from a 30.06—a virtual cannon. And anything less than a 30.30 would only flatten on the skin of a rhinoceros. So, without question, nature had repeatedly demonstrated that the right combination of bone and skin could negate the effectiveness of almost any rifle—except the ultra-high-powered Barrett or a similar sniper weapon.

Hunter looked down to see how the undue excitement had affected the professor. But the old man appeared studious and relatively calm. He stared at the gaping hole left in the distant wood-line where it had fled, and his lips moved in silent thought. His first words came slowly.

"We cannot hold it off," he whispered, almost to himself. "It retreated only because it was shocked. But it will return soon enough ... Yes, but not with a bold attack. It will attack with cunning unless ...unless it is distracted ... by something. But what? Not flame ... no, it does not fear fire. What could distract it long enough for us to realize escape?"

Hunter's eyes narrowed; he looked at the old man. "I know what might distract it," he said evenly. With those words Hunter rose and walked away, knowing. He went directly to Takakura. "I know how we can hold it off for the night," Hunter said solidly.

Takakura stared. "Yes?"

"It uses the element of surprise. Likes to jump on you from trees and shit. We'll take that from him. If we see him coming, then we can open up and drive him back. No matter how many times he attacks, we can give him more than he can take."

"But it will be dark soon," the Japanese responded. "We cannot fight what we cannot see."

"We'll see him," Hunter nodded, angry, " 'cause I'm gonna rig this camp with more than claymores and fancy electronic devices, which it's already defeated too many times. I'm gonna set up some deadfalls, levers and fulcrums. He won't be hurt by them, but we'll know exactly where he is and we can open up. I'll have this place surrounded in twenty minutes."

Takakura s reply was instantaneous. "Do so. Take Buck with you. And Wilkenson. And hurry, Hunter." He glanced at the forest. "Or men will die tonight."

Hunter was in the woods like a panther, knowing every sound, every move, discerning instantly whether the forest told him it was near, knowing whether a broken branch had fallen from a tree, or whether it had been broken by a monstrous, approaching footstep. His skills were supreme now, and he used them supremely. His Bowie knife made swift work of sticks and twigs and the string he had brought by habit was vital. Buck and Wilkenson gathered the larger logs, and within a half hour they had completely surrounded the perimeter with carefully hidden traps that nothing could penetrate.

They returned to camp drenched in sweat, and Hunter knelt beside the fire, warming his bloodied fingers—fingers bloodied because he had worked more swiftly than caution allowed. But it didn't matter. He washed them in the stream and threw a hooked line across to the other side. It wasn't as good as a fish trap, and there was no bait, but should they survive the night, they would have food in the morning. And he knew the professor needed sustenance. For the first time he truly wished the old man had not come along.

Takakura spoke. "It is done?"

"It's done."

"Hat, this is good. At least we can know his direction now from the sound of the traps. We cannot kill him, but we can drive him back with concentrated ordnance."

"I hope so," Hunter threw in. "But we don't know its full potential yet. There's still a chance that bastard, if it's mad enough, can take more damage than we can dish out."

Takakura said nothing. Then Hunter noticed the sword strapped to his back and couldn't help but ask, especially since this might be their last night together. "Tell me," he said, "why do you carry that sword? Seems kinda archaic. No offense."

A soft grunt, perhaps a laugh, made the corners of Takakura's mouth rise slightly. "You are," he answered, "the first man to ever ask me about it."

Hunter waited. "Didn't mean to intrude."

Takakura laughed, actually laughed, as he turned fully to Hunter. Then he reached behind his shoulder and slowly, very slowly, withdrew at least forty inches of the finest steel Hunter had ever seen. It was a beautiful weapon, obviously forged by sword makers who were masters of a craft that the world had long forgotten.

"This sword was my father's," Takakura said, extending the blade so Hunter could behold its purity, its strength, the razor-sharpness. "And before that, it was my grandfather's, who died in battle with the Chinese. And before that, his father's, and his father's. Who also died in battle. It is four hundred years old." He laughed grimly. "Why do I carry it? I carry it because I am born of a warrior clan. And my code is Bushido. I have never used it in combat. And should I, I expect nothing from it."

Hunter blinked. "Nothing?"

"No ...nothing. I do not expect life. I do not expect death. I expect nothing but to fight well. Life and death are the same. The water changes, but the river remains the same. It is the way of all things. And should I face death with this sword in my hand, then all will be good." He waited, staring at Hunter with a strange transparency. "Westerners do not understand such a life, do they?"

Hunter stared into the dark eyes. Takakura brushed his own forearm with the blade, a feathers touch, and a trickle of blood fell to the ground. In a single swift movement he sheathed the weapon. "You never draw the sword without drawing blood."

Hunter waited. "Yeah ... I think I understand."

Chaos!

The creature tripped a deadfall and they turned as one, unleashing a hail of ammo into the foliage that left it on fire. And the barrage continued until Takakura's imperial voice demanded them to cease fire. But none of them could tell if it was still there or not because they had been deafened by the gunfire.

Hunter concentrated, lowering his head, listening not for the creature but for the forest. "It's moving to the south side, where it came before."

"Ready weapons," said Takakura calmly.

And it came again, bowed legs thick with simian muscle, shoulders inhumanly large, almost unbelievably thick with strength, and its fangs were distended to reveal jagged white tusks that announced its intent. And for a split second Hunter had a flash of what the soldiers and scientists at the massacred compounds knew as their last sight. He fired dead into it, the 45.70 hitting it solidly in the chest.

It roared and then Buck fired a grenade from the M-79, but he missed and the detonation disintegrated a tree beside it. Still, however, the concussion hurled it aside, and it staggered up and into the woods again.

Again, fierce and frantic reloading while Hunter counted the rounds still remaining on the strap of the Marlin. He had twenty shots left, and ten more in his pouch. He had never anticipated that it would take an arsenal to bring it down. Then he glanced at Bobbi Jo and saw her, once again, reloading the same clip from the bandoleer across her chest, full of .50-caliber rounds.

And on and on it went, time after time a split-second warning where they would whirl together—a tripped deadfall, a snare, sometimes even one of the electronic aids. Buck, with the M-79, was firing blindly into the forest to light it with a mushrooming flame that set part of the woods afire, and before morning most of the stand around them appeared to be clear-cut land. Broken limbs and blasted trees made this heavily forested" area resemble a swamp in winter. The open area was three times as large as when they arrived, but there was no sign of the creature.

Cautiously, Hunter entered the woods with Buck. Then they walked the entire perimeter, searching for signs of injury. But found only devastation. They returned and delivered the grim news to Takakura, who was silent a moment. "Very well," he said finally. "Break camp immediately. We move."

"I got bad news, Commander," Buck added.

"Yes?"

Buck took a deep breath before he spoke. "We're almost out of ammo. So we can't do this gig again. We could keep it off for maybe an hour with what we got, but ..."

Takakura's frown deepened, then his left fist slowly clenched. He gazed toward the ground. "The radio is not operating correctly?"

"We're having a lot of trouble with it, sir. Wilkenson is working on it."

Takakura scowled as he muttered something in Japanese that Hunter couldn't translate, but he understood the tone. A moment more and the Japanese added, "We move in attack mode. Total silence. Plot a course for the nearest town or research station. A village. Anything. We are leaving this area."

Buck bent to study the map.

Thirty minutes later they were working their way up a rocky stream, feet and socks soaked and burning blisters on their feet, blood filling their boots, but they couldn't stop. They had to move quickly because the nearest civilized location was over forty miles away, and that meant one hundred miles in this mountainous terrain.

Hunter read their mutual fatigue, but revealed nothing. He knew he could have made the hundred-mile run, if he had pushed himself all-out and carried no weight. But he couldn't leave them behind. And he knew what would come with nightfall. His mind was working furiously on a plan to keep them alive when they lost the sun.

As they climbed a steep terrain, boot pressure tearing flesh from already bloodied heels, he began searching for a place to hole up.

And found it.

"Takakura," he said strongly.

The Japanese glared back angrily.

Hunter glanced at the sun. "We haven't gone ten miles, Commander. And you know the professor isn't up to this, and we can't radio for an extraction." He let the implication settle. "We're gonna have to do it again."

The scowl of hate on Takakura's face was terrible to behold. But he knew Hunter was right. That he had failed as a commander wounded his pride. He had led his men—men who depended upon and trusted him— into certain death. Motionless, he lowered his gaze to the ground, shook his head.

"But there may be a way to survive the night," Hunter said, watching him closely. He pointed to a small cleft; it would not qualify as a cave. "That hole in the wall is pretty narrow. Looks from here like only one person at a time can enter. If we can get inside it, and wait, and lay down whatever ammo we still have if it comes for us, maybe it'll think we've still got plenty of ordnance and back off. Buck says he still has two grenades. Taylor has some rounds. And Bobbi Jo alone can make it hesitate." He gave the Japanese commander time to consider it, then continued: "I think it's our only way out, Takakura."

A moment of concentration, a curt nod: "Hat."

It took a tight fit, but they squeezed into the cave and ate some warm MREs while they took turns with the Barrett, watching the entrance. Then Bobbi Jo was finished and took over the cannon.

And darkness descended.

***

Hunter secured Ghost at the rear of the cave with a rope because he knew that after last night's siege, the massive wolf would attack the creature on sight. And what they needed was order. It wasn't long before they heard the quiet but close footsteps approaching their position.

"Unbelievable," whispered Hunter to himself, "it can find us anywhere."

Hunter saw it first, something that didn't seem to move. But he was accustomed to that. He had spent so much of his life watching life in darkness, he knew that if it didn't look like it was moving, it probably was. His tactic was simple: infinite patience. He never took his eyes off the object of his concentration. And after ten minutes or ten hours, if it was an inch to the side, then it was moving.

The distance was fifty yards, but Hunter knew he could make the shot. "Give me the Barrett," he told Bobbi Jo, who obeyed. Hunter centered on the shadow, held his breath, released it, slowly squeezed the trigger.

In the close confines of the small cleft, the detonation was shocking. And it was followed instantly by an enraged roar as the shadow came rushing up the hill while they desperately opened up with the last of their ordnance. If Bobbi Jo had managed a single solid shot at that range, she would have dropped it, but she missed in the darkness and the speed and the blinding blasts of the other weapons, and Hunter knew it would be upon them in seconds.

Frantic, he whirled and saw Buck's small rucksack on the ground and dropped the Marlin. He ripped open the pack and tore out the tent, ripping it apart in seconds to sunder the white mosquito netting.

"Cease fire!" he yelled, and leaped to the entrance, quickly tying the white cloth to either side. And then it was upon them, awesome and raging, eyes glowing with hate. It came to within three feet of Hunter and swiped at him, a blow Hunter ducked as the tremendous gray arm tore thunderously through the air and the claws struck sparks from the flint walls. But Hunter leaped out of range, Bowie knife in hand.

Growling, it stared at the cloth, and reached out as if to tear it from place. But its hand halted, just short. It wanted to tear through, but hesitated again before a bestial growl of frustration shook its head and it raised infernal eyes at Hunter. For the briefest moment, it seemed more human than monster. The snarl that twisted its face embodied an intellectual hate.

Hunter held the glare.

Together, shoulder to shoulder, they paced up and down the flimsy white barricade. And their eyes remained solidly locked. It curled monstrous hands in frustration, claws clicking. Hunter held the huge Bowie knife in an iron grip. Up and down, up and down they paced, defiant glare to defiant glare.

It was the strangest of all standoffs, man and monster, each separated by something that a child could sunder. Then with a final, angry growl of promise, the creature whirled—a movement of tiger-like grace—and was gone.

Hunter stood there, numb, for a moment. His fist was locked so tightly on his Bowie that he couldn't let it go. Then he took a deep breath, and then an even deeper breath, backing away slowly from the thin partition. He turned around to see wide eyes, silence. No questions were asked; everyone was in shock.

Finally, Takakura spoke. "Could you ...explain that, please?"

Hunter looked at Taylor. "Take the entrance. It worked that time. I don't know if it will work again. I doubt it." Then Hunter sat against a wall, staring at the wet limestone. He noticed that his grip on the Bowie had relaxed, and, very carefully, slid it back into the sheath. He licked his lips, took a sip of water, and explained it in a manner that they might understand. He began, "Do you know how they kill a tiger?"

Takakura shook his head.

"They take a piece of white cloth," Hunter continued, bowing his head. "Then they make a V with it in the forest. Maybe half a mile long on each side, but it leads to the place where the lines meet. It's only three feet high. Just a piece of white cloth. Then they drive the tiger into the V with elephants and beaters. And once the tiger is inside the V, they have him dead."

"Why?" Bobbi Joe asked.

"Because a tiger," Hunter continued tiredly, "although it can leap forty feet, won't cross a piece of white cloth that's over three feet high. It scares him, for some reason. And the hunters, the shooters, are waiting for it at the tip of the V. So the tiger is trapped inside this flimsy piece of white cloth, which it could easily leap, but it doesn't. And when it gets to the bottom of the V, the hunters open up and kill it."

Bobbi Jo was staring hard. "Why won't tigers just jump over the cloth?"

"No one knows."

She continued, "And you gambled that somewhere in this thing, whatever it is, are the latent instincts of a tiger, that it would be afraid to cross the white cloth?"

"It has to have some weakness."

A moment passed, and she smiled. "You've got guts, Hunter."

Recovering from shock, he laughed.

"I've been told worse."

CHAPTER 9

They survived the night, emerged into light only to see a darkening sky. Clouds low, black, and sliced by lightning. But the temperature was too high for snow. Hunter didn't care about the rain but knew it would adversely affect the professor, whom Bobbi Jo had tended to through the long night.

They began the day early and covered distance cautiously. Professor Tipler held up well until noon, when the terrain grew steeper and he began to need more rest. Without saying a word, Hunter knew it would be one more night before they could make it to safe ground. His mind began to ponder, but he had no ideas. He knew, somehow, that the trick he used last night wouldn't work again.

It would find a way.

They kept walking until finally the professor sat down, exhausted, on a flat slab. Hunter didn't even have to turn back to know what had happened. He knew everyone's rhythm, gait, shuffle, and Taylor's Frankenstein plodding. He stopped and looked and saw that Tipler was pale, haggard, and sitting with head bent low.

Hunter didn't want to usurp Takakura's authority, so he motioned quietly for the Japanese to join him in a private conference at the front of the line. Together they knelt and Takakura spoke exactly what Hunter was thinking: "Yes, I know. He cannot go much further." There was a decided lack of fear in the statement, and Hunter remembered "Expect nothing."

"I don't think that what we did last night will work again, Takakura,"

Hunter said. "It's getting smarter by the moment. And we're almost out of ammo."

Takakura gazed around, analyzing. "This is as good a place as any to make a stand. We have at least one hundred meters on each side. Perhaps, if we are lucky, we can discourage it with the Barrett."

Hunter released a deep breath. Yeah, it was a good place, but that thing could cover a hundred meters in six seconds. And that was too fast to acquisition for a shot. Still, he didn't have a better idea.

He shook his head.

"It's gonna be a hell of a fight."

***

Hunter gently gave Tipler a drink of water, noticing the ghostly paleness of the old man's face. His hands trembled slightly and he moved with an odd stiffness. Hunter estimated that some of the rigidity was due to the severe testing of muscles, but it could be more.

"How ya feeling, old man?" he asked.

Tipler laughed, "I am feeling splendid, my boy. I just need a night to rest a bit, and then we shall be on our way."

"You bet." Hunter smiled. "But right now all you need to do is rest. I'll be back in a bit to check on you, and Bobbi Jo is gonna be close. She'll be looking in on you, too." Hunter winked. "You just don't go trying to pick her up. She's too young for ya."

Tipler laughed.

Hunter laughed with him as he rose and exited the tent. Then he examined the perimeter. It was a hundred yards across, and Bobbi Jo crouched dead-center in the middle of it, rifle pointed at the sky. She was wearing night-vision goggles and had her back to the fire. She was also wearing what most referred to as "wolf ears"—devices that amplified sound for humans so they could hear as well as a wolf. Hunter had never needed them.

Takakura, also keeping his back to the flame, held the MP-5 close, and was wandering a tight circle while the rest held established positions. Hunter walked directly to him, and Takakura, acutely aware of any movement, turned slowly to face him.

"It has the advantage, Takakura," he said.

"Yes," Takakura responded. No emotion.

"But I think I know how to keep it from attacking."

Takakura stared an unusually long time. The black eyes narrowed. "And what would that be?"

"A challenge."

Consternation in Takakura's face betrayed his confusion. "I believe we have given it as much of a challenge as possible, Hunter. I do not understand your—"

"It's an animal, Takakura, and I understand animals more than any of you. It's the alpha of this forest. The strongest. The ruler of the forest, if you want to put it like that. We're on his ground now, and he doesn't like it. He wants to show us he's boss."

Takakura replied, "And?"

"And so we show him that he's not. That's a challenge he can't resist."

Silence.

"And how would we go about doing such a thing?"

Hunter lifted his head to the darkening forest that surrounded them. "I give it a challenge. It won't be able to resist. If I go out there, I'll be the alpha. It will hate that. It will hunt me instead of you. Then it won't attack the camp."

"You are speaking of ..."

"Yeah. I go out there. Let him chase me instead of me chasing him. Turn things around on him. It'll be surprised at first, but it'll take the bait. I can lead it south."

Takakura said nothing for the longest moment, as if the idea did not deserve a reply. "If you encounter the creature in the dark, it will tear you to pieces."

Hunter bent to retie his moccasins. "That's a big 'if Takakura. 'If bullfrogs had wings they wouldn't bump their butts when they jumped. But I'm taking Ghost with me. And nothing can sneak up on him. Not even this thing. And I can give it a run for its money." Hunter stood. "I can keep it away from the camp until daybreak."

"1 cannot allow this."

"It's your outfit, Takakura. But it's my life. And I'm not under military command. I'm only telling you this ... as a friend. Either way, I'm going out and play a little cat-and-mouse. If I'm not back by dawn, head southwest for twenty miles. Follow the Yikima Creek for five miles, then strike across. The research station is another five. If you push hard, you can make it in six hours."

"The professor cannot make such a journey."

"Build a cot for him and carry him." Hunter removed his shoulder pack and checked his thick leather belt, pulling out a small fist-sized piece of steel with a long thin wire attached to it.

"What is this?" the Japanese asked.

Hunter suddenly grew grim. "A last chance." Then his mood changed and he inserted it back into his belt. He strapped the Marlin to his back, cinched it tight, and turned his face to the almost totally darkened tree-line. "Game time," he whispered.

"Ghost!" he said sternly.

Instantly the wolf was at his side, and Hunter was moving for the darkness.

Takakura called after him. "Hunter!"

He turned back.

"This thing we hunt, it also hunts you."

***

It was a dismal, strangely soundless and chilled afternoon when Chaney strolled casually into the McMillan Deli. It was the habitual watering hole for off-duty, and sometimes on-duty, government agents and was owned by a retired FBI agent named Frank "Brick" McMillan.

"Brick" had earned the nickname twenty-five years ago when, as a deputy marshal, he had been trapped in a house that was fully aflame and all the exits were blocked. Not content to be burned alive, Brick—a former fullback for Texas A&M—just got a good running start from one end of a long hallway and "made" a brand new door in the rear wall of the structure before it collapsed behind him. Somehow, the nickname seemed to stick through the rest of his career.

Chaney sauntered through the crowd with a few handshakes and some smart remarks about how the service was doomed for the graveyard under the new administration. He went back to the kitchen and saw Brick standing over a stainless-steel counter, deftly slicing meatballs and lettuce for a sandwich.

Bricks flattop haircut hadn't changed in thirty years. He claimed he kept it that way because it was "geometrically and theologically correct." And the wide bull shoulders and expansive gut were still present, as were the tremendous gorilla arms and tree-trunk legs. Brick looked up as Chaney walked forward, smiling broadly. He wiped his hands on a rag hanging from his gut and laughed.

"Hey, boy," he said, extending his hand. "What'd they do, make you work for a living?"

"Naw." Chaney picked up a meatball. "I'm faking it. Like always."

"Like I taught you." He laughed.

Chaney looked at the meatball. "Damn, Brick, this is good. Did you make this?"

"Nope. Edna does all the cooking. I'm just a gofer."

"I'll bet she does. How you like retirement?"

"Best of life, kid. Best of life. Just wait 'til you get your twenty so you can tell them to kiss your heinie and they can't touch you. And they still gotta pay. Revenge is best served cold." His square face split in a becoming smile. "But that ain't why you come to see me, is it? Just to see how an old man's getting along?"

Chaney smiled. He shook his head as he sat on a stool. "I guess I still gotta go some to sneak up on you, huh?"

Brick laughed. "Some." He slid the sandwich on the mantle. "Order up!" Turned to Chaney. "Come on. I gotta check the beer anyway. Those CIA goombahs drink like fish. Must be the burden of all their sins."

Chaney followed to the storeroom and Brick continued, "So what you got?"

"Still keeping your nose to the wind?" Chaney sat on a crate as Brick effortlessly shifted four cases at a time.

"Well, kid, I hear things. 'Bout like usual."

"Heard anything about a few stations up in Alaska? Any kind of trouble up there?"

Brick set the cases down with a thump. Turned slowly. "They give that one to you?"

Chaney nodded.

With a grunt, Brick wiped his hands on the apron. "Well, I don't know too awful much. Heard some cowboys got killed. Bad scene. Made me want to stock up the bunker."

"You get that from the Agency?"

A guffaw. "Oh, hell no, kid. You think I trust those goons? You know better than that. At least I hope I taught you better than that. I wouldn't buy an apple from them and I always keep both hands in my pockets when we talk." His laugh was a hoarse rumble inside a huge barrel chest. "No, got it from a friend of mine uptown. Seems like the army, or the marines, were on it. Don't know who had full authority and command. But the Corps ain't too happy about what happened. Seems they lost a lot of recon guys. Tough hitters, 'bout like you used to be before you retired to work for the bleeding Marshals Service. And nobody is talking much, which means there's a lot to say."

Brick focused fully on Chaney, and the full weight of it disturbed Chaney as much as it did twelve years ago when he was a rookie deputy marshal and Brick was his training officer. "What's that got to do with you, boy?" Military affairs ain't your jurisdiction."

Chaney sighed. "I'm supposed to find out what happened, Brick. So, yeah, it's my problem."

"A CIA screw-up ain't your problem."

Chaney didn't blink. "It is now."

There was uncomfortable tension as Brick gazed about. Chaney noticed that Brick seemed as robust as he was over a decade ago. He was a bull-thrower then, he was a bull-thrower now. Brick lowered his voice slightly as he replied.

"You sure you ain't bein' set up? Made any enemies inside the agency lately?"

"No." Chaney shook his head. "Skull is pissed, but that's just Skull. You get used to him. No, he wouldn't do that. Truth is, Brick, I don't know what's going on. Not really. But if there are some dead marines, then one of those leatherneck senators is going to be going ape."

"So you can't use official lines."

"No. This has got to be done quiet. Just like the ol' Reagan days, when we could actually get things done, shake people up. 'Cause if anyone gets wind that I'm sniffing around, they'll just close ranks and start shredding. I can't have that."

"If you want to stay alive, yeah," Brick grunted. "Okay, drop by the house tonight. I'll see what I can get. And don't go acting like an investigator between now and then. Be a good boy. Keep your head down and your mouth shut, just like I taught you. I'll see you later."

Rising, Chaney said, "I owe you, Brick."

Brick winked. "You always will, boy."

Chaney smiled, walked away.

***

"This can't be right," Rebecca whispered. Her eyes narrowed as she stared at a printout of the DNA strand. "No, Gina. This is impossible. This points to something we've never seen before."

Gina shook her head. "I know. But that's what we got. The machine doesn't lie."

Neither of them said anything as they stared at the display on the electron microscope.

"If this is not contaminated, Gina, it's incredible." She flipped a dozen pages of numbers, graphs, curves and comparison charts. "My God," she whispered. "Look at the fibronectin and talin in the inhibitors. This thing ... it has to ... it has to have an incredible resistance to infection. Look at the epinephrine enhancers. Incredible. We've never seen this kind of overabundance of factors." Pause. "Just what in the world is this thing?"

"Well, Rebecca, the DNA go ninety-nine percent Homo sapiens. The rest is as unknown as how many angels can dance on the head of a pin. This particular strand doesn't collate with anything in the bank, but you can see that with all these restrictive enzymes and retroactive proteins this thing has a super powered immune system. I don't know what it is or how it's done, but it's there. I ... well, I really don't know how else to classify it."

For a long time, Rebecca stared at a photon level image of the tendril recovered from the plaster. She had a hard time tearing her eyes from it. Then her mouth tightened, almost angrily, and she spoke. "All right. Record everything. Make three copies. You know where to put them. I'm taking one to the lab at Langley. They need to see this or they won't believe it." She waited. "Hell, I don't know if /believe it, and I'm staring right at it."

It started in the thickest darkness Hunter had ever known, but he knew it was more than just the night. With Ghost at his side, he moved in total silence, alert, sensing every empty shadow. They caught the first hint of it in twenty minutes.

It was about six hundred feet north, and Hunter was west. Calmly, Hunter crouched, studying all there was to see in the silver moon. The night gave just enough light to see the ground. Good enough.

"Come on, boy," he whispered.

It was accustomed to prey fleeing its wrath.

Hunter ran straight toward it, toward the north, closing the gap much, much quicker than it would anticipate. Then he saw the right terrain and leaped high, one foot hitting a boulder that launched him higher to a tree limb, where he leaped onto a slope.

Ghost made the tremendous leap without the advantage of the boulder, landing beside him.

Instantly Hunter angled uphill, running as quickly as the steepness allowed, slowing on moccasin-padded feet as he crested and crouched. Below him, he saw a ravine no more than ten feet wide, and then ... a tremendous hulking shape of a humanoid creature. It was shuffling, confused, and even at that distance Hunter could read the anger in its face, its stance. It turned this way, that, searching with quick, jerky movements. The scent was strong here, it knew, but the prey ...

Hunter smiled, knowing that the very first move he made would snatch its attention. He decided to make it a good one. Backing up a few steps, he rubbed Ghost's head. The wolf knew what he was going to do, was going to do it with him.

Hunter ran toward the gap in the ravine, and leaped, wasting one second to glance down and see the beast whirl as if shot. And he knew what it saw. A man and a great black wolf suspended in the air, soaring across a narrow moon.

Hunter landed lightly on the other side, and Ghost was beside him. Then Hunter was running, running, weaving a complicated path through roots and trees and over boulders, doubling back, avoiding inclines because they slowed him, and then he began laying traps, tricks, immersing himself in a freezing stream and floating downriver until he lifted himself out with a limb and climbed from tree to tree for a hundred yards before dropping to earth.

He stopped in place.

He had landed before a gigantic stone tablet, at least two hundred yards across. It was utterly level, as if ancient glaciers had shaved it. But now it was also littered with boulders, the remnants of earthquakes, volcanic eruptions, flood. Instantly he began a complicated trail, in and out, around good ambush sites, which the beast would approach slowly. He worked for ten minutes, running quickly, crisscrossing a dozen times. He left trails that led into the surrounding forest in a myriad of directions. When he was finished, he was sweating heavily and his legs were numb. But Ghost seemed to have enjoyed it.

Hunter looked at him, smiled. "You idgit-head. All you want to do is fight him, don't you?" He rubbed Ghost's head. "He ain't the alpha, old boy. You are. You always will be."

Afterwards, Hunter floated down a frigid stream, downwind, and finally saw an overhanging limb—too far to reach! In a split-second Hunter had grabbed the snare from his belt and held the steel tube, and as the branch came closer he saw a broken limb, short enough for one good throw. As he passed under it the titanium lasso lashed through the air, silver and spiraling. The loop landed solidly on the projection, tightened, and suddenly cold water was splitting around Hunter.

Hands cutting to the cord, Hunter hauled himself back to the branch, and only by the most extreme strength of his forearms was he able to maintain a grip on the titanium as he hauled himself up. His hand lashed up, settled on the limb and he was clear.

He sat on the limb a minute, breathing heavily, freezing, but he knew his clothes would dry quickly. He could endure. He attempted unsuccessfully to undo the lasso from the four-foot-long limb for five minutes, but the lasso had been designed so that, once closed, it would not open. With his heavy Bowie he severed the limb at the trunk and carried it with him. After another ten seconds of hacking he had severed the limb, unwinding the lasso to replace it carefully in his belt. He smiled to himself; the makeshift device was coming in handy. He climbed the tree to another and then down to the ground at least a hundred yards distant.

Then he sat. Waiting.

Ghost, beside him, listening to the night, was uncannily alert. And Hunter was already exhausted, so he ate some pemmican for strength. Then he gave Ghost a large slab of beef jerky.

If the beast eventually unraveled the trail, Hunter would be able to confirm that it could hunt by scent as well as sight. Every discovery he accumulated about it was important because Hunter never knew what he might be able to use for an advantage.

It was five hours later before Hunter heard distant but determined splashing upstream. He rose, running at full speed, knowing that this thing, as inhumanly strong as it truly was, was not inexhaustible. Nothing was inexhaustible. So he would run it to ground. Would run it until the sun rose in a few hours.

And he knew he stood a chance.

Ducking a low limb with the sinuous grace of a panther, he hit the ground lightly and weaved between rocks, boulders. Some he vaulted, landing only to change direction again, and on and on it went with limbs lashing his face and arms in pitch-dark. His legs and lungs burned, but the land rolled past him. Then he broke the woodland and saw open country, and let out a long, steady, strong stride that had carried him in the past for forty, fifty miles at a time. Five, six, seven miles and he kept the fast punishing pace—noticing without appreciating entire valleys passing or the gigantic stands of timber that loomed up and faded hauntingly into the night behind him. Still he continued. He estimated he had gone ten, maybe twelve miles when fatigue began taking a toll, but he pushed himself harder.

Never before, though he had often run all day in order to cross a forest, had he held such a brutal pace for so long. Sweat poured from his face in a slicing cold and darkened his leather shirt, and his long black hair was laid back with sweat and rushing wind. His blue eyes squinted against both the mist that fogged his vision and the night air that burned his lungs. And eventually, when entire worlds of landscapes had been claimed by distance, even Hunter's arms became fatigued from holding the steady rhythm, and his thighs swelled with irresistible numbness. Beside him, Ghost effortlessly kept the pace, even when Hunter began to stumble slightly with fatigue. Now beginning to fear that he would commit the ultimate mistake and twist an ankle or knee, crippling himself and leaving him virtually helpless in the night, Hunter decided that he had gone as far as he could go. Breath burning, eyes misty and tearful, he stopped and dropped to the ground.

No time for rest!

Groaning, he rose, staggering a moment.

To hear a vengeful roar terrifyingly close.

"Now what," he muttered, glancing around.

And saw a ledge.

What he needed.

Hunter saw the slope downward was like angled granite steps and took the first leap boldly, landing on a slab ten feet below and selecting his next angle of descent. Then down again, not worrying about Ghost's ability to negotiate the steep steps. And as Hunter hit the third slab he stopped fully, crouching like a beast, eyes afire, lips drawn in a snarl, listening. He focused, tried to slow his breath, to think.

The forest was everything to him now, his life, his place, his home. Somehow he felt more animal than man, but he had no time for that. He had to use his instincts but he had to use his mind. He couldn't let the animal out of the cage; he had to use it, control it, retain the human center.

He unslung the Marlin and held it in one hand as a frontiersman would hold a musket when he ran down a deer by sheer strength, exhausting the animal until he could get close enough for a shot. It was a sure tactic but required the endurance of a wolf and the accuracy of a true marksman when sweat was stinging your eyes, and your breath was heaving in hot blasts. And Hunter had practiced it at length when he was young, often running for twelve or fifteen hours before he could make the shot.

Ghost landed beside him without a sound, panting.

Hunter knew it had followed but he hadn't made it easy. Nothing could have followed him easily through the obstacle course of trees and rocks, ledges and ravines that he had leaped and descended, then doubled back to frustrate it.

A twig snapped.

Hunter raised his head, blinking sweat. Less than a minute and it would find him.

Already it was too close, searching now by sight. It was maybe two hundred yards away. Glaring around frantically, Hunter searched for an advantage, a place for an ambush, anything.

He had to outthink it, but the terrain was completely wrong for every trick that flashed like lightning through his frantic mind.

He heard another crash in the woods about fifty yards from the crest of the ridge, then silence. Twisting his head viciously left and right, he searched for some advantage any advantage because he hadn't thrown it off for more than thirty seconds.

He was on a ledge about four feet wide, six feet deep. Another ledge, about two feet wide, ran to the right, disappearing around the edge of the slope. Beneath them was a river, roaring with white water. Hunter scanned it, estimating . . .

If a man fell into that, he would be dead instantly. But this thing ... it would survive. Unless it was badly injured. Hunter debated it and in seconds made the decision because he was in a defenseless position. He moved along the darkened, mist-wet ledge with the utmost caution. Without hesitation Ghost moved carefully behind him. And thirty feet later, Hunter found what he needed.

A narrow niche, a cave of sorts, opened into the wall about halfway down the curve. It was utterly dark and, three hundred feet beneath, the river roared.

It'd have to do.

Ushering Ghost before him into the niche, Hunter slid inside, turning almost instantly as he heard a thunderous impact on the rock far behind him. Then he cocked the hammer on the 45.70, a massively powerful round once used for killing buffalo. Since the demise of the bison, however, the cartridge had been ignored. But Hunter had always preferred its stoutness for felling bear in stride.

Retreating six feet into the niche, he raised the heavy carbine to his shoulder and waited, aiming at the opening.

Last stand ...

His breath, starving and strained, hurt from oxygen loss. And his focus was tunneling, seeing nothing but the target space. He fought it, but the hunt, the chase, the run, and this desperation move had overloaded his system. He tried to eliminate his breathing altogether though, because he knew that its preternatural senses would detect the slight disturbance of air.

Suddenly Ghost tensed behind him and he felt the great wolf move its shoulder an inch forward, as if to get in front of him. Hunter twisted back slightly against it, all he could allow, telling his friend to retreat and be silent. Hunter didn't know if it would be enough, but he knew he couldn't remove his eyes from the—

What dropped dead into the tomblike opening of the niche was beyond horror. It descended from straight above instead of creeping cautiously from the side, and was outlined by a glaring angle of moonlight that captured bristling white hair on huge, hunched shoulders that swelled out from a heavily maned head. Its face was sharp and wedged and monstrously deformed. And it was incredibly muscular in its slouched pose, the thickly corded arms hanging slightly longer than a man's. Then it expanded its chest and unleashed a crashing roar—a vengeful blast of hate.

Talons visible even in moonlight were displayed openly as it unhinged its fangs, glowering and thirsty, and the wholesale murderous gleam in its eyes was shock.

No time for shock ...

Hunter fired almost immediately, not a full heartbeat passing between the horror and the detonation, and the report of the rifle was deafening. Then he glimpsed the huge apelike arms raised in pain and an unearthly, bestial roar of pain that contained bestial rage.

Hunter worked the action and fired again and again and again—six massive rounds as he advanced into it, moving it back on the ledge toward the river. It was swaying on the edge when he ran out of ammo. Then, swinging the butt of the weapon hard, Hunter struck it fully in the face as it fought for balance.

It bellowed in fury and lashed out with a wild blow. Hunter ducked and then returned his own before it swiped the rifle from his hands and caught him across the face with a clawed hand, leaving narrow furrows. It was only a glancing blow, but the force behind it was inhumanly powerful and Hunter was hurled against the wall.

Growling, hands raised, it came for him.

Stunned, Hunter tried to rise, couldn't. But he sensed the immense humanoid shape over him, so large and monolithic that it blocked out the moon and the night together, leaving nothing but itself, master of both.

Hunter clearly recognized its pure, dominating strength, but reached for his Bowie as it prepared, snarling.

It came.

Hunter rose, crouching, squaring off.

What happened next—it was a blur to Hunter—was something that moved with a fury and speed beyond anything he had ever seen or imagined, all coming from a roaring, wild black animal center that exploded from the wall.

Ghost struck the creature fang to fang, colliding against a creature of supernatural strength and rage, and the violence made the night retreat. Snarling and roaring, Ghost savaged it for a fantastic, spellbinding moment before the creature bellowed in pain and twisted as if to hurl the wolf from the cliff.

"No!" bellowed Hunter.

It heard the threat and hurled Ghost into the cleft, turning into the challenge. It slashed at him but Hunter struck first with a purity that merged grace and strength in the unleashed movement, and the blade struck true.

Flashing white in the moon in a crescent that hit the creature full in the neck, the ten-inch blade sliced through the armored skin to exit the other side in a flood of smoking blood and the creature staggered back, holding its throat.

Nothing but this . . .

With his right hand on the hilt, Hunter ducked under the wrathful counterattack—a wild clawed swipe—and slashed backwards to tear a deep slice through its torso, yielding a wild outpouring of blood.

It howled.

Staggering, it grasped roughly at both wounds—mortal for any natural creature—and focused on Hunter with a power and rage beyond anything worldly, staggering forward.

Incredible ...

Hunter staggered back.

Moving with a savagery that shocked even Hunter, Ghost exploded from the cleft once more, roaring in the air, and they collided with a vicious exchange of fangs. Stunned, the creature toppled backwards.

It was too much.

Hovering in midair, the creature wind milled on the edge of the ledge for a long, surreal moment, before the true fall began.

"Ghost!" Hunter screamed as he leaped forward and viciously snatched the wolf by its thick black mane, hauling him from the monster's deadly embrace as it was claimed by space and night.

Only at the last minute did a taloned hand lash out to smash against the ledge with titanic strength and titanic rage before its great weight pulled it down and away, leaving claw marks in the stone.

It was gone.

***

Wind and the last of night enveloped Hunter as he crouched on a boulder, resting on his way back to the ragged campsite. From the stars, he estimated two hours before dawn.

He moved only his eyes as he scanned the broad expanse, patient and disciplined. He felt alive in the purity of it, at home again. But it had been a narrow escape, and even Ghost had not come away unscathed. A series of savage gashes had been torn in the wolf's neck and ribs, slashes that had even torn through the thick fur, though the wolf did not seem to notice. Hunter smiled at the thought; Ghost never noticed anything at all, had never asked a question in his life.

Easing down, Hunter had traveled less than a mile, moving toward a pass that would quickly return him to the camp, when Ghost stopped in place and emitted a single threatening growl. Hunter reacted instantly, swinging the Marlin from his shoulder in a vertical movement.

Immediately Ghost fell silent and Hunter remembered that the big wolf only gave one warning. The next sound Ghost made would be something beyond wild, something that thundered from the center of a blurring black death.

For almost five minutes Hunter held position, conditioned to waiting without sound or movement. Then, in the distance, he saw a black silhouette emerge over a ridge. Ghost lifted his nose slightly to the oncoming wind, tasting a scent as he stood solidly on all fours, head slightly lowered at an intense animal angle.

"Easy, boy," Hunter whispered, noticing the shape was walking slowly and somewhat unsteadily. He squinted through the night, grateful that his vision had improved so much with use, and tried to make out details. He saw almost instantly that it wasn't the creature because it was too small, held too short a stride, and its bulk wasn't right.

Hunter moved to the side without a sound, crouching low, using a boulder to hide his profile against the sky, and then he slid around it and out of sight. He knew that if the man was alert, the width of the boulder would have appeared slightly larger for a split second before Hunter had moved behind it, but he doubted the man had noticed. Hunter gave no concern to Ghost, knowing the wolf would melt beyond the rock with only the faintest flicker of night shadow.

Carefully selecting his ground, Hunter crouched on a slope, still hidden from the stranger's view but bisecting his path. Then, when the man passed beneath him, beyond view but well within Hunter's acute hearing, Hunter stood, staring down.

Instantly the figure whirled, raising a rifle.

Hunter was implacable.

It was an old man. An old Anathasian man.

A hundred years ago, men knew them only by the primitive term "Eskimo," native Indians of the far north. But in the white light of approaching dawn Hunter could identify the style of crude leather clothing, the hair, could almost read every harsh year of survival etched in the gaunt brown face. And he recalled that the Anathasians were once revered as the continent's most accomplished hunters and trackers, even selected their chiefs by their prowess at such things. Those, and war.

It was a warrior race, Hunter knew, and the aspect before him did not belie that suspicion. Slowly, the old man lowered his rifle.

Hunter spoke. "It is too cold to be walking alone in the night, Grandfather, so far from your fire," he said. He knew that, among all North American Indian tribes, "grandfather" was a term of respect.

The old man nodded once. "Yes," he said. Then, "I hunt. Only now I do not hunt so well. Or I would have seen you." He shook his head. "I must be getting very old. I must hunt very badly now."

"Not so bad," Hunter smiled. "Not so old."

Hunter noticed that the gaunt voice, so low against the wind, seemed weary and disturbed. He continued, "Why do you leave the safety of your village to walk alone in the night? And what do you hunt in the night that you cannot hunt in the day?"

The old man hesitated. "I hunt the beast that walks by night," he said simply, unafraid.

There was no need for more. Hunter knew what the old man hunted, alone and helpless, wandering through the hungry cold in the coldest hours before dawn. "Why do you hunt this beast that walks at night?"

The old man bowed his head. "I had a grandson." He waited long, and longer. "I have one no more. He was young. Just learning to hunt. I was there when the beast ..."

Hunter bowed his head. Then, bracing, he looked up. "I am sorry, Grandfather. I am sorry for you, and for your family, and for your people. But I will avenge your grandson."

The old man seemed to stagger slightly. He did a kind of quarter turn, to face Hunter fully. "You ... hunt ..."

"Yes," Hunter said plainly. Up here, he knew, where men were so alone with each other against so much that was not man, there was no need for lies. "Yes. I hunt it."

It was enough. The old man nodded, simple as that. He believed, but Hunter knew he believed for more than the words. A long time in the wild, and a man learned to read the words of other men, perhaps because they heard them so little.

Hunter saw more clearly the old man's withered face as he seemed to somehow step into a fresher shade of moonlight. The countenance was indeed old, but the eyes scintillated with intelligence, keen and quick. "And what is this beast, Grandfather?"

The old man approached the foot of the rock.

Hunter did not move.

"It is not the bear," the old man said. "But it is not man. I do not know ...what it is. I only know that it does not belong."

"Why does it not belong?"

"Because ..." The old man paused. "I have seen pictures of it. Many years ago, when I was a boy, I saw pictures of it in the caves." He pointed to a faraway ridge with his rifle. "Long ago, when my people lived in the caves, we knew the pictures well. The pictures, they were drawn by those who came before us, the storytellers. There were pictures of this beast that walks in the night ... I remember these pictures."

Hunter frowned. "And so what did these pictures say, Grandfather? You said it is not a bear. You said it is not a man. Tell me more of these pictures."

"It is not man ... but it was feared by man," he answered slowly, but his voice seemed subdued, taken by the gusting wind. "The pictures, they spoke of war. War among the natural man and the unnatural man, the Iceman. They spoke of slaughter, and much killing. And they spoke of bones at another place, a cursed place. We do not go there. To the other place." He pointed south with the rifle. "It is at the place the white man calls ... White Mountains. On the river where it bends, beside the water that comes out of the rock. We call it Cave of Souls. There was much death there."

Hunter knew.

"I heard the old people speak of it once. They said that the Cave of Souls is where the Iceman lived long ago, before it no longer belonged, and the forest took it. They say there are also pictures there. And much death. For it is a haunted place. An evil place. But you can find it by following the water that flows from the rock between the two beasts, I have heard. But I do not know. I have never been there."

Hunter said nothing.

Pausing, the old man continued: "When I was a boy, we would find things in the mountains. Weapons not made by my people. All very old. My grandfather told me it had always been that way. And then he would speak of hidden things ... of things buried in the ice. And one day, after we found a bow deep inside the north, he spoke of when he was a young man and they found one of the men of ice. It was very old. Frozen. And when they lifted him from the ice and carried him to the village, his body crumbled like ancient bone. But I remember my father's eyes as he spoke of it, and I know he was very afraid." A pause. "Just as I know that I, too, am very afraid."

Hunter's blinked. "Go home, old man. I will hunt this ...Iceman. I will kill him for you ... for your grandson."

"This I believe." The old man's eyes squinted against a sudden, slicing gust of wind. Hunter knew that what he said next was a warning. "It has killed many men."

"I know," Hunter answered. "And it will kill many more if it is not itself killed. So go home, old man. It is cold in the night. And when you rest beside your fire, pray for me. Pray that I will kill this man from the ice ... before it kills us all."

* * *

Hunter approached the camp from the heights in the last hour before dawn, moving in silence. He didn't worry about Ghost, knowing the great wolf always moved without sound.

He knew the creature had been severely wounded by the fall and the throat cut more than anything else, and knew that they would be relatively safe until dawn, but he still traveled at a relatively brisk pace. Battered and exhausted, he approached the campsite, Ghost trailing beside him, and all of them whirled, alert to the movement. Hunter was also too tired to care if they accidentally fired.

Takakura was the first to reach him. Hunter didn't see where Bobbi Jo was positioned. The Japanese searched his battered form with surprising concern before he hazarded, "And ... so?"

"It's alive." Hunter knelt and picked up a can of MREs, eating a small bite. He made a face and gave it to Ghost, who devoured it in seconds. "I led it west, south, lost it for a while. It caught me. I put it off a bluff. I think we need to get moving. It'll heal up fast."

Takakura's voice had relief. "We will move immediately. But we must proceed slowly. Dr. Tipler is tired. And we would call for an emergency extraction but ..."

Not shocked, Hunter approached him, staring the Japanese hard in the face. He didn't need more to know that the radio was no longer functional. After a second he shook his head, trying to rein in the anger. Yeah, his suspicions had been correct.

"You spoke of this," Takakura said in an unnatural tone. "How did you anticipate this?"

Without even responding, Hunter walked past him, moving to a hastily erected tent where he suspected they had laid Tipler. The old man was inside, and his face was white and sweating. Bobbi Jo was at his side, administering an injection. She tilted her head to indicate they should move outside and discuss the situation just as the professor sighted him.

"My boy!" Tipler cried, overjoyed. "I knew it! I knew you would do it!" He tried to give Hunter an awkward one-armed hug. "Ha! Ha! Ain't no man that ever lived who could ever track my boy!"

The outrageous exclamation was so uncharacteristic that Hunter almost laughed. He moved slowly to the cot, bent gently. His voice was calm. "How ya doing, old man?"

Upon seeing Hunter's battered body more closely, Tipler reached out and gripped him. "You are well?"

"Yeah, yeah, you know me. I'm always fine." Hunter smiled. "A few bruises. But you and me have seen worse." A laugh. "Especially you. I've seen you weather everything."

"Oh, this is hogwash, that's all," Tipler laughed gustily. "I had a slight palpitation. Had them for years. I am about as concerned about it as I am about the fact that my second-grade teacher died forty years ago. You get used to things."

Hunter laughed. "All right, you just take it easy. I'm gonna go outside for a minute and then I'll be back. I'll talk to you in a few minutes. 'Cause we gotta get you out of here." Tipler raised a hand but Hunter said, "No objections, old man." A wink. "You did all you could. Time to rest. I'll be right back."

Outside, a crimson dawn cast a golden halo around Bobbi Jo's silhouette, and Hunter stood motionless—a monument of dignity and strength. He waited only a second before she began. "His blood pressure is lower now than a few hours ago. But his pulse is still in the nineties. He can walk if we go slow, if we don't push him, but we have to get him serious medical attention. He could arrest at any time. I gave him something to thin his blood just a little and to boost his energy. But it's not a good idea to try and control this condition with what I have. We have to get to the research station as fast as we can move him."

"We'll put him on a stretcher," Hunter said instantly. "I'll have one made in fifteen minutes." Then he turned to Takakura. "What in the hell happened to the radio?"

"I do not know," the Japanese commander said plainly. "It is disabled somehow." There was a moment of pause before Hunter turned away and then back again, almost in Takakura's fearless face. "When we get back, I'm going after this thing alone, 'cause something is wrong with this mission. I've seen that from the first. So I'm gonna get you back to the research station, but not for you or this team. I'm getting you back for that old man in there."

He walked into the bushes, past the aristocratic Wilkenson, who said only, "I believe he will be all right until night, Mr. Hunter."

But Hunter wasn't in a mood for replying. He went into the woods, drawing his bloodstained Bowie to swipe two seven-foot length poles of poplar sapling. The trunks were about an inch in diameter, and strong because they were still green. With that and the leather twine in his pack he would quickly have a stretcher constructed.

They had broken camp when he finished gently loading the old man, who protested but finally conceded to Hunter's stern reproof. And then they were walking.

Takakura and Wilkenson guarded the rear. Buck and Riley had the first duty of carrying the professor through the difficult terrain, and Taylor was point. Hunter found himself walking beside Bobbi Jo, lost in his thoughts.

Until she spoke.

"Tell me something," she asked with the tone of someone who wanted to lighten the mood. "How did you get involved in something like this?" she looked at him, clearly curious. "They told us in the briefing that they'd found the best tracker in the world. Said you weren't military, but that you could track a squirrel across rock. But how would they know? Have you worked with them before?"

"No, not really with the military," he said finally. "When I was a kid, I found a place out in Montana. High. Cold. Isolated. Thought I might settle there. I didn't have much, but I could live off the land. So I trapped, hunted, survived pretty well. It looked a lot like this." He gestured toward the woods. "Anyway, I had a ham radio, just in case I was hurt or something. And I was listening to it one day when some kid got lost in this wilderness area below me. It was November, a cold front coming. They had tons of people in the woods, but they couldn't find this kid. I knew those mountains – how cold they got. I knew he wouldn't survive the night."

"And so you went down the mountain and started tracking him," Bobbi Jo said, without doubt or surprise. Hunter grimaced, half-shrugged before he continued.

"Yeah. And it was a tough track. Took me all day. The little kid was so tiny he hardly left a print. And he was wearing these flat-soled shoes that didn't have a pattern. I thought I lost him a dozen times." He smiled, shook his head. "Kids. They're something else the way they wander. You have to be careful. It's easy to lose them. And if you lose them, they'll die quick. They don't know how to find shelter. How to keep warm."

"So, did you find him?"

"Yeah. He was half-frozen, but I built a quick shelter and warmed him up and fed him. Then, the next day, I carried him out."

"He's okay now?"

He nodded. "Oh yeah, heard from him a while back. He's doing great. We write each other pretty often."

Silence.

"That was a lot of pressure," she said. "I mean, to find a little kid lost in a wilderness when the tracks were old, everyone had trampled on them." She thought about it a second. "So little left to go on, you have to get into their mind."

"Pretty much." ·

"And after that?"

A shrug. "Well, after that things just sorta' happened. Whenever someone was lost, they'd call me. Then people in other places started calling me to hunt down camping parties, to find people." He rolled his neck, loosening. "I guess I've tracked just about everywhere. Mexico. Canada. Up north. Out west. It's always different, but the same. I've found most of them. But there were some I didn't find until it was too late."

"And what's that like?" She waited patiently for an answer. "To fail, I mean."

He took a long time to reply. "It's hard when I find the body, and it's too late. But all I can do is my best." A pause. "The first time I found a kid, I knew what I wanted to do with my life. And I was right. Each time is as good as the first."

"I'll bet it is." She smiled. "I wish I could track like that. But that kind of skill is beyond anything you can learn. You have to have a gift. You have to be born to it."

"Maybe," he said. "I don't think about it."

"You just do it."

"I guess," he mumbled, casting a brief glance back to check on the professor. "Something like that."

She paused a long time, smiled. "You're a strange man, Mr. Hunter. You don't seem to like people. Don't even seem to like being around people. But you risk your life to save them. Why is that?"

His face was unreadable.

"Don't know," he said. " 'Cause I like the ones I find, I suppose."

***

Rebecca leaned over the table, attempting to gain the reluctant attention of the CIA physicist at Langley. Tall, white-haired, and aristocratic in attitude, Dr. Arthur Hamilton did not look up from the DNA printout.

"Doctor!" she stressed. "You're not paying attention! Look at the integrin matrix! They're ...they're like ...like scaffolding to an aggregate of molecules that form an adhesion that includes actin, talin, vinculum, and o-actitin. It's not like any regenerative properties we've ever witnessed. Not even in invertebrates that are innately immune to carcinogens!"

Dr. Hamilton's voice was soothing. "And your point is, Rebecca?"

She stared.

"My point?" She laid a hand on the DNA printout. "My point, Doctor, is that this reveals that this creature has a unique ability to activate quiescent integrin molecules so that they adhere to proteins—including fibrinogen—which makes a very powerful bridge for platelets. Then all the systems work together for enhanced healing, no matter the site of infection or injury. It's like this creature's entire extracellular matrix is expressly devoted to some kind of uncanny healing ability." Rebecca went to the edge. "Doctor, I would say that this thing, whatever it is, is completely immune to disease."

Dr. Hamilton stared at her and slowly replied, "That would be presumptive, Rebecca."

"Read the leukocyte level!" She leaned forward, feeling heat from the confrontation. "That printout, which is dead accurate, says this thing has trails to sites of infection like nothing we've ever seen. Look at the reperfusion molecules! The oxidant levels! The molecular adhesion to prevent restenosis! We've never seen anything like this. Not ever! And in that, Doctor, I know what I'm talking about. That's not presumptive!"

He frowned deeply as he studied the printout. "I suppose you have copies of this," he murmured.

"You bet I do."

"Please ensure that you preserve them," he added with greater interest, focusing again on the page. "Will you allow me to run my own analysis tonight? I would like to confer with you in the morning after I have time to collate a breakdown of the D-4 through D-10 to determine a mitosis level."

Rebecca stood back. "All right. Tomorrow. But I want this information in Dr. Tipler's hands by morning. He needs to know."

"Of course. I will see to it personally."

She picked up her briefcase and moved for the door. He spoke after her. "Is there anything the Agency can provide for you, Doctor, while you are staying in the city?"

"No." Rebecca turned back. "I can take care of myself."

"Of course."

Dr. Hamilton watched her close the door quietly and waited a moment before picking up the phone.

***

Brick shut the bank vault and moved with his familiar, unhurried, bull-like stroll, blacksmith arms falling past his sides at slight angles, to a gun crate.

He poured a glass of Jack Daniel's for Chaney, a larger one for himself. Chaney looked bemusedly around the vault as he took a sip, remembering that Brick had gotten it for a song six years ago from a local bank scheduled for demolition. It was the only place in the house where a conversation couldn't be surveilled by electronic listening devices.

"I don't like what I hear, kid." Brick grimaced as he swallowed a large, stinging sip of the whiskey. "Hoo-wee!" He held the glass up before his face, staring hard. "Man, it's been awhile! Must be gettin' old! But better old than dead, I guess." He sniffed, warming to it. "Which is just what you might be, boy, if you poke around."

Silent, Chaney held the rock-hard gaze. Brick usually spoke with a plainness that obtained immediate attention and respect, but rarely with such a dark grimness to the tone.

"Am I being set up?" Chaney asked.

Brick took a smaller sip, shook his head. "I don't know. All I know is that nobody claims to know much. Which means *they do*! They just don't talk about it! If they were ignorant, they'd be asking me questions instead. Yeah, for sure, people in this biz can't stand thinking that they don't know what's going down."

Brick's light-blue eyes, arched by bushy white brows that bristled in the dim light, went dead-flat on Chaney. "Why don't you go slack on this one?" he asked quietly. "Tell 'em you can't find nothing. Give it back and go on to something else. You're G-4, so you ain't gonna go much higher, anyway. You only got eight to fill. It won't hurt you to take a little heat."

Chaney blinked; it wasn't a bad idea. Marshals did it all the time, but something about this affair intrigued him. "What did you find' out, Brick?" He took a larger sip as he listened.

Brick sat on a crate of AK-47's. Thousands of rounds of NATO 7.62 ammo were stacked against the wall behind him. The rest of the vault was similarly stocked with shotguns, semiautomatics, pistols, gas masks, food, emergency medical kits, smoke markers, portable ham radios, and two crates of antipersonnel grenades. Brick's career as a marine, plus two tours in Vietnam, had made him a seriously connected gun lover.

Freshening his glass, he continued, "What I got is sketchy. But I know that two platoons of marines are listed as lost in a 'training exercise.' "

"In Alaska?"

Brick waved dismissively. "Don't matter two frags where. That's just how it's done. But they were marines, don't forget that. Not shake-and-bakes who can't do an air force push-up with a gun at their head. The dutch is that they were assigned a real special tour to guard some kinda research station and got wiped out."

"A military research station? Those are only located along the Bering Strait, aren't they?"

"No, it wasn't military." Brick shook his head glumly. "This was some kinda spook job, up near the North Ridge. I don't know what they were doing. The CIA hasn't had any research stations inside the Arctic Circle in thirty years. I can't even remember when they closed down the last one. Anyway, the word on all that is pretty low. I didn't push it."

For a while Chaney digested it. "That could make sense," he said finally.

Brick grunted over another sip. "To you, maybe."

"No, it does. Imagine this, Brick. Some CIA research station up where it shouldn't be. Okay, but for what? What was it doing up there? How did they get the funding? What could be so important about Alaska's North Ridge that would justify a budget?"

"Cussed if I know."

Chaney stared. "They found something," he said.

"Found something? Like what?"

"Son, I don't know." Chaney shook his head, looking away. "Something they want to keep secret. But something they have to stay close to. Something they're protecting." He strolled slowly around the room. "Were all these guys killed at the same station?"

"No. I did get that much. Seems that there's several of those things up there." Brick paused. Clearly, he didn't like any of it. "Something bad is in the wind, son. And nothing in the news. But somethin' shoulda' leaked. So somebody with power has shut down the pipe." He looked around thoughtfully. "Yeah, I think I'm gonna stock up the bunker."

Chaney laughed, let it settle.

"So, several research stations are attacked," he continued. "Which means that these people, whoever they are, didn't know where to look. They only knew that it was somewhere in one of the stations. I can see how that might make sense. They've got something up there, and somebody else wants it."

"There ain't nuthin' that important, kid. Killing two platoons of marines would be considered an overt act of war. Even though we ain't in the Reagan years no more, there's only so much that folks out there in God's country will take. The people would make us hit back, no matter who it was against. And the good ol' boys would be lining up at the recruiting office, just like they did after we kicked butt in the Gulf."

Chaney hadn't considered that; yeah, killing two platoons of marines probably would be considered an overt provocation act of war unless ...unless. . .

"Unless . . ." he said slowly, "we killed them ourselves."

Brick didn't move.

Releasing a heavy breath, he stared at the wall.

"This is unreal," he said.

CHAPTER 10

Staring intently at the topographical map with Takakura sweating and glowering beside him, Hunter tried to find an easily negotiable route to the research station, located on the south side of the White Mountains, a massive range over thirty miles long and completely impossible to clear in time to help the professor.

His brow hardening, Hunter looked at Takakura, and the Japanese just shook his head, still breathing hard from the last hard knoll they'd had to clamber across carrying the stretcher.

This was obviously not good country for a man to get injured, nor one in which to portage a man out. The terrain was becoming increasingly difficult and rough-cut, and the map indicated that it was about to become even more severe.

As a team, they would have had only moderate difficulty clearing the north ridge of the mountains bordering Fossil Creek, a misnamed river that ran the length of the range. But with a wounded man in uncertain condition this was no longer a strike mission; it was a rescue mission.

They couldn't scale, couldn't push the pace at double time when they mercifully reached a rare level area. So far, the longest level path had been about a hundred yards and ended in a long descent that a strong man could negotiate with caution, but only with the greatest difficulty while carrying a wounded man.

Takakura turned his head. "Riley!"

In a moment Riley was bent beside them, wearily propped on his rifle. Hunter had liked the guy from the first, but had not found a good opportunity to talk to him.

Takakura's tone allowed no room for failure. "We will negotiate this bluff ahead to lower the professor and move for this area known as Windy Gap, which is the only pass through the mountains. Can you rig a harness for which to accomplish this?"

Riley glanced at the map. "That's a one-hundred-foot vertical drop, but yes, I can manage it."

"Good." The Japanese folded the map and rose sharply.

Hunter saw what he meant, knew it was possible. Then he looked up to see Bobbi Jo attentively medicating the old professor through the rough-rigged IV and stood as Takakura continued.

"There is no time to waste. We must move quickly, Hunter," he turned into him. "Are you confident that you and your wolf can detect the presence of the beast, should he approach again?"

Hunter's response was solid. "It hasn't deceived us yet. But it's learning. You can't be sure what it will do next. Confidence can be dangerous."

"How do you know that it is learning?"

"It used to stalk, now it waits in ambush." He paused. "There's other things bothering me about that, too. But we can talk about it later. Right now it's enough to assume that it probably can't move without Ghost hearing it. On balance ... I'd say that, one way or another, either Ghost or I can pick it up. But it's not a guarantee."

Takakura said nothing for a long moment, then turned to Bobbi Jo. "You will take point behind Hunter," he said. "You possess the only weapon which can wound it." He walked away. "Buck and Riley will carry the professor for now. Let's move."

Hunter never ceased to be amazed at Takakura's determination and complexity. On the one hand, the Japanese was patient and courteous and enduring far beyond the rest; on the other he could be as severe as a feudal lord declaring war. But Hunter had come to genuinely respect him; it was enough.

Bobbi Jo seemed to be finally showing the strain of carrying the heavy Barrett and its ammunition. Her face was flushed, perspiration running in rivulets down her neck through a sea of sweat, and her depressed shoulder showed where the strap, though padded, was cutting through her vest. As Hunter walked past her, he asked casually, "Want me to carry that for a while? It's a heavy piece of artillery. And you've carried it all day through some pretty bad terrain."

To his surprise and without blinking she said, "Don't mind at all. It's yours. Here." And gave it to him. Simple as that.

When she let the weapon go, Hunter was shocked. It weighed at least thirty pounds. He couldn't believe she'd carried this weight for so long without ever revealing the effort it took. He put the strap over his shoulder, trying to find a comfortable point of contact, as she worked the action on the Marlin, ejecting a cartridge from the port and then injecting it back into the magazine. Obviously she needed no instruction in how to work his weapon.

She swept back hair from her head, speaking quickly and pointing to the weapon. "There's a round already chambered. This is the safety. It's a semiauto .50 caliber. You already found out that it kicks some, but be ready. You've got five shots but I'll get to you before that." A pause. "*Hopefully.*"

He looked up. "Why hopefully?"

Shaking sweat from her forehead, she smiled, "'Cause I've got the extra clips."

"Oh."

"Let's move!" Takakura repeated, looking more warlike with every step the expedition put behind them. Hunter took point, with Ghost ranging to his left and right, searching, searching, and always ready. Hunter tried to estimate how quickly they could negotiate the expanse between them and the research station before they once again might be forced to try and kill what might indeed be un-killable.

***

Chaney answered the fax, reading it from the screen of the portable laptop. As ever, he was impressed with the modern technology available to modern law-enforcement personnel.

Without shame or concern he considered himself a computer idiot, but he knew enough about technology to remain functional. From the old school, though, he still preferred the old-fashioned snitch and a good fast attack stratagem. However he was not so cowboy-minded that he didn't appreciate fingertip access to information.

Chaney studied the Executive Order displayed on the gray-blue monitor. It was dated one week ago and had authorized the search team in the Alaskan wilderness. And one name in particular attracted his attention: Dr. Angus Tipler, executive director of the Tipler Institute.

Chaney had just learned that Tipler was the country's leading authority on crypto-zoology and ecosystems reputedly on the verge of destruction. In fact, that entire institute seemed dedicated to the preservation of endangered species and environments. Thoughtfully, Chaney studied it. What was this old man doing on what was supposed to be a military mission? Then he saw an obscure mention of the inclusion of a civilian "scout." He focused on the name: Nathaniel Hunter.

Hell, he thought, the army had plenty of scouts; it was a highly recruited MOS. Why would this team need a civilian scout? Did the military not have people who could handle this job? Or was Hunter recruited because he was an expert in the topography, the nature of the wilderness? Was there something more to it?

Question led to question.

What would a half-dozen top-secret CIA research stations be looking for up in Alaska, anyway? What could justify such an outrageous expenditure in an era of wholesale budget cuts? And, most important, who had authorized it? Who was responsible for their activities?

He called the operator for the number of the Tipler Institute, and recorded the address. That would be his first stop. Then he would do some background investigation on this "scout" who was leading the team. It seemed to him for a moment that he had heard of this man, Nathaniel Hunter.

Nothing seemed to come to mind, but he had read it, seen it somewhere. He made a mental note to look into him, too.

Whoever Hunter was, he had to be something pretty special. Because the army didn't normally rely upon civilian "scouts" unless they were operating on foreign soil. And Alaska, though wild and hostile and an easy place to get yourself killed, was still ours.

Then he remembered: yes, Nathaniel Hunter, internationally respected multimillionaire and founder of the Tipler Institute. Chaney understood now why the name had not immediately meant something to him when he recalled what little he had read of Hunter. From all reports, the man preferred the deepest anonymity but was a highly demanded speaker at global events concentrated on the environment and certain ecosystems threatened by civilization.

He was also, as Chaney remembered, a rather generous philanthropist who had funded or co-funded a number of award-winning research and ecological projects—some so complex that Chaney couldn't begin to understand them even when he had tried. Chaney also remembered reading something more obscure—news reports of Hunter somehow aiding in certain rescues. But those had been little more than brief accounts he had occasionally come across in the newspapers. At the time, they had meant nothing, but he had mentally indexed the name.

He wondered: what would this man who was famous for his environmental research projects and enormous wealth be doing wandering around Alaska with a military hit team? Now that, almost more than anything, truly didn't fit. In fact, it seriously enhanced the enigma.

Carefully, he checked the Sig Sauer 226 9-mm semi-auto that was his service gun to ensure that a round was chambered. And he tried to ignore how uncomfortable it made him feel.

Because he had checked it already.

***

Hunter raised a fist, knelt in place.

All the others stopped where they were.

Something—something instantaneous and ghostly—had happened; something that one of his reflexes or instincts perceived but didn't translate to his mind. He stood motionless, head down, concentrating.

As he understood.

There had been a rhythm to the chorus of birdsong, and then it had broken briefly before resuming with a slightly altered cadence.

First, he scanned for bear or elk or something else that may have intruded on the immediate vicinity. But he knew that it was wishful thinking. Even though the team was causing little noise, their combined scents would have scared away every large predatory animal within two miles.

Eyes moving slowly, left to right, Hunter eyed a leveled section of the bluff that ran alongside a series of broken black crags. His gaze roamed up, down, searching without seeing, waiting. He listened, heard nothing. Around them, higher peaks rose to touch a bright blue sky with an almost crystalline beauty, a stark contrast to the vicious battle in which they were trapped.

Hunter turned his head and looked at Takakura, who scowled in silence. Then he turned his face forward, and thought of moving, but something prevented him: Something was wrong here. Something he couldn't place. He remembered the rule: the forest will only tell you the truth, it will never lie.

Almost in the same second, Takakura came up beside him, holding a steady and level aim at the crags. He waited for a moment, and then, "It has not attacked in the daylight yet. Why do you think it might change its tactics now?"

Hunter hesitated, frowning. Then answered, simply, " 'Cause I ticked it off. I hurt it bad and now it wants revenge. Tell everyone to stay a little spread ...but not much. Five feet is good. If it's in there, I think it'll strike from above."

"*Hai*."

He was gone and Hunter motioned for Bobbi Jo to come up. "Give me the Marlin. Time to change."

They exchanged guns and Hunter repeated the procedure she had done, working the action and inserting the cartridge back into the magazine. He ensured that it was fully loaded with a live round in the port. Then he glanced back to see that Buck and Riley were carrying the professor. When he had their attention, he cautiously walked toward the crags. Behind him, everyone followed in silence.

He padded forward slowly, feeling the ground with each step, testing the earth as much as the air, the fowl, the wind. He had six heavy rounds in the Marlin, each hot and hard enough to stop a charging rhino in its tracks, but he knew that they weren't enough against this thing. Nothing seemed like it was enough. They had not had time to logically analyze its native ability to endure small-arms fire, Hunter knew they needed to at the first opportunity. First, though, they had to survive this gauntlet.

He only knew that, unless they caught it with a concentrated burst of fire or unless Bobbi Jo hit it point-blank dead-center with the Barrett and then Takakura took its head with the katana, they were going to be in a big, bad world of hurt. Despite the cold, sweat dripped from Hunter's face.

Ghost, vaguely agitated, stared at the tree-line and shuffled his huge paws on rough, black volcanic rock. The big wolf seemed eager to get on with the fight, but would, as always, wait for Hunter's shouted command.

What happened next made Hunter instantly whirl and trigger the Marlin, ready to shoot anything that moved. In the space of a breath, a terrible silence had struck the entire forest.

***

Rebecca loaded the stat sheets into her car. She was in a mood to do something about this DNA information, and if she didn't get some cooperation fast she would be going to heads of departments that few outside the government could approach.

She had decided all of that during a sleepless night; no, she wouldn't engage in senseless dialogue with low-level bureaucratic morons. Not when Tipler's life was in danger.

She had an easy twenty-minute drive and then she would give this Dr. Hamilton a serious wake-up call. He could react or not. If not, or if he hadn't notified Dr. Tipler of the discovery, she would simply leave without a word. She didn't need the cooperation of the CIA. She had only dealt with them out of good faith.

Angling north toward Langley, she took the curve close and continued moving, enjoying the feel of the road. This was one of the few relaxing moments she'd experienced since the ordeal began.

And then it happened.

She knew.

There was a grating, sliding sound beneath her feet and the automobile lurched. She screamed at the sight of a guardrail speeding under and past her, the car somersaulting violently in the air, ceiling smashing hard and then crashing even harder before she saw stark white and lost her grip, everything lost.... She saw a horrifying steep slope almost void of green—dirt and stone that clung to a vertical face. The car slid backwards, turning again as it struck something hard. She stared wildly at the sky as it passed down and up ...

Ground rushing beneath her.

***

Ghost sensed it and froze.

Hunter didn't blink.

Slowly he turned his head to measure the wolf's motionless stance and saw the bat-like ears standing high to catch the faintest, farthest whisper of movement, but he could see that Ghost was equally frustrated.

It was close to them, so close that Ghost could catch the almost nonexistent sound of soft grass crushed under a padded foot, and Hunter shifted his grip on the 45.70, turning his head to Bobbi Jo. She was already alert, watching him with wide eyes. Silent, he pointed vaguely at a forty-foot section of stone; he was fairly confident that it was somewhere in that jagged darkness. She nodded.

Instantly Takakura followed his direction and Hunter glanced past the big Japanese to see Taylor raise the shotgun from his side, staring into the surrounding dark stones.

Hunter realized that any dark hole in there would be a good place for ambush—which was a likely possibility since it had never attacked them in the day and would likely want the advantage of surprise. But that sparked another idea within him, an idea that perhaps it was hurt more than they had presumed by small-arms fire. Or maybe there was a limit to that healing ability. Impossible to say, and it bothered Hunter for only the briefest of breaths as he poised.

It was so close, somewhere in that jagged fanged mouth of up-jutting stone, that he could almost smell its breath. But it knew that they knew, and it was moving cautiously. Yet Hunter knew also that they couldn't wait all day for it to attack.

Which didn't leave many choices.

For certain, entering the stones to search for it was not an option. Nor was standing here forever, waiting. So he debated and then decided. Raising the Marlin slightly, he took a cautious step, glancing back narrowly to see that the others were following.

He noticed that Taylor had taken a defensive position close to Riley and Buck, who were still carrying the professor; a necessary risk since they might be able to move completely past this position if the beast hesitated too long. But also dangerous because it would take the commandos at least two seconds to drop the old man and raise weapons.

"Ghost," Hunter whispered, but the wolf didn't look. "Find it for me. Where is it?"

Ghost shifted his dark opaque gaze at—

Catapulting from the dark, a blurring shape tore a savage hole in foliage at the rear of the unit and struck like black lightning, a monstrous clawed hand sweeping out with the speed of a lion to hit Buck squarely, it seemed, in the chest. But Hunter saw more clearly what happened next—Buck's head torn from his shoulders—and knew the blow had been higher; head spinning back, long bright blood vessel trailing, eyes still alive—shocked—dead.

"Damn!" Taylor roared and turned as Riley frantically tried to raise his weapon. Then it hit him squarely, a taloned hand tearing away a large section of his ballistic vest to send the commando into stones where he vanished, boots high in the air.

Then it was on top of Taylor, who was already firing the semi-auto shotgun at full-tilt. The creature staggered for an instant, then came on again, unstoppable and un-killable and hell-bent to finish them in one consuming attack. But Taylor didn't retreat an inch, roaring defiance as he fired.

It moved so fast in the next second that Hunter wasn't sure if Taylor was dead or alive, and then it was past the fire-scarred soldier, sweeping up the line and leaping to the side to avoid Takakura's dead-accurate machine-gun blaze before rebounding off the stone like an ape and barreling into Wilkenson, who was blasted far from the path, his rifle sailing high.

Gunfire lit the trees like lightning and Hunter couldn't see or hear in the blaze and chaos and screaming. He tried for a shot but Bobbi Jo was in the way so he jerk-stepped to the left, away from the stones, to fire from the hip and saw it smash into Takakura.

Firing wildly, Takakura ducked away with a desperate shout as the thing—incredibly both humanoid and beastlike and moving with the speed of a lion—lashed out. Takakura managed a last shot as he barely slid wide of the blow, and then it was on Bobbi Jo and Hunter together, smashing Bobbi Jo's rifle contemptuously to the side as it struck her a glancing swipe in the shoulder that hammered her hard to the ground.

Hunter fired point-blank and it twisted with a howl, coming over him. And in that single, unforgettable split-second Hunter met the deep blood-red eyes that blazed with bestial hate, a fanged mouth roaring with arms extended for a murderous embrace, and he twisted, striking it savagely across the face with the butt of the Marlin.

It didn't even seem to feel the pain, returning a backhand blow that hurled Hunter against a boulder, and then Hunter was fiercely angling and parrying to survive. With tigerish reflexes he had developed from a lifetime of deadly survival in the wild, Hunter narrowly evaded a half-dozen clawed blows that struck in one thunderous blur after another, each tearing sparks from the granite around him. Although the attack didn't last more than two seconds, Hunter had never read an oncoming attack so quickly, had never reacted with such perfect speed, balance, and perfect grace—a twist, an angled shoulder, a desperate duck—causing the monstrous hands to miss again and again by mere fractions of an inch.

Ghost, roaring demonically with rage, descended from a leap, landing fully on the thing's shoulder, white fangs flashing.

The next moment was chaos...Hunter seeing angry weapons raised ... Ghost rending ... the creature roaring, tearing savagely as it reached back to haul the great wolf forward ...

Hunter leaped.

As Ghost came over its shoulder, heaved by the immeasurable strength, Hunter caught the wolf from the air and twisted, continuing down and away.

"Shoot it!" he bellowed.

Three weapons erupted in a wall of flame and Hunter wrestled Ghost viciously to the ground to save him from the hail of lead that poured over them both. Then Bobbi Jo gained a knee and, raising the Barrett, managed a single thunderous shot that lit the path with five feet of flame. The beast howled, twisting away from the stunning impact of the, 50-caliber round. Hunter saw it grab at an arm but not its chest.

He made it to his knees as it twisted away and Bobbi Jo wrestled the Barrett's recoil for a second shot. Bellowing and in obvious pain, the beast viciously smashed a wide branch cleanly asunder to gain entrance into the dense woods so close beside them.

"Get it!" Bobbi Jo exclaimed, enraged. "Get it now!"

Takakura reloaded a clip in the MP-5, his dark face glistening with sweat, electrified with rage. He was breathless and fought fiercely to regain a measure of composure.

"Did anyone wound it?" he shouted.

""I put ten slugs straight into that thing!" Taylor snarled as he vengefully inserted another full magazine into the shotgun. "But I ain't sure if they penetrated! I ain't never seen nuthin' move that fast!"

The Japanese commander said nothing, but turned and stared at Buck's headless body lying on the path. Slowly, he walked up and stood beside it, hesitating only a moment to check on the welfare of the professor. He gazed down for a time in heavy silence, then released a deep breath.

His face, unexpressive, contained a deadly element, like dark clouds cloaking a tornado that would soon be unleashed, and once unleashed would deliver death hard and without fear. Then his lips tightened, and calmly—too calmly—he bent and searched Buck's dead body for any evidence of the team. There was no need to search for dog-tags; they did not wear dog-tags on classified missions.

When he stood, the Japanese walked coldly toward the front of the column. And Bobbi Jo knelt beside Tipler, checking the old man's vital signs, speaking to him gently.

Taylor, enraged to madness, kept a hot eye on everything around them. Even his bad eye seemed to glow with a rage that would be quenched only when this beast was meat on his table.

Ghost had not been injured in the brief encounter and Hunter, for the first time, realized it was remarkable that the wolf hadn't pursued the creature into the forest. And the thought occurred to him that perhaps it was because Ghost, on a level that was his alone, was more concerned about Hunter's welfare than he was about killing the thing.

But he also knew that if Ghost chose to leave and roam these hills, only one of them would survive. Ghost would never allow such a creature to live inside his domain. He would hunt it down to fight it, and somehow Hunter knew the wolf would die.

Bending, Hunter rested his hands on his knees, taking a breath, trying to assess his wounds. He knew his back had been torn and bone-bruised when he had rebounded from the boulder, and he had probably sustained a number of torn muscles.

None of the injuries would hurt now. But later, when he rested, they would stiffen. After that it would be a constant battle to stay on his feet.

He looked around, saw a number of floras that he could use for the pain, and walked over. Carefully he picked the leaves and put them immediately in his mouth, chewing them raw.

Taylor, accustomed now to Hunter's oddities, didn't waste a second glance. But Wilkenson seemed intrigued, eyes narrowing in the bronzed, lean face. Badly bruised by the creature's blow, he nevertheless seemed to have recovered his composure. It was clear he wanted to ask what Hunter was up to but the tracker was so enraged by the attack and Buck's death that the Englishman was careful to keep a safe distance.

Bitter and dry, the leaves would have been more effective if they had been boiled, but Hunter had no time. As it was, he would probably suffer cramps later from direct ingestion, but he would have to weather it. He had to head the pain off before it became so distracting that his abilities were compromised. He didn't worry about Ghost; the wolf never seemed to care about any kind of injury.

When Takakura reached Hunter, his face was a mask of pure, almost frightening rage. Hunter stood to face him, heaved a hard breath. For a moment their eyes met, then the Japanese spoke. "We will do as we planned. We will deliver the professor to the research center."

Hunter didn't comment.

"Then," Takakura added, colder, "I will join you on the final hunt. Orders or no orders, we will hunt this beast to the ends of the earth, and we will take its head." He didn't wait for Hunter's acquiescence, nor did Hunter expect him to.

Takakura jerked his head to the side. "Riley! How far to the bluff?"

"Another two hundred yards," Riley answered, still breathless and stunned. Hunter saw that his combat vest, armored with Kevlar and what appeared to be some kind of steel mesh, had been torn like tissue paper. His chest was bleeding—so, no, the beast had not missed completely. The wounds were a deep red-black in the gloom of the ridge.

"Taylor and I will carry the professor," the commander said, allowing no room for contest. "Hunter and Ghost will lead. Bobbi Jo, you will be back-up and Riley will be guard. Beware, Riley! It has struck once from behind. It may again. We go! Now!"

In seconds they were moving more quickly, almost at a trot, though Hunter somehow didn't expect an encounter soon. He didn't know why, exactly; perhaps it was just his forest sense. But he had seen the creature's reaction up close when Bobbi Jo hit it with the Barrett and he had somehow sensed its surprise, as if it still could not believe these pitiful weapons could hurt it.

They reached the bluff quickly and Taylor was the first to rappel down. Takakura was second in order to back up Taylor at the base and then they rigged the professor, who was easily lowered to the bottom. Next, the three of them rappelled down, one after the other, with Riley last.

"What about the rope?" Takakura said. "We may need it. It is still tied to the tree at the top."

"That's why you brought me, Commander," Riley responded. "I lassoed it to the tree."

He pulled on one length of the doubled rope and quickly one end ascended. In seconds, the entire rope came over the summit and spiraled in a slow majestic descent over the climber. "One second," he said, again out of breath; the ordeal was wearing on them all.

That Takakura did not hurry him was a measure of his command ability. In five minutes the gear was stowed and Riley lifted the pack, holding his M-203. "I'm ready," he gasped.

Ghost ranged in front as they picked a path down a slope that bordered a creek running toward Windy Gap, a cut in the mountains. This was their only chance for getting the professor to the research center. It would be the last night alive in these mountains for all of them if they failed to succeed.

Leading, Hunter kept the Marlin ready, for whatever it was worth. When he cast a quick glance back at Bobbi Jo, he saw a vicious edge in the sniper's eyes. She was not just looking; she was hungry. She wanted it in her sights again; she had confidence in both her skill and her weapon.

Then Hunter again remembered the demonic eyes that blazed with malignant intent, heard again the enraged deafening roar hurled from the humanoid face with curved claws weaving a black web of death that he had evaded again and again by the merest margin, escaping death by the space of a breath, and he knew one more thing.

It would never cease this hunt. He was the only one that had beaten it face-to-face, the only one to challenge that dark might and escape. Yes, it would come. And it would come for him.

***

"I can't give it to you on a cellular," Brick growled. "Call me on a land line."

"Give me a number," Chaney said, steering the rented Ford LTD into a gas station. He was less than thirty miles from the Tipler Institute. It was the most likely place to begin.

He wrote down the number Brick gave him and hurried to the phone, knowing he could be racing against a tap. Brick answered before the first ring finished.

"It's only a piece," Brick said hoarsely, "but I found something from one of the snitches injustice. This guy knows somebody who was asking questions about logistics, the satellite support stuff for these research stations. That ain't much, but if someone is poking around, they got a reason."

"Can this be traced back to you?" Chaney asked, suspecting a possible trap. It was the oldest trick in the book; put out false information to a particular person and then wait and see if it surfaces downstream. It was one of the best methods for finding moles and leaks.

"No, this guy is solid," Brick responded. "We go back."

"Did he give you a name?"

"Yeah." He paused, and Chaney heard paper rattling. "He said the guy's name was ... Dixon. Yeah, Dixon. Flashed CIA creds. He didn't mention division. But if it's dealing with this, I'd say covert ops is a good place to start. Want me to check on it?"

Chaney debated.

The Central Intelligence Agency was prevented by law from operating any facilities inside the continental United States, with the exception of a domestic office that they ran at a covert site in New York City. Both the CIA charter and presidential mandate prevented domestic activities. And whatever this would eventually turn out to be, it was definitely a domestic activity. He wasn't sure if he wanted to involve Brick any further.

"No," he said finally. "I can take it from here. I want you to smooth things over. Act pissed off and ignorant. Say you wonder why a bunch of marines got wasted because you're an ex-marine. Make like you're angry about the whole thing. They'll figure, once a marine, always a marine. Take that line. Let them know you don't care who knows you're interested, then they'll think you have nothing to hide."

He almost felt Brick nodding.

"You watch your back, kid," Brick said heavily, his voice deepening. "You're messin' with ... Lord! I don't know *what* you're messin' with! But I know a few tricks that you don't. And I can promise you that they know you're watchin' 'em. So they're gonna be watchin' you back."

"I'll cover my six." Chaney glanced around casually at the highway. "You know me. I always do."

"Yeah. Right."

Chaney hung up and walked back to the car. From the first, he hadn't liked the feel of it. Now he liked it even less. And the questions returned to him: What were they looking for up there? Why did they need one of the world's leading crypto-zoologists, guys that specialize in identifying unknown species?

He opened the car door slowly, completely absorbed by the thought— the military and anthropologists working together in what was essentially a high-tech military hunting party. Which would mean they were, of course, hunting for ...no, not a person. They wouldn't need an ecologist to hunt a—

Chaney stopped in place.

An animal?

He vaguely knew his mouth was hanging open.

Could they be hunting some kind of animal?

He mentally repeated it: an ecologist, a scout, a high-tech killing team ... for an animal? Could an animal have attacked the soldiers? Would that be why they were hunting it, if that's what

166 | JAMES BYRON HUGGINS

they were really doing? Could an animal be responsible for the destruction of the research facilities?

The thought was so outrageous, he went over the facts again, to make sure he hadn't missed a major clue. But he hadn't. And he stood for a long time in silence, trying to accept the possibility of it. He didn't even attempt to measure the absurdity of it. He didn't need to.

He tried to avoid thinking of how incredible a thought it was, concentrating on the hard clues themselves. They had found something up there, he conjectured, something that required someone to name. That explained the presence of the old man. And it was something that was moving—which meant it was alive—and that explained the need for a tracker. And it was something that they intended to kill, which explained the hit team.

Chaney was grateful that that much made good sense, despite the wild-ness of the theory. Then he continued to try to fit in what else he knew.

And someone with power wanted to conceal the operation, which explained the lies. And this agent, Dixon, had reportedly been asking questions about the team's satellite linkups, and that was the factor Chaney couldn't figure. Why ask about communications satellites unless ... unless ... How would you sabotage an attack team?

The answer was easy.

By cutting off their support. By shoving them into traffic and abandoning them.

Chaney frowned. If this thing—an animal, if his theory was correct— could wipe out two platoons of marines, it could easily wipe out a small attack team. But what could do that? What kind of animal could kill all those men in an attack? And why, if you wanted it dead, would you cut off your killing team?

Things just didn't add up.

What could be so important at these sites that they would go to such extremes to conceal? And who would have any motivation to sabotage the operation? And finally, and even more important, who would have the power?

Slowly, turning it over and over, he pulled out from the gas station.

He was even more careful as he exited the ramp, moving north toward the Institute. Maybe he would find the answers there, he thought. But he doubted it. He had a feeling this was going to get a lot worse before it got better.

**

Hunter moved slowly down a gorge that led to a creek. He knew it would lead to an even larger creek. He wasn't consulting the topography map; he didn't have to. From here, his reckoning skills would take them to the gap, though they still had a long twenty miles ahead of them.

Ghost, the only one among them who knew no fear, roamed up the trail and down, always staying close. But Hunter knew it was to protect him, for if Ghost had chosen his preferred action, he would be tracking it even now through this frontier to battle it to the death.

Hunter watched everything, nothing. The forest was quiet, but not un-naturally so, probably due to the uncustomary presence of man in this wooded domain of beasts.

He glanced back—everyone was moving well—so he continued on at an even, measured pace. Not too quick, yet not too slow because they had to make the pass by dusk. There, he knew, they would find some kind of hamlet where they could contact the research station by phone and obtain immediate medical assistance for the professor.

Hunter estimated another five hours on the trail. And, after he released the professor into the care of the army, he would pursue this beast alone and with the means to destroy it.

It was personal now, as when Ghost refused to fall before the wrath of the alpha wolf that he had fought over the dead elk. And there was something more.

Hunter knew this beast would kill forever if it was not stopped. It was like a lion that had become a man-killer. It would return to kill again and again until it was destroyed.

And this creature was even worse than any man-killer. This thing didn't kill for a reason; not food, not fear, not territory. It was simply a mindless engine of annihilation that would continue until it was destroyed.

Hunter knew that nothing like this had walked the world for 10,000 years, if ever. Nor had it long been inside these mountains. For a species this unbelievably savage would have drawn the attention of the entire planet long ago, and quite probably would have been tracked down and killed.

Hunter knew that these "research facilities" were somehow behind this monstrosity. And he decided that, yes, he would fly into the next one ...and he would indeed find some answers to—

Hunter's savage instinct made him whirl.

He twisted desperately aside as the volcanic black shape—a monstrosity of roaring black and red—erupted from a crevice to hurl a clawed hand at his face. The blurring black talons brushed his leather shirt and Hunter, incredibly, hit the ground on balance, spinning back with a snarl.

Yet the blow continued on momentum and hit Bobbi Jo hard, somersaulting her cleanly in the air with the Barrett flung far. Takakura whirled, firing a full round with the MP-5, unleashing a raging clip into its chest as it staggered, striking again to blast the Japanese back.

Driven to the ground by the impact, Takakura slammed into Wilkenson and both of them hit a small slope, a tangle of arms and legs and outstretched weapons rolling hard to collide with a boulder. Moving in a blur, it was on Riley almost instantly.

Without the advantage of Kevlar this time, Riley was virtually armor-less as it swiped out, lifting him cleanly from the ground, its monstrous hand buried to the wrist in a lung.

Riley's face was open in shock for a stunned instant before blood exploded violently from his mouth and he ceased moving. Gloating, almost, it hurled the dead soldier at Taylor, rushing forward almost as quickly as the body sailed through smoking air.

The hulking commando agilely evaded Riley's dead form and quick drew a sawed-off double-barreled shotgun from his waist to fire both blasts in its face.

It staggered, and with a massive roar, returned a murderous blow that should have torn Taylor in half. But, anticipating the response, the big man had ducked, rolled, and come up quick with his shotgun blazing. He hit it a dozen times in less than three seconds and dropped a clip to speed-load another as Hunter fired.

The Marlin's roar was tremendous and the beast winced, staggering back as if Taylor's assault had stunned it. Then Bobbi Jo fired a quick shot that disintegrated a small tree beside it.

For a split second, they had the advantage of distance and acquisition and took full advantage of it, laying a field of fire that hit and didn't hit. Bobbi Jo clambered painfully to her knees, holding her chest. Hunter could hear nothing but the detonation of rifle fire but he saw her attempt to raise the Barrett for a shot. Grimacing at the pain of her effort, she dropped the barrel to the ground. Then, teeth gritted, she tried again.

The barrel rose.

Sensing that Bobbi Jo was about to fire, the thing leaped with superhuman speed, hitting a boulder and clearing the wide stream with a terrific bound before Hunter could raise the Marlin and fire another wild shot, knowing as his finger closed on the trigger that he had failed to lead it enough.

Vaguely it registered to him that a tree somewhere beyond it had exploded from the impact of the heavy 45.70 round, and then the creature gained the ground on the far side of the stream, running.

The entire creek bed was littered with smoking shells and casings, and waves of heat rose from the weapons in the unnatural silence that followed. Hunter could hear nothing but his own labored breath. And then he glimpsed the beast on a nearby hill, charging up the slope as if it had not been wounded at all.

Taylor roared wordlessly, viciously as he opened fire again, aiming high because the beast was well out of range.

Takakura staggered from the freezing stream and cast a single glance at Riley's dead body before whirling toward the hill where Taylor was firing. He immediately joined Taylor, firing hopelessly far and high and wide.

Wilkenson was wounded, blood pouring from his slashed arm, but he raised his rifle at the fleeing shape and pulled the trigger.

Already it was more than a half mile away.

"God Almighty," Hunter whispered. "*Already* ..."

He raised the Marlin and fired, knowing it was impossible but joining anyway. The slug would fall at a quarter mile, probably, and now it was almost a mile away, nearing the top of the ridge.

They were not even close to hitting it as he watched the thing continue to climb, unperturbed by the vengeful rifle fire cascading over it. And he knew that in seconds it would reach the crest, over a mile distant. They didn't stand a chance of hitting it.

Then, snarling, Bobbi Jo gained her feet. Her eyes blazed red and her teeth clenched as she understood the situation. She whipped a machete from her waist and with a single vicious swipe sliced off a nearby branch, instantly slamming it into the ground.

Then she racked a heavy .50-caliber round into the Barrett sniper rifle and laid the barrel through two strong branches that formed a support. She flipped open the scope covers.

Her face grew still and cold. Then her breathing slowed and she threw a lock of hair from her eyes with an impatient toss of her head.

Hunter looked back at the ridge and saw the thing near the crest. Dimly he knew that the rest had stopped firing, finally abandoning all hope with hateful screams.

"Come on ..." He heard Bobbi Jo's soft whisper. "Come on ... I'm gonna reach out and touch ya ..."

She waited with cold fury until it reached the peak of the far ridge. Waited until it turned. Waited until it raised monstrous taloned hands in the air and its glorious bestial roar crashed over them, hurled from the sanctity of safety.

"*Good night*," she whispered.

Fired.

The violent concussion hurled it backward off the ridge. Hunter stared hard but saw nothing more, then dimly heard Bobbi Jo eject the Barrett's five-round magazine, inserting another round from her vest.

Her face was empty, devoid of pleasure or pain. And Hunter sensed that the concentration and cold control required to make such an incredible shot would fade slowly.

She kicked the branch aside and shouldered the strap of the sniper rifle, turning to Takakura. "I hit it low," she said with a surgeon's detached composure. "I was trying for a head shot. But I hit low."

Takakura shook his head in saddened frustration. He cast a single glance back at Tipler, motionless now on the stretcher. "We must hurry," he breathed. "We cannot risk another encounter with the beast. We will not be so lucky next time, I think ... Taylor, help me with the professor. Wilkenson, you can take rear guard."

Hunter's eyes narrowed as he watched the Japanese bend for a second, recovering. He could not imagine, for some reason, Takakura injured or revealing injury. But it seemed for a moment that he would collapse. Then he straightened, a hard frown on his chiseled face, and walked to the professor.

Mile by mile, Hunter thought, they were becoming more ragged and battle-worn. Takakura's short hair was smeared with grime and sweat and his once-impeccable uniform savagely torn by the beast's massive claw. Bobbi Jo's uniform and armor were as devastated as Takakura's, and she appeared haggard, as if the long combat was leeching the life from her. Wilkenson was still holding onto some of his superior attitude, but he too was showing distinct signs of exhaustion and wear. Even Hunter, used to savage encounters and long arduous journeys in uninhabited lands, was feeling the strain. His coat had been shredded by the boulder and the blows of those clawed hands that had only barely missed the skin beneath. Uncounted purple and bloodied contusions lined his forearms and neck, but his face wore the most punishing remembrance of the conflict: the left: side was viciously slashed with four long distinct claw marks that had torn deep furrows from his cheek downward across his chin.

Hunter spoke quietly, Ghost at his side.

"We better get moving." He held the Marlin low, feeling a fatigue that was somehow deeper than any he had ever known before. "It'll be moving ahead of us again."

"*Hai*." Takakura nodded and waved. "Wilkenson will be guard. We cannot afford to lose another. We will return for Riley and Buck ... if we survive."

Bobbi Jo seemed to have recovered somewhat, and turned to Hunter. For the first time, he saw true fear in her eyes. Her voice was soft. "We're gonna die out here, aren't we?" she asked.

She didn't blink.

No lies, her eyes said.

Mouth tightening into a line, Hunter reached up and placed a hand on her neck. He shook his head. "No," he said, "we're not."

She smiled faintly, returned the nod.

Hunter turned: "Ghost!"

The wolf was instantly in a stance, four massive legs solid as iron, ready for any command. His eyes locked on Hunter with a world of love and devotion and fearlessness. Hunter flung out an arm down the trail: "Search!"

The wolf moved away, passing their weary forms as if they were stones. It cleared the small crest before them and hesitated, coming back, always keeping Hunter in view.

"From now on," Hunter said stoically, "we have to move as quickly as we can, Ghost will clear the trail a hundred yards at a time. We'll make the pass in less than four hours." He looked at all of them in turn. "Can all of you handle the pace?"

They agreed and Hunter reloaded the Marlin. He could hear Bobbi Jo's labored breathing from the ordeal, but knew that no one else was qualified to handle the massive Barrett; she would have to endure it. There was no easy way out. Not for any of them.

Always, Ghost roamed ahead, came back, and Hunter knew he was taking a risk with his friend. For even Ghost could be deceived if the creature was downwind and motionless. But he was thinking that the creature would assume they would continue as they had been—moving slowly, carefully, with extreme caution.

And it would surely be wounded somewhat by Bobbi Jo's dead-eye accuracy because she had hit it center-mass. Perhaps, by the time its animal mind suspected the change of tactics, they might have the distance to outrun it, even in this battle-ravaged condition.

Then, when the rest were safe, and he knew what he needed to know—as in who had betrayed them, and why—he would return to hunt it on his own terms.

It was a head he would keep.

***

Chaney didn't like the feel of it.

The Tipler Institute was obviously a prestigious academy for intellectual dialogue. The listing in the lobby was a virtual who's who of scientific heavyweights. Obviously, securing a tour of the privately funded facility was a much desired honor. Although the professor's photo and position were clearly displayed, Hunter's presence was conspicuously absent from the decorations.

He sensed the direct attention of a rather impatient looking young woman approaching him from a nearby hall. Displaying the full scope of his limited charm, he smiled.

"I'm Gina Gilbert," she said, crossing her arms. She didn't seem particularly impressed by his Deputy U.S. Marshal credentials. "Is there some way I can help you? I'm very busy at the moment."

"I understand." Chaney flashed his creds respectfully. "I wanted to talk with Dr. Tipler."

"He's not in the facility."

"Might I ask where I can contact him?"

"He's on an expedition and it might be a week or so before he's near a communications facility," she answered, tilting her head. "Aren't you aware of the expedition?"

Chaney debated for a split second. "Well, I heard that he was participating in some manner with the State Department," he said—without discernible hesitation, he hoped. "And, in fact, that's what I wanted to speak with him about."

"Well," she said, somewhat slower, "maybe I can assist you. What do you need to know?"

"Are you familiar with the nature of his trip?"

"Yes."

"The trip to Alaska?"

She blinked. "Yes." A pause. "What is it that you want to know, Marshal Chaney?"

Chaney enjoyed her using the "marshal." This close to Washington, he wasn't usually given the courtesy. In fact, the closer you got to the capital, the more unimpressed people became with the presence of a federal agent. Whereas in the heartland, say Oklahoma or Montana, flashing U.S. Marshal credentials would get you instant cooperation—or at least a free meal.

"I'd like to discuss Dr. Tipler's role on this expedition," Chaney continued. "If you have the time, I'd like for you to show me anything you have on it."

She was silent a moment, studying Chaney's innocent smile.

"All right, I've got a minute." She turned away. "Follow me, please, and I'll show you what we've been studying."

***

It had been awhile since Chaney had done any hunting, but he could tell immediately that whatever had made the plaster imprint wasn't a bear. It wasn't anything he had ever seen. And if he could believe this woman, he wasn't alone in his belief.

"And Dr. Tipler couldn't identify what manner of creature made this cast?" he asked, bending low. "I mean, isn't he the expert the experts turn to on this kind of thing?"

"He's the foremost expert in the world, Marshal," Gina said as she laid a long printout on the table. "This is the DNA printout that we mapped from a fiber taken from the bottom of the cast. It couldn't be seen with the naked eye but I spotted it on a microscope and we did the test the day before yesterday. Do you understand DNA coding at all?"

"No." Chancy shook his head. All he saw were rows upon rows of repeated letters. It meant nothing. "Can you explain it to me?"

"Not as well as Dr. Tanus."

"And that is ...?"

"Rebecca Tanus. She's in charge of the Institute while Dr. Tipler is on his expedition." Gina folded the printout. "She should be back later if you want to stay around and talk to her. She'll be in Langley until then, if you want to try and reach her immediately."

Chancy tried to keep his voice low and calm. "What's Dr. Tanus doing at Langley?"

Gina obviously sensed nothing sinister about it. "Well, she went down there to deliver these findings. We could have faxed them but we don't have secure lines here. Dr. Tanus was nervous about it."

"I see." Chaney mused. "Does she have a cell phone?"

"Sure." She reached for a book as the phone rang, picked it up as she opened it. "Yes," she said, slowing her movement. "Yes, this is Gina. Can I help you?"

Chaney saw her face open little by little in obvious shock, but barely heard her almost inaudible words when she finally spoke. "Thank you," she whispered. "No. I'll take care of it."

Silently she set the phone on the hook.

Chaney knew.

"Gina?" he said quietly. "Are you all right?"

She didn't look at him.

"Dr. Tanus," she said dully. "She's dead."

CHAPTER 11

Holding a bleeding rib cage with one hand, he followed them on the slope parallel to the trail. He remained on the far side of the river, which provided more cover for his footfalls with the plenteous moss and wet leaves; he was intent on remaining unseen and unheard.

Hunger devoured him, and he realized that he must eat to rebuild his strength so that he might destroy them. But he was concerned. Soon, he was certain, he would find elk, deer, wolf or wolverine. It did not matter; he would consume them quickly, and the nutrients would power his body to transform the flesh into new flesh, strengthening it for the final hunt that lay ahead.

He growled, almost smiling, and leaped from a rock to drop almost without sound between two huge cedars that provided shadowed silence. As he landed, his ribs tore in sharp, lancing pain and he suppressed a roar. Yes, soon he must eat in order to heal, for his body was exhausted. Raising vengeful eyes, he stared at the woman. He wanted her most of all, now, after the man. For she held what could wound him.

He drew a black pointed tongue over blackened gums and his lips drew back in a submerged, vibrating snarl that made his chest close with the effort. The breath he inhaled afterwards swelled the huge nostrils that allowed him to take in oxygen at a rate far greater than these meager humans were capable of doing. He knew what they were doing, and his reddish eyes glanced at the wolf...the wolf. . .

He hated them all ...

He raked the ground as he watched them run, forcing dirt deep beneath his claws; he loved the feeling. So he did it for a while, enjoying the pleasure. And then he glanced down and saw the ragged remnants of pants he still wore.

It mattered not.

He did not feel the cold as they felt it. Did not feel the pain of briar and rock as they felt it. Did not feel remorse at shedding their blood, or ripping their meaty hearts from their chests to squeeze the blood into his mouth like a grape. No, he felt nothing, body or soul.

His mind, or what was there before it had changed, was only some distant half-something, dim and unimportant. Though somehow, he knew, he even yet retained some ability of primitive speech—some unexpected leftover effect of this strange merging of mind and flesh. Yet it had left him with mechanical aspects of his former self. And he might yet tell them, before he killed, that he had purposefully chosen this glorious form, and infinitely preferred it to life in the puny, mortal husks that carried them around.

His mouth twisted as he tried to form words, but his vocal cords had been altered somehow, and the sounds whispered raggedly from his fanged mouth. Yes, he almost longed for the chance to speak to them—especially to the man—and tell them that he would live for ages. That he would be alive when the man's children were dust, and his children's children—that when all this faded, and fell, and rose again, he would still be alive in this godlike form.

As he considered the experience, the thought became as delicious as the flesh and blood he must soon taste.

Yes, he would speak to the man. He would torture the man with the knowledge that he was not simply a beast but that he was far, far more. And that he would always be more than they could ever imagine.

Then he thought of the others, the ones like him who would be there, waiting. And how, when he joined them with his superior mind, they would make war again. Would drive the puny ones into holes where they would feast on their brains.

His eyes narrowed as he smiled.

Yes, they would consume them.

Body and soul.

***

Like a sliver of shadow, Ghost came back over the ridge toward Hunter, pausing and staring, and Hunter hesitated. He turned back to see how the others were keeping up and saw that Bobbi Jo, despite her determination, was faltering badly.

There was no reason for false hope and a suicide run for the pass would only end in doom. No, they would never make it before nightfall. Not in this terrain, and not in this condition. They would be traveling through darkness for at least an hour before they reached the pass.

Too long.

He held up a hand. The professor was lowered to the ground, and Takakura came forward, holding the machine gun. "Why do we stop?"

"Because we can't make it," Hunter responded matter-of-factly. Bobbi Jo opened her mouth in protest but she was so winded that she simply-bent, heaving breath on trembling legs.

Hunter expected Takakura to protest his decision but the burly man recognized the wisdom of the move. He lowered the MP-5 to his waist and shaking his head, he searched the far side of the stream as exhaustion forced him to a knee.

Raising his eyes, Hunter looked at Taylor, who stood in place behind the stretcher, no weapon in his hands. Taylor was staring without expression, but his lack of challenge spoke for him. Whatever the commando was feeling was hidden well behind that fire-scarred face. He was a statue, a stoic image of the professional soldier who knew he would die one day as he had lived, and had prepared for it. And now that the moment had come, he would meet it like a man.

Hunter held out his hand to Takakura. "Give me the map."

Wearily it was presented and Hunter knelt, laying the rifle on the ground as Ghost came up, panting. Without even looking at the wolf he said "Guard," and Ghost began padding in loose circles, checking the wind, the ground, river, trail.

Reading the topography, Hunter searched for any defensible position. He saw a gully—no good; a flat-topped knoll nearby that allowed them to see it coming—no good; not with the disadvantage of night and their wits and senses numbed by the exhausting travails of this seemingly endless ordeal; and then ...an abandoned mine.

Hunter's black-maned head twisted as he sighted it.

A mine.

A mine would have only one point of entry. A mine would be defended on three sides by impenetrable rock walls. Eyes sharpening, Hunter estimated the distance quickly and saw that it was within a quarter mile of their position. He was on his feet as he memorized the easiest and quickest route.

"Let's go," he said. "There's a place near here where we might stand a chance to last the night."

No questions were asked. Together they made a weary pilgrimage to the only site that might provide salvation.

It was late in the day when Chaney checked police reports on the fatal car accident involving Rebecca Tanus. He understood that she had veered off a dry road during a trip from her hotel, plummeting off an embankment only to be killed on impact. No foul play was suspected because there were no collision marks on the vehicle and postmortem blood tests revealed she was not intoxicated. It was listed as an accident caused on the steep downslope when a strut stabilizing the front left wheel—the wheel taking most of the stress on the turn—shattered and caused her to lose control.

Chaney thought about asking to examine the vehicle, then thought better of it. Don't go bustin' no red lights, Brick had warned. Don't go around asking a lot of questions like some hotshot investigator. Don't start attracting attention to yourself

But there was one thing that he could do before he hooked up with Brick later in the evening. He could visit Langley and discover who was in control of these facilities. There was little risk involved because by now—they weren't complete fools—they would have confirmed that this was an official investigation. And not showing up at all would be more suspicious than looking like a guy going through the motions.

It took a single easy—too easy, it seemed—phone call and Chaney was soon admitted into a secure section of Langley. As he walked toward the receptionist in what they call a "white" terminal—a section devoted to research and development as opposed to information gathering—he saw a tall, white-haired man with a clipboard and white lab coat speaking casually with another man. As Chaney stepped to the desk, the man turned.

"Marshal Chaney?" the older man asked pleasantly.

Introductions were simple and Dr. Arthur Hamilton ushered Chaney into his office. Before he even sat down in front of the desk, Chaney knew he was dealing with a heavyweight.

Where the Tipler Institute seemed to have a reserved and somewhat humble tone of intellectuality, there was nothing understated about Dr. Hamilton's office. Obviously concerned about the secretiveness of his own identity, Hamilton had a legion of impressive diplomas on display as well as a polished row of gold-plated awards, none of which Chaney recognized. Graphs and display charts recording geological information were spread on the desk.

"So, Marshal," Hamilton proceeded, "I suppose you are investigating the rather horrendous series of accidents that have plagued our facilities."

Chaney had not expected any stonewalling, at least not recognizable, and played the game. He was glad to see that his instincts had not disappointed him.

"I'm trying to determine the cause of these tragic events at the research facilities, Doctor." Chaney presented the air of a professional—a man who committed himself to an investigation without becoming personally involved. "So I have to ask you a few questions, if you have the time."

"Oh, certainly." Hamilton gestured with concern. "Believe me, Marshal Chaney, we are as anxious as anyone to discover what is attacking our personnel. These are rather expensive facilities and highly trained assistants. Neither are easily replaced. In fact, we have been forced to terminate the research temporarily. But, of course, the greatest tragedy of all is in the truly lamentable loss of life." He paused, shook his head. "Yes, quite tragic."

Chaney cleared his throat. "Just what, Doctor, is the purpose of these facilities? The military has been closing Arctic research stations for years because of the budget. Why is the Central Intelligence Agency funding such an expensive program?"

"Oh, for simple science." Hamilton responded with a wave. "You see, Marshal—and I have, of course, confirmed that you are cleared for this in-formation—those facilities monitor seismic activity in the Arctic Circle. And because of their proximity to the Bering Strait and Siberia, we also can monitor any potential nuclear testing which still might occur." He hesitated. "The cold war is over but vigilance is the price we pay for peace. It is not a mean responsibility, and we take it very seriously."

"I'm certain that you do, Doctor." Chaney glanced at the charts. "So, these research facilities have a printed Mission Purpose?" He knew that a printed purpose of intent was mandatory for all Central Intelligence facilities, just as they were for the Marshals Service.

Chaney also realized that there were few organizations in the world, that demanded as much paperwork and documentation of covert activity as the CIA. It was a remarkable paradox in the agency's pathological quest for secrecy.

Hamilton already had the manual available and handed it graciously to Chaney. Then he sat with utter composure in the larger chair. "You may read it now, if you like," he continued. "Of course you can't make notes or take a copy with you. Even I cannot remove an operations manual from the facility. But you can take all the time you need."

Chaney perused it, noticing that a substantial amount of personnel and equipment were dedicated to advanced sonic measurement of tectonic plates. He also saw that each research station had the same SOP, or Special Operational Procedures.

"Why do these facilities all have the same SOP?" he asked, attempting to appear casually confused. "Seems like one could do the job of all six."

"No, no," Hamilton stressed. "It would appear that way, yes, but that is not the case." He retrieved a series of charts from a nearby table. "You see, each station is situated over the edge of a particular tectonic plate. Each plate, over a hundred miles in width, floats over what is known as the athenosphere, or the partially molten substance that moves the plates from time to time."

Chaney was amazed at how fluidly and persuasively the scientist expounded. He was clearly believable, which told Chaney something more: if the scientist was lying, he was a very dangerous man. He waited until Hamilton completed his lesson in geophysics.

"I see," Chaney nodded. "Then why do you think there have been so many casualties over the past two weeks? Surely this kind of information isn't worth an incident. In fact, our adversaries are probably doing the same to us. Monitoring our activities, I mean."

"Oh, I can assure you that they are," Hamilton said, and Chaney noticed that the scientist was remarkably fit for his age. Although he must have been in his sixties, his face was smooth, almost unwrinkled, and had remarkable color and tone. In fact, Chaney didn't know if he'd ever seen someone of Hamilton's age in such remarkably good physical condition. Even seated, the man had obvious strength and athleticism. He listened patiently as Hamilton described the "nefarious" attempts of our enemies to use satellite surveillance on the facilities.

"Yes, I'm sure these attempts are ... nefarious," Chaney responded. "But that doesn't explain why people are dying, Doctor. I've got a body count of a hundred. Now, surely you have some idea why we have this level of ... of carnage."

Hamilton shook his head. "No, Marshal, I am afraid that I do not. I only know that I have done what I know to do. I have approved a special team, some of which you are already aware of, to investigate this matter." He rose, strolling chin in hand. "I am a scientist, Marshal. Not an investigator, such as yourself. So I can assure you, you are speaking with the wrong person. Oh, I understand nature, as well as nature allows itself to be understood. But that type of knowledge is no assistance in a mystery such as this. In fact, it would be a hindrance more than anything else."

"Why is that, Doctor?"

Hamilton raised his eyes. "Because, Marshal, what I deal with, more than anything else, are mysteries. But mysteries that we will likely never solve." He shook his head, bemused. "Even with something as elementary as geophysics, I consider myself an ignorant man, Marshal, despite all my degrees. Long ago, I gave up being frustrated by the profound mysteries of the universe or even trying to explain them. And if I know so little of my own field, imagine how useless to you I would be in yours."

Chaney wondered for a split second if the good doctor hadn't subconsciously given something away. In a heartbeat he intuited that he might gain more by asking about things not directly related to the investigation.

"Doctor," he began casually, attempting to disarm with charm, "you're obviously a learned man. You could probably explain anything you put your mind to as well as anyone alive."

"Oh, not at all." Hamilton turned solidly, and Chaney was again impressed with the man's muscularity. "I am confident that I can explain many things, Marshal Chaney. But the more one answers, the more mysteries one perceives. I could speak for semesters on quantum theory, for instance. Or the force that holds opposing elements together. Or, perhaps, speculate on the origin of thought, or the soul, or life." He stopped in place, smiling. "But that isn't why you came to see me, is it?"

Chaney realized: Mistake.

"No," he said. "I want to know what you think is killing your people. Or why."

"And in that, unfortunately, I cannot help you."

"Well, Doctor," Chaney sat straighter, "something is for sure killing them. So you might as well give me some ideas."

Hamilton leaned forward. "I can tell you what I have been told," he began. "This...murderer, whatever it is, has literally decimated three of my research facilities. One other remains. But if that installation is destroyed, then the entire program will be terminated. Apparently, this...this thing ... is strong. Extremely fast. Highly intelligent. And I, for one, believe that it may well be an unknown species. Something we have not been aware of. That is why we've gone to extreme measures in hunting it down."

Chaney stared. "Thing?"

"Why, yes." Hamilton's brow hardened. He seemed shocked. Or suspicious. "I ... ah ... don't you know details of these atrocities, Marshal? The accounts of this things inhuman cunning? It's almost unbelievable display of fantastic brute strength?"

"Well, I know that whatever killed your people fought its way through many soldiers at each site, Doctor. But it didn't completely defeat the video surveillance, some of which was recorded at covert sites in Washington. And I believe Washington, specifically the Senate Intelligence Subcommittee, is where this plan to find the creature originated."

"Yes." Hamilton nodded. "We were attempting to deal with the situation internally, of course. But when we were called for conference, we agreed that a highly skilled team was probably the best means of resolving the situation. Obviously, our own efforts had been demonstrably insufficient. In fact, I am on record as saying I had no objections at all to the idea, as long as the National Security Agency could retain full authority and command."

"But the hunting team wasn't your idea?"

"Not originally, no. However, I had no objections."

"Nor was it the idea of anyone inside the Agency?"

"Well, I have no knowledge of that."

"I see." Chaney paused. "And that's when the army and marines got involved? Is that correct? That's when someone from the Pentagon, this Agent Dixon, was assigned to assemble this team?"

"Well"—Hamilton cleared his throat—"there was always a military contingent present at the sites, but only for security. But, yes, they became involved in the more intimate aspects of the situation when this special unit was formed to, ah, destroy this creature."

Chaney carefully analyzed what he had heard. "Tell me, Doctor. I mean, you're a scientist. You know a great deal about biology. What would you make of this creature?"

"Well, Marshal, I would ask you the same thing. After all, you are the one investigating the situation. What do you yourself think of such a creature?"

"What do I think?" Chaney opened his eyes a bit wider with the frankness he felt no desire to conceal. "I would think that he or she, or it, could be classified as a monster, Doctor."

"Yes." Hamilton smiled, suddenly more distant. His ice-blue eyes chilled. "Of course."

The silence was unusual, and Chaney decided to take a different tack. He had already, despite Brick's gold-plated advice, gone over the line.

Now Hamilton knew that he was actually interested and, even worse, serious. He'd decide later how much to tell Brick about his misstep. It probably wouldn't be much.

"Tell me about this team you've organized," he said. "Surely they asked you for input when they designed it."

"Well, my primary suggestion, which I demurely presented, was to include someone of substantial scientific acumen present as an adviser. That, to me, seemed indispensable. The man selected was Dr. Angus Tipler, a scholar of unchallenged genius. I did not participate in the selection of the soldiers; I have little knowledge of them. But I understand they are quite adept at this type of search and ... how do they say it in the military?"

"Search and destroy."

"Yes," Hamilton replied, "a search-and-destroy mission. And we have, oh, some other gentleman who knows something about hunting, or tracking. Something like that. I myself am not so familiar with this last individual. I did not consider him important—not important at all, really. So I only perused his file briefly."

Chaney found that more than interesting: Hamilton didn't consider the addition of Hunter, a millionaire and highly recognized wilderness expert, an important event.

"This man," Chaney said, "is Nathaniel Hunter?"

"Yes, yes, he, uh, I believe he is something of an expert tracker. Somewhat well off financially. Not rich, by any means. But comfortable, and used frequently for finding people lost in wilderness areas. I am not sure that he does much of anything at all except support certain wildlife organizations. So I do not know why he was considered so important. But I have a file here, somewhere, if you would like to peruse it."

"Yes," Chaney said. "I would. But, first, I want an answer to a question that you've avoided twice already."

"Oh, I am sorry." Hamilton seemed sincere. "It was certainly an oversight. And to allay your suspicions, should you possess any, please be assured that I am not attempting to be evasive. Quite simply, I have nothing to be evasive about."

"I understand." Chaney smiled blandly. "Do you think that whatever is killing your people could be somehow controlled by competing foreign interests? Particularly former Soviet or Communist enterprises that do basically the same thing as these facilities? Would the information contained at those centers benefit them?"

Hamilton almost smiled, but it never emerged. "No, Marshal. There is nothing contained within the centers that would merit any kind of foreign attack at all. We monitor tectonic phenomena that have nothing, really, to do with military matters."

"Who is in ultimate command of the hunting party?"

"As I said, the National Security Agency."

"I mean, who's in charge in the field?" Chaney continued.

"Well, that would be Colonel Maddox from the Pentagon. I have spoken to him on many occasions. He frequently calls me for...well, advice, I would say."

"Do you know an Agent Dixon?"

Not even a pause, as Chaney had expected. "Oh, certainly." Hamilton glanced to the side, back again. "Agent Dixon, I believe, is attached to the NSA. He is apparently supervising the operation, according to the mandates of the full command and authority parameters."

"Where can I find him?" Chaney asked.

"Well. . ." Hamilton paused a long time. "I believe he must be in Langley. But I am not certain. As I said, I have only spoken with him on two occasions. He is not, other than the fact that he is supervising the situation for the NSA, awfully important to the execution of this team's activities."

Something about this didn't feel right. Chaney stared for a brief moment, trying to decide how to go into it. "Doctor," he said finally, "surely you know that whoever is ultimately responsible for the team's actions should be closely involved in their day-to-day activities."

Hamilton was either truly ignorant of military operations or feigning with skill. "I ...well, I suppose so, Marshal. I never served in the military. I suppose that is something you should speak with Agent Dixon about."

"I will," Chaney affirmed, and decided to end this charade. He took a while, wanting to leave on the right note. "All right. That's enough. Now I'd like to look at this file, if you don't mind."

Hamilton rose also, lifting some folders. "Well, Marshal, I'm afraid I don't have a file on Agent Dixon."

"I'm talking about Hunter, Doctor."

"Oh, yes." Hamilton waved dismissively. "But as I said, I do not believe that he is important."

Without words Chaney took the file and opened it, seeing a black-and-white eight-by-ten of a man who had obviously known hardship. Eyes as pure with purpose and opaque with instinct as a panther's stared out of the photo. His hair was black, shoulder-length, and ragged. The mouth was neither frowning nor smiling, but, rather, set in a stoic line of indifference. It was a countenance that Chaney could easily imagine as threatening, but threatening didn't seem to fit the broad forehead. No, it was a countenance that seemed to hint more at a quiet command of deep confidence combined with a certainty of extreme ability—as if he knew that he possessed a concentrated purity of will that had been forged with extraordinary and tested skills.

Chaney had a feeling one more thing would unveil whatever was hidden within all this: he had to find out why this man was so damned unimportant.

Hunter led them unerringly to the mine, arriving while there was still enough daylight remaining to prepare for the night.

Chiseled by pickax into the side of a hard bluff, the mine was perfect for the night. Its opening was barely the size of four men standing abreast, and previous owners had closed it with ax-tapered logs that were weathered but still solid and strong despite twenty years weathering. Even better, the logs were buttressed into the side of the hill by steel beams.

For a forced entry, unless the logs were levered over the top of the beam, the creature would have to smash them asunder with brute force. Not an easy stunt, even for this thing. Ripping a steel door off its hinges was one thing; only two hinges of steel had to be shredded and a lock cracked. Smashing a two-and-a-half-foot-diameter log in half was another thing altogether.

Kneeling together, as if in prayer, they discussed the situation beside the professor who, remarkably, seemed to be regaining a little strength. Takakura seemed unconvinced. "It will rip the logs from the foundation," he said plainly.

"I don't think so," Hunter answered. "Those logs won't shatter easily. And if one does, we'll be doing whatever we have to do. This won't be easy for it. And I don't think it will go head to head with us when it sees that it's gonna take at least twenty minutes to break down that wall. It knows we can hurt it."

Taylor looked at the mine and smiled, shook his head. "That's a deathtrap, Hunter," he said. "Anything goes in there tonight, it'll be in there a long time."

Standing, Hunter turned to him. "You have a better idea, Taylor? If you do, I'd like to hear it."

He stared hard at the commando, who looked back at the mine again. Then Taylor shook his head and smiled in the way a man smiles when he's just been told he's about to die. "No, Hunter," he said, a black half-laugh. "I'm completely out of ideas."

All of them were on their feet and Hunter saw that Tipler had raised himself to an elbow. The old man was listening intently, alert once more. He seemed to have recovered somewhat from his attack. He looked at the mine, studious.

"All right." Hunter pointed at an old mining shack, and another. Both of them were still in decent condition; it appeared they'd been abandoned some years earlier. "This is how it has to work." He looked at the Japanese. "If you have any objections, Commander, feel free to share them."

"I have no objections," Takakura said.

"Then we do this," Hunter continued. "But we have to move fast 'cause we don't have much time. First we remove a few logs from the entrance, enough to carry in what we need for a fire. Takakura and I can handle that. Taylor, you and Wilkenson search the cabins for a couple of cots, food, fuel, lanterns, anything we can use. Bobbi Jo, you stay here and watch the professor and guard. You're the only one that can hurt it anyway. Does that sound good enough?"

They nodded.

"Good. We've got an hour and a half until sundown. By then we have to be secure inside the mine."

Together they moved.

It took Hunter and Takakura, working hard, to dislodge the top log. But they were finally forced to lever it over the top of the steel beam that was anchored to the cliff. The second was easier and provided enough room to slide equipment over the top. By then Wilkenson and Taylor had acquired three full lanterns, a half can of kerosene, six blankets and three portable cots.

There was no food, but a small spring coming from the cliff allowed them to refill canteens. Thirty minutes later they were secure inside and with the use of a lever slowly slid the top log back in place, leaving the faintest sliver of light at the top. It was enough for fresh air, but not enough for the beast to get in.

The lanterns were lit and positioned, and MREs were opened. They were all ravenous. Even Hunter ate one, unaware of the taste. Ghost was inside with them, and they lit a huge bonfire outside that would easily rumble through the night.

Now all they had to do was wait.

They ate in silence until Professor Tipler, propped on a pillow, spoke in a low tone.

"I believe ... that I know what it is ... that we face," he said weakly. "If it were not ... for my diminished capacities, I believe I could have told you sooner."

Hunter looked at Tipler, at Takakura. The Japanese had stopped in mid-chew and stared at the professor.

"Finish your meal, please," Tipler continued. "You are ...exhausted. I want to thank you ... for saving my life. And, afterwards, I will tell you who our enemy truly is."

***

"I think," said Tipler, as they finished eating, "that it is time for me to give all of you my thoughts." He coughed hoarsely. "Yes ... time, I believe, while I still ... have time. And you were right, Nathaniel, in having us barricade ourselves within this cavern."

"Sun Tzu said it is always better to take the defensive when strength is insufficient," Takakura muttered. "First to be victorious with your life, then do battle."

Tipler smiled and nodded. "Well put, my friend. And that is why I will tell you ... as best I can ... what you confront. Forgive me, if it seems I do not, at first, make sense. Indulge me. First, listen closely, and hear a small analysis. Nothing I say shall be ultimately irrelevant, as you will soon see. Nor will I test your patience. Nathaniel, do you remember the Arctium lappa on the far side of the stream at our first campsite?"

Scowling, Hunted nodded.

Arctium lappa, or burdock, as it was commonly known, is a bush with a huge dome of head-size leaves elongating to a sharp point. It commanded a large area of a bank, for even one bush of burdock with its mushrooming bowl top of green leaves will usually shade a wide expanse of soil and other plants.

Tipler followed, "And do you remember how this plant aided you when you were sick last year? The time when you were injured and feverish in the Canadian Rockies?"

"Yeah, I remember," Hunter said. "I made tea from the leaves. It got rid of the fever."

"Exactly," the old man nodded. "And do you remember how you used *Euratorium perfoliatum* when you broke your leg near your cabin not five years ago? How the tea you made from the leaves caused the leg to heal twice as quickly?"

"Yes." Hunter had no idea where the old man was going with this, but knew the time was not wasted, especially if it helped them to understand what horrendous force was probably even now pacing around the small compound outside, slavering, searching, staring at the logs and debating its next move.

"Plants, roots, herbs, all of nature is a laboratory," Tipler said, and coughed violently for a long moment before continuing. "If one only knows where nature's secrets lie, the world can provide untold bounties. And that is only the world we know. But ten thousand years ago this area we inhabit was probably the most ecologically diverse land the world has ever known. Yet for years the earth has been suffering the extinction of probably 100 species of animal or plant every day. So the creatures and plants that inhabited this area in that time were far, far more diverse than what we know now. Imagine that unspeakable volume of medicinal qualities? Imagine what secrets they contained? And imagine, what if a race of people, a species similar to *Homo sapiens*, had known those secrets?"

No one spoke.

Hunter and Bobbi Jo exchanged glances.

"Yes." Tipler nodded, smiling. "Already you see. For if some ancient ancestor of man had known which plants enhanced strength, which ones promoted healing, produced paranoia, granted voyages of the imagination, increased musculature and bone density and inhibited aging, what would such a race have resembled after a hundred generations of subsisting on this rich treasury of physically and psychologically altering substances?"

Hunter stared at him. "They would have assimilated some of the qualities into hereditary genes?"

"Exactly!" Tipler snapped his fingers as he laughed. "I knew you would understand, Nathaniel! Variations of a genetic pattern would have developed!"

"So you're saying that thing out there is some mutated form of ancient man?"

"I am saying more, my boy." Tipler leaned forward. "I am saying that that creature out there is a species that was quite probably physically superior to Homo sapiens even without the assistance of that plentitude of nature's medicines. Yet in altering their DNA through dozens of generations of substance usage, in selecting strength and predatory perfection over their higher qualities of reason and conscious thought, that particular species was left with only one thing to dominate their minds." He paused. "And that is the Unconscious."

Hunter squinted. "The Unconscious?"

"Yes, Nathaniel. That part of the mind that responds as it will respond, regardless of the conscious interruption of morality, community, responsibility, love, or temperance. All of the higher qualities that make us men. Those things that have built civilizations and make us proudly human! Yes, I am saying that what lurks for us outside that wall"—Tipler pointed with condemnation at the logs—"is the unconscious mind of man unleashed on the earth in the body of a being that should have been extinct from the planet over ten thousand years ago!"

Half submerged in shadow, Taylor spoke. "So what in the world's it doing here now?"

With a deep sigh, Tipler sat back, raised his brow briefly. "Ah, Taylor, that is a question that we have yet to answer. But I do know this." The elderly professor fixed them all with a penetrating gaze, "What is outside that wall is a being that kills at the slightest impulse. A type of...of proto-human, if you will, that understands neither mercy nor compassion, but will fulfill the slightest whim, the slightest impulse, simply because it is there. It is unrestrained by thought. Unrestrained by the inclination to stay its hand against the most common or meaningless or wanton act of wholesale murder. Its only drive is the fulfillment of subconscious desire. Any desire. And it will fulfill the slightest want. You cannot reach its mind because, frankly, it does not possess a mind as any of us recognize such a thing. It possesses only whatever dark and violent impulses and desires are hidden and repressed in the cerebral cortex—that most primitive form of man. And there is nothing ... *nothing* that it will not do, simply because it desires. And, tragically, because whatever race that bred it used generations of alteration by nature to enhance its predatory powers and unconscious essence, it has the power to do much, indeed."

Hunter felt whiteness in his breath, a slight adrenaline surge. He looked at Takakura and the Japanese was staring solidly at him. They made no gestures, said nothing. With a glance he saw that Bobbi Jo had quietly closed her eyes, was leaning her head back against the wall. Taylor had taken his Bowie knife and was scrawling slowly in the dirt. His bent face was hidden in shadow. He remained silent.

"Professor," Hunter asked, "how do we kill this thing?"

Tipler nodded his head. "We will know, my boy, when we know who created it."

Ghost lifted his head, ears straight. Hunter looked at the log wall. "Game time," he whispered to Bobbi Jo.

He lifted his rifle as he rose.

CHAPTER 12

It was three A.M. when Chaney arrived at Brick's home, located near the diner. But Brick went to work at five, so Chaney knew the retired marshal would be awake.

He parked on the street—a necessity since Brick's driveway was filled with several Lincoln Continentals in various stages of repair. Or, as Chaney often mused, demolition. And once more it occurred to him that the big ex-marshal possessed shockingly little in the way of culture or taste.

He knocked on the door and Brick answered in seconds, already dressed for work in white painter's pants and white T-shirt. He waved as he led Chaney inside, wiping his hands on a towel. "Hey, kid, I was expecting you last night."

"Got held up." Chaney sat down at the table. Without invitation he began finishing an omelet.

Brick looked back. "Want some coffee?"

"Sure." Chaney chewed a moment. He hadn't been aware of how hungry he was.

"So, you ready for a couple things?"

"Sure," Chaney said. "I stumbled over a few things myself. Maybe some of it'll add up. For once."

Brick grinned. "This little adventure up north, it's military, but not really. The military is only present for contingencies." He belched. "Seems that the NSA has been utilizing abandoned army radio posts near the lower half of the Arctic Circle. World War II stuff, mostly. They were closed for a long time, then opened one after the other about six years ago."

"Yeah, but what were they reopened for?"

"Well ..." Brick paused, looked thoughtful. "I heard some street talk. Don't know how reliable. Not my regular people."

Chaney waited. "And ...?"

"Well, I hear that they were doing something that needed some serious isolation, in case of some kind of accident." He looked dead at Chaney "Could be germ warfare, biological warfare, that kind of shit. Maybe some new anthrax or smallpox. Bacteria. Could've even been somethin' dealing with nerve gas or toxic agents, but it was somethin' that they didn't want getting away from 'em in a populated area."

"So," Chaney mused, "that could account for why they wanted these stations as far away as possible. They screw up and they can vaporize any   * mistakes with a couple of fuel air bombs. Not much collateral civilian damage."

"Oh, hell no," Brick responded heartily, "you could fry twenty square miles up there and not hit anything but caribou and trees. Then call it a forest fire, which is what it would be, and play stupid." He grunted. "They'd get away with it."

"Okay" Chaney leaned back. "They wanted containability. But to contain what? What else could they have been trying to contain besides the bacteria or virus stuff?"

"Got no idea."

"Well, hell, Brick, take a guess. You know this business."

Brick sniffed, frowned a little. "Well, everything seems to point to the germ stuff but I can't say for sure. Nobody's talking. So I pieced a lot of this together from gossip." He paused. "Okay, we know the NSA runs the scam, which tells us exactly nothing. 'Bout like usual. I knew that going in. So I checked with a buddy of mine who works the air logs at some airbases up there. I asked him to go back and look at the logs and see what kind of stuff was flown into those areas during the time when the facilities were being reopened. Took him a little while, but he got back to me. Seems there was a company that had a lot of special shipments, and to each facility. That's nothing definite, there were some others. But one of 'em in particular caught my attention, for damn sure."

"What was it?"

"It's called MEAM. Don't know what it stands for. But my buddy tells me that they were shipping ...oh, just weird stuff. Nothing that made any sense."

"What do you mean?" Chaney was intrigued.

"Well." Brick took a breath. "The orders say they were sending perishable stuff that had to be, and this was stressed, 'handled with care.' But the manifests say it was always something like 'office equipment,' or wiring or construction materials. Well, you know right off that that's bull. These goons weren't shipping hubcaps and coffeemakers and marking 'em 'handle with care.' So I did a run on them, and found that MEAM is just a big-ass multi-mother company. Then I asked my buddy to see where the flights originated from, and he finds out that all the special-care flights— and remember that each facility was stocked by these flights—originated from Kansas City."

Chaney knew where it was going. "So what does MEAM own in Kansas City?"

Brick smiled. "I taught you well." He laughed. "Okay, so they only got one place in Kansas City. And you're gonna love this. It's a big-time medical manufacturing company called Bio-Genesis. And they do it all: drugs, hospital equipment. Hell, they supply hospitals and universities throughout the country. There ain't nuthin' they can't get their hands on if they don't make it themselves."

Chaney shook his head a moment before looking away. "Those sons of bitches." He paused. "What about seismological equipment? Do they manufacture stuff to monitor the motion of tectonic plates, maybe subterranean X-ray equipment?"

Brick scowled. "Earthquake stuff?"

"Yeah."

He shook his head. "I don't know. If they do, they can't make too much of it. Seems like they're mostly a medical equipment manufacturer. Drugs. Some of that fancy electron microscope stuff. A first-class outfit."

Chaney knew Brick had probably discovered half of this stuff with a quick trip to the public library. He had simply accessed the variety of electronic services and examined annual corporate reports.

Brick himself didn't even own a computer, considering them unnecessary and intrusive. But when he had to he was a master at obtaining information electronically. And a library was the best place to do it because, if the company was watching closely enough, it would be tracing the identity of the tracker. Now all they would have would be an unknown user at a public library in Washington, a far cry from knowing a particular identity and home address. He took a minute before Chaney spoke, trying to set one piece of information against another, and it didn't fit at all with what he'd already discovered, so it was pretty clear; somebody was lying.

"This thing is ugly, Brick."

"Yeah, kid, I figured that out already." The big man squared off. "Listen—and you know this, but I'm gonna tell ya anyway—sometimes the right answer is the one right in front of you, but you don't see it 'cause your brain is looking for something complicated. It's stuck in grandma' low like an old Lincoln with a bad transmission. So listen to me. What if this is just a legit government enterprise to develop some serums for bacteria or something like that? And somebody wants what they cooked up, up there. So they try and get it covertly, can't do it. Then they try by force, hence all the dead guys. Now, I'm not saying that that is the answer. I'm just saying don't go running off caught up in some big conspiracy theory unless you can back it up with facts."

Brick was probably right; he generally was.

Behind that brutal face, Chaney had learned long ago, was a mind as quick and efficient as a world-class computer. He took a little more time as Brick glanced at his watch; the big man gave no indication he was in a rush. He waited patiently until Chaney spoke.

"Well, I just can't buy it, Brick. I know what you're saying, but something here doesn't make any sense. Why is a medical manufacturing company supplying equipment for what is supposed to be a station monitoring seismic activity?"

"Is that what you heard they was doing?"

"Absolutely," Chaney said hotly. "I was at Langley and that's exactly what the head of the program said."

"Well." Brick paused. "I didn't look up everything they sold. There might be a division like that. Or they might have gotten some of that stuff on other flights. Even if they did, they still have to have some reason to be ordering all this bio-med stuff. Anyway, it does back up the street talk, for what that's worth."

Yeah, Chaney thought, it did. Sort of.

"But if these guys were conducting research in germ warfare, then they couldn't have done it without classified materials," he continued. "You can't just go down to the library and pick up specifics for those bacilli, and you don't want to waste time duplicating twenty years of research. So you start where others have left off" He felt solid in his suspicion. "What if they really were developing new means of germ warfare instead of a means to counteract it?"

Brick smiled wryly. "It'd just shock the hell out of me."

Shaking his head, Chaney paused. "But if they were doing that, they'd be in violation of an Executive Order."

"Well, ain't we a young Sherlock." Brick laughed, setting down his coffee cup. "Look, kid, the United Nations treaty, which the United States never got around to ratifying, by the way, prohibited the development of germs for warfare. Everybody agreed to destroy what they had. End of story. Except you know that if we think some goombah out there may have something, then we might need a serum for it. Can't be playing 'catch-up* in a war, right?" He shook his head. "No, they don't want to shamble around like some drunk in the dark trying to catch up to a bug some Middle East moron drops into a lake or water tower and we got cities going out left and right. No, we want to be ahead of the game. Always. We ain't never stopped developing them after the treaty. Not completely, anyways. But we slowed our butts down a lot until we got that wake-up call from the Gulf."

"Saddam," Chaney said.

"Yeah, and that's why they don't want to play catch-up again. Saddam could have hit us with something as simple as anthrax and wiped us out. And that, my friend, scared the bejeepers out of everyone from the Pentagon to the White House to Ma and Pa Kettle in Podunk. Or he could have used other kinds of germs and caused a world of hurt, 'cause we weren't prepared. The only reason he didn't is because he suspected—and rightly so— that we would vaporize his heathen butt and turn Baghdad into a sheet of glass. End of story. And since then, I know as fact, we've been putting heat on developing something that is resistant to the more dangerous forms of bacterial attack. So, then, these places might not have been dedicated to the development of more biological weapons as much as they were dedicated to developing the countermeasures. The only bad thing about that is you can't develop serums without bacilli and virus to test them on. But, if it was legit, then why all the secrets? And what I just said, despite what I might be inclined to believe, doesn't explain the deaths of marines. I don't know the details, but I heard they were cut down pretty bad."

Chaney paused. "Which ...which just leaves us with a few obscure facts. One is that the NSA handed this company millions for medical equipment. Second, that whatever these goombahs were doing was important enough to have a Ranger platoon at each site." He was silent a long time. "Brick, do you think someone is running black operations under government sanction, but the op's gotten out of hand? Maybe this *thing* – whatever it is – is just a disguised attack so people can reach whatever these fools have developed up there?"

Brick was studious a long time. "Likely," he said at last.

"That's what I'm beginning to think," Chaney mused softly, almost to himself.

Seemingly morose, Brick began wiping his hands on a dishrag. "Well, you ain't got the nuts and bolts to make that call. You gotta have more hooch. You know that."

"Yeah," Chaney mused. "I know."

Brick grabbed his coat. "You listen to me, kid." He didn't smile. "No matter what, always remember one thing. You don't run into a fight. You walk into it. And there's bodies enough already on the ground that they won't hesitate to lose you, too. Remember the rules. Three-call everybody. False ID. Watch your back. Change cars every day. Stay off the cell phone. Land lines only."

"Yeah, I know." Chaney smiled. "I remember, Brick. I ain't a geezer yet."

"Yeah, well, don't underestimate a geezer, either." Brick reached the door. "Hey, I just got a new crate of brand-new M-1 Garands yesterday. Best battle rifle ever made. Want one?"

Chaney laughed. "Brick, what do you need all those guns for? You can only shoot one at a time."

"Huh," the big man grunted as he closed the door. "Guess 'cause I'll never know when some boy that I turned into a United States Marshal might get his butt in the wringer. Something like that, it might make ol' Brick mad."

Laughing, Chaney walked toward his car. "I appreciate everything, Brick."

"What's your next stop, kid?"

"A junkyard. Then the CIA."

Brick stared after him.

"There's a difference?"

***

Together they were on their feet.

The first sound they heard was Ghost growling.

The second sound was a subterranean rumble.

Immediately it was followed by a raging, almost reptilian roar on the far side of the wall that seemed to hang in the air and then closed with a horrific impact that struck the wall like a truck, bringing down dust from the roof. A concussion, hurled by the incredible collision, swept over them in what felt like a sonic boom.

"Good God," Taylor whispered, stepping back.

They took a line behind the wall, and the next impact was equally as titanic—a thunderous, wrecking-ball forearm brought down with unbelievable force on the reinforced logs.

They edged back.

It continued again and again, a ceaseless uninterrupted crashing that would occasionally halt for the briefest heartbeat with a shrieking, outraged roar only to be followed by another thunderous impact that reverberated like a gunshot through the mine.

Hunter noticed they were still backing up.

"Hold it here," he said angrily. "We can't give it any more room."

"Maybe we should give it something else to shout about," said Taylor.

Only one of them possessed a weapon capable of penetrating those logs. Hunter glanced at Bobbi Jo. She raised the Barrett.

"My pleasure," she said.

She waited until the next colossal impact and then, with a surgeon's detachment, tracked the barrel a foot to the right. Bracing, she pulled the trigger of the .50-caliber sniper rifle, hurling a three-hundred-grain solid-steel bullet from the barrel at over four thousand feet per second. The blast itself was tremendous, blinding and deafening them together. And a large section of wood splinters shot over them at the impact, exploding from where the Barrett penetrated the logs.

On the far side a haunting pause was followed by an enraged scream. And then an even more monstrous blow was hurled against the barrier. It cracked the third beam—positioned at chest level—down the middle.

When Hunter saw it crack, he knew what would strike the mind of the beast. He was right.

It had found a weak spot, and it would seize the moment.

There was a short pause with a spiraling roar of victory, and then an incredibly colossal blow, and another, and another, and with each one the log cracked deeper with a sound that was even louder than the primordial howling that preceded it.

"Get ready!" Hunter shouted.

One final blow followed, and two cleanly split pieces fell into the mine in a swirl of dust.

Two red eyes glared at them from the darkness, white fangs distended in victory. Then, as it screamed mockingly, they opened fire together, filling the tunnel with fire and splintering the wall with the cascade.

Hunter saw it stagger back. But he could see nothing more, and they continued firing until the rifle barrels were dangerously overheated. Then they paused together, as if afraid the weapons were about to melt down.

There was a faint ringing, the choking scent of cordite in the air, thick smoke carried from the entrance by the out draft of the mine, and Hunter saw nothing in the space of the severed log. Nothing but darkness.

Together they edged slowly forward, not trusting their hearing since they were temporarily deafened by gunfire in the enclosed space. Hunter held up a hand after a dozen steps, motioning for the others to stop, and edged another step.

The logs were shredded by the rounds, an awesome sight of long splintered holes torn into the massive logs. Even the logs were smoking from the impact of so much lead in so short a period of time. Hunter took another step, almost within arm's reach, then stopped cautiously.

He waited, listening, but heard nothing on the other side. He began to take another step when he heard an approach behind him, saw Ghost running forward. Bobbi Jo made a leap for the wolf but he was past her and Hunter commanded: "NO!"

He sensed it, just as he sensed the Siberian that had come up behind him in Manchuria—how it had vaporized out of utter gloom and silence to be gigantically, horrifically there as he slowly turned.

It was the same instinct, a different foe.

The creature came on with a roar, thrusting a long arm through the shattered space and seizing Hunters leather shirt, jerking him toward the wall with titanic strength.

Instantly Hunter's leg lashed out, his moccasin smashing against the wall, and the thing was stalled for the briefest moment before its left arm also lashed out, a massive clawed hand grappling.

Enraged white fangs beneath glaring red eyes were visible as the beast strained to pull him close, and then the leather shirt began to tear. Hunter heard the leather ripping as he felt its breath on his face. Struggling with all his might, he measured the incalculable strength surging deep within that bestial chest, the inhuman will to kill, kill—*fangs close!*

With a roar Hunter surged back, the shirt ripping at the sides as the beast at last slammed the Marlin out of the way, lashing out for his throat in the same movement. Hunter dropped the rifle and caught the arm by the wrist, digging his fingers hard into the incredible rhino-like skin.

Arm to arm they struggled, Hunter straining to push the poised taloned hand from his throat. Then, holding tightly to his shirt with its right hand, it hurled itself away from the wall and Hunter's leg caved.

In the blast of power Hunter flew toward the wall but his left hand lashed out to smash against a timber, still holding him from the wall at arm's length. And in a shuddering, straining contest of strength they hung there, only a few timbers separating them as they surged face-to-face— Hunter trying to escape whatever monstrosity of nature was attempting to haul him within reach of those gaping fangs.

For a spellbinding moment each endured, resisted, and then Hunter felt his strong right arm—the one holding its left arm at bay—losing to the might of something he could never approach, glimpsed the long curving claws coming closer as—

A white vise of fangs flew up from beneath, smashing against the beast's right arm with such force that it rocketed off the top timber and down again.

Hunter saw a furred demon savaging the creature's bicep, fangs buried deep in muscle and twisting viciously, jerking, tearing with a low roar smothered by the dark flesh.

Clawing backwards against the wood, Ghost surged with his full weight of incredible strength, seeking to tear the arm from the beast's shoulder. And for a moment they were fang to fang, red eyes glaring into the wildest untamed black, and Hunter couldn't tell which was the more savage.

Its taloned left hand scraped his neck.

Straining violently, shuddering with the incredible effort, Hunter pushed it back an inch ...

Hunter only glimpsed the flash of silver that passed him, barely sensed that it had come from above, descending with a flicker to strike the beast's right arm. And up it came again in the same flickering movement to hit the arm again and Hunter knew: a sword!

Yet again the blade descended and the arm was jerked back through the wall. And, understanding instantly, Hunter fast-drew the Bowie at his waist and stabbed upward, viciously plowing the wicked ten-inch blade completely through the forearm so close to his face and saw the red eyes blaze in pain.

Vengeful, Hunter mercilessly twisted the blade lengthwise, slicing a long twisting path through bone and muscle, and with a terrifying roar the hand released and rocketed back through the gap, tearing its grip from the wolf and vanishing into darkness.

Hunter was already rolling back as he hit the ground, holding his massive Bowie. His rifle lay on the floor beside the wall and at the moment he couldn't care. He crawled back gasping for breath, sweating, and collapsed on his back, trying to recover.

For a moment he knew nothing but red light and the merciful absence of a roaring attack, and it was peace to him. Then Bobbi Jo was there, bent, checking without asking. She moved his torn leather shirt, felt his neck. He heard her voice through a fog: "There's some deep cuts! Get me my kit!"

She was shouting encouragement at him, and he was grateful for it. But he could barely hear, with the blood pounding in his ears, the roars still reverberating in his head, adrenaline making his vision blurred and cloudy with sheer fear and exhaustion.

He took a deep breath; it seemed to help.

Bobbi Jo had her medical kit unfolded and was working on him delicately. At first he couldn't feel anything at all. She washed the deep wounds with an antiseptic, and then he felt a faint stinging that was somehow good.

"Oh, man," he managed, finally, raising a hand to his head. "How ... bad?"

She spoke quickly. "It gouged your sternum and your right second rib. No major veins. But very deep cuts. But it's gonna be all right. It ... I think it was trying for your throat. But you were too quick. You moved before the arm came through the wall."

"I didn't know that."

He was beginning to recover as she worked on him. He clenched his teeth as he felt her scraping the bone, cleaning. "I have to," she said gently. "Too great a chance of infection. It'll only take a minute."

As she worked, Hunter glanced toward the wall and saw Takakura, sword in hand, beside Taylor and Wilkenson, a human wall. They stood stoically at ten feet, facing the broken portal, weapons ready. Then Ghost was beside him, sniffing. Hunter looked at the wide black face, the coal-black eyes, and shook his head. He reached out, rubbed the blood-soaked mane of the wolf that had saved him.

"First you almost get me killed," he mumbled. "Then you save my life." He ruffled the gigantic wolf's mane, looked into the eyes, now gentle and concerned.

Hunter laughed. "Make up your mind."

Chaney bought an afternoon beer in a mall off Pennsylvania Avenue and sat staring glumly at the huge arched copper fountain, pondering. The sudden rain that had blown up from the river had turned the day to doom and gloom. It didn't help his mood at all.

Some things fit well, but some of it was wildly out of kilter. Taking a meditative sip, he analyzed it: There were NSA research stations supposedly dedicated to watching seismic activity near the Arctic Circle. Already he didn't believe that one. Call it gut instinct, professional suspicion, whatever. He didn't know for certain. He just had a bad feeling about it. And not because it couldn't be possible, but because it didn't fit well enough with anything else.

Nobody was going to kill a ton of soldiers to get into what was basically a glorified radio tower. Not for any reason. Nor were they going to destroy them by running monstrously throughout the entire facility, killing with the ferocity of a lion.

Second, the street gossip Brick had picked up was right; the biotech stuff backed it up. He thought of the rest.

All right, there was a hunting party with a professor and a legendary tracker hunting a beast that had decimated some research facilities. And at these facilities, which no one was willing to admit, was a probable experiment in biological or germ warfare. Where this creature came from, or what it was, was still a mystery. Why Hunter was so unimportant was a mystery.

He knew now that the Agency had never really wanted the hunting team—they had been forced into the procedure by others—and that explained why they were secretly trying to sabotage it. But then that brought it back to ...what? To protect this creature? Which brought him back to ... the secret reason for the installations ...

"No ... there's no way," Chaney muttered, closing his eyes as an idea came to him.

No, he thought, shaking his head. That's impossible. They couldn't have done that. They couldn't have been that stupid.

There is no way, his rationality told him, that they had infected, or altered, or in some way changed something, like a bear, with some wild experiments and created this fiasco. But if they had done it, and it was loose, they sure wouldn't want anyone to know about the disaster, which would explain why they would try and sabotage the hunting party. Nor would they want anyone to know the true nature of the research facilities, which explained the recalcitrance.

He thought about the cold rationality he had cultivated during twelve years as a Deputy United States Marshal, and he laughed. With a smile, he took another swallow.

Yeah, he was certain how that would look when he gave it to ol' Skull: "Well, boss, there's this mutated son of a bitch up there in Alaska, see, and he's meaner 'an a junkyard dog, and that's what's killing all these good folks. No, don't have any proof. And then these guys have this germ warfare gig going... no, don't have any proof of that, either, but. . ."

He figured that'd be about as far as he got before Skull threw him out of the office and then out of the service. Then he thought of the murdered colleague of Tipler, Rebecca Tanus.

It was murder, obviously.

Only he could never prove it because the strut was so expertly cut. He had stopped by the junkyard just long enough to examine the car, and found what he'd expected. The left front strut had been very carefully filed away until there was only a thread remaining. And on the downhill slope, when the entire weight of the car was centered on that single point, it snapped. Artistic work.

With a gathering fear, Chaney glanced around. He attempted to appear casual, but felt twice as conspicuous. Shrugging, he sat almost upright, utterly alert.

Professional hitters. Illegal biological warfare. Some mutant killing people left and right. A hit team that was doomed from day one. Dead folks that shouldn't be dead.

He shook his head.

He should have known it would come to this. It took him awhile before he conceived something even faintly resembling a respectable plan. And he played it out slowly to measure the good and bad, weighing the value of the information he might obtain against the risk he'd have to incur to gain it.

He knew that, first, he would have to discover what was really going on inside those research stations. That would be the crux, give him something to work with. But to do that he would have to do some very covert work, probably even illegal.

Then he thought of all the good men that had gone down in this, men who were good soldiers, husbands, fathers. And, as an ex-marine, it affected him.

His mouth tightened slightly.

Let's go get 'em.

He was rising as his beeper went off, and he scowled as he looked down. He was on special assignment and shouldn't be disturbed for anything less than an emergency. Then as he saw the callback he knew that it just might be an emergency. It was Gina Gilbert at the Tipler Institute.

He left the mall quickly and walked outside into a hard rain.

CHAPTER 13

Submerged in gloom, he collapsed within a dark leafy silence, holding his hideously injured right arm. The man had stabbed and twisted. He had viciously severed muscle, vein and nerve, and carved into bone.

He had been so close.

He snarled with rage as he breathed heavily, truly wounded for the first time. He had never known pain like this, not ever. The rest, the guns, they could not hurt him. But this had hurt him. He did not understand. The fang—the knife, as his mind remembered it—was dangerous.

It was the same with the wolf.

The fangs tore through his flesh as bullets and blade never could. His arm ached where the demon had savaged him, and closing eyes to rage, he remembered that great weight straining against him, his shoulder twisting beneath the surging strength and the crushing fangs that numbed his arm and would not let go.

Yes, oh yes, they would die for this. If he had to track them to the ends of the earth to kill them all, he would do it.

Once he rejoined his brothers he would return, and together they would destroy them all, eat their brains, and rejoice in the blood. They would hunt them as before, in the night beneath the moon through the shadows of the forest, howls haunting the night as they caught them in the woods and valleys. As they cracked their bones for the marrow and sucked out the delicious black juice.

He attempted to rise, to return to them, to slay . . .

Collapsed upon the ground.

Breathed deeply. Shuddered.

A red moon ... black lines against sky.

Almost nothing of what he had been could be remembered, but he did not suffer from it. He was content to be what he had become, content with the killing.

Yet he remembered another time, a time now dim but still there; a great darkness...something he could not define, could not see ...screams and howls, roars of pain and rage and vengeance and defiance and surrender that died ... the wildness, the purity, the ecstasy ... another hunt, a different hunt. And the weak ones had not been the prey ...

But there was blood, always blood.

He could not remember more.

Red moon ...

He closed his eyes.

Silence and quiet repose followed horror in the mine. Tipler had passed out, and Bobbi Jo had carefully monitored his blood pressure, pulse, and breathing. She had administered something to help him relax, then sat down beside Hunter.

Stoic, Hunter was staring at the Magellan Satellite Phone case. Inside was the radio phone that was supposed to be able to reach any location in the world from any other location by sending a signal that triangulated off three satellites to its destination. It was not a line-of-sight megahertz radio as used by most field units. This was a specially modified device that utilized ultra—high frequency modulation and even offered a screen for graphic communication.

If needed, it could provide a visual depiction of weather, troop movements, climatic conditions, and other factors for as much as one-quarter of the earth at a time. It could, if it were working, tell them to within a distance of five feet exactly where they were standing on the planet, and the terrain around them. Seeing it unusable only reinforced for Hunter the reasons why he had honed his skills at dead reckoning to a fine art.

His face was studious, but he cast a discreet glance at Takakura, who rested against the wall on the far side of the professor's cot, and Taylor, who hadn't moved in over an hour, the shotgun laid casually across his legs. Hunter couldn't tell whether he was asleep or not, but the commando was unmoving, his face hidden in shadow.

Bobbi Jo's voice was gentle. "Talk to me. Tell me about someplace that's not this place."

They were sitting side by side. He glanced over and saw her eyes closed, her face tight. Her head was bent slightly forward, as if in sleep, but like the rest of the team she was too stressed to sleep. The team was alive because of her skills with her rifle. That was as it should be; this woman was a warrior. The surprise was that his friend, the professor, was alive only because she had given him such tireless attention despite fulfilling her combat responsibilities. Now that she had a moment to rest, he was more than willing to offer her some relief.

He leaned back, relaxed.

"Okay," he said gently. "Well, let's see. I guess I could tell you how, under a big, white full moon the Grand Canyon looks like a dream might look, and how, in firelight, you can feel like an angel walking the crest of a mountain. Or I could tell you about how the woods of northern England are so quiet and mossy and peaceful that it's like walking through time, to the days of kings and queens, and princesses waiting for their princes. Or what it's like to finally find a kid that's lost and scared and cold, and how they love you for it. What it's like to see their face when they see yours. All of that shared at once, and how it lasts forever. All that happiness, all that joy brought out of fear." He smiled. "Maybe that's the best."

She smiled gently at him. "I would like to know that feeling," she said quietly. "I could use that feeling."

"You could do it," Hunter said, holding the Marlin easily. "You're as good as anyone I've ever seen."

"Not as good as you."

"Sure you are."

"Nobody is as good as you, Hunter. And you know it." She smiled with it, meaning it. Of a sudden, Hunter was surprised that they were so physically close. He hadn't really been aware of it until her eyes closed and her head leaned against his chest.

She continued, "I've never seen anyone like you. I've never seen, or even heard of anyone, who could see so much. Who understood so much." She paused. "Is it like that for you in everything? Is that why you don't like to be around people? 'Cause you see so much?"

Hunter paused, shrugged. "Could be. Never claimed to be too sharp. Maybe it's just that I don't need much."

"Just that crazy wolf."

He laughed. "Yeah, he's crazy all right. But he's my friend."

"Is he the only one you trust?"

He shook his head. "No."

"The doc?"

"Yeah." Hunter looked at the professor. "Yeah, I trust him. Always have."

She was staring at Ghost. The big wolf was resting without removing his coal-black eyes from the shattered wall. "You know something, Hunter. You and that wolf are a lot alike. You both like being alone. You're both quiet. And you don't play games. But you're always there when someone needs you." She paused. "I could stand being like that."

Absorbing the words, Hunter studied her face. She continued to stare at Ghost for a moment, looked at him close. "Do you always want to be alone?"

Hunter waited, let the silence speak for him for a moment.

"No," he said, and she smiled. He looked away, sniffed. "I guess I'd like a family. Always have, I suppose. I ... I really love kids. I just never got around to it. Not the right person, whatever." He laughed lightly. "Wouldn't be so easy for a woman to live with me, anyway."

"And why is that?"

"Oh," he began slowly, "I don't know. I travel a lot. I prefer a hard life to a soft one. The things that matter to me aren't money and power. I got plenty of that, but it ain't life. I guess what I call life are kids, love, a family. Old-fashioned stuff. It don't go over too good nowadays when people think life is jet-setting and doing as much as they can as fast as they can."

"Tell me about your place in New York," she said. "Why don't you stay there more?"

"Oh, I stay there a good bit," he answered. "That's where I have my equipment. Sort of like a base. When I'm dealing with all the environmental agencies, or the Institute, I generally stay there. Got all my computers, my library."

"You read a lot?"

"I don't know. I guess I've got a few thousand books, maybe more. Read all of them. And I've collected some things, mostly art. I like art. And I've got some work from the Baroque period, some Neoclassical and Romantic period work. I ...you may have never heard of him, but I have some bronze work by Antoine Louis Barye."

She laughed. "You're right. Never heard of him."

They smiled.

"Well, he was a French sculptor. He primarily portrayed animals in tense, dynamic situations. His bronze work is his best, and I invested in a few pieces in Paris. His romantic works, his strongest images of the wild, usually depict one animal struggling against another for supremacy." Hunter paused a long time, as if even he wasn't exactly sure why he enjoyed the work. "That might be why I like them so much," he added softly. "The reality of the struggle."

"But you don't like the struggle, do you?"

He shook his head lightly. "No ... no, I don't."

"That's why you're so good at it. Did you know that? Because you really don't like it. To you, it's a terrible thing. So you do it quick. Get it over with."

He raised his brow slightly. "Could be." Smiled. "You're pretty smart, girl."

She laughed. "And something else. I know that, inside, you're really soft. You don't want to hurt anything, or see anything hurt. That's why you repeatedly risk your life tracking these kids, Hunter, when you're their only hope. You care. It's also why you stay away from other people, really. It's not because you're a hard man. It's because you're a hard man who has a gentle heart. It's not that you don't care. It's that you care too much. And that's not so bad, either." She smiled gently. "Seems like a good place to be."

Turning to her, Hunter gazed seriously a moment. "Some things aren't so hard."

She met his eyes, silent.

A long time passed, no words spoken, then Hunter added, "You know, when this is over, maybe you'd like some R and R." He hesitated, easy with it. "I know a nice place where you could relax."

She laughed softly. "After this, I might retire for some permanent R and R, Hunter." Silence. "Do you really think we're gonna make it out of here?"

He frowned, knowing it was the second time she had asked, and she wasn't someone prone to doubt. She was a professional soldier, trained to fight to the last, no matter what. But as he considered his answer it was clear that she had her reasons; good ones.

They were cut off from support and hunted by something that couldn't be stopped by small-arms fire. They were alone in a million acres of wilderness and nobody knew where they were. Plus, they were handicapped with the burden of carrying Dr. Tipler, unable to leave the old man or move quickly as they carried him. Except for the fact that Bobbi Jo possessed a weapon powerful enough to injure the creature, they had no advantage. He had set out to track it; he had succeeded too well.

His eyes settled once more on the Magellan Phone Satellite System. Something within kept piquing his attention, drawing it back again and again to the instrument.

It was odd that the Magellan had become inoperative almost immediately, when it was a highly dependable communications instrument. He had used one himself on several occasions without complications or glitches. Something wasn't right; so much didn't fit together.

Hunter's eyes narrowed as he leaned forward. Slowly, he reached back and removed a Gerber all-purpose pocket tool from a pouch on his belt. Moving quietly, so as not to attract more attention than necessary, though he knew he would, he knelt over the satellite system. Takakura's voice came from the gloom. "What is it, Hunter? The system is inoperative. Wilkenson already attempted to fix it."

"Yeah." Hunter nodded. "I know."

He opened the case and then the system, which resembled a portable laptop with a phone built inside it. Instantly a screen lit up, stark white. He shut the monitor and flipped it on its face. Then, carefully, he removed the screws holding the back-plate in place.

"What are you doing?" Takakura asked again.

"I'm gonna take another look," Hunter said, indicating that he wasn't asking permission.

In ten minutes Hunter was staring at the guts of the machine.

"Wilkenson already did that, Hunter. I even attempted myself." Takakura seemed less patient. "I have already told you this."

"Yeah, I know." Hunter took his time, scanning the interior. From his pouch he took out a small flashlight the size of a cigar and shined it over the schematics. "Well, if Wilkenson took a look at it, and you couldn't fix it either, then it must be seriously broken. I can't do any harm taking another look."

Hunter studied the transmitting panel, examining each aluminum thread and solder joint, each matrix configuration as he slowly worked his way through the printed circuit cards. He was dimly aware that Takakura had stood up in the half-darkness of the cave and was staring at him curiously. The Japanese spoke.

"What are you doing?"

"Just looking things over again," Hunter replied absently. "Wanted to make sure."

"You can do such a thing?"

"Well, I pick up a little here and there. I might be able to help."

In truth, before taking one of these machines into the field, Hunter had devoted hours to learning the mechanics of the sophisticated communications system, imagining every conceivable worst-case scenario and what might be required to correct the malfunction with the meager tools he regularly took with him.

Bobbi Jo was leaning close to him, on one knee, the other shin flat against the ground. Her arms were wrapped around her front leg. "Where did you learn to do this, Hunter?" she asked so quietly that no one else could hear.

He winked, smiled. "Survival is a habit of mine."

She smiled back and he continued to work patiently, thoroughly. He didn't blink as he followed the circuits, his hand moving fractions of an inch. Minutes passed and then his hand stopped, eyes narrowing.

Stepping forward, Takakura indicated he noticed the change in countenance. "What is it?"

"I don't know," Hunter said. He removed his pocketknife from his waist and gently touched a small circuit board. Without effort he lifted a tiny aluminum wire no thicker than a slender thread of hair. The wire bent easily beneath the blade. Hunter pushed it back down into place, a humorless smile twisting one corner of his mouth.

"You have found something," Takakura said, stepping forward again.

"Yeah."

A pause. "Well?"

Hunter's voice was distant, still in the board. "It seems that a connection between the voice receiver chip that takes sound received and converts it has been severed."

He removed the circuit panel from the machine, holding it high, in the full illumination of the flashlight. "Yep," he added. "Severed."

"How?" Takakura asked angrily. His hands were clenched.

"No way to know." Hunter shook his head. "Could have been anything. Or nothing. The cut...it's clean. But that doesn't mean anything. The wire is thin, so it's impossible to tell whether it broke or was cut."

Silence.

Hunter noticed that Taylor hadn't moved, hadn't said a word. Then Takakura was standing over Hunter, glaring down. The Japanese—and Hunter had expected it—was incensed. Takakura despised disloyalty, but even more than that he hated treason. Hunter could see the rigidity in his stance, could almost feel the cold aura. Takakura, in turn, cast glances at Taylor, Wilkenson. He held the look on Wilkenson a heartbeat longer.

"There will be an investigation into this," he said stonily. Then, turning to Hunter, "Can you repair the damage?"

Hunter studied it. The line was so thin it would have been impossible to see if not for the mini-light. He saw where the connection was broken, wondered how to solder it back in place. He tried to recall the melting temperature of aluminum, could only remember that it was relatively low, under a thousand degrees. Okay, he thought, let's see what we can do.

First he would need heat, a lot of it, and he didn't have much to work with. He looked around, searching. Surely there was something he could use to pull this off. He saw the medical kit, spoke softly to Bobbi Jo. "Do you have any alcohol in that?"

"Sure." She looked at him strangely.

"Give me some. You have any ammonia?"

"Yeah, it's standard for rashes. It's an antiseptic."

"Give me some of that, too."

In a moment he had both bottles and removed a lamp from the wall. After setting it on level ground he removed the glass and turned up the wick until the flame was burning brightly. Then he removed the metal container of the alcohol bottle and poured a little into it, then some ammonia. He carefully positioned the cap at the very tip of the flame, the place where it was hottest.

"Find me a cotton swab," he said quietly to Bobbi Jo.

As he worked, he slowly turned the tip of his huge Bowie in the bottom of the flame, heating it red. After a few moments, the combined chemicals in the cap were bubbling. Hunter spoke distinctly. "I want you to dip the swab in the lower part of the cap. Get some of the gel at the bottom, not the thinner liquid on top."

She did, carefully holding a hand under it as she lifted it from the cap. Hunter could see the glistening clear residue on the swab and knew what would happen when it came into direct contact with flame, or in this case, the edge of his knife, now reddened, almost glowing.

Then he took a 45.70 bullet from his strap, and in a few seconds was emptying its powder on a small piece of wood. Without looking at her he said, "Give me the swab."

She complied silently as he took it and very lightly dusted the thick transparent gel with a thin layer of gunpowder. Then he bent carefully over the monitor, again focusing on the severed aluminum strand.

He would have less than a tenth of a second and there was a danger that the intense heat could melt surrounding circuits as it fused this one.

"Hold the light for me," he whispered, and slowly lowered the tip of the knife to the circuit, holding the severed sections in contact. Then he lowered the swab, and as it touched the white-hot blade there was a brief flash of brilliant light. Hunter slowly removed the knife, pressing down just once, to ensure solid contact.

He looked close.

Yes!

He had done it. He leaned back, wiped sweat from his face. He didn't look at Takakura as he spoke. "We'll give it time to cool, but I think it worked."

Takakura offered a slow nod, obviously pleased but still troubled. "Wilkenson!" The voice left no room for misunderstanding. "Why is it that you could not find this severed wire? You are our communications expert, are you not?"

"Nobody can see everything, Commander." Wilkenson seemed offended, but not overmuch. "Hunter found something I missed. Simple as that."

"Men died because you missed . . ." Takakura let the words settle. "There will be an investigation to see if you are only a fool or something worse."

"Investigate all you want, Commander," Wilkenson said evenly, holding Takakura's gaze.

Leaning back against the wall, Bobbi Jo beside him, Hunter was faintly startled to see that Taylor still seemed not to have moved. But now, instead of a shotgun, he held his knife in his hand, tip buried in the dirt at his side. Though Taylor's face remained hidden in gloom, Hunter could tell that the commando was glaring at Wilkenson.

***

Chaney arrived at the Tipler Institute to find Gina Gilbert waiting in the lobby with slender arms crossed over a white lab coat. Her dark-rimmed glasses—a curiously outdated style—framed wide and anxious eyes.

He began, "I received your—"

Then she was moving, hand on his arm, ushering him toward a pair of white double doors located toward the rear of the small entranceway.

"You've got to see this," she said breathlessly. "I found something else on the electrophoresis that—"

"On what?" Chaney managed as she ushered him into the room he had seen earlier, locking it behind them even more quickly. She moved him forward as she continued, "I think I may have found something very important and I don't know who else I can trust."

Releasing him, she sat in the center of a large concrete slab that dominated the lab. On two twenty-inch computer monitors in front there were a series of horizontal lines, moving upward off the screen. Behind the lines were a series of little sparks that seemed to blink and disappear, then reappear where they had been.

"Have a seat," the slightly built woman said, staring intently at the screen. Or, rather, she had seemed slightly built in the open air, where Chaney felt a comfortable familiarity with his authority and natural physical presence. But in this small, well-insulated cubicle with millions of dollars' worth of machinery, he felt distinctly inadequate.

Quietly he took a seat, casting a single narrow glance to see the dual monitors' display reflected on Gina's wide, oval glasses. The dark eyes were unblinking as she manipulated the controls with a deft, gentle touch.

"There," she whispered, pointing to the screen, and did something else. In a moment Chaney heard a printout of the image kicked out on the table beside them. He gazed at the screen a long time, not having the foggiest idea what had just happened.

"I see," he nodded finally, turning to her. "And just what am I looking at? I hope you understand that this is not my forte. I barely passed high school biology."

His attempt at humor never penetrated. "This is an electron microscope and you're watching mitochondrial DNA in action," Gina said. "It's the small globs of molecules in a cell that are like the batteries of life. Each has its own DNA, separate from the cell itself. Mitochondrial DNA is what most institutes use to study evolution."

A pause, and Chaney asked, "Evolution? Did you say 'evolution'?"

"Yes."

"And why, exactly, would you study evolution with this DNA, Ms. Gilbert? You were a little excited and—"

"I still am," she broke in.

"Yes," Chaney said, watching her closely now, "and so you didn't tell me if this was the DNA you removed from the cast. But I assumed that it was. So ... if it's a modern creature, then what's the purpose of studying it for evolution?" He waited; she didn't reply. Then: "Am I missing something here, Ms. Gilbert?"

"This!" she said quickly and hit the display for a printout again. And again the machine hummed and a long paper copy of what was reflected on the screen—it looked like a Fourth of July fireworks demonstration to Chaney—was printed.

Crossing his arms, Chaney leaned back. Maybe it had just been the excitement of the day's events, but he had half-expected some kind of smoking-gun revelation when he arrived.

At the moment, however, he wasn't even sure why he was here and, outside the higher realms of academic guesswork, doubted that any of it would forward his investigation. He wondered what else Brick might have turned up with his street goons when Gina returned with the printouts, laying them on a desk.

Rising, he placed hands on the table as he leaned over them. After a moment, he nodded studiously. "Uh-huh," he said as politely as his meager inspiration allowed.

"I know you don't understand yet," she said, drawing lines on the paper with a pencil, almost like connecting dots. "But listen closely. A quick lesson. I can make it very simple for you. Okay, DNA has four chemical bases. It's not important to know what they are. But when DNA reproduces itself, each chemical base also reproduces itself. The order by which the chemicals do the reproducing creates proteins, which are made up of amino acids." She looked dead into Chaney's eyes, which were concentrated on the page. "Are you following me so far, Marshal? Don't hesitate to tell me if you're not."

Chaney smiled, somewhat grim. "You're doing well, Ms. Gilbert. It's not easy explaining DNA to someone like me."

She flipped a hair from her face. "We learned it from Professor Tipler," she said offhandedly. "He says that if we can't explain the most complex molecular process to a six-year-old child, then we don't really understand it."

Chaney laughed, knowing what she meant and not offended. "Good enough. Go ahead."

"Okay." She pointed to the print. "Now, when these proteins separate to reproduce, they act like a mirror. They're constantly checking the new strand of DNA to ensure that it exactly mimics themselves. Sort of like you painting yourself with a mirror. It's a built-in safeguard so that impaired DNA molecules aren't reproduced. Follow me?

He nodded.

"Okay," she continued, "so each dual strand of DNA has the same chemicals, the same proteins and amino acids . . ."

She drew a dramatic hard line to a rather spectacular display of lines and sparks on the far side of the spreadsheet. Drew a circle around the center. She seemed to have somehow captured something important with the movement.

"And this doesn't have A, G, C or T factors of the dominant DNA found in the cast!"

Despite himself, Chaney was beginning to get the idea. "Altered DNA ...," he mumbled before he realized he'd said anything.

"No, Marshal. Not altered. It's something else."

Chaney looked up at her. "Something else? Like what?"

Her mouth was tight. "Like a mutation that is completely different from the host DNA!"

Chaney stared. "Yes," he smiled, calm.

"You don't understand!" she shouted. She drew vicious lines across the paper. "This DNA could never have come from this DNA! They were fused, Marshal! Someone, or something, fused them into a hybrid DNA strand that is this! It's a created creature!"

Staring a moment, Chaney didn't know what to say.

"A fused creature?" he asked.

"A created creature!"

He shook his head, raising his hands. "Well, Gina, no offense. But what the hell is a . . ."

"Marshal," she was smiling now, "this thing was created by someone up there! It is not a mutation! Not really! It might look like it. Yet its DNA is fused. Which means that someone had to take"—she used her hands as if she were moving stacks of money—"human DNA, move it here. Then take some other kind of DNA, and move it over here. And then fuse them together to make a completely new creature! A creature that was created in some kind of matrix that didn't allow the proteins to splinter off!" She leaned into him. "I'm certain of it, Marshal! And you have got to believe me. This is what Rebecca was killed for. Because they were afraid that we were about to find out what they'd done!"

"Well ... what the hell does that *mean*?" he asked after a moment.

"I think," she looked straight at him, "that you're dealing with a creature that has been scientifically created in some kind of electromagnetic matrix. Possibly it was a human being at one time, but it's not anymore. Now it's an impossibly strong thing that can heal itself almost as fast as you can hurt it as long as it has something to eat. And the alien DNA that was fused to the host is slowly taking over the host system. Like a parasite. It just keeps growing and growing, multiplying at an incredible rate because the human DNA doesn't see it as an invader."

Chaney didn't understand that one either. He did, remarkably, know a little about how an immune system responded to bacterial invasion. He asked, "Why wouldn't the host see it as an invader since that's basically what it is?"

"Because this alien DNA is so closely related to Homo sapiens DNA. It ... it's just assimilated so easily by the host. I actually think the human immune system sees this fused DNA as part of its own system. It doesn't register it as a threat." She paused, her eyes narrowing. "Where this DNA strand came from, I don't know, but it was from something very closely related to homo-sapiens. "

Frowning, Chaney stared at the charts. "But, really, what would that be?"

She emitted a brief bark of harsh laughter. "Marshal, you're in some kind of delayed scientific shock at all this. There is more difference in the DNA between a sheep and goat than there is between a man and an ape, or a chicken for that matter. Most creatures on this planet are compatible with the DNA of man up to ninety-five percent. An ape is ninety-nine percent. Only one percent of its DNA is non-man. That's a fact. But that one percent is everything. Somewhere within it is intelligence, emotion, egoism, self-conscious awareness. Basically, the mind. This is no different. Somewhere in this one percent is something else— something that's not even close to man. And, degree by degree, it is slowly infiltrating the entire host organism, slowly gaining complete control. If it doesn't have complete control of its mind, it will soon."

Chaney stared at the graphs. They meant little, since he couldn't understand them at all. But he understood everything Gina had said, knew that there was far more going on in those research stations than anyone would admit. He didn't take the time to formulate a plan. He knew vaguely what his first move would be; the rest would decide itself for him.

"Okay, I want copies of these," he said. "I want a copy mailed to the White House, a copy mailed to my boss, a copy sent to an e-mail address that I'll give you, and a copy mailed to a friend of mine for safekeeping."

"And you, Marshal?" Gina stared at him. "You want one for yourself?"

"No." Chaney shook his head as he stood straight. "I'm going somewhere else for answers. And they ain't gonna be glad to see my smiling face, I can tell you that for nothing."

He started for the door.

"Marshal?"

Chaney stood in place, staring at a very small young woman surrounded by a billion dollars' worth of science that he couldn't master in a lifetime. Her voice was hesitant. "Please get the people that killed Rebecca. Make them pay."

Now that was his world.

Chaney nodded.

"You can count on it, Gina."

CHAPTER 14

Birdsong heralded morning long before first light, and Hunter could tell from the cadence how long until dawn. Outside, it was still dark but he knew, or felt, that the creature wouldn't be attacking again tonight.

For one reason, they had, for the first time, truly injured it, and he turned the episode over and over in his mind, trying to conclude why bladed weapons had injured it when bullets didn't. He couldn't come up with a reason; it didn't make sense.

A knife traveled with far less velocity than a bullet, struck with less impact; there was no explanation why he had been able to savage the creature's arm as he had with a blade. Finally he let it go and turned his attention to Bobbi Jo, who had at last fallen into some much needed sleep. Her head rested on his shoulder and he was careful not to move, so as not to disturb her.

Looking across the narrow corridor he could see that Taylor was wide awake, as always. The commando was lazily scrawling images in the dirt with the Bowie knife, his shotgun laid against the wall. He had loaded each clip with depleted uranium slugs for deadlier contact, and he seemed eager to get on with it.

Ghost was asleep, lying on his side, a good sign of safety. And Takakura had spent the last hour sitting in isolated silence, though Hunter occasionally saw the Japanese gazing bitterly at Wilkenson.

The SAS agent did not seem to notice the attention. And if he did, he hid it masterfully, appearing completely unperturbed. He had spent the time cleaning and oiling the modified Heckler and Koch 7.62mm fully automatic assault rifle and sat patiently without expression, glancing only occasionally at the rising chorus of morning outside the wall.

Finally Takakura stood. "It is daylight," he said in a stronger tone than he had used through the night. He looked at Hunter.

"We must go outside in order to transmit a direct signal to the satellite. The phone system cannot penetrate rock."

Hunter rose, fatigue and soreness assaulting him in a wave of stiff muscles and pain. "I know."

His chest ached from the deep furrows torn by the creature s claws, and he knew he'd been lucky. He didn't know what had warned him, didn't think about it that much. It was enough that some primal instinct that he could barely comprehend had acted for him.

Now they were all staring at the wall, unmoving. Then Takakura turned to Bobbi Jo. "If the creature is waiting outside, the only chance we have is for you to shoot it point-blank with the Barrett. If one of us is in the path of the bullet, you must not hesitate. You must fire. Do you understand this? A team member, balanced against the survival of the rest of the team, must be considered expendable. There is no other way."

Expressionless, she nodded. Racked a round into the Barrett.

Hunter had no doubt that she would do it. Now, he understood that later she would pay more dearly than others with the nightmares and regrets, but the job would have been done.

It was a simple matter to remove the third log, since the second was shattered. Then they removed the fourth and hesitated.

"Remain inside the mine," Takakura said. Without waiting for a reply he took his sword in one hand and one of Taylor s shotguns in the other and slid through the narrow opening.

He vaulted softly into azure light, alert and careful, glancing above, left, right. He stood for a moment in the middle of the small clearing, but nothing happened. Finally he turned back and motioned for them to follow.

They quickly removed the remaining logs, keeping their weapons near, and Hunter helped the professor from his cot. He sat the old man on a chair they had gotten from one of the cabins. Wilkenson activated the Magellan System.

Hunter heard the movement in the trees, the wind swaying branches, the breeze rushing over the stream located at the bottom of the slope, the musical sound of water trickling from the limestone cliff, a distant chattering woodchuck, and somewhere in the far distance a moose calling for its mate.

After being shut into the mine all night, every smell was fresh and distinct: rotting vegetation, green pine, old wood, even the earth itself. He inhaled deeply, relaxing, and released the breath as Wilkenson seemed to finally make contact.

He listened intently as Wilkenson requested an emergency extraction. The reply was negative. They were instructed to move at least a quarter mile downstream where a Blackhawk personnel helicopter could airlift them back to the base.

With a faintly perturbed expression, Wilkenson closed the case and gazed somberly at a frowning Takakura. "Well," the Englishman began, "seems we are still on our own, Commander."

"As I anticipated," Takakura growled. He turned to Hunter. "You are more familiar with the terrain than anyone. Can we make it?"

"We can make it," Hunter replied, steady. "Now we know how to kill it." Moving forward without words, he began down the slope. He held the Marlin lightly, knowing it was useless. The only weapon he possessed that could penetrate the Kevlar-like skin of the creature was the Bowie knife on his waist. The problem was that in order to inflict a wound, he was bound to receive one. A wound, or death.

Roaming ten feet ahead of them, Ghost led the procession.

Hunter heard Takakura order the Englishman and Taylor to carry the ailing Tipler on the stretcher. Then he ordered Bobbi Jo to back up Hunter at point while he took rear guard, and they were moving slowly, carefully, fearfully.

In a half hour they reached the path—it seemed to require far less effort than the climb to the cliff—and moved west toward the pass. It would take two hours, he estimated, to reach the clearing where the Blackhawk could pick them up.

And until then they would remain in danger, as anyone in these accursed mountains was in danger. But Hunter had steeled himself to it; there was nothing that could surprise him or shock him now, and he somehow despised the fear, knowing it would make him weaker, slower, less instinctive and less ready.

Casting an obscure glance back to see the formation of the unit—their positioning and readiness—Hunter heard Bobbi Jo's quiet voice. It was so soft he could barely make out the words, and he knew she had spoken only to him.

"Thank you for last night," she said without overt emotion. But it was there, somewhere beneath the words, in the tone. And in the fact that she had said it at all.

He nodded without looking back, knowing she was watching him, and they continued on, Hunter leading with winter in his veins and a cold wind in his face.

***

Chaney had left the Tipler Institute in a scientific fog. Without question, Gina knew her discipline, though he wondered if she might not be somewhat unsettled by the death of Rebecca, and whether it could be influencing her theories.

He knew all too well how emotional content often shaped rational thinking—one reason why the Marshals Service prevented agents involved in a shooting from pursuing the suspect.

No, they were routinely reassigned to another case because supervisors feared that causes of vengeance and anger would shadow logic at the moment of apprehension. Chaney had never had a problem with it; he had a pretty broad disposition toward vengeance, so it generally worked in his favor by keeping him out of prison.

He hadn't told her it was murder, but Gina had assumed it. But, then, he hadn't corrected her when she herself used the term, so that was a confirmation of sorts. He wondered if he might not need to order some protection for her as he made his way to the car and headed it toward Washington.

The game was getting more complicated, but it was adding up quickly. He knew that the government had done something far outside the known perimeters of science and law and probably of ethics as well.

What, exactly, was hard to discern. But something had happened up there and had gotten out of control. And now they were trying to mop it up before a public relations fiasco broke loose that would make the Bay of Pigs look like a carnival.

He headed across town toward the installation at Langley, calling Brick on the cell phone to leave a coded message that he would meet him later in the day. He had one other appointment he had to keep—maybe two— before he was finished.

Somehow, he was looking forward to them.

***

He felt his energy building as he raced to catch up to the team, and then he saw a dark moving speck on the far side of the stream, far up the trail. He moved faster, forsaking absolute silence for speed as he raced through the forest, leaping from boulder to boulder, hurtling fallen trees and vaulting small streams with ferocious strength powered by the sustenance he had consumed.

The caribou had fallen as if struck by lightning and he had lifted his fist from its shattered skull, his taloned hand groping for a split second to withdraw a ragged portion of the brain, which he had eaten first. Then he had ripped huge chunks of meat from its flanks and consumed them voraciously, growling with primitive pleasure.

He had not taken long before he noticed his arm healing far more quickly, even the searing scarlet scar fading moment by moment until he was whole again. He could feel his body utilizing the nutrients, strengthening him, making him once again what he had been: the ultimate beast of prey.

As the sun crested fog-shrouded trees, he had consumed enough and turned, running quickly and with purpose. He had hoped to be there when they emerged from hiding, but he had been moments too late, though it had been easy to discern their tracks. As a precaution, since he had come to more deeply respect the strange man who led at the front, he had crossed the stream to avoid detection.

Yet as he closed on them, his strength rising to match his rage, he began to lose his fear degree by degree, imagining the man's blood in his mouth.

Oh, yes, the man would die, though now he might save him for last. To torment him, to torture him, to make him afraid. Through with the thought, as he placed a broad black hand on a fallen tree that he vaulted without effort, he knew the man would never be truly afraid. No, he would die as the old ones had died, fighting till the last, though they had ultimately died.

Such glory ...

Days of blood, nights of cruelty and screams in the dark as they had hunted the weak ones, finding them in the shadowed forest to leap with a scream from above. He remembered the ecstasy of falling, killing before he touched the ground. And then rising slowly, so slowly, to behold their horror, to see the rest run.

Grinning, he increased his speed.

* * *

They knelt together before the cleft, and Hunter cast a tired glance at the professor, who was again sound asleep. Hunter was grateful for that. He hoped that when Tipler awoke again, they would be at the clearing where the Blackhawk would airlift them to the last surviving research station.

Takakura was studying the cleft closely. His dark eyes were narrow as he spoke. "It is the perfect place for an ambush," he said slowly. "But there is no other path we can take. The rock"— he pointed to the sheer cliff that descended like a wedge to the stream—"blocks any other line of advance. We must take our chances."

He turned to look directly at Hunter, but Hunter didn't acknowledge it. His mind was already inside the cleft, imagining the best method of negotiating that long walk in darkness. For they had lost most of their equipment in the pell-mell of the retreat, often casting off load-bearing vests in the heat of combat so they could move with greater agility and stay alive. But they could have used a major light source. All they had was Hunter's mini-light. Not enough.

Hunter stood. "Give me fifteen minutes and I'll make some torches," he said. "We can't go in there without light."

Taylor pulled a machete from his waist. "I'll help you."

He followed Hunter off the trail and into the woods. In minutes they had cut branches of dry pine into sections four feet long that Hunter slivered at one end into twigs as thin as toothpicks. Then he ripped up what remained of his T-shirt into tiny ribbons, stuffing them deep into the thin splinters.

Hunter had the torches burning in ten minutes, and turned to the rest. "Okay, I think we should stay close. We know bullets don't hurt it. But a blade will, so this will be face-to-face. We don't know yet how it really reacts to fire. If it's more man than beast, the torches could hold it for a second. But it might not. Just tell me, Takakura, if you don't like anything I'm saying."

A curt shake of his head and the Japanese answered, "I disagree with nothing." He lifted his eyes to the cleft. "We must negotiate the pass. That is all. We will deal with what we must deal with."

Again, Hunter was struck by the stoicism, and he remembered what he had read about the code of Bushido: expect nothing—not victory or defeat—and live knowing only death.

Hunter shook his head silently at the thought. He understood it, and he respected it, but he had found a different path through life. Neither was superior, he thought, as he rose with two torches in each hand, passing them out, but what he had come to know as life embraced life. It wasn't life focused on death. But that, too, was part of Bushido, the way of the warrior.

The torch didn't seem as bright as he stepped into the cave.

***

He had been forced to move more quickly than he had thought possible to get ahead of them, for he had spied the cleft far away, emerging high on a cresting knoll to see the black ribbon stretching down from the cliff.

He had leaped right, dropping thirty feet to the ground and rising to run through the forest with enormous leaping strides until he reached their stream. There he had launched himself viciously into the air to land catlike on a dry boulder where he had continued his momentum, casting himself high into the air to gain ground on their side. Then he had moved uphill and west, passing them far on the ridge and down again, where he had entered the cavern before them.

Now he rested on a ledge, breathing heavily from the tremendous exertion but feeling his monstrous body galvanized by the flesh of the beast he had slain. He was strong, stronger by the moment, and a trembling set into his arms and legs, an anticipation of slaying them in the dark as they wandered unknowingly into his path.

From his narrow view, he had watched the man fashion the torches— the fire—and knew they would bring the fire with them.

Creeping silently back until he was well out of whatever meager light the pitiful fire would hurl in the narrow rock-walled corridor, he threw back his hideous head and laughed.

Yes, bring your fire to me ...
We will see who is afraid ...

***

"Are you Dixon?"

Special Agent Dixon of the Central Intelligence Agency looked up at the sharp rap on the door, his eyes flicking down to check the valid pass and the United States Deputy Marshal credentials the man casually presented.

"I'm Dixon." He rose with the words. "I assume you're Marshal Chaney."

"I'm Chaney. I'd like to talk to you."

Dixon smiled, reaching out to shake. "Sure. Have a seat."

Chaney had already moved into the room, noticing as he shook hands that Dixon was a typical-appearing career man: white shirt, dark coat, dark tie, short-cut hair swept back, pale from too many hours under fluorescent lights, and eyes that seemed none too friendly. Chaney took a seat opposite him. He had been careful not to bring any notes, nor did he indicate that he would take any.

Reasons for that were twofold. First, Chaney wanted to scare Dixon, if he were truly involved in the subterfuge. And second, he wanted Dixon's immediate attention and respect. He had learned that other federal agents who didn't bother with recordings scared Agency people.

Chaney settled back into the chair, almost relieved at the atmosphere, though he knew he was on hostile ground.

With Gina he had been woefully, inadequately out of his league. But here, surrounded by policy and procedure, rules and regulations and the aura of secrets, clearances, and easy betrayal, he was at home. He waited for a moment, just to see what Dixon would do, measuring the man's temperament. But Dixon only leaned back and gestured casually.

"Well, Marshal," he began, in a cooperative tone, "I'm at your disposal and I'll help anyway I can. Of course, you're aware of restraints placed by Article 2453 negating any—"

"I'm aware, Mr. Dixon."

Chaney accented his response with a curt nod to indicate that he wouldn't allow the direction of his investigation to be derailed by regulations or policy. Nor would he allow his concentration to be distracted by protocol.

With Dixon, Chaney felt, it was best to play from strength.

"Ah, good." Dixon leaned forward, aggressive. "Then how can I help you?"

Chaney wanted to set the board up clean, so he didn't hesitate, didn't use a friendly tone, didn't couch anything in polite or tactful terminology. "Tell me about these so-called research stations that run under this program from the Arctic Circle," he began. "The ones where all the soldiers and personnel were injured or killed. I don't have to tell you that I'm investigating them."

Dixon opened his eyes wider and released a deep breath. He shook his head. "Frankly, Marshal, I'm as confused as anyone else. I don't know what is happening, really. All I know for certain is that the program has suffered setbacks due to the violent interference of some type of animal that is attacking our personnel."

"Yeah, I know that much." Chaney held the CIA man's eyes, watching for the slightest flicker. "What, exactly, are these stations designed to achieve?"

"Just geochronology and monitoring of tectonic plate movement." Dixon was all business. "It's a simple affair, really. Virtually every major country has some type of research station in the Arctic. Some are in international territory. Ours are on our own turf, in Alaska." He leaned back, shaking his head with more emphasis. "I can't really tell you why this bear or tiger or whatever the hell this thing is has singled out the stations. I've had people working on it. They say it might be related to radiation, or low-frequency sounds that could be attracting it, but that's all I can tell you. I'm not a scientist."

"Neither am I, Dixon," Chaney answered, purposefully dropping the "Mr." Then: "I only know that the information I've dug up so far indicates that these ... facilities ... are engaged in something more than seismic monitoring."

Dixon tilted his head. "Oh? And how would you reach that conclusion? Because that's certainly beyond any information that I've obtained."

"I can't reveal my sources," Chaney said, finding faint pleasure in the baiting. "But I believe the stations are engaged in some sort of biological research."

There was no hesitation at all in Dixon's reply. "Really?" He followed with a deliberate pause, as if he were seriously absorbing and considering the weight of it. "I did not know that. Just how accurate do you believe this information is, Mr. Chaney?"

"Accurate enough. It fits."

Silence.

"I see," Dixon responded at last. "So ...biological research, you say. Now ... of course, you know I can't move on that information unless I have corroboration."

It was the moment Chaney had been waiting for, but he didn't know it until it came. "You don't have to corroborate it. I already have. And I don't care for you moving on it, either. I'm gonna do that personally." He leaned slightly forward. "Tell me about this hunting party you have up there, Dixon. Certainly that information is not classified under the *Posse Comitates* threshold of Top Secret and Above! "

"Well," Dixon responded, tapping the desk with a pencil, "I believe that they are an elite unit of specially recruited soldiers highly qualified for jungle survival and experienced at hunting both animals and men. They are all experts in small arms, veterans of combat, decorated to a man, or woman, and possessing appropriate security clearances."

It was just what Chaney had expected to hear; there had been no mention of this man named Hunter.

"What about the guide?" he asked.

"Who?"

"Nathaniel Hunter."

"Oh, yes." Dixon waved vaguely. "According to those who selected him for the mission, he is the best wilderness tracker, as they call it, in the world. Seems like he can find anything in the jungle, the forest, the desert, wherever, and capture it or kill it. I didn't have the responsibility of verifying his credentials, so

I really have no idea. Nor did I select him. That was beyond my pay grade."

"Did you ever meet him?"

"Oh, yes, but only for a moment. And it wasn't the type of engagement where you can make a studied analysis." Dixon's face and eyes revealed nothing. He could have been reciting a laundry list. Chaney was impressed. "But in the few moments I shared with him," Dixon continued, "I came to appreciate his understanding of these things. I had no objection to allowing him on the team. We did, after all, need someone who could hunt this bear down and kill it before it caused further damage to the program."

"You keep saying that." Chaney didn't blink.

Seemingly surprised, Dixon looked straight at him, innocent. "Saying what, Mr. Chaney?"

"Saying it was a bear."

Dixon blinked, studious. "Well, what else could it be? Unless a tiger swam the Bering Strait—unlikely—then it would have to be a bear. I have, after all, read reports on the attacks." He shook his head, a jerk. "The loss was ...horrendous. Nor am I a man easily disturbed by carnage. It is my profession to remain dispassionate and unaffected by such things. They color judgment. But upon reading the descriptions of such wholesale murder, I knew that we were facing a beast of incalculable strength. As only a bear would possess. And a rather large member of its species, at that."

Chaney decided to change tack; this was going nowhere. He decided to fall back on one of Brick's oldest rules: when lying doesn't work at all, try using half the truth. Just remember to always mix it with enough lies to keep them off balance.

"Do you believe this creature might be a mutation?" he asked.

Dixon gazed at him, open and honest. "Mutation?" He let the question hang. "Well, Mr. Chaney, I believe I already told you that I don't know anything about any ... mutations or experimentation ... at those stations. However, I do not rule out the supposition. I have been in intelligence too long to doubt any concept, however illogical and bizarre it may seem."

"Is it bizarre?" Chaney said, deciding he wasn't going to let up. "What would be so bizarre? 'Cause these stations are perfect for it. They're isolated, easy to quarantine. The area is largely unpopulated, and far beyond executive supervision. Anything is possible in those backwoods, especially if the U.S. government is picking up the tab. Surely, Dixon, you're aware of that."

Dixon was nodding. "Yes, yes, Mr. Chaney, I am aware of the theory, and the history, of similar events. But that is not to say that I will believe it unless I have incontestable proof to present to my supervisors. They are not men ...who suffer fools. And they consider anyone who makes an unconfirmed estimation of a crisis as an ignorant man—the kind of agent that is never promoted or trusted."

Chaney's eyes were focused like lasers, unblinking and sharp. "Have you investigated to see whether there were other forms of research beyond seismic monitoring occurring at these stations?"

He nodded. "Yes, according to policy our sanitation crew always performs analysis on disks, records, logs, and military reports. We operated according to the procedure, and found nothing to convince me that there were anything but legitimate tasks being performed by the personnel and their on-site supervisors."

"I want to see the records."

"That is not possible."

"I can obtain a subpoena."

"Well," Dixon replied, "you must do as you see fit, Mr. Chaney. But I assure you that those records, which are highly classified, will reveal nothing to you." He paused. "If you are insistent I can ask the director for permission, and perhaps in three or four days you can peruse the less classified sections."

Chaney knew not to go for that one. In three days they could manufacture any kind of false records about the activities of the installations. Then he remembered what Brick had said about realigning a satellite and decided instantly. He moved to the heart of the situation.

"I want to make contact with this hunting team."

"Impossible." Absolute certainty in the terse reply.

"Why?"

"Because we cannot reach them."

Dixon looked at him as if he were content to let the silence linger forever. Chaney tilted his head, almost unable to believe that the team had been totally cut off from support. But he knew it in his soul.

"What did you just say?" was all he could phrase.

"I said, Mr. Chaney, that we have lost contact with the ...the hunting party ... as you term them." Dixon leaned forward. "Under law I am obligated to remind you of your secrecy pact. What I'm about to tell you requires the highest clearance."

Chaney said nothing.

"We lost contact with them two days ago," Dixon continued blandly. "They advised us that they were beginning the hunt, leaving the installation. And later that day when we attempted a status check, we received no reply. This ...beast...was in the area, by last reports. It is quite possible, even probable, that they are all dead." No betrayal of remorse. "We launched an air search and have yet to turn them up, even though we've used infrared and starlight scopes. So at the moment we are debating our next move."

"So, I suppose, you've fortified the last installation?"

"Absolutely. We have doubled the Ranger contingent, now at almost seventy men. We have increased voltage in the perimeter fence and reinforced external doors. Plus, we have backed up all information at the station in case of attack. Nothing that has been recorded, including an illegal underground nuclear blast performed by the Soviet Union three months ago, shall be lost in an attack."

"You don't seem too emotionally upset over the possible fate of this hunting party, Dixon." Chaney was casual. Curious.

Dixon stared at him in sullen silence for a moment. "Mr. Chaney, I am always upset when I lose an operative. But it is my job to send men on missions, and to their death, if the mission requires. Long ago I became inured to the hardships of this job. If I seem insensitive, then it's because I probably am. You can only see so many men sent to their death before you begin to develop a very thick skin. And if you can't do that, then you eventually become an alcoholic or a drug abuser or insane." He waited a moment. "I believe you understand what I'm talking about."

Silence.

Chaney rose. He nodded as he extended his hand. "I appreciate your time, Mr. Dixon," he said curtly.

"Whatever I can do, Marshal. And, if you don't mind me asking, how is the investigation coming along? I'm still rather confused why they gave it to the Marshals Service and not our own people."

Chaney smiled slightly. "Well, you know what they say," he answered, "don't ask the fox to guard the chicken coop." He walked toward the door. "Nice meeting you, Dixon. I'm sure we'll talk some more."

"So where are you off to next?" Dixon leaned back, cradling his head with his hands, utterly relaxed. He was a man who recovered quickly and completely; Chaney surmised he could conceal just as easily.

"I'm going to have a little conversation with Dr. Hamilton," he answered. "Gonna have a little skull session with him."

"Did you say Dr. Hamilton?"

Pausing, Chaney studied the face. "Yeah."

"But I thought you knew."

Chaney took a step back toward the desk that would have seemed overtly threatening if he had not stopped a good ten feet away. "Thought I knew what?"

"Dr. Hamilton isn't here."

"Where is he?"

"Well, he's gone to Alaska. He's at the last research station. I believe he said he'd be out of touch for at least a week. If not longer."

Chaney could tell from the all-too-obvious consternation and concern in Dixon's expression that, in that moment and that moment alone, the CIA man had seriously overplayed his hand. Because he was actually trying to appear helpful.

It was a strange and uncanny moment as they stood torch in hand outside the cleft, staring silently into gloom cast by giant granite slabs sliced from the mountain during the Ice Age.

Hunter bent, studying the ground, and saw the tracks of a host of animals from bear to wolverine to squirrel. Obviously, nature knew that this was the only way from this side of the cliff to the other. And if the animals, who were wiser, relied upon it, he was certain they would be forced to use it as well. Especially with the burden of carrying the professor, because they couldn't haul him in his diminished condition up that almost sheer face.

If Riley had not been so viciously slain they might have rigged something, and Hunter even now carried the rope across his chest, but he wasn't skilled enough to negotiate that climb. Also, he had failed to obtain the chocks and levers necessary for anchoring himself to the wall.

The torches burned brightly and Hunter knew they would burn for another thirty minutes before the twigs were exhausted. Hopefully, by then, they should be safe.

"I say we just make a run for it, "Taylor rumbled. "Just start running and go through it like hell, not stoppin' for nothing. Then when we get to the other side we rig a satchel of C-4 to a trip wire and let it come after us." He glanced behind them. "Let's see the mother follow that."

In a smooth motion of solid purpose, Takakura slung the MP-5 onto his back and unsheathed the katana. It was a solemn moment—the long curved blade, razor-sharp and at least a quarter-inch thick, glistening in the afternoon light. Then he inserted the black-lacquer scabbard into his belt, medieval-style, holding the sword loosely in his right hand. After a moment he looked down at Hunter, who had watched without expression.

"Only a blade can injure it," Takakura intoned. "We have learned this much. Its skin is impervious to bullets, unless they are traveling at sufficient velocity."

"Like 4,000 feet per second," said Bobbi Jo.

"Yes," he continued. "Perhaps the uranium slugs which Taylor is using can injure it. We will see. But for this I prefer the sword. If it conies to us inside the dark, and if fire fails to deter it, then we will be fighting face-to-face. In this, a sword can be superior to a rifle."

Hunter lowered his head. It was amazing to him, all at once, how much a man could consider in a single moment in time. He saw his life, what he had lived for, all he had learned, his hopes, his unfulfilled dreams, his sorrows. It seemed that all his skill, his knowledge, his understanding and wisdom had brought him to this place in time.

And he still didn't know what they faced, still didn't know how to destroy it. He only knew that he had overcome in the past simply because he had never surrendered to the pain, though he had bled with it.

Feeling a wrong kind of tired, he raised his head. He turned toward Bobbi Jo, smiled slightly, but she only looked sad. He glanced at the professor, sleeping, and nodded to himself.

It was time.

A tough man with a gentle heart ...

Slowly, hiding any hint of the fear he felt, he stood and expelled a hard breath, staring at the cleft.

"Let's assume the worst," he said. "It's waiting for us in there. Assume also that it's not afraid of fire. Which it probably isn't. How, exactly, are we going to respond as a unit to an attack inside an enclosed space?"

"With any means possible," said Takakura.

"We blow the hell out of it," Taylor added.

"No." Hunter walked forward a pace and knelt, trying to feel what was there. He didn't expect success, and he wasn't disappointed. After a moment, knowing he was wasting time, he walked slowly back.

"Here's my plan," he began. "I'm gonna climb high, about twenty feet, and make my way through the higher tier of the crevice while you guys carry the professor through the passage. I'll lead, and if I sight it, I'll hit it with the rifle. It won't hurt it, but you'll know what to do. Retreat and blow the crevice behind you and then hold the position outside." He looked at Bobbi Jo. "If anything comes out or over that opening that isn't me ... kill it."

She asked, "What will you be doing if we retreat?"

Hunter slung the Marlin on his back, began to free-climb the broken ridges that bordered the crevice.

"Probably fighting for my life," he said.

He gained a foothold and lifted himself with the strength of his legs to save his arms. "The main thing is to get you guys out of there before it can run you down, which it'll do quick since you're carrying the professor."

"Hunter—" She stepped forward.

He paused, looked down. Winked.

"Hey," he smiled, "you just make sure you don't miss that chopper."

***

Wearing attire appropriate to the landscape—khaki pants, a khaki shirt and a wide-brimmed fedora—Dr. Arthur Hamilton de-boarded a Ranger helicopter and loped, head low, from the landing pad, holding a black briefcase tightly under an arm.

Behind him a small entourage carried baggage, equipment, his parka and their own belongings.

At the edge of the pad, beyond the reach of the slowly rotating rotors and the dying whine of the engines, Colonel Maddox stood holding his hat to his head. "Nice to see you, Dr. Hamilton!" he yelled above the whir of the chopper. Then: "I can't say I'm surprised, though! I'm amazed you didn't come earlier!"

Hamilton nodded curtly and kept moving as Maddox fell in beside him. "We've done everything you ordered, Doctor! I don't know exactly why you wanted the equipment removed, but we flew it out this morning on a chopper!"

"Good!" Hamilton responded as they were finally out of the chopper's annoying range. "Did you follow all of my instructions to the letter, Colonel?"

Maddox nodded. "Right to the letter, Doctor. We shipped it by Sea Stallion to the installation in Los Angeles. Even the pilot doesn't know what he's flying."

"Good." Hamilton moved for an oversized steel door and in moments was at a sub-basement two levels below the visible facility. He inserted his chin into a small cup as a scanner read the blood vessels of his left eye, and then a steel vault opened, allowing entrance.

He was greeted by a tall woman—black-haired, thin pale face with two crescent moons of dark skin sagging beneath her eyes. She smiled as he neared and Hamilton raised his eyes to a glass tube suspended in the middle of the laboratory.

The tube, as large as a sarcophagus, floated in an electromagnetic field. It touched neither the floor nor ceiling and was filled with a liquid that allowed small air bubbles to rise to the top where they disappeared in a lace of reflective mesh. Green light cascaded down over the figure in a halo; it was an aura of holiness.

Hamilton smiled, almost reverent.

For within that liquid, equally suspended, was a thing such as the world had never seen and never imagined. Its head hung in death, hair all but gone to ten thousand years of ice, but its body preserved, almost fossilized by the intense pressure and cold of a glacier melted by an oil fire that had decimated Alaska's North Ridge.

Magnificent, terrifying, and godlike, the humanoid shape floated alone in its own dead space. Its chest was enormous, huge cords locked into the sternum like unbreakable iron cables stretching out to connect with Herculean shoulders. Its arms— heavy and thick and overly developed— ended in large powerful hands tipped with black curving claws. And its legs were equally dynamic; the legs of a hunter, of a creature that could run for days or even weeks without rest or respite only to ferociously attack and feast, and run again, leaping, climbing, attacking and attacking. Though dropped forward in death, its face was surprisingly visible on an imposing mound of neck muscle. The brow was broad and low beneath withered white hair, its nose broad also and flattened with wide nostrils. And its wide mouth, uncannily open in death, revealed fangs as long and deep-set as a tiger's. Then the primitive face ended with a square, solid chin with knotted muscles set deeply in the hinges and high in the cheeks to indicate a uniquely formidable countenance. It was the image of what Homo sapiens might have been if he had possessed the strength of a dinosaur, the mind of a man and the terrifying aspect of a tiger.

Hamilton gazed upward in awe.

"Surely ... the purest of all beings." He stepped forward softly. "Surely it ruled the world like a god."

Consumed by the sight, Hamilton lowered his head, a faint smile on his lips. His voice was hushed. "And so, my dear friend Emma, have you managed to finish analysis of the sequencing?"

Dr. Emma Strait, holding a clipboard to her chest, took a slow step to stand beside him. "It was as you suspected, Doctor," she said in a low voice. "Its protein levels were clearly regulated by a long version of the genes that control dopamine and serotonin. But we also found something we hadn't expected."

Hamilton gazed expectantly. "Yes?"

"It's rather complicated, and unexpected, and we don't even understand it ourselves yet." Nervously she glanced at the suspended dead form. "There are variations—some severe—

in the regulatory regions for the transporter genes. We haven't mapped the entire genome, but the reconstruction we've managed to produce allows us a hint at its makeup. The D2 Dopamine receptor gene is at least thirty times as large as modern Homo sapiens. Apparently a product of heredity. Or a mixture of heredity and environment. So you were correct in surmising that extraordinarily oversized genes regulating emotional and intellectual control faculties had been severely metamorphosed by some unknown outside influence. Possible diet, climate. It's unknown. Quite possibly we will never know unless ... it's captured."

"Something we are hard at work on, I assure you," Hamilton answered. He turned back to the mummified giant. "Yes, it is as I assumed. Its genetic coding prohibited the manufacture of those very chemicals which give modern man control, consciousness, morality, and mercy. A creature that lived forcefully for itself and nothing else. A creature that by its genetic structure was incapable of caring for anything but its own self-serving goals. And look what it became. The strongest of its kind. The strongest of *our* kind."

Dr. Strait took a breath. "The ... triggers ... you could call them that ... which buffer the genes are fantastically rapid in response – fifty to a hundred times more rapid than normal human DNA. We've concluded that they allowed receptors to relay impulse, reaction to hunger or threat or anger, to activate adrenaline and other proteins which in turn gave it a spectacular propensity for violence." She glanced again at the corpse, as if glad it were dead and entombed. "Something it was quite capable of even without the proteins. But its genomes made it basically a creature that moved on any impulse – any impulse at all, regardless of consequences. I don't think it was capable of understanding the concept of consequences, actually. According to the specs that we've mapped so far, all its physical attributes from cardiovascular fitness to strength ratio were at least thirty times that of Homo sapiens. And an ocular check revealed that its powers to discern color and see movement were approximately five times greater than that of modern man. It may have even possessed a type of telescopic vision, like an eagle."

Hamilton shook his head in unconcealed admiration. "And don't you see the beauty of that? Even without the mutations which eliminated serotonin and dopamine from its system, chemicals which were in some way compensated for by other unknown segments of the DNA strand to prevent compromised cerebral capacities, it was the most perfect predator of all time. As I assumed. And ...," He hesitated, "was my other assumption correct as well?"

"Yes." She nodded. "The immunity segment of the strand, and remember that we haven't finished mapping it, split in quadrilateral pairs. Its mutation somehow allowed it to heal up almost instantly from wounds or disease. Its lymphatic system, which we were lucky enough to stumble upon by mistake, indicates a set of reflectors and transmitting genes that far surpass anything we have ever seen – even in sharks. It was, for all practical purposes, immune to any invading bacteria or viral agent. The genes that we tested on the computer matrix revealed that its lymphocytes and white cells suffered no delay at all in identifying an invading molecule. Even something so small as the single molecule of a virus. It's really ... quite fantastic. I've never seen anything like it. None of us have."

"Nor have I," Hamilton breathed. "And now we can begin to isolate the specific genes which buffer that incredibly robust immune system. Isolate them, and bring them into the present day. Within a few years, those selected for the glory will know what it knew. A life span of hundreds of years. Immeasurable strength. A hardiness that has been so jealously claimed by a forgotten age. Soon we will have the same fearlessness at the approach of old age or disease or frailty. We shall be untouched by sickness or feebleness, and laugh as all those around us are ravaged by time. Yes ... that was my dream: immortality."

Nothing was said for a moment. Then: "Dr. Hamilton," she began, "the search team ... they made contact with the facility an hour ago."

Hamilton's suddenly darkened presence was chilling. He turned to her slowly. "What did you just say, Emma?"

She took a deep breath, bracing. "The search team is still alive, Doctor."

"That is impossible," he scoffed. "They have been alone in the forest for almost four days, battling the creature. No one could survive such a conflict."

"They radioed in, Doctor. They're still alive, somehow. They survived, and they're being picked up by helicopter within the hour."

"It seems my young protégé, Luther, disappointed me. Hmmph. Well ...nevertheless. Until I see them alive before my eyes, I will not believe it." Hamilton barked a short laugh. "Luther, the young fool, was impetuous and paid for his arrogance. The matrix had not even been tested when he injected himself with the serum alone and unsupervised. He should have died, but he did not, and became what he has become. I consider his transformation ... a blessing, of sorts."

"Will we try and help him if we capture him?"

Hamilton seemed astounded. "Help who, Doctor?" He waited to no reply. "Help Luther? That is truly amusing. No, we will not help Luther, Emma, because Luther no longer exists. Except, perhaps, in some dim half-dream within the creature's mind. Luther is gone forever. Only his body remains. Transformed. Mutated into the mightiest, the fiercest and most predatory beast to ever walk the face of the earth. And in this diluted canard age of evolution, where the true beasts have fallen to fire and ice, and expendable man is the reigning species, he will enjoy his feast."

Dr. Strait's face tightened. "Then what will the creature do?"

"It will do as it has done," Hamilton answered calmly. "It will come for the rest of the serum, for Luther used an inadequate amount for complete replication. There are other genomes which it must absorb to perfectly mirror this indestructible coding. This much, I am certain, he remembers. Though I am sure that, in shape and form and ferocity, it is almost the equal of this magnificent ancestor, and may even retain some of its memories."

"Memories, Doctor?"

"Yes, of course." Hamilton smiled. "Memory is encoded in DNA, just as the manufacturing for particular proteins that decide a propensity for violence or pleasure. There are clearly areas of the DNA strand—imperfectly decipherable to us as of yet—that grant such a faculty. And as Luther's body and mind are overwhelmed, so too I believe are his memories disappearing under the onslaught of the memories of another time, another race."

Dr. Emma Strait stepped close. "And what of the facility if Luther, I mean ... the creature ... comes here for the rest of the serum as it's done at the other installations?"

"Oh, we are well protected, my dear." Hamilton smiled. "I have no fear that it can penetrate this vault, and our means of communication are self-contained. If it does indeed destroy the base, just as it has done, we shall be quite safe within the vault. Even the creature's terrific strength cannot tear that twenty-ton vault from the passageway. It is only an animal, after all, though magnificent and manlike in structure." He released a deep breath. "So, we shall continue our research, and when we are quite finished, I shall allow you and all those who have labored so diligently to join the new society—a society which will never grow old, and will accumulate power century after century until we are princes on the earth. You and I, Emma, will rule nations, enjoy the feasts of kings, and live for centuries with perfect health, perfect strength. All that remains is to isolate the immune strands and the receptor genes and leave the genes regulating instantaneous replication, as Luther so foolishly did not, from the serum."

A tense moment followed, and Dr. Emma Strait responded, addressing him by his first name. "Arthur, the staff ... is concerned. They don't want ... well, they're worried. I know what you say, but Luther, uh, the creature, it's killed so many people and—"

"Emma, Emma." Hamilton spoke indulgently. "Rest assured that we are all quite safe. I created this. I know quite well what it is capable of accomplishing. I am as familiar with its glory as with its corruption." He smiled—a spectacular smile. "A terrifying beast it is and shall remain. But even a beast of such incalculable power must die one day. As it surely will."

***

Crouching in darkness, lifting the torch high, Hunter scanned the jagged, broken ledge that stretched out before him. Twenty feet above the passageway, carefully balanced on a granite slab, he saw nothing but shadows leaping before the flickering flame.

He leaned his head to the side, attempting to discern a better angle, but saw nothing more. And he tried to ignore his racing heart, the adrenaline that surged from his chest with each thunderous beat of his heart. His hands were sweating and he wiped them on his dirt-grimed pants, licking his lips.

He knew fear now, true fear, because he had stood alone on the ledge in the dark with nothing but flame and steel, and should he fight it face-to-face, Hunter knew it would be a swift end. He didn't have the advantage of a barrier, couldn't move with that fantastic speed, and would be quickly overpowered by its irresistible strength.

Thinking of the power that surged to pull him into those monstrous fangs, he shivered before turning his will, shutting down emotion. He had to concentrate; he couldn't let horror cloud his judgment however terrible the price. And after a moment of cold concentration he inched forward, trying not to reconcile himself to the fact that he was as good as dead.

He had told Takakura to wait for his signal before they entered the crevice. And Hunter was certain that they would; the commander was too cautious and professional to alter a plan once it was decided upon.

Then Hunter remembered how Taylor, in a remarkable display of friendship, had come up to him at the last minute and handed him a rectangular canvas-covered satchel about a foot long and six inches wide. Without asking permission Taylor had pointed to a looped handle on the top and said, "Pull this and you've got five seconds, buddy. It'll blow anything inside that cave to hell and gone. And once you pull it, run your butt off, 'cause there ain't no stopping it."

Shocked for a moment, Hunter had nodded, then set the satchel in his pouch, the only other thing he wore on his upper body beside Riley's rope, looped shoulder to hip.

Shadows moved weirdly before him. And with some unconscious instinct he withdrew the Bowie, holding it close as he inched cautiously forward.

His breathing, despite his iron control, was heavier and faster, making him feel almost light-headed. He released a long, slow breath and tried to keep himself from hyperventilating. Then he shook his head sharply, as if to physically throw off the chimeras dancing like vapid ghosts before his eyes.

"Come on," he whispered, "get a grip ..."

Another ten feet, twenty, and still his senses revealed nothing. And despite his fear he felt a descending sense of security, perhaps because some unconscious part of him hoped that, since he hadn't been attacked so far, he wouldn't be. But his mind told him better. He knew that, if it were here, it would be waiting patiently, fearing the blade if it feared anything at all.

He made another ten feet, glancing at the torch to see another fifteen minutes remaining. Eyes flashing in the gloom he continued, searching, thrusting the torch around a corner and withdrawing it quickly, tempting an attack. It never came.

In another ten feet he would tell them to proceed.

It was a flickering shadow ahead of him that made him tense as if he'd been struck, instantly rising to his feet to place them fully across the four-foot crevice, straddling the long drop to the floor with a foot on opposite ledges.

He watched the shadow ...rise?

Fall?

"What—" he began.

And knew.

Electrified with thrilling breathlessness, slowly moving only his head, Hunter turned cryptically to gaze behind.

Glowing red eyes, fangs distended, it stood gigantically less than five feet away. It smiled.

Its arms, so incredibly huge, hung almost to its knees, and Hunter noticed a difference in its face, as if it were more grotesque, more deformed with a heavier brow brooding over the baleful glare. Claws clicked as it moved its fingers in a rapid, staccato flexing that was almost too quick to follow. It seemed to laugh.

Slowly, Hunter turned toward it, saying nothing, doing nothing, prepared to drop cleanly to the floor and take his chances. And what happened next almost caused him to stagger. His eyes opened in shock as strength flowed from his form.

Fangs laughed beneath glowing, blood-red eyes.

"You cannot escape me," it growled.

In a truly foul mood, Chaney parked and walked slowly toward Brick's diner. For once, he was actually hungry as he neared the doors, but his mind was so preoccupied that he knew he couldn't eat. He had played out whatever meager hand he'd been dealt. And for the time being he didn't know what to do next. This thing was going down like nothing he had ever seen.

He didn't mind putting on his real mood for Brick; Brick wasn't affected by anything and had seen him like this before. He supposed that's why he always liked stopping in on the retired marshal when a case was going to pieces.

Chaney would stop by, complain and curse, and Brick would go on calmly cutting meatballs and filling orders and occasionally nodding to indicate that he wasn't completely ignoring him. Chaney would feel better having vented and go on his way with a beer. It was a system he liked, even if it was predictable—a danger in this profession.

He walked through the door at midafternoon to see the place fairly crowded. Without announcement—he had never announced himself— Chaney went through the swinging doors and saw Brick sitting at a desk surrounded by his uniquely personalized system of chaotic organization.

Watching over bifocals, Brick followed him as he half-collapsed in a chair. Chaney said nothing. Brick said nothing. Brick's face was bland. "I seen you look worse," he said.

"Really?" Chaney answered wearily. "When?"

"When you had that accidental discharge as a rookie and shot the front windshield out of your car."

Chaney paused. "Oh ... yeah, well, that was a bad day."

"You're telling me." Brick went back to the calculator. "I'm the one who had to do all the paperwork." His fingers flew over the pad with remarkable dexterity. "So what you got besides what I gave you?"

"I'm not sure, really. This scientist, a smart gal, says that this ...creature, whatever it is, is off the charts. Says she doesn't have anything to match its DNA." Chaney paused before continuing. "She said that it's got some kind of immunity to disease, injury, anything. It was weird."

Brick stopped adding, stared dead at Chaney. His gravelly voice held an equal amount of amusement and disbelief and intrigue. "You don't say?"

"Yep," Chaney answered as he opened a beer from a nearby case. "Brick, this is out of my league. I ain't no scientist. And the only person I might have nailed down has gone to Alaska. To the last research station."

"So?" Brick began adding again. "Doorstep him. He can't get away from you. I learned a long time ago that you had the tenacity of a bulldog and half the brains. Follow the mother to the ends of the earth. Make him nervous. It's called 'harassment 'til you spill your guts to me.' " He looked pleased at the number he had reached. "That's what I'd do."

That option hadn't occurred to Chaney, but the more he thought of it, the more it seemed appropriate. He did, after all, have an unlimited budget and the right to commandeer a private jet at his discretion, though there might be hell to pay with Skull afterwards.

Yet all of it kept coming back to Alaska, the research station, and the man most responsible for whatever was going on inside that facility had gone there ... to hide something? To finish something?

"You might have an idea there, Brick," Chaney mused after a slow swig of warm beer.

"I know most of the games, kid. Heck, I invented a few of 'em myself. He's ducking you and you know it. Best way to rattle his cage is to show him you can't be ducked." There was a long pause. "You should go just to let that scientist fella know he can't get away. Sometimes it's the principle of the thing. But I'd do something else before I went hightailing after him."

Chaney knew what he was talking about. "A little extracurricular activity?"

"You got it."

It was a phrase Brick had invented in the old days for serving search warrants on dangerous felons.

The night before the scheduled raid, Chaney and Brick would illegally break into the suspect's house and search it for guns, weapons, anything that might endanger them in execution of the warrant the following morning. They wouldn't ask permission and wouldn't tell anyone what they'd done. And if they found a weapon they would disable it—remove the firing pin, jam it, remove the barrel, or something else equally as effective—so they didn't have to worry about being shot the next day.

It was a well-known if unconfessed practice and nobody asked questions about it. But everyone, including supervisors, expected it to be done in order to insure the safety of fellow marshals.

At the briefing before the execution of the warrant, a fellow marshal would inevitably ask Brick, "What did you do last night?" To which Brick would casually respond: "Nothing. Just a little extracurricular activity."

It wasn't a guarantee of safety, but it worked well enough. And now Chaney knew Brick was recommending that he break into Hamilton's home, glean what he could from what he could find, and leave no trace that he had been there. Chaney had already thought of it, but it helped to have someone reinforce what could be considered a wild idea. He took another sip before he spoke. "Yeah, but I don't think this guy takes his work home, Brick."

"He takes his life home, kid." Brick leaned forward on burly forearms. "Don't worry about his computer. It won't be there. Or in the files. Go to his bookcase. Study what he's got. A bunch of literature on earthquakes? Is that his interest?" He nodded hard. "Or is it something else?"

Chaney knew where the old man lived. "All right. I'll take a little look-see tonight."

"Where does he live?"

"A town house, not far from here."

Brick's square head, vaguely resembling a heavyweight boxer's, nodded with each word. "Remember, son, don't mess up the alarm, just disable and pick the lock. Nothing disturbed. Nothing broken. No prints. Don't forget to fix the alarm on your way out. Any fool can break into a place. The trick is breaking in and leaving without anyone ever knowing you were there."

"Yeah, I remember." Chaney hesitated before he brought up his most disturbing thought. "How would you cut a team off from support in the field, Brick? What would be the best way of doing something like that?"

"What do you mean, 'support'?"

"Put them in a position where they couldn't call for backup."

"Well," he responded, concentrating, "I guess the easiest way would be to disable their communications equipment. Wouldn't be all that easy, since everyone is trained to fix the radio, but it could be done if you didn't have a replacement part. In fact, back in 'Nam I heard some war stories about it. They called it a high-tech frag. Guess they figured it was more creative than rolling a grenade between the lieutenant's legs while he was taking a crap."

Chaney pondered; disabling a radio was certainly easier than altering a satellite, which required NSA approval. And a realignment wasn't all that easy even with that.

He knew that a satellite occupied a stationary orbit, which means its orbit coincides with the rotational speed of the earth, keeping it in the same relative location at all times. For instance, the satellite over Alaska was forever directly over Alaska, and retro rockets had to be fired in controlled bursts to either speed or slow the satellite's trajectory. And any mistake with the rockets could destabilize its orbital distance, which could cause it to fall and disintegrate on reentry.

Chaney trusted that Dixon had asked about altering the orbit of a satellite, figured he knew which one, and may have even done it. But somehow Chaney suspected that Dixon would want things quieter. He wouldn't chance a high-risk maneuver as potentially scandalous as a re-alignment if it wasn't absolutely necessary. Whatever this was, and. Chaney knew it was something, was too unstable. They couldn't endure the attention.

Chaney set the beer down and rose. "I've got work to do. Might see you later. Or I might be out of town ... way out of town, in fact."

Ponderous forearms on the table, Brick said nothing for a moment. Then: "Boy, I think you're in way over your head on this. I don't like it. Some ... what did you say? Creature?"

"For lack of a better word."

"Whatever," Brick continued. "This thing is up there, and you're going up there, and you don't even know what it is, where it came from, where it's going, what it's doing. You gotta think this stuff through." He raised a hand. "Now, I know what I said. But that's in normal situations. Not in situations where some monster is running around knocking down electric fences and tearing people's heads off." He paused, shook his head. "Now, I must say, I seen a lot in my time, but that's a real unusual situation. And now you're thinking of going up to where this creature has killed all these rangers and marines which, by the way, ain't all that easy to kill. Now, I don't know and I ain't gonna try and tell you what's the smart thing to do, but if I was you I'd do a little more homework with that smart lady scientist before I went off into the wild blue."

Chaney laughed, shook his head. "You always did have a way of putting things, Brick."

"Comes with old age."

A silence.

"All right," Chaney said. "Tonight I do a little snooping. I'll see what I find. I'll make a decision after that."

Brick nodded. "You let me know."

"You bet."

"And one more thing, Chaney."

Pausing, Chaney said nothing. It was rare that Brick ever called him anything other than "kid," although he was almost forty years old. But Brick, at sixty-three, had the right in more ways than one.

"Yeah?" he asked.

"This thing up there, it's up there," Brick said slowly, in a voice he used when he was dead serious, "it ain't real. Whatever it is, I don't know. Probably nobody knows. But you don't need to be playin' no hero. You shoot it on sight. Fair ain't part of this. 'Cause it'd do the same to you."

Chaney nodded. "Brick, whatever that monster is ... it could kill anyone."

Staring dead into its eyes, Hunter didn't move.

Neither attempted to retreat or close the distance.

The creature was slightly hunched, as if preparing, and even in its stillness it seemed to be drawing closer. But Hunter knew it was an illusion caused by adrenaline and fear. He had been in this situation before, so he tried to control his sudden lack of breathing caused by the shock of its words.

"Last night"—its words grated over smiling fangs—"you fought well."

Hunter braced himself, testing his foothold, and mentally measured the drop through darkness to the pathway beneath. He knew he couldn't make it unless the creature was distracted. But it was twenty times faster than he was.

He couldn't retreat, and a frontal attack was suicide. The only chance he had was that he might hit it hard, then drop, because it couldn't drop any faster than he could. But when he hit the floor he'd better come up running and use what Taylor had given him. It was a risky gamble, and probably suicidal, but he was determined to not go down without a fight. Despite all his torn, sore muscles, he didn't feel any of them at the moment.

Gathering his courage, he frowned and spoke. In his mind, somehow, he couldn't reconcile himself to the possibility that it would respond. Part of him hoped it wouldn't.

"What do you want?" he asked.

A voice like dirt shifting in a grave: "You."

Hunter was shocked that it was hesitating at all. But there was obviously an unexpected measure of intelligent cruelty buried in that primitive mind, enjoying his fear.

"How can you ... how can you speak?" Hunter asked, watching it sharply as it lifted taloned hands.

"Humans," it said, laughing, and Hunter perceived that its vocal cords were never designed for this manner of articulation. "You are all ... so helpless."

Shifting his foot less than an inch toward the edge of the ledge, Hunter tried to engage whatever mind it possessed. "Why did you kill those people?"

"Because they are prey. *You* ... are prey. You have always been prey."

That left nowhere to go; Hunter tried something else.

"So where did you come from?" he asked, closely watching its eyes. "You haven't always been here. I know that much. Before you kill me, you can at least tell me that."

"From inside you."

Hunter assumed his shock must have been revealed.

It laughed, genuinely amused.

"Oh, yes," it whispered. It held up its talons. "Look at these hands. Monstrous ... are they not?" Dark laughter. "What would your hands be like if you had my freedom? My strength! My power!" Silence. "Let me tell you. Then you would be like me! Yes! What do you see when you look at me? What do you see?" It nodded with a whisper, "You see *yourself.*"

Hunter shook his head, almost brought into the conversation, though his mind was flying behind his calm countenance.

"I would never be like you."

"You are already like me," it rasped, bending as if to charge. "The beast within you ... is all that I am. You think you are so noble – so righteous. But you are nothing more than me beneath what you call 'human.' ' Its laughing found expression in a grating growl. "Yes, I am what you truly are. And you know it's true ... I am only what you are deep inside ... what you fear you are. What you know you are."

Hunter's foot was at the edge.

"You're insane," he said, calm. "Listen ... listen carefully to me: Let me take you in safely. We will not hurt you. But if you don't come with me, others will come for you. More men. More weapons. You are strong. But they will hunt you down. You can't beat the entire world. Sooner or later, they will corner you. And they will kill you. Don't be insane."

Roaring in a black and measureless mirth, it threw its head back, lost in the glory of its matchless might. "No, no ..." It lowered its head, smiling malevolently. Then it exhaled, releasing an impression of terrifying power. "No ...*not insane* . . ."

Hunter remembered what he had discovered at the research station, what he had suspected all along with the repeated attacks. Take a chance, he thought.

"What are you searching for?" he asked, giving no indication that he was split seconds from making a desperate attempt at escape. It stared at him a long moment, as if Hunter had abruptly distracted it from its intended thoughts.

"The other," it rumbled.

Hunter stared. "The other? The other ... the other one like you?"

The red eyes dimmed. "Yes."

Silence.

"And ... where is the other one like you?"

The fanged visage seemed to withdraw, somehow, within itself. The alien glow in its scarlet eyes verged on madness.

"I must find him. I must ... find him."

"Why?" Hunter never expected a chance question to carry him this long.

"To be complete."

A strange, wild theory struck Hunter. "Who did this to you?" he asked, himself incredibly caught up for a split second. He stared intently with the question, as if to read the truth in its eyes. "They did this to you, didn't they? They made you into ...this. You were a man, weren't you. And now ...you're this."

A blazing roar of laughter caused the corded neck muscles to bulge like hot iron. Hunter saw the veins, twice as thick as a man's, pulsing fiercely with that savage blood, and then it stared upon him once more, seeming to revel in the garish moment of mirth.

"Foolish, foolish mortal," it whispered with spite. "No ... *they* did not do this to me ... *I did this to me!*" Its chest rumbled with a strange growl. "I had the power to become a god and so ... *I became God!*"

Now, with true horror, Hunter understood.

"What was your name?" he asked, somehow enlivened with an even sharper revulsion. He couldn't imagine that this monstrosity, with all its viciousness and blood thirst, had once been a human being.

"My name ... was Luther."

"Luther ... why did you do this? You're not a god. Nobody lives forever.

Fangs parted in laughter, but it was silent. No sound, not even breath, whispered forth for a still moment.

"To become as them" it answered finally, with a short bark of laughter. "To become as god on the earth. Unkillable. Because I am the strongest. Yes, the strongest. Nothing can destroy me. And I will live forever."

It was insane.

Hunter knew he couldn't reason with it.

"So you sacrificed your humanity for this," he said, edging toward the drop. But there was a trace of contempt. And remarkably, it noticed.

It smiled, and taloned fingers clicking once in that eerie, uncanny flexing that made them flicker and relax. Although subtle, it was horrifyingly threatening.

Hunter knew he was out of time, it was about to attack. Almost because he had to know, because he knew how this would end, he said what he truly felt.

"You're an animal now, Luther. Not a god."

Hunter steadily held its contemptuous stare.

As it paused, Hunter suddenly saw Bobbi Jo, the rest, moving silently from the far end. His heart raced but he concealed his alarm. He raised his eyes, measuring; they would need fifteen seconds at a full run to clear the tunnel. He had to stall it for at least ten.

It shook its head, and Hunter could sense something volcanic building within it; a tightening of its chest, the slight rising of the enormous shoulders and an almost invisible shift of balance. It didn't come closer, but it was only seconds away.

"If you only knew the power," Luther growled, despising. "You consider yourself ... human. Not ... animal. But I am more human than you. I am only what you are ... in the darkness. I am what you hide in the light. I did not lose my humanity. My humanity is purer, and stronger, than yours. Because I do not hide what I really am."

Bobbi Jo and the rest were almost directly beneath, and the creature seemed not to have yet noticed. He was too involved with Hunter.

"I only wanted you to know this," Luther continued, and breathed deeply, as if the intellectual labor of speech had fatigued it. "I will kill you. I will kill all of you. And I will live long. Far, far longer than men. And when your children are dead ... I will still rule this world ..."

Bobbi Jo and the rest passed beneath.

"Now," it said, smiling, "you die."

"One last thing!" Hunter shouted, knowing he had to demand its full attention. "I want you to know something!" It paused.

"This!" Hunter roared, cocking and firing the Marlin in a single one-handed motion.

The creature recoiled, almost as much from the blast of light as the impact. Hunter leaped into him, viciously swiping across its ribs with the Bowie and then descending into the darkness.

He kicked the wall to send himself across, striking the granite hard, and again kicked to take another four feet out of the fall by bouncing back, and then he was sliding, falling, lashing out once with the Bowie for a grip—a terrific stabbing blow that struck sparks from the granite, grinding, before he crashed numbingly hard.

He was dimly aware of torches vanishing at the far end of the tunnel— they understood, were running. Then he was on his feet, ignoring the numb feeling in his side, staggering forward knife in hand as a colossal weight crashed onto the path behind him with a vengeful roar.

Light was before Hunter, the end of the passage. He pulled the cord on the satchel: five seconds!

He heard it charging with the force of a rhino.

"Shoot it!" he screamed.

Instantly Hunter dropped and in the next heartbeat five .50-caliber rounds from the Barrett laced a destroying path down the crevice, powering above Hunter's prone form. He heard them hit with a sound like an ax being buried in flesh and then he was on his feet again, running.

Hunter threw the satchel as he exploded from the tunnel and violently grabbed Bobbi Jo around the waist.

"Everybody gel clear!" he screamed.

Holding her tight in his arms, Hunter leaped far to the side, carrying her. She screamed as they landed on a downward slope, and he kept them rolling, gaining distance.

The rest had moved as one; no questions.

An eruption of flame like a dragon's wrath thundered from the entrance. The blast flattened them to the ground grinding and rumbling, punishing.

Smoke, trembling ... echoes.

The light was gone—the spectacular red-orange and crimson that Hunter had seen through closed eyes—to gray silence, a ringing stillness in deafened, superheated air. Clouds of black rolled from the tunnel.

Bobbi Jo, still holding her sniper rifle, didn't move. Suddenly concerned, Hunter bent over her, gently removing a lock of hair from her face. His voice was soft. "Hey ..."

Her lips trembled. "Jesus," she whispered. "Jesus ..."

Hunter smiled slowly, hand on her shoulder, before he looked over the slope of the bank, squinting into the burning smoke. The professor was far to the side, safe, and Takakura was lying atop him, covering the old man's body with his own. Wilkenson was on his back, clearly stunned, not recovering.

But Taylor was already on his feet, peering cautiously into the crevice, shotgun ready. Then he saw Hunter's concentrated frown and shook his head: nothing there.

Nodding, Hunter lifted Bobbi Jo to her knees and she raised a hand, slowly rubbing her eyes. "Oh ...man," she whispered, shaking her head. "That was ... way intense. I should have been a plumber ... or something."

Hunter laughed lightly. "Yeah. Or something."

Looking at the roiling blue-black cleft in the cliff, she added, "Did we get it?"

Hunter's smiled faded slowly. "I don't know. Would have been hard to survive. Maybe."

"Yeah?" She struggled to her feet and walked to the top of the slope, letting the Barrett hang on the sling. She stared into the passage a moment. "How could it have survived that?"

"I don't know," Hunter answered dully, glancing at Takakura, who now knelt like a boxer waiting out a count. The Japanese shook his head angrily.

Hunter continued, "It couldn't have escaped the explosion. It was too close. Almost on top of it. But it might heal up faster than we expect. It's already healed up from what we did to it last night. I could tell that much when I saw it."

"How close did you get to it?" Taylor asked.

"Too close." Hunter picked up his Bowie from where it had fallen, wiped the blade on his grime-smeared pants. He knew they needed to move soon. For the moment, he didn't feel his wounds much—a gift of the high levels of adrenaline coursing through him. Hunter knew this pain block was part of an involuntary survival mechanism and he couldn't consciously turn it on any more than he could shut it down. He also knew it wouldn't last more than an hour or two before he would be hobbling in agony. They had to get to the Blackhawk, and quickly.

"Can the professor be moved?" he asked Takakura.

"*Hai.*"

The stoic Japanese had gained his feet, sword held hard in his strong right hand. Then, casting a single glance at the cleft, he sheathed the awesome weapon without looking. "We have no choice. He will die if he does not receive medical attention."

Time to move.

Hunter lifted one end of the stretcher and Takakura the other, and with Taylor at point, they began moving forward. Bobbi Jo and Wilkenson were rear guard as they began their last walk through soundless black hills inhabited by the most terrible of all nightmares and fears.

He crawled, twisting and writhing on rotten leaves, coughing, gasping, dazed and breathless. He rolled down a short slope, found himself up against rock and water, his mind alive with fire and pain.

He remembered crawling on cold dirt, rising, falling, unable to cease moving because of the pain. He was blinded and he stumbled, roaring and striking in rage until he fell again, not to rise.

Now he lay in shadow, staring up without seeing until he remembered his strength. And with memory his hands closed, pain lancing his body as the claws touched boiled flesh. He screamed, and screamed again, twisting his head in rage and frustration before rolling to a knee and stumbling on, unable to remember ...what?

As the hours passed he sensed a lessening of the pain, as he had vaguely expected, and as he felt the lessening he remembered more and more, but his strength was insufficient. He stumbled over a root and rolled down the hill where he now lay, breathing heavily.

His deep-born animal mind told him to rest, to drink, to wait, and, with dark, to kill and eat and heal. So he lay silent, letting his body do what it was so magnificently designed to do. And within hours, he knew, he could rise to feast again, restoring his strength.

Then he would go back, and he would kill them.

He would kill them all.

***

It was ridiculously easy to enter the professor's town house. Chaney walked through it, impressed by the rich mahogany desk and bookshelves in the den, the living room's light-brown leather couches.

The kitchen and dining room were full of black-lacquered hardwood and stainless steel. Chaney thought that the professor may have spent too much time in the lab.

He found an extensive amount of health food, herbs, vitamins and a full array of prescription medicines on the kitchen shelves and in the refrigerator. He moved to the bedroom.

It was even more impressive than the den, with a huge oak four-poster bed covered with a dark blue spread. He walked over to the bed, opened a drawer in the nightstand. He found a book on nutrition, a flashlight and a gun.

Brow rising slightly, he picked it up; a Smith and Wesson .38-caliber revolver with a four-inch barrel. With his gloved hands Chaney opened the cylinder, found six hollow-point rounds. He put the gun back and looked around again. Then he searched the closet, found a number of dark suits, blue, black or gray. All expensively tailored.

In a corner of the closet he found some mountaineering gear. Well-used crampons, an ice ax, expensive Gore-Tex jackets, masks, a helmet, gloves, pants, boots—enough gear for a serious expedition in the Arctic.

Moving into the den again, he examined the bookshelves. He searched by sections: philosophy, classical literature, modern literature, history separated by epoch, anthropology, archaeology, a large selection of medical journals, catalogued indexes of medical periodicals, a smaller section comprising medical and foreign language dictionaries, and finally reference manuals and biographies.

Chaney perused the wall and occasionally opened a book to glance through it, but despite the range of interest apparent here, he found nothing on biological warfare, military research or its history. He was about to walk away when something caught his eye.

He saw the slightest sliver of yellow protruding from a magazine in a binder. He removed it from the shelf: North American Anthropology, June 1975.

Chaney opened it to the yellow bookmark and studied the pictures first. They revealed a creature classified as *Homotherium*.

The illustration featured a skeleton of this ferocious-looking beast that looked to be equal parts man and saber-toothed tiger. It was standing on hind legs, forelegs reaching down to its knees. Its fangs, incredibly long and deep-set in the skull, were viciously distended. Alongside the skeleton was a fleshed-out and rather spectacular portrait of what it might have looked like. It seemed exquisitely designed for fighting, for predation.

Chaney was impressed.

That's what guns are for, he mused.

He read the article slowly, wondering if it related to the case. He read the caption beneath the skeletal display: "This body of a Homotherium, one of the rarest of all prehistoric predators, was discovered on Alaska's North Slope in 1974 by an Idaho archaeological team. Remarkably preserved, it was discovered beneath the body of an early relative of Homo sapiens that scientists have so far failed to classify. Experts believe the second set of bones belongs to a distant cousin of Neanderthalis sapiens, which possibly migrated from Siberia to Alaska in 12,000 B.C. across islands in the Bering Strait."

Chaney looked again at the photo of the excavation. It was still clear and had lost little detail over the years. Then he glanced at the reconstructed model of the creature and back at the skeleton as it lay in the ground. Back and forth, he studied the two photos a long time. He couldn't find a photograph of the second skeleton that had been uncovered with the tiger-like beast.

"This thing was found beneath the body of a man?" he asked aloud. "What does that mean?"

He listened to the steady drone of traffic outside the town house, kept staring at the pictures, perused them all, read the article again. His mind kept coming back to the second skeleton, which wasn't mentioned anywhere but the caption. And then something caught his eye.

The skull.

Chaney turned the magazine in his hands, as if he could get a better angle. He couldn't. He moved it directly beneath the light, angling it so there wasn't any glare, and lowered his face only inches from the page. And he noticed something intriguing.

The entire skeleton of the Homotherium, almost complete and undisturbed, was intact. Only two ribs had been broken by the pressures of the glacier. But the skull had a deformed, strange indentation to it, and splintered cracks trailed down the temporal regions as if the head had exploded from the inside. It wasn't the kind of damage that would have been caused by crushing, Chaney knew enough about pathology to determine that.

No, this was different, as if the top of the creature's skull had been struck with a sledgehammer. Although the angle of the photo wasn't perfect for analysis, it appeared that there was a fist-sized hole in the crest of the skull.

He slowly closed the magazine, vaguely disturbed, and placed it back on the shelf. He knew he would find nothing more, and moved slowly for the door. A quick look confirmed a mostly empty street. He set the knob so he wouldn't have to risk another moment resetting the deadbolt, then went outside. He was down the steps and moving in five seconds, just another person out for the evening.

It was a mystery to him, this beast and whatever had so ferociously crushed its skull. And why Hamilton had, of all his periodicals, marked that particular one. Or kept it since 1975.

But a mystery was better than nothing at all.

Remaining carefully aware of everything around him, Chaney stepped cautiously outside.

***

With Wilkenson guiding them via radio, the Blackhawk finally swept in over the trees slightly after dusk. Hunter had built a huge bonfire, burning logs to light up a space the size of an amphitheater, and the four-rotor chopper had no trouble landing.

Hunter turned away, watching the trail behind them as the professor was carefully loaded onto the chopper. Then Takakura was bellowing at him.

"Hunter! We go! We go! Come on!"

Hunter turned and loped toward the rest who were gathered at one of the open doors. As he reached it he grabbed Bobbi Jo's shoulder and pushed her ahead. Ghost was at his side as he leaped into the bay and one of the crew gave thumbs-up to the pilot.

They rose above trees, shifting slightly as they entered blue sky and stars and black claimed the trees beneath. As they reached altitude, Hunter released a breath but revealed no physical sign of relief as they gained speed, angling higher and higher, heading south.

One of the crew, obviously a trained medic, was administering an IV to the professor, injecting something into the tube. Hunter watched for a moment and then nodded, bowing his head. Then he reached out to ruffle Ghost's mane. But the black wolf only looked tiredly at him, and Hunter knew that Ghost, like all of them, needed food and rest.

As they left the valley behind, Hunter gazed back somberly. Still, he could not believe it: It had spoke to him ...

It had *spoke* to him ...

CHAPTER 15

Chaney had parked his car a few blocks away, near a corner. As he walked toward it, he kept wondering what in the hell that article had to do with anything. He knew it was important but it didn't make any sense. Whatever beast was captured in those pictures was long dead. But clearly it meant something to the good doctor. Maybe it would mean something to Gina.

A couple, arm in arm, passed him.

Chaney nodded, hands in pockets, and continued strolling. He passed a group of older guys playing basketball, engaged in trash talk. He laughed, remembering the days.

The city was slowly coming alive with those who tended to wake up at night, like vampires. Already, in the few minutes he'd been walking, it had grown more congested. Not bustling by any means, but not as dead as it had been in late afternoon.

Two guys off to the side were doing what appeared to be a drug deal. Chaney glanced at them, grunted, let it go.

The pieces were beginning to fit together—the creature, the killing team, the betrayal. The one thing that didn't fit was the death of Rebecca Tanus. She had discovered something important about this creature's genetic structure. But what would be so important about DNA that it would justify murder? He just couldn't understand a professional hit that—

Shadow—

Something happening—

React!

Chaney went for his gun without seeing an enemy and sensed what was coming a second before it hit. He knew what it was by feel, by the glimpse of gray and steel beyond his head. A pipe. He went down—arm dead—and they were on him but his arm wouldn't work and the Sig .45—a black matte weapon useless on cement—was at his feet as he rolled to avoid a second blow.

The pipe, crashing down beside his ear in the hands of a huge black man, sent fragments of cement across his face and Chaney kicked up, trying for the groin. But the man was an experienced fighter and blocked the kick with his thigh as the second man swung another pipe, glancing the steel off Chaney's cheek before it crashed across his chest, doubling him in breathless shock.

For a moment Chaney knew nothing, no breath, not even pain, though he knew he was hurt bad, and then the bigger one grabbed his shirt, Lifting him half from the ground as he stretched his arm back, pipe tight in a square fist.

Chaney didn't have time to be afraid of the glaring eyes and the rage. At the moment the swing began he withdrew the concealed .38 from his ankle and, like a boxer throwing an uppercut, brought it up under the man's chin and fired. At the shot the second man jumped back and Chaney swung fast, still breathless, targeting. The attacker leaped and ran.

"Don't!" Chaney shouted.

The man ran faster and Chaney took careful aim with the last of his control, pulled the trigger. It hit dead-center in the spine and for a suspended slow-motion moment the man was bowed in the air, arms outstretched to nothing before he landed on his feet, took another step, staggering, and fell to the sidewalk facedown.

For a second Chaney lay back, pulling, pulling for breath, and finally caught one, paying for it with a sharp pain in his ribs. Struggling, he rolled to his side, then crawled to his knees, breathing slowly, painfully, trying to concentrate.

He crept over the dead black man and reclaimed his Sig, put it back in his hip holster. But he held the revolver as he rose—he didn't know why—and walked to his car. He didn't notice that the basketball court was empty or that the streets had suddenly become deserted as he fired the engine and pulled away.

He couldn't wait for police, couldn't go to a hospital, couldn't make himself visible or vulnerable again. They had anticipated this move, he suddenly realized, holding a hand across his chest, sweating and trembling.

He groaned as he turned a corner, and knew he'd be caught if police spotted the car because he wasn't in condition to out-drive anyone. He had to ditch it, but he was too injured to steal another one. His mind raced, searching for ...

He saw a familiar street sign and hung a sharp left, praying that nothing was coming, but he had to move fast because he could feel something coming on, something that would put him out. He knew he was only awake because of shock and fear and adrenaline, but that would wear off quickly enough and he would crash hard. He had to reach a safe house, a place where he could hide.

Fighting fiercely to stay conscious, he drove toward Brick's.

***

Gina Gilbert, hair stringy and plastered with sweat from working nonstop for the last forty-eight hours, stared at the electron microscope monitor. The screen was littered with the strands of the DNA sample that she was working her way through.

As she identified even the most basic characteristics, like eye color or pigmentation, she would move on, searching for something unusual. She knew, in general, what she was searching for, but it was difficult to discern.

What she sensed was that this seemingly endless DNA strand contained something that would reveal the secret of this creature's identity. She didn't know what it would be, but she was certain she would recognize it when she saw it. She turned a large black dial and the screen flickered, revealing another molecule.

Empty boxes of Chinese and Italian food—take-outs—littered the table behind her. She folded her arms across her chest and watched, studying the movement, counting the electrons and calculating their molecular weight.

It was something unknown—part of the alien DNA. She leaned forward again and studied the strands, and saw that it had enhanced transmitters, or reflectors, that sped the production of proteins.

She smiled.

"So," she whispered, "now I got you."

It took another hour to analyze the proteins. She compared them to those from a gorilla, a tiger, and finally from Homo sapiens. But she found no corresponding genetic formation. Then she went back to the readout and repeated the entire procedure step by step, counting the molecules, verifying the enhancers that connected the molecule to the more familiar human DNA. And again, the results were the same.

There was an unknown protein—some kind of powerful mind-influencing chemical—generated from the strand segment. She knew it would take hours and hours to discover what protein or enzyme was being generated, what effect it had upon the creature, and what secrets it might provide to the beast's identity. But that didn't bother her. She had all night. She felt a wave of sadness at the thought, remembering . . .

Rebecca had no time at all.

"God Almighty!" Brick shouted as Chaney, bloodied and sweating, collapsed through the back door.

Brick, who had answered the door eating a meatloaf sandwich, pulled Chaney into the kitchen and rolled him over. Even before he examined Chaney to determine his injury, Brick tore the Sig from Chaney's hip holster and leveled it at the open door. Enraged, the big ex-marshal searched left and right, gun leading and all the slack taken from the trigger, but he saw nothing.

Turning on the floodlights, he shut the door hard, threw the deadbolt, and bent, feeling over Chaney's chest.

Groaning, Chaney coughed, spoke with difficulty. "They ... after the search ... they were waiting."

Brick muttered a stream of obscenities, lifting Chaney by the arm. He held the Sig in his free hand as they stumbled across the kitchen. "Good thing Edna's out of town this weekend," he muttered. "She'd be going nuts seeing you like this. Come on, let's get you down into the basement. Don't you worry 'bout nothin', kid. I got ya and I got what ya need. Yeah, ol' Brick's gonna fix his boy up."

Together they stumbled down the stairs and Brick laid him on a cot. Then he unfolded a large green Special Forces emergency surgical kit. He tore open a packet with his teeth, gave Chaney two blue pills and water, then felt his chest.

"You got some hematoma there in the ribs, boy," he grunted. "Somebody whacked you good with a bat, or pipe. Can't tell. Doesn't matter. You're hurt."

"A pipe. Two of them. They're dead."

"I ain't sheddin' no tears," Brick said as he helped Chaney out of his coat and shirt.

Chaney sank back and Brick gently felt the ribs. "Man, you got some swelling here, kinda high. Probably just cracked 'cause I don't feel no break. Hurts bad enough, though. Cracked hurts as bad as broke, no lie." Quickly he felt Chaney's neck and shoulder. "You got some bleeding, here," he added. "I'll fix that up."

"You got the house locked up?"

"Always."

In short order, Brick cleaned and bandaged Chaney's shoulder and face. It was an efficient, professional job and Brick's hands moved with surprising tenderness. Finally Chaney felt the painkillers kicking in, the pain fading so softly he could barely feel it diminishing. But it was leaving, and it made him feel stronger. Still, he knew it was a deception; he wasn't stronger, so he didn't move.

His breath was regular, measured, and he tried to replay the scene in his mind, cursing himself for his carelessness. He had been so distracted by his theories and discovery that he had failed to remember the elemental rule of a hitter: they almost always waited for you to come to them, and he had walked right into it.

"Stupid," he muttered to himself.

"Did you recognize either of them?"

"No."

"Sure you got 'em?"

"Yeah." Chaney rubbed his bandaged face. "I got 'em."

"Good," Brick muttered, removing a syringe from his case. He inserted the needle into a small vial of Lidocaine. Then he removed it and inserted the needle under Chaney's arm. With the painkillers, Chaney hardly felt the sting. Closing his eyes, he floated on the drugs and the fatigue from the fight.

He felt like his mind was returning from panic and stress overload.

"A little something to kill your side while I sew up this gash." Brick removed a curved needle with black thread dangling from it. In his other hand he held forceps. Then, deftly and without hesitation, he began an efficient, circular movement with the forceps as he inserted the needle in Chaney's side and withdrew it, tying a quick knot every two seconds. In less than thirty seconds it was over and Brick snipped off the thread, laying the instruments to the side.

Brick nudged him until he opened his eyes. "You're gonna be all right, kid. You got a couple burst blood vessels in the skin, some bruised or cracked ribs, and a three-inch cut in your side that I stitched up. But you came out pretty good, considering."

Chaney didn't say anything, closing his eyes again, as Brick rose and^ walked swiftly to the vault. In seconds he had opened the gigantic steel door and walked inside.

He heard Brick moving equipment, shuffling, then the familiar sound of a rifle chambered. Almost instantly Brick emerged carrying an AK-47, a large thirty-round clip inserted in the port. Three more full magazines were in his hand, and a Colt 1911 .45-caliber semiautomatic pistol was stuck in his belt, pressing against his gut. He came straight to Chaney and bent.

"You're safe down here," he grunted, a bit breathless. "Ain't but one way in or out. I'll be upstairs watching for 'em. Get some sleep. We can talk in the morning."

Chaney attempted to rise. "My gun ..."

"Right beside you." Brick gestured. "Right here. But don't reach for it unless you hear shooting upstairs. Those are morphine tablets I gave you. Pretty strong ones, too. I don't want you holding that Sig while you're high unless you have to. But if things get that bad, if they get past me, then there ain't no wrong you can do. Just shoot whatever comes down the stairs and keep shooting 'til you're empty. You still got the clips on your belt. Understand what I'm saying? If they get past me, it's Dodge City as far as I'm concerned."

Nodding with the last of his control and strength, Chaney closed his eyes. "Yeah, Brick, I got it. I ..." He felt sleep coming over him, soft and comforting. "I got it."

Without another word Brick rose and Chaney heard him hurrying up the stairs. Somewhere, far off, he heard a series of thumps, Brick running across the ceiling above him, and knew the old marshal was making certain that the house was completely secure. Chaney glanced to the side, made sure the Sig was within reach, and as he passed into unconsciousness he suddenly remembered Gina Gilbert, and knew she would be next ...

He began to rise, to warn her.

Collapsed back.

***

Despite his exhaustion, Hunter felt himself stiffen as the Blackhawk swept in over the last knoll separating a windswept field from the surrounding forest. And as he sighted the facility from high, he knew instantly that this one was not like the rest.

White cement walls enclosed a four-acre facility that vaguely resembled a squared fortress. The roof was a forest of antennas and satellite dishes and wiring and cooling equipment—an impressive piece of architecture for the middle of nowhere. He noticed at least a hundred fifty-five-gallon drums, perhaps holding coolant, to the side of the building beside a wide set of double steel doors, and three enormous ten-thousand-gallon fuel tanks beside the back fence.

There were no windows; only large steel doors guarded by two sentries with M-16's at port arms. He scanned the brightly illuminated compound further and saw light transport vehicles and at least fifty military personnel. He estimated there would be at least a third more inside.

The chopper set down on a pad and a team of EMTs met them, instantly entering the bay as the team members slipped out. In seconds they had loaded Professor Tipler on a gurney and were rolling him into the complex, already checking his vitals.

Though he was almost too weak to stand, Hunter refused to show fatigue or weakness. He frowned as he saw Maddox approaching. "What about the rest of the team?" Maddox asked, incredulous.

Takakura's tone was not friendly.

"Dead," he said simply.

Maddox paused. His shock was apparent as his eyes moved from Hunter to Takakura, then to the rest of the team. "All of them?"

Takakura walked past him without reply.

As the rest fell in silently behind Takakura, Hunter waited. Then he walked over to Maddox, staring into his eyes.

"I'm gonna talk to you in the morning," Hunter said menacingly.

Maddox glanced down at Ghost. The wolf was fixed on him with mesmerizing intensity. "Of course," he managed. "This is

... *Good Lord*! ... A great tragedy!" He managed to recover. "But then not as bad as I feared. When we failed to make contact with you, I had assumed you were all casualties. At least some of you have survived." He looked at Hunter. "And the creature?"

"We don't know."

Maddox glanced toward the fence. "I see."

Closing on him slightly, Hunter whispered, "Let me tell you something, Maddox. You see those men at the fence?"

"Certainly, yes."

"Well, get them inside that fence and close that gate. Pump up the voltage as high as it'll go and break out every dog you've got. Keep 'em moving night and day. And take your men off those M-16's and put 'em on whatever elephant guns you've got. You have some M-60's around here?"

"We have two positioned on the roof."

"Put all of 'em up there. As many as you got. Snipers, too. 'Cause I think that that bastard is comin' this way and right now you've got nothing that can stop it. It's gonna hit that fence at a dead run, take the charge, and tear its way through. Or it's gonna just leap clean over it."

Maddox was incredulous. "That's a twelve-foot electrical fence, Hunter."

"Maddox," Hunter growled, "that thing could leap that fence with you in its teeth. Do as I say and you and your men might live."

"You are certain of this?"

Bending over him, Hunter stared him hard in the eye.

Maddox recoiled and nodded. "I'll follow your ... advice."

Feeling exhaustion claiming him, Hunter walked toward the infirmary. Ghost fell in beside him.

Maddox called after him, "You probably know this creature better than anyone!"

Luther, Hunter thought.

"You could say that," he said.

***

Dr. Arthur Hamilton, bent in concentration over a microscope, raised his head as a white-shirted lab technician approached.

Neither friendly nor indulgent, the doctor's tone indicated that he wished not to be disturbed.

"What is it?" he murmured.

"They're here, Doctor."

Hamilton absorbed it with the greatest calm.

"I see," he answered. "Very well. I will deal with them when they are rested and fed." His demeanor was that used when dealing with animals. "See to it that they are airlifted on the first helicopter returning to the air-base. Their mission is officially over."

"Sir, they're pretty badly beaten up," the technician said, with a hint of fear. "I don't think they're in condition for flight just now. And they seem ...well, angry. The old man, the professor, he's just regaining consciousness. His heart—"

"Yes, yes, I'm certain they had a difficult time." Hamilton rose up straighter on his chair. "But nevertheless, their job here is done. This afternoon the NSA, which retains full authority and command, issued the ruling. Therefore they have no further authorization to remain on the base. In the morning, when they are prepared, I want all of them transferred." He did not blink. "Do you understand?"

"Yes, sir. I understand."

"Good. Now, if you please ..."

He bent over the microscope.

The technician turned without a word and walked out of the laboratory. As he vanished, Dr. Strait, having witnessed the conversation, approached and stood in silence.

"Yes, Emma?" he said, still intent over the microscope.

"We have it," she said.

Her voice was oddly cautious.

Hamilton raised his face, a flush rising in his cheeks. His mouth was open a moment as he stared at her. "You have isolated the gene which allows the immunity, the longevity, and separated it from the transmitters which promote cellular domination and absorption?"

She nodded faintly. "Yes."

Hamilton was instantly on his feet as she handed him a printout. Then he scanned the pages, flipping them rapidly, reading just as rapidly until, finally, he lowered the pages to his side and raised a fist before his eyes. He slowly turned, staring at the ancient man suspended in the electromagnetic matrix, and he smiled.

"At last," he whispered. "To be ... immortal."

Silently he gazed. Finally he turned back. "How long before we can isolate the genomes and prepare buffers for human DNA?"

"Perhaps by tomorrow night. But we'll need ... human test subjects. We'll need to be sure that the serum doesn't kill outright or cause another severe mutation."

Hamilton's face froze. "Test subjects," he said softly, lifting his eyes to the ceiling.

Above them was the first subbasement, filled with equipment. And above that, the ground floor: the commissary, the barracks and offices.

And the infirmary.

A grim frown became a satisfied smile.

"I believe I know just where to find them," he said.

Hunter was so exhausted that he had trouble thinking coherently. His entire body felt like a mass of contusions, strains, sprains, and twisted joints.

He had been hurt and exhausted before, but rarely anything like this. He revolved his head, moving it slowly, but it didn't do anything except cause him more pain and make him worry that he had somehow permanently crippled himself. He figured that he'd know soon enough; they were all being examined by the medical team.

Tipler was in ICU on an IV and a number of medications. He was still unconscious but Hunter knew the old man stood a much better chance here than in the mountains. He wasn't as worried as he had been, even feeling some sense of relief that they had been given a brief respite from the ordeal.

He would finish this hunt, but he would be better armed on the next expedition. What weapons he would carry had dominated most of his thinking since they had landed, but he hadn't decided. There was time for that later.

A doctor removed the blood-pressure cuff and listened to Hunter's heart. Very military looking with short-cut black hair and a smooth-shaven face, the physician was in his early thirties. He spoke precisely and confidently: "You have the innate constitution of an ox, Mr. Hunter. Your heartbeat is strong, your blood pressure is perfect, and your pulse is close to normal. You are extremely fit. Perhaps the strongest man I've ever examined. But you're also badly traumatized and dehydrated. Even for someone as strong as you, your body is on the verge of collapse."

He took some time examining the sharp incisions on Hunter's chest. "Hmm, that one's deep," he said. "What did this? A bear? I've never seen a bone scar like this."

"Something like that," Hunter mumbled, rubbing his head. "A bit more hostile."

The physician raised his eyes at the enigmatic remark, turned to the table. "Well, there's no infection. Your medic did a good job cleaning out the wound. So I've given you a tetanus shot and something to stave off any alternate infections. And it wouldn't hurt to have a couple of stitches. It's swollen, but not yet healing."

"Go ahead. I'm not going anywhere."

He performed the antibiotic injections easily and quickly, then prepped a needle with Lidocaine.

"Forget the painkiller," Hunter remarked absently. "Just stitch it up. I can find what I need later, if it hurts that much."

The physician stared at him. "Are you sure you don't want something for the sewing? This will not be pleasant."

"Most things aren't. Just sew it up."

A slight moment of hesitation, and the physician made an expression of "whatever you say" and began. Hunter felt the prick, the needle drawn through flesh, and the stinging of the thread as it was quickly tied off and cut. After five minutes it was over and the doctor dropped the needle and unused silk into a trashcan.

"Took twelve in your chest," he said. "You were lucky it wasn't an inch higher. It could have severed an artery." He wrinkled his brow. "I'd say you were lucky on that one. Lucky or good. Doesn't make much difference. You'll be fine in a few days but I'll need to see you in the morning. Same as all your friends."

Hunter nodded and looked around, wondering how long it'd been since he was in an emergency room; figured it was three years ago when he broke three ribs in a fall. It was a quick trip, in and out, and he had gone back to the search.

Hampered by the pain and lack of mobility, he had nevertheless eventually found the lost party, a hunter who had become lost in a January cold. When Hunter finally found his dead body, he saw that the man still had a backpack of food, a fully loaded rifle, and enough ammunition for a week. A tragedy.

The man had possessed everything he needed to weather out a week in the cold. But he had panicked and, eventually, after burning up precious energy stumbling blindly through the woods, had simply sat down and fallen asleep in the sub-zero temperature.

Hunter had seen it on many occasions—strong men who could have survived for weeks if they had used their tools and remained calm. Yet upon fearing that they were lost, they committed themselves to a senseless stampede that left them too exhausted and shocked to do the very few simple things that would have preserved their lives in even the harshest conditions.

Thoughts like that often gave Hunter pause because he sometimes forgot—so native were his skills to him—that some people simply had no concept of wilderness survival.

Hunter rarely measured his skills against anyone; it was not in his nature to compare himself at all. But in rare moments he appreciated the skills that allowed him, with nothing but his knife, to survive anywhere for weeks or months or years.

Part of it was skill and knowledge, and part of it was years of conditioning, but there was more—a certain hardiness of spirit or soul that reinforced his will in times of physical suffering or fear. It was that part of himself that didn't rely upon intelligence or mind for strength or direction—an ability to allow his lower mind to compensate for whatever his higher mind could not provide, carrying him past the point where most would surrender to pain or cold or hunger and, quite simply, die.

He had seen the phenomenon at work within himself before, and knew that he had the ability to live almost as an animal—hunting, tracking, and killing with that ferocious mind-set of surviving no matter the amount of physical and mental suffering he must endure. It was a certain purity of being—a surrendering to the most basic animal instinct and force of will—and he could turn it on or off, almost like a light switch.

The drawback was, quite simply, that when he gave himself to it he also gave himself to an utterly cold ruthlessness that could be somewhat unsettling.

It made him remember what the creature ... what Luther ... had spoken of. And he knew that, despite the lies surrounding what the beast had said, there was a grain of truth to it.

Deep inside the heart of man, there did lay a great darkness. Something to be feared even by man himself. It was the place where darkness reigned. Where killing was no more emotional than eating. Where a man could submerge his soul in the blackest sin and feel no guilt at all. Where life was nothing more than the satisfaction of what he desired, and the fulfillment of that desire. It was a place where ruthless strength fed dark desires—the heart of the beast.

Now the dark heart of man had been given indestructible, superhuman form, and was loose in mankind. And Hunter knew he would have to kill it.

And to kill it, he feared he'd have to become it, to release that darkness inside himself.

Hunter didn't want to think about it. When the time came, he knew what he would become. He just hoped it wouldn't be so difficult for him to shut it down when, and if, he destroyed it.

He did know that if he gave himself to the animal within, he would have to be alone. Because no one could keep up with him if he went into it. He would move with astonishing speed, easily covering fifty miles in a day and killing as he moved, eating the meat raw and still moving, killing again, hunting, always hunting—the animal within him selecting the most perilous and difficult of paths as his gray eyes read the faintest faded track.

Athletically, he would be a human tiger—-jumping, running for hours, or descending from boulder to boulder in sinuous leaps that never seemed to pause as he hit one granite slab only to descend terrifically to another before he struck the ground to continue running.

Until now, he had been holding back because they couldn't have remained at his side if he had traveled with even half of his true ability. But the time had come to unleash a little of his true strength, and they would have to remain behind unless they were ready to follow in a helicopter.

He glanced up to see Ghost lying atop a heavy stack of blankets. Violating regulations, the medical personnel had wisely decided it was more prudent to allow the wolf a quiet corner in the ICU than a space in the hallway.

From Ghost's quick notice of the faintest sound or movement, it was clear that he remained alert. His ears stood straight, quick to catch the faintest rustle of cloth, and his obsidian eyes carefully followed the actions of everyone in the room.

Bobbi Jo emerged barefoot from an isolated trauma room wearing a dark-blue surgical shirt and pants. Her hair was stringy and matted, and she rubbed her eyes sleepily as she walked slowly to Hunter. He watched with a faint smile as she sat down beside him on the table. Gently, she reached over and touched the stitches in his chest.

She laughed. "A good job. Tidy. I guess you'll have to add those to your list."

Hunter laughed with her. "I don't keep track anymore. Gave up on it a long time ago. Ran out of fingers and toes."

"Oh, come on, Hunter." She smiled. "Even though you've been frozen, starved, cut, smashed, knocked off cliffs, mauled by wild animals, and sewn back together with all your body parts in the wrong place, you've still got a few good years left. I asked the doc and he showed me your warranty card."

He found himself laughing—rare for him—and glad she was so close. After a moment of enjoying her presence, he asked, "So, what'd they tell you? You come out of it in pretty good shape?"

"Oh, I'm kinda beat up." She shrugged. "They told me I'm dehydrated. I've got a torn muscle in my shoulder. But it's not a rotator cuff, so it won't need surgery. Then, oh, I've got a mild concussion and I've lost twenty percent of the hearing in my right ear. They say it's probably only temporary. Got a ton of contusions, too many to count, and about three bruised ribs." She smiled and winked. "But they gave me some great painkillers." A pause. "Then my right shoulder has a bad bone bruise from not having the Barrett set tight enough on that shot beside the creek. But other than that, I'm just fine and dandy."

Laughing, Hunter shook his head. "Yeah, seems like you came out all right. What about the professor?"

"I don't know." She shook her head. "They told me he's not in a coma, but he's unconscious. I guess we'll know by tomorrow. They say he can't be moved."

"No," Hunter rumbled, "I'm sure of that. And I ain't leaving, either, 'til he can be moved. I guess the rest of them are all right."

"Oh, yeah. Taylor is already gone. Said he was hungry. Wilkenson is still in there, they're working on some bruises. He got a flash burn from the explosion in the cave. And Takakura ... well, you know Takakura. He's the curse of doctors everywhere."

With a smile, Hunter said, "Yeah, he's tough. He'll be okay. Guess all we do now is sit and heal up a little. Get some rest."

Silent, she stared at him intently.

"You're going after it, aren't you?" she asked finally.

He said nothing.

She shook her head. "Don't do it, Hunter. Just let it be. I know how you feel. I feel the same. But if you go out there, alone, it will kill you. And you know that."

"Maybe," he replied, stoic. "Maybe not. But if it's not stopped, it's gonna keep on killing. And who's next? Some old woman? Some kid? A village?" He stared at her. "You know it's not gonna stop. Not ever. It's gonna kill until someone stops it."

""It doesn't have to be you."

"So who's it gonna be?" Hunter held the moment with his conviction. "You? You know you can't track it. Not like I can. The army? They've already tried. So who's left?" The silence lasted. "There's nobody, darlin'. Nobody but me."

She didn't say anything, staring into space. Then: "You won't come back."

It was said with a professional warrior's objectivity, but there was an imploring look on her face.

Hunter grunted. He slowly lifted a hand and flexed it, testing its strength. He was hurt bad, but he could continue. Yet he somehow felt that he'd lost something of himself in this hunt—he had had some deep, untapped reserve of endurance or ultimate physical might that, once spent, might be gone forever. Some challenges took away a measure of what you were, and the body could never replenish it.

"Probably," he replied finally. "But I don't have a choice. If I walk away from this ...life won't be anything but regrets and ghosts and guilt."

Watching him steadily, she said, "And you couldn't live like that."

"Couldn't be called living," he grunted. Then he shrugged. "Seems like it's always like this. Seems like there's always someone who can do some ... special thing. They have a skill. A talent. And they find themselves in a place where this ability is needed. And something deep down tells you what you have to do. That you were meant to be here, to do what has to be done." He shook his head. "Like I said, an old story. But true, I think."

She didn't blink. "I understand," she said at last. "And, I thought I'd let you know, I'm going with you."

"No, you're definitely not coming with me."

"Why not? This is still a military operation."

"Not for me." Hunter rose, loosening a shoulder. "I'm done with the military. They're lying to you. To me. To everybody. They always were."

"Think I can't keep up with you?" she asked.

He smiled lightly, touched her cheek softly. "No offense."

A pause.

"You're not gonna hold back this time, are you? You're not gonna let us catch up to you?"

"It's the only way," he said softly, gazing out the window at the spot-lit night of the compound. "I have to run it to ground."

"And when you do? What are you gonna do when you corner it or it corners you? Just the two of you alone in those mountains? How are you gonna kill what can't be killed?"

"Anything can be killed," he said, sullen, and his face darkened as his suddenly cold blue eyes seemed to behold something beyond the compound. "Anything."

CHAPTER 16

Brick came down the stairs in a rush, the AK-47 slung around a bull shoulder, barrel bouncing on his hip. He walked wordlessly into the vault and came out with three hand grenades hung on his belt. He held a large starlight scope—a night-vision device for the rifle.

He glanced at Chaney, who now sat upright on the bed, testing his arms for injury. Chaney eyed him and knew, from the old days, that Brick was ready to deal out some serious hurting.

He asked, "Anything out there?"

"Not that I can see, kid." Brick adjusted the night-vision scope and mounted it carefully on the AK with a small screwdriver. "But I can't see so good in the dark. They could be laid up in the shadows." He took a moment, adjusting carefully. "Good thing I picked up one of these starlight scopes at the last gun-and-knife show. Figured it'd come in handy one day. Better to have it and not need it than to need it and not have it."

Chaney lowered his legs over the edge of the bed, rubbed his head. "Thank God for morphine," he mumbled. "Listen, I've got to make a phone call. Where's the horn?"

"Upstairs," Brick grunted. "But I don't think you're in shape for walking."

"I better be." Chaney rose with the words. "I've got to get in touch with a girl at the Tipler Institute. She's in danger." He picked up the Sig, moved the slide enough to ensure it was chambered, checked the .38 on his left ankle, and slid it back into the concealed holster. Mechanically, he moved the Sig to his left hand.

The semiautomatic pistol didn't have a safety, all it needed was four pounds of pressure on the double-action trigger to fire. He had fifteen rounds to a clip, and two backup magazines. Strange, but before tonight he always figured forty-five 9-mm rounds to be sufficient for any gun-fight. Now he knew they weren't.

"Come on, then." Brick held him by an arm, moving to the stairs. If you gotta go, let's get upstairs."

* * *

Hunter awoke as a hand touched the doorknob to his room, but he didn't move. Only his eyes, gleaming in the dark, shifted as he watched the darkened portal.

They had all retired to quarters, Bobbi Jo in a room next to his, the professor still in the ICU. Takakura was across the hall and Taylor was also in the wing. Wilkenson was down the corridor, near the exit. And for the longest silent period, nothing happened. Then the door opened, just a crack, and a sliver of light cascaded through the gloom.

Without making a sound, Hunter found the Bowie knife and, even though the move almost made him groan in agony, lowered himself into a crouch beside the bed. He didn't look but knew Ghost was also crouching, poised to attack. He waited and a shadow slowly, almost tentatively, entered and stood motionless.

Bobbi Jo's silhouette stood in the narrow portal.

For the first time. Hunter saw Bobbi Jo the woman, instead of the warrior. Her hair was loose, and she wore blue jeans and a white T-shirt. Silhouetted against the light, she was more beautiful than any woman Hunter had ever known. She didn't say a word and didn't move, only stared at him.

Hunter laid the Bowie on the table. Then he walked forward, stopping close in front of her. He reached out to touch her cheek softly, and at that movement she reached up, grasping his wrist, leaning her head slightly into his hand, closing her eyes.

He gazed silently at her.

Her eyes opened and stared into his.

"At least we have tonight," she whispered.

Hunter paused, then reached out and lifted her from the floor. He closed the door softly and carried her slowly across the room to the bed.

* * *

Dr. Hamilton, tirelessly overseeing every aspect of the isotonic distillation of the serum, studied the technicians who were preparing the first twenty cc's. Drop by drop, the serum fell into a glass vial that slowly began to fill. The processing had progressed slowly, but after three hours there was almost enough for the initial test.

Emma was beside him, holding her ubiquitous clipboard. "After we do the electron scan and cross-check it with the receptor and transmitter genes and insure that there's no reopening or cyclization, we can proceed."

"Yes," he said thoughtfully. "You have ensured that the linear itrons are still intact?"

"Yes, sir." She nodded. "It's four hundred and fourteen nucleotides long. The same as before. But we've removed transgressors and progresses to stop the mutated cyclization rate. Now, when the molecule splits off a fourteen-nucleotide share, the split will multiply no faster than human DNA. The RNA is no longer self-replicating and tetrahymena has been molecularly spliced to normal human DNA to neutralize any mutation splicing. So basically there will be no rate of mutation at all. No way for it to overtake the human system. And yet it still contains the RNA itrons and RNA-related proteins that provide the healing and longevity factors." She paused. "I believe we've arrived, Doctor."

"Good." He seemed pleased. "Then it is time for our first laboratory test."

"Doctor, I know what... what is at stake. But we have already had one catastrophe already. Do you truly think that it's wise to risk the same dangerous results without the necessary precautions in place? I mean, shouldn't we isolate the subject somewhere?"

Hamilton smiled, his native charm and confidence awesomely displayed. "Emma, Emma," he answered, "there can never be surety of results. That is why we use test subjects. Now, granted, this is an unusual scenario. And because it is an unusual situation, it requires creative thinking. Surely you don't expect us to quantify results with mammals that have less than ninety-nine percent mutual strands with Homo sapiens, which leaves us with man. Now, should the test be a success, no harm will have been done. And should it fail, then we will know more precisely how to alter the serum to achieve our goal."

"I'm speaking about the danger of another monstrous mutation, Doctor." She seemed firm. "I'm speaking about Luther."

He laughed. "Now, surely you don't expect me to proceed without safeguards. Every contingency has been considered, every measure put in place to ensure the safety of both our team and the facility. These measures have not escaped me. Do not trouble yourself."

Emma glanced back at the lab personnel. "I'm saying this, Doctor, because some of the lab techs are terrified. I'm worried that their work will suffer, that we'll make a mistake in the isolation process. You have to remember, Doctor, they've been working almost nonstop in an attempt to compensate for the data lost at the other facilities. They're tired and frightened and I fear they're going to make mistakes."

"That's the reason that I am personally overseeing every aspect of the distillation process," Dr. Hamilton said, nodding sagely. "By noon tomorrow, we will have the first experimental serum, and the day after that, we will know if our efforts to synthesize this gene have been successful."

Emma didn't move. "And if this serum causes another monstrous transformation? Like the last?"

"As I said"—Hamilton turned back to his work—"those contingencies have been addressed. If there is a transformation even slightly similar to the initial reaction, we will be quite capable of killing it and performing an immediate autopsy to study the electro-molecular phenomenon." He shook his head, as if dealing with a disturbed child. "Emma, trust me. No one else shall be injured, except the initial test subjects. And then, when we have perfected the serum, there will be many who will be greatly aided."

Silent, she stared at him.

"Just imagine it, Emma," he continued. "Imagine what miracles reside within that blood. The complete cure for every disease known to man. All the flivo viruses, utterly incurable until now, will fall one by one. The devastation of HIV shall be no more. None of the great killers, from anthrax to Marburg, will be able to overcome the unconquerable strength of this immunity factor. And, finally, with the endless regeneration of cellular structure, we will live for hundreds, possibly thousands of years. For all practical purposes, Emma, we will be immortal.

"Do you understand what I mean, Emma?" he finished, unmoving.

Emma Strait found herself nodding. "Of course, Doctor. I just ... I just thought I'd make you aware of a few things. I didn't mean that we should postpone the tests."

"Of course you didn't," Hamilton replied, more distant. "And now ..." He turned back to the microscope. "I must verify that these serum samples have not developed mutations which would allow the extraordinary transmission of qualities that destroyed our expendable Luther—these base animal faculties that transformed him into a creature which ... we may yet be able to use."

***

Chaney received no answer at the Tipler Institute, and set the phone down. This was bad. But who could he call? The police? Hardly. His own people? Even more dangerous.

No, he had to avoid all government or official lines of communication. No matter how he handled it, he had to do it alone. He put on his coat, groaning. The stitches were in tight; Brick had done a good job. But the morphine was wearing off and he was feeling a multitude of sore muscles and contusions that he had been mercifully spared until now. Brick saw him moving, spoke from his position beside a window.

"Where in the hell do you think you're going?" he rumbled.

"I have to reach this girl," Chaney replied, trying to conceal the pain. "If she's not dead already, she will be. These people are thorough."

"You ain't in shape for it."

"Doesn't matter. I gotta go."

Brick bowed his head for a moment. His chest expanded as he took a deep breath and lifted the AK from the wall. "I don't like this at all," he said. "First, you get waylaid. Now you're going out in the middle of the night to find some woman who's on a hit list. You're busted up. I'm old and slow and out of shape. We don't know who these goons are, how many of 'em are out there, or what they're willing to do."

"They're willing to kill us." Chaney put the Sig in his hip holster. "That's all we need to know."

"Wait a second." Brick disappeared down the stairs. In five minutes he emerged in different clothes. Now he was wearing brown pants and a heavy shirt, and Chaney could tell he had put on a ballistic vest underneath. He also wore a thigh-length coat, and when the flap opened Chaney saw two Uzi submachine guns on dual shoulder holsters. The remarkably compact weapons hung on carefully designed hooks that allowed Brick a fast release.

"Now we're ready, boys!" Brick shouted. "Let me get us a car."

Chaney figured the retired marshal was carrying enough firepower for two or even three gunfights because Brick had only one rule: "It's better to have 'em and not need 'em than to need 'em and not have 'em. Just remember: ammo is cheap, your life ain't."

Brick fired up a Lincoln that was still mostly intact, and they drove across town. Morning was only hours away. Chaney watched the passenger side mirror for a tag but didn't see anything. Brick noticed his casual glances and commented, "Ain't nobody on us yet. But you've talked with the girl before, right? The brainy one?"

"Twice." Chaney winced as Brick took a corner.

"Once is enough," the retired marshal rumbled. "They could anticipate you doing this. Might lay up for ya. And you know that if it burns down, all you got is that Sig and the .38. Not much for a setup like this." He debated. "When we get there, we'll get a couple of CAR-15's from the trunk. I put 'em in there before we left."

"Doesn't matter," Chaney replied, glancing left, right, searching. He was painfully fatigued. "We'll go in heavy, but we're going in. Because that girl is next; I guarantee it."

"Probably. They've already killed just about everybody else. Might as well do her, too. Sanitize the whole thing. And if they're pros, they ain't gonna leave no smokin' gun. They'll be in, out, gone, and laughing in a bar when the locals call her folks."

Chaney said nothing, but he knew there were some things you just didn't do unless you wanted to provoke a little righteous retribution. And deep down, Chaney wasn't sure if he could stay on the right side of the law if they killed Gina. Whatever was going on, she was clearly innocent.

As the Tipler Institute came in sight, Chaney studied it, brightly illuminated in the harsh white glow of security lights. Even at this late hour there were still cars in the parking lot.

"You see anything?" Chaney asked quietly.

Brick studied the grounds; the building itself covered at least four acres and rested on a large, conservatively landscaped lot. There was ample parking space; no one was visible.

Reaching down, Brick removed a pair of binoculars from beneath the seat. He stared over the grounds, moving the lenses slowly, pausing, moving on. "You got two security guards up front. Uniforms. Looks legit." Another pause. "The place is tight. Ain't sure how we'll get in."

"We'll just flash our creds," Chaney said, removing the Sig to again ensure that a round was chambered. "If that doesn't get us in, we'll call Gina up front. She'll take care of it."

"Sounds like a plan."

"Best I can come up with."

"Just walk right in, huh?"

"Yep."

Considering it, Brick shook his head. "Something don't seem right, kid. How come they got two security guards up front? 'Cause that ain't normal. Usually one guy does the desk, one patrols. Then they shift out. That's the way it's done."

Chaney thought about it, knew Brick was right. That's how it was usually done. And the Tipler Institute, despite their delicate research materials and equipment, wouldn't normally violate such a fundamental and simple rule of security.

"You're right," he muttered, suspicion low but rising. "That's how it's done." He wondered if the morphine had dulled his edge to make good field judgments. "What do you figure?"

"Well," Brick said, hunkered over the steering wheel, "I figure if there's two, there's probably four. Or six. We won't see 'em, but they'll be close. If they're waiting to open up on us, they'll be coming out of the woodwork. This could get ...mean."

Chaney frowned. He expected to be upset that he might be walking into an ambush. And, strangely, he didn't care. He figured that he'd already been through so much that another gunfight wasn't enough to arouse his emotions.

He put the Sig back in the belt holster, but didn't snap the hammer guard. It wasn't much of an advantage, but it would allow a speedier draw by a split second. "Let's do it."

Brick cocked his head as he put the Lincoln in gear. "You're the boss."

In five minutes they were walking very, very slowly across the parking lot. Chaney kept his hand casually on his concealed pistol, scanning everything without appearing to. Then they reached the door and Brick put his back to it, staring over the lot. His burly arms were crossed over his barrel chest, and to anyone else he would have appeared perfectly harmless. Only Chaney knew that each of those huge hands were settled tight on Uzis.

The door opened cautiously.

"Yes, sir?" asked the guard.

Chaney didn't ask permission as he shoved the glass door open and motioned the man aside with his credentials. "I'm Chaney, United States Marshals Service!" He pointed at the man with authority. "I want you beside that desk. Now."

"But—"

"Now!"

Complying instantly, the man joined the second guard— mid-thirties with reddish hair. Chaney saw that they both carried Smith and Wesson Model 19 revolvers. The Model 19 was probably one of the finest out-of-the-box weapons available, and was chambered for either .357-Magnum or .38-caliber rounds. A dangerous weapon.

Chaney didn't trust either of them.

"Both of you, take out your guns real slow, lay them on the table. Then take three steps back and don't do anything stupid. We may have a crime in progress and you'll get them back as soon as I verify that the situation is not an emergency."

Brick had taken a position where he could simultaneously watch connecting hallways and the lobby. He had removed the Uzis and held one in each hand as he looked continuously around the perimeter, scanning. Chaney heard the sharp crack of the safeties as Brick flicked them off, preparing to fire at the faintest warning.

In the brightly illuminated entrance, Brick seemed distinctly out of place: a burly prizefighter type holding submachine guns while surrounded by prestigious peace awards which lauded the Institute's global attempts to save endangered species.

"I don't see nothing, kid," Brick said, still searching.

Chaney emptied the revolvers and tossed them onto a couch. "Get Gina Gilbert on the line right now," he said, motioning to the phone with his Sig. He followed with, "Before I lose my patience!"

Instantly the first guard was ringing the laboratory. Chaney had the guard wait a long time, but there was no reply. Brick cast him an ominous glance and Chaney shouted, "Page her, boy! Just get her up here right now! I don't care how you do it!"

The guard, galvanized by the imperious tone, tried a host of lines paging one area of the installation after another. After five minutes Chaney knew they'd have to make the long walk back to the laboratory. He reached over and grabbed the first guard by the shirt. "Come on," he whispered. "We're walking."

"B-B-But ..." He pointed to the desk. "I have to watch the—"

"All you have to do is what I tell you." Chaney cut him off, feeling remarkably stronger as the tension spiraled. "We're going to the laboratory and see if we can—"

It was a sudden movement—an out-of-place quickness—that made Chaney hurl the man to the side. As he did, he saw a shotgun coming up in the hand of the red-haired guard, but he knew it was too late. The barrel of the weapon had already cleared the desk.

Brick opened up with both Uzis, tearing through the guard and devastating the wall behind him, the desk, pictures, and computer equipment. Chaney knew what would happen next and didn't hesitate.

Holding the Sig in his right hand he reached across, thrust the barrel under his left arm, and fired as his former prisoner lunged. The round hit dead center, and to make sure Chaney fired three more rounds before shouldering the corpse aside, knowing there would be more.

Almost instantly he glimpsed the door behind Brick open a crack. He spun and fired the bullet, missing the retired marshal by inches. Brick, knowing the point of impact and understanding, also whirled, firing hard and long into the panel, which shut slowly.

For a moment they were shooting and then Chaney dove and rolled over the desk, fiercely exchanging a clip as Brick slammed into a wall, eyes blazing, searching. He dropped the long clip in one of the Uzis, slammed in another. His face was red and sweaty, and his eyes flashed as he scanned the room. For a long time they heard nothing and then there was the faintest rustling sound from a connecting hallway.

Chaney turned his head toward it, knew Brick would watch the rest of the room. It had been five years since they were in the field together, but it was like yesterday. Without words, each knew what to do. Chaney raised a hard aim on the corner, waited, and tried to slow his racing heart. He knew what separated him from his prey—plaster, two-by-fours, more plaster. Not enough to stop a supersonic 9-mm hardball round.

He fired ten rounds through the wall, moving in a quick pattern, then moved his sight alignment again to the corner, ready for an attack. Then there was a stagger, a groan, and the clattering of an M-16 hitting the floor. He saw a form fall, a blood splash erupting across white tiles.

Brick looked up. "You getting help off the psychic hotline? Good shot!"

Chaney grinned mirthlessly as he mentally counted his rounds—six left in the clip, a full clip with fifteen, and two left in the emergency reload. He decided to stay with the six rounds, moved from behind the desk with Brick moving back-to-back, staying tight.

"Just like the old days, Brick," he said. "Same routine."

"Two by two on doors without any crossovers and don't get fancy on me," Brick rumbled, holding the Uzis at chest level. His dark eyes, quick and wide open, read everything.

Chaney had the impression that the old man hadn't lost that much after all. And in ten minutes they were near the door of the silent laboratory. Chaney swung the Sig left to right as they entered quickly, in more than a hot-enough mood to kill another one. But there was nothing; the laboratory was deserted.

"Don't relax," Brick rasped, scanning the mezzanine that ran the length of the facility. "Just keep looking like you know they're here. Which they are."

Chaney crouched beside a computer base. He was out of breath and tried to calm down. "The guys ..." He swallowed, took another breath. "The guys up at the front, they weren't wearing mikes that I could see."

"They weren't," Brick confirmed, turning to look behind them. "Don't mean they ain't got friends."

"So ... how do you want to do this?"

"This is where she's supposed to be?"

"Yeah."

A pause.

"All right," Brick began, "we'll do it by the numbers. Room by room. Stick to the routine."

"Real methodical."

"Slow and careful."

Chaney sniffed and thumbed back the hammer of the Sig. "Okay, I know this place so follow my lead," he said as he rose and walked slowly forward, watching everything. Brick was close and turning, looking behind, above, reflexes sharp and poised. And in five minutes they forced open the door of the lead-shielded electron microscope room to find ...nothing.

Chaney's sweat-streaked face twisted in frustration.

"They had to have gotten to her before we did," he whispered. "They already did her. Carried her off."

Brick, bent like he'd heard something, was silent. "Did you hear that?" he whispered.

Chaney paused, listening.

"No," he replied softly. "What was it?"

Shaking his head, Brick continued to stare. Then he moved slowly for the door, one Uzi at shoulder level, the other low. He did a slow scan, inch by inch, of the room. "I don't know," he said. "Sounded like ... something hitting something."

Chaney walked into the room, moving ahead of the bigger man. Caution was good, but he was losing patience and quickly nearing the point where he was going to start kicking in doors to find some answers.

The pain and the violence and the medication had given him an edge of indifferent recklessness. If they wanted to leap out right now and begin firing, it was fine with him. He would give as good as he got.

Chaney jerked his head

"There." Brick raised the aim of the Uzi and together they were moving toward a wall of yellowish white refrigerator doors. There were about twenty separate doors that fit neatly into the wall, the panels flush with the plaster. Chaney stood a long time, and this time he heard it.

Together they targeted on the door and Chaney moved behind it, Brick taking aim with both Uzis. Then—on a practiced count of three— Chaney ripped it open and Brick tensed dramatically. The Uzis dropped to his waist as he leaped forward.

Even as Chaney turned the door, Brick was hauling Gina Gilbert from the refrigerator and ripping off the plastic bag wrapped around her head. Her hands were tied to her feet. Chaney didn't even check her condition as he ripped out a knife and slashed the ropes.

Her face was white and tinged with blue. Then she made a choking, guttural, frightened moan, half raising a hand like someone returning from the dead. She rolled over, inhaling deeply, wrapping arms about her chest.

Brick grunted, "Get her a blanket!"

They managed to warm her quickly—Chaney knew it wasn't the best medical treatment, but they were in a tactical situation—and she slowly regained the power of speech. She weakly acknowledged Chaney and Brick, and asked, stuttering, "They ... they t-t-tried t-to kill me. The men ..."

"It's all right." Chaney nodded.

She seemed to notice the heavy smell of gunpowder permeating both of them. Confusion was in her face.

"We had it out with them in the lobby," Chaney said evenly. He shook his head. "You don't have to worry about them."

Revealing no remorse at their deaths—understandable—she said, "We'd better get out of here."

"Wait a second," Brick asked, a hand on her shoulder. "How many did you see?"

"F-five."

Chaney raised his eyes at Brick.

"That leaves one," the big man said.

"We gotta get her out of here, Brick," Chaney said as he dropped the six-round clip and loaded a full fifteen-round mag. The big man nodded with a frown.

"Can you walk, Gina?" Chaney asked as he lifted her, but she fell limp.

He picked her up in his arms, holding the Sig in his left hand. He looked at Brick cautiously. "You know that you're gonna have to spot him and take him, don't you?" he said.

With a quick nod Brick turned and went to the door. He stepped out, came back. "Okay, it's clear to the hall. We'll do it in sections."

Section by section they carried her through the building, moving for the exit nearest the car. Chaney had thought of taking the closest exit but that would have meant going around the building, exposed and without cover or concealment. Better to take a chance in the hallways and office rooms where they could quickly find cover.

They reached the main lobby, second-guessing that the last hitter wouldn't expect them to leave through the scene of their earlier firefight. Chaney glanced over the long lobby, mostly open floor, and blew out a hard breath; there was no way to do this safely.

With a coordinated glance at Brick, they opened the door and began the only act left to them: they started walking slowly across the open space. Every two steps they turned, moving in circles; slow, cautious, open-eyed movements. Chaney had the Sig leveled at the waist, holding the girl. Brick had two fresh sixty-round clips in the Uzis.

Cautious, slow ...

Gina screamed.

Chaney didn't even think. He spun in the direction she was looking at. Everything in a micro-second coordinated in his mind, his body moving three to four moves ahead: Throw her out as you spin and get the Sig from under her legs, take one step to the left, protect her with your body and fire fast to rattle him. Then acquisition and open up with everything you've got—

Everything erupted.

Chaney fired while Gina was still in the air.

Brick had already opened up, tearing up a counter on the far wall. Chaney hadn't heard a shot from the hitter but he had felt the whip of a bullet passing by his ear. Something in Chaney s mind told him silencer. When Brick roared and went back something changed in Chaney's mind.

He stopped shooting, took an extra second to take dead aim.

No time for Brick ...

A silenced shot cut his right arm.

Not enough.

Chaney had sighted solid and steady on the counter. Breath stopped, no wavering, excitement forgotten, becoming cold as death to wait for the shooter to come out and try again ...

He did.

Chaney pulled the trigger ten times, the first hitting the counter, the next nine hitting the assassin. Chaney continued until he felt the man wasn't just dead, but good and dead.

The corpse slid to the floor.

Chaney didn't change clips; he still had four rounds left.

Reflexively he turned to Brick, who was already up on an ox-like arm, tearing at his vest. His face was flushed, angry and sweating. He pulled violently until he could slide a hand beneath, feeling for a wound. When he found only a bruise, he turned to look at the far wall and then at Chaney.

Chancy nodded.

With a tired nod back, Brick rose. "Let's get the hell out of here," he muttered angrily, moving for the door. "We ain't got much time."

Together they entered the Lincoln and were clearing the lot as they saw distant code equipment approaching down the only road leading to the Institute.

Brick, cold as ice at the wheel, killed the headlights.

Chaney had a moment of panic as the codes drew closer. Brick increased the speed of the twenty-year-old tank up the mountain until there was only a single curve left between them.

A dirt road that Chaney had never noticed presented itself.

Brick took it quickly and slowed just as quickly. He eased down thirty feet, stopped with the parking brake to avoid setting off the brake lights. It was a trick Brick had taught him a long time ago, which Chaney had forgotten.

In twenty seconds the patrol units sped on behind them, burning into the Institute to shut off all exits.

Brick backed slowly onto the road, Chaney holding Gina quietly in the backseat, and in another half hour they were at Mercy General Hospital.

Exiting the car at the Emergency Room entrance with his credential boldly displayed, Chaney helped the attendants load Gina onto a gurney. She grasped his hand as they swirled around her, and Chaney shoved back an overzealous orderly who attempted to raise the handrail.

"Gina, you can hear me, right?" he said loudly.

She nodded.

"You have to contact the United States Marshals Office in Washington!" Chaney shouted. "Tell them you want to talk to Marshal Hank Vincent! You got that, Gina? Hank Vincent! Tell him everything you know and tell him to alert the marshals in Alaska! Tell him I might need them and soon! Tell him to stay alert on the beacon! Just tell him that! Stay alert on the beacon! The beacon!"

Gina took a second, gripped his hand harder.

"I'll tell him," she whispered. "Be careful."

Standing back, Chaney was fierce as they gathered around her. Surprised medical personnel stared as if they expected him to escort. Chaney threw out an arm, pointing. "That is a federal witness! Notify Washington PD and the marshal division! Tell them Marshal Chaney delivered her!"

Stunned looks as they backed away from his fierceness.

With that, Chaney was back in the car and Brick was speeding down the ramp to hit the road with a hard right and then another four turns as they headed back for the house.

* * *

Stronger with each moment, he leaped from the ledge and hit the ground running, moving swiftly through the night with a surety of direction that he could not explain. Nor did he try. To know—by some dark and un-nameable instinct beyond anything he could explain—was enough as he devoured long miles on seemingly endless endurance.

He had killed again, snapping the neck of a bull elk before he feasted heavily on the deep red meat. Then he had continued, feeling his almost inexhaustible reservoirs of energy pooling, gathering, and swirling as he drew upon them. Even as his lungs burned with each breath, he felt stronger, a power building layer by layer, fed by the nutrients he had consumed.

Occasionally he would chance in the utter dark upon a plant that reached out to him on the wind, and he would crouch, ripping the root from the soil to devour it, soil and all. And in this way he continued to enhance his fantastic abilities—healing, speed, strength, his very perception of reality His eyes dilated until he could see almost as in the day, and still his metamorphosis continued until he was again a humanoid shape moving with the speed of a wolf, fangs hot against a cold night, black eyes blazing and clawed hands tearing bark from trees as he continued to run, always running.

He must find the man that had injured him; that was all he knew. He would find the man and the wolf, no matter where they had fled, and he would eat their hearts, their brains, just as he had done to those who had come before him. Then he would be reunited with his brothers, for they were waiting. And together, with the night and the forest and their strength, they would consume puny man.

Etched horrifically against a haggard moon, taloned hands outstretched to grasp a rising night wind, he howled in glory as he descended through darkness.

***

Bobbi Jo's face was soft against his chest, and Hunter found himself gently stroking her blond hair, a soft mass in his fingers that he lazily caressed, over and over. She had said nothing, but he knew she was thinking—and probably sadly.

Their moment had been passionate, but slow, and when it had ended she had settled over him, tired and exhausted. He, too, had been exhausted and had lain on his back, eyes closed as he cradled her in an arm. After a while she had spoken and he listened patiently as she talked of her life, her training, her fear, and how she had never known terror as she had known it in these past days.

For a long time he had said nothing, but listened and continued to touch her. Then she had asked, "You're afraid of it, too, aren't you?" Pause. "You're scared ...like me."

He smiled as he touched her face, a caress.

"Yes," he said.

"But you're still going out there."

Silence.

"Yes."

She said nothing and they rested in a comfortable silence until she spoke again, this time touching the scars on his chest—scars gained in hard adventures of survival that he could scarcely recall. She traced a long, ragged scar that joined his heavy arm to his massive chest.

"You don't care about pain, do you?" she asked.

He laughed lightly, hugged her neck. His voice was gentle. "Sure I do. I'm just like you. I hurt the same. I feel the same. If you cut me, I bleed."

"But you don't care. You've survived too much." She paused. "Your luck, your skill, even your strength won't be enough one day, Nathaniel."

Hunter was deeply touched. She had called him Nathaniel.

"You're not un-killable," she said, with a distinct sadness. "And that's what will kill you." A pause. "It's out there ... waiting for you. And you know it ... And if you go out there and you'll fight it, you will be fighting a beast no human being was ever meant to fight."

Hunter was silent; her words were a murmur.

"Why do you have to do it?"

"We've talked about it, darlin'." He kissed her face. "And, now, you need to get some sleep ... sleep."

"I can't sleep."

He smiled gently. "Sleep, darlin'. You've earned it."

Her eyes closed.

Silence joined them.

"It's afraid of you, too," she added softly. "That's why it has to kill you. Because it's afraid of you."

Hunter slowly caressed her cheek. "Sleep ..."

She pressed herself more firmly, snugly, into his chest and arm and her eyes closed. Her breathing deepened and her face relaxed as she began to surrender.

"Kill it, Hunter," she whispered faintly, "before it kills us all …"

***

It was a long while before Bobbi Jo rolled softly over, curling away from him with the covers tightly around her neck. He rose from bed, staring back to ensure that she was in the grateful sleep of exhaustion. Something in his heart made him content and peaceful that she could sleep so blissfully in his bed. Then he dressed slowly, in silence.

He glanced back at her as he neared the door, mentally assuring himself that he had brought everything required for this dangerous, but necessary, task. At the last minute, as he touched the door, Ghost rose from the floor. Hunter motioned sternly for silence, and pointed at Bobbi Jo. Staring a moment, the wolf padded over and lay obediently beside her side of the bed, acutely alert. Hunter knew the wolf would guard Bobbi Jo until his return. The best bodyguard in the world.

In utter silence he opened and closed the door, ensuring that it had not disturbed her, and stood quietly in the corridor, listening. But nothing was moving close; he could determine that much beyond what he could even see or hear.

He knew the complex would be alive with guards, all of whom he'd have to stealthily evade. And then he'd have to take the most daring risk of all—searching the room of the person he trusted least.

Hunter stared into the hallway, remembering every turn and hallway and corner and alcove. He moved with a plan, but a plan he could change at any moment. Animal cunning awakened, and he let it gain control.

Silence …

With a wolf's strides, he loped down the corridor.

***

"They *must* pay," Brick growled as he drove the Lincoln through the predawn light. Already, faintly above the river, the sky was a light yellow, the sun rising into a gathering cool breeze that smelled faintly like rain.

They had made an anonymous call to local police to ensure that they responded to the Institute. It wouldn't take much for them, looking inside, to see the devastation and decide on a forced entry.

It would be quite a scene, for certain, with confused uniform officers and then a full-blown building search with canine units and SWAT. All the bodies would be located and identified as well as possible, and then everyone would be looking for Chaney because his prints were all over the spent cartridge cases. It wouldn't take long for the FBI to close that noose. But by then Chaney would be well on his way to bringing this entire thing to an ending. So whatever interference was thrown up from inside the NSA or even from the Hill would be too damn little and too damn late.

Chaney was in a bad mood, and he let it ferment inside him, building in rage. He would need it when he landed in Alaska at the last research station. He would put the good Dr. Hamilton on ice until he cracked and told him what he wanted to know.

Might be complicated, legally, to get away with, but Chaney knew he was already so far out in the badlands that he couldn't really endanger himself too much more. He just hoped Skull would cover him long enough for the stunt, but there was no guarantee on that, either. He was in the black hills now, but that was all right with him.

"Brick, I'm going to Alaska."

"I'm going with ya."

Shaking his head, Chaney glanced out the side window, searching by reflex for a tag. "Brick, this ain't your fight. We already got dead bodies stretched halfway around the world. You did your time, man. You don't need to go out on the line again."

Brick turned solid. "Let me tell you something, boy. I was a marshal when you was still in junior high school. And you're all by your lonesome, just in case you ain't noticed. You think I'd let you go up against these goombahs without another gun?" He barked a laugh, utterly without humor. "The day I'd let you do that is the day I'd strap a grenade to my head and pull the pin." He shook his head again. "No, sir. We're in it now. Both of us. Up to our necks. You think I spent all those years keeping your butt alive to see you get it wasted by some godless heathens that tried to kill a little girl like that? Yes, sir. We're gonna take it to 'em."

Chaney stared, shaking his head. "Like how, exactly?"

"Well, first, we ain't taking no commercial flights. I got a buddy of mine that can get us on a military flight—no names, we'll just tell 'em we're gofers on another hop—and then we can scramble a chopper around Anchorage. You figured on a chopper, right?"

Smiling, Chaney said, "Yeah, I did."

"Yeah, I know you did," the big man replied. "I heard what you told Gina. Stay on the beacon. Yeah, I ain't forgot." He hung a hard right. "You still know how to dog one of them things?"

"Been awhile," Chaney continued to check for anyone following, but Brick was doing a good job. "They're not using Hueys anymore. Now it's Blackhawks." He thought about it. "I think I can handle it. A chopper is a chopper."

"Good enough, then. So we get back to the house, load up what we can carry, get our gear stowed, and we're airborne by midday. It's a ten-hour flight, so we land, regroup, arm the chopper and we pay this Dr. Frankenstein a visit. I've got my old creds, and you've got the documentation for running an investigation on a federal reservation. We'll get this done before somebody tries to shut us down." He hesitated. "I tell you one thing, though; we'll have to work fast. We won't have more than a day. Maybe two if we're lucky."

"Yeah," Chaney nodded, more tired now by the moment. He could use a few hours of sleep on a flight. "I figured that much."

"But don't you worry, kid." Brick finally turned onto his street. "I'm gonna break out something special from the vault. Yes, sir. I got the cure for what ails 'em."

***

Hunter was back long before dawn, and awake again, leaving Bobbi Jo sleeping contentedly. Dressing in his freshly cleaned clothes, a black combat shirt procured from the military, he entered the hallway to get some food. He had gotten a good feel for the installation last night.

Where the others had been crudely designed with cement walls and an almost depression-era air of construction, this one had stainless-steel walls, well-lit corridors and an almost antiseptic atmosphere. It was luxurious compared to the substandard building requirements of the others. Its layout, as far as he had learned, was a series of circles with intersecting lines drawn to the center of something he had not seen. But in essence it resembled a large spider web.

He assumed the center of the facility was some sort of laboratory, but he had somehow caught the scent of fresh earth somewhere, and suspected that the heart of the station was underground. Possibly several layers beneath the surface. Every door was a metal he had never seen, but seemed impregnable. The hinges were concealed and protected by stainless-steel walls.

The Ranger contingent was at least seventy men, possibly a hundred. They were exceedingly well armed with heavy weapons—Barretts and single-shot Grizzly .50-caliber rifles— very unusual—and wore a sort of high-tech body armor that Hunter had never seen before. It appeared to be molded plastic, but upon closer observation, even without touching, he could tell it was a space-age blend of ceramic and metal, molded in a unique wraparound protective shell. They wore kneepads and elbow pads and specialized helmets that appeared to have night vision built into a visor that could be lowered, as a pilot lowers a visor on his helmet.

Despite his fatigue, Hunter was impressed; whoever these guys were, they certainly had the best equipment. And he knew something else; they were expecting something big to go down here, and were well prepared for it.

Wearing his wool pants, knee-high moccasins and a black BDU shirt, Hunter walked casually through them as they changed shifts. They gave him little attention, but he knew that the easy atmosphere was the result of a well-arranged briefing. If someone without clearance had stumbled into this complex, they would have been arrested before taking three steps. Then in a moment he was inside the commissary, Ghost moving close to his side, and settled down to a relaxed meal while Ghost devoured four large steaks.

He noticed that anyone entering or leaving the chamber had to run an ID card through a wall-mounted security device. And he was intrigued that all the doors between his chambers and the commissary had been wide open. Yeah, they would let him wander, but only where they allowed him to wander. He thought back on the cat-burglar stunt he had pulled last night and smiled. Even technology could be defeated.

He heard an approach and knew who it was from the stride. He didn't turn as he addressed the intruder. "Tight outfit you have here, Maddox. Real secure place."

The colonel sat down before him with a nod, a smile. "We do our best, Mr. Hunter. You're certainly up early."

"I don't need much sleep."

"I can see that." Maddox placed his hands openly on the table, conversational. He smiled. "So, how are your friends?"

"I don't know. How arc my friends?"

The colonel opened his eyes a bit wider. "I talked to the night shift and they said that the professor is much stronger. And, as you know, Takakura and Taylor are fine. Minor burns. Some cuts and bruises. They'll live. Wilkenson was rather badly burned in that explosion, but he'll have a complete recovery, I'm told. They're flying him to a hospital this afternoon." Maddox cleared his voice, hesitant. "I suppose you wonder what the status of the operation is?"

"Haven't thought about it."

Maddox seemed taken aback. "Well ...don't you know what we're going to do with you and the team?"

"Couldn't care less what you do with your team, Colonel. I'm done with the army and this so-called mission. Soon as the professor is all right, I'm going."

"Going where?"

Hunter stared him in the eye. "I think I'll do some hunting."

Clearly, Maddox wasn't sure how to respond. Finally he seemed to craft a careful reply. "You, uh, you realize, of course, I could place you under arrest for interfering in a situation of national security."

It wasn't anything Hunter did purposely—it could have been initiated by his sudden stillness—that brought Ghost fully to his feet. But before Hunter could stop him the black wolf had emitted a low, threatening growl that seemed to blacken the atmosphere until it vibrated with the soul of the purest animal viciousness and power. No fear, no pain, no regret, and no hesitation could be known in the rumbling aura that made the entire chamber seem to fade away.

Maddox paled, lifting a hand. "Now ... now ... I didn't do anything, Mr. Hunter. I, ah, I was just ... just thinking out loud. And ... and for your own good, I wanted to tell you."

Without a glance at Ghost, Hunter said, "Don't ever threaten me again, Colonel."

"B-B-But ... I didn't!"

Maddox was trembling now, and Ghost's low rumbling had faded to an even lower growl that was, incredibly, even more menacing. Hackles had risen on his back, and his canines, more frightening than knives, were out in the open. Hunter knew he would have to restrain him in a moment but he let the wolf make a point: it was enough.

"Ghost," Hunter said, a sharp glare.

Sullenly, the wolf settled back. But his eyes remained fixed on Maddox.

"Good God," the colonel whispered, wiping sweat from his brow. He appeared chilled. "That was quite ...quite unnecessary, Mr. Hunter. Quite unnecessary."

Hunter had resumed eating.

"It was you that did it, Maddox. Not me."

"But I didn't do anything!"

"Well," Hunter said slowly, "he's sort of sensitive to someone's attitude."

Maddox took a moment to compose himself. He didn't look at Ghost as he resumed, but Hunter could too easily read that the colonel was following the wolf intently.

"Hunter, what I was ...attempting to tell you ... is that this is a matter of national security. When you operated under our supervision, you were restrained by a contract of security. If you operate independently, you won't have support."

"Never did."

"But...but if you attempt to hunt this creature alone, then you will surely meet the same fate as your team members who were killed in action. Clearly, no man is a match for it."

Hunter took a slow sip of coffee. "My load, Colonel, not yours." He set down the cup with deliberation as clear as his words. "Whatever I'm gonna do, Colonel, Ghost and I do alone. So you keep your military boys under your command, and leave us the hell alone. I'm gonna stay until the professor is shipped out on a med flight, then I'll be thanking you for your courtesy."

Maddox had composed himself; Hunter knew he was no fool. There was simply something about Ghost's terrifying presence that chilled the colonel to the core.

"Hunter," he began, "I want you to know that I have been honest with you since the beginning of this assignment. Whatever happened out there, it was not my doing. A man in my position has to make hard judgments at times, and sometimes I must send men on missions that I know they will probably not return from. But I have never, nor will I ever, send a man out on a mission that I myself have sabotaged. I have gotten full reports from Takakura and Taylor and Wilkenson. Bobbi Jo refused to be debriefed. I only came over to tell you that, if indeed there was sabotage, I will do everything within my power to discover who it was and bring them to justice."

Hunter had always trusted his instincts. So he paused, listening to that inner voice. For a long time he was still. Then he looked up. His face wasn't pleasant, but his tone was friendly.

"Colonel," he said, "I honestly believe that you don't know what the hell is going on here. I think you're an honest man. But you've been used. And you don't have the foggiest."

Maddox looked at him, puzzled. "What do you mean?"

Without intention, Hunter realized that the conversation had turned into an interrogation, with Maddox being the interrogated.

"Colonel, just what do you think these facilities are used for?"

"That is classified, Hunter."

"Secrets work both ways, Colonel."

"What do you mean?"

"I mean it hurts you and helps you. Too many secrets, too many lies, and eventually even the good guys—the guys who keep it all together— don't know what's really going on." He stared. "How often have you visited the laboratory here, Colonel?"

"I don't believe that information is within your need-to-know," Maddox replied.

"You've never seen it," Hunter said bluntly.

"And ... if I haven't? Do you have some point?"

"Yeah." Hunter shifted. "My point is they're doing something here that you don't know about. Something nobody knows about, really. And, because of all these secrets and need-to-know, you're helping protect a lie."

"A presumption, Hunter."

"Have you tried to gain access to the laboratory?"

"No," Maddox answered solidly. "I am under specific orders not to interfere in the laboratory."

"Why?"

"That's classified."

Hunter took a moment, pondering. "You know, Colonel," he began thoughtfully, "I didn't ask you to come over here and sit with me, and it's amazing how things happen. Sometimes a chance meeting can change everything. Why don't you do something for me, Colonel? And for yourself." Hunter paused to allow time for any objection; it never came. "Why don't you try and gain access to the laboratory under some pretense. Just ... make it up. Anything at all that would keep you out of trouble. I guarantee you that they won't let a lieutenant colonel of the United States Army into a facility he is bound by duty to protect with his life. But they will let civilians in there, Colonel."

Hunter let that settle.

"You're the top man at this facility, Colonel," he continued. "If anyone has a right inside that facility, it's you. You don't work for the damn NSA. You work for the United States Army, and it's your responsibility to ensure that this entire facility is safe. And that includes the laboratory."

A long silence followed.

"What is your point?" Maddox asked, at last.

Hunter felt genuine sympathy.

"My point, Colonel, is that Dr. Hamilton, whatever his real name is, has played you for a fool."

Maddox's face froze.

"My point," Hunter continued, knowing he couldn't hurt the man any more deeply, and not enjoying it at all, "is that Hamilton is performing experiments in there that are illegal and immoral and unethical and against presidential mandates and you are unknowingly aiding him in his crimes. My point, Colonel, is that if you, with the full power of your rank as a colonel in the United States Army, a colonel who is risking his own life to protect this facility, are not allowed into any area of a facility that you are assigned to protect, then someone is attempting to usurp your rank and play you as a fool, sir."

Maddox's face went scarlet with rage. Rising from the table, he casually straightened his coat.

"We shall speak of this again," he said coldly.

Walked off.

***

Hunter didn't find any portals sealed between the commissary and the infirmary, but every doorway had two uniformed guards with M-16's at port arms. They didn't say anything to him and he said nothing to them. He entered the ICU and found the professor sitting on the edge of the bed. Tipler raised excited eyes as Hunter paused, but a quick glance at the heart monitor told him the beat was steady. Tipler gazed at Ghost and smiled. Yet when he looked back at Hunter, his expression instantly altered, hardening until the pale blue eyes burned in a bloodless, exhausted face.

"We must leave this place, Nathaniel," he said, heaving a single deep breath. "If we do not, we will be dead by morning."

Hunter approached the bed. He grasped the old man's arm and squeezed it. "Listen, Professor," he began, "there's nothing you can tell me that I don't know. I know more than even you do, at this point."

Tipler stared.

Hesitating, keeping the heart monitor in view from the corner of his eye, Hunter said quietly, "It spoke to me, Professor. It spoke. No matter what it is now, once it was a man. Something ... happened here."

Hunter had expected surprise, shock. Instead, Tipler's mouth closed grimly. He nodded almost imperceptibly. In a moment he gazed at the wall as if he were gazing at the whole facility.

"Those fools," he said.

Relieved that he didn't have to explain, Hunter leaned farther forward. "You know, just like me, that it's coming here." He waited until the professor nodded. He added, "I'm going to try and get you out of here. The rest of the team will fly out with you. They'll protect you."

"And then you will go out to meet it," Tipler replied.

Hunter's face was cast in stone. He said nothing.

Tipler looked away. "Yes," he said, a sad nod. "I knew ...and I knew it earlier." He paused a long while. "You have been compelled your entire life, Nathaniel, to protect those who couldn't protect themselves. It is something I have always admired in you. It will always be the greatest, and is the rarest, of all human qualities. But...yes, I knew what you would do. It is no surprise. You needn't be concerned at my shock. Because there is none."

Hunter's brow hardened as Tipler smiled. "You expect me to say that it is suicide, and that you cannot survive," he said, smile turning to frown. "But you, alone of all men, may be able accomplish this. And if you cannot, then no one can." He paused. "I feel a measure of guilt as I say this, my boy. But if you cannot stop it—and it must be stopped—then nothing can stop it. I would, I admit freely, sacrifice both our lives if we could destroy it. But I am old, and weak . . ."

Hunter smiled, pushing him slightly back on the pillow. He shook his head as Tipler began to speak. Neither did Hunter say anything to end the discussion. He simply nodded, turned, and walked to the door. Then he looked at Ghost—so large he filled up a quarter of Dr. Tipler's cubicle.

Glaring down sternly, Hunter pointed at Tipler.

"Guard!"

Ghost padded over to Tipler, then placed both paws on the bed and stood up. Even bent on hind legs, staring down on the professor, he was nearly six feet tall. Obviously happy, Ghost panted, glad to see Tipler again. The professor laughed.

As Hunter tilted his head, about to tell Ghost to get down, Tipler raised a hand to cut him off.

"Leave him be, leave him be," he laughed, rubbing the huge black head. "I am glad to see my old friend."

CHAPTER 17

Chaney descended into the guts of the C-141, a jet-powered transport plane with double bays and a lower tier that cached all small arms and equipment, to see Brick bent over an ammo box normally reserved for rifles.

Brick was obviously running an inventory on the contents, counting and clearing weapons. His hands moved with professional familiarity and a quick dexterity as he cleared, worked the bolt, reset the weapon and obtained another, repeating the procedure with a reflex of trained muscle memory that was impressive.

Chaney realized it had been a long time since the old man had seen any real action, and he was as impressed by Brick's familiarity with the weapons as he had been as a rookie U.S. Marshal. He knelt beside the older man as he silently studied the crate's complete arsenal. Brick's lips moved as he counted to himself.

Chaney saw two M-79's—shotgun-type grenade launchers. They resembled a large single-shot shotgun and had a row of grenades attached to a sling.

On the black market, where Brick had no doubt purchased them, each of the grenades would have cost at least fifty dollars, if they could be obtained at all. Then Chaney saw two larger rifles, huge oversized weapons like double-barreled shotguns. He pointed to them.

"What the hell are those, Brick?"

Brick picked up one of them and Chaney saw that the wood was highly varnished, almost a collector's item. Yet the double bores were gigantic. No, not a shotgun.

"These babies are Weatherby .454's," Brick said in his heavy voice, cracking the breach. "They fire a .454-grain slug from each barrel at a velocity of four thousand feet per second. At a hundred yards the bullet will break the spine of a full-grown bull elephant. At closer range, if you get a shoulder shot, it would go completely through 'em, come out the other side and keep going 'til it hit a tree big enough to stop it. I worked with 'em last summer and, just for fun, put one round through four solid feet of oak. There ain't nuthin' made by the hand of man that hits harder at close range."

Staring at the weapon—heavy steel construction, peerless wood stock and handle securing the two twenty-inch bores—Chaney believed it. "But it only gives us two shots, Brick, before we have to reload. What if we have to tight this thing at close range?"

Brick grunted and pulled out a large revolver. Chaney knew what it was when he saw it: a Casull .454 caliber.

It appeared to be just a normal six-shot revolver at first glance. But upon closer observation it was obviously a beefed-up version of the Colt Peacemaker. The cylinder was modified and heavier and only held five rounds with a six-inch barrel to allow a longer powder burn.

Chaney knew from his limited knowledge of weapons that it was a favorite defensive sidearm of back-country Alaskans because the Casull could drop a Grizzly or a Kodiak brown bear with a single round. According to experts, it was the only handgun for practical self-defense in a wilderness inhabited by large predators.

He hefted the Casull when Brick handed it to him, instantly impressed by the exacting craftsmanship, the perfect alignment and tightness of the cylinder and barrel. He remembered that it had a reputation for being one of the finest handcrafted handguns in the world and was exceedingly reliable in adverse weather conditions.

"Nice piece of work," Chaney murmured, leveling and sighting on a piece of cargo to obtain a feel. "Good god, Brick, you've spent some money on this stuff."

"Not so much." Brick gestured, organizing. "You pick up a piece here, there, and after a few years you'll be surprised what you have. And the money is gonna be spent anyway, sooner or later. Might as well get something you enjoy. That's the way I look at it." He laid a box of .454 Casull rounds beside Chaney. "Anyway," he added, "how many armored cars you ever seen at a funeral? You can't take it with ya."

Chaney studied the rest of the contents of the crate. He saw a collapsible grappling hook with a thirty-foot knotted rope, ammo and ammo belts for the massive Weatherbys, hip holsters for the Casulls, straps for the M-79's, two pairs of black BDUs with black combat boots, and two load-bearing vests to carry the equipment efficiently. Then there were canteens, compasses, survival kits with sutures, morphine and adrenaline injections, uppers, downers, an amazing assortment of knives, and two pairs of night-vision goggles.

After checking and cleaning the weapons, Brick stood and removed his shirt. After five years of retirement, Chaney could see that he had lost none of his bull strength.

"We'd better get outfitted," Brick said, slipping on fatigues. "Then we can settle in and hit the rack. We got a ten-hour flight and we'll eat twice. But we'll need some sleep before we hit the deck and requisition another bird."

Chaney glanced over the crate and felt a slowly growing sense of security. He didn't know if it was caused by Brick's cockiness or the awesome collection of hardware. But whatever it was, it felt good.

In twenty minutes they were outfitted for bear. In addition to the Casull and the double-barreled Weatherby, Brick had the M-79 slung across his back. At least ten M-79 grenades were on the sling. Chaney was amazed at how well he slipped back into the mode. It was as if he had never ceased being a marine, which in truth he hadn't. He remembered the code: once a marine, always a marine.

Chaney had opted to carry the grappling hook, thinking the extra weight would tire Brick out more quickly. But upon observing how easily the retired marshal moved about, fully armed and prepared for a meal, he realized that it had been a useless concern. Together they locked the crate and moved upstairs.

"All this recondo makes ya hungry," Brick grunted. "Let's grab some chow."

Chaney was behind him as they reached the short ladder that led to the storage bay of the jet. He was thinking about apologizing to the old man for dragging him into harm's way when Brick said, "Ain't nuthin' makes you feel alive like this stuff. By God, I'm in the field again."

***

Light splintered and beamed through trees and he moved with more caution, so close to the township. He could smell, even at this great distance, the stink of oil and electric circuits. He could taste their scent on the wind that lofted gently through the moving green leaves, and he angled for the deepest of day shadow.

It was not difficult to remain in stands so thick that no one could have seen him. The trunks were large and long, and provided thick cover as he moved, still unexhausted from his long, fierce run through the night.

Several times he had imagined what he might have looked like: a leaping piece of the darkness, fangs and feral eyes dancing in distant shadows, closing, grinning, passing, vanishing.

His mind envisioned the man—the hunter—who had tracked him so relentlessly. He imagined, over and over, the man's throat in his hands—as it had almost been but for the man's uncanny reflexes—and knew that he would not make the same mistake twice. Next time, he would strike with utter ferocity with nothing between them.

His passion compelled him to run—always run—as he closed on the last research station. Yes, the man would be there . . .

As the hours wore on he felt the first faint lightness in his stride. He did not leap and climb so easily, and realized without conscious thought— for he had little—that he must eat. Yes, kill and eat quickly, and continue. For the night would be upon him soon, and with night he must be strong so that he might feast on even more delicious flesh.

***

Dr. Hamilton was enjoying the sunlight, staring at the rapidly setting crimson orb, when he heard the crunch of gravel behind him. He turned with a pleasant smile that faded instantly.

Stopping shoulder to shoulder, Nathaniel Hunter gazed silently into the mountains. He said nothing. Seemed as if he never would. And after a moment, Hamilton seized the opportunity.

"Well," he said pleasantly, turning away, "I suppose I should return to work . . ."

"I know what you did," Hunter said, not looking back.

Hamilton turned, smiled. "Excuse me?"

Hunter said the word solidly: "Luther."

The sun seemed brighter of a sudden, burning down from a wintry sky. Hunter listened but heard no retreating footsteps. Then there was a soft crunch. He waited.

"I'm sorry?" Hamilton asked, staring down.

Hunter was several inches shorter. Hunter didn't look up as he said, "I was talking about Luther. An old friend of yours. Talked to him the other day. He's having something of a midlife crisis. Said to say hello."

Hamilton thought his smile was unreadable—a self-deception he had unconsciously developed from years of conceit, when he assumed his charm and intellect were swaying his listeners.

"Young man," he began, "please make yourself clear."

Hunter turned to him. "He's an old friend of yours. He's changed a little over the years."

"You are mistaken. I do not know this man."

Hunter laughed. "I think you're going to, Hamilton."

A long pause. Hamilton smiled faintly. "You are on dangerous ground, Mr. Hunter. Very dangerous."

Blue eyes smoldering dangerously, like a storm sweeping in from an angry sea, Hunter spoke with cold contempt.

"You know who I am, Hamilton." He glanced to the side, ensuring that they were alone. "And I know what you've created. I've seen it, spoken with it, fought with it. And now you've put me in the position where I have to kill it. So I hold you responsible. I just thought you might want to know that. And something else. When this is over, I'm going to destroy everything that your work has brought. Because you've done something no man had a right to do. You set something free that should have never been set free. It had its time. Its chance. But it was over. It should have stayed over. Your arrogance brought it back to where it doesn't belong."

Hamilton was leaning back slightly. His smile was ultimately arrogant, even genuinely amused. He laughed.

"What. . ." He faltered. "Please, Mr. Hunter, what can a man such as yourself do to someone like me?" He enjoyed it. "Son, listen, you are stressed. I understand. You have suffered a terrible ordeal. I can easily arrange for you to have a – "

"Luther is as good as dead, Doctor," Hunter said. "Everything that you've done is dead." He shook his head at the facility. "All this. It's gone. I'll see to it."

Hamilton, despite his arrogance, knew enough to be shocked by this open defiance. His face changed almost instantaneously. In an eye blink his amusement was transformed into chilling hostility.

"You don't want to do that, Mr. Hunter."

"Oh, I do. And I will." Hunter smiled. It was his turn to be amused. "When I'm through, you'll be lucky if *all* they do is send you to prison."

Hamilton regarded him narrowly. "You realize, of course, that I am a very powerful man."

Hunter laughed. "So am I, Doctor – very powerful. Maybe you want to see how powerful."

A pause hung between them.

Hamilton reassumed an air of ignorance. "Really, Mr. Hunter, I don't know what you mean. Denial, you know, is quite an efficient defense. Especially when there is no evidence."

"There'll be evidence, Doctor. There'll be Luther's dead body."

Hamilton smiled. Nodding, Hunter walked away. He was ten feet gone when Hamilton tried to get the last word.

"Situations like these can get persons killed, Mr. Hunter."

Hunter turned back. He smiled, but the smile vanished as he spoke.

"Nobody lives forever."

***

It was a strange gathering, Hunter contemplated, as they surrounded the professor's bed. Takakura and Taylor stood on one side, Hunter on the other. Wilkenson had been flown out for injuries, and they were grateful. For although none had spoken it aloud, they somehow knew that all considered him guilty of sabotage.

The professor began with a statement that reminded Hunter of the old man's wise perspective, his maturity and dignity. His voice was heavily laced with sadness as he spoke.

"I, for one, will greatly mourn the loss of those brave men who accompanied us into the mountains." The statement was followed by a pause, like a moment of silence to honor the lost. "But there is nothing we can do for the dead. The living are our concern. And that is why I have called you together."

Together, they stood in patient silence, awaiting the professor's direction.

"Chromosomal manipulation, my friends," he said.

Hunter and Bobbi Jo exchanged a glance. Takakura's burning black eyes never left the professor.

"That can be the only explanation," he continued, perilous fatigue in his voice. "I suspected it but was uncertain until Nathaniel told me that it spoke to him, even as we speak to each other."

Knowing of the meeting, Hunter had already briefed the others so that there was no shock. Hunter regarded the old man. "But it seemed to have trouble communicating, Professor. It knew, or part of it knew, what it wanted to say. But it had difficulty."

"Yes, that is to be expected." Tipler nodded. "Yes, to be expected." With visible effort, he composed himself. "My friends, again I thank you for your risk, and your sacrifice, to remove me from those mountains. I know that you engaged in extreme and unnecessary risk because you would not leave me. I remain in your debt. And now the time has come for me to tell you what this creature is, and where it came from, though I can provide no proof. But we are all weary, and perilously short of time. Forgive me if I may seem presumptuous."

Takakura spoke softly. "Speak, Professor. Among ourselves, we make our own rules."

With a smile Tipler nodded, seemingly pleased at the acquiescence. "My friends, I believe I know who, or what, this creature is. And you may find my theory both irrational and unbelievable, but I beg you to listen to me fully before you deliver judgment. And, perhaps, when I am done, you will be satisfied that my reasoning merits some small measure of consideration."

"Go ahead, Professor," Hunter said. "So far, you're the only one that has made sense."

Tipler laughed, then his face grew intense. "This creature that we have tracked and joined in combat again and again, it is not a creature that has ever before walked the Earth. It is ... how do I describe it ... an *artificial species* – a monstrous amalgamation of science and ancient man which should have been the work of God, not humankind. And I will explain to you how I have arrived at my observation. Clearly, the creature's habits, his faculties of strength, speed, need not be addressed. We have all observed them. That is sufficient. However, his faculty of speech is not in keeping with prehistoric man, as his physical attributes clearly are. Thus the mystery. Unless the creature is, in some dark manner, the genetic recombination of both ancient man and the modern mind." He gazed at each of them in turn.

"You see," he continued, "we now believe that ancient man was more beastlike than human. There is still a beastlike aspect to our nature, but it has been smothered and controlled by our higher faculties. No, this creature we now confront is not constrained by conscience or morality like modern man because, quite simply, it has none. Consequently it obeys all that it knows, which is the beast within. It is unhesitating, unconscionable, unrelenting, unafraid and unstoppable. It is the purest of all beings because it is totally unrestrained in its determination to fulfill its lusts for blood, or flesh, or vengeance, or any other motivation. Yet"—he waved a hand—"it speaks our language, which means it is not prehistoric or ancient man."

There was a long silence.

Takakura broke it. "And how would you explain such a phenomenon?"

The professor gazed at him. "Quite simply, I would surmise that DNA from prehistoric man survived in an icy tomb and was discovered in this barren land. It was somehow reconstituted and then implanted into a modern man."

Tipler allowed that to settle. Hunter said nothing. He wondered how complicated this would become. He was no scientist, but he had little trouble believing it.

"That is the only explanation," Tipler said. "I have looked at the facts, simply and dispassionately gone where science inevitably led, and arrived at this bizarre conclusion. I believe, my friends, that this creature was once a modern man. And these ... these research stations ... conducted an experiment which transformed it into what is neither ancient nor modern, but a hideous blasphemy of the two. It retains, however, somewhere within its once-human mind the power of speech, of primitive communication, and the emotions of vengeance, rage, and lust. It is totally dominated by the bestial character of man that was overcome ten thousand years ago." He stared at Hunter, focusing. "You do not merely challenge a beast, Nathaniel. You challenge the darkness within us all. A darkness that man overcame eons ago because it only wrought destruction, and death. Except, now, that darkness is coupled with a dark and terrible intelligence. Its rage has not changed. It is the same. Pure. Undiluted. Yet stronger. Because its major cerebral faculties are aided by some form of modern knowledge, however weakened by its transformation."

Hunter said nothing, holding the professor's stare.

He didn't really know what to say, except that he believed the old man's theory. Nor was he certain what the next course of action should be, since the professor was clearly too ill for an air transport. In a full-blown emergency, Hunter would risk it, but only then. Because the old man's heart would probably not endure the strain. Then Tipler relieved him of the burden of reply.

"Fantastic science is often difficult to believe, my friends." He lowered his head slightly, staring between them—at nothing. "But one tenet is certain: some things do not belong to man. And changing the fabric of humanity—the very stuff of which man is made—is a task best left to God."

Releasing a deep breath, Hunter stood off from the wall, met Takakura's glancing eyes. Focused again on Tipler. "Professor," he began gently, "you can't be moved. You said you want to leave, but to move you now might precipitate another—"

"I know what you are thinking, Nathaniel." He raised a hand. "But this is what I surmise. This creature, it will come. Probably tonight. Because it has been methodically assaulting these facilities, one after another which, in turn, means there is something it is searching for – something its human mind still seeks. And when it comes, it will leave no living thing in its wake. So anyone deciding to remain will be in grave danger with nightfall."

Hunter leaned closer. "Professor, I'm not leaving. I'm staying here because you have to stay here. So is Ghost. And these other people aren't going to abandon the facility either. They think they can defeat it and ...I don't know ...maybe they can. They're heavily armed with high-caliber rifles, and this facility is far more secure than the others. It won't be easy for that thing to get in here."

Glancing at the rest of them, Hunter continued, "I'm gonna find out what's so special about this place, Professor. And I will be here until I can get you out. Takakura and Bobbi Jo have my respect, no matter what decision they make."

"I'm staying," said Bobbi Jo squarely.

Takakura didn't even reply. His chiseled face and resolute gaze said it for him.

"Yes," Tipler responded. "Just as I presumed." He shook his head lightly. "Sometimes it is unfortunate to possess strong faculties for anticipation. It makes life so much more painful. But, nevertheless, this creature is coming, and each of you will be forced to battle it once more. So you must make yourselves ready, and remove my welfare from your mind so that you are not distracted. In contest against such a beast, who has already decided what it will do and is moving upon that impulse while you are debating the proper reaction, you can tolerate no hesitation. No fear. No mercy. You must become just as merciless, just as instinctive. Equally as animal. And you must accomplish all this without losing your faculties of higher reason, which may yet defeat it. Yes, you must be what it has become, and more, in order to destroy it."

Bobbi Jo stepped from the wall and laid a hand on his. Her smile was radiant. "That's okay, Professor. We're ready for it. You just rest and leave the killing to us." She winked. "Hell, that's what I look forward to!"

A slight raising of his eyes and Tipler made a compassionate sound—something between agreement and amusement. His voice was raspy when he replied, "Leave the killing to you – yes, it is beyond me now. But I wonder ... What destroyed this creature before, for surely stood at the top of the ecosystem, virtually without enemies. And yet it was, somehow, wiped from the face of the Earth overnight. I wonder: What could have been its doom?"

Hunter said nothing, because he had nothing to say. But he raised his eyes to gaze out the window and measure the sun's dying arc. He didn't have much time to prepare, so he reached out and laid a strong hand on the professor's shoulder.

"Get some rest, Professor," he said confidently. "We're ready for it. And ...it's like you said; something killed this thing before. Something can kill it again."

***

Takakura and Bobbi Jo entered the Armory after preliminary identification was made according to rules and regulations. Takakura wore jungle fatigues but Bobbi Jo had switched to solid-black BDUs. Her blond hair was pulled into a tight ponytail and she wore dark glasses to prepare her eyes for night vision; the less light she perceived between now and dusk, the sharper her eyesight would be in shadows.

Takakura's eyes raked the weapons as the master sergeant looked on, waiting. Finally, the Japanese spoke. "Give me the M-14 on the wall, the one with a Kreiger heavyweight barrel, a belt for ten twenty-round magazines and a .45 with four extra clips."

The sergeant laid them out on the counter. The M-14, a preferred weapon of navy SEALs because of its accuracy and formidable stopping power with the .308 round, was almost a work of art.

"It's glass bedded with a titanium firing pin for faster contact," the sergeant said easily. "And the .45 is broken in. You won't have any trouble with either of them."

Saying nothing, Takakura lifted the weapon and cleared it. He inserted an empty clip and removed it. "Where can I practice with it before nightfall?"

"Got a firing range at the back of the base. It's supposed to give one minute of angle at a hundred yards. That's as far as the course goes. You want a scope?"

"The eyes which I possess are sufficient," Takakura muttered, outfitting himself with belts, clips, strapping the .45 on with a thigh holster. When he was finished, Bobbi Jo said simply, "I need thirty .50-caliber rounds loaded hot for the Barrett. Seven extra clips. And give me a cleaning and gauging kit."

"No problem," the sergeant replied, and in a minute they were ready.

"I will meet you at the range ," Takakura said to her. "I do not go into battle with an untested weapon."

"I'll meet you in a half hour." Bobbi Jo placed the ammo and clips and kit into a small duffel. "I've got to clean and oil the Barrett and gauge the headspace and scope mount. I think all the jostling has it out of alignment."

"Very well. I will await you. After we check the weapons we must prepare for tonight."

"How much time till sundown?"

"Three hours."

"That's enough. Thirty minutes."

As the big Japanese vanished out the door, Bobbi Jo scanned the racks for anything that might penetrate the creature's bullet-resistant skin. "What did the other team member, Taylor, acquisition?" she asked, unable to find anything that might prove useful.

"The big guy?"

"Yeah."

"The one with the scar on his face?"

"Yes," she replied, slightly perturbed. "Do you remember what he took?"

Lifting a clipboard, the sergeant loosed a long whistle. "Man," he began, "that mother cleaned us out. He got fifty depleted uranium twelve-gauge shotgun rounds, took the only .50-caliber Desert Eagle we had in stock and forty rounds for it. Then he checked out ten antipersonnel grenades." He looked up, fear in his eyes.

Bobbi Jo was reminded that the team, and what had happened to it, was not a secret among the rangers. By now, everyone would know that this thing had almost wiped them out in the mountains. She had noticed that everyone on the base was very heavily armed with large-bore rifles and handguns. Just like the master sergeant, who wore a .45 in a shoulder holster, another one in a hip holster.

Beside him, leaning against the wall against regulation, was a World War II Garand, probably the most powerful self-loading battle rifle ever designed. Yeah, everybody knew what had happened to them, and the rest of the stations. This place, if it went down at all, would go down hard and slow.

"Is this gonna be bad as all that?" the sergeant asked, his eyes narrowing.

Bobbi Jo paused, a frown lowering the edges of her mouth. She didn't look up as she nodded. "Worse than you can imagine." Then she looked at him. "And that old Garand ain't gonna help you, Sarge, if you want to know."

He was shocked.

"Well, what will?" he asked nervously.

She shook her head.

"Prayer."

The sergeant's mouth hung open.

Bobbi Jo turned away. "Save the last one for yourself. You don't want it to get its hands on you while you're still alive."

Dr. Hamilton stood outside the glassed-in ICU, staring at the sleeping form of Dr. Tipler. The old man was completely unconscious and heavily sedated so his blood pressure and breathing could be more carefully regulated.

Moving his hand slowly, a smile creasing his face, Dr. Hamilton carefully removed the syringe from his right pocket, feeling the plastic safety cap.

It would be over quickly, and no one would know, he told himself. He would simply inject the experimental serum into the professor's IV and then wait, observing the results. If the serum was perfectly isolated from the receptors and transmitter genes that caused monstrous mutation, then the professor's health would improve immediately. If not, then the genetic transformation would require that they kill the old man. It would be the loss of a human life, but a significant gain for science. Nor did he have any compunctions against sacrificing a few for the greater good of others. Namely himself.

When the serum was perfected, they would never release it to the masses, to the world. No, they would conceal its greatness in the corridors of power, where those who were chosen could become immune to disease and decay and even death.

Yes, it would be easy to build unconquerable power in such a time, to gain control over entire continents, living from century to century consolidating forces, laying plans and pursuing them with cunning determination to actualize a kingdom without peer in history.

Moving through the almost abandoned ICU—a single nurse sat at the monitor desk recording vital signs and making notations—Dr. Hamilton approached the room where Tipler lay sleeping. He nodded to the nurse and she smiled, returning to her work. She would notice nothing, so quickly would he work, and then time would be his only enemy because he did not know how long it would be before the serum assimilated the indigenous DNA.

The creature might, indeed, penetrate the compound and kill many. It might even be sufficiently powerful to shatter the steel portals above and massacre those within the facility, but his team would be well beyond its demonic reach within the vault.

With soft steps—he did not know why he was moving with such stealth because the old man was sound asleep—Hamilton entered the room where he lay and with his thumb carefully removed the plastic cover on the syringe.

Four seconds ... that's all I need ... four seconds ...

He reached up to grasp the IV and found the injection port. He was smiling as he—

A blackness moving silently and quickly around the foot of the bed, a wild shape low and massive, made Hamilton turn and gasp as he saw a huge dog head leading a gigantic body. He took the sight in at once; black eyes blazing over shockingly white fangs already distended, ears standing straight and hackles rising on broad, thick shoulders. Huge and powerful, it stood solidly before him. An ungodly subterranean growl made the tiles tremble.

Already sweating and trembling, Hamilton backed away, attempting to call for a nurse but again found that he had no voice.

"Good ... good God," Hamilton whispered, hands trembling violently. "I ...my God ..." He patted the air, slow and careful. "Stay, boy ... Stay! ... Good dog!"

It didn't move.

The opaque eyes glowed like a leopard's.

Finally, since it had not killed him outright, Hamilton realized that it might not, and he found the courage to reach over and quietly press the switch summoning the nurse. In a moment she was at the door.

She focused on the wolf.

"Ghost!" she said sternly.

Not immediately, but within a minute, the wolf backed away the slightest bit, though the uncanny eyes never left Hamilton. The small retreat returned some of his courage. "Nurse," he managed, trying not to appear overly rattled, "what . . .just what ... is that dog doing in the intensive care unit?"

"Orders, sir."

"Whose orders?"

"The orders of Colonel Maddox, sir."

Hamilton paused, taking deep breaths. "Is there some reason, I ask you, why the colonel ordered you to violate hospital safety standards and endanger your job by allowing a dog into ICU?"

"It's a wolf, sir."

"I don't give a damn what it is!" He glared at her. "What is a dog or wolf or whatever it is doing in ICU?"

A commando appeared in the door behind the nurse; a woman heavily armed with her blond hair pulled back in a ponytail. She was dressed in black fatigues, two pistols on her belt and a massive black rifle slung from a shoulder. She stared at Hamilton.

"Can I help you?" she asked.

"No," Hamilton said sternly. "You cannot help me. I will speak to the colonel of this intrusion of the ICU and this blatant violation of hospital procedure."

"Ghost," she said, looking at the wolf. "Down."

Ghost didn't remove his eyes from Hamilton. And Hamilton seemed to know without doubt that if he moved one inch toward the old man, he would die horribly.

"Ghost!" the commando repeated. "Down!"

The wolf didn't move.

Her eyes narrowed on the great black form. "He doesn't like you, Doctor."

Hamilton's face twisted in true fear. "I am the senior medical staff member at this facility ... uh ..."

"Lieutenant," she said.

"Lieutenant," he provided. "Yes, well, Lieutenant, I am the senior medical supervisor at this facility, and I will instruct you that if that animal is not immediately restrained, I shall have him shot." He reached out, slowly, to grasp the phone.

Ghost growled.

"You would do well to restrain him," he added in a low, non-threatening tone, "before the guards arrive."

Bobbi Jo measured the raised hackles, the growl that continued to make the air shudder. For whatever reason, Ghost was fully aroused and she didn't know why.

"No, Doctor," she replied with the faintest worry, "I think it's a very bad idea to touch him right now."

The commandos eyes watched him closely as he dialed the phone. She looked at Ghost again, slight fear in her eyes. "Ghost!" she said sternly, "Go lie down! Go lie down, boy! Do it now!"

Ghost stood unmoving.

Hamilton spoke quietly into the phone and then hung up. His gaze switched between the two of them and he managed a thin smile. "Do not worry, Lieutenant. I have summoned someone to help with this situation. They should be here in thirty seconds. And they will promptly kill this animal."

A squad came through the door with rifles ready. Bobbi Jo jerked her head and saw six of them, fully armed with M-16's, running to Tipler's cubicle and sighting Ghost still poised.

She didn't move from the doorway and felt a wave of panic. As they reached the door she lowered her head to the side.

"Stand fast. Sergeant," she said. "I'm senior officer here."

"But ..."

"But nothing!" Bobbi Jo shouted. "I'm senior officer! Get Maddox on the horn and do it now!"

The sergeant, a powerfully built soldier with the emblem of the 82nd Airborne sewn onto his left arm, stared at the wolf and jerked his head hard to the side. "Do as she says!" he ordered another guard and the soldier was instantly on the radio, calling for Maddox.

Then another form parted the soldiers like a ship slicing through water. Without announcement or permission Hunter boldly entered the cubicle and Bobbi Jo turned her head at the approach.

He passed her without a word. He didn't ask questions and paid no attention to the soldiers as he reached Ghost and grabbed the huge wolf by the scruff of the neck, forcibly pulling him back.

Ghost strained against the granite physical control for the briefest moment and Hunter bent, eye to eye with the wolf, before he spoke in an imperious tone: "No!"

Ghost did not move, so Hunter lifted him from the floor by the scruff of the neck and moved him to the foot of the bed. Then Hunter pointed at him, locking eyes.

"Stay there! Stay!"

Glaring at Hamilton, the wolf growled once more and shook its head in frustration.

Without a wasted second, Hunter approached Hamilton and stood in amused silence. He noticed the syringe, still exposed, in Hamilton's trembling hand. Then he reached out, slowly removing it from his grip. Eyes narrowing, Hunter raised it before his face, studying the amber-colored liquid.

"What you got here, Doc?" he asked with a wry smile.

"It is something for pain."

"Really?" Hunter smiled, glancing at Tipler. "The professor doesn't look like he's in too much pain right now." The smile faded. "Maybe I'll keep this for later."

"And you are qualified to make such a medical judgment?" Hamilton's force of personality was instantly enlarged. "For this interference in the treatment of a trauma victim I could have you forcibly removed from this facility. I could even, if I so chose, have you locked up in the brig."

"Oh, I doubt it." Hunter casually handed the syringe to Bobbi Jo. "But you could give it a try. Unfortunately for you, this facility is still under military jurisdiction. So I can't be removed without the approval of Colonel Maddox."

Hamilton was easily taller, though Hunter had the advantage in sheer muscularity over all of them. The physician used it to his advantage, stepping closer. "I want you to know that that animal attacked me. And for that, he will be destroyed."

Hunter laughed out loud. "If he had attacked you, Doctor, you wouldn't be standing in the ICU. You'd be lying in the graveyard. And if Ghost came to visit you at the cemetery, all those dead folks would be leaping out of their graves."

"It is a vicious dog."

"He's a wolf."

"I don't give a damn what he is! He interfered without cause or provocation in the performance of my duties. He is a dangerous animal and he'll have to be destroyed or removed from the base."

"Oh, he'll be removed, Doctor. Just as soon as I'm removed. Just as soon as the professor is removed. And, until then, he'll do just as he's told. He'll stay in this room and guard Dr. Tipler."

Hamilton sneered. "We already have guards, Mr. Hunter."

Hunter smiled.

A moment passed, and the physician's eyes narrowed. "So you are the one who led a team of professional soldiers into a massacre." He shook his head. "I cannot say that I am surprised by your recklessness. As I said, we already have guards but you insist on this insanity."

"You don't have a guard that never sleeps, Doctor," Hunter half-laughed at the ludicrous insult. "And if you have a problem with it, take it up with Colonel Maddox. He's the one who approved it."

"Be assured, I will."

Maddox came through the door, slightly winded. His face was flushed, as if he had raced from the other side of the compound. "Then you can speak to me right now," he said, coming forward. "What is the problem, Doctor?"

Pointing solidly at Ghost, Hamilton spoke with anger. "That animal is the problem, Colonel. This is a hospital facility, not a kennel. Certainly I need not remind you that it is both unsanitary and dangerous to have a wild animal inside the compound, and even more dangerous to contain it in a trauma facility. I advise you, as senior medical supervisor, to have it removed or destroyed immediately."

Maddox looked at Ghost, at Hamilton. "You don't appear to be injured, Doctor."

"The guards arrived in time to prevent an attack."

"I see." Maddox lifted his chin slightly. "So you were in fear of an attack?"

"Of course I feared an attack." Hamilton seemed offended at the tone. "Just as any reasonable man would have been in fear of an attack. Clearly, that is a dangerous animal. A wild animal. It belongs in a cage, not in an infirmary."

"Which is precisely why he is to remain beside Dr. Tipler until we airlift the hunting party from the facility, Doctor."

Maddox stopped Hamilton as he opened his mouth to reply. "There will be no more discussion on the subject, Doctor," he stressed with military bearing. "This is my command. And the wolf remains as a personal bodyguard to the professor until I receive contrary orders from my superiors. If you wish, you have my permission to contact them and discuss the situation."

Hamilton was enraged but spoke coldly. "I will, indeed, speak with them immediately, Colonel. I can assure you of that. We will see who is truly in charge here."

"You do as you see fit," Maddox replied.

Hamilton walked past him. "Believe me, I will."

Almost out the door, he stopped before Bobbi Jo and extended a dead-calm hand. "The syringe, Lieutenant."

"I'll take it," Hunter said as he gently removed it from her grasp. "Maybe the professor would like to take a look at it when he wakes up." He gazed, unblinking, at Hamilton. "Unless it's something you don't want anyone to see."

Hamilton's face flushed.

Without a word he walked out.

Watching him exit the trauma unit, Hunter's brow hardened. Bobbi Jo stepped up and looked thoughtfully at the syringe, at him. "Why did you do that?" she asked.

He once more raised the amber-filled syringe before his eyes. "Just thought about something an old man once told me about how I can tell if something is right or wrong."

"Which is?"

"He told me that if you can't tell if something is right or wrong, ask yourself if you mind people seeing what you're doing. If you'd rather keep it a secret, then maybe it ain't so right after all."

***

A crimson sun rose higher in the sky as Chaney lifted off in the modified Blackbird from Sparrevoh Airbase. He was immediately struck by the crimson dawn that domed the horizon in scarlet tatters and an atmosphere of eternal day.

But he knew it was an illusion created by altitude. For as long as they remained high, the day would last. It was only when you were trapped in the deep valleys and ravines that night settled so early and without warning.

Located ten miles from the closest township, the four-hundred-acre airbase was still more than five hundred miles from the as-yet unnamed research station. But the helicopter had a range of fifteen hundred miles at its maximum speed of three hundred miles per hour, so they would be there soon enough.

It had been surprisingly easy to commandeer the attack helicopter after the base commanding officer telephoned Washington to verify Chaney's orders. Then he and Brick had quickly loaded the chopper.

Chaney had used ten minutes with a qualified pilot to re-familiarize himself with the updated flight control panel and was impressed with how modern technology had changed what was basically a Huey into a flying limousine.

It was a well-crafted machine with a muffler that could be hydraulically lifted to virtually silence the twin turbos and engine. He also learned that, when cloaked, the only sound the chopper made in flight was that of rotors slicing air. It was also armed, doubling as a gunship. Yet Chaney didn't expect he'd need the 30-mm cannon so they had lifted off with only the armaments they'd brought, which seemed formidable enough.

They easily cleared the first jagged whitewall of mountains at nine thousand feet and the Magellan Navigational System kept them on a steady course. Chaney glanced at the displays as they gained even more altitude to ensure the craft was operating smoothly and not approaching the twelve-thousand-foot limit because the cabin wasn't pressurized. Plus, unless you were on oxygen at twelve thousand feet, a sudden loss of consciousness was a possibility.

With only a quick glance he saw that hydraulic pressure was steady, no overheating or cooling, and that the rotor speed and pitch were appropriate. Rear automatic stabilizers were computerized, and they automatically adjusted to wind and climatic changes.

Chaney had never flown a chopper with computer-enhanced rear rotor blades or anti-torque control, but it was easy to become accustomed to. He realized that he felt a sense of calm because, overall, the Blackhawk was a much easier chopper to fly than the crude but effective Huey.

"How long before we deck?" Brick spoke into his mike.

"It's five hundred miles ... maybe two hours," Chaney replied into the headset. He could have used the cloaking device to dull the roar of the engine and the drone of the turbos, thereby making conversation easier, but the ceramic shields also increased hydraulic temperatures. He remembered that the sound-dampening system couldn't be used for more than fifteen minutes at a time because overheating, and possible engine damage, could occur.

"Good enough," Brick replied, eyes centered steadily on the vast mountains that reached up to the horizon. "We'll still get there with a couple hours of daylight. We'll use it to get a good feel for the place before you get down to your little chit-chat."

"Yeah, well, if I get the chance," Chaney responded. " 'Cause if they know we're coming, they're gonna be prepared. And I don't think the good doc is gonna take it lying down. He'll be on the horn with Washington at the first available opportunity and get some interference runnin'. And he'll probably make up some shit about how I'm hampering their precious research with my inane questions." He cocked his head. "As it is, we're already in trouble. They might throw us in jail for leaving that scene in Washington."

Brick grunted. "Yeah, they'll get us for that sooner or later, kid. Believe me. They'll have to. But don't worry about that now. And, in any case, we were smart to hit the road. If you'd stayed in Washington they would have tied you up for days or weeks with bullshit statements and forensics and probably a suspension 'til a shooting review board could be arranged. So you did the right thing. And when this little gig is over, I'll be there to testify for ya. I was a witness to the whole thing, so it won't be so bad. Really, we had no choice. We just didn't go by the book on the aftermath."

Chaney shook his head and frowned. "It doesn't really matter to me, Brick. Whatever's up here is a hell of a lot worse than whatever's back there." He paused. "But all things considered, I'd rather be in Philadelphia."

Laughing gruffly, Brick took a second before he focused hard on Chaney. "Just remember your job, kid. We ain't here to kill that thing. We're just here to find out what's going on, document it, and send paper up the ladder. All this hardware is for defense. Let them settle it out with lawyers and depositions and hearings." A pause. "But, then again, we do have a score to settle. 'Cause somebody needs to hang for what they did to those poor girls, and the hit on you. So once we got a good lead, or a head in our hands, we're outta there."

Chaney answered, "Might be easier to get in than out." He paused. "But I've come too far to back down, old man. Too far by half. Going back would be twice as bad as finishing this out. What do they call that? The point of no return? The place where going over is easier than to go back?"

Brick nodded his agreement and leaned back in his seat, closing his eyes as Chaney stared at the white-capped mountains looming up and surrounding them. He was reminded once more how harsh a land it was, how easy it was to die inside those valleys and ravines, snowfalls and glaciers. Then he thought of this man named Hunter who was reputed to be the greatest tracker in the world, the greatest wilderness expert in the world—a man who understood the wild like no other. And somehow, he sensed, Hunter just might be able to answer some questions.

Only one thing was certain: the enigmatic Dr. Arthur Hamilton would not have mentioned this mysterious tracker—who was so "unimportant"—if he had not, for some reason, feared him.

CHAPTER 18

Hunter raised his eyes to the horizon to measure how much light remained. There would be a pale moon tonight, but the base would be brightly illuminated by the thirty-million-candlepower spotlights strategically positioned along the perimeter and inside the compound itself.

From their angle and proximity, Hunter estimated there would be very little shadow, though he doubted that it would deter the creature from attacking. It had attacked them in daylight already, indicating that it did not fear the light so much as before. They had convened on the range so Bobbi Jo and Takakura could sight in their weapons.

Takakura had been especially diligent, firing over a hundred rounds through the M-14 in thirty minutes to break the weapon in and gain confidence in its reliability. But Bobbi Jo had only fired thirty rounds before she was certain that she had the scope adjusted for close-quarters battle.

Strangely, the Barrett was less accurate at a hundred yards than a thousand. Nothing severe, perhaps only a half inch off point of aim, but enough for a sharpshooter to notice.

Bobbi Jo explained the differential in accuracy by saying that, at a hundred yards, the supersonic bullet was still "washing" in the air, or swaying slightly. Then, when it stabilized at two or three hundred yards—a distance reached in one-tenth of a second—it settled down and flew true, stabilized by the rifling-induced spin.

Hunter was impressed by Bobbi Jo's skill and mastery over the huge sniper rifle from the beginning. But as she honed the scope and rifle into a unit, he was even more impressed as she talked, rather abstractly and with remarkable emotional detachment, about how the rifle had to perform.

She spoke about shots fired in past combat situations. Such as scoring a headshot on a Palestinian sniper at nine hundred yards as he risked a quick glance over a wall. "It was like hitting the stamp on a postcard at three hundred yards," she remarked casually.

Then she had spoken of how she once decimated all ten members of a Shining Path death squad with a hail of .50-caliber rounds fired at twelve hundred yards from an elevated position. Even with a 12 X 3 Tasco sniper scope, it had been akin to shooting flies at fifty feet.

When she was through reminiscing, Hunter held her in high regard not only because of the professional manner in which she described the acts, but because of her almost encyclopedic understanding of ballistics, windage, bullet speed, placement, and fall.

Seated side by side on a table while she cleaned the Barrett with easy familiarity, Hunter wondered how she felt about last night. He wanted to ask, but found himself silently watching Takakura finish his last twenty-round magazine. He was uncomfortable—mostly because love was something he had never known before, but also because he felt himself becoming more and more dependent on her.

Although he had never known a woman with her background and training, he had discovered that beneath her professional veneer, she was, indeed, very much a woman with the same softness, eagerness for intimacy, intuition, and sensitivity as other women. He contemplated where the relationship would proceed, or if it would at all, and felt a pang of loss at the latter. Then out of his peripheral vision, he saw a slight grin cross her face. She spoke as she continued to clean and oil the Barrett.

"You were all right last night, Hunter." She smiled mischievously. "Especially for a man who was all beat up, physically exhausted, emotionally wasted and wounded." Then she laughed; a good laugh. "Yeah, I'd give you a ten, all right. Ha. Dead drunk, I'd probably give you a ten."

Raising eyes slightly, Hunter smiled. "I thought it was a good idea to do my best. Didn't wanna get whacked in my sleep."

She was enjoying it, and Hunter could see she had no regret.

"And," she added, "I don't know if you know it, but you talk in your sleep."

Hunter froze. "What?"

"You talk in your sleep," she repeated, enjoying it more and more. "Gotta tell you, it was pretty interesting, too. You've led quite a life."

"Well, uh ... what did I say?"

"Oh, you talked about hunting. About tracking, about how you won't let this person die, or that person die. You talked to some of the kids that you rescued. 'I got ya, kid, I got ya ... It's okay.'" Smiling slightly, she began inserting the six-inch-long brass rounds into the oiled magazine. "Then you talked about blond hair. And love. That kind of thing. Kept me up, for sure."

Hunter realized his mouth was open.

"So." She laid the rifle against the table and propped her chin on her hands as she gazed at him with mock seriousness. "When do you want to get married?"

Hunter laughed and glanced away to see Takakura walking toward them. The M-14 was smoking from heat and the Japanese seemed pleased. Hunter looked back at Bobbi Jo: "How about today? Or is that too soon?"

Her open laugh joined his. "You know, Hunter, I never figured you for a romantic. But you are, in a way."

Shaking his head, Hunter understood that she was relieving some of the pressure from last night, and the night to come. She was not relaxed, she was only trying. He knew too well from experience that it was impossible to stay at a high pitch of concentration constantly. Everyone needed a moment to breathe easily before an unavoidable battle.

Takakura arrived at the table and reached for the cleaning kit. "It is sufficient," he said, and noticed their sudden silence. "I ... uh, did I disturb something?"

"Not at all." Bobbi Jo smiled. "Did you sleep well?"

The Japanese cast a narrow glance at Hunter before he smiled openly. And it got Hunter's instant attention because it was only the second time he had observed anything other than duty or obligation on the sharply chiseled face.

Dark eyes narrow with amusement, Takakura added, "Not, I suppose, as well as some whom I know. But, then, I had nothing to distract me." He nodded to himself, as if he had discovered something profoundly pleasing. "Yes," he added, "it is amazing how the crucible of war can bring hearts together. For you can discover more of a person in a few hours of combat than in years of casual acquaintance. And when the battle is over you realize that you have glimpsed into a heart. I have seen lives forever changed by such things."

Bobbi Jo said nothing, but her smile didn't fade.

Glancing over at her, then at the range, Hunter said, "Guess you're right. Never really thought about it."

"Until now," Takakura said, finishing disassembly of the M-14. "But it is a lesson worth learning, and remembering. I can tell you that the closest friends I possess are those who fought beside me in war. And the only people I truly trust are those who have, out of honor and courage, risked much for me.

"Anyone can be brave in the day, when you feel warm and safe and protected. But one must first walk in the night, alone and unaided, before he can say he is not afraid of the dark."

Without another word he began cleaning the weapon. Even at a distance Hunter could feel heat emanating from the barrel and receiver, but Takakura seemed not to notice as he efficiently swabbed the bore. In fact, the Japanese seemed not to be thinking of anything at all as they tell silent.

A distant drone coming out of the southwest caught Hunter's attention and he turned his head, searching the sky. Then a small speck like a metallic dragonfly rose from the far side of distant bluffs and he looked closer, recognizing the distinct forward silhouette of a Blackhawk flying fast and low.

"Looks like we've got visitors," he remarked.

Bobbi Jo rose, shielding her eyes from the light of the dying sun. "It can't be more troops," she replied. "They've already got almost a hundred guys here." She was quiet, gazing steadily. "It's not a gunship. They're not racked and they're not carrying missiles. I wonder ...you think it's another hunting party?"

"No," Hunter answered, "they're not going to do that again anytime soon. They've already got some kind of plan for capturing, or killing, this thing. I figured that much out. I don't really know what they would need ...unless it's some VIP."

Takakura had ceased cleaning the M-14. He scowled as he watched the chopper close on the compound and then set down gently on the pad. A moment later, two men, one big and heavily armed, the other smaller but obviously in good condition, exited and walked slowly toward the station. After flashing some sort of credentials that demanded immediate respect, they gained entrance and vanished within the steel door.

"Curious," Takakura mumbled. Clearly, he did not like what he had seen. "Two soldiers to add to a hundred. It is not enough to make a difference, should the others fail to defend the compound."

The Japanese scowled, eyes squinting at the helicopter as the four-bladed rotor finally stopped spinning. Abruptly he looked at Hunter. "Perhaps we should investigate this," he added. "Clearly, we are among those that we cannot trust."

"Where's Taylor?" Hunter asked as he picked up his Marlin. "He'll need to know about this."

"You think they're hitters or something?" Bobbi Jo asked as she lifted the massive sniper rifle. "They didn't look too friendly, for sure. In fact, they kinda looked like professionals, if you ask me."

"Professional what?" Hunter addressed her.

"I'm not sure." She shook her head. "But they sure know how to handle themselves. Plus, that Blackhawk isn't a Chevy. It takes six months to learn to fly one and the only ones qualified are military. Marine or army."

Hunter analyzed the situation before addressing the Japanese commander. "Why don't you find Taylor? Bobbi Jo and I'll try and find out what this is all about."

"*Hai*," Takakura replied, reassembling the M-14 before he had completed the cleaning. "I will notify him. Then we will meet back in the intensive care unit in thirty minutes. No more."

"Sounds good," Hunter walked forward. "See you in thirty minutes. And it might be a good idea to look sharp. This place is dangerous, but what's out there"—he lifted his chin toward the darkening forest—"is more dangerous. As dangerous as anything gets. And it's coming. Coming tonight."

***

Eyes slitted like a cat's, he watched the helicopter descend. His vision, almost perfect even in total blackness, followed the two of them until they were inside the building, and then he looked over the rest of the expansive, fenced-in compound.

There were more soldiers, dogs, and guns here than at the others. He considered the large contingent that was visible and searched for a suitable place of entry. Then, as twilight faded to what would soon be night, and the huge lights ignited to blaze as day, he knew that there would be only one means of penetrating the complex.

He was grateful that he had fed, for he could feel his fibers absorbing the nutrients, making him stronger by the minute. Yes, he was at the peak of his strength, and would need eat no more until he attacked. Then, as before, he would devour as he slew, methodically working his way through the compound until he shattered the steel portals and gained entrance, slaying still.

Rising on legs thick and hard as oak, he stood in shadow. His hands, clutching involuntarily, made sharp clicking sounds as the long talons grazed each other.

Soon ...

By the time he had crept close enough for exposure to the bright lights, which he would have to disable, the darkness would be complete. And after he cast them into darkness he would become their lord, master, and destroyer. As always.

He did not recognize fear as they recognized fear. No, he could feel nothing but the super-oxygenated blood coursing strongly from his chest, providing him with enhanced and all-but-matchless might. His shoulders swelled with chemicals that accelerated his speed and dulled whatever pain he might receive. His bare feet pawed the ground, toes clenching cold dirt and the decayed, cast-off leaves of many seasons.

Glowering, he bent and glided over a hidden grassy path, using the trees to disguise his silhouette from their night-vision devices, for he still understood these things somehow—how they used things to see in the dark. These things would not be enough to stop him.

Even darkness was as day to him, now that he was almost complete. And with the moon, the woods were white fire and pale shadow. And the presence of every living thing that had passed this way for weeks, and even months, hung heavy in the air.

And yet, still, he was not perfect.

But he knew what was protected within that facility—the purest part of his blood that would make him even greater than his brothers, would complete the transformation. Yes, greater, for then he would have the full power of the ancients plus the higher faculties of man himself—enhancing his glory.

And when his system reached its zenith he would be as nothing the world had ever seen, or wanted to see. He would be without limits, an indestructible and wrathful god come to deliver a dark judgment upon the earth. Their flesh would be his for the taking, their lives and their deaths existing only for his amusement, the brutality of his pleasure.

Hiding his steps under the whispering wind, he crept on monstrous strides—a Goliath etched against skeletal trees, shadow moving from shadow—fangs distended in a hideous smile.

Soon, he knew, he would not need the wind.

***

"So," the man introduced as Chaney said with guarded interest, "you're Nathaniel Hunter."

Measuring the man while he searched for whatever truth might be revealed in the stern eyes and face, Hunter answered, "Yeah, I'm Hunter. What can I do for you?"

Facing each other squarely, they stood in the ICU where Professor Tipler, having regained consciousness and refusing to take medication to ease his pain, lay listening.

Despite his agony and obvious exhaustion, the professor maintained an expression of keen concentration. His pale eyes never left Chaney's face, nor did he move. The heart monitor beeped regularly, no trace of arrhythmia.

"I'm glad you asked, Mr. Hunter," Chaney responded. But Hunter detected the faint edge of caution in the reply and the pause that followed, as if the U.S. Deputy Marshal wasn't exactly sure whether Hunter could be trusted. "The truth is that I've come a long way, and I've been through quite a lot of trouble, just to ask you a few questions. I hope I haven't wasted my time."

Hunter cast a glance at the professor, who said nothing. "Well, I don't know if any of us can help you, Marshal ..."

"Just Chaney."

Hunter nodded. "All right, Chaney. Like I said, I don't know if any of us can help you, but we'll do what we can." He glanced at Bobbi Jo. "We're probably the only ones here that don't care much for secrets. Ask whatever you want. But, first, why don't you tell us who your friend is. Looks like he's loaded for bear."

Smiling slightly, Chaney gestured to Brick. "Forgive me, that was an oversight. This is a friend of mine. He a retired marshal. But he's temporarily reinstated until I close the investigation. As far as what to call him, you can just call him Brick. Everybody else does. Anyway, we're working together."

Brick nodded pleasantly to Hunter and Bobbi Jo. "I'm just along for the ride," he said. "Any of you folks want me to step out, I'll be glad to. Don't want to ruffle nobody's feathers."

Studying him a moment, Hunter shook his head. "No, I was just asking. Glad to meet you."

"Same here, Hunter," Brick replied, and smiled. "I figured you didn't care much for the 'mister' part."

Hunter laughed. He sensed nothing suspicious about either man, only honesty and frankness in their voice and expression and an unspoken but inflexible air of duty.

The fact that Brick was heavily armed with a wide array of weapons seemed to indicate that they could skip the preliminaries. Obviously, both men had a rudimentary understanding of the situation, and had come well prepared.

Nor did their posture indicate an air of superiority or command. Rather, it seemed as if they were in the dark even more than Hunter and the team. On first impression, Hunter liked them both.

"I'll do what I can for you, Chaney," he said. "What do you want to know?"

Chaney sat back easily on the edge of a table, crossing arms over his chest. The sleeves of his black BDUs were rolled tightly to the elbow to reveal his forearms, and Hunter could see that no matter how many hours Chaney spent behind a desk or in court, it was clear that he kept himself in excellent physical condition. And Hunter respected that, because it indicated a practical man who knew that survival in combat, and even life, very often hinged on pure physical strength, endurance, and skill.

"I won't waste your time telling you things you already know as well as I, and probably better than I," Chaney said frankly. "In a nutshell, I've been assigned to discover what this thing is that's been destroying the research stations. And why it's doing it. Basically, the same mission you've been given."

Chaney gazed without blinking, as if to make a point. "I know what happened to your team, Hunter. I got that from the CO when I landed." He paused. "I'm sorry. I've led men in combat, and I know what it's like to lose one. It's something you never forget."

Hunter replied, "I appreciate that, but it wasn't really my team. Takakura was in charge, and he did the best job any commander could have done. I was just there to track. I suppose you know already that I'm not current military or under any kind of military jurisdiction."

"I know."

"All right, so, again, how can I help you?"

"Well." Chaney cleared his throat, took a sip of coffee. "Can you tell me how many times you've made contact with the creature?"

Hunter was cognizant that the marshal didn't want to control or command; he simply wanted information, honest and complete. And because of that, Hunter was disposed to cooperate.

"Three ... maybe four occasions," he answered.

"And they were all combat situations?"

"Yes."

After a careful stare—as if wondering how Hunter had survived the encounters—Chaney added, "How is it that you're all still alive? From what I understand, this thing ... well ... not a lot of folks walk away from a fight with it."

Hunter held the marshal's stare. "Some of us didn't, Chaney. And, frankly, I don't know how the rest of us did either. It attacks and retreats guerrilla-style. So we never had a prolonged battle with it. It toyed with us, and when it finally got serious, it was too late. We were airborne."

Chaney didn't reveal any surprise; instead he appeared intrigued. "You say these confrontations were quick but intense, and it would retreat before you could kill it?"

"Well, Chaney, I don't think we had the ordnance to kill it, anyway. Its skin is resistant to small-arms fire, to a degree. The professor can explain it better than I can, but it's not easily hurt by bullets. Only the Barrett seemed to affect it, but we're not sure if even the .50-caliber rounds really cut through its skin. To make it brief, I'll say the fights were ... I don't know, vicious but quick. Maybe sixty seconds."

"Yeah." Chaney seemed intrigued by that aspect. "You said before that it retreated. You said it was playing with you. But animals don't do that, Hunter. And you know it."

Nothing was said for a moment.

"Seems pretty damn curious," Chaney added finally. "There's no reason I can see why it wouldn't have attacked and killed and then eaten someone and moved on. Like a bear. A tiger. Something like that."

Neither Hunter nor Bobbi Jo volunteered any information. Hunter was tempted, briefly, to say that the creature had somehow taken Hunter's dogged search as a personal challenge. But he reasoned that it would sound too bizarre. He didn't say anything and Chaney continued to speak, almost to himself.

"So it attacked time and time and let you live.... There has to be a reason why it could change its methods. It's an animal, and they're creatures of habit. It wouldn't do something differently unless it had a damn strong motivation." He looked hard into Hunter's face. "Tell me the truth, Hunter. Take a chance. I'm asking you."

Hunter's eyes were flat. There was a long silence.

Chaney didn't move at all.

"All right, Marshal," Hunter said finally. "I'll tell you something honestly. It's not an animal. And I don't care if you believe me or not. But it's not an animal."

Chaney didn't seemed shocked

Brick grunted, an unpleasant scowl clearly visible on his beefy, squared face. And, though he did not reveal quite so much, Chaney also allowed his curiosity to surface.

"So what in the hell is it?" he asked.

The question reinforced Hunter's initial impression that the deputy marshal had nothing to hide and wasn't here to command or intimidate. Hunter blinked, and decided to cruise truth, and if Chaney had the instinct to accept it, Hunter would tell him everything.

"I think," he began slowly, "that it could be an undiscovered species, Chaney. It's manlike and tiger-like in how it stalks and kills, but it's also like a man. It obviously anticipates, and it's exclusively bipedal, but it has the stalking method of a quadruped. It has no territory that I could identify but it doesn't wander, either. So it's unlike a bear or tiger in those aspects. It prefers to attack in the night but it'll also attack in the day if it's presented with the opportunity."

Chaney made no movement. Didn't even blink. "Hunter, have you ever encountered anything remotely similar to this?" he asked finally. "Anywhere?"

"No."

"Have you ever heard stories of something like this?"

"No."

"Well, then, how do you explain it?"

"I don't explain it, Chaney. I'm just telling you what I think."

Chaney pursed his lips in thought. And Brick, having listened to the entire enigmatic conversation, lowered his gaze at nothing. His visage hadn't altered, but from the depth of his frown it was obvious that he deplored the sullen direction of his private thoughts.

Shaking his head, Chaney said, "Hunter, I know you haven't lied to me. You've told me what you think. But I don't think you've told me everything. And ... that's smart; I can understand, after what you've been through, why you wouldn't trust anyone in a uniform. But the situation has become more serious than you know. I'm afraid ... that I've got some bad news for you." He paused as Hunter froze. Then: "I'm afraid that one of your employees, Rebecca Tanus, has been murdered. They tried to kill Gina, too."

Hunter didn't move, but his mouth opened slightly and his eyes turned dark. Slowly he moved away from the table, approaching Chaney with a single step. It was an unthreatening action, and Chaney seemed to understand. He waited patiently until Hunter asked in a hushed, clear voice, "Who killed her?"

"They're dead," Chaney replied. "Brick and I did 'em in."

A moment, and Hunter nodded gratefully. "Good. And Gina?"

"In the hospital. And she's the one who led us here. She indicated you might be able to tell us the plain truth without all the wildlife bullshit."

"All right, Marshal, let me tell you exactly what you're looking for.

And no bullshit. But get ready for it, and if you don't believe me, I don't give a damn." Hunter was solid, his eyes unblinking. "You're looking for a genetic freak. Something that is half man and half monster. Something that can speak. Something that can move like lightning and has skin that is, for all practical purposes, bulletproof." Hunter watched the amazed reaction at that. "We hit that thing with enough ordnance to kill a hundred men, and it kept coming back stronger than it was before. No wounds, no nothing. The only way we've been able to hurt it is with knives."

"With knives!" Chaney exclaimed. "How in the hell could a knife injure it when a bullet wouldn't? And how did you get that close to it, anyway? From what you said, nobody would stand a chance against it with a knife."

From his glass cubicle, Professor Tipler responded. Weak and light at first, his voice grew in strength and tone as he continued. "It is quite possible, Marshal Chaney. It is only a simple matter of engineering stress."

Chaney gazed at the old man.

The professor added in a low drone, "This creature's epidermal molecular structure is, ah, probably similar to a rhinoceros which, incidentally, has the thickest and most densely designed epidermal surface on the planet." Gesturing as if it would assist him in framing the concept, he continued, "You see, a blunt object such as a bullet or shrapnel cannot penetrate its skin unless the leading point of impact is a cutting edge. This phenomenon does not necessarily reflect the thickness of the skin, however. Merely the composition."

Chaney moved closer. "Explain that to me, Professor."

With a nod, Tipler answered. His energy seemed to build with each sentence. "It is easy enough to understand, Marshal, if you think of it in terms of analogy." He drew a deeper breath. "First, we will remember that there are only two means of neutralizing the force of a bullet. Both methods, however, involve the same rule of physics, and that is to absorb, rather than resist, the force. In the first method, the bullet simply cannot make sufficient contact to actuate the intended trauma. The struck substance surrenders so completely that contact, if any, is so insignificant as to be nullified. Perhaps an example would enable you to visualize that type of situation." He paused, then: "Ah, yes. For instance, if one would suspend a silk handkerchief in the air by two corners and then fire a bullet at the hanging portion, the silk would surrender so completely and quickly, even matching the velocity of the bullet, that there would be almost no contact at all.

"This method, of course, is not an option for a target which, because of immutable physical laws, cannot surrender with such alacrity. Now, the second method involves a partial surrender, or absorption of the force of a bullet's impact. For, upon contact, the shock is dispersed or spread in a pattern over resilient, multi-flexed fibrous tissue that removes the bullet's force. Needless to say, this fibrous material would have to be exceedingly intractable, similar to substances utilized in the manufacture of ceramic-steel plating. An example would be ... ah ... oh, yes; let us imagine that you tossed a bulletproof vest in the air, and shot. Now, the vest would absorb far more of the impact than a scarf because its weight would negate complete surrender. But it would surrender nevertheless and the impact suffered would be dispersed across the fibers, as I've already mentioned, in shock waves. Not unlike ripples created when one tosses a stone into a calm pool. The surface absorbs the impact and sends the resulting trauma out in waves. Now, for the optimistic analysis. This creature, as you said, Nathaniel, is essentially exempt from injury from small-arms fire. However, if you possessed a weapon that could fire a projectile at far beyond supersonic speed—a speed that would not allow its fibrous molecular epidermis sufficient time to absorb and disperse the shock on impact—you would be able to overcome this spectacular defensive faculty. And, in fact, you have almost done this exact thing. Bobbi Jo's weapon—" He gestured toward her.

"The Barrett." She smiled.

"Yes, yes, the Barrett. That very large gun that she utilizes with such effectiveness does this. Although it has not yet devastated this animal's epidermis, it has obviously wounded it. What, may I ask, is the velocity of those bullets that you are using, Bobbi Jo?"

"They're three-hundred-grain bullets loaded with 1110 Hodgdon powder. The ones we chronographed before the mission began were ranged at 4,372 feet per second. It was a hot load but I've boosted the power with some CFI for more explosive detonation. I'd say they're pushing five thousand feet per second because I also dropped to a 195-grain Teflon-tipped bullet. A smaller bullet allows higher velocity as long as it's not so small that it's affected by windage." She paused, shook her head. "I'm probably pushing the gun to the limit right now."

"Yes, yes." Tipler nodded. "Exactly my point. Certainly, if one calculates the velocity, size and form of the other bullets fired at the creature against the damage resulting from Bobbi Jo's vastly more powerful weapon, you can acknowledge that the creature does have a threshold of tolerance. Subsonic ammunition probably has no effect whatsoever, but when a projectile's speed is faster than the faculty of the epidermis to disperse the force, then it can be injured by weapons. Unfortunately, I fear, a majority of those weapons that protect the complex are useless against it."

Chaney spoke in a thoughtful voice. "That would seem apparent, Professor. But even if the shock of a bullet was ... was dispersed, as you said, this creature would still suffer a blunt trauma, wouldn't it? Something like bruising?"

"In a sense, yes," Tipler answered, eyes closing suddenly to a sting of deep pain. "But if the creature possessed an enhanced healing factor, then any resulting blunt trauma would be quickly erased. So the only advantage we would gain would be through its pain, and the consequential distraction, both physical and mental. For even a short-term and superficial wound would reroute its chemical reserves into the laborious act of healing, thereby subtracting these same substances from its superior strength and endurance. Quite probably, the lack would consequently weaken and slow it, which would be another advantage.

"This is why, after Bobbi Jo struck it with the sniper rifle, it retreated. It was not wounded, merely shocked." Holding a hand briefly to his chest, Tipler inhaled deeply before continuing, "Yes, it had to retreat because of the loss of strength, and the distraction of pain. But when the pain subsided and it replenished itself with nutrients to replace those used in healing, it returned even stronger. You see, its body was learning, conditioning itself to the phenomenon of injury, probably even mutating to compensate for the new threat. As it will no doubt continue to do. For its spectacular proclivity for enhanced evolution within hours seems to pace the evolution Homo sapiens experience in as many centuries. I do not doubt that, shortly, if it is not destroyed, there will be no weapon powerful enough to defeat it."

Chaney had approached the bed as the professor spoke, and Hunter could clearly see that the marshal wanted to continue. "Are we exhausting you, Professor?" Hunter asked. "We can continue later, if you wish."

Raising a hand weakly, Tipler answered, "No, no, I am fine. Hear me out...before I rest, which I must do shortly." He took another deep breath. "So, that is why bullets fail to sever its multi-layered epidermis. However, and remember this, an edged weapon provides the very opposite kind of force. An edged weapon, such as a knife or sword, reinforces speed and structure to create what is known as 'pyramidal penetration.' Which is exactly ... as it sounds. You see, instead of the base of the pyramid making impact, allowing a dispersion of force created by the combined factors of velocity and form, a pyramidal impact delivers a singularly focused edge of contact that multiplies weight and velocity into a razor's edge. And by this means the fibers are unable to disperse, share, or otherwise escape the trauma. So this, in a simplistic way, would explain the creature's near-invulnerability."

Chaney said nothing, seeming to realize that the professor had reached exhaustion. Then with a nod he murmured, "Thank you, Professor. I appreciate your help." He walked slowly over to Hunter.

He didn't look Hunter in the face but stared at the closed room of the infirmary; the nurse had been ordered outside so that they might talk in private. Bobbi Jo was monitoring the displays at her station. Finally Chaney said, very quietly, "Hunter, tell me something. Just how strong, exactly, is this thing? Don't tell me that 'strong as a gorilla' stuff. I want an exact estimation."

"Strength?" Hunter returned the question. "I would say that nothing short of a bank vault, and I mean a big one, could stand up to a full-scale assault from that thing, Chaney."

Chaney grimaced. "You're sure about this?"

"I'm sure." Hunter nodded curtly. "I've tracked it. I've fought with it. And the only reason I'm standing here is because I'm lucky. I can tell you about many who weren't. And I can tell you something else. Whatever this thing is, it was created. That much

I'm certain of. Somebody, Chaney, with a secret agenda wanted that thing to live, so they made it happen."

Chaney frowned.

Hunter's conviction was complete. "Chaney, if you can handle the truth, this isn't some undiscovered species. It's an extinct species. Its time came and went. There is no way that a race of these things could have existed in those mountains for the past ten thousand years without somehow revealing themselves. Even if they had stayed in the mountains or high on the North Ridge, there would have been occasional sightings, the discovery of bones or tools, campsites or caves. Something. Anything. But there's nothing. Not a trace. Not even a footprint. This land, this territory, may have been its haunt once, but not for a long time. Like ten thousand years."

Hunter leaned closer as Chaney recalled the magazine article from Hamilton's town house. It was all coming together, now. Almost to the last. Then Hunter added, "The only thing we don't know is who found the relic of this creature, how they used it somehow to re-create it, and what their intention was."

"And something else," Chaney said, staring with anger and a tinge of fear. "What their intention is."

"That, too. And when you figure out who ultimately created this monster, and why, you'll know why they killed Gina and Rebecca. And so will I. I already have an idea, I just can't prove it yet."

"Dixon?" Chaney asked.

Hunter shook his head. "Hamilton. 'Cause this isn't a government issue. It's private, and has been from the first. The government only got involved on some kind of convoluted sublevel to cover various incompetent butts. I don't what unit is ultimately responsible but I know that Hamilton is the brains behind it. And he's civilian with a lot of interest in a lot of things."

Cocking his head, Chaney had no reservations that Hunter, no matter what form of justice was meted out by the system, would apply his own brand of wrath to those responsible. Although Hunter would probably not kill them, he would certainly use his considerable talent and awesome power to make their lives a living hell.

Brick came to life with that.

"Time's getting close for a killin'," he said abruptly.

Together they turned as the ICU door opened and Dr. Hamilton approached. Strolling slowly, hands comfortably cradled in the pockets of his white lab coat, he gazed with unconcealed amusement from Chaney to Hunter, as if he were singly master of the situation and always would be. Halting, he waited in silence.

Hunter knew it was a power display and he remained silent as well, despising the arrogance. Chaney, obviously, also knew that it was a manifest display of authority but wasn't in the mood for mind games. Staring hard into the scientist's eyes, he stepped close.

"Tell me something, Doctor," he almost whispered. "Why is it that a physician, a healer of men, is heading up an operation far better suited to geologists or computer geeks? And what was of such vital import that demanded your immediate presence here when I hadn't completed my investigation?"

In lieu of an immediate answer, Hamilton pursed his lips. He cast a brief, bemused glance at Hunter before saying, "I see that you have been listening to Mr. Hunter's outrageous speculation." His smile was tolerant. "To be truthful, I myself am in the dark as to the creature's past and his existence. However, I must disagree with the theory Mr. Hunter expounds."

"Which theory would that be, Doctor?"

Hamilton's eyes opened wider and he glanced briefly at Hunter, who remained stoic. "Why, I assumed, wrongly it appears, that Mr. Hunter would have already indoctrinated you about his 'creationist' theory."

"Which is?"

A laugh, and Hamilton gestured. "I'm certain that Mr. Hunter can far better illuminate you on that scenario, Marshal. I myself had trouble completely following it when he graced me with his advanced scientific perceptions."

None of the disparagement seemed impressive to his listeners. Hamilton recognized his diminished status.

"Yeah, he mentioned it." Chaney leaned back on a table. "But I'm not a scientist, Dr. Hamilton. Why don't you explain to me why the theory is so unsound."

"Well." Hamilton raised his eyes, quite humble. "I am not formally trained in anthropology or genetics, Marshal, as Mr.

Hunter may be. I have only a rudimentary understanding of these things. But, and please correct me, Mr. Hunter, if I inadvertently misspeak your hypothesis. But I believe that Mr. Hunter suspects that this creature is somehow, ah, a product of science. He even intimated to me that perhaps these stations which are singly devoted to monitoring seismic activity might be somehow involved."

"And that's an outrageous theory?" Chaney stared at him.

"Oh, yes—well, I do not mean to insult Mr. Hunter—but yes, I would categorize it as a bit farfetched. Even if—and I remind you that it is not the case—these facilities harbored the undocumented goal of creating a .. . uh, a creature such as this, what would be the point? This creature has destroyed three facilities already and almost terminated the program. We will never recover from the episode because the congressional funding was a onetime venture that was almost vetoed in the line-item budget. No, for us to create such a thing only so it would cause the expiration of the program would be the most foolhardy of all endeavors." Hamilton's confidence, if Hunter hadn't seen what he had seen, would have been contagious.

Hamilton continued with only the faintest air of superiority. Apparently he knew he'd overplayed his hand and had quickly and gracefully retreated to a pedantic analysis of the theory. He could have been teaching a biology class at a university.

"Further, I have no idea how, in according with the laws of genetics as I understand them, such a thing would be possible." He hesitated, as if someone might offer an idea. "DNA, under perfect conditions, may sustain its molecular structure for two or three thousand years," he continued. "And, in fact, there are documented instances in which it has. However, if I am correct, this is a creature which Dr. Tipler presumes to be from the Pleistocene epoch, which dissipated an incredible ten thousand years past. Now, that is an amazingly long period of time for DNA to withstand destruction. And to be brutally frank with you and Mr. Hunter and, of course, Dr. Tipler, whom I hold with respect, I find it inconceivable that DNA, or even heme units of blood, could survive half that time."

He shook his head, as if estimating.

"No," he added firmly, "think what you will of me, gentlemen. I know that you hold me in suspicion of untoward activity. And, in a sense, your suspicions are correct. There are, indeed, some classified purposes of these research stations which I cannot reveal. Why else do you believe its supervising administration is secreted at Langley?" He smiled warmly before continuing. "However, there is nothing that involves the scenario I have perceived from Mr. Hunter. The most I can do for all of you is offer my opinion on the probability of such an event transpiring, and I would have to say that it is beyond calculation. It would be odds of one against many tens of billions that heme units would survive such a period of time. Then, again, it would be odds of trillions against one that these units could be reconstituted in some speculative, and probably quite immoral, adventure of science with such startling success. No, I begrudge Mr. Hunter nothing. We had a disagreement of minds, and for that I apologize. I will admit that, with a rude presumption of my own superior learning in the sciences, I treated you with arrogance. I am a man disposed to such arrogance, something I must constantly guard against. But to imagine such a phenomenon is...well, it is simply beyond me, gentlemen. I am at your disposal to assist in whatever means are necessary. But I cannot in good conscience agree with a theory for which I do not have verifiable evidence or even theoretical explanations."

Hunter half-smiled, shook his head. "And then there's common sense, Doctor."

Turning his head, Hamilton again appeared to raise an invisible guard. "Common sense," he said. "And why, Mr. Hunter, would common sense lead me to believe that something which I believe is scientifically impossible could occur?"

Hunter tilted his head toward the window where a gathering dark had already activated automatic security lamps on the wall. It would be another thirty minutes before it was dark enough for the gigantic spotlights that would sweep the compound through the night. He looked back at Hamilton without emotion.

"In the last week, Doctor, you've lost three one-million-dollar installations. Several hundred personnel. Some creature—and it's not an animal—has been searching one research station after another, looking for something that you have. Now, common sense tells me that these research stations are important to it. And so far, Doctor, you're the only one who has told me that these installations aren't so important. Why is that?"

Hamilton's anticipated line of retreat was more polished on its execution. "Mr. Hunter, I know you are not a fool. You are a learned man, a philanthropist, an expert on ecology, and an internationally respected survival expert. I am none of those. I am simply a scientist—nothing unique or special—who operates under a policy of full disclosure to the Senate Intelligence Subcommittee. To whom I report four times each year. You have theories, and they may be good theories, and you may even be correct. But the simple truth—if you accept that as common sense—is that I personally find your theory inconceivable and therefore honestly voice my disagreement." He accented it with a stare. "If you had one shred of evidence to support such a fantastic proposal, I would listen most passionately. However, you only have a suspicion for which I find no verification. We may not practice full disclosure, Mr. Hunter, but we are not mad scientists conducting some irresponsible genetic experiment gone so terribly wrong that it cost several hundred innocent men and women their lives!"

Hunter said nothing, and Hamilton's expression revealed that he was finished, both listening and expounding. After a moment of dull silence he turned to Chaney. "Do you currently have any questions for me, Marshal? I came to ensure the welfare of Dr. Tipler, who appears to be recovering nicely. If you do not, then I shall return to the lab. They are conducting classified experiments which require a supervisor for verification."

"Just a couple," Chaney replied. "But I'll make it quick. How many floors are there to this complex, Doctor?"

"Well, there are three floors aboveground and one below, Marshal. It is only a storage area, or warehouse, you might say, for the facility. All of the scientific equipment is located on this floor, and the other floors are dedicated to offices and barracks for the military personnel and medical...uh, I mean, staff personnel."

"I'd like a tour of the basement," Chaney said. "I want to see what kind of equipment you're housing."

"Of course, Marshal. I have nothing to hide. I can also provide you with a tour of the barracks and science facilities if you so desire. I assure that you will have no suspicions afterwards." He lifted his wrist to examine his watch. "I still have a little time. If you like, we could do it now and get it over with."

"Right now is fine."

Hamilton exhaled, as if he were dealing with children that he must reluctantly indulge. "Very well, then. Though I doubt that you'll be able to conduct a full inventory. No matter; we can complete it tomorrow." He raised an arm to invite the tour. "We can begin now if you wish."

Chaney walked forward.

Hunter caught a momentary grimace on the doctor's face. A flash - less than a tenth of a second – that was subdued by the friendliest of smiles. "It will no doubt be brief because there is nothing to see," he added. "Unless, of course, you enjoy skulking about seemingly endless rows of cardboard boxes filled with computer equipment, food, blankets, or replacement parts for vehicles. You can understand that, up here, so far into the mountains, we must remain quite self-sufficient. It is necessary to keep at least a six-month supply of everything available at all times." He focused with the air of a busy man too long detained. "Could we begin immediately, Marshal?"

"That's fine with me." Chaney nodded and looked at Brick. "Get a feel for the place. I can handle this."

Hunter turned his head to Ghost: "Guard."

Ghost rose on hind legs and put both paws on Tipler's bed, staring down, panting. The old man laughed, and the great black wolf began pacing back and forth before the door opening. Nothing mortal was coming inside without permission.

Hunter turned to Chaney. "If you don't mind, I'd like to go along. I wouldn't mind taking a look around that place myself."

"Got no objections at all," Chaney said, lifting the Weatherby .454 from the desk. He snapped open the breach to make sure two mammoth brass shells were chambered and closed it with a sharp iron click. Holding the weapon midway, in perfect balance, he said, "Let's go, Professor. You're the tour guide."

"I'm gonna stay with the professor," Bobbi Jo said to Hunter alone. "And when the nurse returns I'm going outside to take up position. Probably on the roof."

"All right." Hunter followed Hamilton from the room, but turned backwards for a single step—he didn't know why—to see her staring intently after him. Then she moved her lips to frame a silent sentence and Hunter knew exactly what she said. With a slight surprise, he realized that he'd expected it.

"Be careful. "

Takakura and Taylor scanned the compound, roaming. They checked the fence at one point with a small piece of steel, laying one end on the ground and letting the other end fall over so that the current grounded out. A split second later the automatic breakers reset and they knocked the steel aside with a long section of a severed two-by-four—a safe thing to do because wood can't conduct an electrical current—and resumed roaming.

Taylor had spent most of the afternoon, or what time was left after his debriefing by army intelligence, arming himself for the expected battle. Two bandoleers of shotgun shells, at least fifty per belt, crisscrossed his barrel chest. A semi-automatic street-sweeper—a short shotgun with a cylindrical twelve-round magazine—hung heavily on a sling. And he had a sawed-off double-barreled shotgun in a hip holster. The side-by-side barrels were barely eight inches long; the stock had been sawed off and sanded to allow a firm and comfortable pistol grip. He also had a .50-caliber Desert Eagle semiautomatic on his right hip with clips attached to his combat belt. Night-vision goggles hung on an elastic strap from his neck.

Takakura carried the katana on his back and the M-14 in his arms. He also was heavily armed, with a .45-caliber pistol on each hip and at least eight antipersonnel grenades in his pockets. He had used a thin strip of white tape to doubly secure each pin, thereby preventing the pin from being pulled prematurely. Although the tape made it twice as difficult to pull the pin, a man in combat, hyped on adrenaline and fear, might disregard it.

Glancing down, Taylor noticed the combat trick.

"Nice gig, securing pins like that," he said. "Reminds me of Panama when we were hooching the worst bush you'd ever seen. And some green puke, about two months in, was trying to work his way through a jungle of 'wait a minute' vines. I was at covering distance right behind him, maybe fifteen feet, and he was almost through the wall when the pin on one of his grenades got jerked loose by a vine." He cocked his head sympathetically at the memory. "Never did trust grenades after that."

Takakura grunted. "Precaution is always wise, especially in combat, where surprise is the last thing the dead realize. I suppose we will discover if we have taken enough of them."

"You really believe it's coming? Tonight, I mean?"

"Yes."

Silent for a moment, Taylor then asked, "What makes you so sure? I mean, look around you."

Takakura lifted his eyes to the ceiling and angled them to the darkened hills outside the compound. A stygian cloak seemed to absorb the light rather than be illuminated by it. "It will come," he frowned. "It comes for him."

"For Hunter?"

"Yes," Takakura said with subdued emotion. "For Hunter."

***

He had discovered the outside listening post by scent, disappointed that it had been abandoned. Then a distant, mournful howl carried through the night and he raised his head, laughing.

Yes, the wolf he had slain with a single slashing blow, severing the head and consuming the brain just for the primitive pleasure of it, had been discovered by its mate.

Killing was such sweet pleasure.

Feeling again the physical release he had felt when the wolf's body had fallen, so slowly, to the ground—its eyes blinking in shock as the head hung suspended in the air before it landed on a slope—he growled and turned back to his task, studying the structure.

Wooden logs covered with a thick layer of dirt and brush would have concealed the bunker from a visual search, but human scent thickly marked the air.

Only a small slit cut into the hill had allowed a narrow view. He knew that the entrance and exit would be in the back, also concealed. Yes, they were wise to withdraw within the safety of the fence, a fence higher than any it had yet encountered.

Crouching in darkness three hundred feet from the compound, he saw the soldiers, dogs, guns, and armed vehicles, the heavily manned towers in constant movement.

Frowning, he studied all that was here, memorizing the routine, the location of troops. With narrow red eyes he spied a large building located at the back. Even across the distance he could hear the drone of machinery as the machine powered the fence, the lights. Without the machines, they were helpless in the dark.

Rising slowly, apelike arms hanging with a fullness of refreshed strength, he inhaled, and his mammoth chest swelled gigantically. Snarling, he prepared himself, rising on an internal tide of empowering rage, knowing this would be the most difficult of all.

And yet fear did not enter his animal mind as he turned, loping high across the surrounding ridge, constantly searching for the tiny wires that had injured him once before, because he had not known the danger. And quickly he was close to the building that roared with the turning electrical thing that he would destroy.

Creeping soundlessly across waist high bush, he moved in.

***

"What's this, Doc?"

Chaney's voice echoed across the near-silent underground chamber and Hamilton moved slowly toward him.

"Oh, that is a backup electromagnetic monitor," he answered. "We are trying to correlate any sunspot activity with the change in the tectonic plate shifts. So far, we have been unsuccessful in tracing any coordination. But it was an interesting theory, nevertheless."

Rising slowly, Chaney removed a crowbar from the wall. "Let's have a look."

"Of course, Marshal, you are in authority here. Feel free to examine anything you wish."

In a minute Chaney pried off the wooden lip and removed the cushioning Styrofoam and cardboard. He didn't lift it from the box, but felt the back, the front. Then he walked inside to examine the seemingly endless rows of food, fuel, spare parts, weapons, clothing. It was a virtual harbor of goods, and Chaney wore a displeased frown as he wandered about.

On the far side of the room, Hunter was utterly still. He hadn't moved more than thirty feet since he'd entered the lower level, though Chaney thought Hunter was also checking inventory.

No, he hadn't moved, nor did he plan to blindly wander the storage aisles looking for what he knew was not there. He was confident Hamilton would have never complied with their request if there were any evidence of guilt.

For certain, whatever they were searching for would be better concealed. And so he turned his mind to role-playing the prey, attempting to think as Hamilton. It was a trick he used when hunting elusive animals; he hoped it would help him now.

Think like a tiger ...

Like a wolf ...

Like a fox ...

What did an animal do when it wanted to conceal something?

He knew most of the answers without effort: An alligator would shove the body of its prey beneath a stump, allowing it to rot before it fed. A bear would cover his prey with dirt, all the while hovering nearby and eating the carcass at its leisure for days at a time. A fox would cover his food inside a log close to the den and bury it with leaves. But never too close, lest the dead prey lure rivals into a fight for possession of the hard-won sustenance. A tiger would simply drag his prey into a secluded location where he would bury it under leaves and eat for a week, never leaving the slaughter for more than an hour at a time. A quick review, and Hunter realized that the same instinctive practice was occurring again and again, though in varied form.

Bury it.

Yes ...

Bury it!

As Chaney opened another box before the patient and endlessly indulgent Dr. Hamilton—arms crossed in calm cooperation—Hunter placed a hard hand on the concrete floor.

Cold, smooth, and ... something else ...

He frowned as he studied it, wondering.

Cold, smooth, and ... what?

Time passed.

Hunter scowled, unmoving, and concentrated. He closed his eyes, letting it speak to him, searching.

Cold ... smooth and ...

What did he feel?

He shook his head, frustrated.

Before he understood.

Vibration.

Hunter didn't open his eyes, revealed nothing in his repose. Then, slowly, he raised his hand until only the tips of his fingers—a place where the nerves were clustered closer than any other place in the body—were touching lightly. He relaxed and closed his eyes, feeling, reading, waiting, and he noticed that the infinitesimal vibrations were rhythmic.

So slight as to be unnoticeable to anything but the lightest touch, they continued without respite. And Hunter looked around, searching and wondering. Upstairs, he knew, the second story of this facility was fed electricity by massive generators housed in the tin shed at the back of the complex. Too far, he knew, to make the cement floor beneath him vibrate with the labor.

No, this was something different. It was from the machinery housed upstairs or from something ... beneath.

He opened his eyes to see Hamilton aiding Chaney once again in the examination of yet another ubiquitous military crate. In the space of a breath Hunter rose and walked toward them. When he was close, he spoke loudly to Chaney with a trace of carefully constructed frustration, of defeat.

"I'm outta here, Chaney," he said, waving as he turned away. "We're not gonna find anything. I'm gonna check on Bobbi Jo."

Chaney scowled. "We haven't had a chance to check this place out yet, Hunter! Why don't you look on the other side? See if you can find anything that doesn't have shipping orders attached to it!"

"No time!" Hunter threw up a hand. "I'm going up top to make sure we've got our ducks lined up and check on Bobbi Jo! You can finish this!"

He had walked ten feet when Hamilton called after him. "You needn't worry about the elevator!" he instructed. "It will automatically stop on the first floor! I'm sure you will know your bearings!"

Hunter said nothing—don't overplay stupidity—in reply as he reached the elevator and entered, hitting the button and waiting as the doors began to shut. He had a moment of panic as Hamilton continued to stare at him and then the doors began to slide. At the same instant, Chaney said something to the doctor and Hamilton glanced down.

Years of split-second decision-making gave Hunter the edge to slide with animal grace out the doors as they closed. He moved with the stealth of a panther, flattening himself against the end of a shelf along the wall. He was almost completely submerged in darkness.

Carefully glancing over the crates, he saw Hamilton turn to the elevator. The doors were closed completely and for a second the doctor frowned, as if he had been denied the pleasure of observing Hunter's departure. Then Chaney was moving again and Hamilton—ever too eager to assist—was beside him.

They walked farther into the warehouse as Hunter bent and crept in the opposite direction, stooping occasionally to feel the floor. But the vibrations became weaker as he worked his way to the west end of the building, more powerful as he stalked toward the east. Concentrated on the task, he could almost hear the dim subterranean drone when he sensed shadows approaching.

It wasn't so much sight or sound as that nebulous and unexplainable "something," warning of another's presence that caused his face and narrow eyes to rise.

Hunter had learned how to obey the sensation instantly and was moving slowly and silently between two huge crates that might have housed refrigerators when they rounded the corner where he had been. He heard rather than saw Chaney and Hamilton at the elevator cargo doors, and followed Chaney's every word.

"We're not done here, Doctor," he said with obvious displeasure. "We'll put off the rest of the search until morning. But we'll continue. So plan for it."

"Of course. Anything you wish, Marshal."

Then they were gone and Hunter emerged, gazing at the empty warehouse. Every fourth overhead fluorescent light remained lit, and Hunter assumed they were on all the time.

Step by step, he worked his way closer to the heart of the vibration, eventually locating a section near the east wall. He knew only one thing: if it was a cooling system, it would require ventilation because it couldn't circulate either cool or warm air without evacuating it as well.

Searching the floor, Hunter found two small vents. But he discovered a much larger vent not far away. He knew the two smaller vents were for heating and cooling. This big one was something else: it was an exhaust vent for the floor below.

It took him another ten minutes to move a heavy crate away from the wall, and he frowned grimly at the discovery.

Holding his open hand before the ventilation grill, Hunter clearly felt warm air expelled from the lowest and unmentioned level of the research station—a level that the cooperative Dr. Hamilton had somehow forgotten to name. He waited, letting his senses speak to him, and found that what was below was scented with heat, electrical circuitry, paper, people, science . . .

He shook his head, saddened at what he knew lay beneath.

"No more secrets, Doctor," he said aloud.

***

A gigantic ray of light, so intense that he could feel the heat of it, passed over his head, but he did not move. Motionless behind an outcropping of rock, he waited patiently until it reached beyond him to starkly illuminate a barren slope.

Closing on the deserted area behind the shed had proven more difficult than he'd anticipated. Four times already dogs on patrol had stopped and stared directly over him, but he knew their limitations, knew they could not see him behind the rocks, nor could they scent him because he was downwind. After a moment their handlers had prodded them to continue moving, though the patrols were so close together he could only gain a few precious feet before he was forced to lie still once more.

Somewhere within him there arose a fear: a fear of the man. Then he shook his head to clear it and continued, crawling closer.

He knew that what this body had once been was almost completely consumed. And he was pleased. Because for so long now, in the most un-expected moments, a flare of past awareness would spark white through the lower depth of his darkest being, remembrance of a consciousness not completely destroyed.

It was of no matter. For in time he would completely overcome the vestiges of whatever this being had once been.

He was already as pure physically as he had been in his lost age, though he yet continued to mutate, each change enhancing and enlarging his strength, endurance, or cunning—all the faculties that made him the greatest, and the purest, of all predators.

Without effort he could catch the scent of a wolf when it was yet miles distant. And as he loped with unending endurance through the mossy dark forest, the leaf-strewn floor buried beneath countless seasons of decayed vegetation, he could effortlessly identify plants that he could barely see in the gloom.

Yes, he knew which plants yet survived and thrived beneath the loam, and whether they would heal or hurt. He knew what animals had been this way, and when, and what lay dying or dead on the farthest surrounding hill. He could hear the faintest broken twig that filled the silence, and knew whether it was from wind or decay or another's presence. There seemed no end to his strength, his rage, his glory, and he reveled in it.

He knew that if others had seen him as he made this dark journey—a spectral image of fangs and monstrous talons, tirelessly, relentlessly closing the distance to his prey—they would have beheld the purest image of physical perfection, of ultimate predatory might.

No, he told himself, he was not afraid of the man.

The man had wounded him, but he would wound him no more. For when he had the man in his grasp again, the end would be quick. And the man would know he had been defeated; he would know true fear. As all of them had known fear before ... before ...

Again, images came to him.

Screaming/descending through night to crush flesh/brains, hot blood, wet fangs, red throat/consuming, consuming/war that was won/glory, leaping, ecstasy/green forest in sunlight, others who challenged and were defeated/red-white images on stone with shadows dancing before flame/ blackness burning/roars/fear and screams, fleeing, descending/confusion within/war within/ turning, war within/fighting, hurt, fleeing/anger, cold, fear/ white blood/war-death behind him/tiger beneath, kill, eat/ falling together, white ice/white . . .

He had forgotten where he lay.

War?

A long time he waited ...

No answer came.

He drove the images from his mind, attempting to remember where he lay beneath this cold cloud dome of bright white, and it returned to him. They could not see him yet, he knew, but soon he would be observed. But it would be too late.

Humans ... so frail.

They could never be as he was. Because they would never know the night as he knew it with the rage and the flame and the hunger that was satisfied only by the blood.

Yes ... the blood.

Their blood ...

CHAPTER 19

It required ten minutes to remove the screws attaching the aluminum ventilation cover to the smooth cement wall. When he had finished, Hunter stared down into a long square shaft. It was easily large enough for a man and he had a fairly good idea where it led. But he didn't know if he had time for a thorough inspection of what lay below.

Hunter raised his face to the tiered ceiling, listening, but he heard no sounds of gunfire, no alarms—nothing. Yet the lack of declared, open combat was not comforting.

He was confident that the creature would attack tonight, cunningly and quickly. He suspected that when the alarms sounded, the battle would already be half lost.

As he stood there, Hunter contemplated every aspect of the situation. He dissected each incident from the first research station destroyed to the dispatch of the hunting team, the suspected sabotage, the creature's manlike intelligence yet feral nature, and its passionate search to find an unknown treasure.

And he knew whatever lay below held the answer to all those questions together, was confident that the secret hidden there would be the nexus of a mystery that had cost so many lives, and still threatened the world.

If he was going to move at all, it must be done quickly.

Hamilton—no fool, though Hunter held him in contempt—would doubtless soon notice his absence and order a search. It was a chance that he'd have to take. He'd deal with that complication when the time came.

By instinct or habit—it didn't matter, he knew the purpose—he felt for his Bowie knife, half removing the wide ten-inch blade before sliding it downward into the sheath.

He had no other weapon except the device he had constructed in secret before the track had begun, the snare that had already twice saved his life. And even now he carried the slate-gray stick of steel with its killing loop of titanium wire in his belt.

If the moment came, he would use it, though he doubted a situation requiring that desperate measure would end in survival.

Descending the shaft like a mountain climber, wedging his body into the corner, Hunter silently lowered himself into the darkness.

The updraft was colder than he had anticipated, and he suspected that the computer equipment hidden below required an uncomfortably chill atmosphere. It took him less than a minute to cover the distance in absolute quiet—and he found himself staring through the grill at the back side of a large off-white computer.

Unlike the floor above, this grill could be pushed out without the removal of screws, and Hunter entered what he knew already was a vast, open laboratory. The air was still. And although he had not yet looked, he knew it was one enormous chamber.

There was an unmistakable sense of space in the way the air hovered – of a room high and deep – that he hadn't encountered anywhere else in the complex.

He bowed his head and listened, hearing the drone of numerous terminals. And somewhere in the distance, measuring the length of the room by sound alone, he discerned soft voices.

Angling toward the far end of the computer, away from the voices, Hunter looked into the room and saw only random equipment—it could have been any science complex. Then he looked more boldly and there, with their backs turned to him, were four white-coated lab technicians revolving around a multi-monitored computer dais. In the center of the room, a long cylindrical tube rose from the floor almost to the stark-white ceiling. Although it was filled strangely with darkness, it was clearly an object of importance. The entire chamber seemed designed around it.

Conditioned to avoiding the uncanny instincts of tiger and bear, Hunter effortlessly avoided the dulled, civilized senses of the technicians as he covertly crossed the chamber. And for a split second he imagined how truly easy it had been for the creature to slay them—civilized weaklings with senses atrophied by disuse and insulation. If it were not plainly before their eyes, they would not see it.

Trapped in their routine, they would not notice him or his actions. The only thing that could make them notice would be one of their machines. These were men and women who had surrendered to machines the very abilities and responsibilities that had once made them superior. And if he had been the predator and they the prey, he could have ended it quickly. How much easier it had been for the beast when it had stalked the corridors of the other facilities, effortlessly snatching them from futile hiding places into a roaring world of fang, blackness, claw, and death.

Kneeling behind a black computer terminal—several monitors built with sophisticated networking into a polished altar-like display system—he studied it carefully. He saw blood-analysis charts, the complex breakdown ratios of heme units, electrolytes, receptor cells and genomes, and nodded.

Yes, of course ...

Years of association with the world's greatest scholar of genetics allowed him to understand the data easily; it was a molecular diagram of a DNA strand.

Hunter lightly touched the keypad, scrolling the information, analyzing the coding sequence, and estimated that the dual strand of DNA was predominantly human. Moving carefully to avoid sound, he typed in Directory/pause. And instantly—damn fast computer—he was staring at a screen-sized list of file names with a breakdown of subtopics included in each. He moved the cursor to the file named "Species" and hit enter.

What greeted him next, in full color and with amazing accuracy of detail, was a computer simulation of what he had hunted and challenged and fought through the mountains for the past three days. Nor was it a placid picture, but rather a moving image of primal power, muscles tensed in rage, hands clenched in irrepressible contraction with claws upraised—an image he knew all too well.

Alert to the location of everyone in the laboratory—some had strolled closer and were seated less than twenty feet away—Hunter scanned the files one by one, searching. He opened up a search mode, grateful that he had taken the years to familiarize himself with computer technology, and typed in HD-66.

What opened to him was no surprise:

Prototype of unknown species' DNA synthesized at North Ridge Laboratory for purpose of injection and experimentation. Unsuccessfully tested on species N-5, N-6, and N-7 with molecular breakdown of host indigenous DNA recorded at 9:31:23 hours of implementation. HD-66 serum refined with molecular removal of 91.3 identifying Homo sapiens dual-strand proteins and isolation of transmitter molecules and receptor genes.

IMPLEMENTATION: 00:00:00 Hours
IA Injection unrefined HD-66 serum at 11:29 A 6 Hours into host organism.
2B Successful absorption of refined HD-66 serum by indigenous host DNA at 28:41:34 Hours: 0 percent.
3C Destruction of host indigenous DNA by refined HD-66 serum at 31:54:25 Hours: 52 percent.
4D Complete molecular breakdown of host indigenous DNA to HD-66 at 45:52:03 Hours: 100 percent.
FINALIZATION: All host systems terminated and destroyed in accordance with Level IV Biohazard Containment Procedures 0-010-000. Experiment terminated with nitrous oxide and host organisms destroyed at 72:13:43 Hours.
Refinement of HD-66 re-implemented at 13:00:00 Hours . . .
Hunter read more, a percentage analysis of lymphocytes, T-cells, granulocytes, monocytes, a diagnostic of the response neural network to generate white cell production ...
Following every movement in the room by sound, Hunter returned to subject listings and something caught his attention. An instinct, almost like a ghostly touch on his shoulder, caused him to wonder what the video file "Security Video, Station One" contained.
The decision was made as he saw it, and he opened the file to a grainy black-and-white projection with the time—45:14:42 hours—displayed prominently in a lower corner of the screen. Sweating with the stress of hovering so close to the lab personnel, Hunter saw a security video of a large laboratory similar to this one bustling with generic technicians who seemed so nameless, faceless, and lifeless. But on the far side was a glassed-in chamber—a cell of sorts—where a man sat motionless and alone on a blanketed cot.

Without Hunter's direction the camera switched angles to show the man more closely. And for a moment Hunter stared, all the while following with his eyes two more personnel who had walked across the room and now stood six feet away.

He blinked sweat from his eyes.

What happened next made his skin crawl, chilling him even as he felt his heart rate increase, his breath deepen. For the man had fallen onto his face, writhing in pain. Then he clawed at his shirt, his eyes, and his face and began screaming, howling. He tore off his shoes and for a moment vanished beyond the camera angle, and when he writhed back into view Hunter was horrified . . .

Slowly at first, and then with appalling acceleration, the man's face altered, widening and distorting—transforming—and his hair fell in clumps and waves as he continued to scream and claw at himself. And then, in a maddened frenzy of rolling, beating upon any inanimate object that touched him as if it burned with fire, his body was grotesquely twisted by some tectonic collision of cells, hideously deforming him before he ...before it...lay in a stillness far deeper than death.

Hunter recognized the primordial outline of that form, though far smaller in this video than it had since become. And he knew his enemy. Knew finally where it had been spawned, and how.

Recovering consciousness and breath, the creature rose slowly, sullen and sneering, from the floor.

On the left side of the monitor, the glass wall was visible, and Hunter saw innumerable technicians staring in horror, holding clipboards close. He did not need to see their faces to read their fear. And as the creature inhaled deeply, almost with savage satisfaction at his altered state of being, there was an unnatural stillness in them all. Then, striding forward with remarkable slowness, it simply walked into the six-inch Plexiglas, shattering it spectacularly with a hammer-like blow, and was among them.

Hunter did not need to see what happened next.

One less mystery.

Hunter raised sullen eyes to the suspended cylindrical type that hung inside an electromagnetic field—he understood the process because the bare copper wiring that domed the top and bottom of the cylinder fairly hummed with energy—and knew that inside that darkness lay another answer.

He had followed the movement of the four technicians, and rose as they came around the display where he crouched. He knew that they would have cried out if he had allowed them the chance, but Hunter instantly seized one by the throat, shoving him against the chest-high computer terminal. And before the other could react he pinned him also with his Bowie knife. Holding the blade against the technician's neck while easily controlling the first man who, not unsurprisingly, did not resist, Hunter spoke with threat to the others.

"Stay where you are!"

Already on their feet, they moved no farther.

"Don't touch anything!" he continued. Then he shoved the two male technicians toward the other man and woman, crowding them for control. He pointed to the cylinder. "Turn on the lights. I want to see what's inside the tube."

The woman, not removing her eyes from Hunter, reached down carefully to the computer dais. When her hand was close, she cast a quick glance and slowly pushed a switch, and Hunter stepped away from them, staring upward at the tube. His knife hung forgotten in his hand as the image emerged before him, green light washing slowly over a bowed, monstrous head, ragged wisps of hair floating in jade liquid.

The light flooded downward—shaggy gray hair doming a broad deep forehead above a heavy brow that shaded dark eyes, high cheeks that protruded stone-like on either side of a broad, flattened nose; then a wide mouth—a wicked, frowning gash with the pinpoints of long fangs visible through the jade—hanging open. And the hugely muscled, apelike neck and gorilla chest that swelled as thick twin shields beneath the chin, and, finally, to the knotted, powerful arms, matted and dark with coarse hair. And even farther the light descended to reveal long muscular legs—not like those of an ape, but of a man, yet so overdeveloped and powerfully defined that they could have undoubtedly propelled this colossus of human evolution to shocking heights or hurled that hulking weight with a cheetah's speed across the vined and tepid slime morasses of a world long buried beneath the awesome weight of time.

It was dead; Hunter needed no one to tell him that. And from the withered facial features, the smoothness of its flesh, he knew it had been dead for eons. Almost as an afterthought, he studied the large, powerful hands. Even the centuries had not dulled the fiendish aspect of those blackened claws.

Inhaling deeply, Hunter shook his head at the foolishness of man. Not anymore did he need anyone to tell him what they had done. Now the only question remaining ...was why.

No alarms had sounded above; he felt no compulsion to rush. Nor had the laboratory technicians moved to flee, although he would have allowed them. Rather, they stood in absolute stillness, apparently fearful that he meant them harm, which he did not.

He heard the elevator open behind him, listened calmly as suppressed footsteps approached and counted their number: six pairs of military boots and the squeak of foam-soled working shoes—the kind that Dr. Hamilton habitually wore.

Sheathing his Bowie, Hunter continued to stare with amazed disbelief at the entombed monstrosity until, ever so slowly, Hamilton halted beside him.

Absolutely no registration of anger or disappointment was visible on the scientist's face; obviously, he was a man rarely surprised. His arms were crossed casually and his posture was that of a man admiring a fine painting. And when he spoke, a glimmering smile raised one corner of his mouth in what seemed to be admiration, even amusement, at what Hunter had discovered.

"And so," Hamilton began pleasantly, "now you know."

Hunter almost laughed, but it was more of a disbelieving grunt. The situation was so insane, so beyond the realm of reason and responsibility, that he didn't know what to say. He shook his head and looked at Hamilton.

"How did you ever think to keep a thing like this secret?"

Nonchalant and amused, Hamilton smiled. "But I have kept it a secret, Mr. Hunter."

His confidence, again, was supreme. Hunter wondered how Hamilton truly looked upon others.

Hunter glanced around casually and counted six black-clad soldiers. "I suppose," he said, "that you intend to kill me."

Hamilton said nothing, and his aspect did not change.

Hunter had never seen the uniformed soldiers aboveground and reasoned that they weren't regular military but a special contingent designed to protect this hidden level. Escape was paramount in his mind, and then he thought of Bobbi Jo above with the rest, waiting for the attack. He looked at Hamilton, shook his head.

"You really are insane, you know," he said.

"Hmm?" Hamilton raised his brow, undisturbed. "Well, of course, there are those who might think so, Mr. Hunter. But I disagree. And, as regarding my plans for you, I believe that is self-evident. After all, we are both men of the world. We are both reasonably experienced, each in his own way, with illegal, dangerous, and dark oceans of secrets. Further, I do not wish to be indelicate by stating what is both obvious and unavoidable. And I hope you understand: I really have no choice in the matter."

If Hamilton expected to see fear in Hunter, he was disappointed.

Hunter smiled.

"You know, Hamilton, in all my traveling, all the places I've been, the things I've done, I've never actually killed a man."

Hamilton took it as the insult it was intended to be. His face tightened, eyes crinkling with the sting. He didn't attempt to polish his tone as he replied.

"Really? A shame I can't say the same."

***

Standing on the edge of the roof, Bobbi Jo had positioned the Barrett on a large crate, bipod extended. The huge rifle dominated the weapon-heavy environment, making the M-16's seem like toys. Two freshly loaded clips were set on a table. She had positioned a bench behind her so she could comfortably pick off the creature with one well-placed shot after another when it penetrated the perimeter.

She had refused binoculars but held a Generation III NightQuest starlight scope in a hand. Hardly larger than her fist, the two-pound monocular allowed light amplification 45,000 times greater than what was visible with the naked eye. At intervals of two to three minutes, she would raise it and scan the fence, the brush, and surrounding trees before lowering it in stoic silence.

There were perhaps twenty personnel positioned on the building's four sides. Most of them carried lightweight automatic weapons, but there was also an M-60 armed with a gunner and a second soldier, a belt runner, on each wall. The compound itself swarmed with four- and six-man attack squads, and canine units were working in pairs, patrolling the fence line.

Measuring the multilayered security, Bobbi Jo knew that, if she were attempting to defeat the security, she would have called it a "no-go." Nothing, surely, could either steal or fight its way through that hive of dogs, guns, and soldiers. Not to mention the steel-mesh fence powered to twenty-five thousand volts; the generators in the back shed roared with the maximum electrical output. And a ten-thousand-gallon tanker "was parked close to ensure that the two-ton machines had enough gasoline to last the night.

No one spoke to her because it was understood; snipers preferred to work alone. Utter concentration was paramount in the job, and distractions were despised. Without facial expression she wondered where Hunter was, and if he was safe.

The eerie atmosphere of secrets combined with the forthright promise of impending mortal combat continued to wear upon her emotional control. She was trained to control her feelings. She was all too aware that, for him, her control was vanishing.

A voice came from behind her.

"Have you seen Hunter?"

Bobbi Jo turned and saw the marshal, Chaney, with the big man called Brick. They were carrying the Weatherby .454 double-barreled hunting rifles, and each sported a bandoleer of the five-inch-long brass cartridges. Brick also had an AK-47 slung across his back, and six full magazines and four antipersonnel grenades strapped on his regulation-issue gun belt.

"No." She frowned. "I thought he was with you, Chaney."

"No." Chaney shook his head, brow hardening. "He said he was coming up to check the roof, to make sure you were okay. Then I think he said he was going to walk the perimeter."

Bobbi Jo's eyes narrowed in worry. "No. I haven't seen him. How long ago was that?"

"Twenty, thirty minutes."

Brick grunted, soft and low, turned his head in thought. No one spoke for a time and then Bobbi Jo added, "Maybe somebody should go look for him. It's not right for Hunter to say he's gonna do something and not do it." She paused with heat. "He's not like that."

Chaney nodded.

"All right," he agreed, making a half-turn. "I'll go take a look around."

"I'll do it," Brick broke in, placing a beefy hand on Chaney's arm. "I know this kind of setup. Worked one in the Philippines, and there's lots of places a guy can get confused, especially back there around the motor pool. If he's doing some real serious checking, I could speed things up for him and then we can all rendezvous back here."

"Sounds good," Chaney acquiesced. "But tell Hunter to get back here as soon as he can. He understands that thing better than anyone. We can use him to anticipate its attack."

Bobbi Jo spoke up. "Hunter doesn't want to be on a roof, Marshal. He'll want to be out there with it, hunting it just like it's hunting him. That's what he's best at."

"What he's best at, Lieutenant," Chaney responded with an edge of im-patience, "and what we need are two different things. Hunter is the only one that can get inside that thing's mind. So if we have him coordinating our counterattack, we might fare a damn sight better than the other installations that went to ground. Colonel Maddox is in charge, but I think he'd agree with me. The more we can anticipate what this creature is going to do, the better our chances are of countering. And maybe, if we're lucky, we might just survive this goddamn fight."

Brick was walking away, head down in intense thought. "You guys settle it. I'm gonna do some looking." He turned back with an agility that belied his considerable bulk. "You said Hunter told you he was coming up top?"

"Yeah," replied Chaney.

Brick nodded. "Where was the two of ya when he told you that?"

"We were in the basement, looking over the inventory. But he came up before I did."

"Huh." Brick turned back to the sniper. Chaney opened his mouth to continue but Bobbi Jo cut him off. "Listen, Marshal, I'm not in the mood to argue with you. I just take orders. I don't give them. Whatever suggestions you have for Hunter, you can settle them with him."

"Good enough." Chaney nodded and walked across the antenna-strewn roof toward Colonel Maddox, who had taken position in the command center. Field telephone lines hooked with numerous lights were manned by a sergeant, and a young communications officer was dispatching on UHF radios.

Maddox, hands clasped behind his back, paced back and forth in their midst. " 'Evening, Marshal," he said distractedly as Chaney arrived. He signed a clipboard that was presented and absently checked the .45 at his waist. It was the first time Chaney had seen him in battle dress. Chaney wasted no time, saying, "Colonel I think it would be advantageous if we had Hunter in the command center instead of on the grounds."

Maddox looked emptily at him. "Hmm?"

"I said," Chaney repeated, "Hunter is the only one who can anticipate what this thing might do, and we might be able to use him in the command center."

Maddox was nodding, but Chaney wasn't certain if the colonel had heard what he said. It was to be expected; Chaney had seen the same look in 'Nam when a battalion of Viet Cong would have an isolated firebase surrounded, waiting only for darkness to fall so they could launch a merciless, scorching series of attacks that would continue until dawn. Once the battle began, Chaney never had time or emotion for fear; he was too busy staying alive. But, in the long period when they would be waiting together for nightfall, they all had too much time to contemplate the oncoming horror and knew nothing but terror. Those were the times, Chaney often thought, that he had hated the most and remembered the most. He decided to try communicating with Maddox more forcefully.

"Colonel," he said, stepping up, "we need someone in the command center who can help us anticipate what this creature might do! I suggest we ask Hunter to come up here as an adviser!"

Maddox waved. "Oh, yes, of course. Uh, tell Mr. Hunter his presence is requested in the CP." He glanced nervously at the surrounding trees. "And do it quickly."

***

Maintaining severe emotional control, Hunter mentally pictured what he knew about the room—the locations of various equipment, doors, cables, terminals.

He didn't know what, exactly, he was going to do. But he had already decided that Hamilton was not leaving his side. He tried to delay what seemed inevitable and, as he spoke, realized that he truly wanted an answer.

"I suppose it was you all along?" he asked.

Hamilton laughed dismissively. "Of course not, Mr. Hunter. It was never 'only' I. In fact, the tentacles of this exercise reach deeply into a dozen, oh, how shall I say it ...domains?" He paused. "Yes, domains. Seems a strange word. But many are involved. Men of unlimited wealth, some in government, some in the private sector, all wishing to inherit the benefits contained within this fantastic specimen of evolution. Strange how I never sought to classify those who have labored beside me, until now. I merely considered them part of a higher system, or the heart of the system, you might say."

"And what system would that be?"

Hunter actually wanted to know, now that he had come this far and was likely to pay a severe price for the knowledge he obtained. He added sullenly, "Sounds like a good crew, Hamilton. A system of rich sleazeballs that murdered a young woman to protect some apeman that died ten thousand years ago." He shook his head.

The scientist's entire body shook with an explosive laugh, and Hunter instantly checked his mercurial impulse to kill Hamilton with a single move. But even as the reaction seized him, Hunter had already shut it down. His hand never moved.

"Really, Mr. Hunter, I may have overestimated your worldliness," Hamilton responded. Although the smile failed to fully fade, he grew still, staring with that impenetrable arrogance. "Do you really presume that all ...this...could be the work of a single man? Or even a single agency? No, Mr. Hunter, it was a coalition, you might say. People who forever remain in the shadows."

Hunter frowned, stoic.

"Really, Mr. Hunter, you disappointment me and surprise me simultaneously. First you deduced, and correctly I might add, that there was a hidden level to the institution. And other deductions you reached regarding my poor ..."

Hunter interjected: "Luther? Your poor Luther?"

Hamilton's smile was benign. "Yes, Mr. Hunter – my poor Luther. Or the creature, as you now call it, who was once a respected colleague of mine. Yes, his name was Luther Friedkin." He shook his head in the mildest remorse. "Poor Luther, he did not know what manner of game he played. Always impetuous. Always rushing ahead of where science had conclusively led. And he was quite brilliant, you know. But—and I assume you have watched the video since it continues to replay the ghastly carnage of that night— Luther impractically moved ahead of safeguards and injected himself with the cloning serum which he himself had ionized from ..." Hamilton lifted his hand with reverence. "From one who was like a god."

Hunter didn't look at the creature. "This man must have had a good reason to take a chance like that," he said. "Why don't you tell me about it?"

With the most minute shrug Hamilton said without emotion, "Well, in truth, who will ever know for certain? Luther's genius was, indeed, unparalleled. And perhaps he concluded, erroneously, that he had perfected the serum." He paused. "Earlier tests on his serum, which were conducted on baboons, were spectacularly positive and so Luther bypassed human testing and volunteered himself. Perhaps Luther was simply too impetuous to seize the power, the pure physical might and the immortality that man has sought since time began."

Hunter was dead-steady. "It's a fantasy, Hamilton. Nobody lives forever."

"Oh, on the contrary, Mr. Hunter, I believe that our species is capable of exceeding long life spans. We have simply not isolated the means of rejuvenating cellular structure as the body ages. An enigma since, scientifically, there is very little definition except the loss of cellular modules to explain why we age at all past maturity; an unexplainable phenomenon. And for many years now it has been my goal to uncover that mystery. You see, I am almost sixty years of age. Not old by any means. But I am haunted, more and more, by the specter of my mortality. It is an old story: a young man thinks not of death, the old think of nothing else. And you would represent yourself well if you did not consider me a monster, Mr. Hunter; a man who betrayed his oath and his profession to cheat death. Or, if not to cheat, then to delay interminably."

Hamilton hesitated, and some of his arrogance seemed to subside, as if the contemplation had made him more honest. Hunter allowed him to ponder in silence while he slightly bent his head, observing the exact location of the guards.

Still ranged in a tight semicircle, they held M-16's at port arms. Each of them wore black battle-dress uniforms with black balaclavas that hid everything but their eyes. For a surreal moment, Hunter wondered if it was their duty to keep intruders out or the research personnel inside.

Hamilton beheld him with eyes that seemed strangely more pale. "In truth, those of us who have crossed this ethical and scientific void to realize what has escaped man since Eden should be lauded for our courage, our vision, and our sacrifice. For not in a thousand years, since man accepted that he is not the center of the universe, has the world faced so great a revelation as we have unveiled. Yes, I know what you are thinking, Mr. Hunter. Quite probably, there is nothing you can say that has not already crossed my mind. You are thinking that the loss of that young woman, as well as the deaths at these installations, were too great a price for success."

Hunter was stone-faced. He revealed nothing in his expression as he unblinkingly held the older man's gaze.

"But I tell you that all of these people, to the last one, would have died within the next one hundred years." Hamilton held himself as if the incontrovertible statement would settle the dispute. "And the scientist that was dispatched at your institution because of security reasons ...well, the loss of life is always tragic. But that situation was, in truth, beyond my control. Really, how long do you believe it would have been before that woman would have succumbed to the ravages of old age or some vampirish illness that leeched the strength from her soul? How long before she would have prayed for death to cease the multitude agonies? Ten years? Twenty? Fifty?" He shook his head. "You know the answer as well as I. But what if that same woman could have been given the elixir of eternal health and life? Would she have refused? No, Mr. Hunter, I sincerely doubt that. No, she would have gratefully accepted the gift of the gods; immortality, for all practical purposes, and eternal health. Of course, no one, not even with the elixir, truly lives forever. But a life span of a thousand years is incomparably better than a life span of a hundred."

Hunter gazed up somberly at the muted giant, monstrous head bowed so that the square chin rested between huge pectoral muscles thick as armor. "And him?" he asked. "You call that human?"

"No," Hamilton answered frankly. "It was a beast. Half man, at best. And, in truth, we never categorized him. Once his fantastic qualities of rejuvenation and enhanced longevity were discovered, a classification became needless. It was enough that within his bones lay the remnants of *heme* units that provided the magical coding, which we attempted to duplicate. It was only Luther, the fool, who moved too quickly, precipitating this incident."

"Incident?" Hunter asked coldly. "Several hundred men and women are dead, Hamilton. I wouldn't call that an 'incident.' I would call it a disaster."

"And that is where your mind fails to seize the opportunity for turning a disadvantage into an advantage." Hamilton's tone was dead-steady, certain, and convinced. "You see, in any experiment there is always the danger of compromised security. It wasn't until the creature had struck for the second time that I was inspired to turn this ... disaster ... into a positive force."

Hunter was appalled. Feeling a rush of warm blood to his face, he spoke: "You let them die." It wasn't a question, and he repeated it. "You're worse than your monster. When you got what you wanted, you let those people die so you could contain your secret."

Hamilton's expression was bland.

"As you said, Mr. Hunter, no one lives forever."

***

"This is *un*good," Taylor muttered.

Bending his head inside the listening post they had established in the motor pool, Takakura spoke in a low tone. "Use your night visor. You should be able to see easily in the shadows."

"The night visor don't see through solid steel, Commander. I've already checked the treeline and the rocks, and it ain't there, far as I can tell. But I know it's somewhere. I can smell it."

Takakura held the M-14-A1 close, a pistol on his chest and thigh. Anti-personnel grenades and extra clips for the M-14 were staggered on the left side of his gun belt. Taylor, as always, was armed with a variety of shotguns. The street-sweeper was loaded with twelve depleted-uranium shells. It fired as fast as the trigger could be pulled. It would be his primary weapon.

The headphone Takakura wore suddenly squawked with a static burst before the Japanese frowned. Watching, Taylor listened to the muted replies: "No ...no, we have not observed him ... *Hai* ... I will inform you." He returned to observation.

"What was all that about?" Taylor asked.

"It was the marshal, the one called Chaney." Takakura frowned. "It seems they are looking for Hunter. They do not know where he is."

Studious, Taylor squinted. "You know, now that you mention it, I haven't seen him around. That ain't like him. Usually he's on the front line. Where's the wolf?"

"Guarding the professor. I stopped in ICU and checked on them before we took listening-post duty." Takakura's pause was long. "You are correct. It is not like Hunter to vanish."

Taylor didn't like it either. "Maybe we oughta' go find him," he muttered, but even as he said it, he realized it was impossible. Every listening post was vital; it was the first line of warning, and their best defense. Plus, the CP didn't have either the time or manpower to reassign the duty. An alarming thought settled over Taylor as he pondered possibilities.

"You don't think Hunter went into the woods, do you?" He hesitated. "I mean, like he did before?"

"No," Takakura answered with confidence. "What he did before, effective as it may have been, was from desperation. Hunter is a brave man, but he is also wise. He does not risk his life unless it is necessary, or unless he consciously forfeits it for what he has decided is a greater good. No, he would not have gone out alone. For with this electrified fence and this much armament, we might have a chance of resisting the beast until dawn. Then, hopefully, we will airlift from this facility and leave it to the creature."

"We should have done that today," Taylor grunted. "But so what. They ain't gonna do it tomorrow either, Commander. 'Cause they're stuck between a rock and a hard place. They have something to do with that thing out there, I guarantee it. And they can't let it roam around killing innocent folk. Word might get out, and then they'd be toast. No, they gotta kill it or capture it before the press and public get wind, one way or another. And that's what all this is for. Man, the brass is briefed on the fact that we don't stand a snowball's chance. But that ain't their problem. 'Cause we're just grunts; we're the ones who are supposed to be doing this stuff while they sit on their butts making their oh-so-smart political decisions. And plus that, we know too much. I don't know what's going on here, but I know it's heavy. And if I know those buttheads in Washington, they ain't gonna want too many witnesses walking around when this is over. Heads have a habit of talking." Anger shook him. "No, they're gonna leave us hanging here until that thing's dead or we're dead. I know that score."

Frowning, Takakura nodded. His expression was stoic, the image of a man who accepted pain without complaint, a professional soldier, a man who intelligently measured risks before a battle yet joined the battle nonetheless. When he looked back at Taylor, his expression altered slightly, and there was a glint of humor in his dark eyes.

"You know, there was a time," he remarked, "when I dreamed of honor in battle."

Taylor stared. "And now you don't?"

"Not for armies," the Japanese whispered. "Just for men."

Quiet for a time, Taylor finally added, "Well, we might be able to put its face in the dirt. We're loaded for bear, we're rested, and we've got the home-court advantage. It won't be easy to take this place."

A grunt, and Takakura glanced at him, the frown returning.

"We shall see."

Words in a moaning wind floated to him as he lay concealed behind more rocks, almost lost to air that vibrated with the roaring engines contained within the building.

He still had a short distance to crawl before he was close enough to vault the fence—he knew from the distinctive feel of invisible fire in the surrounding air that the barrier was dangerous—and the battle would begin.

There was something familiar in the subdued tones that reached out to him over hundreds of feet; a tone or...emotion. He could not be sure, except to know that he had somehow known the tone before. The sensation caused him to lie very still. But he heard the voices no more.

Scowling faintly, he gazed up, staring through spaces in the rocks, watching the patrolling guards. Their weapons were meaningless. He did not see the woman, whose weapon had blasted the breath from his lung and ripped open his ribs, allowing the black blood to flow hotly over his side. Yes, the woman could injure him, and the fact that he did not see her aroused his anger.

But he was not afraid. He would never be afraid. And if she challenged him again he would hunt her down with singular, undaunted rage and kill her quickly, for she had injured him enough. For the pleasure of that blood, he would ignore the rest of them, would ignore what he sought until it was finished. Then he would continue as he had continued before, stalking, slaying at will, enduring their pitiful resistance until they fled screaming into the roaring night, where he would hunt them down still, slaying one by one.

A growl that began deep in his chest was choked in his throat, because he was too close. He would make no sound until he struck, would give them no warning until he was among them. Then their fear would be his ally, his weapon.

Moving only a muscular forearm and foot, he inched forward. He did not feel the impulse to rush, so complete were his stalking skills. Just as he knew he had the patience to wait for days, if necessary, waiting for a single chance to ambush his prey. With either means of attack he was skillful, though he enjoyed much more the glaring triumph of descending from above, beholding the terror in their eyes as they screamed and raised hands for mercy ... before he feasted on their brains.

***

"So it was Luther who injected himself with the serum," Hunter said, unimpressed by the egomaniacal arrogance. "And that thing out there . . ."

"Is no longer Luther," Hamilton added without emotion. "No, I'm afraid that nothing of poor Luther remains. But it was his own hand that destroyed my colleague. I shed no tears. And it was not a complete failure, in any case. For although Luther's physicality was monstrously transformed into the living representative of this unknown species, he also retained the healing and longevity factors. Yes, Luther—or whatever remains of him—will live for quite some centuries, although in that irreversible, bestial form. And since his impertinent adventurism, which ended so tragically, we have gloriously completed what he began. For we have isolated and removed the genetic transmitters that allowed the creature's DNA to transform Luther into a likeness of itself." Hamilton's eyes gleamed. "Yes, we have the serum, Mr. Hunter, and the long night is at an end. We have the sentient qualities, those that grant immortality without the lamentable curse of the primitive mind. And soon a select few will be ...immortal." He smiled.

Unimpressed, Hunter asked, "You never really planned to kill the creature, did you?"

Hamilton blinked. "Hmm? Oh, yes." He placed hands behind his back, as if lecturing. "Yes, Mr. Hunter, at one point it was considered. And, for prudence and diplomacy, we were certainly required to display some confusion and concern about the recurring attacks. But before your team was dispatched we had already decided to let the creature do our work for us in order to ensure containability of our secret enterprise. By that, of course, I mean allowing the creature to silence the research and military teams, an unexpected effect. And then ... who knows? Perhaps we might have terminated him, and may yet do so. Or we might attempt to capture him. Frankly, I have not turned my mind to the matter in some time."

Eyes narrowing, Hunter saw a shadow move—or seem to move—on the far side of the room. He didn't look toward it again as he took a wild chance, moving slightly to the side. Hamilton angled his eyes to follow Hunter's slow step, but he did not reposition. And none of the soldiers advanced, though Hunter saw hands tighten on rifles.

"No more secrets," Hunter said, facing Hamilton squarely. "I know what it's looking for. And I know you could have stopped the killing at any time. But you didn't."

Hamilton displayed rare surprise.

"You are an exceptionally astute individual, Mr. Hunter." For a moment, he appeared to regard Hunter with awe. "Yes, exceptionally astute. What was your first clue that it was searching for something? It could have been wreaking vengeance, you know. Moreover, it could merely have been exercising animal savagery against the only populations that its diseased human mind could recall. And yet...your certainty is complete. You know, indeed, that it was searching and, even, what it was searching for. But how? Would you tell me? I am most curious."

Even without looking for it, Hunter saw a shadow on the floor adjacent to a large computer terminal. But there was no sound. And he tried to follow the almost imperceptible shifting with peripheral vision because he didn't know whether it was Chaney or Bobbi Jo or the creature.

There was always a chance the military might have missed something, some hidden tunnel or gateway that wasn't recorded on the blueprints. His toes curled slightly down within his moccasins as he tensed, preparing to move in any direction at a split-second's warning. And in the short pause he decided to tell Hamilton what the scientist so badly wanted to hear, buying precious time, finishing the charade.

"It was at the research station," Hunter said, with the faintest shadow of a mocking sneer. "That was your first mistake."

Hamilton stared. "Yes? Well, what was there to find? Our sanitation team, and this is no empty boast, are quite thorough about removing evidence, ensuring our secrecy. We use them all over the world for a number of situations. And they thoroughly swept the station long before you arrived."

"I know," Hunter said, unimpressed. "And they did a good job; there was nothing to find. And that was their mistake, Doctor. They did too good a job. And in the wrong places."

"What do you mean?"

"It's the same with men as with animals, Doctor. Nothing moves in the world, anywhere, without leaving a sign—a trace of itself. The same rules apply in civilized environments." Hunter searched for the shadow, saw nothing. "This creature attacked the station, the soldiers, and he left traces of himself. Then he attacked the personnel, the lab techs, and left more traces. Tracks, claw marks, blood that told me where he was going, where he'd been, what he was thinking. And then he attacked the installation it-self, leaving even more traces. All of it like pages in a book. Everything that happens is told in the tracks, or in the pages. All you have to do is know how to read them."

"Yes," Hamilton responded, "I follow your reasoning. But that still does not explain how you deduced that the creature was searching for something, which I myself find quite fascinating."

"It's just like I said, Doctor. Every room in every installation told a story." Hunter paused. "Except one."

Hamilton seemed to perceive it.

"The vault," the scientist said simply, with a faint smile.

"Yeah. The vault. The only chamber that that thing didn't destroy. And yet it destroyed everything else. So there was a page missing from the story." Hunter caught a glimmer of response in the doctor's eyes. "It's fairly simple to follow a track, once you know where to begin," he continued. "So after I searched the vault and didn't find any traces of the creature, I knew something was wrong. So I searched it again, and found some lines where your crew, probably wearing biohazard suits, had worked the most diligently at sanitation. I suppose you know where that would be."

"Oh, yes." Hamilton smiled, clearly enjoying the endgame. "At the refrigeration module."

"Where your crew removed every trace of its entry," Hunter continued. "And I wondered: why remove traces of this thing's entry into that one chamber while ignoring what it did throughout the rest of the complex? And the answer seemed fairly obvious."

Hamilton almost spoke, some fevered dimension of his personality taking pleasure in this spirited contest of intellects, but with visible effort he restrained himself.

"So I located the module's manifest and ran an inventory, and I located all of the serums that were supposed to be there," Hunter continued, allowing Hamilton the juvenile pleasure of finishing.

"Except one," the scientist contributed magnanimously.

"Yeah. Except one."

"HD-66." Hamilton shook his head, a slightly satisfied smile.

"Exactly. Which didn't mean much to me at the time. But I knew it would mean something sooner or later. Then, when the third facility was destroyed, it was the same thing. HD-66 was missing from the serum module with the area swept clean. No traces, no tracks. Another missing page. So I knew that this entire scenario somehow revolved around HD-66. But, still, I didn't know what it was. I didn't even know enough to run it past the professor because it was just numbers on a page. Its existence had been erased." Hunter stared evenly. "Sometimes by erasing tracks, Doctor, you make them more visible."

Undaunted, Hamilton beamed. "And yet, Mr. Hunter, despite your amazing deduction, you were still unenlightened as to the specific purpose, and salient characteristics, of HD-66."

"At the time." Hunter opened his eyes wider. "But with what I've seen, I believe I understand, at last."

"Really?" Hamilton was openly amazed. "Well, why don't you tell me? Because, as much as I would like to believe you, I find it an incredible suspension of reason to imagine that you could somehow deduce the purpose of a substance that you have never seen or studied. In truth, the only means by which you could understand the properties of HD-66 would be through a diagramed molecular synthesis. Which, of course, you do not possess."

"There are two ways to understand something, Doctor. You can know the thing itself. Or you can understand the world around it."

Hamilton seemed abruptly lost.

"I don't quite ..."

"It was you, Doctor."

Hesitation.

"You say it was I?" Hamilton repeated. "How so?"

"Your pride was your downfall, Doctor. Your arrogance. Your self-righteousness. Your greed. Your self-serving satisfaction of your dreams of grandeur. Your maniacal pursuit of scientific glory at the expense of human dignity."

Hunter could determine by the furrowed brow and utterly confused expression that the eminent Dr. Arthur Hamilton was dumbstruck. He decided to end the mystery.

"While you were sleeping last night, Doctor, you weren't the only one in your rather opulent bedchamber. The fact is, I was with you for quite some time."

For the first time, fear was visible in the scientist's pale eyes.

"Yeah, I was there," Hunter repeated calmly and matter-of-factly. "And I searched the entire room, but I didn't find any solid clues. You're quite disciplined at leaving all research materials in the laboratory."

"Yes," the scientist acknowledged, recovering from the shock of Hunter's unknown intrusion. "I am, indeed. And what did you find during your nocturnal skulking, Mr. Hunter? There is no documentation whatsoever in my personal quarters."

"That's what I mean." Hunter almost smiled, but restrained the impulse. "But it's like I said, everything leaves a trace of where it's been, where it's going, what it's thinking. And you're no different from the rest of us. A person just has to know how to read the signs."

"And what was this trace of the truth that you keep mentioning with such obscurity?"

"You, Doctor."

Slight surprise glimmered in the narrow eyes.

"Please elucidate," he said.

Hunter half-laughed. "Like I said, I already knew a great deal. I knew that you had somehow created this thing—a creature that once belonged on the earth, but doesn't anymore. And I knew that it was searching for the rest of the serum. The only question left to answer was why." A pause. "After searching your room, I was about to leave when I noticed the book you'd been reading before you'd fallen asleep."

There was concentrated remembrance, and then the scientist slowly nodded. "Yes," he mused, a thoughtful pursing of the lips. "Heart of Darkness. How observant."

"One of my habits."

"Of course." He laughed with a mocking mirth. "But, please, continue. I am fascinated with your deductive abilities and am well on my way to genuine admiration."

Hunter sensed the shadow glide another few inches. It appeared to be slowly working a path through the computers and desks to a flanking position on the guards.

"So," he added, "I saw that you were reading Heart of Darkness. Joseph Conrad. And that was curious to me, considering the gravity of our situation. Because usually, in times of crisis, a man will focus his entire energy and attention on the situation until it's resolved. Especially a man such as yourself. A man consumed with his work, and with himself. So I picked it up and paged to a well-worn section that had a single sentence underlined. And in that entire book it was the only sentence emphasized. I know, because I checked." Hunter recited from memory: " '*The mind of man is capable of anything because everything is buried inside it – all the past as well as all the future.*' "

Hamilton's smile was approving. "And then you knew."

"Yeah, I knew," Hunter said, with no tinge of pride. "I had decided a while back that HD-66 was a serum. But for what, I didn't know. Just like I didn't know why the creature wanted it so badly. All I knew for certain was that it wasn't going to stop until it found it. And then, with that, I understood why."

Hunter, although he was virtually unarmed and outnumbered, controlled the atmosphere now with the straightforwardness of his will, his utter lack of fear, and his unflinching moral courage in the face of insurmountable odds. He could read their reluctant respect in their posture and silence, though he knew it would not alter their intentions for him. He finished his thought.

"That thing out there, which you're responsible for, wants to remember all that it was because its past is somehow genetically remembered in its DNA coding," he concluded. "But the serum that transformed your colleague wasn't only imperfect, it was incomplete, wasn't it?"

Hamilton shrugged. "It was ...experimental. At that stage, we were still fundamentally unaware of what, exactly, we were dealing with."

"I know. So, not only did the experimental formula transform your friend into something that was neither animal nor man, the DNA had insufficient coding to fully restore the creature's genetic memory." Hunter was so confident of his reasoning that Hamilton's assertion, or a dispute if it had come, would have meant nothing at all. "Its genetic memory is and always has been incomplete, and it knows that. So it wants the part of itself that's missing. And whatever remains of your colleague knows where to find it. And that's why it's been destroying the research facilities. It's searching." He shook his head. "Yes, Doctor, it wants HD-66, its own heart of darkness, so that its cellular memory will be restored. It wants the serum so that the transformation is absolute."

Hamilton stared for a moment, a condescending grin spreading slowly, before he clapped his hands. "Bravo, Mr. Hunter!" He laughed. "And I had categorized you as a base wild man filling an inconsequential existence with inconsequential thoughts. But you have truly astounded me— a rare pleasure for a man such as myself." He nodded curtly, dropping hands to his sides. "I congratulate you. This was a remarkable intellectual accomplishment."

Despite the steel reasoning required to assimilate all he had learned into a definitive explanation, despite the haughty harassment of Hamilton, despite the finely focused attention of the guards, Hunter had not failed to follow the shadow of the still-unknown intruder as it maneuvered into position behind the masked soldiers. He knew from the lack of overt aggression that it was not the creature; the beast used no subtlety in attacking. So he felt certain that it was someone from upstairs. But whether that person intended to assist him, or not, remained a mystery.

"And now"—Hamilton turned his head to the guards, nodding curtly—"I am afraid that—"

Hunter moved.

Exploding in a violent movement not telegraphed at all, he leaped forward and collided hard with Hamilton to take them together over a computer dais—a wild and twisted tangle of arms and legs—to the other side. Paper and laboratory materials scattered chaotically at the impact and reckless descent, and Hunter was first on his feet, volcanically heaving the scientist around as a shield, his Bowie knife already at Hamilton's throat. Before Hunter spoke a single word Hamilton's upraised hands halted the onrushing guards.

"Stay where you are, you fools!" he bellowed, suddenly graceless. Hunter was amazed he had swung the situation around with a single dynamic move. He pushed the old man forward, hoping to control the situation by ruthlessly taking advantage of their temporary confusion and emotional shock.

Then the large figure of Brick erupted on the far side of a bookcase— the soundless shadow Hunter had followed so long.

The big man held the large, double-barreled Weatherby in both hands with pistols and grenades and extra ammo attached to his brown vest. A leather bandoleer of huge bullets was slung from shoulder to hip, and in a flashing glance Hunter registered yet another rifle—some kind of semiautomatic—slung across his back.

"Drop 'em!" Brick bellowed and two of the guards, quicker than the rest, spun with rifles raised. But before the first guard had completed the turn Brick fired, the enormous expanding flame of the Weatherby reaching out six feet, and the guard's chest exploded with the impact. Then Brick swung the barrel and fired again, thunderously lifting the second guard off his feet as Hunter threw Hamilton to the ground and the laboratory was ripped by gunfire.

Chaney was becoming more frustrated as the moments passed, moving in and out of the trucks, Humvees, tankers, and transport trucks at the motor pool. The area was checkered with pits of black that could have contained anything: he had left his night-vision device in the facility, not reckoning that he would need it.

Despite stumbling on a dozen listening posts that denied seeing Hunter—he had not chanced upon Takakura and Taylor— he was certain that Hunter said he was moving outside to check the perimeter. He was loping at a respectable gait across the yard, passing the front of the shed containing the two-ton generators that were powering the facility, when he caught a slowly moving form high in the air.

It was a bizarre floating, grayish image—like a ghostly apparition emerging from fog. It came across the earth without touching it, hanging in the air, arms outstretched.

Chaney looked curiously, and although he was among the most controlled of all men, shouted something incoherent.

For, seemingly suspended, neither rising nor descending, the beast was nearly twenty feet in the air, hanging for what seemed an impossibly long time before it came down hard, its stone-heavy impact sending a gunshot effect that made a hundred heads turn together.

So shocked was Chaney that he didn't immediately open fire, somehow doubting against reason that it might turn and flee. Then it leaped again, angling for the domed hull of the green tanker parked beside the shed. Immediately Chaney raised the Weatherby and fired.

He had no idea if he connected as it completed an arching descent to vanish from view, landing without sound on the grassy area between the truck and building.

"HOLD FIRE! HOLD FIRE!" a commanding voice boomed over the intercom system. And Chaney needed no one to explain why. It would be simple for panicked troops, some having never seen true combat, to open fire in fear and accidentally detonate the ten-thousand-gallon tank. Chaney himself had recognized the threat only at the last moment and purposefully shot high, hoping to catch it in the shoulder, virtually assuring that he had missed.

Chaney stared in shock.

Nothing could have prepared him for this.

For what he had seen suspended in the night air made all human conflict seem insignificant. He had almost not believed it even when it landed with such fearless intent, and cursed himself for his hesitation. For he had had one moment for a clean shot and might have caught it as it stood gloating.

As an afterthought, remembering the hulking might outlined by the fog-shrouded skylight, he was glad he had brought the Weatherby and quickly replaced the spent round, clicking the breech closed.

Soldiers in teams of ten and thirty ran past him, taking lateral and frontal positions on the motor pool. Officers bellowed commands to compete with the roar of the generators, and Chaney ran down the line of Jeeps and trucks, hoping for a glimpse. Whatever it was, they had it cornered in the twenty-acre lot of automotive vehicles.

A hideous scream that rose in volume erupted in the night for a split second, then died abruptly. A wild rattle of M-16 fire was followed by another and even shorter shout of panic. Then silence. Chaney knew what it was doing; it had located the first listening post situated in the pool, killing both soldiers like lightning.

One platoon, close and tight with weapons ready, moved into the south end of the motor pool. Two more teams of thirty, one in the center and one on the north end, moved with them, a hundred men spreading into a skirmish line as they crossed the first line of vehicles.

Carefully, alertly, they moved forward, the instructions of sergeants and lieutenants to "look sharp and fire on acquisition" repeated over and over in the semi-darkness.

Chaney scanned the vast acreage, and in the distance, at the eruption of another frightful scream, saw a brief blurred shape of black moving left to right in a frenzy. Chaney's teeth came together in frustration and rage: two more down.

It was moving quick, slaughtering methodically.

The skirmish line had covered about a third of the distance when more screams echoed violently in the night. Chaney remembered Taylor and Takakura. He keyed his throat mike and tried to raise them, repeating their designation in order to warn them.

But they didn't reply.

Taylor glanced up and saw Takakura's sweating face silhouetted by a stadium-like display of floodlights. The Japanese was bent, sword in hand and a .45 pistol in the other. His eyes were feral, staring with rage, and his teeth shone white in the pale light that made his dark face glisten. He stared high and then dropped, silently searching underneath the truck beside them. When he rose he shook his head in frustration, snarling as he spoke: "It is working its way to the north end, away from us. It is methodically working its way through the listening posts."

"You wanna go after it?" Taylor asked, tightening the bandoleer so it wouldn't slide from his shoulder in violent movement.

Takakura shook his head sharply. "No ... I don't think so. Then again, it will find us soon enough. As it has found the others." He calculated, his eyes blinking hard and quick. "Yes, it will find us. But not as it found them."

"You wanna set an ambush?" Taylor whispered.

"There remains one more listening post between us and the creature. If it continues to kill methodically and is not somehow deterred, it will finish them next." His face hardened, dark eyes narrowing into slits. "It will be our only chance. It will be upon us in moments." He wasted a single second. "Do you believe those depleted uranium slugs will penetrate its skin?"

"I don't know. It'll penetrate the armor of a tank. But I don't know if these magnum shells give 'em the velocity it's gonna take. I'm damn sure it's gonna feel it, but to kill it ... I don't know." He shook his head, sweat dripping from his scarred face as he took a breath.

"It will have to suffice." Takakura crouched, peeking around the front of a transport.

Frantic rifle fire tore through the night at the other end of the field, a wild continuous blaze of at least twenty rifles on full automatic. A bestial roar rose above it all, and there were the horrifying sounds of men dying in fear, and then the firing became wildly unorganized and sporadic. Even from a distance Takakura could tell from the white muzzle blasts that some of them were firing in all directions or into the air, lost in war madness and fear.

"Now is our chance," he rasped. "While it is engaged we will take up a flanking position near the right listening post. If it comes for them next, then perhaps we can make contact with it before it hits. We must move quickly."

Forsaking greater stealth for speed because the far end of the field still thundered with rifle fire and an occasional bellow that could only have come from a man knowing death was upon him, they located the listening post without being sighted and took up a discreet flanking position. Takakura laid the M-14 across the hood of a Humvee, turning on the starlight scope. And Taylor angled across to the back, securing himself inside the rear of a tent-covered transport truck with a thirty-foot clear range at the probable area of contact.

Startlingly, the next chaotic cries and rifle fire erupted behind them, near the front of the lot.

It was incredible; the thing had traveled the entire expanse of the twenty-acre pool in fifteen seconds, effortlessly bypassing a thirty-man platoon securing the center, to launch an attack on troops searching the south end.

"God help us," Taylor whispered. It seemed incredible that they had survived it in the mountains—unless it was becoming stronger, more cunning, and more powerful as it continued to mutate.

Broken rifle fire over a hundred yards behind them erupted, as if they couldn't acquire the target and were simply firing into the darkness. Then the truck, a ten-ton rig with a twenty-foot wooden bed suddenly tilted toward the hood—silence, staring, not moving, staring—and with lionish velocity and grace the massive manlike shape sailed over Taylor's hidden form, landing fully ten feet from the fender, hurling itself forward as it struck the ground.

Almost before Taylor could rise to his knee and fire, it had struck the first man in the listening post, a sweeping blow from a taloned hand that finished the scream. But the second man managed a quick shot that went wide before the same hand struck his chest, smashing through the Kevlar vest like straw and—

Taylor pulled the trigger.

The blast was blinding. Taylor leaped from the truck to see it leaning back against the door, holding a hand to its shoulder. It gazed at him in anger, but without pain, and opened a fanged mouth, unleashing a roar that felt like a hand pressing against Taylor's armored chest.

Taylor roared and pulled the trigger again, only dimly aware of distant shots that told him backup was coming fast. But not fast enough.

As the bestial image of death rushed forward on horrible bowed legs, arms outstretched beneath glaring red eyes, Taylor pulled the trigger again and again, focusing all his skill, all his will, all his training and experience to make certain each of the twelve rounds hit solid. He sensed rather than saw Takakura's leaping shape as he emerged from behind a Humvee and dropped to a knee, instantly sighting and firing. Then the creature was upon him.

Taylor fired his last round.

He saw a depthless wall of gray might that blocked out the night and sky and stars and light; taller, inhumanly massive and indestructible with awful glee glaring from the purest bestial fury. Then it seemed to angle left, its right arm raised high, and Taylor leaped into it, roaring in rage as he reached for his Bowie knife to—

"NO!" Takakura shouted as Taylor, standing for a strange moment, fell back before the beast. In the shadows Takakura saw that a wide portion of the commando's chest had been torn cleanly away, leaving half a man falling backward to the ground. The creature tossed a black mass to the side, and turned its grotesque face toward Takakura.

Fangs parted in a menacing smile.

Takakura saw the other soldiers converging on the site— twenty seconds—and dropped to a knee, firing all that remained in the thirty-round clip at the creature as it strode slowly forward. So contemptuous was it of the Japanese and the rifle that it did not rush at all, but came with thundering, remorseless strides that closed the distance in horrible certainty.

Somewhere in the last few rounds Takakura understood its inhuman pleasure at a slow kill and spaced the bullets, firing the last one—it was still moving slowly—when it was five feet away. It opened its fanged mouth in an explosive roar.

Gambling that it would expect him to react as the others had reacted at its horrific image and approach, Takakura lifted the rifle in a frightened stance, feigning shock. Gloating, growling, it raised its right hand high, fangs wide with a hellish smile.

Takakura moved.

With the speed and skill perfected from a lifetime of kendo he dropped the rifle and quick-drew the long katana, angling the sword through a cross-body cut with all the strength of his back and arms and wrists. The entire movement, from the time his hands left the gun until the momentum of his cut carried him to the side, had lasted less than a second.

A normal man would have been cut cleanly in half through the hips. But the thing staggered forward a space, glaring down at the deep gash torn in its chest, blood already descending in dark rivulets. Then it turned slowly in a tight half-circle, staring at itself, then at Takakura with an odd mixture of shock and anger.

Takakura knew he would not be so lucky next time. He had deceived it with its own pride. But now it knew it could be injured by the katana. It would not make the same mistake twice.

The other platoons now reached the site and opened fire. Takakura ducked away as they unleashed hundreds of rounds at the creature. Glaring back in the deafening smoke-choked atmosphere Takakura could see the lead impacting against the thick skin, bouncing or flattening and utterly failing to penetrate.

Yet its rage ran deep, for despite the concentrated attack it came for Takakura again, who stood sword in hand. Takakura knew it would kill him this time; if his first masterful blow had not been enough to finish it, then he could not kill it at all. And although the Japanese moved as quickly as he could, far quicker than most men, it was on top of him as he hit the ground, rolling under a thirty-ton Dooley.

Charging at the last, it struck the gigantic transport vehicle in the door with its shoulder—a thunderous impact that shattered glass and half-lifted the Dooley from the ground—and a split second later Takakura saw the wide steel door ripped away and hurled into shadow.

It reached beneath the cab to snatch him and Takakura scampered to the far side, narrowly avoiding the reach of that colossal arm and rending talons.

But he knew he couldn't keep up the game; sooner or later it would get him. Then the entire night was a wall of rifle fire, illuminating everything—the Dooley, tires, vehicles, lights, the fence, and the creature, screaming and roaring in the apocalyptic night. And with a hideous bellow it charged fully through a line of soldiers, hesitating only a heartbeat to kill anyone in reach, and was lost.

Stunned, breathless, and shocked, Takakura rolled onto his back, feeling his chest, checking for injury. As caught up as he was in battle, he knew he could be hit in half a dozen places and not notice. After a moment, as scattered fighting continued to rage— the creature continuing to play its game of devastating guerrilla attacks—he rolled out from beneath the truck and wearily gained his footing.

He searched for his rifle, saw a dozen slaughtered troops in the smoking opening. Then he staggered forward as an invisible fist whistled in from the darkness—a rocket he did not see but sensed—and an unseen baseball bat hit him hard in the chest, fully flattening him back against the ground.

Groaning, rolling, fighting violently for breath, Takakura knew what it was: a stray .223 round had found him. He had not been the target, but so many rounds fired in so small a place would eventually find friendly casualties.

Breathless, dazed, and nauseated, he managed to detach the bulky load-bearing vest, dropping it to the ground. Then, eyes blurring, he ripped away two of the Velcro straps securing the bulletproof vest, feeling his sweat-slicked chest beneath.

He groaned, too tired to feel relief.

No, it hadn't penetrated.

As he struggled to rise, he felt the night whiter, lighter, warm, and hazy. He took one staggering step ... two ...

Blackness rushed up.

***

Hunter heard Brick hurl the elephant rifle violently across a desk and began to rise when, on impulse, Hunter whirled, swiping with the speed of a leopard with the Bowie. The butt of the hilt caught Hamilton, also attempting to rise, square on the cluster of nerves located midway up the neck, and the physician fell limp to the tiles.

Reorienting, Hunter saw the second guard's rifle lying close but still too far to reach without exposing himself. So he risked a quick glance and saw that the other four had opened up on Brick's position with fully automatic fire, apparently forgetting him in the presence of an armed and obviously very dangerous intruder firing upon them.

Launching himself forward, Hunter dove and snatched up the M-16 as he sailed over the cleaved body of the second soldier. Then he hit the ground and rolled, instantly finding cover behind a thick metal desk as one of the guards glimpsed the bold move and fired, bullets tearing through the steel panels.

Moving quickly, Hunter rounded half a dozen corners and threw his back against the wall as he ripped out the magazine. Shaking his head to clear his face from the sudden eruption of sweat, he saw that it held thirty rounds. So he set the selector switch on fully automatic and chambered a cartridge, insuring that the safety was off. Holding the rifle close, he angled back to the firefight.

Brick had obviously hurled the Weatherby aside after the first two thunderous rounds—there had been no time to reload—and was using the semiauto. Listening and catching quick glimpses of desperate black shapes outlined by a strobe of gunfire, Hunter targeted two of the guards. He lowered the barrel around a corner, taking time to adjust for elevation, and pulled the trigger.

Recoil was greater than he'd anticipated and he lowered the aim quickly, striking both guards, the equipment around them, and the floor, losing a number of rounds into the ceiling before he completely adjusted. But when he turned and retreated, breathlessly selecting a new line of attack, he had acclimated. Not as bad as a 30.30, the M-16 nevertheless became quickly unmanageable on fully auto if a firm grip wasn't applied to the stock. With no backup magazines, Hunter realized he would have to conserve rounds.

Raging, firing, cursing, and roaring, Brick was holding his own against the surviving four, and Hunter located him by the distinctive sound of the rifle. It was a louder, booming blast that by comparison made the M-16's sound weak and wispy. Then the shooting stopped—stopped all at once to a ringing silence—and Hunter froze.

He had been halfway to his intended location when somehow, somewhere far above they heard the report of a tremendous explosion, followed by a subterranean vibration that rattled the floor and walls and ceiling.

Hunter knew it had begun.

He had to get up top.

He had to reach Bobbi Jo.

***

"No," Bobbi Jo whispered as the tanker exploded, engulfing a third of the compound in flame.

It had finally happened, as she knew it would. The wild and erratic rifle fire of the troops had found the gasoline tank, and now the compound roared with the inferno. Night rushed over her head, sucked into a firestorm that created its own wind.

She saw probably thirty troops fully aflame, rushing blindly around the motor pool. Other soldiers grabbed them and threw them to the ground only to have their arms and legs light up from the rain of fire still spiraling from the sky. She shook her head, shocked at the carnage.

Never had she seen anything like this. This was the end of the world, a war fought in hell with the devil among them. They would die tonight, she thought. Every one of them. They would die.

Her attention was snapped awake as she saw a Herculean form striding, neither fast nor slow, from behind a Humvee, moving for the back of a soldier assisting a burn victim. She didn't need any more to recognize that Goliath-like profile—the shaggy squared head with gray hair sweeping back—and her eye was at the scope. She had instantly flicked off the safety, sighting solid.

She knew the range by heart: 120 yards.

Point-of-aim contact.

It raised wide hands when it was ten feet away from the unaware victim ...

Bobbi Jo fired.

The incredible blast of the Barrett blinded her for a split second and she blinked. A moment later she saw the unwounded soldier already on his feet, firing his rifle at the creature, prostrate beside the Humvee. The burn victim had ceased moving, lay still in the flame.

The next explosion, from generators overheated by the burning tanker, rocked the mountains around them. Thousands of gallons of gasoline stored in the shed for emergencies went up with a small nuclear-shaped mushroom cloud of fire that scorched her face though she was three hundred yards away. The roar of the explosion continued on and on into the distant cold night, reverberating from mountain to mountain, over the world.

Bobbi Jo shouted at the secondary concussion, a breathtaking shock wave that shook the building. Blasted-out windows and rocketing antennas clattered behind her as they fell.

She was instantly up and searching, flicking on starlight illumination to acquisition the creature in the flame-lit night. She didn't find it beside the Humvee where it had fallen. It wasn't finishing off the wounded from the explosions. It wasn't slaughtering the last group of unwounded soldiers huddled tightly in the middle of the compound. Struck by quick fear she swung the scope, searching desperately for that terrifying—

"No!" she screamed.

It landed with solid intent on the cab of a truck less than twenty feet away and she fired. But even as the Barrett discharged she knew she had missed and set her shoulder tight against the butt, forgoing the scope; at this range she didn't need it.

Ten soldiers stationed on the roof opened up with her, a cascade of lead pouring defiantly down, but it leaped forward and at the ground launched itself powerfully forward, running full speed—a wild bull with the speed of a cheetah—to smash with awesome force into the steel door securing the rear of the building. Following its lightning-quick strides they tracked a devastating deluge of lead, centering on its mutated form until it burst the door from its hinges and bolts and vanished.

Soldiers on the roof, already electrified with panic at the horrifying slaughter in the motor pool, erupted in confused panic and contradictory orders. Then Maddox, fear and desperation strengthening his spine, bellowed for them to lay down a cross fire with the M-60's—heavy-caliber, fully automatic machine guns that were the major small arms of the Vietnam era—on the single door leading to the roof.

They moved with the efficiency of action inspired by life-and-death situations. In quick time they had the door covered. If it could walk through that concentrated barrage, there would be no stopping it. Ever.

Crouching behind the short wall that hid her profile from the ground, Bobbi Jo reviewed what she knew about it, tried to remember what Hunter had told her. It was difficult to think but she concentrated, closing her eyes briefly to regain control. A few breaths, and she analyzed what it had done . . .

Would it simply come up the stairs?

Did it ever attack as they anticipated?

Flashing through every confrontation that she'd suffered with the creature, she knew that only one thing was indisputable. It never attacked like you anticipated.

"Not this time, no," she whispered, running to the south side of the building, searching down. Nothing. She ran to the east, behind the cubicle that housed the stairway, to the warning cries of soldiers. They were simultaneously screaming at her, ten voices bellowing the same thing, colliding with each other for supremacy; "Bobbijo! Get out of the way! If it breaks the door we'll have to shoot you, too!"

Grimacing with physical exhaustion and ravaged nerves, she searched over the edge. Nothing.

"Get out of the way, Bobbi!" a soldier bellowed with concern and rage.

Sweat pouring, Bobbijo ran for the north side as—

She saw it emerge, backlit by roaring flame that reached hundreds of feet into the air, and it did not see her. And she knew; it had simply leaped, as before, clearing the twenty feet to land on the edge of the roof. It landed hulking and bent, broad bowed head glaring at the backs of those who'd been deceived. As she stopped and spun the Barrett, sighting from the hip, it noticed her and turned its head slowly.

Snarled.

What happened next could only happen to those who knew they would surely die, here and now, if they did not reach deep within, to that place where even professional soldiers rarely went, for that last measure of courage.

Bobbi Jo fired and the impact was high in its torso, slamming it back against the wall. Mentally she calculated how many rounds remained in the magazine: two. She fired the next as it leaped, and she hit it again, center chest contact. It staggered a step before it fell onto its face, folding slowly to its knees, a hand rising with a growl. Bobbi Jo dropped the near-empty clip and did a tactical reload, slamming in a new magazine of five rounds.

The rest of the platoon, well aware of its surprise attack by now and having adjusted to swing aim, opened up together. And at the irritating impacts, bruised and burned and somehow bloodied, the creature rose and ran toward Bobbi Jo.

Standing solid, Bobbi Jo frowned: there was nothing else to do,

She fired, teeth emerging in a snarl, the six-foot flame almost joining them past the long barrel. It roared, grunted, staggered, and she raised aim, hitting it again as the Barrett lit the rooftop with its devastating muzzle blast. She hit its chest, heart, placed another round to the heart, saw her last bullet tear off a chunk of its neck.

It stood, staggered off balance, as if in shock. Apparently deeply wounded, broken, it twisted slightly away from her, placing a monsters hand against its savaged throat.

Frowning—with nowhere to retreat to, anyway—Bobbi Jo dropped the clip and inserted another in less than a second, racking the six-inch bolt almost for the sheer pleasure of letting it know what was coming. But her action didn't get its attention. It staggered away, clutching its throat, groaning.

"Hey!" she shouted. "We ain't finished!"

The thing staggered toward the platoon.

"Bobbi Jo!" they screamed together. "Get out of the way!"

It closed on them.

They were in each other's line of fire. The platoon couldn't shoot the creature without also shooting her, and she couldn't open up with the Barrett with them so close in front of it.

Ten more steps and it would be on them.

She didn't have time to run to the sides.

She read the panic on their faces: God help me, they have to be able to shoot. . .

Twisting her head, she glared over the edge of the roof, saw a twenty-foot drop to a rusty brown gazebo above the kitchen door. Trash cans littered the tiny area. Only for a tenth of a second did she consider the possibility of a safe descent. Then, Barrett in hand, she placed the other hand on the waist-high wall and vaulted into the night.

"Kill it!" she screamed as she was claimed by the fall.

Behind her the sky was instantly lit by strobe and roars and wounded rage. It continued as white flashed past her and she struck something hard that shattered, surrendering, and closed.

She struck again, harder.

She lay there, hair across her face.

Then darkness.

Clenching his teeth with heated emotion and adrenaline surging in his system, Hunter narrowly suppressed the impulse to rush, knowing it would be a mistake. Then, moving carefully but wasting no time, he rose and continued forward.

As quickly as the gunfire had halted it began again, Brick viciously returning as good as he got, and then Hunter had come up behind them, more worried about Brick's unceasing wall of lead than the two soldiers yet unaware of his presence.

Just as Hunter edged carefully around a concrete pillar he glimpsed Brick's flattop-gray image—an old, big guy with teeth clenched in rage firing a fully automatic rifle with beefy arms—erupt from behind an overturned desk. Ducking back instantly Hunter evaded the cascading round that ripped steel and plastic and buried his section of the room in rifle fire. He waited until the barrage broke, then dropped the barrel of the M-16 around the edge and fired.

One guard went down as the other turned, raising aim. Hunter ducked back again as cement was reduced to chalk, and then Brick's enraged voice cut through the booming chaos.

"*Vis a vous, darlin'!*"

Hunter didn't look but knew who had fired first. Then he peeked out to see Brick standing coldly over the last guard. Massacred by a long stream of 7.62's fired from what Hunter now recognized as a cut down AK-47, the guard was unmoving. Brick dropped a banana clip and withdrew another from his vest, racking the slide. When he looked at Hunter, his face held no remorse, no emotion.

"I think we got 'em all," the big man said.

Even so, Hunter knew what he had said more by vision than sound because he was temporarily deafened. He shook his head a moment and dropped the clip from the M-16, pausing to remove a bandoleer from one of the dead guards that had another six full clips. He inserted a full thirty-round mag and racked the bolt, rising as Brick approached carrying the Weatherby. The big man snapped the breech shut as another explosion rocked the laboratory.

"They started without us." Brick looked up, his voice low and controlled. "We'd better kick in and join the party."

"Yeah," Hunter mumbled, moving away quickly. He opened the door of the vault—a refrigerated, lead-reinforced chamber about twenty by twenty—and walked inside. In reality, it was simply a large freezer, and nitrogen-cooled mist rushed into the brightly lit room as he searched through the cold white atmosphere.

"I don't think I'd go in there without one of them blue suits, kid." Brick stood at a respectful distance, watching. "I heard everything, know the score. And we can take 'em down without the serum. There's enough proof, or there will be, once this is over. Come on," he added anxiously, "we're missing the fireworks."

Ignoring Brick's plea, Hunter located the serum module and spun the smoothly designed cylinder until he saw it: HD-66. It was surprisingly slim, a plastic bag filled to the top with an amber liquid. In appearance it was not unlike a saline bag used to rehydrate hospital patients, and Hunter slipped it in a small black canvas bag as he crossed the lab, moving for the elevator. They had used the ventilation shaft to descend, but they'd make it public when they re-emerged.

"You got anything else to do?" Brick shouted.

Frowning menacingly, Hunter walked toward the cylinder.

"Just one thing," he said.

He stopped directly in front of it and fired the M-16 from the base of the magnificent cylindrical sarcophagus to the crest and down again. Glowing green phosphorescence exploded into the electromagnetic field and the copper coils erupted violently with electrical discharge.

The proto-human body hung for a moment before its great weight completely disintegrated the glass coffin. Hunter held aim, continued firing until the entire atmosphere was heated by the holocaust and the body pitched forward in an ages-overdue death.

It was shredded by the unceasing assault before it crashed into the copper and exploded instantly into flames, ignited by the spiraling electrical surge loosed by the short-circuited wiring.

Merciless, Hunter watched the body consumed by flames.

Turned away.

"Let's go," he said coldly.

Shocked at the carnage, Brick turned with him.

"Jesus, Hunter," he whispered.

Knowing it was likely their emergence would go unnoticed as the fight raged aboveground, Hunter speed-reviewed everything he had just learned about the creature. That it had once been a man was of no use; what it had been and what it had become were as night and day. He was already familiar with its enhanced healing ability. Only the revelation that it had a life span over ten times that of man had been new, and that had no bearing on the battle.

The elevator doors opened to a night already torn with flame and smoke and colliding sounds of rifle fire. Soldiers sprinted chaotically through the blackness and, somewhere in the distance, the louder roar of something huge surrendered to an inferno. Hunter felt a brief moment of panic.

But you have what it wants ... it will come after you.

Use it ...

Brick was at the door, almost filling it with his bulk. He pressed his back pressed against the frame as he glared outside, turned his slag face to Hunter. "Can't see jack in all this smoke!" he coughed. "The thing musta' knocked out the power! Look, I'm gonna partner up with Chaney if I can find him in this mess! Where're you gonna be?"

Mounting stairs that led to the roof three at a time, Hunter called back, "I'm going high to get a visual! If I can get its attention, I think I can lure it away from the complex!"

Brick barreled into the night as Hunter turned on the stairs, ascending quickly as the howls and cries of the wounded and dying followed him.

***

Stunned almost into unconsciousness, Bobbi Jo rolled slowly across something flat and hard before realizing it was a section of tin. Blindly reorienting, she reached out and felt for the Barrett, found a section of severed steel.

With a groan that emerged as a curse, she brutally forced herself to a knee. The shock of plummeting through the overhang had numbed her entire body. She knew she might have numerous broken bones or other serious injuries, but was thankful that for now the volcanic adrenaline would prevent her from feeling them.

Acclimating to the reduced light, she found the Barrett and attempted to lift it, but failed.

Taking a deep breath she looked around and saw that no one else had made the jump. The roof above was silent while the grounds on the far side of the building seemed to reverberate with chaotic cries and panicked howls. Gritting her teeth, she slung the heavy sniper rifle from her shoulder, poised to fire from the hip, and racked the bolt to chamber a round.

Instantly she was moving at a fast walk, uncertain of her injuries. But she found that she could move well enough, and rounded a corner to see the storage shed in back fully ablaze.

From skills honed in a thousand training missions, she felt her load-bearing vest for the extra five clips and confirmed they were still in place. She reached the back of the building and boldly stood in the open, searching coldly for the humped silhouette. She saw nothing but scores of wounded, some with their limbs torn from sockets and rolling in abysmal pain, others clutching huge empty holes in their body where the clawed hand had struck a fiendish blow.

Eyes narrowing, she searched, but it was not there. Nor was it on the roof. But it was somewhere close; the German shepherds were frantically howling and barking, each of them confused by terror and pain and the alien creature that strode with demoniacal power and wrath among them, leaving devastation and death in its wake.

A large figure came around the fir end of the complex and she swung the Barrett, finger tightening hard to—

Brick saw her outlined against the raging flame of the shed and waved hard, signaling. She ran as hard as her bruised body would allow, painfully halting before him as he gasped, "I think it may have gone ...inside." He breathed hard a moment, face contorted with the effort. "How many still alive?"

She found the strength to shake her head. "Not ... not many. Most of them are dead, the rest are dying. Their wounds ... God, I've never seen anything like it ...we can't do anything for them." She lowered her head, fighting the pain of a possible concussion. "Where's Hunter?"

"He's alive," Brick responded as if that in itself were a miracle. "But he won't be for long if we can't put this thing down. They're going to go head-to-head."

"I know," Bobbi Jo whispered, and together they ran for the side door; it was locked. Without words they loped as fast as possible to the front and it was Bobbi Jo who saw it first, Brick close behind. What happened next was chaotic—a glimmering black monstrosity holding the ravaged body of a soldier. The victim's entrails hung long and black and glistening, trailing into the night as the thing gloated at the feast. The soldier bore little semblance to a human form: its arms were severed at midshaft, its trunk had been eviscerated, and its shattered head fell backward on a broken neck.

It sensed their presence, turned its hulking torso.

Dropping the soldier, it leaped forward, hurling its monstrous form across the compound, the long legs covering the distance with superhuman strength and speed.

Savagely raising the Barrett with a vicious scream, Bobbi Jo fired instantly and the night was rocked by the thunderous blast. Then Brick had dropped to a knee and targeted as the massive black form seemed to stop magically in midair, held suspended above the ground, before it landed solidly. And in a space of time that had no true measurement, both of Brick's .454-caliber rounds hit it solidly, staggering it backward.

Not waiting to see the result of the shots, Bobbi Jo had cut loose with the Barrett, the .50 shells hurled thirty feet from her position as she pulled the trigger again and again, firing from the hip, each bullet flying true to hit the pectorals before it raised gorilla arms in front of its face and turned, running with long leaps that seemed to barely touch the ground. Brick had reloaded and his third round hit it squarely in the wedged back, propelling it forward. Roaring in rage, it staggered slightly as it rounded the corner, and the ex-marshal's last bullet pulverized a foot-wide section of cement.

Already Bobbi Jo had speed-changed clips, chambering another of the five .50-caliber magazines. She expelled a hard breath and waited for Brick to rip the smoking brass cartridges out and insert two more from the bandoleer. Then he snapped it hard and nodded. She didn't need more communication than that.

As they began to move forward a hand snatched her from the shoulder to pull her back. Brick whirled, prepared to fire from the hip before he recognized the flame-etched profile.

Bobbi Jo leaped into him. "Hunter!"

"Come on," he whispered, "we can't fight it like this."

Instantly, wasting no time on preliminaries, he crept back down the wall and Bobbi Jo asked no questions, though she recognized a fullness that had erupted in her breast at the welcome sight of his face. They edged carefully around the corner, separated only a few steps, and closed on the open rear entrance.

"We've got to pull back," Hunter whispered. But his eyes, constantly scanning, never looked at them. "If we try to fight it in the open, we'll lose. We have to trap it somewhere and then open up on it with all we've got. If we can hit with enough heavy rounds in a short enough period of time, we can put it down."

Despite the sweat that masked his face and plastered his ragged mane back over his head, Hunter appeared to be suffering little from exhaustion. His words were terse and his balance and poise perfect as he led them silently closer to the steel portal.

Brick's hoarse voice reached forward.

"Where's Chaney?" lie gasped. "And the Jap? They were securing the motor pool and back fence."

Turning her head briefly, Bobbi Jo stared at him. "Taylor, he's dead. I saw him go down. And then Takakura went down but I don't know if he's dead." She bent forward in a sharp surge of pain before shaking her head wearily. "I ... I don't know where Chaney is."

"Okay, this is how we're gonna play it," Hunter whispered, glancing inside the doorway to note the red glare of emergency lights. He looked at them. "I'm going out there to try to find anybody that's still alive. Did you say Chaney and Takakura were at the back fence?"

"Yes." Bobbi Jo nodded as she wiped sweat-plastered hair from her forehead.

"Good. All right, secure this door. It's the only door that's open and the rest are welded shut. I've checked." He gave them a moment, but there were no objections.

"So give me ten minutes or until you see that thing coming again. Then you've got to shut and somehow bolt the door whether

I'm back or not. The bolt is busted so you'll have to somehow wedge it and keep firing to keep it away from a rush. Weld it shut if you can. And once the door's shut, it stays shut. Get on the radio if you can find it and call for an emergency extraction . . ." He glanced at the Blackhawk—unmolested by the beast's rage as if it did not understand the importance of the machine—before he looked at Brick. "Unless one of you can fly that thing."

Bobbi Jo shook her head, drawing deep breaths.

"Not a chance in hell," Brick rasped.

"That's what I thought," Hunter responded, revealing no trace of disappointment or fear as he moved away from the wall. "Look sharp and use your ears. And don't forget to keep checking the roof up there for silhouettes. It might climb up the other side and attack you from above. Look quick."

"You'd better take this." Brick handed him the Weatherby and bandoleer. "You got two fresh rounds. They hurt him, but it ain't gonna put him down for the count."

Without another word or expression, Hunter loped quickly and lightly across the yard with silent, tiger-like leaps. He did not slow down until he reached the motor pool, engulfed in darkness.

CHAPTER 20

Hazy lights came slowly into focus, and Dr. Arthur Hamilton stared, unknowing. He saw a white ... ceiling? ... Slender white rods ... Fluorescent lights ... Tiles ... Black pinholes in chalky white ...

The laboratory!

It came to him.

"What the – ?" he shouted, rolling painfully to a knee and reflexively reaching for something, anything, for balance. His knee and shoe crunched fragments of broken plastic, glass, paper, and other debris. He crouched like a boxer, staring in a daze. Speechless, reviewing the situation as he could re-member it before he lost consciousness, he was appalled at the carnage, understanding with raw emotion the consequences of what lay before him.

Hunter had survived!

"My God," he whispered. "My God ..."

He turned toward the back of the laboratory. "Come out, you cowardly fools!" he called, not troubling to disguise his anger. "Come out before I come back there and drag you out!"

A moment of silence passed.

Then Emma Strait's black-haired head peeked timidly around the corner. A male and female assistant looked out from behind her shoulders, holding onto Emma as if she were their security. Emma's face was fearful.

Dr. Hamilton regained enough emotional control to hesitate, drawing breath. He would have to ignore the stiffness in his neck, the strange lightness in his step. Understanding that Hunter had apparently struck him across the neck, he motioned with forgiveness for Emma to step forward.

Then, to further ease her fear, he leaned back heavily on a computer terminal and rubbed his neck. And as she watched him so closely, he made a smooth display of interpreting this event as a tragic but expected occurrence. His act was polished brilliance, even without words: a madman was in their midst, and he had done this ...

Not appearing so agitated as to seem unhinged, he looked back at her and nodded. "Come, Emma, we must nevertheless deal with this unfortunate situation. Nothing can be gained by securing yourselves in the bunker. Although I'm sure it was a prudent measure at the time. Yes, we are fortunate, very fortunate, to be alive."

On an impulse that he wished he could have avoided he glanced at the tube and saw that the creature's coffin was shattered by rifle fire, the body disintegrated. Nothing remained but a smoking mass of liquefied flesh and starkly visible bone. Hamilton could not conceal the bitter grimace that twisted his face. When he glanced back at Emma, she had stopped in stride.

"Oh, it is nothing, Emma." He gestured, trying to maintain a smooth manner. He tried to close his mind to the horror of all his great effort, now destroyed by this base wild man, this nobody, this tracker who would not surrender to superior forces. "I ... I was simply wondering how much damage our complex had suffered in this ... this gunfight ... which I seemed to have missed entirely."

"You ... you missed it?" she asked.

"Oh, yes." Hamilton made a great display of rubbing his neck: you must make her sympathetic. "I'm sure you and the others were secured safely in the bunker—I'm glad that I included it in the budget—but I was out here among them, trying to reason with them.

"The intruders, apparently renegades from this hunting party, surreptitiously stole in here to either injure us or acquire something. The guards caught them, and I attempted to negotiate, in order to avoid senseless injury. Then one of them—this madman called Hunter—struck me unconscious. I suppose I am fortunate to be alive." He grimaced. "Yes, I need medical attention, but now is not the time. A cursory examination will have to suffice as long as we remain under his attack."

Emma, followed closely by the rest, had cautiously moved closer to him. But Hamilton attempted to make it seem of no importance, as if saying, "Of course you would stand beside me. Why not? Have I not protected you thus far? Am I not your colleague? Your teacher?"

He gestured to indicate that he had no doubt of their loyalty. "Now we must discover if any of the data have been stolen."

Bending to indicate pain beyond what he truly felt, Hamilton continued, "Please run a file check, the times and user, to determine what has been examined in the past three hours. Then do a physical inventory of the vault, and determine if any materials have been removed."

Unmoving, they stared.

"Well, come on!" Hamilton used his authoritative tone, knowing that by now they had been properly prepared; their suspicions were dulled, their fears assuaged by his honest appearance of his own pain and shock. He added more angrily, "We have work to do!"

Swarming like worker bees who knew their responsibilities without instruction and were willing to drive themselves to death in order to fulfill their roles, the crew assumed their shattered work stations. Some of the terminals were still smoking, and the ten-man technical team immediately initiated undamaged backup systems housed in adjoining rooms.

Hamilton's last orders were all but lost in the activity as he turned to Emma.

"Please contact Mr. Dixon on the NSA satellite immediately," he instructed calmly. Then, as an afterthought: "And, just in case, have someone lock the entrance to this level. I believe it is time to secure the vault."

***

Hunter moved stealthily and silently, knowing the creature would be forced to track by scent in this chaos. Frowning, angry and fearless now, he'd make it work.

Hesitating beside the body of a dead soldier, he reached out and touched the man's gaping wound, feeling compassion. Then he rubbed the blood on his boots and continued moving, crossing the path of a dozen more slain soldiers, repeating the procedure, mixing his scent with the scent of the dead.

It was impossible to remain in the darkness because blazing orange light from the inferno of the tanker and disintegrating shed threw dancing diagonal shadows across the motor pool. So he kept loping, going high over the roofs of trucks and descending to the ground again.

He held the Weatherby close as he threaded a path through an army of dead men. But he saw nothing, heard nothing, sensed nothing. Then, heart flaming, he heard a low moan and whirled, searching with narrow eyes.

In the distance, perhaps thirty feet away, he saw a hand weakly raised in the air and loped easily toward it, all the while alert to any movement or sound beside or behind him.

It was a young soldier. Almost a boy.

Hunter almost groaned at the sight, and knelt beside him.

A slashing blow had torn away part of the boy's chest. Blood had matted in the wound, concealing its depth. He grasped Hunter's hand weakly, and Hunter knew he could do nothing for him. The creature's blow had torn away ribs, leaving the chest cavity exposed; it was a matter of moments.

Gasping, the boy spoke.

"Did we ...get it?"

Hunter grimaced. "Yeah, soldier. You got it."

There was almost a smile, then the boy took another breath and was gone. Slowly, Hunter stood, staring down. His rage was channeled now, and he stood like a monument of judgment. It would die for this, he swore to himself. As surely as he lived, it would die.

Hunter gazed about, knowing exactly what had happened, though he had seen none of it.

It had chosen its terrain well, using their fear, and they had fallen into the trap. If he had been here, he was certain, this never would have happened. At least not on this scale. But they had allowed themselves to get caught up in the chase. Had lacked the patience to pick their terrain more carefully and wait with infinite patience until the prey was close and vulnerable. He shook his head.

Here, with shadow and light crossing like a chessboard, it had been able to move only a step before it disappeared, only to re-emerge from complete blackness to kill with a blow before moving on, vanishing again into darkness, stalking.

Such a loss ...

It was a battlefield, a graveyard of dead men that might have won, but for want of his direction. He cursed himself silently as he heard a sound.

Whirling, he had the Weatherby centered.

Takakura ...

The Japanese commander was holding his chest, sword in hand. And his face was slack, sweating, while he stared down over the boy, as if the soldier were somehow different from the multitude surrounding him, or if he somehow epitomized the score of dead. Then the Japanese simply shook his head, bowing wearily to lean on the hood of a Humvee.

"Come on," Hunter said, not wasting time on questions. He put his arm under Takakura s shoulder, supporting him, and they began to move.

"We've got to get inside the building before it finds us. Which it's going to do fast enough."

Takakura, a true soldier, merely frowned at his injury. He asked no questions as he stumbled alongside Hunter, his sword dragging a narrow trail in the dust. Hunter knew the Japanese was badly wounded but never asked how or where; this was no time.

A cacophony of explosions erupted in an area near the shed and Hunter froze, lifting his head. He saw blasts of gunfire and heard heated shouts from the glowing devastation. The gun blasts continued, broken only by short pauses of cursing before they resumed once more.

Hunter glimpsed a distant silhouetted figure moving back and forth and saw it raise a rifle, firing two rounds that were followed by a heated curse that carried across the compound. In the next moment the figure ran to the right and vanished.

Hunter leaned Takakura against the front grill of a troop carrier. The big truck easily supported the Japanese, although Takakura's head was bent forward in exhaustion and shock. Hunter pushed him back and spoke close to his face.

"Takakura!" Hunter pointed to the installation. "Can you make it to the building? Bobbi Jo and Brick are at the side door!

All you have to do is get to the building! It's not that far! Do you understand me!"

A slow nod. "*Hai.*"

Grimacing stoically, he pushed Hunter's hand aside and staggered forward. Hunter moved toward the place where he had seen the gunfire. He glanced back once to see Takakura moving slowly and slightly off balance, but with determination. It might take him longer to make it alone, but Hunter believed he would. And, although Takakura was easy prey in his wounded condition, Hunter didn't think that the creature was an immediate danger to him. No, he was confident that the man at the far end of the motor pool, the one firing the gun and raging at the night, had sighted the thing and was trying to finish the fight.

Hunter had a good suspicion who it was before he ever reached the liquefied remains of the tanker.

Even 150 feet away, the heat was blistering, and Hunter glanced to the far right to see Chaney raise the Weatherby against a shoulder, firing twice. Obviously getting more skilled with the double-barreled rifle, Chaney had ejected the spent rounds and inserted two more in the blink of an eye. As quickly as Chaney had performed the action, he might as well have been firing a semiautomatic.

"Chaney!" Hunter yelled from behind the protection of a Humvee. As enraged as Chaney was, Hunter was taking no chances that he might accidentally shoot him.

Chaney paused before he called out, "Hunter?"

Instantly Hunter was out from behind the Humvee running forward, searching the area where Chaney had been shooting. And they began the conversation long before they stood face-to-face, Hunter alert to everything, close shadows on the right, distant shadows beyond flame on the left. He raised an arm briefly against the tidal wave of heat pouring from the ruined tanker and shed.

"What do you have?" he shouted to Chaney above the roaring inferno.

"I near tripped over the thing!" Chaney yelled back. "Somebody finally hurt it! I don't know who! It was on the ground and I just shot it point-blank!"

Hunter knew before he even asked. "Did you kill it?"

"Hell, no!" Chaney glared at him, sweating. Hunter saw that he had used about a third of the cartridges on the bandoleer. "But I sure got it mad." He grimaced, catching his breath. "I hit it again as it got up off the ground and then it was gone! I chased it across the compound, hittin' it every chance I got! Then it vanished over here! I got a glimpse of it a second ago and sent two over there!" He pointed to the far side of the flames, shook his head. "Haven't seen it since!"

Another time Hunter might have congratulated him, but there was no time for praise. Then a voice roared from the flames on the other side of the shed.

"Hunter! I know your name! I will kill you for this!"

It was the beast.

Still alive ...

Hunter debated a reply, and shouted back, "Then come and kill me! Do it now!"

"No! Not now! But soon! Soon! You think you have won but you have won nothing! Because I am more than man!"

Hunter snarled, "You're an animal, Luther! An animal! You'll always be an animal now!"

"Tell me that when I eat your heart!"

Chaney shouted, "Eat this!" and fired the Weatherby blindly toward the voice before Hunter grabbed his arm.

"No!" he said. "We've got to get back to the building. It's our only chance. We can't stop him with these weapons. Come on! Let's move! We gotta get everyone into the building and wait for it to come to us!"

Frowning with anger, Chaney raised his head to search briefly over the flames before he grimaced, turning. Hunter saw that, as fired up as Chaney was with the close combat, his fever had not overridden his tactical judgment.

"All right!" He loped forward, holding the Weatherby. "Let's get back!"

Holding his heart, Professor Tipler sat on the edge of the bed, bathed in red light flooding out from the corners. The emergency lights had kicked on and he had heard the roar and clash of battle in the motor pool, the howls of wounded men, the screams of the dying.

Even from this great distance, secured within cement walls, he had discerned frantic orders, endless gunfire. And now that the gunfire had ceased, except for scattered resistance, he presumed the battle had been lost.

Standing monolithic in the gloom, Ghost filled the narrow entrance of Tipler's cubicle. True to his loyalty and love, the great black wolf had not left Tipler's side since the ordeal began. Like a great unsleeping spirit of flesh and fang cloaked in black, he fearlessly stood his ground.

Tipler smiled. He knew Ghost would never leave his side. Not until Hunter gave the word. And he wondered what would happen if he told the noble wolf to find his master. Tipler closed his eyes as the possibility entered his mind that Hunter had been killed by the beast. Again, he shook his head; so little an old man can do ...

Raising his eyes, Tipler regarded the ever loyal Ghost. Perhaps, if all was lost outside, the wolf could yet escape. He knew that Ghost would easily survive in these mountains, which were his true home. Or he might find Hunter, still alive, and fight beside him. Surely, though, he was not needed here. Not any longer.

Tipler could feel a chill in his spine, an emptiness in his chest, that assured him – *No, not much longer.* He nodded, firm in the conviction. Then he pointed to the open door leading from the ICU.

"Go!" he shouted. "Find Hunter!"

Ghost's alertness at the words was complete. The ears were straight black angles against red light. And although Tipler could not quite see the eyes, he knew from the quick blinks that made the shining obsidian orbs fade in and out that the wolf had focused on him completely. There was a new tension in his stance.

Tipler repeated the command, shouting to fill his voice with anger.

Still, Ghost did not retreat, held his guard. But the wide wedge-shaped head tilted, confused.

"Go!"Tipler roared, and stood away from the bed. He pointed thunderously. "Go and find Hunter!"

Ghost retreated before the great enraged voice and looked at the door. Then he looked back at Tipler, clearly unsure. Tipler picked up a plate from his tray and flung it high, scattered utensils and roaring with his command. "Go, Ghost! Find Hunter! Find Hunter! Go! Go! Go!"

Ghost was halfway across the intensive care unit, standing his ground and glancing with confusion at the door, at Tipler, the door, and back again. And then Tipler's strength faded with a washing, light-headed announcement. Still standing close to the bed, he leaned and reached out, falling lightly onto his right side ...

"Go, Ghost," he whispered. "Ghost ..."

Ghost stood his place and watched, head tilted, until the man was utterly still. And after a moment, when the man had not moved at all, he wandered close, sniffed, and caught the scent of death. With a whine, he stepped back, still holding his place. Then, finally, with a solemn turn he moved across the antiseptic room into the red-shadowed darkness of the door, turned and was gone.

***

Chaney had no trouble, uninjured as he was, keeping pace with Hunter. But as they cleared the motor pool they saw Takakura struggling, only halfway across the compound. The Japanese was moving more slowly with each step and Hunter instantly angled to the side, making for him. Chaney, understanding instantly and too conditioned to the wild unpredictability of combat to waste breath on questions, followed with strong strides.

Hunter glanced to the left to see Bobbi Jo on one knee, the bipod of the Barrett resting on a crate. Her head turned as she searched everything around them, and Hunter knew the creature couldn't come upon them without her hitting it with the sniper rifle. And even if the massive round couldn't stop it, the impact would slow it down, possibly giving them time to reach the sanctuary of the complex. In any case, a little hope was better than no hope at all.

Takakura fell forward as Hunter reached him. Hunter heard heavy approaching footsteps in front and raised the Weatherby, turning the Japanese aside.

Brick.

Breath heaving, he came up with the AK-47 slung on his back. His hands, beefy fists as large as rocks, worked rhythmically over his chest as he covered the last few yards. He bent and slipped his head under Takakura's left arm. With Hunter on the right, they hoisted him and Chaney took rear guard, running backwards with the Weatherby held close across his chest.

Bobbi Jo heard a shuffle and whirled.

Her intellect instantly assured her that it couldn't have been the beast but her reflexes made her react as if it were. She stared for a long silence and then saw a creature, utterly black and moving with effortless grace, around a far corner. Pausing, it saw her and without hesitation or sound loped quickly forward.

She smiled. "Ghost ..."

The wolf came up slowly and pressed his nose against her face. Bobbi Jo touched the rough black fur, smiling. Her next thought was of Hunter as Ghost swung its huge head to gaze out over the compound, and her hand closed tightly on its midnight mane.

"Ghost!" she yelled suddenly. "Stay!"

Ghost surged forward as he saw Hunter but she held him back, both hands locking around the neck as she spoke sternly, trying to push him against the building. It was desperate enough with the three of them out there; the wolf would only complicate the situation, and would probably refuse to retreat at all if it sighted the creature.

But without really even moving, Ghost brushed off her attempt, merely shifting his stance to make her slide awkwardly down his side. To him it was merely play, nothing that required conscious effort. But Bobbi Jo was struggling with all her strength and skill to control the wolf's twisting, powerful form.

Bobbi Jo's hands scraped and grasped at the body and mane, trying to find a grip that he could not easily escape when Ghost, rising suddenly on hind legs, roared with a rage and fury that sent her sprawling wildly back. She glimpsed the savagely separated white fangs, black eyes blazing in a fury beyond anything mortal, and twisted her head to the side.

She screamed as she saw the creature almost upon Hunter and Chaney, hurtling across the compound with the speed of a lion.

She dove for the Barrett but knew she'd never target it at such velocity.

She screamed a warning.

And Ghost was already forty feet from the building, silently hurling its magnificent black shape forward with a speed that rivaled the beast's. Another volcanic stride and it vanished into darkness.

"Ghost!"

***

At Bobbi Jo's warning scream, Hunter raised his head and saw Ghost's black form racing across the compound. But the wolf wasn't directly running for him so Hunter dropped and spun, understanding instantly. The Weatherby rose as he hurled Takakura roughly back.

Chaney was slower, but not by much. Before Hunter had fired he had already turned, saw it all, understood, and the stock was at his shoulder when Hunter pulled the trigger.

The four barrels blazed as one and the creature staggered aside, hurt and slowed. It raised its face as it launched itself forward again. An explosion erupted at the door of the faraway complex and it was hurled onto its back, rolling with the wrecking-ball impact of Bobbi Jo's .50-caliber round.

It rose snarling wildly, glaring at Hunter.

Fangs displayed, it charged again.

Chaney's breech snapped shut and Hunter remembered that he hadn't reloaded. He cracked the breech, burning fingers on the spent cartridges. He speed-loaded two more cartridges as Brick targeted with the AK-47—not a damaging round but certainly more painful than the meaningless .223's—and fired, the lead bouncing off the creature's ballistic-resistant skin.

Chaney had fired both rounds and reloaded again as Hunter raised aim. And the creature still staggered forward, relentless.

Its nightmarish face twisted in pain and rage, striding through the onslaught as if the sole reason for its being was to kill and to kill more, to endlessly kill and kill and kill.

And in that surreal moment, Hunter saw it as it truly was.

The professor's words descended through his mind like a tilted water tower, the deluge disgorging everything inside with a single titanic blast. It took no time, and it was there in all its complexity.

Here, before Hunter, was the deepest, darkest mind of man; without conscience, without mercy, without pity. Untouched by compassion or regard or restraint, it was the center of what man once was before he rose above blood and mindlessness, to become man. For in those scarlet eyes and gaping fangs lay the black heart of death and murder and destruction for the sake of destruction alone, impulses felt and fulfilled for nothing other than the satisfaction; nothing to question or challenge; no reason to stay its hand when it might shed the blood it craved. It was a creation that lived—that existed—only for the physical expression of the darkness so deeply buried within man that even man feared to pry away the stone and see the horror within. As Chaney speed-loaded the Weatherby and Brick frantically dropped to a knee, exchanging a clip, Hunter stared at the epitome of human evil.

It stalked forward, a growl building within, and it sprang upon them, its terrible strength carrying it in a long twenty-foot arch. Then Hunter glimpsed the blinding streak of black racing from the side. He turned and screamed.

"Ghost! NO!"

The gigantic black wolf struck the beast in the air, and they instantly locked in a thunderstorm of blows thrown and blows returned, fang to fang, spinning through red darkness until they crashed to earth together, savagely fighting to the death.

Scattering blood with each blow they revolved through the dark. Ghost hurled himself with unimaginable force against the monstrosity to blast it away from Hunter.

Again and again the great wolf struck, tearing savage gaps in the creature's arms, chest, and neck that brought forth rivers of blood. The beast returned the same, hurling vicious swipes of its clawed hands in a devil's battle that wounded Ghost with equal violence.

It was the heart of fury, the place where savagery and rage were conquered by something greater, something even more furious. The beast hurled a clawed hand that struck Ghost's shoulder, ribs glistening white at the impact, and Ghost came off the ground like a rocket, hurling himself from the bloodied earth to hit it full force. Together, they smashed into a truck and then they hit the ground again, revolving and wrestling with fang striking fang.

Hunter didn't know he had leaped forward until Brick's massive form tackled him from behind.

Falling forward, he felt a wet collision with the earth. Then, with a roar—a roar that surged from a sacred and unknown place—Hunter volcanically pushed himself up from the ground and flung the larger man off like paper. He spun to the rest of them and said nothing, communicating only with the fire of his eyes.

Ghost and the creature raged against each other almost fifty yards away. And Hunter saw, even in the half light, white streaks in Ghost's side; ribs exposed to the night. But the wolf held his ground, his hideous growls and roars vibrating in the atmosphere.

Yet the creature was severely injured, clutching ravaged red gaps torn in its chest and neck, its forearm savaged with bone shining reddish-white in the semi-darkness. Retreating slightly, it circled, cautious now, with taloned hands threatening.

Frowning, Hunter raised the rifle and fired.

Both rounds hit true, and the creature howled in rage and pain. Then Hunter hurled the rifle aside, drawing the Bowie as he ran forward.

He never saw what happened behind him, but knew. He hadn't taken five steps when he heard a stampede of angry voices following. Even Takakura was there, all of them charging the last remaining feet to close on the creature.

Chased no longer; hounded like sheep no longer; fighting now, taking the battle to the beast, refusing to retreat and choosing the moment of their death, if need be.

Ghost leaped to attack as Hunter closed the last stride. The creature caught the wolf in the air, then hatefully hurled him aside, and Hunter hit it full force.

Lashing out quicker than the eye could follow, his knife was nothing but light in the gloom as Hunter hit it clean, deep and out again to leave a furrow through the ribs. But, quick as he had moved, he could not escape the beast's retaliation.

It whirled in a backhand—a blow that would have killed a normal man—but Hunter saw it, turning into it with both forearms to defy the attack that struck like a mountain. The forearm met his and Hunter was flung through the night air.

Brick, four feet distant, squared off and fired both barrels of Hunter's discarded Weatherby. The double impact of the mammoth rounds made the beast bend double at the waist. A second of raging pause, and then Takakura leaped to the side, the katana flashing down—a heaving vertical strike—to catch the creature solidly across the back of the neck.

And at the impact of the blow the creature came from its bowed posture like a rocket, instantly grasping the sword and twisting to hurl both it and the Japanese far and away. They crashed painfully against a Humvee and fell to the ground.

As it turned back to Chaney and Brick, almost with contempt, Brick's feet had left the ground. His body, twisting volcanically, had spun, holding the barrels of the Weatherby in huge fists. The wide wooden stock of the rifle swung like a baseball bat to strike the bowed head with incredible force. And at the impact the sound of pulverized flesh echoed like a gunshot across the glade. But the stock shattered, leaving Brick staggering back holding a broken rifle, gazing upward into the face of the beast.

Shaking its head in contempt, it started for him.

Hunter was on his feet, roaring as he moved, and Ghost moved with him, each attacking the creature from opposite sides. Hunter saw Chaney take aim and hit the beast solidly in the head with two .454 rounds of the Weatherby. A blinding burst of white came from the side—Bobbi Jo joining us—that made Hunter reflexively bend away before he hurled himself forward and slashed at the neck.

Sensing his approach, it flung out its left arm to hurl him back hatefully. The blow caught Hunter's shoulder as it roared with rage. Then—

A Japanese cry ... sword flashing, slashing across, back again ... explosion before them, gray shape falling upon Hunter ... Bowie slashing up to hit gray flesh, down quick, stabbing ... black wolf across, white fangs lashing out ... spiraling blood ... explosion in his face, blinding ... Bobbi Jo, Chaney ... DUCK! ...Clawed hand lashing viciously over his head ... returning ... blade moving on weight ... come back to me to hit ... weight and body behind the blade, slashing hard ... stabbing deep ... that's it ... bring the blade down and put your body into the ... blade stabbing deep, rising, falling with weight, rising volcanically ... steel vanishing into gray, ripping away ... animal roaring ... Brick struck and flung ... hurled through air bellowing, striking wildly at air ... *Chest*! ... Leaping forward blade poised to strike upward now! *Opening*!

Roaring, Hunter uncoiled like a rattlesnake, the blade flashing before him to AHH!

Darkness.

Roars, orange flashes in the blackness, spotlights in the sky.

Lowering ... so cold ... to him.

Rising slowly, Bowie knife hard in a clenched fist, Hunter stood, raising his face to the strange silence as it registered that all of them, even Ghost, were motionless and prostrate on the wet ground. Brow hardening, knowing that a half-dozen helicopters were settling in the glade, Hunter gazed about curiously, fist tightening even more on the huge Bowie.

He saw nothing.

The beast was gone, though in the stillness he knew where he would find it. He raised his head wearily; he was covered in blood and it didn't matter. Enough was enough, they had come too far. He even knew who the undisclosed men in the helicopters were, and didn't care. Nothing would stop him now.

This belonged to him, not them; it had changed hands a long time ago, when they had sent him out to die. He had already destroyed the relic, and now he would destroy the living embodiment of this primordial evil.

Hunter could not accept the possibility that his colleagues were dead, and regretted hurling himself into the battle. But he had done it out of love. And that he did not regret.

As the helicopters landed and scores of black-clad soldiers leaped out, guns poised, running across the glade, Hunter knelt beside Ghost. The wolf, sensing his presence, blinked, and Hunter smiled, sitting gently on the ground beside it, stroking the thick, bloodied black fur.

The wounds torn into its muscular body were deep and terrible, but Ghost revealed no pain.

"It's gonna be all right, boy," Hunter said quietly.

Ghost blinked again, silent in his pain.

A team of soldiers, locking and loading automatic weapons, surrounded them.

At the sounds, Ghost tried to rise. But Hunter placed a hand on him, continuing to speak in soothing tones. He talked about everything, about nothing, about what they would do when they went home. And he talked until the awesome, courageous black eyes glazed over, and the huge chest fell still. Hunter waited another moment, his hand soft on the mane, stroking his friend. Then he solemnly bent his head.

A frown twisted his brow as he rose, staring darkly at the weapons, the men. He feared none of them, and never would. Death would be welcome to him now. He almost invited them to shoot. Glancing across the faces, he found no leader.

"Where's Dixon?" he growled.

"Get on the ground!" a soldier bellowed.

It took a single long second for Hunter to turn his head to the voice. His countenance was deadly.

"Make me," he said, low.

The soldier stepped back.

Orders were barked, and Hunter glanced to the side to see Chaney rising, holding a hand to his bruised forehead. And Takakura was stirring, clumsily and painfully. Bobbi Jo lay where she had fallen; she made no movement at all.

Hunter moved for her, and a cacophony of voices and orders thundered in the air; he didn't give a damn. He reached her and rolled her over gently, checking the wounds.

A large blue-red welt on her head revealed where she'd been struck. And a narrow gash—the wound of a single claw—streaked her forehead, the blood already drying. Another clawed blow had split her Kevlar vest at mid-torso. But after carefully removing it, Hunter saw that the claws had only barely touched the skin, though she bled heavily from the cuts.

Despite the shouts behind him, Hunter turned to them in a low voice. "Do you have a medic with you?"

They cared nothing for his words. Nothing for his needs.

Bellowing now with authority, they told him what to do.

He stared at all of them: if dying was this, so be it. He would obey no one and nothing until he had helped his friends. Ignoring the conflicting orders, he looked to the side to see someone obviously in charge striding through the detachment: Dixon.

Hunter squared into him.

Without expression, Dixon came up, hands clasped behind his back with a hundred rifles trained on Hunter. Smiling faintly, Hunter communicated that he knew who had true courage.

Dixon was unfazed. He spoke boldly, frankly, and with a complete lack of concern or compassion for the suffering and sacrifice that Hunter and his colleagues had endured in the last three days. It was an attitude that Hunter had expected, but even he had not anticipated such a perfect, superlative level of pure arrogance and apathy at the death of so many; deaths that could have been prevented. Bowing his head, eyes hidden in shadow, Hunter didn't reply.

"Mr. Hunter!" Dixon kept his distance with the words. "I feel that it's only right to tell you: if you do not discard your knife in the next three seconds, my men will shoot you and everyone with you stone-cold dead! You are not a soldier! I am! Believe me, I say what I mean!"

Hunter looked into his eyes. Laughed.

"Three seconds?"

"Three seconds!"

"You won't give us more?"

Dixon laughed. "You're such a fool, Hunter. I am about to count. Remember. Three seconds."

Hunter nodded vaguely, understanding. "Okay. Count."

"One ... two ..."

Hunter lifted a hand from behind his back and the Bowie knife at the same time. Dixon's eyes widened as he saw the only bag of HD-66, the source of all they sought, poised at the tip of the blade. The slightest movement, even by accident, would split the bag and spill the precious liquid on the ground, costing them all they had schemed and worked toward for so long.

Instantly Dixon extended his arms, his words soaring over all else as he bellowed, "Hold fire! Hold fire! Hold fire! No one is to fire! Is that clear! No one is to fire! No one is to fire!"

Confused looks were cast at the CIA agent, and Dixon stretched out his arms as angry figures rushed from the complex behind them. Hunter recognized Hamilton. The rest, he didn't know. He stared back at Dixon as they neared, his hands dead-steady despite the adrenaline surge he felt in his system.

Chaney came up beside him, staring at the troops. He shook his head as he muttered, "America's finest."

Hunter heard Takakura rise, gain balance. Then the Japanese bent to help Bobbi Jo to her feet, lifting her gently to sit her on the fender of a truck. She didn't take the Barrett with her, even in her confusion knowing it wasn't necessary. There was a pause, and then her voice cut through the tension.

"I figured it would end in something like this," she muttered.

Hamilton halted, breathing heavily, beside Dixon.

"These ...these are the men," he exclaimed, pointing. "They are guilty ...they are guilty of sabotage!"

Dixon never removed his eyes from Hunter.

Smiling, Hunter never removed his eyes from Dixon.

"I think the right of decision has passed to Mr. Hunter, Doctor," Dixon said with cold assessment.

Hunter looked into his face and knew that Dixon would murder them instantly if Hunter gave them the serum. Only the threat of its destruction was keeping them at bay. He lifted his chin.

"Get everyone back into the choppers," he said. "Now."

Dixon shuffled and glanced at Hamilton, who now noticed the amber-filled bag in Hunter's rigid hand. The doctor's face blanched and he extended his hand: "You took it! You stole the serum!" He swayed a moment, shaking his head. "Was it from ingenuity, Mr. Hunter?" he added with hate. "Or was it the vengeful motivation to kill this magnificent creature?" The doctor laughed. "Yes, I know. You did not expect to use it in this manner, but neither did you hesitate."

Hunter shifted his eyes from Hamilton to Dixon.

"Tell you what, Dixon," he said softly. "You've got three seconds to lay down your weapons and get out of here. Your men fly. You stay."

Shocked, Dixon blinked. "You can't be serious."

"One ..."

"Back in the choppers!" Dixon whirled, cupping his mouth for volume. "Get back in the choppers! All of you get back in the choppers! Move! Move! Move!"

They hesitated.

"*Two ...*"

"Get in the choppers!" Dixon hurled an arm out, motioning violently. He grabbed the nearest soldier and flung him toward the Blackhawks. "All of you get in the choppers now! Do it now-now-now!"

Disciplined, they dropped their rifles and ran across the short space to the choppers. Then, as a helicopter filled with unarmed soldiers, the Blackhawks lifted off one after the other until they stood alone in the glade listening to the vanishing whirring of blades in the invisible night. Angry, Hunter focused fully on Dixon.

"Well, Dixon," he said, "I guess this is what they call 'reality.'"

Dixon smirked; he had had several minutes to collect himself. In turn, he glanced at Takakura, Brick, Bobbi Jo, and Chaney. When he looked back at Hunter, he revealed a rich amusement.

"Not much of your crew is left, Hunter." He almost laughed. "You go in with seven, come back with three and now you are trapped with nowhere to go even if you wanted to escape. My men are not fools, you know. They are waiting for you to attempt escape. And then, quite simply, they will blast you out of the sky."

"That's not your problem, Dixon," Hunter responded, stone-cold, with a hint of malice. "Right now you need to be thinking about how you're gonna get out of this alive."

Dixon glared into Hunter's eyes with scorn.

"You're lost, Hunter." He shook his head. "You're just out of your league, man. How do you think you can compete with us? We know everything. We're locked into everything ..."

"What are you locked into, Dixon?"

Dixon started to reply; something real. Then he dropped his hands to his sides as if he never could.

"Just ... everything, Hunter."

"So this is what it comes down to, huh?" Hunter shook his head. "Hundreds of people die so a handful of the privileged can live. Doesn't sound like much of a tradeoff, Dixon. Especially for the people you pushed into traffic."

"You and I don't make those calls, Hunter."

"Who does?"

Dixon stared. His expression was honest. "I have no idea."

Having already lowered the serum to his side, Hunter held his Bowie in a loose fist. He would use both when the moment came. And the words of the old Indian returned to him, more meaningful in the last six hours than they had ever been.

He understood, now, where it was going. And he knew he would have pieced it together a long time ago, if they had only been honest. But he had been forced to discover the truth for himself beneath layer upon layer of lies and deceit and betrayals.

Somber, he turned to the forest. The far horizon was touched with a steel-gray dawn that matched his mood.

The beast was wounded, and retreating.

It knew, now, that it would never obtain the serum; whatever remained of its human mind would convince it of that. But the animal would rule as it always ruled. So it would do what an animal always did when it was wounded. It would retreat to where it could heal. It would go to its lair. And that's where Hunter would find it.

Time to finish this ...

"You're not listening to me, Hunter," Dixon implored. "The best thing you can do right now is just hand over the serum. Listen, I know you destroyed the relic. So all we have left is that bag because the ...the elements ...whatever they're called ...can't be synthesized. It has to come from the source."

"There's still him," Hunter said stoically.

Dixon paused. "Yeah, there's still that ... *thing.*"

"And what if I capture him for you?"

A laugh.

"I don't think I can authorize that, Hunter. Things are too out of control."

"It was authorized before."

"No," Dixon shook his head, "not really. That was just smoke and mirrors. You were there to make it look official." He sighed, "We never really wanted you to find it. But we never wanted you to kill it, either. We just wanted it to look like we were doing our best. And it worked." Impressed with his own genius, Dixon nodded. "Worked pretty well, actually. Answered a ton of questions and everybody thought we were doing the right thing. We'll never catch any heat. Because we used the best tracker in the world, hired the best hunting team in the world, and you guys did all that anyone could do, so no matter who wants heads roll after this, I'm covered like a blanket." He smiled. "I'm a pro at this, Hunter."

With no hesitation Hunter drew the Bowie and smoothly slashed the serum bag, spilling the precious liquid onto the dirt. As he dropped the bag to the ground, Dr. Hamilton gaped.

Shocked, Hamilton stood in place, mutely extending arms to where Hunter had trashed his life's work.

Dixon, disappointed, shifted slightly in his stance, staring at the ground. It was a moment before he could find the appropriate words, but his tone retained an air of professional calm.

"You know, I figured you were gonna do something like that," he commented.

Hunter controlled the moment, nodded.

"And then there was one."

"Aaahhh..." Hamilton managed, arms extended in mute protest.

Dixon cast the scientist an annoyed glance before focusing again on Hunter, the team. He looked over all of them for a long moment, shaking his head in amazement. "You're really planning on taking this crew out one more time?" he asked. "Have you looked at yourself lately, dude? You're wasted! Your team is wasted! All of you, especially you, look totalled. Yeah, I know you're a tough guy, survival is an art you cultivate, all that. But you ain't gonna last three days out there. All of you belong in the hospital, man, not some jungle. And I've got more happy news for you."

Silence, as Dixon smiled.

Chancy walked up. "No," he said. "You can't be serious." He searched Dixon's face as he stopped, standing beside Hunter. "You can't tell me they're that crazy."

"Oh, yeah, they're that crazy," Dixon confirmed, casually glancing at his watch. "We've got ... oh, about twenty-six minutes, I'd say."

Hunter laughed brutally; he didn't have to be told.

A moment of strange silence reigned.

Dixon was impassive, and the rest were too emotionally burned out to feel anything at all. Only in their minds did they dispassionately realize that this entire area was going to be vaporized by an air attack, erasing any traces of the research facility, the records, the dead, the creature, the earth itself.

What would remain here in half an hour would be a blasted piece of planet that would burn for days until only ashes smoldered in the midst of a strangely silent and deserted wilderness. There would be nothing for prosecutors to examine, and nothing hidden. It would be as if it had simply never existed at all. And any investigation, should it happen, would die with nothing but innuendo, suspicions, and questions easily deflected.

"The lab is two stories belowground," Chaney said. "How are they gonna blast something that's forty feet down?"

"Oh, I ain't sure," Dixon responded casually, lighting a cigarette. "I suppose they'll use a fuel-air bomb. It was the only thing strong enough to destroy underground bunkers in Iraq." He shrugged. "Doesn't matter, really. Fuel-air. Sidewinders. Dragons. Whatever. But they'll do the job right, I guarantee you. So in less than half an hour, gentlemen, and lady, this glade will be a solid sheet of glass. No experiment. No facility. No evidence. No monster. No nothing."

The CIA man maintained his casual air. Hunter knew Dixon was certain that he and the others would be airlifted out on the single remaining Blackhawk as quickly as possible. Dixon believed they wouldn't leave him behind to die.

Bobbi Jo walked past them. "I'm going to get the professor," she said to Hunter. "We have to get out of here."

Watching her lope with amazing strength—considering her injuries— across the compound, Hunter judged her strong enough for the task. He turned back to Dixon. "That was your plan all along, wasn't it?" he asked. "You were gonna perfect the serum, trap that thing in the complex, then raze the whole place. Perfect containment. Everyone is dead. You've got what you want. And there's no evidence at all that anything happened." He shook his head. "Almost the perfect plan, Dixon."

"Almost?" The agent smiled. "I'd say it was perfect, Hunter. Except for you." He cocked his head. "I must admit, I never figured you would muck things up the way you did. My fault; I underestimated you. But, well, that's what happens when you make last-minute changes to a perfect scenario. Guys like you get involved. And you think you got it all figured, but this guy, whoever, turns out to be some kind of war hero. Just won't lie down and do as he's told. And then ..." He motioned around him, "you have gold-plated FUBAR."

"I die hard," Hunter said.

Dixon acknowledged it with a nod. "Obviously," he replied, spitting out a piece of tobacco. "Too hard, it seems. But I don't think you're gonna survive the firestorm that's gonna be dropped on this area in about twenty minutes."

"You still don't have the serum, Dixon."

At the mention of "serum," Hamilton groaned and closed his eyes. His hands had fallen to his sides and he stood in awful silence, head bowed in misery. Hunter ignored him.

Dixon was angry. "No, Hunter, we don't."

"Well, then"—Hunter stared at him—"I guess it all comes down to you and me. What are you gonna tell your bosses when they see how you messed this up? Think they're gonna be happy that, after this 'perfect scenario' of yours, they're out a billion-dollar facility, have to answer a congressional investigation and still don't get the serum?" He nodded. "I think Siberia is in your future, Dixon."

"Well," the agent answered calmly, "you may be right. I don't think they're gonna be too pleased at this end result."

"So what about it?"

"What about what?"

"What about letting us go after it?"

Dixon's eyes narrowed, calculating. "I must say, destroying the serum was a masterstroke, Hunter. But there are other trackers. And I'm sure we can find someone as skillful as you. Perhaps even more skilled." He spat out another piece of tobacco. "No, you're not irreplaceable, son. And when things calm down, we'll locate and capture the thing." He smiled. "Hope is not lost."

"You're deluding yourself, Dixon, and you know it. There's only one person in the world who stands a chance of finding it, and that's me. But I have to move fast." Hunter used his trump card. "If you cooperate, I'll have it for you in six hours."

Dixon laughed. "You've had a week, Hunter! How are you gonna find it in six hours?" He raised an arm to the forest. "Hell, it could be anywhere! Look around you! Look at yourself!"

Confident and smiling, Hunter stepped closer to the CIA man. "I know where it's going, Dixon," he said quietly. "I know exactly where it's going, so this won't be a track. You give me six hours, and I'll have your serum for you. But you have to give me six hours. Then you can go back and tell your boss that everything went according to plan. They're in the clear. You're in the clear. They have what they want. The evidence is destroyed. And you get kudos and a pat on the back."

Clearly it was tempting. Gazing solidly at Hunter as if to discern a lie, Dixon released a long, slow stream of smoke, rolling the cigarette in his fingers.

"Six hours?" he asked.

"Six hours."

"And then?"

"Then you have what you want," Hunter nodded. "And we go free."

Silence, minutes ticking.

"You're gonna try and do something, Hunter," Dixon said, absolute suspicion in his eyes. There was no doubt, and it disturbed him. "I don't trust you."

Hunter's smile was dim.

"Okay, Dixon, hire another hunting party." He turned and walked away. "Good luck."

"Wait."

Hunter hesitated.

"I want some insurance," Dixon said. "I want the woman to stay with me. Then I'll know you won't break our deal."

"Negative. I'm gonna need her."

"You're planning something, Hunter!" Dixon walked closer, glanced at his watch. "You think I'm not used to this? This is all I do! Of course you're planning something! You don't want that creature alive! You want to kill it! And then you want to destroy it so we'll never have the serum!" He raised his hands, as if in divine supplication. "Hunter, I have got you figured out! I've had you figured out! You're a very self-righteous kinda guy. It aggravates the hell out of me. The only thing I was wrong on was how hard it is to kill you." He blinked, utter frankness in his demeanor. "To tell you the truth, son, 'cause there's no love lost between us, I thought all you guys would be dead by day one.

No offense, but that was the plan. But noooooo ... you're just like the bloody Energizer bunny! You just keep going and going and going! Except that I'm not as stupid as the good doctor here. And I'm not gonna let you go after that thing unless I've got some pretty good insurance that you'll bring it back."

"Okay," Hunter replied, smiling. "You can come with us."

Stunned silence, and it lasted. But Hunter did give Dixon credit for a quick recovery.

"No way," he said.

Hunter had watched Bobbi Jo approaching, and his eyes focused hard on her as she stopped, head bowed. He didn't need her to say it, and he bowed his head, too.

The professor was dead.

Something in Hunter told him that everything, his whole life, all he would ever be, had come down to this. He had lost the only two creatures he had ever truly loved, and in the same hour. Death didn't seem so bad now. But he wouldn't go out defeated. He turned his head briefly to Chaney.

"Fire it up," he said, and grabbed Dixon by the collar, hauling him across the compound.

"Jesus, Hunter!" Dixon shouted.

For a frantic moment, suddenly reduced to using primitive physical force instead of calculated threats and the power of an invisible empire of espionage and secrets, Dixon was dumbstruck. For all his brave talk and sinister promises, he had been heaved, in the space of three seconds, into a world where civilization and its power could not help him. He was talking fast, hearing himself protest as he was dragged along.

He stumbled but Hunter's strong right arm hauled him to his feet, the tracker never breaking stride as they closed quickly on the chopper. "Come on, Hunter!" Dixon pleaded. "You gotta believe me! They'll shoot us down!"

"Then they'll shoot you down, too," Hunter snarled, using the pain of the professor's death for strength. He violently hurled Dixon into the bay and was instantly on top of him as the rest grabbed seats and Chaney took the controls. Brick glanced at his watch, at Chaney.

"Two minutes, kid," he said.

"We'll make it."

Hamilton was at the bay, scrambling to enter.

With Dixon under control, Hunter turned on the no-longer-dignified physician. He spoke quietly. "Doctor, you might want to get some distance from your facility before they incinerate it. A lot of distance."

Hunter closed the bay in his face.

A muted scream of horror penetrated the steel door above the sound of rotors and twin turbos. "Everybody hang on!" Chaney yelled over the intercom. "I'm gonna have to try a cold takeoff. It might be rough!"

It was.

Without sufficient hydraulic pressure the Blackhawk pitched hard to the left, swinging across the field at an almost vertical angle before Chaney managed to stabilize the rotors, bring the nose up sharply. Then, rising hard, they cleared the edge of the forest and swept into roaring gray light.

Gazing down into Dixon's terrified face, Hunter took a moment to make it more real.

"This is what it comes down to, Dixon," he whispered, leaning close. "Death ... is that what you're scared of?" Hunter frowned. "Well, you've sent hundreds of people to their deaths, Dixon, so you should be used to it! And let me tell you, you're gonna know exactly what they knew! You're gonna know what it's like to stare that thing in the eyes!"

Trembling, Dixon raised his hands. "Hunter, listen, man, you've lost it ..."

"It's gonna be in your face" Hunter whispered. "And if you live ..." He laughed, "... you'll never forget the face of each and every one of the people that you sent up here!"

Dixon, trembling uncontrollably, closed his eyes, hands raised plaintively.

Remorseless and still emotionally traumatized by the professor's death, Hunter threw him back and turned angrily. A mushrooming orange balloon rose silently in the distance, a sphere of pure white fire expanding, rising, fading to red as it topped the trees.

The air filled with the roar.

"Hang on!" Chaney yelled.

The concussion struck them like a physical wave and the Blackhawk was hurled into a turn, whirling crazily as the helicopter shivered, quaking and trembling, spinning wildly.

Chaney s choked cries from the cockpit rose above it all and Hunter, thrown to the panels, saw the marshal struggling madly to regain control of the craft. He attempted to rush forward to help, knowing he couldn't, when a secondary shock wave—a wall of heavy air rushing overhead to fill the vacuum created by the explosion—smashed them from the opposite side and the helicopter pitched again.

With a curse Chaney righted the Blackhawk as the sky behind them brightened brilliantly, flame expanding to rise higher and higher, mushrooming in fire that only at the last darkened the horizon at once, fading slowly to silence with the dimming echo of roars rippling over unseen mountains.

Silence ...

And finally – steadiness.

Flying steadily, Chaney was rigid and possessed at the controls, utter exhaustion evident from his profile. He said nothing on the intercom, nor was it needed. They were safe, and it was enough. And the suicidal atmosphere in the cabin was grim with exhaustion, relief, and a slowly gathering rage that each one of them fed in silence, knowing what they had to do.

Dixon, relief expressed in his slow words, spoke. "Where are we going, Hunter?"

Groaning, Hunter reached back and pulled a headset from the wall. He mounted it, adjusted the mike. "Punch in White Mountains Park into the Magellan," he said. "There's a creek there; it's called Fossil River. It runs between the north and south sides of the range. We need to head upriver to find a cave. I'll tell ya more when we're closer." He paused. "Are the others following us?"

Hesitation as Chaney checked the radar.

"Radar says some of 'em have decked for refueling," Chaney said. "But there's a shitload on our tail, just the same. I'm tracking about seven Blackhawks and six A-14's circling. Damn, they musta' had a cruiser off the coast or something. They ain't doing nuthin', though. Just circling. I guess 'cause they don't know what we're doing, yet." He paused. "Want me to tell 'em something?"

"Yeah. Tell them we have Dixon. Tell them to give a message to whoever's in charge that we know where it's gone. And tell 'em we're gonna put an end to this." Hunter blinked; so tired now, so deathly tired. "Tell them that if they want this thing brought down quiet, they need to leave us alone 'til it's over."

Staring at Dixon, Brick suddenly rose, grabbing the CIA agent and tossing him roughly to the front of the bay. Then the hulking ex-marshal felt along the back wall, searching.

"For combat missions," he whispered to himself, though Hunter somehow heard, "these things always got a stash."

Chaney's voice came over the headset: "They say they're just doing surveillance! But I gave 'em the message! Everybody knows the score! They ain't gonna do anything!"

Hunter lowered his head, almost laughing at the absurdity of it. They had sent him out to die and he had survived, and now they both cursed and feared him. But this was the last of the game. Either *he* would die or *it* would die; there was no other way for this to end. Then remorse and affection struck him at once, and he gazed at Bobbi Jo.

She was waiting for it, was already staring at him.

What was spoken—and Hunter knew that she utterly understood, and agreed—was done without words or expression. Then she smiled—a sad smile—and he bowed his head.

Yeah, they'd finish it.

"I got it!" Brick shouted, and the back panel of the bay fell; a wall of steel lowered to reveal an entire arsenal of weapons.

Hunter saw stacked grenades, a flame-thrower, M-203's, rocket-launched grenades and two extra Barretts. The lower half of the compartment was packed with crated ammunition and extra napalm canisters for the flame-thrower.

Smiling or frowning, Brick looked down.

His voice was grim.

"Let's see the son of a bitch survive this," he said.

CHAPTER 21

A vast wall of rolling gray storm followed them through the canyon as if to terrify and isolate them during their final battle against the beast.

The air rippled with ceaseless lightning, causing the chopper to tremble with thunder, as the Blackhawk descended into a jagged valley of broken stone cut deeply by a river that whitened over rapids and swirled into strangely cut eddies that disappeared beneath heavy overhangs of stone.

Inside the craft they defiantly loaded weapons, each of them committed to the last battle with this creature that they had come to understand too well. Beaten and bloodied, they paid little attention to their wounds, taking time only to staunch the bleeding of their most serious injuries.

Hunter wrapped Bobbi Jo's torso in heavy gauze, using most of the surgical tape. Then she replaced her shredded vest with another, tightening the elastic straps to further secure the dressing.

All of them were covered with dried blood from their own wounds and the creature's, but Hunter was the most seriously marked, with uncounted contusions and abrasions.

A wide cut on the right side of his face—a vicious injury he didn't remember receiving in the last chaotic exchange—still bled. But there was no way to bandage it without compromising his vision, so he had cleaned it and left it alone.

His forearm where he had blocked the beast's last thunderous blow was severely slashed and blackened with blood, as if the creature's skin alone were a weapon. He wrapped the forearm with what remained of the gauze and taped it; it would have to suffice. If they lived, he could attend to it more carefully later.

Rising from the bay, Hunter took the seat beside Chaney. He mounted the headset, dimly hearing the rest of them loading and preparing weapons.

Chaney was keeping steady distance on the storm, flying low and level. The radar revealed that the rest of the helicopters had detoured south, still close but avoiding the lightning-slashed sky behind them. His voice reached Hunter over the intercom system: "Could it have gotten this far so soon?"

Hunter barked a humorless laugh. "Yeah, it could have. Believe me."

Chaney took his word. "All right. So where is this cave that we're trying to find?"

"Further upriver." Hunter pointed. "It's probably somewhere around that bend. We're looking for a waterfall that comes out of a cliff face. And on either side there will be two rock faces that resemble ... I don't know, something like wolves. Tigers. It shouldn't be too hard to find."

Chaney continued in silence for a moment. "Tell me something," he said finally. "If this thing was around ten or twelve thousand years ago, how did it survive the Ice Age?"

"Lots of species survived the Ice Age," Hunter responded, searching the cliff walls intently. "And this ... this species, if it's as intelligent as it seems, could easily have found shelter in these mountains. Something like a cave where it could have weathered it out. Plus, it has a high degree of adaptability." He considered it. "Yeah, it could have survived easily enough. It probably thrived when the rest of this region was dying out. That's why they wanted it. For its ability to adapt to disease, its immunity factor, its genetic mutation factors. They wanted a species whose genetic superiority made it basically un-killable."

Chaney grunted. "They did too good a job."

"What they didn't understand was that they had to take the bad with the good," Hunter said more slowly. "They wanted something that was un-killable. And what they got was something that lived to kill." He was silent a moment. "Stupidity. They wanted to live forever. And they killed hundreds to obtain it."

The helicopter moved upriver.

"Well," Chaney responded, "if these things stood at the top of the food chain, with no natural enemies, then why did they ever die out?" He stared. "I mean, something had to kill them off, right? But what could have done something like that? According to what I've seen, nothing that ever walked or crawled could have even killed off one of these things. Much less a whole race of them."

Meeting his gaze, Hunter said nothing. After a moment he stared away, considering. "I don't know," he said finally. "Maybe we're gonna find out."

"There it is," Chaney said suddenly, bringing the chopper to almost a dead stop as he swung it smoothly to face the south wall.

Hunter saw it instantly.

A waterfall at least three hundred feet from the valley floor cascaded heavily from the cliff side. And above that, slightly to the side, a fissure disappeared into darkness. On either side of the cleft, larger than he had anticipated, two jagged outcroppings seemed unnaturally cut into protruding stones.

Studying them closely, Hunter could imagine that thousands of years ago the fixtures had indeed resembled either tigers or wolves, but time and erosion had faded the finer features. A large section of the wall was completely smooth, and, gazing down, Hunter could see where it had broken away from the cliff long ago. Crumbled sections of granite, some weighing hundreds of tons, lay scattered across the valley floor.

At first glance the cave seemed inaccessible, but Hunter could see the remains of a trail, now unusable without climbing equipment, that had once led to the opening. Yet, while it would doubtless be a difficult climb for them, Hunter knew the creature could have easily clambered apelike to the entrance.

Rolling thunder rumbled over them and Hunter glanced back to see the storm approaching more quickly, streaking the black-gray wall of cloud with hazy lightning.

"We'll rappel from the top!" Chaney shouted, bringing the Blackhawk to a steady climb. "Looks like it's only about eighty feet, and we have gear for that!"

Removing the headset, Hunter walked into the bay to see Bobbi Jo and Takakura sitting somberly, holding fresh weapons. Bobbi Jo had armed herself with a dozen new clips and a Beretta 9-mm pistol. Hunter knew the sidearm would be all but useless against the creature, but he understood her thinking.

All of them were taking whatever they could find, mainly because they had little choice. Brick still carried the Weatherby, but the big ex-marshal was conspicuously low on rounds, with the bandoleer already half emptied. Still, he compensated for the shortage with the huge sidearm—a Casull .454—that would undoubtedly penetrate the creature's armor-like skin.

As the helicopter settled smoothly on the summit, shuddering slightly at a blast of gathering wind, Hunter turned to Takakura. He saw that the Japanese was armed as before. The katana, now well-used and proven to be an effective weapon against the creature, protruded from behind the Japanese's powerful right shoulder, and he carried a variety of primary weapons—a Beretta semiautomatic pistol plus at least six phosphorous hand grenades and a heavy rifle that Hunter didn't recognize.

Chaney angled into the bay and Brick threw open the port. Then Hunter bent, roughly lifting Dixon. Frowning with terrifying menace, Hunter reached over the CIA man's shoulder and lifted an M-16 and clips. Then he gave them to Dixon, knowing he wouldn't be stupid enough to attack them.

"It's game time," Hunter nodded, ignoring a half-spoken protest as he roughly shoved the agent out of the bay.

Hunter quickly grabbed a large Harris M-98 .50-caliber Browning sniper rifle from the bay. Similar to the Barrett, the Browning was a devastating weapon, easily capable of hitting targets at well over two thousand yards.

The .50-caliber rounds left the barrel at five thousand feet per second, and could penetrate an inch of steel plating. Plus, the gun's lethal effectiveness with the creature had already been demonstrated. But it was at least four feet long, with two-thirds of that in the barrel, so he had to make it more manageable for the close confines of the cave.

Reaching into a toolkit, Hunter lifted a lug wrench and unscrewed the bracing, sliding out the last seventeen inches of heavy barrel. The rifled extension is what provided long-range accuracy, but that kind of accuracy wouldn't be needed. The heavier section that was forged to the receiver would be sufficient for this kind of close-range fighting.

Then, working efficiently though it was an unfamiliar weapon, Hunter removed the scope and shoulder stock, leaving only the pistol grip. It took him two minutes, and when he was finished, he had a compact weapon that still held devastating power. As an afterthought Hunter reached back and attached two thermite grenades—phosphorous-fed incendiaries with a five-second fuse that vulcanized anything they touched—to his belt.

"Let's go!" Chaney said, quickly tuning the radio to a frequency beacon. "We need to get in there before this storm comes down on us! Everybody knows how to do this so we won't waste time! I'll go down first, and Dixon, you come down right after me! Hunter, you come next and let us know real quick if that thing is close or if it's even in there! I don't wanna be down there with my thumb up my ass when it walks up behind me!"

Slinging the Weatherby, Chancy shouldered a small Alice-pack loaded with flares and lights and was gone, descending over the ledge as if he'd done it every day for years.

It took them almost no time and then Hunter was standing deep inside the cave, staring at a tunnel that seemed to lead deep into the mountain. Behind him, flares burned red to the strong smell of sulfur, hissing loudly in a darkness made moist by mist.

Gazing down, Hunter saw where the shale had been disturbed by something passing this way. And he reached out, lightly touching the ground to discern the faint indentations.

Yeah, it was here . . .

He grinned faintly; he'd taken a chance, but he'd been right. It had retreated to the only place that it thought it could rest without being hunted and hounded. But they couldn't let it escape. For if they did, then it would only continue to kill without end or reason, feeding its lust for blood with more and more blood.

It had to end here. For each of them.

Chaney s voice was unnaturally subdued. "What do you think?" he asked. "Is it here?"

Hunter looked ahead into the darkness. "It's here. It didn't beat us by much. It's gone into the cave."

From the rear Brick growled, "How could it know the way?"

"A lot of animals can find their way back to where they were born," Hunter said, concentrating. "It's like they have some kind of genetic code that compels them to return to a certain place at a certain time. I've seen it before. It's nothing new." He rose and they moved forward, careful to keep the light as far ahead as possible.

As they moved, the tunnel widened, some corridors branching off into inky blackness. But Hunter could read the tracks now, even in the flickering half-light, and knew it was moving on a true course, deep into the vastness of this abyss. Its trail, occasionally marred by blood, was uninterrupted as the tunnel took a downward slant. No, the thing wasn't veering from side to side, distracted or confused by the connecting passages; it was holding a certain path.

Hunter realized vaguely that the thing's nocturnal vision was even more extraordinary than he'd guessed. And, unfortunately, that gave it a distinct advantage in this gloom.

"Wait," he said, lifting a hand.

No one moved or breathed.

"What is it?" Chaney whispered.

Hunter said nothing, staring hard into the darkness, and still they didn't move. Rising, moving along the walls, shadows lent an eerie atmosphere to the broken stone. No sound but the hiss of flares weighed in the air. Hunter finally spoke.

"It's there," he whispered, lifting the Browning. "Somewhere far ahead. I heard it."

Takakura had edged forward. He didn't look at Hunter as he spoke quietly. "What did you hear? I heard nothing."

Shaking his head, Hunter scowled into the vast dark ahead of them, stretching out infinitely to defy their torches. "I don't know. It sounded like ... I don't know ... like it was *attacking*. Something like that, and it wasn't close. But it wasn't far." He paused. "Another mile. Maybe two. We'll find out."

Dixon's voice was tremulous. "Jesus Christ, people, this is seriously not a good idea ... Look, let's just blow this place and bury the thing! You know, we *seriously* don't have to go *mano a mano* with this thing again!"

"I do." Hunter looked at him for a moment. "And that's what I've never liked about people like you, Dixon. You sent hundreds of people to their deaths, and yet you don't have any idea what death is. Do you know why you kill so easily, Dixon?" Hunter let the question settle. "It's because you do your killing with machines – with *numbers* so you can spare yourself the blood and the horror and the work. And that's why you don't appreciate anybody's skin but your own." Hunter shook his head, leaning closer. "Whoever or whatever gave you the right, Dixon, to decide who deserves to live? That decision belongs to God – not man. And especially not you!" Hunter leaned back, openly revealing his contempt. "Fool."

The silence that followed was more condemning than Hunter's tone. And, shaking his head once more, he added somberly, "No matter what, Dixon, I'm gonna see that you're held responsible for everything you've done. That's a promise."

Turning away slowly, Hunter heard Brick grab the CIA man's shoulder and move him forward. The ex-marshal's burly voice had a grim intonation of doom. "Move on, boy," he growled. "You signed up to serve your country, didn't ya? So serve it."

Eventually the passage became almost like a shattered stairway, narrower and more defined.

Leading cautiously and in complete silence, Hunter no longer searched the shadows because the connecting corridors had faded. Now they were on a definite pitch that was carrying them directly downward, and in the distance Hunter saw specks of white light on the wall where the tunnel bent into blackness. Approaching stealthily, he lifted a flare and saw tiny leechlike creatures clinging to the moist stone.

The air was warmer, and utterly still. Hunter realized they must be at the base of the mountain, if not beneath. Yeah, they had come at least three miles through the cavern and were probably at the final chamber; this didn't appear to be a maze cave. Rather, the entire serpentine structure indicated that it led inevitably to a cathedral-like cavern.

Hunter had explored similar caverns and knew from experience what could be expected. And then, as the path turned sharply around a huge stalagmite, they saw it.

What was more amazing—the faded, titanic images painted on the sweeping cathedral walls, the underground lake that burned with a strange green tint, or the last and most terrifying discovery of all—Hunter could not say. But the last was, without question, a sight that chilled his blood and made his skin tighten.

Heaped in endless dunes and mounds and bleached crests, scattered across the vastness of the underground mausoleum, were hundreds of thousands of stripped bones—skeletal specters of some hideous subterranean slaughter. The scent of ancient decay, of old death, hung hauntingly in the blackened atmosphere, and as Hunter stared over the skeletal underworld he could almost count every bony finger pointing motionless into a dome of darkness, could almost register every crushed skull, shattered spine, or splintered bone.

To himself, he nodded.

Yes, it made sense at last, and he understood completely. Just as he knew that this ghastly tribute to mindless savagery was all that remained of the greatest predators ever to walk the earth.

Together they stared over the ghostly remains of a long-ago carnage that must have been the ultimate of horrors to behold. None of them broke the silence.

Scattered across the shadowed chamber, bony arms stretched silently from heaps of twisted, shattered skulls and taloned hands even now locked in combat—all that remained from a ten-thousand-year-old rampage that had decimated a nation, an entire species, in a single devastating battle.

Staring somberly, Hunter could read the scene, knew what had happened in this dark moment of history. Without equal in might or ferocity, this predatory species had stormed without rival to the height of the food chain, conquering all the world as they knew it, fearing nothing. With physical supremacy rivaled only by their inherent savagery, they had killed all that could be killed, leaving only themselves. Hunter saw the severed heads and dark skulls shattered by the sweeping black claws still buried in bleached bone.

It was a war, but it was only themselves that they destroyed.

Insatiable in their lust for blood, uncontrolled because the nexus of mind that powered their ferocity had no restraint or regard even for their own kind, the predators had eventually directed that unlimited thirst for blood and physical rage into this.

Hunter imagined that it had begun with a single attack that had somehow spiraled through the cavern like a forest fire. For once the rage was fueled it had met no barriers of consciousness. No, it had been pure and unbridled, and it had caught and spread as they blindly turned one upon the other, each rending and striking with that inhuman strength to slaughter the next.

Head bowed. Hunter imagined the wholesale battle as it must have been—monstrous forms slashing to dismember and slay only to be slain in turn. And he thought, dimly, that it had probably happened in the space of a few hours. The remorseless conflict had raged until there were only three, two ...one.

Finally the wounded survivor, if any, had perhaps wandered into the mountains and died or simply remained here and perished from age or some pestilence. It didn't matter; what happened here had been their death. Their own ferocity had been their doom. There were no questions remaining.

Chaney's voice was strange.

"Well, now we know," he said in an unnatural voice. He shook his head, attempting to control his tone. "They actually killed *themselves off*! And all at once!" An awed pause; "Must have been a hell of a fight."

Takakura shook his head, frowning across the ghostly maze of shattered bone, the slashed or shattered skulls staring emptily toward the torches. He gazed somberly upon a twisted heap of slender skeletal arms and legs that lay in a larger dune.

"Such stupidity," he said.

"No," Hunter remarked. "Not stupidity. They were never mindful enough for that. They were without minds, really, as we understand it. They were just creatures of impulse. They killed on a whim, a thought, the slightest inclination. Whatever controlled them wasn't the conscious mind. It's what all of us fear inside ourselves. The beast, the rage we control because it terrifies us." He nodded. "We've evolved beyond that. But they hadn't. They were the closest thing to the unconscious mind of man that this world will ever know."

"And look what it got 'em," Brick grunted. He, too, revealed astonishment, but was recovering quick. "Guess it goes to show you; be careful what you ask for."

A moment passed, and then Takakura walked forward, igniting another flare and tossing it onto a ledge where it cast a higher angle of light across the room. Shadows vanished at the elevated illumination and, slowly, they moved forward.

Then a familiar scent reached Hunter and he bent, examining a black pool. Vaguely the size of a man, the depression was heavy and stagnant, and he felt the thick liquid with a hand, slowly raising it to his face.

"Oil," he whispered, as Bobbi Jo knelt beside him. "Here," he added, "let me see your flare. Stand back." He touched the wick to the pool and it ignited explosively.

The mushrooming blast swept past Hunter's face before he could jerk back. Shocked, Hunter felt his face for a moment, reflexively checking for injury. But there was none and the fire burned bright, dulling the light of their flares to insignificance. Now the entire room was brilliantly visible, and they saw cave paintings that had endured the centuries.

Faded red images of creatures that had ruled this region long ago were inscribed on the stone—images of beasts running, leaping, hunted, slaughtered. And as Hunter turned slowly he saw that the entire mammoth cave was decorated in the primitive art. Entire frescoes of huge animal hunts— whole herds of buffalo and deer driven from cliffs by hunters in ragged clothing—occupied vast spaces before another image, some kind of cleaning and gutting, was detailed.

Almost every image involved hunting, killing, slaughtering, as if that had been the dominating force of their existence. There were no displays of family or play or societal rights—not anything that would indicate culture or civility. It was simply the bestial exultation of carnage – of slaying and gutting and feasting. And as Hunter saw it altogether he was overcome by the wild, barbaric atmosphere.

Dark images of their own dead were displayed on a nearby wall. He saw the mangled image of a severed skull and felt an undeniable sensation of revulsion.

So, they were also cannibals.

He felt no surprise.

It would only be right. For they had no consciousness, no sense of morality or regard for life. So one of their own dead would naturally be as welcome as another creature's. Flesh was flesh, and any blood was warm enough if drunk quickly.

Staring about, he saw that the cave emptied into a dozen large tunnels that doubtless led into lower levels, possibly more lakes or even to the outside. He didn't presume that this was the only entrance. In fact, he reasoned that there would probably be much more accessible openings, but most had been half-buried or obscured by the mountain's changing geology over time.

Everyone was fairly scattered now and Hunter searched the ground, looking for tracks. He saw where the creature had entered, how it had hesitated, as if in shock. And he began to wonder about the scream he had heard.

Could it be that whatever genetic memory the creature possessed didn't contain any memory of the war that destroyed it? Was it possible that it had come here expecting to be received by its own kind? He wondered; this scientific madness had created something that was in essence the equal of this ancient species, but it was also the twisted manipulation of nature. It seemed possible that genetic coding, distorted and erased by the unnatural transmutation, had been lost.

It had come here expecting its own species, and had found nothing but a bone-littered tomb. So its rage had been expressed in the only manner it knew—by an unchecked release that would have destroyed any living creature, if it had been present.

Hunter nodded; he could use that to his advantage.

Rising slowly, feeling the stiffness in his limbs from the brief respite, he wiped his brow. The heavy humidity, probably close to a hundred percent, was making all of them perspire heavily. Already Bobbi Jo's hair was plastered back across her head. She had ripped a piece of clothing from her shirt for a headband, and her battle-dress uniform was blackened with sweat. The rest were equally suffering.

"All right," Hunter said, turning to them as he racked the bolt on the Browning, slamming home a six-inch, .50-caliber cartridge. "I can track it, but we're gonna have to stay alert. This is its home ground, and it's gonna use it. So look high, and get a shot off quick if it charges. The rest of us will back you up."

An animal roar, angry and wounded, bellowed from the depths of the cavern, enlarging the room with an astounding bestial fury that smothered them together. Hunter raised his head at the thundering rage and frowned before casting a glance to Bobbi Jo. She revealed nothing as she chambered the Barrett.

Haggard and pale, she carried the huge rifle on a shoulder sling, the long barrel leveled at her waist. Her finger was curled around the trigger and her poise was solid. But Dixon trembled, backing away from a huge yawning tunnel that echoed deeply.

Hunter grabbed him by the shoulder, pushing him forward as they advanced. "No place to go, Dixon," he said. "This is where you learn all about eternal life. And the lack of it."

The tunnel was wide enough to accept all of them with a separation of ten feet. But its vastness defied both their hand-held light and the illumination of the burning oil pool.

Staring steadily into its depths, Hunter understood why the creature had chosen this terrain.

Ledges loomed, unseen in shadow, along the tiered stone walls. And the floor, flat and level, was unencumbered with crumbling rock, allowing rapid movement. Other, higher tunnels disappeared into the uppermost reaches of the passageway—blackened eyes that could conceal anything. Hunter moved forward carefully, alert to the slightest sound. But he knew this was more of a wait than a search.

No, he wouldn't see it first, and knew it would come from a ledge. It would descend into them furiously and hope to finish them quick. And if it hit the ground before they could target it, Hunter recognized that they would be seriously handicapped. For it would move fast, in and out and back again, and they'd have to be careful not to shoot one of their own. He blinked sweat from his eyes as all of them moved in painful silence, the lights revealing their position to the beast.

Brick spoke from the side.

"This thing, it's gonna try an ambush, right?"

"Yeah," Hunter said, raising eyes to a submerged ledge.

"Then why don't one of us stay a little farther back?" the big ex-marshal asked. "If it's directly above you, you won't see it coming down. But somebody a little farther back, they'll get the angle on it."

Nodding, Hunter knew it was a good idea. In fact, he had already considered it, but discarded the tactic because one man isolated as a rear guard would become more vulnerable. He explained the objection to Brick.

"Yeah, it's a risk." The big man breathed heavily. The suffocating humidity was affecting them all. "But I'll take the risk. If that thing lands in the thick of us, we're gonna be shooting each other, son. I know what I'm jawin' about."

Hesitating, Hunter looked at Chaney, who nodded. "Let Brick take rear guard for a while," Chaney suggested, swiping his face. "But I'll flank him. That leaves the three of you up here, two of us in the back. It won't be that easy to get the drop on us."

Hunter stared, finally nodded. He wondered when it was that he had somehow taken military control of the situation, then forgot it; it didn't matter. Takakura acknowledged his agreement and they divided forces, Hunter leading a wary wedge.

Behind him Brick and Chaney had the double-barreled Weatherby poised high as they searched the ledges, ready to shoulder as if shooting clay pigeons. And Hunter felt safer with them guarding the upper tiers, but slowly began to sense a vague, intensifying nervousness that he couldn't lock down. It was a sensation that whatever should have happened by now hadn't happened.

He quickly analyzed all his former battles with the creature, reviewing its tactics, instincts, habits, and almost unconscious inclinations. More than anything, it used the same tactics over and over again. It ambushed from high ground with a directness of action that capitalized on the prey's limited reaction speed. It never attacked directly unless it was in the open field, always used darkness or broken terrain for short, devastating assaults before seizing solid cover from small-arms fire. It also preferred to use the advantage of confusion, but that wasn't an option for it now, so . ..

No, there was no question: It would come from a ledge.

With a hundred yards of tunnel before him, an abyss where the light was absorbed by the gloom, Hunter turned and raised a hand. He knew it was close because it wouldn't be able to restrain itself for a more distant attack. And, in that, its maniacal desire to kill worked against it. Made it predictable.

Hunter knew, somewhere above, it was lying in wait.

Close and silent, it was pausing for them to pass so that it could either emerge for a silent approach or attack with that lightning speed and a roar to stall their reaction by fear. Neither of them, Hunter decided, was going to work. He was in a killing mode now, and there would be no hesitation.

Everything he knew—everything he had ever experienced in the wild—would be used in this encounter. There would be no attempt to wound or capture, nor would he have compassion. Then, raising his eyes to the walls, Hunter declared, "Light more of the flares. I want to see everything."

There was no dispute as Brick and Chaney, close but still forty feet away, ignited a half-dozen flares and tossed them in a wide uniform pattern, illuminating a large section of the passage. Although the ledges were deep in shadow, the red-whiteness of the light burned the darkness from every other crevice to leave a stark dead-white. The passage was fully visible in the steadiness, and Hunter almost smiled as his next tactic came to him.

Yeah, it might wait until the light died down, hoping that darkness could return so it could initiate its preferred plan. For it would expect them to search defensively, afraid of its overwhelming power. But Hunter would take that from it.

"Look sharp," he said as he stepped onto a boulder, slowly climbing toward the upper regions of the cave. "I'm gonna try and flush it out."

Shouldering the elephant gun, Brick cocked both hammers without a word.

Chaney spoke, swinging aim to the opposite side. "Hunter, be careful. It moves fast."

"I know." Hunter rose sharply above a ledge with the mini-light, targeting everything instantly. He turned the light to shine back across the passage, spying the opposite ledges.

Nothing.

A grim commitment to the task twisted his face into a frown. He knew that he'd come upon it soon enough, initiating a wild fight that would cause the cavern to explode in a haze of gunfire and chaos; a horrific battle once started that would rage with suicidal courage and adrenaline-white excitement to a savage end. Climbing onto the altar-like stone, he walked slowly forward, flicking off the safety of the Browning.

Still nothing, but he knew it was here ...

Crouched like a lion, Hunter stared at the blind wall and considered waiting it out. But without even a glance at the flares he knew they wouldn't last another fifteen minutes. No, he had to find it, force it out. And when that happened he would have to survive the first blurring rush, try sending it into the passageway where they could target and fire freely. He knew without asking that, despite their courage and skill, they wouldn't chance a round if he were close to it.

The edge loomed before him, darkness beyond.

Hunter watched and waited, utterly cold. If it waited on the far side of the outcropping, he might be able to wear on its nerves, make it careless.

Seconds slid in silence, drops of sweat falling from Hunter's brow as he blinked. Still nothing.

Just do it!

Get it over with!

He rose, eyes narrowing as he approached the corner. Then he paused as his hairs stood on end at an impression, sharp and distinctly dangerous. Instinctively he had frozen.

Knowing that he might have only seconds, he continued to extend his arm, keeping the illumination moving forward as he settled slightly back, leg caving on his weight. If it was not on the other side of that wall, then his instincts were woefully wrong and he was unsure what to do. Then he decided, knowing that only elemental wildness could answer elemental wildness, and advanced with three quick strides.

On the edge of air and darkness Hunter dropped to a knee and raised the Browning from the hip to fire mid-waist into the air, not taking time to search, not knowing what lay ahead. The explosion of the cartridge was tremendous—blinding and stunning—and he brought the rifle out from a hard recoil with a roar. It took him a few seconds to realize that there was nothing ...

No ...

It's here.

It was the sense of certainty a man possesses when he feels a familiar sickness closing its grip on it. He knows the signs, can measure how long before he is broken and weak. Although it may be hours away, it is already present, his body warning him with subtle signs. But Hunter gave no overt sign of surety as he walked forward. He feigned confusion with consummate composure.

Moving a dozen steps into a collapsed alcove—a chamber domed by a ceiling whose stones were slowly breaking loose—he saw a dozen possible hiding places. Almost immediately he decided to use its own instincts against it. For he knew that, if it could not attack from ambush, it would strike from behind, as before.

Lowering the rifle to his side, Hunter turned his back to the chamber and took one step forward in absolute silence. Almost instantly he felt a tingling in his arms, neck. Knew he couldn't wait more than a few seconds . . .

Two steps.

It's gonna try for absolute silence ...

Three.

Hunter wasn't breathing with his next step.

Turn!

NO!

Hunter gritted his teeth; it preys on weakness ... Wait until you hear it or you can't wait anymore ... Wait ...You know how to do it. You know how to wait. So wait ...

Wait!

At the last step, the ledge loomed before him. But it was a step that never happened as Hunter felt a sudden thrill that he couldn't suppress and turned into the threat.

Mammoth, crouching with arms hooked to grapple, it was creeping forward. Poised on one leg, it was almost laughing in its silent rage. The other foot was lifted in a step that would have placed it on Hunter in another second.

Hunter roared as he brought the Browning up and fired point-blank into its chest, fire joining them in the darkness, beast to beast, and it screamed in rage as it raised an arm. Then it drew back for a blow but Hunter had already leaped high and far, aiming for a sloping boulder ten feet below the ledge. He hit hard and rolled, avoiding the trigger of the Browning in the bruising concussion and descent until he crashed painfully against the jagged floor.

Chaney—everyone—had opened up, devastating the ledge in a thunderstorm of massive rounds that pulverized stone and seemed to hurl the creature back. Only as they frantically reloaded did it launch itself far from the stone, sailing cleanly across the corridor where it struck the opposite wall and rebounded, landing with terrific force beside Chaney.

Whirling, Chaney raised the rifle with a shout as a hammer-like fist descended to hit the Weatherby, shattering the stock and sending him back. And in the brief collision Hunter didn't need to ask; no, not dead, but the marshal was injured by the blow. Enraged, Hunter hotly exchanged clips as he rose.

Brick managed a clean shot, an almost point-blank exchange that made the monster twist away before it returned the violence with a sweeping right hand too quick to follow. Hunter saw it as it began, a great clawed hand drawn to the waist before the beast uncurled with that vicious velocity. And then the blow had passed—only a glimpsed flicker in the light—and Hunter stared numbly as a gory remnant of a human being fell back, Brick's face completely torn away as bone and blood rained through the haze.

Hunter saw it was wounded deeply now and fired. Bobbi Jo and Takakura were also shooting, and the passageway was lit by the deafening extending flame.

Staggering and howling, rocked by rifle fire, it unleashed a bellowing defiance of pain, then turned with that uncanny quickness and leaped for Takakura.

As if he'd long anticipated the attack, the Japanese reacted even as it began, diving and rolling under the blow and rising with drawn sword to slash a backhand blow that struck solidly across its spine. Injured yet again it whirled and hurled out a hand, tearing deep furrows across Takakura s chest, and he shouted in defiant rage as he went to a knee. Face twisted in pain, he returned the violence with a vertical blow of the katana, the blade cutting deeply through its ribs to enter the air with a wake of fiery blood.

Hunter's next thunderous shot hit it cleanly in the sternum, propelling it powerfully toward Bobbi Jo where, sensing rather than seeing her, it struck even as it staggered—a wild, almost desperate move that she easily sidestepped as the Barrett continued to explode. She hit it solidly, each shot erupting in a shower of flesh and blood. But its next blow was not so wild, and with a tiger's viciousness its hand tore away her vest to send a ragged shield of armor sailing through lightning-struck air.

Hunter hit it again and again with the Browning, each wound mortal but for the creature's immortal vitality. Bobbi Jo, recovered, opened fire, and for a spellbinding moment the holocaust continued, two titanic tongues of flame that stretched through the corridor toward a monstrosity that staggered, bending and rising with forearms raised across its face, bellowing in defiance.

Its arms were uplifted as it twisted between impacts, and the fanged mouth was open in a roar that thundered from its chest though the sound could not be heard above the detonations of the .50-caliber weapons. Then with a sudden decision it turned, hurling its hulking shape over a stone and into darkness.

Seized by the impulse to rush after it and finish the kill, Hunter managed to calm himself, steadying his adrenaline. Laying the rifle to the side as Takakura advanced, aim centered on the corner, he bent to Bobbi Jo.

She had fallen to a knee and the wounds on her chest were opened, now crossed with another set of deep furrows. She gasped several moments to regain breath, then lifted a hand to her chest and coughed, closing her eyes tightly in pain. A low moan escaped.

Experiencing a heated rush of emotion, Hunter laid a hand on her back, letting her know he was there. He didn't attempt to talk to her, knowing she was incapable of speaking.

Takakura's voice reached from the gloom: "Hunter."

Raising his head, Hunter focused on the Japanese.

Takakura stood stoically over the body of Dixon. He had been slain so quickly in the blazing chaos of the gun battle that no one had even seen the creature's blow. Hunter blinked, sniffed; he had not meant for the CIA agent to die. He had simply chosen not to let him escape without punishment for the carnage he'd created. But it was over; at the moment he had more demanding priorities.

Rolling to both knees, Chaney finally gasped: "Jesus!" He shook his head angrily. "What's it take to stop that thing?" Then his eyes settled on Brick and he grew utterly still. He stared with remorse at the gaping face, jagged skull glistening in the light of the flares.

"Oh, no," he whispered.

No one spoke as Chaney reached out, holding the big ex-marshal's shoulder for a time. His face was bent, concealing his expression, but he shook his head slowly as his hand tightened. After a moment he patted Brick's arm, nodding. Then he lifted Brick's cracked Weatherby and inserted a new round, violently snapping it shut. When he turned to Hunter, his expression was death.

"Let's finish this," he said stonily. "This beast is going down."

Hunter spoke gently to Bobbi Jo. "How ya doin', babe?"

She coughed again. Her hand, when it came away from her chest, was heavy in blood. "I'm okay." She rubbed a forearm over her eyes. "Just let me change clips. I just need ... a second."

"We can turn back," he offered.

"No!" She raised eyes on fire. "*We finish it*!"

Hunter studied her resolve, nodded. "All right, but let me take a look." A quick examination of her chest revealed that the wounds, while bleeding profusely, had not penetrated muscle. "You bring anything for pain?" he asked.

"Yeah, but by the time they kick in, this'll be over. I'll go just like I am."

"All right. Stay close to me."

She nodded, silent in her injuries.

Hunter stood at the sound of Takakura's voice. But the words were cloudy and buried, or submerged somehow, by the dark atmosphere. Hunter realized that the rifle fire had temporarily deafened them.

"It is gravely wounded," the Japanese said stoically.

Hunter's voice was angry. "Yeah, well, wounded is one thing, dead is another." Gently, he helped Bobbi Jo to her feet. Then he lifted the Barrett and she took it in bloody hands.

"Still, though, it is badly wounded," Takakura intoned, staring at the tunnel with the sword stretched before him. "And the blood trail is wide. It will not retreat far."

"No, it won't," Hunter said, knowing it already. "It's hungry to kill us now. It has to. We've hurt it, and it knows that it can't survive more damage." He racked a fresh round. "The next time is the last time. Nobody is going to walk away if we don't put it down fast."

Locking and loading, they entered the long tunnel.

It was a labyrinth of sorts, far different from the steady certainty of the passageway above and inviting a new kind of nervous fear. But Hunter was too exhausted by battle to be nervous. His steadiness was fed by cold determination to destroy this creature; he felt nothing at all.

In fact, there was almost a recklessness in his approach now, as if he was more than willing to go face-to-face one more time in order to deliver all the damage it could endure. But only the most acute awareness of those beside him could have discerned that he moved with a lesser edge of caution.

The tunnel began to curve away, angling gradually until Hunter sensed that they were retreating along the same general direction. In the distance, flares burned to a small circle of light, and Hunter steadily followed the splashed blood trail until they saw a bright glowing dome before them.

It was the central chamber of the cave littered with the bones of ages. Hidden in utter darkness for centuries, the skeletons glared white in the flame. And Hunter knew that the beast had returned here to finish the battle.

The damage they had inflicted upon the creature had finally reduced its almost measureless strength. So, no, it no longer trusted its superior senses without relying upon sight. And it had circled back to this place, where it would launch a last ambitious attack. But Hunter never assumed anything. Cautious as a wolf, he moved slowly into the cathedral chamber of bleached bone.

Leading, he studied the endless expanse of dunes and crests and mounds. And with each uplifted clawed hand he saw the creature—a merciless and malignant power that knew no restraint. Only the darkness of its own mind had been its doom. And yet, despite the gigantic strength, Hunter felt no fear because it had so maliciously killed those he loved: Ghost by violence, the professor by its very existence.

Yeah, you're gonna die . . .

"It'll probably do the same as before," he said, organizing them, "though there's no way to be certain because it's always learning. So just put as many rounds into it as you can." He paused to study their tense faces and read the evident fear. Even Takakura seemed shaken. He added, "Listen, this thing isn't unkillable. We've already hurt it. Now it's dying time."

Silent consent, and they continued.

Fanning out, they entered the cathedral. Slowly, Hunter walked past a high, heaped pile of skeletons and studied the dust, searching for any area where it might have concealed itself. But he saw nothing. Not even blood, and it disturbed him.

Nothing moves without leaving a sign ...

What was he missing?

The doubt tugged at him, distracting and alarming.

Suddenly seized by it, he paused and knelt, carefully studying everything he could see. Concentrated, he tried to read any sign of disturbance, of moment, and again saw nothing. And with each second, his alarm increased.

It's there ... It has to be ... Trust what you know ...

A cavern silent with centuries-old dust stretched out before him. He saw the smears of where they had entered and left, the faint traces of track where it had staggered through, the minute claw marks on stone. But there was nothing more.

There should at least be blood ...

Frustrated, Hunter rose and stared over the room. He trusted his skills and knew it couldn't deceive him. He had tracked this thing across an entire wildness scarred by animal life and weather. He had defeated it again and again with his knowledge and experience. No, it couldn't defeat him here. Not when he was this close.

Steadily he allowed his vision to roam, absently noticing the creeping silhouettes of Bobbi Jo, Takakura and Chaney. They were holding a close formation as they advanced in a solid line, searching. But he knew in his soul that something was wrong.

Nothing moves without leaving a sign ...

Hunter turned back to the tunnel they had just quit. There was only darkness there, and he had followed the blood trail into the cavern. He walked slowly back toward the corridor, and with each step felt a rising fear—a sharpened instinct that told him to beware. He halted twenty feet distant of the entrance, staring into the circle of blackness. Experience and instinct decided for him, and he went with it.

"It's backtracking on us," he said to the rest, not removing his eyes from the corridor.

Chaney's voice boomed from across the room. "What?"

"I said it's circling!" Hunter shouted, taking a hesitant step as he cast a careful glance at another darkened corridor. "All these passageways interconnect! It's trying to come up behind us!"

Takakura scowled. "I thought you said it came in here!"

"Oh, it came in here, all right," Hunter answered more quietly, moving to the side as he searched another tunnel, rifle leveled. "It couldn't fake that. It just didn't stay long. It went back into the tunnels to come up behind us."

"You're sure about this?" Bobbi Jo asked incredulously. "It was hurt pretty bad, Hunter. I don't think it could have gotten very far. Not bleeding like that."

"It didn't have to." He shook his head, maintaining their location by voice. "It wouldn't have taken it more than thirty seconds to backtrack into the tunnel and let us pass it by. Then it turned around and went back the way we came." He stared. "Yeah, that's what it's done. It's scared now. Knows it's hurt. It's waiting for us to come to it. But it won't fight us again if we're together. It senses that it could lose, so it laid low while we passed it."

"We could flush it out again," Chaney said, disturbed.

"No," Hunter responded with certainty. "It won't do that this time."

"Why?"

"Because it learns from its mistakes, Chaney. It's savage, but it's not stupid. This time it'll keep moving, trying to avoid a trap. We have to cut off its lines of escape."

"Cut off its lines of escape?" Chaney answered. "Hunter, that'll mean splitting up! We can't split up with the thing out there! Hell, even together we might not be able to put it down!"

"It's either that or we lose it!" Hunter turned his head into the words, then calmed. "Listen," he continued, "there's only one way to corner this thing, and that's by cutting off every line of retreat simultaneously. It's like driving a tiger. You beat the bush until you've driven it from hiding and into a kill zone! And remember: this is that thing's home ground! It may have come here on instinct, but by now it knows this cave like the back of its hand! So if we're gonna get another shot at it, we have to force it into the open!"

An uneasy stillness settled over them.

Bobbi Jo was the first to lift her rifle. "I say we go for it. We've come too far to walk away now." The entire front portion of her uniform was blackened with blood.

"We'll split into two teams," Hunter said. "Me and Bobbi Jo will take the passage we just quit." He nodded to Chaney. "You and Takakura take the bigger passage that runs to the right. We'll meet where they converge. Remember that we have to check all the ledges. We can't give that thing the slightest chance to come up behind us."

They nodded together.

"All right," Hunter finished, "let's move. If you can get it on the run, drive it into this room, we can kill it. It won't survive another exchange like that last one."

Bobbi Jo advanced beside Hunter as they neared the passageway. Then they were submerged once more in the enveloping blackness, walking silently. The flares revealed them but they didn't want the sounds of their own footsteps to muffle the stealthy approach of a rear attack. Within minutes they stood at the intersection of the first passage.

Perilously fatigued, Bobbi Jo wiped sweat from her face. Hunter stared as she leaned her back against a wall, recovering breath in the intense humidity and thick air of the cavern. He knew the accelerating blood loss was also draining her strength, but he didn't know what he could do for her at the moment.

"Good God, Hunter," she gasped. "This thing has got to be hurting. 'Cause we're dying."

Grim, Hunter nodded. "It's dying, Bobbi."

She swallowed hard. "How do you know?"

"I just know, darlin'."

"Tell me how," she grimaced," 'cause I could use the encouragement."

Gazing back at her, Hunter smiled. He reached out, touching a stone. He lifted his fingers away, blackened by the diseased blood of the beast.

"That's bright blood, Bobbi Jo," he said. "Somebody hit an artery, and it isn't healing like it was. We're finally wearing it out." He nodded slowly. "Yeah, it's weak. Probably dying. But we still have to finish it. And it ain't going down easy."

She stood away from the wall; the Barrett was beginning at last to wear her down, but she held it firmly. "Then ...let's finish it," she gasped. "Before it finishes us."

Hunter smiled. Nodded.

"Whatever made you so tough?" he asked softly.

She laughed tiredly.

"It must be the company I keep."

Chaney paused, hastily wiping sweat from his brow.

It was stifling work, working a slow path up the passageway. His entire uniform was drenched black with sweat and blood from a ragged and profusely bleeding cut on his forehead—the chance result, he had surmised, of the shattered stock arching from his hands when the creature had hit the Weatherby. But, although irritating, the wound was not incapacitating, so he continued.

Takakura, alertly scanning everything, stood on guard as Chaney attempted briefly to adjust his clothing, seeking to find any level of comfort. But the BDUs were so ragged and torn—stretched by perspiration and blood—that it was impossible. Chaney motioned in frustration, straightening.

"Forget it," he breathed. "It's not worth the—"

Slowly the hands extended behind Takakura, emerging with ghostlike silence from the utter darkness of a crevice. It was a terrible image: demonic claws reaching from blackness only inches from the unknowing Japanese.

Chaney raised his rifle instantly at the sight but words froze in his throat because, in the wild moment when he had seen and reacted, he didn't know whether to tell Takakura to leap away or risk a wild shot. Yet the Japanese, a true warrior, somehow realized and in the same breath had moved, diving and rolling forward.

Chaney's blast from the Weatherby illuminated the crevice to reveal the beast, its face distorted by a hideous scream. Then Takakura fired. Light again, then in the next second a creature possessed of a prehistoric rage erupted from the dark, instantly beside them.

Its roar was a physical force, slapping Chaney in the face and chest, and then he was lost in a frantic turning, twisting battle, his rifle erupting again desperately.

Takakura, rifle flung away wildly at the creature's first swiping blow, returned a crippling wound with a flashing slash of his sword, hitting it solidly across the chest to draw a sweeping stream of blood that trailed the katana into darkness. Then it turned fully into the Japanese, who met it force to force.

Chaney shouted as Takakura leaped, hurling the full weight of his body—everything he possessed—in a stabbing lunge that drove the steel blade into the tremendous muscular chest through and through to send a foot of steel out its back.

It was a blow of artistry, of poetic movement made savage only by the definition of its delivery. Then Takakura—not wasting time or motion to appreciate the perfection of his skill—shouted and turned, viciously jerking the blade clear and spinning. And as he came around the sword again caught it, crossing his earlier blow into its chest. And yet again the Japanese hit as Chaney finally reloaded, blasting two deep furrows into its back.

Takakura leaped forward again, striking for the arm, but it recovered from Chaney's shots and leaped into the Japanese, furiously blasting the blade aside.

Its clawed right hand snatched Takakura by the neck as Chaney was hurled wildly back, somehow struck by a backhand. Then the creature ignored Chaney completely as it turned fully into Takakura, viciously driving its hand into a blow that struck the Japanese hard, disappearing into the chest of his torn uniform.

Dead ...

Chaney knew it.

Takakura, standing his ground to the last, was dead.

Knowing its incredible speed, Chaney was already on his feet and running, hurling his wounded body up the passageway with all his strength. He knew that he retained the revolver and debated turning to fire the remaining rounds, but realized it was futile. Feeling a sudden dissipation of strength as he staggered into the central chamber, the light casting monstrous shadows upon the walls, he careened forward and slid down a slope, crashing to a graveyard of bones that wrapped around him sharp and tangling, tearing at his skin with a thousand clutching claws.

Glaring back, too shocked to be astonished, he saw the creature standing imperiously on the crest of the slope. And, staring upon it, Chaney looked steadily into the glaring red eyes. Although pained, they reflected a purity of purpose—the awesome rage that had fired it to kill so relentlessly, so many times.

It was a moment of silence, each regarding the other.

Chaney rose amid the skeletons, refusing fear.

It smiled.

Strode slowly down the slope.

Only a split second for Chaney to notice the bloodied, ravaged wounds marring that monstrous strength—the bestial body, separated fangs, clutching talons. He never glanced again into the laughing red eyes that focused on him with such purity.

Raising his arm, his finger tightened on the trigger of the Casull. Then twin eruptions—or one; Chaney couldn't be sure—blazed from behind it to hurl it from the surface of the slope.

Roaring, it arched painfully in the air. And the attack it had suffered propelled it past Chaney to the cavern floor where it disintegrated in a dune of bones with a cascading, continuing crash.

Without even a backward glance it rolled, smashing a pathway through the grave mound, scattering bones that lanced the apocalyptic atmosphere like spears. Ducking away reflexively, Chaney avoided most of the projectiles before, stunned, he could turn back to target the creature.

It had vanished among the debris.

Hunter changed clips before he reached Chaney, gripping the marshal strongly by an arm.

"I'm all right," Chaney gasped. "Takakura ..."

"We know," Hunter replied without breath. His expression was heated as he glared out. "It's wounded! Just kill it on sight! Kill it like an animal!"

He moved over the skeletons. "Everybody stay close! We'll have one more—"

Rising volcanically from a mound of bones it struck out with awesome accuracy at Hunter, and it was only the lion-like reflexes of the tracker that saved him.

Its first blow was a thunderous sweeping hand that Hunter ducked with pantherish speed. Then it struck with the other taloned hand, aiming to take his head at the shoulders but Hunter threw himself inside the blow, striking it solidly with his shoulder.

Together, fighting savagely to the death, they rolled down the skeletal slope in a whirlwind of blows and roars, each wounding and being wounded. At the base of the mound, Hunter was first to his feet, feinting a move to the left that it took, and Hunter leaped wide to the right, gaining quick distance.

Bobbi Jo fell to a knee, centering on it with the Barrett. And as it closed on Hunter she fired two more rounds that ripped wild surges of blood from high in its chest. Chaney was firing every round he had remaining in the Casull, hitting it over and over before he dove madly from the mound, rage carrying him beyond reason in the consuming heat of the battle.

It saw him descend and turned with clear contempt, a backhand sweeping out to blast him from the air like a fly. Crying out in pain, Chaney devastated a pile of bones as he exploded into a slope, sliding shocked into the skeletons.

Distracted by the marshal's meaningless attack, it raised red eyes to Bobbi Jo, who struggled to remove a jammed clip from the Barrett. Growling, it focused on her with special intensity. Then, as if in hated remembrance, it gazed downward at its body, frowning over fangs, and lifted a bloody gaze to her once more.

Bobbi Jo stared. "Oh my god ..."

Suddenly ignoring Hunter, it took its first ascending step on the mound.

Its eyes blazed with inhabited darkness, the mouth turned down in a terrible promise of doom. And, electrified by the horrifying image, Bobbi Jo tore fiercely at the magazine. But it was twisted; the metal wouldn't surrender.

She hurled the rifle in its face as it reached the crest and leaped away but its long arm lashed out, snatching her back by the hair to hurl her into a heap.

As it moved over her, hands flexing, she searched for a weapon but in a moment of horror knew there was none ...

***

Knowing the danger, Hunter rose, searching desperately for the rifle, but it was gone. He cast a single glance to see the creature cresting the mound, moving for Bobbi Jo, and then he was moving with it, climbing and reaching inside his belt for what he hoped he would never be forced to use.

He saw them together as the slope flattened and Bobbi Jo screamed, raising an arm in futile defense. The creature roared in glory and raised a monstrous arm, talons black-red with blood.

"Luther!" Hunter roared.

Utter stillness held.

The creature did not initially move, and then clawed hand relaxed and, glaring with red eyes, it turned.

A wall of flame rumbled behind Hunter.

Darkness highlighted the might and fury of the beast as it beheld him. Cold and contemptuous, it dropped Bobbi Jo to the bones, advancing into the challenge.

Stepping to the side, angling on the dune of bleached bones, Hunter held the titanium tendril behind his back. And it matched him step for step, walking slowly forward, squaring.

"You are a fool," it growled.

"Who's the fool, Luther?" Hunter shouted, still angling. "Somebody who sacrificed their humanity for this?" He flung out an arm. "Look! Look around you! What do you see! You sacrificed your humanity for nothing!"

Hands clenching, the beast took a step forward.

"Never call me Luther," it snarled. "Luther is dead."

Hunter shifted his hand on the handle, the snare.

"Your *immortals* killed themselves, Luther!" Hunter said as he retreated a half-step, trying to draw it from Bobbi Jo and Chaney. "There's nothing left! That's what you traded your life for! So who's the fool! You were a man! And you gave it up for nothing! For nothing!"

"We ruled this world!" it bellowed as it advanced a wide space in a breath. And at the move Hunter reflexively bent, preparing. His mind raced as he circled to his right.

"You returned to a graveyard, Luther!" he said. "Everything you thought was glory! Look! You've returned to hell, Luther! They're gone! You're the only one! So how long will you last? A week? A month? A year before they hunt you down?"

It roared—a soul-searing rage extending from greatly distended white fangs—and it suddenly seemed to stand closer and more terrible and infinitely more threatening. Monstrous taloned hands clenched as it slowly advanced.

"I'll kill you for this!"

"For what, Luther? For showing you the truth?"

"For challenging me!"

Hunter cast a glance at Bobbi Jo to see her still trying to dislodge the clip; no time for it.

He stopped retreating, knowing he had to move now or it would move for him. Steadying, he focused on it, shifting his stance for perfect balance. Behind him, he felt the heat of flames. Beyond the creature, only darkness. No more games.

"You were doomed to lose, Luther."

Luther raged, "I am immortal!"

Hunter shook his head. "Nobody lives forever."

It leaped upon Hunter as he angled smoothly to the side. In his wounded condition he should have been struck but the beast was not so fast as before, injured as it was with open wounds shedding that titanic strength into the grave.

It was over him but Hunter was already wide of the impact and he twisted back on the skeletal hill toward its hurtling bestial form. Then his arm uncoiled with smooth skill that sent a flashing silver thread through raging red air.

And what he had hidden for so long was unleashed ...

Staring in horror, Bobbi Jo saw the charge and leaped to her feet. And then Hunter was outside it and she saw a silver line lashing through flame.

It was almost beautiful in its symmetry—reaching, spiraling out in a white, waving line that straightened and tensed at the last moment. It hovered almost magically before it settled in a noose that descended smoothly over the neck of the beast.

Hunter twisted his arm; it closed.

Twisting powerfully, he hauled backward and the monstrosity straightened, clawed hands reaching instantly for its neck, but Hunter wasn't finished. Again he whirled to heave the creature off balance atop the haphazard heap of bones.

Hunter's next explosive twist sent it over his shoulder, and as the creature crashed on the bluff it tore at the restraint and hauled, and Hunter was suddenly airborne. He hit the creature squarely and together they tumbled down the slope, with the beast grasping at the sinewy strand snared so tightly around its thick neck.

As it reached the base it angrily regained balance and turned into its greatest enemy, grabbing the noose that it could not escape and whirling to send Hunter crashing into a skeletal hill.

Bones scattered spectacularly at the impact, raking the cavern in ribbons of white. But Hunter used the momentum to his advantage, turning once more into the defiant contest of strength and skill to hurl it beyond himself yet again.

And together they spun, each punishing the other with volcanic efforts that sent them revolving through red-darkness, screams, the horror-filled cries of slaughter that echoed from the fallen bones of its victims and their own defiant roars that collided and died with each impact, only to be reborn as they violently gained their feet.

Hunter was at the disadvantage as he barely avoided a bull-like charge by the beast. But at the last moment he turned its superior weight to an advantage by twisting away and hauling it cleanly over his shoulders with the cord.

Mesmerized, Bobbi Jo watched as they spun chaotically through the dark, each shattering skeletons and stone with the merciless impacts that carried them at one point past the burning pool.

For a heartbeat she saw them silhouetted against flame, fighting viciously to the death. Then Hunter's free hand held his Bowie—nine inches of wide razored steel—and he leaped, closing the distance before the creature could react. The blade struck true and tore away, a gout of blood erupting from its ribs. But the wound came at a price as the beast, hovering in midair, lashed out to tear four vicious claw marks across Hunter's face.

Yet as vicious as the creature was, Hunter matched it dark measure for dark measure. The Bowie swept out in a backhanded blow that caught it cleanly across the neck, severing muscle and armored skin with an explosive crack and a cascade of blood. Then, not hesitating to measure the extent of damage, Hunter roared and turned, catapulting it into a stalagmite that shattered at the terrific impact.

There was a moment of stunned silence as it rolled and then it rose, blood flooding from its fanged mouth and throat. It struggled savagely to draw breath, staggering again. For a strange, eerie moment, neither moved, each attempting to draw breath. Then the monstrous face twisted in rage and it charged again, colliding hard with Hunter. They grappled— a fierce, volcanic intertwining of arms before Hunter leaped clear, hauling hard on the wire to send the beast sprawling once more in a mound of skulls that scattered wildly.

The next engagement was a vicious dance of blows thrown and blows evaded, some that struck to leave a scarlet trail in their wake and others that missed cleanly to slash through smoking air. Neither retreating, they attacked and counterattacked, struck, blocked, and angled, striking from fantastic angles with fantastic skill. Heedless, they stumbled through a burning sea of bones, ignoring the surrounding flames as they fought on and on, each as merciless and savage and determined as the other.

Hunter leaped and angled with the grace and strength of a lion to evade its most devastating blows, returning two wounds for every wound he received. Fatigue and blood loss were slowly claiming it now—it could feel the uncountable injuries only vaguely, but knew it was dying. Then it caught him hard, leaving another set of claw marks across shoulder and chest where he partially blocked the killing move.

Just the shock of the blow would have slain a normal man but Hunter was in killing mode now and felt little pain. He took the force of the impact and hauled it forward a step. Then he twisted violently back with the Bowie to gouge a deep crevice through its ribs. The blade sank to the hilt and Hunter twisted it sideways as he withdrew it, causing even more damage. And as he did the creature stumbled, obviously reduced by the injury.

Still, it would not die, and threw a wild backhand that Hunter ducked at the last second.

Without surrendering hold of the coil that was slowly choking out the creature's life, Hunter leaped forward—a desperate move—and kicked violently to send a shower of burning oil into the air. And the blanket of blue-tinged fire hit the creature in a roar to set it fully aflame.

It staggered back in shock, but it did not last.

Its rage was immeasurable as it charged Hunter with a scream.

***

Hunter saw the fire and made the decision instantly, only the dimmest, most overwhelmed region of his mind telling him that, if he made this desperate move, he would have to kill it quickly. Because its pain would be without end. And the pain would drive it forward, far past any pain that it now sought to escape.

Moving almost as quickly as the beast, Hunter drew tension in the coil as he turned and heaved with all his strength, taking its balance to drag it from its feet. And in the next instant he glimpsed a humanoid monstrosity fully aflame, soaring beyond him in a vengeful roar before it crashed heavily into the flames.

It landed and erupted with the same heartbeat, gaining the edge of the pit before Hunter had a chance to leap away. Even now, injured as it was, its speed was surpassing.

Live or die now!

Hunter had no thought for Bobbi Jo or Chaney or the rest as he crouched like a boxer, waiting.

Even the fangs were aflame as it closed the remaining distance with three rushing strides, reaching him in a horrifying image of death. Glaring through the wild flame, its blazing red eyes focused on Hunter with a deathless intensity. Hunter waited a final second—waited until the apelike, smoking arms had reached out to encircle, drawing him into the gaping jaws.

Leaping forward with a terrific lunge, Hunter collided hard against it and stabbed outward in the same movement. And, tight in his fist, the knife was a silver blur between the outstretched arms, aimed dead for the chest.

There was a flicker in the half-dark and then the huge blade hit solidly between the thick shields of its chest, disappearing into the beast with a thudding impact. Hunter instantly released the blade, ducking to survive the crushing arms as they closed.

For a moment there was an impression of being torn apart by two mountainous forces, each seeming to rip Hunters shoulders from their sockets, and Hunter resisted with all his strength. Pushing back against the monstrous arms, he separated a small space as talons tore deep grooves across his back and spine. Then he felt the talons lock deep in muscle and his back bent, closed in a force beyond imagination. A moment later, to his surprise, he found himself sprawled on the dusty cold floor, dazed but alive, struggling to regain consciousness.

Rolling painfully, he saw that the creature had collapsed onto its face, rising for a brief instant on a gorilla arm to grasp painfully at the protruding Bowie. Lifting its head with gaping fangs, it pulled at the blade, finally hauling the steel from its chest. Then it slumped back before struggling, far more slowly, to its feet.

Frowning, death in his eyes, Hunter stood to meet it.

Glancing behind the monstrous shape, he saw the flaming oil burning bright in the serpentine atmosphere. And, still hanging from its neck, was the snare that he had designed. Though designed from the simplest of tools—the tools of a simple man— the weapon streamed heavily with its blood.

One last move to make ...

Hunter stepped forward and anticipated its reaction. He timed it— purposefully slow—in order to draw it into moving too early, and the blind, backhand blow missed by six inches. Then Hunter leaped forward quick, snatching the bloody steel tube of the snare.

Whirling instantly, all the strength of his devastated body behind it, Hunter twisted to hurl the beast in an arch. It was a final finishing move but carried it fully into the flaming pool, where it crashed in a screaming mass of pain. Knowing that everything— their lives and the lives of everyone else—had come down to this moment, Hunter pulled the thermite grenade from his waist and pulled the pin with his thumb to spin back instantly.

Screaming within flame, it rose.

Hunter opened his hand; the clip flew in red light.

Staggering, howling, and seeming somehow to understand, it straightened and gathered itself for the briefest moment to focus absolutely on Hunter. Immeasurable hate blazed in the bloodied countenance as it snarled, striding forward.

Staring it hotly in the eyes, Hunter tossed the grenade and dove away, hitting smoothly to roll clear and then diving clearly over a second dune of skulls before the thermite exploded within the flames.

It was a lifesaving move. The resulting explosion bathed where he had stood in phosphorous- and flame-washed oil that lit the cathedral like lightning. And Hunter was moving again as he narrowly gained balance in the tumult, leaping to place another mound of skeletal refuge between himself and the heart of the storm.

Subterranean thunder shocked the struck cavern, shattering longstanding stalagmites to send them crashing to stone. Reverberating through rock a long while with white sheets of flame descending wildly through the atmosphere like fallen ghosts, the thunder continued until the doomed cave abruptly collapsed with deep trembling.

Stunned, shaking his head, Hunter glanced back.

Only seconds passed before the flames engulfed the entire cathedral-like cavern, eerily igniting a wide spiraling funeral pyre that blazed with bones and skulls blackening in flame.

Slowly, attempting to clear his vision, Hunter stood and stared over the burning monument to such a black, savage empire. But he did not have long to contemplate anything at all as his attention was drawn away.

A consumed, red-black shape shambled from the flames.

Hunter turned his head, disbelieving.

Rising vengefully from the inferno, the creature even yet struggled to survive, to attack, to kill. It rose from the purest liquid fire, swirling and crackling with the holocaust, and finally gained a foot, an edge, before stumbling—falling to a knee.

Hunter picked up his Bowie, walking forward.

Luther glared at him, smiled insanely.

"I ... am ... immortal ..."

Hunter reached out and grasped the burning hair, ignoring the flames that curled around his arm. He frowned, a force deeper than himself emerging.

"No, Luther," he said. "You're not."

He twisted violently and the Bowie came across and struck, and the blow continued without hesitation through flesh and blood and bone to finish the fight, the battle, and the beast. And the monstrous, headless body fell forward to the bone-littered ground.

Still ignoring flames that spiraled upward over his forearm, Hunter glanced into the now lifeless eyes. And if he had possessed the energy, he would have felt relief. For so long he had known only fear, desperation ...rage. Now there was nothing within him but immeasurable tiredness.

He tossed the head aside.

Hunter raised his eyes to the heart of the cavern and saw Bobbi Jo slumped on the hill of bones. Beside her, Chaney rested, collapsed on a bloodied, determined arm. His head moved slowly with each exhausting breath; he didn't look up. Yeah, they were hurt, but they'd survive.

Hunter held Bobbi Jo in his strong arm, and as Chaney stumbled alongside them, stoically enduring the pain, he slowly led them up the mountain and into the world.

EPILOGUE

Hunter, bloodied and savage, was the last to crest the summit, his Bowie the only weapon he retained as he emerged upon the sloped red rock. He was greeted by innumerable black choppers, soldiers, United States Marshals, some unidentifiable civilians, probably CIA, and two army medical helicopters.

An angry debate seemed to be raging between the leader of the Marshals Service and the army. And then there was Dr. Hamilton—he had obviously somehow survived the obliteration of the installation—standing beside a major.

Hunter ignored them all as he knelt beside Bobbi Jo, brushing back a lock of blond hair from her eyes.

Sitting tiredly on a white gurney, she was a mass of cuts and bruises and claw wounds. Her head was bowed in extreme fatigue while the medics gently dressed the furrows raked across her face and chest. As they started an IV, she spoke softly to Hunter: "Don't let them take you in. You'll...disappear."

Kneeling to meet her low gaze, Hunter smiled. "Hey, don't worry about me. You just get some rest. I'll see you at the hospital." He winked. "You still got some R and R to spend with me, remember?"

She laughed faintly as they laid her back on the gurney. In a moment they had her in the first medical helicopter, which began a cautious lift from the smooth, flat summit. Vaguely, Hunter wondered that so many choppers could be crowded into so small an area. Then he gave it no more thought as he walked stoically forward to find Chaney beside a tall, gaunt figure he was calling "Skull."

Hunter heard Chaney speaking quickly, alert and logical despite the distraction of his wounds. "Skull, listen, he's lying. It was all a lie. All of it. And I've got all the proof we need. About two miles beneath us in that cavern. Trust me, boss. I'm right on this one."

"Never doubted you for a second, Chaney," the man replied, staring hard at Hamilton. "Doctor," he continued, "I believe you have a lot to answer for. And I'm gonna be asking the questions."

Tension, already high, spiraled.

The military behind Hamilton seemed strangely uncertain, but they were obviously instructed to back up the doctor. And the U.S. Marshals behind Skull seemed ready, to a man, to defy them. When an army official, Hunter guessed a major, instructed Skull that Chaney and Hunter were under arrest, Skull laughed out loud.

"They're under arrest, Major," he retorted, leaning into it, "when I say they're under arrest and not a moment sooner. Your jurisdiction under *Posse Comitatus* has been withdrawn and I, notwithstanding the Second Coming of Jesus Christ, am now in charge of this situation." He looked at Hamilton. "You, Doctor, are hereby placed in federal custody for concealing vital information from the United States Marshals Service, for murder, for conspiracy to commit murder, for obstruction of justice, for the violation of civil liberties, and for the violation of federal law prohibiting experimentation in biological weaponry. And if that's not enough, I'll think up some more in a few minutes."

Chaney, too tired to laugh, shook his head.

Then Hunter stepped into it, shouldering his way between Skull and Chaney to engage Hamilton's enraged glare. The physician appeared unhinged, and seemed not to recognize his brutal, bleeding countenance for a moment. Then, pointing a trembling hand: "It was this man!" he shouted. "This ...this animal! He is the one who destroyed my facility!"

"And your life," Hunter nodded coldly. "Nothing left but the truth, Hamilton. And, just so you know, Luther is dead. He's lying two miles beneath your feet with his head cut off."

Skull nodded curtly to the marshals behind him and a team began rappelling over the edge of the cliff, headed down to the cave. Hunter knew they would retrieve all the evidence, the bodies of his compatriots, and what was left of Luther. He didn't know if any of it would ever see daylight, but it would be enough to put away the guilty for a long time.

Grimacing in pain, Chaney added, "You picked the wrong man for the job, Hamilton. That's why Hunter was so damned unimportant, wasn't it? He was the wild card. The rest of them, they were soldiers. You knew they didn't stand a chance against Luther. But you weren't sure how Hunter would react. What he would do. That's what scared you from the first, but you couldn't figure a way out of it 'cause you had to put on a good show. Well, I'm glad to see he disappointed you." Chaney turned in beside Hunter as they walked away and then called back: "See you at the arraignment, Doc."

As they walked to the second medical chopper, Skull began giving terse instructions for documentation of the scene and preservation of the beast's body. Hunter glanced back to see Hamilton, arrogant and despising to the last, being led away in cuffs. Although both of them were so wounded they could barely walk, now that the abysmal pain of a dozen serious injuries was emerging from beneath the stress, the sight brought a smile to Hunter's face as he spoke quietly. "You gonna be all right with the way this burned down?"

"Oh, yeah, no problems," Chaney said, obvious pain making his voice chipped and brittle. "How about you?"

"I'll be fine, I think. I just want to get to the hospital and check on Bobbi Jo. She was hurt pretty bad."

"Yeah, but she'll be fine, Hunter. She's strong. Got a strong spirit, too." He spoke slower. "I'm sorry about Ghost. And about the professor. He was ... a good man."

Moving another step, Hunter was silent. Then he stopped and slowly turned, staring back at the cliff. The marshal's team had already descended, and he was briefly immobile. After a moment he shook his head.

"Killing it don't seem like enough," he whispered.

Chaney, still holding his broken shoulder, let the moment last. "Come on, Hunter," he said finally. "You're hurt. I'm hurt. The rest are dead and that thing is dead. It's over. Now it's up to you and that body of yours to make sure something good comes out of this. Skull and I'll clean up the rest of the mess."

Frowning, Hunter paused, then began walking beside Chaney up the hill, toward the descending sun.

"So much for immortality," he said.

For More News About James Byron Huggins,
Signup For Our Newsletter:

http://wbp.bz/newsletter

Word-of-mouth is critical to an author's long-
term success. If you appreciated this book please
leave a review on the Amazon sales page:

http://wbp.bz/huntera

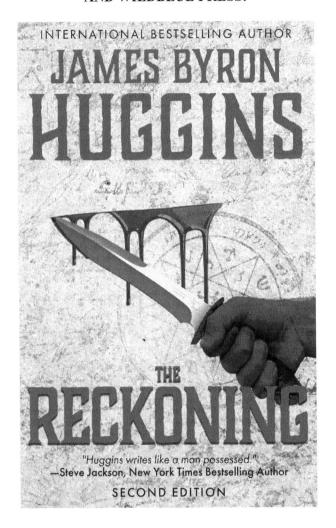

THE RECKONING by JAMES BYRON HUGGINS

http://wbp.bz/reckoninga

Read A Sample Next

ONE
Westchester, New York

"Is he dead?"

Father Stanford Aquanine D'Oncetta shook his head patiently as he casually removed a cigar from the darkly-illuminated Savinelli humidor.

"No, Robert, he is not dead," replied D'Oncetta calmly. "But there is no need for emotion. He will be dead soon enough."

"Not soon enough for me."

Stately and imperious, D'Oncetta laughed. Drawing steadily upon a vigilance candle to light his cigar, the priest leaned back against a mahogany desk, slowly releasing a stream of pale blue smoke.

Separated from D'Oncetta by the length of the library, Robert Milburn regarded the priest in the dim light. Reluctantly impressed by D'Oncetta's authoritative appearance, Milburn noted the deeply tanned hands and face of a man who had actually spent little of his life in dark confessionals or chapels.

The face of this man commanded true power and feared nothing at all.

Above the clerical collar and the black, finely tailored robe, D'Oncetta's straight white hair laid back smoothly from his low forehead, lending him the demeanor of an elder statesman. Everything about the priest was richly impressive, dignified, cultured and refined - an investment banker wearing the robe of a holy father.

"What are you so afraid of, Robert?" D'Oncetta laughed in his voice of quiet authority, a voice accustomed to controlling and persuading. "How many men is it that you have stationed outside?"

"Eleven." Milburn met D'Oncetta's steady gaze.

"And is that not enough to guard a single, isolated mansion in Westchester, especially with the noble assistance of New

York's vaunted police force that even now has a priority patrol on surrounding streets?"

D'Oncetta smiled reassuringly and exhaled again, savoring. Then he looked down at the cigar, turning it in his fingers with familiar approval.

"A Davidoff," he remarked fondly. "Rich and complex. Always the result of superior breeding. And it's not even Cuban, as one might presume, but a product of the Dominican Republic."

D'Oncetta's satisfied gaze focused on Milburn. "Would you like to try one?"

"No."

Turning his back to the priest, Milburn moved to the uncurtained picture window. He stared past the mansion's carefully manicured lawn and into the shadowed night beyond.

"I just want that old man upstairs to die, so we can all get out of here." Control made his voice toneless. "I don't like this, D'Oncetta. If Gage is really out there, like your people say he is, then we should just leave the old man alone. Because if Gage claims the old man as family ... If he's put Father Simon under his protection, then Gage will come for him. And if that happens..." Milburn paused, turning coldly toward the priest. "You don't have any idea what you're dealing with."

"But that is why you are here, isn't it, Robert?" D'Oncetta responded tolerantly, and Milburn suspected a faint mocking tone. "It is your solemn responsibility to deal with such matters. And there is much that remains, for this is simply the beginning. There are even more delicate tasks which will require your skills in the near future. Tasks which, through the centuries, have always demanded men such as yourself. Men deeply inured and intimately familiar with the higher arts. Men who can insure the success of our plans while simultaneously protecting us all from this individual whom you seem to respect, or fear, so profoundly."

Milburn's face was stone.

"Yes, Robert, that is why we need superb field operatives such as yourself. And that is why you and your men will remain here, guarding us all so efficiently, until Father Simon is dead. We do not want him disturbed in his final, tragic hours, do we?"

Milburn took his time to reply.

"I'm retired," he said finally.

D'Oncetta nodded magnanimously.

"Of course."

Milburn looked again out the window. Shadows completely cloaked the darkened wood line, untouched by the security lights illuminating the surrounding lawn. Training told him not to look for the faint outline of sentries concealed within the obscured trees, so Milburn allowed his gaze to wander, unfocused, receptive to discerning movement where shape could not be seen.

But there was nothing.

He turned nervously toward D'Oncetta.

"How much longer will it take?"

Black and stately, the priest shrugged.

"An hour," he said with supreme composure. "Perhaps less. The chemical is quite painless and, I might add, undetectable. Not that we shall have to worry. Validating documents have already been executed. There shall be no confirmation of peculiarity. So it will be tragic, but natural. For, as you know, Robert, all of us are destined to die."

D'Oncetta released another draw from the Davidoff and smiled again, this time plainly amused. And Milburn made a decision, releasing some of his tension by taking a slow and threatening step across the library.

Toward D'Oncetta.

The priest watched Milburn's measured step with calm detachment. And when Milburn was face to face with D'Oncetta, he stopped as if he had always intended to stop, emotions tight once more. But as Milburn stood close to the priest he felt a sudden strangeness in the moment, in the tension, and he heard the question coming out of himself before regret could silence it.

"Who are you, D'Oncetta?" he asked quietly in a voice of unbelief no matter what the answer.

D'Oncetta laughed indulgently.

"I am a priest, Robert."

Milburn's face was a rigid mask. Slowly he turned away and lifted a small radio from his coat: "Command post. Perimeter check."

One by one, unseen guards responded.

"Position one, Alpha clear ... Position two, Epsilon clear," until finally the code words, "Position eleven, Omega clear," emerged from the radio with startling clarity.

"Command clear." Milburn lowered the radio to his side, refusing to look at D'Oncetta again. But he knew the priest maintained his air of amused calm.

"There, you see, Robert. We are all quite safe."

TWO

The pale figure lay silently beneath the white shroud that stretched, thin and veiled, from the vaulted ceiling.

Darkness cloaked the room, leaving the dying man within a single white space claimed by the lampstand, a separate light that removed the old man from the shadows with a deep and glowing authority.

He laid with eyes closed, as motionless as he would lay in true death. But he was not dead, for the ashen face would sometimes tighten, stirred from within some abysmal pain, to release a low moan.

Watching in silence, the stranger stood in the shadows, far from the dying man, sweat glistening on his darkened face. Only moments after the priest had departed the room, he had stepped from the curtained balcony, moving without sound to shut the wide, double doors behind him.

Now he studied the room. And after a few moments he slowly removed a thick, black visor from his waist-length coat and raised it to his eyes.

His head turned with a mechanical, trained precision as he scanned the room, concentrating longer on areas that separated him from the dying man. Then he placed the visor again within his coat and eased into a crouch, feral and wary, an animal approaching a trap baited with what could not be resisted.

A long time he poised, as if searching for something that should be feared but could not be seen. Then in a slow, fluid movement he rose and stepped lightly upon the floor. At home with the darkness, he threaded a careful path through the shadowed furnishings to approach the dying man.

With reverence, with tenderness, the stranger reached down to clasp the man's trembling hand. The dying man weakly turned his head to behold the ghostly image and through clouded eyes, he smiled. Then he returned the stranger's grip with a strength that made death seem suddenly more distant. For the briefest of moments the hands held strong, encouraging, delivering and receiving with the familiar measure of firmness known only to old friends. And the weakened eyes looked up warmly into the shadowed face.

"I knew you would come. My son ... I knew you would come ..."

Silently the stranger nodded. Then he lowered his head even more, his face close to the dying man, a strong hand on the white softness of the bed.

"I'm taking you out of here," he whispered.

The old man shook his head. "No, no, it is too late for me – far too late." He drew a painful breath. "Quite effective, this pestilence. And ..." He laughed softly, "I am too old to run."

The stranger searched the fading eyes. Then he shook his head and moaned softly.

"I know ..." The old man squeezed the stranger's hand. "But you will do well without me ... You are strong, now ... Strong! ... *You are not the man you were!*"

After a moment the stranger raised his head, but his countenance was changing with each breath, eyes narrowing slightly with a bitter frown turning the corners of his mouth. He gazed upon the pale hand held within his.

"What is happening?" He leaned closer to the old man, eye to eye. "Why have these people done this to you?"

The dying man shifted suddenly, remembering something that resurrected horror in the unseeing, widening eyes.

"It has been taken!" he rasped. "They have stolen the prophecy!" He rolled his head from side to side, grieved. "I cannot believe they would commit such sacrilege! Surely it is mortal!" Trembling, he paused. "Clement would have destroyed it in time. He scorns their secrets and has always stood against them." A mournful breath escaped the sunken chest. *"They will destroy us all!"*

"Who are they? Tell me! Who are these people?"

The old man stared blindly into the surrounding darkness. "No, no, I do not know who they are ... But I knew you would come ..." He focused again on the stranger. "Yes, it was ordained long ago ... And now the Hour of Darkness has come – the Hour where *you* must take your place!"

The stranger's brow hardened in concentration. "What would you have me do?"

"Destroy the prophecy!" the old voice hissed. "Destroy it! It has cursed us for too long!"

With compassion the stranger's hand settled on the old man's chest.

"Rest, old friend," he said.

"No, no, there is no time," the dying man whispered. "I wish I could tell you more. But there is no time ... no time. But I knew you would come, so I prepared a letter for you. It is hidden in the cathedral. You know where to look." A sudden thought and he found a defiant strength, struggling to rise. "Ah, only know this, my son. Their victory is not complete. For Santacroce repented of his sin! Yes! He repented! And he buried ... he *hid* the prophecy in the tomb of his father! You can find it before they do! You can destroy it before their Evil claims it once more!"

The stranger gently pushed the old man to the bed.

"Rest. I know what to do."

The dying man hesitated, staring, and was quiet. And the stranger watched as the thin, dry lips moved in an unknown supplication, before the prayer fell still.

"I've loved you like a father," the stranger said.

Old eyes laughed. "And I have loved you as a son. I am sorry that I did not tell you more. I feared that this would come one day. But I wanted you to forget that world. To forget ... I know you have seen too much ..."

"I have forgotten," the stranger said.

The old man shook his head. "I know better. I know the faces still come to you in the night. But you are not what you were! The Dragon is dead, my son ... He is dead."

Abruptly the old man stiffened, face pale with pain.

A frown hardened the stranger's face.

"Do what you can for Sarah," the old voice whispered, and the stranger perceived that he heard a faintness behind, or within, the words, as if they were spoken from within some invisible mist. "Malachi is prepared to die. He is a good man. But Sarah has done nothing! She does not even know their secrets!" He shook his head. "She was there when we found it. But she does not know what it contains!"

"No one else will be hurt, my friend." The stranger placed a hand upon the old man's brow, gently pushing back the wispy, white hairs now damp with sweat.

"I'll bring an ending to this."

Nodding, the old man began to speak again, but the thought was lost as the clouded eyes saw something in the surrounding shadows. The stranger didn't turn; he knew there was nothing there that human eyes could see.

"Yes... an ending," the dying man whispered. "At last ... an ending."

It happened quickly, peacefully. The stranger knelt in silence, waiting, holding the weakened hands until softness faded from the pale face beneath him, and a brittle coldness settled upon the brow. Then, breathing deeply, he slowly rose, stepping back from the light to gaze mournfully upon the still shape.

A long moment passed before the first, violent shudder stiffened him and his fist clenched. Though his gaze remained focused on his silent friend, his fist clenched tighter, trembling, bloodless, a force struggling to find release and he shut his eyes, fiercely resisting a hated passion.

Then, after a moment, the cold gray eyes opened again and turned to gaze, malevolent and measured, upon the bedroom door that led to the hallway, and to the stairs beyond that led downward.

To the library.

And finally, though the stranger continued to stare at the door, the trembling fist slowly relaxed, was lowered to his side.

Frowning, breathing heavily, he turned back to the still form on the bed.

He nodded; "An ending."

Shattering the solemnity, static emerged from the radio concealed within the stranger's coat. An authoritative voice, tense and harsh, requested yet another perimeter check and unseen guards responded with clearances and codes.

Impassive, the stranger reached into his coat and removed the radio, along with the bloodied headset that he had chosen not to wear during the final, cherished moments with his friend. And he remembered the shocked expression of the guard now lying coldly beneath the shadowed wood line.

When it was the guard's turn to respond, the stranger engaged the device, speaking softly.

"Position eleven, Omega clear."

"Command clear," came the reply.

The stranger waited, gazing quietly upon his friend. Then he slid the radio into his coat, wearing the small, wireless earphone for silent monitoring. From his side pocket he removed a pair of black gloves and put them on, tightening a strap at each wrist. When he finished he was again completely cloaked in dark, somber hues.

He crossed the shadowed room with movements made profound by sadness, solid with purpose until he reached the balcony doors.

Was lost in the night.

THREE

Shadow in shadow, the stranger crouched on the balcony outside the room, opening his mind to the night to search by sound, sight, or scent. But he sensed nothing beside him in the dark. There was only the cool breeze, the sound of wind rustling the autumn leaves, distant traversing of traffic.

Moving slowly, carefully, the man reached back and removed the continuous circuit device that had bypassed the contact alarm on the double doors, placing it again within his coat. He turned, allowing his gaze to wander across the estate.

Almost completely concealed behind the balcony wall, he studied the surrounding grounds. He didn't center his gaze but scanned vaguely, knowing that in the darkness he would recognize shape by peripheral vision before he could discern it from middle focus.

He wondered if the slain guard, or the dog, had been quietly discovered and a trap set. He suppressed the violent urge to rush; it was always a mistake.

Soon.

He took a slow, deep breath and repeated the procedure to slow his pulse, waiting until the trembling stopped.

He shook his head.

Three years ... a long time.

Too long ...

Cautiously he took out the night-visor, a compact device resembling welding glasses that intensified ambient light sources for night-vision, and slid it over his head. Starlight luminosity registered sixty-four percent, easily allowing him to penetrate shadows of the distant tree line. He could also discern the faint outlines of three sentries, still holding the standard separation of one hundred feet.

No movement.

Suspicious, always suspicious, he attempted to scan along the tree line for other guards hidden behind the foliage.

He hesitated. Cautious. Uncertain. He initiated a switch on the upper right side of the visor, and the green-tinted screen was doubled over a thermal imaging detector that registered differences in air temperature.

Able to read through fog, windows, curtains, and rain, the heat sensor could detect heat variations as minute as one degree Fahrenheit. Instantly the three sentries were outlined in a reddish-yellow glow of body heat, while the remainder of the field was projected on the green rectangular screen in starlight, everything clear.

With the thermal imaging-starlight synthesis, he again scanned his field of observation. But he saw only the three sentries. He knew the rest would be stationed to the west and north of the estate, or roving.

That would make it more difficult.

Through an internal gauge in the night-visor, he saw that the batteries were nearly depleted and calculated that the double read-out mode was quickly exhausting remaining power. He switched off the heat index, leaving only starlight for visibility. Once more he scanned the layout of the surrounding terrain and streets, drainage pipes, hedges, and other areas that allowed limited visibility. And as he had done for the past night, he mentally familiarized himself with the architecture and landscape of the sprawling manor, preparing his mind for the instant rejection of any escape plan and the immediate selection of another.

Before entering the estate he had predesigned three various lines of retreat, with the last and most desperate being the initial line of entry. But he had never been forced to leave an objective along the path of entry. Never. It was an unbreakable rule, though desperation in past missions had taught him no rule was truly unbreakable.

On penetrating the security he had noted the roving patterns, the equipment, of the teams. He knew that whoever controlled the grounds had also hired military expertise for the job. Even after only a single night of surveillance he had determined that everything was done by the manual: listening posts directed outward, night-vision equipment and microwave transmitters for communications, patrol teams two by two roving interior grounds with dogs on the inside and perimeter.

Standard Operational Procedure ...

Night concealed his dark frown.

None of you can stop me ...

Automatically his mind locked into a familiar mode—fiercely focused, emotionless, concentrating his fear and rage and pain into physical strength and skill. A thousand calculations were formed, all turning intuitively in simplifying combinations: the mechanics of movement, light variations, background and cover, sound factors and noise discipline, tactics of evading detection while maintaining observation.

Then, remembering and ruled by the knowledge, he closed his higher mind. His training, sharpened and alive with instinct, would direct him. The science, the art would automatically select the tactic that his physical conditioning would reflexively execute.

Black gloves absorbed the moisture on his palms, but he wasn't accustomed to wearing gloves and unconsciously shook his hands, as if the cool night air would dry the sweat. Scowling, he noted the wasted movement, and his abrupt anger broke him from his heightened state.

Three years ...

I've lost my edge ...

Shut it down, he thought, shutting his eyes tight.

Concentrate on what you have to do ...

He expelled a slow, quiet breath, and focused.

Opened his eyes again.

No movement in the tree line, all visible listening posts facing outward.

Clear.

Silently, careful to keep his profile low, he moved slowly over the balcony, descending a thin rope he had lashed to the stone railing. When he reached the ground, he eased against the most advantageous background, a trellis of broken ivy and high shrubs that profoundly compromised security, partially concealing him from even ambient light devices. Then, patiently, he moved forward, coldly channeling feverish adrenaline and raging emotion into silent stalking.

An instinct, hot and fresh, that was the center of him, flowed through him. And he was hot with it; - thirsty, predatory, finding a familiar way with it.

But he knew he would not surrender to it.

Not like before.

Get the book at: **wbp.bz/reckoninga**

ONE

Sitting upon a bough, the raven watched.

In the dying of the light the little boy swung slowly from the tree, his body broken, a noose around his neck. And at the edge of the forest a car burned and the raven watched as flame rose from the heat like hate rising from the heart of the sun.

The raven and the boy were together as the fire burned and burned and began to fade in the last of the day but still the raven did not move. It stayed upon the bough and did not leave the boy alone until the sun had descended, and was gone.

The raven watched as the boy was claimed by the darkness of the night. It watched as the fire smoldered and the smoke vanished in the evening gray that overcame the day. It watched and it watched and it watched and it watched until something else had begun to burn in the dying of the light ...

Fire rose in the raven's eyes.

* * *

Joe Mac felt the gray November cold more completely than he'd ever felt it before because he could no longer see the leaves fade from rust to gold or gaze upon the skeletal silhouettes of trees etched against the gray November sky.

Now he lived in the world of the blind, so feeling the cold was all that remained. The rest was darkness and he would inhabit this darkness until the day he died and they buried him in the dirt and this darkness.

The raven came as it always came; it descended with the sound of enormous wings to land with a thunderclap on the home Joe Mac had built for it.

Three years ago they met as Joe Mac was first learning to live in the world of the blind. The raven had come to him every day as he sat alone in the back of the barn and Joe Mac named him "Poe" after the old poem. And every evening they would sit together in the back of the barn in Joe Mac's eternal night.

Poe did not rise or even seem to notice the familiar Mrs. Clemens as she approached but then Poe rarely flew away when someone came close. Rather, he seemed to know the exact distance for danger and ignored anything else.

Mrs. Clemens brought Joe Mac his supper – an act Joe Mac reckoned to her uncommon human kindness – and spent a moment to inquire about his health. But Joe Mac sensed something different in Mrs. Clemens tonight. Her steps were halting and seemed to wander before she laid a hand on his shoulder.

Lifting his face, Joe Mac asked, "What is it, Mrs. Clemens?"

Mrs. Clemens shuffled and Joe Mac felt the strength lessen in the hand; it was not much of a change, it was true, but a hand with little strength is even more revealing when what little strength it possesses is diminished ever more.

Joe Mac repeated more sternly, "What is it, Mrs. Clemens?"

"Oh," moaned Mrs. Clemens, "it's horrible, Mr. Joe Mac. Just horrible. Oh, god, I don't know how to tell you."

"Just say it."

She faltered, "It's about your grandson, Mr. Joe Mac. It's about Aaron. The poor thing disappeared from daycare today."

Joe Mac's left hand tightened on the arm of the chair. "How could they lose a four-year-old boy? Have they called the police?"

"Your poor daughter has called everyone! We're all scared to death something terrible has happened!"

With a shrill cry Poe erupted into the night sky as Joe Mac stood pulling his wool coat more tightly across his chest; he snapped his cane to length. "Why didn't someone tell me about this earlier?" he demanded.

"They've been too busy searching for him, Mr. Joe Mac! They've looked everywhere! And you can't even …"

She let the sentence die.

"Take me to my daughter," said Joe Mac. "And compose yourself, Mrs. Clemens. We don't know that anything terrible has happened. Compose yourself! Stay calm. And take me to my daughter."

TWO

"Here's the case file on that little kid."

Jodi Strong raised her eyes as the file was laid upon her desk. The veteran New York City detective, Thomas Grimes, who delivered the file pulled up a chair and leaned back, folding hands on his chest.

"What do you want with this thing, Jodi?" Grimes asked and didn't attempt to conceal either his curiosity or confusion. "There's already a million cops on this and we got twenty cases of our own to work."

"I took the original call last week when I was in uniform," said Jodi. "I interviewed the day care workers, the mother, the father. And then they found the little kid but he was already dead. Just like the others."

Grimes spoke in a weary monotone, "Jodi, it was your case when you were in uniform. It was your case when you took the missing person report. But you got promoted to detective three days ago and it ain't your case no more. It belongs to the task force and you ain't on the task force, neither. So what are you doing?"

Jodi shook her head, "Grimes, I know it's always a mistake to get personally involved in a case but –"

"Then don't."

"But that scene at the house really shook me up," Jodi continued. "I saw the little boy's room. I saw his picture. I felt like I knew him. And then he ends up … like he ended up." She slapped the file. "I'm tired of this psycho!"

Grimes sighed, "Jodi, the FBI has a thousand people on this. We've got about a million. One more cop ain't gonna make no difference in this. And we need you here."

Jodi made a slight sound as she sucked breath through her teeth. Then she said, "He's made a mistake, Grimes. They're just not finding it. Nobody's perfect."

"Well, this psycho is pretty close to perfect because right now the task force guys tell me they don't have a clue. One of 'em told me they're no closer to catching him now than they were four years ago."

Jodi opened the file and leaned back; "Aaron Roberts. Four years old. Abducted from the playground of his daycare. His body was found one hour after sunset –"

"Same as the rest of 'em."

Jodi continued reading as Grimes stood and leaned over her desk.

"Jodi," he began in a patient tone, "listen to me; I'm glad you made detective. I think you're a natural. But you're wasting your time. Whatever mistake this guy made ain't gonna be in no file. There's no fibers, no hairs, no prints, no DNA. There's no witnesses, no video, no tracks." He pointed toward the door. "This guy has killed twenty-four people and he could walk through that door right now and confess to everything we've got and we wouldn't be able to pin him to a single thing. He doesn't take anything. He doesn't leave anything. He has no motive. He has no face. He has no name. He's a ghost."

"Excuse me."

Jodi lifted her face to see an exceeding large man standing on the far side of her desk at the same moment she realized he was blind.

The man was slightly less than six feet but built like a brick. His body seemed one uniform size from his linebacker shoulders down through his barrel chest to his waist and weightlifter legs. His head was a square granite block set on a short neck. His white hair was standard military high-and-tight. His arms were heavy and the hand holding the cane was thick with strong-looking fingers although he held the shaft with a fisherman's touch.

Jodi was instantly curious why the man's presence gave her a palpitation of alarm. There was certainly nothing obviously threatening about him. And yet an aura of doom seemed to cloak him even more than the knee-length undertaker coat or the impenetrable black glasses; it occurred to Jodi that his appearance could not have been more unsettling if he'd been wearing a black funeral veil over his face. In all he reminded Jodi of a Texas tombstone she'd once seen that read, "As you are, I once was. As I am, you will be…"

Jodi whispered, "Good god …"

Grimes turned, gaped, and grabbed one of the man's blacksmith arms. "Joe Mac Blake! I haven't seen you in years, Joe! How ya been, man?"

"You're lookin' at it," said Joe Mac. "They still got you in robbery, Grimes?"

"Same 'ol same." Grimes theatrically lifted a hand toward Jodi as she rolled her eyes; he's blind, you dolt. "Jodi, this is ex-homicide detective Joe Mac Blake. Joe is a legend! Joe, this is Detective Jodi Strong. She's the newest member of the team." A laugh. "Well, this is a blast from the past, buddy. What are you doing downtown, man?"

Joe Mac lightly tapped the desk with his cane. "Got a seat for me?"

"Sure." Grimes pulled up a rolling chair. "Sit down."

Joe Mac felt, found the chair, and sat. He turned his face toward Jodi, "Nice to meet you, Jodi. Grimes is a good man. He'll help you get the lay of the land around here but it won't take you too long." He paused. "Can one of you tell me who's handling the Aaron Roberts case? He was the little boy that got killed last week."

"Officially that case belongs to the task force," said Jodi. "He's another victim of a serial killer we've been trying to catch for a long time."

"The Hangman?"

Jodi stared, then, "We've been ordered from on-high not to use that phrase but, yeah, it was 'The Hangman.'" She glanced at the file. "But as it happens, Joe, I've got a copy of the file right here."

Joe Mac lifted his face. "Have you had a chance to look at it?"

"No. I just got it. What can I do for you, Joe?"

"Aaron was my grandson." Joe Mac's face was stone. "I know I can't contribute to the forensics, but if you have any personal questions about Aaron, maybe I could help you out a little bit."

Jodi stared. "I'm sorry for your loss, Joe."

"Appreciate it."

After expelling a long breath Jodi said, "Look, Joe, they've got a task force briefing in about twenty minutes. Why don't you come with me? The FBI will be there along with Captain Brightbarton. He's in charge."

"I don't have a badge anymore."

"You're with me. You'll be okay."

Joe Mac rose, his hand moving his cane.

"Let's go."

* * *

Joe Mac knew he was seated in the third row from the back, the second chair from the right side of the room. He'd been here many times during his thirty-five-year career as a New York City uniform patrol officer and then as a gold shield homicide investigator and he knew every line of this place.

He also knew that the front few rows would be filled with investigators and uniform patrol supervisors. The next rows would contain FBI personnel. And the last few rows would be filled with forensics experts, psychologists, and people like himself.

Captain Steve Brightbarton announced, "All right, gentlemen, you've all had a chance to review the forensics on four-year-old Aaron Roberts. As of this moment we can confirm that Aaron was killed inside that warehouse. The suspect used blunt force trauma to break all his bones – the same thing he did to the other victims – and then he hung him by a noose around his neck. Same as the rest. Forensics says the tool used in the attack was a club coated in bronze so keep your eyes open for a plain-view search. Crime Scene didn't recover any DNA. No hairs. No fibers. No prints. Not even any touch-DNA. We don't have him on video. We have no witnesses. The car was stolen from a police impound lot and that's all we got. At this time I'll turn it over to FBI Special Agent Jack Rollins."

There was little to hear besides the rustling of clothing as Jack Rollins stood and Brightbarton took a chair.

"Afternoon," Rollins began, "you all know me. But for the uninitiated my name is Jack Rollins and I am the Special Agent in charge of the FBI task force. Everything Captain Brightbarton just told you is accurate. I'll only add that the murder of Aaron Roberts is consistent with the twenty-three murders preceding this, so confidence is high that we're dealing with the same suspect.

As usual, the suspect left nothing behind. The rope he used was standard clothesline that you can purchase at any hardware store. He torched the vehicle with a half-gallon of gasoline inside a one gallon milk jug armed with a two-dollar off-the-shelf egg timer so we have no prints, no fibers, and no DNA.

"We have nothing further on a description. We know he uses disguises and we have him on traffic cameras as an old man, a young man, a poor man, a rich man. The only thing we know for sure is that it's a man. We have isolated no salient physical characteristics that would make him easier to identify. He could be me. He could be you. All we can tell you is that we believe he's a white male in his mid-thirties. He's about six foot, 180 pounds. He very, very strong physically and we believe he has a superior IQ. So our strategy is for the NYPD to continue their stop and frisk strategy of any and every person of interest. We want you to continue priority patrols and stakeouts of secular daycares, church daycares, schools, malls, playgrounds, parks. Meanwhile, we at the FBI will continue to work forensics and continue our enhanced surveillance of every name the computer spits out. Now, we do not know if this psychopath is armed but, of course, you know to approach him as if he is." He paused. "I know I certainly will. And now I'll turn this over to Dr. Marvin Mason. He's assistant senior anthropologist for New York's American Museum of Natural History. He also has a doctorate in archeology and he is continuing to work with our Division of Behavioral Science to keep an up-to-date profile on this guy. So, Dr. Mason? Would you, please?"

The chamber was subdued, which allowed Joe Mac to hear Dr. Mason's soft steps and then the microphone was turned, apparently to accommodate his height.

"Thank you," said Mason.

Imperceptibly Joe Mac nodded; yeah, from the depth of his voice Mason wasn't big but he wasn't a lightweight, either. Joe Mac estimated him at a few inches less than six feet, about 170 pounds. His accent was native Long Island.

"All I can tell you what I've already told you," Dr. Mason began. "As you know, this subject takes the time to break every bone in a victim's body and then he hangs them by the neck from a tree. We've done extensive research and we have found this manner of human sacrifice, or punishment, to be so prevalent in ancient cultures that we can't isolate any specific cult or religion or sect or civilization as the primary instigator. He could have taken it from the Jews or the Gaelic tribes or the Vikings or various Asiatic cultures. All we can say is that we believe you're looking for an individual who kills in this highly methodical manner because he is motivated by some kind of pathological religious psychosis." He paused. "We know you guys are working hard and all of us at the museum want to help. But that's all we've been able to come up with. There's just nothing exotic enough about what's he doing to narrow it down to any one culture or religion. It's barbaric and savage. But it's not exotic. Throughout recorded history it's something that's been done by almost everybody."

Jodi said, "Dr. Mason?"

Mason paused. "Yes?"

Beside Joe Mac, Jodi stood; she was leaning on the chair before them. "Doctor, how long is he going to keep this up?"

"We believe he's going to keep it up until you catch him or kill him."

"Why do you say that?"

"Just like we don't know what kind of obsession is motivating him, we can't say with any certainty when this obsession will be fulfilled," Mason answered. "I think it's safe to say that you're dealing with someone who is very smart and very cautious but also completely insane and I see no reason why he will stop doing what he's doing."

"History doesn't suggest a motive?" Jodi asked.

Mason sighed; "The closest thing we've found to a motive are rituals used in turn-of-the-century Europe to destroy werewolves." He cleared his throat. "In Europe, when they caught someone they suspected of being a werewolf, they would put them on a rack, break their bones, hang them and set them on fire. They did the same thing to people suspected of witchcraft. Even in this century. Even in this country. But we don't think he's doing all this because he suspects someone of being a werewolf or a witch. We think he's doing it because he's afflicted with a bizarre religious psychosis that is totally beyond the understanding of any sane person and probably beyond his understanding, too. We don't think even he knows why he's doing what he's doing. He doesn't know why he's doing it but he can't stop himself. That's how crazy we think he is."

"But why do you insist it's a religious psychosis?" Jodi pressed.

"Because breaking someone's bones and hanging them from a tree are traditional religious punishments. Both of them are in the bible. Both of them are in the Koran. Both of them are in the Torah. In a nutshell, they're universal religious means of punishment for someone breaking a religious law regardless whether that law comes from Yahweh or Allah or Shiva. Does that answer your question?"

Jodi nodded, "Yes, thank you."

FBI Special Agent Jack Rollins stood – Joe Mac heard the scrape of chair legs – and asked, "I'm sorry but I don't know your name Detective –?"

"Detective Jodi Strong, sir."

"Are you on the task force?"

"No," Jodi answered firmly. "I worked the original missing person call on Aaron Roberts when I was in uniform."

Hesitation.

"I see," said Rollins. "Well, the fact is that we don't know any more about who killed Aaron Roberts than we know who killed the rest of the victims, detective. We know this guy's methods. We have no idea who he is or why he's doing this."

"I understand," said Jodi.

She sat.

Joe Mac followed Mason to his chair on the back of the dais and listened as Brightbarton approached the podium.

"That's it, gentlemen," said Brightbarton. "Check your boxes at the end of shift for any updates. And remember: Approach this guy with the most extreme caution. And that means approach him with your gun out and shoot him graveyard dead if he even looks at you funny. Be careful out there. Dismissed."

Joe Mac didn't move as everyone rose and began filing out the three doors. He lost contact with any presence on the podium in the mulling of footsteps and conversation like one might lose sight of an eagle against the sun. He did know that Jodi hadn't moved. Neither had she opened the file she'd brought from the office. He would have heard the rustling of paper and there wasn't any.

"I checked up on you," said Jodi.

Joe Mac's voice was a soft growl; "When'd you have time to do that?"

"When I went to the bathroom. You're a legend."

Joe Mac revealed nothing.

"The lady in the bathroom told me that you solved over a thousand homicides. She said you were a detective first grade with a gold shield and you were one of those real guys always out there, always hunting. Then you lost your eyesight when you rescued that little boy from that house fire. And I know it sucks – I mean, don't get me wrong; I would never say I know how much it sucks – but you did save that little boy's life. And I bet you're still a great detective."

Joe Mac lifted his chin. He seemed to hear better that way; he didn't know why. He didn't care. It worked and if anything worked at this stage of his life it was good enough. "Are you thinking you might could use some help?" he asked.

By the scraping in her seat Joe Mac knew she turned. "Well, Joe, you knew Aaron. And I've already talked to your daughter. She's in no shape to help me or anybody else right now. So what do you say we ride out to that daycare center and take a look around?" She stood. "Anyway, the daycare's right down the road from your daughter's house. And you live close by, don't you?"

"I live in the barn out back," said Joe Mac. "They sort of turned it into an apartment." He shrugged. "It's good enough."

"Then let's take a ride, Joe. If nothing else, I'll take you home."

Joe Mac stood.

"Bring what you got on this case."

* * *

Joe Mac didn't need eyes to know exactly where they were at any moment. His soul knew this terrain by neurological imprint. He imagined that he might have driven much of it by himself even now.

"I don't know if I told you how sorry I am about Aaron," Jodi said – the first time she'd spoken in her squad car. "I know that nothing is fair in this world but this truly wasn't fair in an ungodly, horrible way that should be damned to Hell."

Someone once said the greatest sound is silence but Joe Mac couldn't remember who it was. He only knew he had nothing to say until Jodi finally turned the squad car slowly to the left and announced, "Here we are, Joe."

She parked and Joe Mac could feel her stare.

"You ready for this?" she asked.

Joe Mac nodded and opened the door.

"Let's do it," he said.

He extended his cane though he hardly needed it; he could remember every inch of this daycare since he'd seen if often enough when he could still see; it was a compact one-story building with three wings like a T. There was a playground with brightly colored plastic equipment out back. It was surrounded by mesh fence about four feet high that had a gate leading into the building. There was one exterior gate on the left. The entire facility was a half-acre surrounded by pines.

Joe Mac had already moved to the front of Jodi's car as she walked up and said, "Do you remember the layout?"

"Yeah."

"Wanna go up to the fence?"

"All right."

Joe Mac had no problem negotiating the sparsely occupied parking lot. He felt the curb with his cane and stepped up knowing the feel of grass beneath his feet; it was a half-inch deep with dry ground beneath. He estimated three steps to the fence and he was right. He placed a hand on the top of the steel mesh and lifted his chin.

He became aware that he was waiting for … something ….

"Those pine trees back there," said Jodi. "Do you think he could have come in through those? They would have hidden him from view until he came right up to the fence."

"He could have." Joe Mac turned his face toward the back acreage as if he could still see. His voice was faint. "Still green up top. Thick enough. Dead pine needles don't make a sound when you walk on 'em … Yeah. Let's go back there. I know the crime scene boys went over it but it won't hurt to do it again."

"I'm game," Jodi said and they turned to walk along the fence line.

The front easement had been mowed up to the steel mesh so Joe Mac didn't have to worry about weeds. Then he felt Jodi's hand at his left elbow, guiding him gently, and he wasn't offended. Guiding a blind man by a light touch at an elbow was something people just seemed to do by instinct.

Joe Mac was accustomed to the drag of his cane on grass; it was much different than the steady, balanced, light touch he used on concrete. He had to lift it higher and touch more quickly; it was more like stabbing fish than the smooth side-to-side he normally used.

Joe Mac estimated twenty steps to the end of this fence line and he was right. They turned to the left and resumed walking when Jodi said, "I think he used this side. The other side faces the road and I don't think he'd use that. He'd have to stop his car on the road, jump out, run up to the fence and try to grab one of them. And the kids would have probably run away from him, screamed for their teacher, and they would have called for a unit. He would have never been able to get out of the area before one of us caught up to him. I think he knew that."

"You're right," said Joe Mac. "He wouldn't do that."

"This guy doesn't leave anything to chance." Jodi's voice took a tinge of impatience. "Sometimes it amazes me how crazy people can be so smart when it comes to killing other people. It's almost … cosmic."

They reached the section furthest from the building and Joe Mac said, "Stop here. What do you see?"

Jodi said, "Well, this is the farthest point of the fence and they don't mow the grass back here. It's about waist high right up to the playground. But it's been stomped down a little by the search party."

"How big was the search party?"

"It wasn't all that big. There wasn't enough time to organize a big search party or even get the word out. Aaron was reported missing at three in the afternoon and they found his body at seven-thirty." A pause. "If he'd been missing for a whole day I'm sure we'd have had thousands of people walking the woods out here. But all they had that day was a few cops and some neighbors.

Then they found Aaron's body beside that warehouse and there was no more reason to look."

"Keep moving," Joe Mac motioned. "Keep looking down. Tell me what you see. It doesn't matter what it is."

They strolled and Jodi began "Looks like we got one rabbit hole ... Rabbit tracks ... There's a fresh mole hill ... A coke can ... "

"Bag it."

"Got it."

They continued.

"We got another mole hill ... A blue leaflet ... Bagging it ... A candy bar wrapper ... Bagging it .... I don't know why those guys didn't bag all this stuff ... Amateurs ... I should have come back here myself but I was at your daughter's house ..."

"I appreciate it. Keep looking."

"I don't think this is going anywhere, Joe ... This coke can and candy bar wrapper look really old ... I don't think they have anything to do with what happened ..."

"Never assume anything, kid. Keep going."

"Okay ... Well, there's some kind of dead thing ... Looks like it used to be a bird ...There's a piece of white string ..."

Joe Mac stopped. "What?"

"What?" Jodi repeated.

"A what?"

"A string?"

"Did you say 'white string?'"

"Yeah. It's white."

"You wearing your gloves?"

"Yeah."

"Pick it up."

Jodi led him to the wood line, bent, and straightened. After a pause, she said, "It's just an ordinary piece of white string, Joe."

"Follow it."

After a moment, Joe Mac felt a tug on his arm. "This is kind of tricky, Joe. Stick close to me. It ..." They took several steps, "... it leads into the woods."

Get the book at: **wbp.bz/darkvisions**

ALSO AVAILABLE FROM WILDBLUE PRESS!

AL SHABAH by A.E. SAWAN

"A haunting, harrowing story of civil war … written by someone who lived it." – Raymond Khoury, New York Times bestselling author of The Last Templar

http://wbp.bz/alshabaha

ALSO AVAILABLE FROM WILDBLUE PRESS!

HARD DOG TO KILL by CRAIG HOLT

Hardened mercenaries Stan Mullens and Frank Giordano are fighting their way across the Congo jungle to kill a charismatic diamond miner, Tonde Chiora. But their victim is full of dangerous surprises, and the jungle offers more opportunities to die than to kill. Struggling to survive in the dark heart of the Congo, Stan begins to question his old loyalties – and his tenuous belief that he is still one of the good guys.

http://wbp.bz/hdtka

33390824R00279